BANE of ASGARD

THE RUNESTONE SAGA

Also by Cinda Williams Chima

THE RUNESTONE SAGA

Children of Ragnarok

THE SHATTERED REALMS SERIES

Flamecaster

Shadowcaster

Stormcaster

Deathcaster

THE HEIR CHRONICLES

The Warrior Heir

The Wizard Heir

The Dragon Heir

The Enchanter Heir

The Sorcerer Heir

THE SEVEN REALMS SERIES

The Demon King

The Exiled Queen

The Gray Wolf Throne

The Crimson Crown

CINDA
WILLIAMS CHIMA

BANE of ASGARD

THE RUNESTONE SAGA

HARPER
An Imprint of HarperCollinsPublishers

The Runestone Saga: Bane of Asgard

For information address HarperCollins Children's Books, a division of HarperCollins Publishers, 195 Broadway, New York, NY 10007.
www.epicreads.com

Library of Congress Control Number: 2023936890
ISBN 978-0-06-301873-0

Typography by Laura Mock
24 25 26 27 28 LBC 5 4 3 2 1

First Edition

To my grandsons, Jack Archer and Isaac Williams Chima.
May books take you to all the magical places and open your hearts to the people and possibilities just beyond your grasp.

THE MIDLANDS
NEW JOTUNHEIM
Tar Pits
Temple Ruins
Orchard
Iron Furnace
Foundry
BONDI VILLAGE
Folkvangr
Barracks
Riftwall
RYFTHOF
Elivagar
Serpent's Spine
SUNDHAVN
VIGRID
Bainahruga
Mosifell Mtns.
Moderlund
NAGLFAR
ITHAVOLL
The Grove
Langadale
Langa R.
LUNDHOF
AUSTHAVN
VESTHAVN
Snaefell Mtns.
BRENNABY
VESTHOLM
Jarnfen
WETHERBY
BRENNAVIK
ELMYRJAR

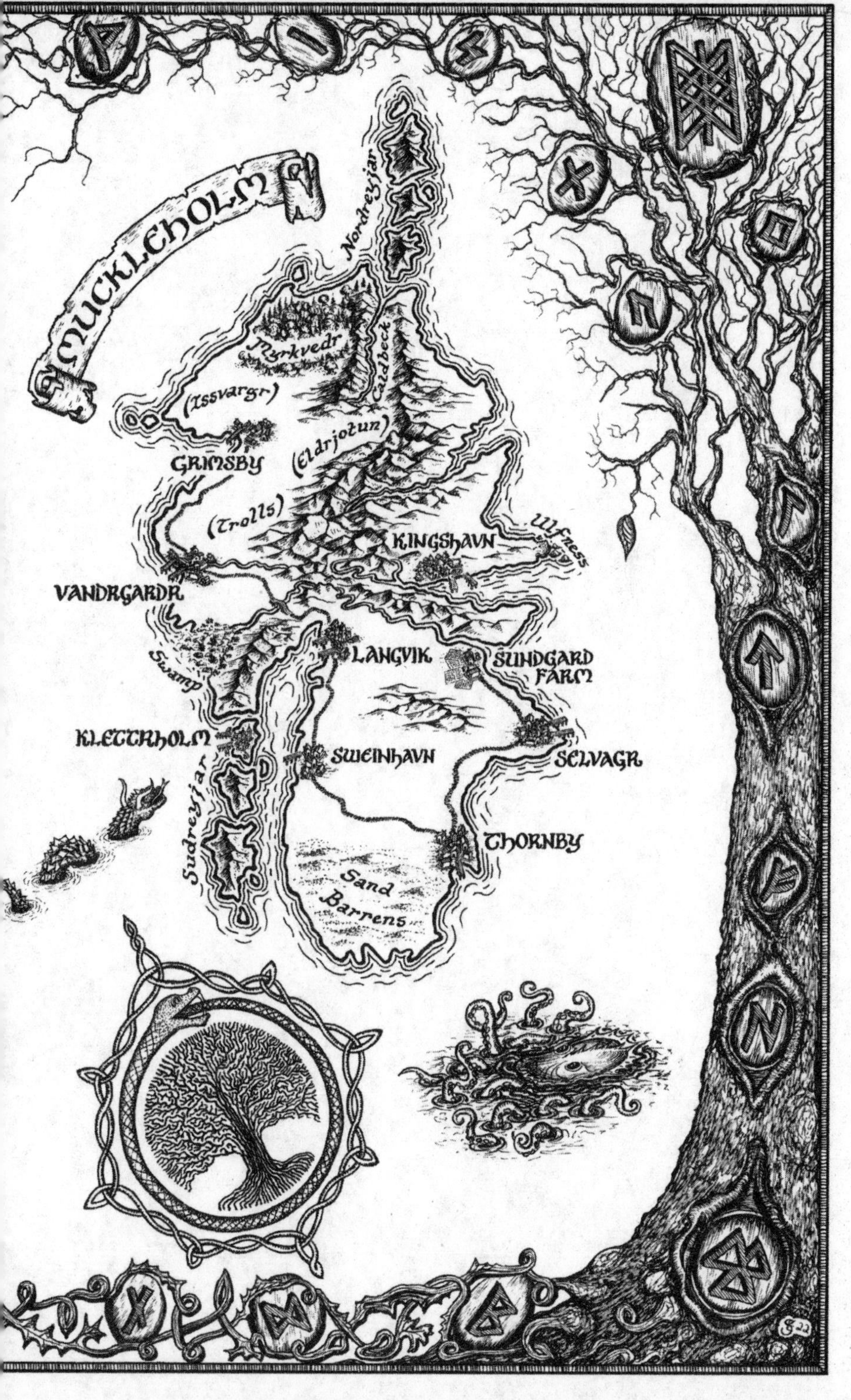
MUCKLEHOLM
Nordreyjar
Myrkvedr
Caldbeck
(Issvargr)
(Eldrjotun)
GRIMSBY
(Trolls)
KINGSHAVN
Ulfness
VANDRGARDR
Swamp
LANGVIK
SUNDGARD FARM
KLETTRHOLM
SWEINHAVN
SELVAGR
Sudreyjar
THORNBY
Sand Barrens

1

AT ANCHOR IN ROUGH SEAS

FOR DAYS AFTER THE REUNION with Liv at the executioner's block, Eiric roamed the nightmarish realms between waking and sleeping. Once, he opened his eyes to find Modir Tyra leaning over him. When she noticed that his eyes were open, she thrust the glittering head of her staff into his face, sending his thoughts into a whirlpool that sucked him into the screaming blackness.

Or maybe that never happened. Maybe it was a dream.

His mind was a mingle of old stories and new, some his own, and some unfamiliar. Whenever he tried to sort them out, he encountered barriers and bridges that he couldn't cross. One thing he knew—he'd done something unforgivable, and he deserved to die for it.

He heard Liv's voice, felt her calloused hand on his forehead. He opened his eyes, catching a glimpse of blue silk before his head went spinning and he closed them again.

"What's wrong with him?"

"I don't know, dottir," Tyra said. "I have tried to restore his wits, but he's unreachable. This must be the result of his time in the deadlands. No one has ever gone there and survived. It explains his attack on the council and the keeper. He will never be the brodir you remember."

Liv's breath hissed out in frustration. "It's not his fault."

"Maybe not, but in his present state of mind, he poses a danger to us all." Tyra paused, lowered her voice. "You shouldn't spend so much time here, Firebird. It serves no purpose, and it only breaks your heart."

Liv straightened the bedclothes around him. "I hate to see him like this."

"Which is why you should have let the execution proceed."

"No," Liv said flatly. "I am not giving up on him. There has to be something that can be done."

"He will betray you, Heidin."

"He is my brodir. He will not."

"He cannot help it. It is in his nature. Your fadir betrayed us, and his son will, too."

Heidin? Her name was Liv. A memory pricked at him. A little girl on the beach, clutching her amulet, saying, "Liv is not my name."

Tyra's voice again, like syrup of poppy dripping into his ears. "You must let go of him. There is too much to do." After a brief pause, she said, "I have something that will ease his path. He will feel no pain, I promise."

Maybe that would be best, Eiric thought. No guilt, no pain. No chance he would kill again. And, since he didn't believe Bjorn's stories about Valhalla, no penalty for dying in his bed.

But Liv wasn't having it. "Without Eiric, I never would have made it home," she said. "In the Archipelago, we looked out for each other. If he is in this situation, it is because of me."

"Even if he recovers, he cannot be allowed to return to the Archipelago, Heidin."

"He can stay here," Liv said. "Who wouldn't choose New Jotunheim over Muckleholm?"

"You cannot keep an Asgardian warrior like a pet," Tyra said.

"Don't forget—my fadir was Asgardian, too."

"Yes," Tyra said. "He was. He provided the spark of divinity we needed. We've all made sacrifices so that you can ascend your rightful throne. I worry that you are not taking the long view, that you are blinded by an affiliation that—"

"Do *not* force me to make a choice, Modir," Liv said in a voice as brittle as ice at midwinter. "You may not like my decision. And if anything happens to Eiric–anything at all–I will lay it at your door."

After a long, charged pause, Tyra said, "Very well. We'll hope for the best."

That was the end of that conversation.

He remembered little about the days that followed, beyond the dreams that came and went. A few times, he was aware of Liv in the room, glaring at him as if she could will him back to his senses.

There was a kind attendant who bathed him and washed his hair and tried to persuade him to take a little broth, a bite of porridge. She was wary as a skogkatt, but when he tried to speak to her, to reassure her, it came out all wrong.

Other times, it was Tyra, stirring his thoughts like a poisonous cauldron.

You are a danger to your systir. People blame her for what you did. You stand in the path of her ascent to greatness. The days of the Asgardians are past. You must step aside.

I would never hurt Liv, Eiric said.

You already have. The best thing you could do for her is to leave this world for the next.

He couldn't have said for how long he drowned in an ocean of regret, with some consciousness of people coming and going. Liv. No, Heidin. Liv was gone. Tyra. Once, Eiric opened his eyes to find a soldier leaning over him, elderflowers pinned to his tunic, a dagger in his hand and death in his eyes.

"Troels!" someone hissed. "Leave him be. It's not worth it. He'll be dead, soon enough."

Eiric closed his eyes again and waited for the prick of a blade that never came.

Until one day a mix of familiar voices called him up from the depths. Liv's and . . . one other. He swam desperately toward the light. He'd nearly broken the surface, when all at once he startled awake, feeling as if someone were running a lit taper over the skin at the base of his neck.

He opened his eyes.

She leaned over him, her finger on his collarbone, tracing a design. Her hair smelled of flowers, and flame, and flint against steel. Her face was familiar, bringing memories of healing and kisses and goodbyes.

But who was she?

"Please," he whispered. "Stay." He grabbed her wrists, so thin and breakable, afraid that she would fade away like every good dream. This was one dream he wanted to live in a little longer.

"I'm not going anywhere, Eiric," she said. "But you must let me go."

Eiric. Was that his name?

"Who are you?" he said. "I think I know you, but I can't remember."

"My name is Reginn," she said. "We met in Langvik."

He whispered her name so he wouldn't forget.

Reginn.

She tried to pull free, and he tightened his grip. "Don't leave," he said, as if she were a raft in a killing flood.

"I will come back," she said, "if you let go. You're hurting me."

"I'm sorry," he said, finally releasing his hold.

He settled back, overcome with weariness, and fell into a sleep more peaceful and healing than any he'd had since he'd awakened on the beach on Ithavoll.

At first, she came nearly every day and sometimes twice a day. Often she would sit by the side of his bed and bring out her flute. Sometimes that was the only thing that would quiet the waking dreams that ambushed him constantly.

Each time, when she left, he would whisper, "Don't go."

And Reginn would say, "I'll be back."

Liv came less often now—she seemed to be busy day and night. He missed her fierce and disappointed gaze.

And still, nearly always at night, Modir Tyra came. She looked disappointed, too, though he guessed for different reasons. Several times, he heard Liv and Tyra arguing in the hallway outside his cell.

Nobody could argue like his systir Liv, but Tyra came close.

He was aware of time passing, of rising and falling like a boat anchored in rough seas, the winds shifting constantly. He didn't seem to be improving. He knew, better than most, that the best-made craft would founder eventually, if left to the mercy of the weather.

2
COUNSELOR

FOR THREE NIGHTS RUNNING, REGINN had been chasing sleep with no success. On this night, as on so many other nights, she gave up.

She sat up in bed, wrapped her arms around her knees, and glared at the battered old staff in the corner. Its amber eye glowed, forcing shadows into the corners and gilding her skin like a courtesan's. It demanded her attention like a splinter under the skin—one that was beginning to fester.

She occupied herself during the day, like a rat in a labyrinth, racing toward exhaustion.

Twice a day, she went to Eiric's cell, which was an exercise in frustration. She would see a glimpse of the coaster she knew in a gesture, a smile, a hint of recognition in his eyes. The next day, it was gone. It was like rolling a boulder all the way to the top of a hill, only to lose hold and have it careen back to the bottom.

Twice a day, she walked to the dining hall, which seemed cavernous in its emptiness. The other members of the new council were rarely there—either detailed to Ithavoll or choosing to eat in the private dining room in the council house. It was surprising how much she missed them.

Why can't you just fall in line, like everyone else?

Is it all right to do evil as long as everyone joins in?

Even the library was not the refuge it had once been. At least once a day, she checked the message niche to see if Trude had left a message. At least once a day, she was disappointed. She felt abandoned.

What she needed to do was enter Brenna's tomb, something she hadn't done since the day she'd met up with Heidin and Asger in the tunnels. She made excuses. She might be followed. Tyra might find out, and be reminded that Reginn had entered the tomb once, and could open the door to the secrets Tyra seemed to think were inside.

The real reason was that Reginn was a coward.

Brenna had called her Aldrnari, that her magic was elemental to all others. Had told her that she was dangerous, that she had the power to destroy the only one of the Nine Worlds that remained after Ragnarok.

She remembered Brenna's warning.

Raising the dead is an elemental gift.

One Ragnarok is enough.

When Reginn had asked if there was any way to use her power safely, Brenna had suggested that a staff might help.

Just choose carefully.

Brenna had tried to deny Reginn entry to the tomb. But Reginn had the key from Trude, and she entered anyway. And took up the founder's staff.

Her presence did not go unnoticed.

She heard the voices.

Hear us, Aldrnari. We would rise.

Raise us, Aldrnari, that we may blood our blades again.

Lead us, Aldrnari, that we may leave the field with honor.

When she'd encountered rampaging boars in the tunnels, she tried to wield Brenna's staff and found that it had a mind of its own, scratching VAKTI into the dirt. To awaken.

Then the aurochs came.

Reginn was haunted by the memory. What if Brenna had set her up somehow? The founder had reason enough to seek revenge. What if the founder's staff was wielding *her*?

Sliding out of bed, she approached the staff warily, closed her hands around the shank and rolled it between her palms, feeling the grit of rust against her skin.

What would happen if Tyra knew that instead of being the hero that rescued her long-lost dottir, Reginn had unleashed the beasts in the first place?

What if it happened again?

Too many questions, not enough answers. And with Trude unavailable, Brenna was the only person to ask. Perhaps the founder would be willing to train her in the use of the staff in order to prevent further disaster.

Well then. So much for sitting and waiting for the bad things to come to her.

The moon had not yet risen when Reginn Eiklund slipped from her suite in the House of Elders, padded down the common hallway, out the front door, and into the lush night air.

The guards posted on either side of the door nodded to her and murmured, "Highest." They were used to her comings and goings at odd hours. No doubt the sighting would be included in their duty report.

It didn't matter. She was an elder now, and not subject to curfews or answering to guards.

Reginn crossed the hushed quad, her staff lighting her way, like a star traveling a dark path. As the Memory Tree came into view, she paused, squinting in disbelief. The tree appeared to be in bloom, swathed in a haze of purple.

Ash flowers *were* purple, but really not that showy. And it was too early for an ash to be blooming anyway.

Reginn kept walking, and as she drew closer, she realized that the tree was covered with elderflowers. She wondered if they had been tied there. She approached one of the branches that hung close to the ground and fingered the clusters of flowers hanging from it.

No. They were growing from the tree–some still in bud, and some fully open. On impulse, she plucked one of the elderflowers and pinned it to her overdress.

Who would have done this? Who *could* have done this?

The only person to come to mind was Shelby. But that seemed unlikely. Last she heard, he was in Vesthavn, teasing giant oaks from the ground to supply the shipyards.

Who else, then? Who besides the bondi would honor the keeper in this way?

It was Brenna–it must have been. Honoring the mortal she'd loved.

"Beautiful, isn't it?"

Reginn spun around, heart pounding.

It was Tyra, dressed in black edged with sapphire blue, an elderflower orchid pinned to her shoulder.

"Kennari!" Reginn said, trying to catch her breath. "I am surprised to see you out so late."

"I could say the same thing to you," Tyra said, "but I know you are a creature that loves the night."

Eager to change the subject, Reginn waved her hand, taking in the canopy above. "It *is* beautiful," she said. "I've never seen anything like it. Has it happened before?"

Tyra shook her head. "Never. It looks to me like a tribute to Amma Inger."

"Who has the power to do something like this?"

"Who, indeed?" Tyra said. She took Reginn's arm. Firmly. "Come. Let us pay our respects. It's time we had a talk."

They descended the steps together, into the cool damp of the caverns lined by the roots of the great tree.

Here was the familiar space before Brenna's tomb, where Reginn had sung herself hoarse, trying to engage the founder. And finally succeeding.

Tyra sat on the low bench facing the tomb, motioning for Reginn to take a seat beside her. The large garnet ring on the middle finger of her left hand glittered in the torchlight.

The ring the keeper used to wear.

Reginn sat, her staff clenched between her knees. She closed her right hand, to hide Trude's key. She wondered if Brenna was listening.

That's when she noticed that the inscription on the stone had changed.

Beneath Brenna's name, lines had been added.

Inger Lund, the Keeper of Brenna's Heart

Be at peace.

How could the change have been made so soon?

Tyra followed her gaze. "Yes," she said. "Amma Inger was the most faithful servant the founder ever had. In this time of heartbreak and tragedy, I hope she has found the peace that she deserves."

Reginn groped for an answer. Certainly, the bodies of the council and the keeper had been disposed of quickly, as was the custom. The council members burned together in the temple grove, with no mourners in attendance, but the keeper's pyre was tended by volunteers from all over Eimyrja, who kept it going for three straight days.

When Reginn said nothing, Tyra continued. "The rest of us must move forward. The best way to honor their memory is to protect the sanctuary they built together and take revenge on those who shed blood on this hallowed ground." She took a breath. "And, yet, the Asgardian still lives."

Tyra paused, as if awaiting a response, but Reginn had none to give. She was learning that if she never said what she was thinking, Tyra would tell her what it should be.

It's been centuries since a student challenged her, Reginn thought.

"The good news is that Heidin is here to lead us."

"What a blessing that your dottir has come home," Reginn said.

"Yes," Tyra said. "Now. Tell me about the day you rescued Heidin."

Reginn wet her lips, acutely conscious of who might be listening. "I think you know most of the story already."

"Humor me," Tyra said. "I've only heard it piecemeal."

That's the way I like it, Reginn thought. That makes it easier to hide the gaps.

Still, Reginn was used to lying on the fly. "Well, as usual, I was trying to persuade the founder to respond to my questions and allow me into the tomb. I'd been working on that for months, with no response. But on that day, she seemed especially distracted."

"How could you tell she was distracted, if she never responded?"

Reginn breathed in. Breathed out. Tread carefully. This is not your typical alehouse audience.

"Although she hadn't spoken, up to then, I'd begun to feel a consciousness, a presence. That was the only thing that kept me going sometimes."

Tyra sat cross-legged now, resting her chin on her laced fingers, head tilted slightly sideways, like a child eager to hear more.

She was so young, and yet–so very, very old.

She was so beautiful–and yet so ugly under the skin.

"So," Tyra prompted, "the founder was distracted."

"I could feel the–the rage and chaos within the tomb, and the founder's growing agitation, as if something was wrong."

Reginn had made that part up, but now she felt it for real–a tidal wave of anger under stone. She pressed her back against the bench, wishing she could crouch behind it.

"And then–?" Tyra said impatiently.

"And then she spoke to me."

"The founder spoke to you?" Tyra breathed, captivated. "That's what I've hoped for. How did you know that it was really her?"

"I had no reason to think it was anyone else."

Tyra nodded. "That makes sense. Go on. What did she say?"

"She said, 'Dottir, hurry. They are killing her. You must stop them.'"

Liar.

Brenna's voice rang out like a bell, causing Reginn to flinch.

"Killing who?" Tyra whispered. She obviously hadn't heard.

"Well, I didn't know who she meant, but then the tomb opened."

"That must have been frightening."

The ground trembled beneath them. Soil sifted down from around the roots of the Memory Tree. Death berries fell from the vines overhead, bouncing across the stone floor.

Tyra didn't notice.

"I *was* afraid, but the founder motioned me forward. And so I–"

"You *saw* her? You saw Brenna Wayfinder?"

"Oh. No. That was–that was just a figure of speech. She urged me forward." Reginn was usually a talented liar, but it was hard to concentrate while being pelted with pebbles, with fissures opening at her feet.

"What was it like–inside?"

Reginn swallowed. "There were bones," she said. "And, um, rats. There was a large room with bins of weapons and spinner staffs."

"Did you see any runes?" Tyra said.

"I didn't have a lot of time to look, because then I heard screaming."

"By the Lady," Tyra swore.

"Brenna said, 'Hurry, or you'll be too late!' And so I scooped up the nearest staff and set off running toward the sound."

Tyra gestured toward Reginn's staff. "And that is the one you chose?"

Reginn nodded. "I can't say I chose carefully, but this is it."

"It bears a striking resemblance to the one the founder brought from Muckleholm when she first arrived in these islands."

"Really?" Reginn pretended to study the staff, tracing its twisted iron frame with her fingers. "It's not much to look at, but I was in need of a staff, and it seems to suit me well."

"It does, Counselor," Tyra said. "I'm sorry that I keep interrupting you with questions. Please, go on."

"The screaming continued, and the founder was shouting at me to hurry, so I ran forward–"

Liar.

Reginn broke off and looked around. "Did you hear something? A voice?"

Tyra shook her head, brushing dirt from the bench. "The tree shifts sometimes, when it's windy. We should have the stonemasons reinforce the foundation."

Reginn was in too far to stop now. She shook dirt and death berries from her hair, hunched her shoulders against further attack, and went on. "By the time I found Lady Heidin, she was already injured and the demon was holding off a pack of wild boars."

"The demon?" Tyra said, confused. "Oh. You mean Asger Eldr." She paused. "You don't trust him."

"I have no reason to trust him."

"Do you think he poses a danger to Heidin?"

A dark spirit within her wanted to say, *Yes! Banish him immediately.* Or, *Ask him to meet Grima in the courtyard. That would be an interesting matchup.*

"Dottir?" Tyra said. "I asked if he–"

"No," Reginn said. "They–ah–seem to have come to an understanding. It depends on how long their interests continue to coincide."

The floor seemed to shift beneath her feet so that she all but slid from the bench. Now larger stones were falling. It might have been Reginn's imagination, but it appeared as if the stone face of the founder's tomb was bowing outward.

The air was suddenly too thick to breathe.

"Forgive me, Kennari," Reginn gasped, surging to her feet, "but I have to get out of here."

She raced up the steps from the crypt, stumbling, nearly falling, until she burst into the fresh air. She sat, then, leaning back against the trunk of the tree, heart pounding, the founder's staff lying next to her.

A few minutes later, she heard Tyra's light tread on the steps. The glow from her staff leaked through the open doorway, and then her teacher emerged herself.

Tyra sat down beside her, draping an arm over her shoulders.

"I'm sorry," Reginn whispered. "I never expected that to happen."

Which was certainly true.

"I don't want you to think I'm a weakling–I'm not," Reginn said. "It's just–it all came rushing back to me. And I've never been good with tight places."

"I'm so sorry to have put you through this," Tyra said. "I should have known better. The experience you've had would make anyone claustrophobic. I just . . . felt the need to know the details."

"It's all right," Reginn said. "There's not much more to tell." She'd already decided not to mention the aurochs. "So after we drove off the beasts, we carried Lady Heidin to Brenna's House. Fortunately, Bryn was there, and we treated her wounds." Reginn paused. "Your dottir is strong. Her wounds have healed unusually fast."

Tyra nodded. "She will need all her strength to survive the days ahead. I am sorry that the arrival of my dottir and preparations for war have prevented me from devoting as much time to your training as I would like."

"That is understandable, Kennari," Reginn murmured. "There is so much to do."

"The important thing is, you've been into the tomb and returned alive. Do you think you can do it again?"

Reginn sighed. "To be honest," she said, which is what a person says when they are not being honest at all, "I don't know how it was that I was able to enter after failing so many times before. I believe it was because the founder knew that Heidin was in danger and acted to save her."

Tyra appeared to be charmed by that notion. "That must be it," she said.

Reginn killed the charm right away. "Unfortunately, I've attempted to enter the tomb several times since, without success."

The smile faded from Tyra's face. "Well," she said. "You'll just have to keep trying. Perhaps the three of us can return to the tomb together."

Well, that's a terrible idea.

"As you wish, Highest."

"One more thing," Tyra said, lowering her voice as if the dead might hear. "I know that my dottir has been exerting considerable pressure on you to find a way to cure the Asgardian."

"You mean her brodir?" Reginn couldn't help saying. *That Asgardian?*

Tyra nodded, seeming unaware of the prick of the blade. "I worry that he presents a danger to everyone in New Jotunheim, but especially to Heidin."

"He's never harmed her or threatened to do so," Reginn said. "She loves and trusts him."

"That is precisely why he presents such a threat," Tyra said. "I have not been able to convince her to be careful. She should never have been allowed to form an attachment to him. In fact, she should never have been allowed to mingle with the people of the Archipelago. It will make it difficult for her to do what she has to do."

"Are you talking about the war?"

"Among other things," Tyra said vaguely.

"And, yet, at one time, you had a connection to Eiric's fadir," Reginn said.

"I did what I had to do," Tyra said. "As I always have done. If coupling with a barbarian was the price to birth a dottir like Heidin, I was willing to pay it."

"I see," Reginn said. "It seems to me that mingling with the people of the Archipelago can cut both ways, depending on what you experience there. You and I left the Archipelago holding a grudge. From what I hear, Heidin experienced some of the same things we did. She harbors no illusions about Muckleholm."

Tyra was studying her, head cocked, in the way she had. "You are different from the others," she said. "Stronger, more streetwise. You, too, are a survivor. That is why I named you my counselor. I will need a strong, savvy partner in the days ahead."

"You give me too much credit," Reginn said.

"Heidin will need a little time to get to where she needs to be," Tyra said. "In the meantime, there are tasks that you can do that she cannot."

Maybe dangerous tasks, too risky for Heidin.

"Of course, Kennari," Reginn said warily. "I will do what I can to help."

"Good," Tyra said. "It's time you had a broader view of what's going on. I'll be returning to Ithavoll next week. I want you to come with me and review our facilities there. Sistkyn Durinn is commander of our army. I would like your opinion on how preparations are going and what can be improved. I believe Durinn has some questions for you about Muckleholm."

Skita.

Reginn was reluctant to leave Eiric unprotected while she was gone, especially since it was likely that Heidin would be away as well.

"Thank you, Kennari," Reginn said. "How long do you expect I'll be away?"

"It should be no longer than a fortnight," Tyra said.

“I’ve been eager to see Ithavoll,” Reginn said, trying her best to look eager, “only–I wonder if this is good timing. I’ve been hoping to reestablish communication with the founder, and–with both of us gone, there will be no one to tend to Eiric.”

Tyra laughed. “I know you’re eager to return to the catacombs,” she said. “The Asgardian can wait. This war cannot.” Reaching into her carry pouch, she produced a small, corked bottle. “Keep this hidden and safe,” she said, putting it into Reginn’s hands and closing her fingers around it. “When the time comes, I will tell you what to do.”

3

THIRD TIME LUCKY

EIRIC WOKE IN THE DARK, gripped by many hands, feeling the burn of ropes at his wrists and ankles. He bucked and struggled, heaving some of his assailants off him, but others crowded in. His knees connected with a bearded chin with a satisfying crunch. He bit down on someone's ear and blood spattered over Eiric's face, but the man ripped free, cursing. They stuffed his mouth with rags, pulled a bag over his head, wrapped him tightly in blankets and strapped him to a plank like a baby on a carry board. With considerable effort, he could wiggle his toes. That was it.

He was lifted and carried up a twisting staircase. He breathed out the stale, damp air of the prison and breathed in the scent of the forest. He could hear the clatter of branches overhead and twigs cracking beneath the feet of his abductors. He could smell the scent of the ancient wood–sap rising, decay, the living above and the dead beneath. Somewhere ahead, he heard the sound of the sea crashing against stone. It grew louder and louder, and that's when he knew that he was being carried to the edge of the cliffs overlooking the sea.

Eiric could guess how it would go. He would end up broken on the rocks at the foot of the cliffs, with no one the wiser. That was the one argument that nobody could answer. At long last he was returning to the sea.

Did Liv know? Had she approved it? If she had, who could blame her? It would simplify her life in a big way.

Still, he held on to the hope that she didn't know, that she hadn't given up on him. That she might seek revenge when she found out.

After all that, they did not pitch him into the sea. Instead, they turned away from the clifftop and into a building, the walls muffling the wind and the sounds of the sea. Huffing and puffing and cursing under his weight, they climbed several flights of steps. He heard the rattle of a key in a lock, metal scraping on stone. Finally, they deposited him on a sleeping bench and left, locking the door behind them.

After that, for what seemed like a long time, nobody came. Finally, the caregiver, Sibba, came and cut away the ropes, removed the hood and gag, and chafed his wrists and ankles so the blood returned.

After that, there was no one but Sibba. She returned several times a day, bringing him food and drink and taking away the used chamber pot.

That was when he began to mend. Gradually, the dreams came less frequently, and his mind cleared. He began to take more interest in his surroundings.

This cell was larger than before, with a window overlooking the sea, though too small to force his shoulders through. At least he could see the horizon, hear the sea crashing on the rocks far below, and smell it, and taste it on his tongue. So near, and yet unreachable.

Slowly, Sibba seemed to gain confidence that she could safely turn her back on Eiric without risk of attack. One day, along with the nattmal, she brought him a bundle of clothing and a stick hanging from a chain. It was about the length of his middle finger with symbols carved and painted into the wood. He turned it in his hands, running his fingers over the symbols there. Familiar. "Where did you get this?" he said.

"Elder Reginn sent it," Sibba said. "She said it might help you."

"Reginn," Eiric whispered, a few gaps in his memory closing. Memories of healing. Magic. Kisses. A demon.

A demon?

"But . . . I thought the elders were dead," Eiric said. "I killed the council. Right?"

Sibba hesitated, as if afraid of revealing something she shouldn't. "Yes," she said. "She's a member of the new council."

They didn't waste any time, Eiric thought. He let the chain run through his fingers, then held up the runestick. "This was mine–wasn't it?"

Sibba shook her head. "I don't know."

Eiric dropped the chain over his head. The runestick lay against the skin of his chest, thrumming with power, picking apart his tangled thoughts. "But there was more–wasn't there?"

"I don't know, Highest."

Eiric rummaged through memory. "There was a pendant, too. And weapons–a sword and an axe."

"It's possible," Sibba said, her voice gaining an edge. "I just don't know."

"Where is this Elder Reginn now?"

"Nearly everyone is on Ithavoll, preparing for war."

"Who are they fighting? Ithavollians?"

"Barbarians," Sibba said.

Eiric thought about this a bit. As far as he knew, he was the only barbarian around. "Why am I still alive?"

Sibba was beginning to look as if she would prefer to go back to the prisoner who couldn't put a sentence together.

"Well. I don't know for sure." Then, taking pity on him, said, "I think it was Lady Heidin. She won't give you up. When she returns, I know she'll be glad to see that you are better."

"Why did they move me?" Eiric asked, adding quickly, "If you know."

She hesitated. "I believe that Elder Reginn thought you would be safer here while she was gone."

"Safer from who?"

Sibba shrugged. "You'll have to ask her. But nobody is supposed to know that you're here."

"Do you know when she'll be back?"

Sibba shook her head. "Soon, I hope." As if eager to change the subject, she thrust the bundle of clothing at him. "I brought you some fresh clothes. Would you like to bathe before you put these on?"

Eiric rubbed his bristled chin. "Is that possible?" He'd hoped that he wouldn't die stinking. Even a basin and rag would be helpful.

Sibba crossed to a small alcove next to the hearth. Drawing a key from a pouch that hung from a cord around her neck, she dropped to her knees and unlocked a large wooden hatch set into the floor. She lifted it to reveal a small pool, already filled with steaming water. She set a piece of rough soap next to it.

Eiric knelt on the stone floor next to the tub, breathing in the scent of sulfur. He'd caught whiffs of sulfur before now but hadn't located the source. He tested the temperature with his hand, then shook his head in wonder. "What kind of magic is this?"

Sibba smiled. "There's a hot water spring beneath the foundation that flows into the sea. The founder diverted some of the water to serve this building."

"Pretty fancy for a prison," Eiric said.

"I don't believe it was a prison originally," Sibba said. "I think it was used as a school building." After a beat, she said, "Do you need help with your clothes?"

He shook his head. "I'll manage." He stripped off everything but the runestick and eased into the water.

She watched with no trace of embarrassment. "I've never seen anyone heal so quickly."

"Everything but this," Eiric said, tapping his head.

"Even that seems to be improving now." She stood. "Will you need anything else?"

"This is fine," he said. "And thank you for having the courage to talk to me."

He waited until she left, then worked the soap into a lather and scrubbed it into his hair. When he'd attended to every part of his body, he lay back, his head resting on the pile of clothes, and soaked.

He felt better on the outside, but the hollow inside him seemed impossible to fill. Every memory that surfaced represented loss. His weapons were gone, the sunstone was gone, the pendant he'd inherited from his fadir, Leif, was gone. All he had left was a bad headache, crushing remorse, a new set of clothes, and too many questions.

And the runestick. He touched it like a talisman. Liv was still protecting him. Reginn was healing him.

Once again, Eiric had women looking out for him. But how long could Liv afford to speak up for a brodir so unpredictable and dangerous he had to be locked up?

And, once again, he heard Bjorn's voice in his head–something he hadn't heard in a while.

A man cannot choose his fate–that is determined at birth. But he can choose how he meets it.

Well then. His body had never failed him, and his mind was clearer than it had been since the night in the Lundhof. Give him a weapon–any weapon–and an opportunity, and soon he'd be in a position to look out for himself.

4
ITHAVOLL

WHEN REGINN SAW THAT THE visit to Ithavoll could not be avoided, she had persuaded Heidin to arrange to move Eiric to a new lockup in a secret location so that he could be kept safe while they were gone. The only person who would interact with him would be Sibba, who seemed to know how to keep a secret.

Reginn still worried that this plan might provide an alibi for Tyra and an opening for an attempt on Eiric's life. Grima wasn't on Ithavoll–she often disappeared for months at a time.

Tyra's bottle was a weight in Reginn's carry bag. Naturally, she'd opened it at the first opportunity. It contained a thick red syrup that smelled of cherries. She recalled what Tyra had said in the catacombs, when she'd warned her away from the mourner's tears.

Sometimes poisons are useful.

How could one man make so many enemies during his short time in New Jotunheim?

Eiric Halvorsen cut a wide path, wherever he went.

The kennari had asked Katia to show Reginn around Ithavoll.

Katia was a good and chatty guide, full of information. By the end of Reginn's time there, she'd been to the iron furnaces, where sweating men and women loaded charcoal, iron ore, and limestone into stone chimneys, tapping molten iron from the bottom of the shaft onto the cooling floors, where other workers with pickaxes broke it into bars.

They'd moved on to the foundry, where the bar iron was melted and poured into molds for weapons, wheels, and other uses, or processed further into steel.

In the horse barns, Stian's team was hard at work, training young horses to submit to saddle and exposing them to some of the sights and sounds they might encounter on the battlefield.

"I'm so glad you're here," Stian said, several times. "I'm so glad you're with us."

Why? Reginn thought. Why are you glad? What do you know that I don't?

She'd spent a day in Eira's workshop, where adepts and bondi created magical tools and weapons under the elder's direction. Eira seemed pleased to share her work with the kennari's counselor, though she was constantly besieged with questions and requests from those she supervised.

Many of the items were unfamiliar to Reginn. In one locked shop, workers wearing heavy clothing and thick gloves painted a dark substance onto arrow points, hanging the finished work in racks to dry.

"What's this?" Reginn said, picking up an arrow by the shaft.

"Be careful with that!" the fletcher said sharply, so that Reginn all but dropped it. "Make sure you don't touch the edge."

"Why? What is it?"

"A tiny scratch is painful enough to drive a man berserk," the fletcher said. "He'll be no good to anyone for days."

Reginn carefully returned it to the rack.

She picked up a bottle of a luminescent liquid that swirled and shimmered as she turned the vessel. "What's this?" she said, wondering if it was another kind of magical paint.

"That's Heidin's Fire," Eira said. "All but impossible to put out. The demon, Lord Eldr, assisted in the manufacture of it. The barbarians won't keep their advantage at sea for very long."

Reginn shuddered, recalling the night she was trapped aboard the burning skiff, forced to choose between drowning or burning. She wondered if that had given Asger the idea.

"Is someone building the ships you will need for the crossing?"

"Fortunately, I'm not in charge of that," Eira said, rolling her eyes. "It's difficult to find skilled shipbuilders, because there has been little need for them here, except for fishing inside the boundary. We've brought in some shipwrights from the islands, and we are hoping to recruit more in Barbaria."

And how will they be recruited? Reginn thought. As thralls, or bondi?

"We have been able to produce a large supply of kynstones," Eira said, reaching into a barrel and pulling one out. It hung, spinning, from a plain bronze chain. "We found a supply of the gemstone that the founder had stored on Ithavoll. The plan is that everyone deployed to Barbaria will have one, so that we can easily sort out enemies and friends."

"Could I see that?" Reginn said.

Eira dropped it into her hand. "These are crudely cut, compared to the originals, but they will serve the purpose."

The stone *was* rough-hewn, but it turned the same golden-amber color she was used to. The color that signified that she was different.

"Do you mind if I keep this?" Reginn said. "I've never had one."

Eira laughed. "Take two if you'd like. We have plenty."

So Reginn did, stowing them away.

"What we don't have enough of are sunstones," Eira said. "There are only three that we know of, plus one that is being used by our spies in Barbaria. We know we'll need more of them in order to move an army of this size."

"Oh!" Reginn said. "The thing is–" She stopped, reconsidered. "Is somebody working on that?"

"We have a team on it, but because both the wind wall and the sunstones were made by Brenna Wayfinder, we don't know if we'll be able to replicate them in time for sailing." Eira paused, and when Reginn asked no further questions, they moved on to another small studio that housed equipment for metalworking, woodworking, and gem-cutting.

"This is my space," Eira said, "though lately I haven't been able to spend much time here."

"What are you working on?"

"Mostly staffs," Eira said. "I either modify existing ones, or build new for those who have none." She paused. "I couldn't help noticing the one you carry. May I see it?"

Reginn extended it toward Eira, somewhat sheepishly. "It's very old. I haven't really cleaned it up."

Eira grasped the shank of it, then quickly let go. "It's telling me to back off," she said. "Curious."

But Reginn was no longer listening. She was distracted by something she saw on a nearby table that sent shudders through her.

It was a plain gold torc, apparently seamless.

"What's that?" she said, pointing.

"This?" Eira scooped it up. "It's a collar that collects magic from the wearer." She extended it toward Reginn, who flinched away.

"Why would you need something like that?" Reginn said.

Eira set it back down on the table, eyeing Reginn as if perplexed. "It's something Grima requested. She's been working in the Archipelago, locating the gifted and sending them here, before the coming war."

"Looks like a thrall collar to me," Reginn said.

"Oh! No!" Eira said, shaking her head. "This is just for everyone's safety, until the–ah–candidates can be evaluated. Then it comes off." Reading the suspicion in Reginn's eyes, she added, "Look, have you ever seen a thrall collar made of gold?"

"Yes," Reginn said. "Those are the worst."

* * *

Now Reginn and Katia sat their horses on a small rise overlooking the military complex at Ithavoll. Below, waves of soldiers clad in dun-colored tunics ebbed and flowed across the plain like a muddy sea.

"It's impressive, isn't it?" Katia said, as proud as if she'd recruited and trained them herself.

"I've never seen so many soldiers in one place," Reginn murmured, shifting uneasily in her saddle.

"And all equipped with the latest weapons, thanks to Elder Eira and her team." Seeing Reginn's expression, Katia leaned toward her and squeezed her shoulder. "Be at ease. I know you went through terrible things in the Archipelago, and you must be worried about the coming war. Modir Tyra thought you would find this reassuring."

"Oh, it is," Reginn said hastily. "Very reassuring. It's just . . . surprising . . . and impressive . . . to see so many soldiers, weapons, and military facilities that I didn't even know existed."

Even Reginn could tell that this was more than a defensive force, and it had not happened overnight. Someone had been making plans for a while. Now they were watching hundreds of soldiers on foot and on horseback engage in complex maneuvers.

"How long has this been going on?" Reginn said, sweeping her arm toward the deadly dance below.

"The council has been building this army for years," Katia said. "Modir Tyra has been heavily involved in training them, but she's been worried for a long time about their intentions. After the old council–ah–died, she spoke of disbanding the army, but, given the coming threat from Barbaria, decided that would be foolhardy. So. It is our hope that a tremendous show of force from the beginning will keep bloodshed to a minimum. Come on–I'll introduce you to Sistkyn Durinn, the commander." She heeled her horse forward, down the track to the drill field, with Reginn following after.

Durinn had been riding up and down the field, calling orders to the troops in the field, putting them through their paces. When they spotted Reginn and Katia descending the trail, they rode to meet them.

Durinn was a weather-beaten officer of uncertain age. Their fair hair was threaded with silver, their face broad and seamed from long days in the sun.

"Elder Katia," Durinn said. "I thought you said you wouldn't be back this week."

"Change of plans," Katia said. "This is Elder Reginn Lund, counselor to the kennari and our Lady Heidin. She is here to review our military preparations."

"Perhaps *review* is too strong a word, Commander," Reginn said. "I'm here to learn."

Katia waved that away. "We've already toured the barracks, the lockup, the horse barns and smithy, and the commissary."

"Welcome, Counselor," Durinn said. "I understand that you grew up in the Archipelago. I would like you to review our maps for accuracy, and advise us on possible points of vulnerability and a strategy of attack."

"Oh! Well, ah, I don't know how helpful I would be," Reginn said. "I can tell you a lot about the best alehouses and meaderies, where to find a privy in a pinch, and what streets to avoid after dark in every village in the Archipelago. I'm just not used to assessing defenses."

Then she rushed on. "But of course I will help in any way I can. Right now, I'd like to know more about your strategy, weapons, and like that."

Durinn seemed pleased at Reginn's interest. "Well—with Elder Katia's assistance, we can provide a demonstration of how our infantry and cavalry coordinate with the landvaettir. Would that be of interest to you?"

Katia pretended to scowl at Durinn. "I should have known you would put me to work."

"Oh!" Reginn said, recalling the faerylike creatures that had watched over her the first night she arrived at the Grove. "But I would love to see that."

Katia sighed. "All right. Let's do First Flight. I'll call the dreki while you give the troops a heads-up."

Dreki? Gooseflesh rose on the back of Reginn's neck. *Dragons?* When Katia had mentioned using the vaettir in the coming war, she'd imagined tiny, birdlike creatures doing reconnaissance, or message-carrying.

Maybe they were small, friendly dragons? Or maybe *dreki* meant something else in New Jotunheim?

Durinn walked back to where the army was gathered and spoke to some of the officers, gesturing toward Reginn and Katia.

Katia whistled, high and piercing. A moment later, two spots appeared against the setting sun, rapidly growing larger as they approached. Reginn squinted but was unable to make out details until they circled overhead and landed lightly just above them on the slope of the hill.

"*Those* are the landvaettir?" Reginn said, taking a step back.

"Amazing, aren't they?" Katia said.

They were dragons the size of longships, pale as wraiths, and just as terrifying, because they resembled the draugr—the undead.

Reginn breathed in the scent of sulfur as they both turned their heads toward her. Their eyes burned like coals set into their skulls, and they released a stream of smoke and flame with every breath through what appeared to be razor-sharp teeth. And yet their blue-white scales reminded Reginn of layers of sea ice that clattered as they moved.

Their scent reminded her of Asger. They eyed her in much the same hungry way.

Fire and ice. Life and death entwined.

Laughing, Katia waved away the fumes. "Breathe on somebody else, please. Neither one of us wants to smell like a foundry for the rest of the day."

Then something strange happened. Both of the dreki, still focused on Reginn, lowered their massive heads in a kind of bow.

"Well!" Katia said. "I've never seen them do that before. You don't happen to have a dead sheep under your coat, do you?"

Reginn shook her head, not sure she wanted the dragons' attention. "I did wash up after the dagmal, I really did."

But now Katia's attention was focused down the field, where Durinn was shouting orders to the assembled soldiers. They quickly formed a shield wall at the far end, facing the open field. The cavalry formed up behind the line, the horses snorting and rearing at the sight of the dreki.

"Now imagine that the enemy is lined up midfield, behind a shield wall of their own," Katia said. "This is how we plan to use the dreki to break the enemy lines before we engage, which we hope will save lives."

Whose lives? Reginn thought. And, then, to herself, *Whose side are you on?*

A question all but impossible to answer.

"Here we go," Katia said, sweeping her hand forward.

The dreki launched from the side of the hill, the slope allowing them to gain altitude quickly.

The dragons swept back and forth across the field, their flaming breath scorching the ground, every green and living thing shriveling under the blast.

Reginn was no military strategist, but even she could see that a shield wall was no defense against this.

The dreki made several more passes before Katia called them off. Sweeping low over their heads, they disappeared over the edge of the escarpment, leaving a faint trail of smoke in their wake.

Durinn's soldiers rushed forward, wielding their swords in a pantomime of battle, their boots smoking as they hit the still-smoldering ground.

"We had to redesign their boots so they wouldn't burn through while they finished off the survivors," Katia said.

"Good thinking," Reginn murmured, feeling a little queasy, imagining what it would be like to wither under that torrent of flame.

When they burn you . . .

The infantry parted, and the cavalry charged in, exploding through the smoke like the flaming horses that draw the sun across the sky.

When the demonstration was over, Durinn heeled their horse toward them, joining Reginn and Katia on their side of the field.

"You can see the idea," the commander said, "even if it's just a war game here. What do you think? Do you have any suggestions?"

They directed this at Reginn, who shook her head. It was as if they assumed Reginn must be skilled at fighting, coming as she did from a violent place. "I don't know much about battle strategy, but I cannot imagine any army standing up to that." After a pause, she continued, "Do you think all this is necessary? I've never seen more than a handful of soldiers in the Archipelago, and those were some jarl's personal guard drinking in the alehall."

"You saw the barbarian who slaughtered so many of our soldiers," Durinn said, their face grim. "If they're all like that, even a few are a threat."

I've never seen anyone like him, Reginn thought, before or since.

"Hopefully, the barbarians will surrender immediately and there will be no need for fighting," Katia said, reading Reginn's expression.

Turning to Durinn, she said, "Thank you, commander. I wish we had more time, but I promised to show the counselor the riftwall and the temple before we return to Eimyrja."

Durinn saluted and turned away. Reginn and Katia watched them ride toward the assembled troops.

"What's the matter, Reginn?" Katia said, once Durinn was out of earshot. "I know the dreki are intimidating, but they're on our side."

"I know, but . . ." Reginn lifted her shoulders, then dropped them with a sigh. She was not doing a good enough job of maintaining her performer's face. "All of a sudden I'm going to war against the only home I've ever known. There are barbarians on Muckleholm, but there are good people, too."

"Those good people are not at risk, I promise," Katia said. "They will be welcome in New Jotunheim."

Everyone has a role to play, whether spinner, slave, or sacrifice.

Fortunately, it wasn't far from the drill field to the rift. Reginn had seen the fault line from Mosifell when she'd first arrived on Eimyrja, but she'd never seen it up close. The scent of sulfur stung her nose long before they arrived. They had to fight their horses to get close.

Finally, they dismounted, tethered their horses, and continued on foot until they reached the low stone wall that ran along the cliff edge.

A sulfurous mist boiled up from below, setting Reginn's eyes to watering, making it difficult to get a good look. She took a step back from the edge.

Katia pointed across the abyss. "That is Vigrid, the site of the Last Battle of Ragnarok. We call it the deadlands these days. It is the final resting place of the gods, humans, beasts, and demons of the old world. They are said to be eager to return to the world of the living."

Vigrid appeared to be a rather unremarkable plateau that stretched into the distance. Yet as soon as Reginn laid eyes on it, she reeled backward, struck by a tidal wave of emotion–mingled grief, regret, and frustration, the memory of valor and cowardice, loyalty and betrayal, the shield-biting madness of battle.

Raise us, Aldrnari. . . .

She tripped over a root and ended up down on her backside with a bruised tailbone.

"Reginn!" Katia said, squatting next to her. "Are you all right? What happened?"

"It's the fumes," Reginn said, blotting her streaming eyes. "Is it always like this?"

Katia nodded, extending a firm hand to help her up. "Sometimes it's worse, depending on the way the wind blows."

"What's down there?" Reginn said.

"They call it the Elivagar," Katia said. "I guess it's named after one of the eleven frozen, venomous rivers in the sagas."

"That seems apt," Reginn said. "How do you get across?"

Katia shook her head. "We don't. Nobody goes there and survives."

"And yet–didn't you say that Halvorsen came from over there?"

"That's what he said, if he was telling the truth."

Reginn rubbed her forehead. "But if he didn't come from the deadlands, then how–?"

"By the time I arrived, he was standing right about here," Katia said with a flicker of irritation.

"I'm sorry to be so persistent," Reginn said. "The reason I'm curious is that Lady Heidin said that she had landed in the deadlands, too. I found her badly injured in the catacombs, but she doesn't remember how she got there."

"Maybe she was confused," Katia said. "Maybe her divine nature offered some protection."

"How did Halvorsen seem when you spoke with him here?" Reginn said. "Was he confused, disoriented, out of his head? Covered in blood?"

"Not at all," Katia said. "I was the first to speak with him. He said he was looking for his systir, that she'd been washed overboard in a storm." She smiled, remembering. "He was actually pretty funny. And charming. When we asked for his weapons, he gave them over.

Not willingly, but he did. He asked to go to the Lundhof and speak to Amma Inger."

"Did he?" Reginn murmured. "Did he say why?"

Katia shook her head. "Given what's happened, he must have planned to murder the keeper all along."

This was new. Reginn compared this account to the story Modir Tyra had told on the day of the "incident." Tyra had suggested that Eiric's time in the deadlands had driven him mad. But it sounded as if he'd been lucid when he arrived at Ithavoll.

"I appreciate your explaining that," Reginn said.

"Anyway, Captain Yrsa locked him in the guardhouse and sent a messenger to Elder Scarlet. It didn't seem right, so I went and told Modir Tyra right away. When she went to the elders, Scarlet wasn't there, and none of the other members knew anything about it. It seemed that Scarlet wanted to keep him to herself. The kennari got permission from the council to bring Halvorsen back to Eimyrja to stand before the full council.

"Shelby and I rode to Ithavoll with Modir Tyra to fetch him. When we arrived, he had already killed large numbers of our soldiers and was holding Elder Scarlet hostage." Katia paused. "To be fair, she'd taken him into the temple and tried to throw him in the rift." She pointed to the temple cantilevered over the edge of the cliff.

"Why would she do that?" Reginn asked, though she thought she knew. She'd seen the blodkyn rune carved into Eiric's flesh.

Katia gazed at her, eyes narrowed. Then said, "I guess we'll never know now." She gestured toward the horses. "We'll need to hurry if we want to make the crossing."

5
CONVERSATIONS IN LOCKUP

LIFE IN THE PRISON AT the cliffs settled into a routine. Sibba brought food several times a day. It was plentiful, and varied. Still, Eiric really missed eating torrfisk and porridge every day.

Actually, that part wasn't true.

Sometimes he would grip the iron bars on the seaward side, lean his forehead against the grate, and dream of fair winds and following seas and journeys to faraway places without spinners who twisted the threads of mind and memory into a tangle.

To be honest, having a clear mind made imprisonment worse.

On the opposite wall, a heavy iron door stood between him and the outer room, where Sibba slept. It had a small window with a slider that a person on the outside could open and speak to him or slide a meal through or see if he was up to any mischief.

He seemed to have the building to himself. Maybe this was the prison of no return, where you stayed until you crossed the boundary.

Then one night he awoke to the sound of activity next door—hushed voices, a rattling of chains, growled orders. Eiric found himself putting his ear to the wall to try to overhear the conversation. He couldn't make out much, but from the voice, the new prisoner might be a woman.

Where once the corridors had been silent, except for Sibba's comings and goings, now he could hear voices in the hallway, the tread of boots, and the sound of metal on metal as a meal was delivered to his new neighbor.

When Sibba brought Eiric's breakfast, he nodded toward the door.

"What's going on out there?"

Sibba set the food down on the small table by the window, turned, and rested her hip against the stone ledge. Her face was pale and drawn. "I wish Reginn were here," she said, voice trembling.

"Why? What's wrong?"

"Another prisoner was brought in last night and put in the cell next door. Now there are guards posted in the hallway day and night."

"Who's the prisoner?"

"That's just it–usually guards are loose-lipped, but nobody's saying. It must be somebody important. They're trying their best to keep it all quiet."

"Just like us," Eiric said, but received no smile in return. "Don't you think it's an honor to be in the very-important-prisoner lockup?"

Sibba chewed her lower lip. "I'm just afraid all this traffic will make it more likely they'll find out you're here."

"Do you know when Reginn will be back?"

"Soon, I hope. In the meantime, try not to draw the attention of the guards."

That very night, just as Eiric was trying to decide whether to sleep facing the wall or on his other side, the music began–a stringed instrument, skillfully played. It was coming through the window, from outside.

He rolled off the sleeping bench and crossed to the window. He wasn't sure what he expected–a small boat anchored offshore, with a band aboard? A kraken with a harp? But, of course, all he saw was the ocean, stretching to the horizon, the scalloped waves gilded by moonlight, foam rolling away from the foot of the cliffs.

The music was coming from the cell next door, the sound pouring out one window and into his.

When the prisoner began to sing, Eiric knew for sure that it was a woman.

One song followed another. Eiric sank to the floor and sat with his back to the wall, listening. The songs were mostly blood-stirring, pick-up-your-axe-and-fight songs, though there were a few put-down-your-axe-and-kiss-your-sweetheart songs, all of them sad. He sat, half dreaming, until, eventually, the sounds of the strings died away into silence.

By sitting on the window ledge, he managed to maneuver his head through the bars so that he could see the window of the next cell over.

"You play very well," he said, shouting out the window, hoping to be heard over the crash of the surf.

There was no reply.

"What kind of instrument is that?"

Still no answer.

"My name is Eiric Halvorsen," he said, before he remembered that he probably shouldn't be telling her that. "Why are you locked up?"

A head poked out of the window of the cell next door. It was a girl, fair hair peeking out of the scarf around her head. Her face was blackened and bruised, one eye nearly swollen shut, as if she'd taken a hard beating. Or several. She eyed him for a moment or two, then said, "My name is Naima Bondi. I killed someone."

"Me too," Eiric said.

"So I hear," she said. "You're the barbarian that killed the rest of the council."

"The rest of the council?"

"I killed Elder Skarde. The chair," she said. "You finished the job."

There, now, Eiric thought. We have something in common. Maybe we can be friends. Briefly.

"It looks like you've taken a beating," he said.

"They think I have accomplices that I will name. I do not."

"Are you one of the temple witches?" he asked. "A spinner?"

She snorted. "I'm a cook," she said. "A gifted cook, I guess you could say." She laughed, as if this was some kind of a private joke.

Eiric digested this. "Did you poison him, then?"

"Did I poison who?"

"The head of the council. Skarde."

"Men always think that poison is the only weapon a woman is capable of wielding," Naima snapped.

"I *know* better than that," Eiric growled, thinking of Liv. "I was just thinking, you know, a cook would be in a good position to–"

"I stabbed him," Naima said. "I aimed straight for the heart, pushed the blade in all the way to the hilt, and then twisted it for maximum damage." She paused, as if expecting a horrified reaction. Receiving none, she added, "Cooks always have the best knives."

All right, then. Good to know.

"Why did you kill him?"

"You first," she said. "You're a stranger here. Did the jarls in Barbaria really send you to kill the council?"

Eiric shook his head. "I came here to find out what happens to the children taken from the Archipelago."

Startlement flickered across Naima's face. This was not the answer she was expecting.

It wasn't the only reason, but after what he'd seen so far in New Jotunheim, it had elbowed to the front. And it sounded better than *I came as a sell-sword to pay off the blood price for killing my stepfadir.*

"What do you care?" she said.

"They're *children,*" Eiric said. "They're carried off, and never heard from again. We have no way of knowing if they are sold off as thralls or–or what."

Naima studied him through narrowed eyes. "And what have you learned so far?"

"I've learned that this place does not welcome uninvited visitors," he said.

She laughed. He could tell she didn't want to, but she did. "What exactly happened?"

Eiric explained how he'd been up for execution on Ithavoll, but Modir Tyra and two of the temple dedicates had intervened and brought him to the temple grove. "She gave me a room in the temple and said she would try and convince the council to spare my life." He paused. "After that, things get blurry. Tyra woke me from a sound sleep, saying that she'd failed to convince the council, that they were going to sacrifice me to the gods to assure victory in the coming war."

"Sacrifice . . . *you*?" Naima said, as if he would be a less than impressive gift. "Why you?"

"Why not offer up an unwanted visitor?" Eiric said. "Someone they already hold captive?"

"That's not much of a sacrifice," Naima said. "Someone you want to get rid of anyway."

She had a point, though Eiric couldn't claim to know the rules of blood sacrifice. "Well, anyway. A barbarian in the hand. They made do. Tyra hid my weapons in the temple, so when they took me there, I killed them."

"Nobody mourns the council," Naima said. Then, after a heartbeat of silence, her words came in a rush. "What I don't understand is why you would kill the keeper."

Eiric had asked himself the same question. Why would he go after an old woman on the say-so of a stranger?

"Modir Tyra told me that the keeper was a powerful sorceress who ruled New Jotunheim with an iron fist. That she was the greatest threat of all. That the oppression of the council wouldn't end while the keeper was alive."

"Modir Tyra told you to kill Amma Inger," Naima said, as if making sure she'd heard correctly.

Eiric nodded. "I tried. I went in to do it, but she started talking and I couldn't."

"She's dead," Naima pointed out.

"She killed herself," Eiric said.

"She stabbed herself with your sword?"

"No," Eiric said, confused. "She drank poison."

"She was found stabbed to death, your sword lying beside her." For a prisoner, Naima seemed to be extremely well-informed.

Eiric shook his head. "If that's true, would I be stupid enough to leave my sword behind?"

Naima shrugged, as if to say, *How do I know how stupid you are?*

A memory surfaced, like a bubble in a stagnant pond.

This sword is Gramr—given by Odin, won by Sigurth, mended by Regin of the dwarves, and used by Sigurd to slay the dragon Fafnir. Now it is yours. It brings good fortune to those who honor the gods.

When had he last seen Gramr? He just couldn't remember.

"No," Eiric said flatly. "I would never do that. That sword belonged to my fadir. It came with a story and a name."

"Well, however it happened, the matrona is gone," Naima said. "Every bondi in Eimyrja is in mourning. You'll find elderflower orchids pinned over every doorway in our neighborhoods. She was the only one who ever lifted a finger to protect us."

"Protect you from . . . ?"

"For a barbarian, you ask a lot of questions," Naima snapped.

"My grandfadir always taught me that was the way to learn," Eiric said. He tried to think of a more acceptable question. "The council tried to sacrifice me. Is that common here in New Jotunheim? Human sacrifice?"

"Yes," Naima said evenly, in a way that invited him to ask the obvious question.

"Who would they typically choose, then, if not prisoners?" Eiric said.

"Children," Naima said.

For a moment, Eiric thought that he had misheard. "Children? They sacrifice *children*?"

"Bondi children, and the children brought from the Archipelago. It's the secret everyone knows, but no one speaks aloud. Children disappear. Those whose gifts aren't viewed as valuable, so their only gift is their potential. The younger the better. To the council, they are worth more dead than alive."

That was the same thing they'd said about him.

He recalled what the keeper had said after he'd told her the council was dead.

I have never seen a more repulsive pack of hyenas in my life.

"Is that why you killed Skarde?" Eiric asked. "Because of the children?"

"Mainly," Naima said. "Not that it will do any good." The onshore wind teased a lock of hair free, and she brushed it out of her eyes. "Tyra calls you the Asgardian. Is there any truth to that?"

"Don't believe anything Tyra says," Eiric said.

"You must be good at fighting," she said. "Killing, anyway."

"There is more to a man than fighting and killing." It was as if Sylvi's voice was channeling through him.

"Is that so?" Naima said, cocking a skeptical brow. "For instance?"

"My fadir and grandfadir taught me to sail and navigate, how to train a horse to saddle, build a boat or a house, put meat on the table, and where to take shelter in a storm. What a man needs to survive." These were skills he'd always valued, but, spoken aloud, it didn't sound like much.

Eiric raked his fingers through his hair. "Here's what I don't understand–it sounds like killing the council was a good thing."

"Some would say that." Naima paused, then added, "*I* would say that, but my opinion doesn't carry much weight."

"So, if the council deserved killing, and Modir Tyra wanted me to kill the council, and I did, and now she's in charge, then why . . . ?"

"Then why are we locked up?" Naima cocked an eyebrow. "A very good question." She lowered her voice. "And why would she ask you to kill the keeper? The answer is that Modir Tyra has her own agenda that does not include having us walking around telling our story. If you want my advice, try to make her think you're still muddleheaded."

"I don't know how much longer I can play that game," Eiric said.

Naima studied him, as if debating whether to say more, and deciding against it.

"Do whatever you want," she said, turning away. "It won't make any difference to me. I'll be dead within a week."

6

REUNION

REGINN WAS GLAD TO BE out of the seething cauldron of Ithavoll—where it was impossible to ignore the fact that war was coming—and back in the familiar Hel of Eimyrja. She hoped to find that Eiric had improved in her absence.

Her room was on the ground level at one end of the House of Elders. She'd chosen it for its small, walled garden. She didn't know who had occupied this room before the slaughter in the temple. She'd scrubbed everything down, twice, and burned herbs to purify the air. Still, it would be a long time before she felt comfortable sleeping under that roof.

Brigida had filled a large tub with water and set out bathing supplies. Reginn dropped runestones into the water until it was steaming, stripped off the stinking blues she'd worn for three days, and scrubbed off a week's worth of sweat and grime. All the clothes she owned were dirty, save the ones she'd worn when she arrived at the Grove. They'd been cleaned and mended, so maybe they would do.

But when she opened her wardrobe, she discovered that her old clothes were gone, and several other garments had been added. There were three overdresses she hadn't seen before, all of heavy, rough-spun silk in vibrant colors—one blue and one purple, and one in a coppery red-orange.

There were also several new linen underdresses.

She fingered the silk, tempted. But should she be wearing new clothes when attending a patient?

If not, then when, exactly, should she be wearing them? In the dusty old library or the musty old crypt?

Reginn dropped one of the new underdresses over her head. It felt like a whisper against her skin. She followed with the sunset silk overdress, strapped her remedy belt over top, and finger-plaited her hair. Finally, she picked up her staff and her flute, armed for a certain kind of battle.

When Reginn left her room again, she heard the sounds of a party getting started in the back garden. Every night, a party. Katia had tried to persuade her to come, but she'd begged off, saying she had too much to do after being off-island for more than a week.

As she walked past the end of the elders building, she saw a shadow detach itself from the shrubbery path to the garden and pad silently after her. She was being followed.

Eiric would be safe only as long as nobody knew where he was housed.

Reginn made a sharp turn off the path and waited, knife in hand, until her stalker passed by. Then she stepped out behind and said loudly, "Hello!"

The figure visibly jumped and turned around.

"Grima!" Reginn said. "I didn't know it was you. Are you coming to the party?"

Grima looked her up and down, taking in Reginn's new clothes. "Actually, I–"

"Come on," Reginn said. "It'll be fun. We can walk in together."

She went to take Grima's arm, but the executioner flinched away. "I–ah–have something to take care of first. I'll be there later." She hurried away in the opposite direction.

This might mean that Grima had already taken advantage of Tyra's and Heidin's absence to access Eiric's old cell in the House of Elders. If so, she knew he'd been moved.

Out of an abundance of caution, Reginn walked back to the garden, passing through the throng of elders and guests. "Reginn!" Katia called from a crowded table. "I thought you couldn't come!"

"Just here for the wine," Reginn said, scooping a cup from a sideboard on her way out.

Heidin had claimed that Eiric had had no unsupervised visitors while imprisoned at the House of Elders, and that Tyra wouldn't dare harm him, but given Eiric's lack of progress, Reginn had her doubts. She was eager to see if he had improved in her absence. What if he was worse? One thing she knew–if anything had happened to Eiric since the move, Heidin would blame her for insisting on it.

Worse, Reginn would blame herself.

She'd had Eiric moved to an upper floor in the old academy building. It was a gutsy choice.

While it had once served as an overflow space for long-term prisoners, it was rarely used for that these days. Most wrongdoers were redeemed through mind magic and released, or executed after any useful information was wrung out of them.

The only prisoners housed here were the condemned, all on the first floor, an easy walk to the central courtyard where Grima carried out those executions with ruthless efficiency. Reginn could not forget Grima's eagerness to take Eiric's head off his shoulders and her visible disappointment when Heidin intervened.

Eiric's cell had once been used as a faculty office, so that it was actually a suite of two rooms–a larger room with a window overlooking the ocean, and a smaller front chamber that must have been a receptionist's or clerk's office. Reginn had arranged for a sleeping bench and washbasin in the outer room so that Sibba could have some rest and privacy. It provided a double layer of security against intruders in the corridor.

Before she left for Ithavoll, Reginn put out word that she was using the space to experiment on cadavers from the execution yard, trying to bring them back to life, dumping any remains off the cliffs and into the sea. Any screaming and shouting from the inner office would reinforce that story, and hopefully keep the curious away.

On this night, though, when Reginn reached the floor where Eiric was being held, she froze on the landing, swearing under her breath. Three guards stood watch in the corridor, one of them just outside the door to Eiric's cell. Inconvenient, at best, but it might signify something much worse. Gathering up her elder arrogance, she strode toward them.

"What are you doing here?" she demanded. "Didn't anyone tell you this floor is off-limits?"

"My pardon, Highest," the guard said, bowing. "But we're holding a prisoner here temporarily." He nodded toward the iron door next to Eiric's.

"Why is that?"

"It is rumored that there might be an attempt to break her out of the stronghold beneath the House of Elders. Elder Grima ordered that she be moved here."

Elder Grima. Reginn's heart skipped a beat, then accelerated. "Who's the prisoner?" she asked, though she already had a suspicion.

"Naima Bondi," the guard said. "She's the one who–"

"I've heard of her," Reginn said, thinking, *She's alive!*

She covered up her joy with irritation. "When I moved my workspace over here, I was told that at one time this building was used to hold overflow prisoners, but that the upper floors hadn't been needed for years. Now I come to find out that one of the most dangerous prisoners in the realm is being held next door to where I spend a good part of my days. How do you think that makes me feel?"

"I can only imagine, Highest," the guard said, his gaze shifting to her staff. Reginn read his expression as *A powerful sorceress is intimidated by a cook?*

"I am not worried about my own safety," Reginn snapped. "My

chief concern is that something may go amiss with my work, putting all of you at risk. The borderlands between this world and the next are a dangerous place. When you punch a hole in that boundary, there's no telling what might barge through. That's why I like to keep this area clear."

Now she had the guard's attention. He wet his lips and stole a glance at the door to Eiric's cell.

"How long will your prisoner be here?"

"Not long, Highest," the guard said. "I believe that her execution is planned for later this week, down in the courtyard."

"Is she in good health otherwise?" Reginn found herself asking.

The guard gave her the look that question deserved. "The prisoner has been undergoing intense interrogation. That takes a toll. Otherwise"–he shrugged–"she'll have no problem making it to the block."

Yes, Highest, the prisoner was doing well right up until her execution.

"Would it inconvenience you to take up your stations at either end of the corridor?" Reginn asked. "That will give you room to maneuver and time to react if anything happens."

"Of course, Highest." The guard bowed and turned away.

When Reginn opened the door to the outer office, Sibba was just inside. She had obviously been listening.

Reginn noticed that she wore an elderflower orchid pinned to her tunic.

"Welcome back!" Sibba said, and they embraced, Reginn being careful to avoid crushing the flower. "I am so glad to see you!" She took a step back, looking Reginn up and down, reaching out to touch the silk. "You're all dressed up."

"All my other clothes are dirty."

Taking Sibba's arm, Reginn walked her to the rear of the chamber, where they would be less likely to be heard by someone in the corridor. "So you already know," she said, gesturing toward the door.

Sibba nodded. "When I went out to fetch the dagmal yesterday morning, they were out there," she said. "They gave me a fright."

"Did they ask what you were doing here?"

Sibba nodded. "I told them that I was working on a project with you. When I asked why they were here, they gave me the same answer they gave you. I didn't know what to do."

"Have you heard anything from next door?"

Sibba shook her head. "Do you think they'll really execute her?"

Recalling what the guard had said, Reginn nodded. "Yes, I think it's highly likely they will execute her."

"Couldn't—would Lady Heidin intervene? I mean, she spoke up for her brodir."

"With everything that's going on, I suspect she might support a hard hand when it comes to putting down anything like a rebellion."

"Who said anything about a rebellion? She was saving a child."

Reginn sighed. "To people in power, killing a council member for any reason looks like rebellion."

"You're a council member," Sibba said, scowling. "Is that what you think?"

"Sibba," Reginn said, stung. She suspected that her fancy new clothes played a role in this. "I am the poorest excuse for a council member that you've ever seen. If anyone deserved killing, it was Skarde. If I had my way, Naima would be given a medal."

"But Eiric killed the rest of the council, and the keeper," Sibba said. "Yet nobody's talking about executing him."

"Oh, they are," Reginn said. "Just not in Lady Heidin's presence." She looked away from Sibba's disappointed expression. "Speaking of Eiric, has there been any change?"

Sibba blotted at her eyes with her sleeve. "Come and see for yourself," she said.

* * *

Eiric stared out the window, toying with the runestick, which had become a habit again. He hadn't heard anything more from the prisoner next door since the "concert" the night before. He'd leaned out the window and called to her once, but received no answer. He left it at that, not wanting to draw attention.

By now he'd grown used to hearing voices in the corridor outside, so he didn't realize at first that the voices he was hearing were in Sibba's quarters. When the door banged open, he swung around, reaching for a weapon that wasn't there.

Eiric recognized her immediately, despite the months and miles since their first and only real meeting, despite the fact that she was dressed very differently from the spakona gear she'd worn that night in Langvik. Her silk dress was the color of a sunset on a horizon he could never quite reach. It must have been made to measure, because it fit her small frame like a courtesan's glove.

Red sky at night, coaster's delight.

Her hair was plaited and entwined with fire lilies–Liv's favorite flower. Every spring, they bloomed on the hillsides above the sound–a signal that it was time to put the boats into the water for the coasting season.

She wore the familiar remedy belt slung low over her hips, but also carried a staff he'd never seen before. Unlike the elaborate jeweled staff Bjorn had left to Liv, this one was bent, twisted wrought iron, resembling one of the stunted trees along the coastline, battered and shaped by centuries of wind and spray. A chunk of raw amber glowed in the cage at the top.

Even more than before, she resembled the fine lady he'd once taken her to be.

He looked and looked, and only wished he could look harder.

Reginn ran her eyes over him in a deliberate way that set his heart to hammering. Probably just assessing him for new damage, but still.

"Halvorsen," she said finally, nodding, "you're looking much improved."

And Eiric Halvorsen, coaster, notorious pirate, heartbreaker of the Archipelago, could not manage a word to save his life. He might have been a fish, gasping on the beach.

Sibba had come in behind her, and Reginn turned back toward her. "Does he speak?" she whispered, as one might do with some mute elder relative.

"Yes," Sibba said, staring down at the floor, unimpressed by Reginn's attempt at humor. Eiric sensed a tension in her that hadn't been there before.

Maybe Reginn noticed it, too, because she turned back toward Sibba and touched her shoulder. "I can stay over tonight," she said. "Why don't you take a break from this place for a little while?"

"Are you sure?" Sibba said, looking from Reginn to Eiric.

Reginn nodded.

"As you wish, Highest." She backed out of the door, closing it behind her.

For a long moment, Eiric and Reginn stood looking at each other, breathing and yet breathless, their aloneness sucking all the air out of the room.

He cleared his throat. "Thank you for . . . all your kindness," he said. "I won't try to explain the things I've done. All I can say is, I'm sorry. I wouldn't blame you if you–" He broke off, startled, as Reginn's staff clattered to the floor.

She barreled forward and slammed into him, all but knocking him off his feet. He braced himself as she wrapped her arms around him as far as they could reach and buried her face in his shirt. He could feel her warm breath through the thin fabric. "I'm so glad you're still alive," she whispered.

That was the last thing he expected. He stood frozen, afraid to move. Maybe she didn't know.

"Didn't they tell you what I–?"

"Yes," she said. When she pulled back, he could see that her cheeks were wet with tears.

Eiric plowed on, like a farmer with one furrow. "It was as if–I was in a berserker trance, killing people who never did me any harm. I'm . . . I can't be sure it won't happen again."

"It was not your fault," Reginn said.

Whether it was true or not, it was good to hear. But–

"Still," he said. "You'd better keep your distance. I don't want to risk–"

"Oh, shut up," she said. "This is probably the least risky thing I've done all day." Standing on tiptoes, she laced her fingers around his neck, pulled his head down to her level, and kissed him.

Eventually, she broke it off and said, "I'm afraid I may be rusty. I haven't had much practice since Langvik."

He couldn't help himself. Cradling her face between his hands as if it were made from Frankian glass, he kissed her back, gently, carefully. Even so, it was the single best thing that had happened to him since he landed on Ithavoll. One tiny part of the cavern within him filled with gratitude. He had this, at least.

"I thought you were dead," he said, his voice thick, eyes stinging. "I saw the alehouse go up in flames, and I assumed . . ." His voice trailed off.

"Asger waited until I went out to the privy, then torched the inn, believing you were still inside. I let him continue to think that, so that he wouldn't go looking for you."

No wonder he was surprised to find me alive and well in Selvagr, captain of the ship he wanted to crew on.

Reginn picked up her staff, took Eiric's hand, and tugged him toward his sleeping bench. "We need to talk," she said. "Let's sit." Leaning the staff against the wall, she sat down on top of the bedclothes. He sat next to her.

Reginn kicked off her red boots. Then she stood again, unfastened her remedy belt and dropped it to the floor. She followed this by peeling off the red silk overdress and draping it over a chair.

Eric watched this with growing interest and some confusion.

Now clad only in a linen underdress, she sat next to him again, her hip touching his.

"That's better," she said. "I've grown impatient with uncomfortable clothes. Besides, I keep ruining them."

The underdress was light, loose, but he could see the form of her body underneath. The neckline was tied with a silk cord that invited untying.

The memory of the night in Langvik came boiling up–her sharp wit, her gentle hands, the feel of her lips on his, her body pressed against him, breasts, belly, hips–fingers in his hair. His body remembered what his mind forgot.

He remembered what she'd said to him when they parted.

Just know that this is the first time a man has touched me and it hasn't caused me pain.

It was like a gauntlet thrown down between them that he didn't dare pick up. There was just too great a chance he would hurt her.

He inched sideways, putting a little distance between them.

"You really should be more wary of me," he said, looking down at his hands, fingers laced to prevent them from getting into mischief. "At the best of times, I am undisciplined. I am used to taking what I want. And, now . . ." He shook his head, having no words to finish it.

"You'll fit right in here," Reginn said, as if murders were as common here as rats at the market.

"I'm confused," Eiric said. "This is supposed to be a paradise, right?"

"It is," Reginn said. "Look around. The weather is fine, and everyone has enough to eat." She pulled her knees up, wrapped her arms around them, and wriggled her bare toes. "Frankly, there is no one in New Jotunheim that either one of us can trust."

"Then why do you trust me?" Eiric said, trying to ignore the bare toes.

"Who says I do?"

Eiric laughed. "I deserved that." Then, moving on to safer ground, he said, "What about Liv? Shouldn't we trust her?"

Reginn rocked her hand. "You would know better than me."

Eiric sighed. "She's changing. One moment she's the systir I remember, and the next–she's a stranger. I don't know what to think."

"I believe she loves you and wants to protect you," Reginn said, "but she also wants a relationship with her modir."

"It's true, then? Tyra is Liv's–Heidin's–modir?"

"I know less about that than anybody, but they both seem to think so," Reginn said. "There's something else, though. Part of this story is missing. What happened between Tyra and your fadir?"

"I think we *know* what happened between Tyra and Leif," Eiric said. "One thing, anyway." He stopped, mortified to have brought up that topic in this charged atmosphere.

Good going, coaster. Is that all you are–lust in a pretty package?

He cleared his throat. "The keeper said that my grandfadir–Bjorn–and Leif sailed here a number of times."

"So you spoke with Amma Inger?" Reginn said.

"She said Leif couldn't–" He strained to remember. "She said Leif couldn't resist Tyra's mind magic, that she should have provided better supervision."

"And yet your fadir returned to Muckleholm?"

"My fadir never stayed more than a season with any woman, except my modir," Eiric said. "He left Sundgard every summer, but he always came back in the fall." He smiled. "I suppose my modir had a magic of her own."

"How old was Liv when she came to Muckleholm?"

"She was eight," Eiric said. "I was five."

"Why did your fadir go and fetch her?"

"Somehow, he or Bjorn must have learned that she was in danger. She was scarred when she came. It looked like she'd been badly burned, several times, but no one spoke about it. My fadir–" Eiric thought for a moment, netting memories from his murky mind. "My fadir said that her modir was dead, but Liv called that a lie and demanded to go back. She couldn't, though, because my modir took the sunstone that my fadir and grandfadir used to travel here."

"So it's true–you had a sunstone," Reginn said.

He nodded. "Later on, Liv told me that she never felt safe here at the Grove, that she was surrounded by enemies."

"So Liv didn't feel safe here, but, still, she wanted to come back," Reginn said thoughtfully.

"I had the idea she had unfinished business here. My systir has never been one to shrink from a fight."

"An eight-year-old had unfinished business?"

"Welcome to my family." Eiric rolled his eyes. "There is always unfinished business, grudges, and debts to be paid."

"How did you and Liv come to sail here?"

Eiric told her about the council's verdict, the jarl's intervention, and the service he required in return.

"So you *did* come on behalf of the jarl?" Reginn said, looking disappointed, as if her suspicions were confirmed.

"I came on behalf of keeping our farm and staying alive a little longer," Eiric said.

"Why was he interested in Eimyrja?"

"He said he was concerned about what the spinners wanted with the children they collected in the Archipelago," Eiric said. "Though he's also heard rumors about the treasures to be found here. He thinks our troubles at home might be due to a lack of magic. He's worried that magic is draining out of the Midlands and being hoarded over here."

"It didn't just 'drain' out," Reginn said, hackles rising. "It was driven out."

Eiric raised both hands, palms out. "It was driven out. Bear in mind that Rikhard has no love of magic–it's just a means to an end. What he's really hoping for is the return of the old gods."

"Is he now?" Reginn snorted. "Which gods?"

The question took Eiric by surprise. "I don't know–the usual. Thor and Odin, Freyja and that lot, I suppose."

"The gods of Asgard," she said, nodding, as if that confirmed something.

What other gods are there? Eiric thought.

"Oh, and he wants to be a king. I guess he thinks it will help to have the gods on his side."

"Is that all?" Reginn said dryly. "Ambitious, isn't he?"

"At least he knows what he wants," Eiric said, thinking that it seemed like he was doing all the talking. "Now you," he said. "Is it true the spinners kidnapped you from Langvik? That's the story Karlsen and Asger were pitching."

Reginn shook her head. "That's not true. Modir Tyra and Amma Inger saw me perform in Langvik. They offered me a place at the academy here. At first, I was afraid to accept, but the same night Asger tried to kill you, he murdered another friend of mine. It was just–it just tipped the balance. I just couldn't live like that anymore." She paused. "How did Asger talk himself onto your ship? You didn't recognize him from the inn?"

"He looked completely different," Eiric said. "He said he was someone else–a thrall named Thurston."

Reginn's face darkened. "That bastard," she whispered. "That *bastard*!"

Eiric waited, but if he expected an explanation, none was forthcoming.

"It wasn't until we were on our way to the Grove that he confessed who he was," he said. "That's when I finally figured out that Karlsen and Asger must be working together."

They both fell silent, each occupied with their own thoughts. When Eiric looked up, Reginn was gazing at him with mingled longing and regret. Like she was watching a ship, sailing away for good.

"What is it?" he said. "What's wrong?"

Reginn huffed out a breath, as if coming to a decision. "Nothing's wrong," she said. "I'm just tired of talking about Asger." She shifted onto her knees. "I could really use more practice at kissing." Planting her two hands on his chest, she pushed him flat. Then crawled forward until their faces aligned. "Is it all right if I kiss you?" she whispered, her breath warming his cheek. Without waiting for an answer, she covered his face and neck with kisses, each more incendiary than the last. Every few kisses, she whispered, "Was that all right? How about now?"

So much for self-discipline. Eiric's body had decided that it was fully recovered and ready for action. He drew her close, returning her kisses one for one. She rolled onto her back and pulled him on top of her so that he had to brace his weight on his knees so as not to crush her. Her hands slid under his clothing, exploring. He tugged at the cord at her neckline and whispered, "Is it all right if I–?"

"Yes," she said, helping him with the knot.

He slid the dress from her shoulders and down to her waist. She lay back on the rough bedlinen, flower petals scattered around her head like a crown. He planted kisses along her collarbone, then moved down, brushing his lips over her breasts, her rib cage to her belly. Her skin glowed like amber in the light from the lamps, each curve highlighted, each hollow a mystery to be explored.

He reached under her, tracing her spine with his fingertips until it reached the swell of her buttocks, his hands overlarge and rough against her skin.

As if awakening from a spell, he realized that she was fumbling with the cord on his breeches. He knew where this was going and it would be there in a heartbeat.

Gently, he gripped Reginn's hands, pulled them away from the ties, and enclosed them in his own. It was, possibly, the hardest thing he'd ever done. "What's going on?" he said.

She blinked at him, as if confused. She couldn't have been more confused than he was himself.

"What do you mean?"

"What's the hurry?"

For a long moment, Reginn was too flustered to speak, her cheeks stained with color. "Don't you want to?"

"Of course I want to," he growled. Shifting forward, he kissed her, long and fierce and deep. Kissed the hollow of her throat and buried his face between her breasts, felt the wild thump of her heart against his cheek.

Gently, she ran her fingers through his hair. "And, so?"

He propped up on his elbows, looking down at her. "Because there's something you're not telling me," he said. "Because this feels like good-bye."

Her stricken expression told him he'd hit on the truth. She closed her eyes, and tears seeped out from under her lashes.

He wiped them away with the edge of his thumb. "Tell me," he said. "Am I to be executed tomorrow?"

She opened her eyes, her wet lashes framing a well of despair. She reached up and caressed his cheek. "You need to leave New Jotunheim. If you stay here much longer, they will kill you."

7
DIGGING A HOLE IN THE OCEAN

TOVE OFTEN SAID THAT TRYING to persuade an obstinate person is like digging a hole in the ocean. Dig until you're too exhausted to dig any more, and when you stop, it will be as if you were never there.

Reginn expected that Eiric Halvorsen would resist the idea of leaving, that he would see it as running away from a fight. He did not disappoint.

"Why would I leave?" he said. "I've only just arrived."

She rolled her eyes. "How's your visit so far?"

"I must admit, the hospitality isn't what I'd hoped for, but I came without notice, after all." Eiric paused and, when Reginn said nothing, he continued. "I'd like to meet more people."

Reginn just gazed at him, lips pressed together.

"Who will kill me?" Eiric said, looking around as if the assassin might be lurking nearby.

"Everyone," Reginn said. "Or anyone. But Modir Tyra will be behind it."

"I'm not afraid of Tyra," Eiric said, his jaw set.

"No? Well, you should be."

"She won't take me by surprise again." He still sat astride her, still held her hands, but it was as if he'd forgotten what they were up to. Every time he shifted his weight, Reginn lost her train of thought.

Having given up on kissing for the moment, Reginn said, "If you insist on talking, then get off me. You are a very distracting person."

Eiric released her hands and rolled to the side. He slid back so that he was sitting next to her, hip still touching hers, his back propped against the wall. He was a person who took up a lot of room, and not just physically.

So close. So impossible to ignore. After weeks in lockup, he still carried the scent of blood and steel, mingled with the scent of the sea.

He was studying her, too, blue-green eyes narrowed, as if trying to read her thoughts. "You don't give me much credit," he said. "I can take care of myself." He grimaced. "Despite what you've seen so far."

Reginn tugged her underdress back into place, taking her time. "I give you credit for being smart enough to know when you are playing in a rigged game. Tyra is unlikely to come after you herself, at least not when you're clearheaded. She won't want Liv to know. It will be someone else, someone you think you can trust, or a person you have no reason to fear."

"Like you?" Eiric said, sliding her a look.

"At one time, maybe," Reginn said. "Probably not now. She doesn't seem eager to get into my head these days. Apparently, it is not a very friendly place." She put her hand on his thigh. Then removed it. "You should know that the only reason we are able to have this conversation is because Tyra doesn't know where you are. That could change at any time."

"Look, if Tyra is that powerful, that means Liv is in danger, too," Eiric said.

"Maybe," Reginn said. "But she's Tyra's daughter, and Tyra seems almost . . . deferential toward her. I'm still trying to figure out what's behind that."

"Naima told me that they're killing children," Eiric said.

Reginn's racing thoughts slammed into a wall. She twisted around to look at him. "Naima? You've seen her? You've spoken to her?"

"Briefly. Through the window last night. Is it true–about the children?"

Reginn sighed. "That's true." She stared down at her hands. "That's why Naima is in prison. She intervened."

"And you knew about this?" Eiric said, his voice rising, his expression mingled shock and disappointment. "You're *in* on this?"

"No, I am not *in* on this," Reginn snapped. Or was she? Could she have done more to put a stop to it? After all, Naima had acted, risked everything, and now she was facing execution. Naima was a cook. Reginn was counselor to the kennari and a member of the new council. Not only that, she seemed to have some resistance to Tyra's mind magic. What *had* she done?

She read that question in Eiric's face, and had no answer that she wanted to say aloud.

She'd kept her head down and her mouth shut because she was determined to survive. It was what she'd always done.

"Does Liv know?" Eiric asked, his voice cold and clipped. Then he shook his head. "No. I know Liv. She wouldn't allow that."

It was painfully obvious that he didn't have the same confidence in Reginn.

Why would he? He really doesn't know me that well.

Maybe he sees me more clearly than I see myself.

"I don't know what she knows," Reginn said. "I do know that there's an army on Ithavoll preparing to sail for the Archipelago. They've been told that you were sent here to assassinate the matrona and the Council of Elders in preparation for an invasion by the jarls."

Eiric stared at her. "What? But . . . why would they say that? It's not true."

"It's a good excuse for launching a war," Reginn said.

"But why would they want war with us? What do we have that they want?"

Reginn just looked at him without speaking until the confusion cleared from his face, replaced by revulsion. "The children," he breathed, as if he didn't want to be overheard by the gods who judge such things.

Reginn nodded. "But not all the children. The spinners are the descendants of the Jotun, the enemies of Asgard."

Eiric frowned. "The Jotun? I've heard of those. But weren't they monsters and giants and trolls?"

Reginn laughed. "Spoken like a true Asgardian, based on history handed down by supporters of that pantheon. The Jotun are just another tribe of gods. The Asgardians were always fighting them because they were competitors. Co-equals. According to the Jotun, every good thing Asgard has was stolen from them. Including magic, and the secrets of the runes."

Eiric seemed to be trying to organize his skeptical expression into something more positive. "So the Jotun survived and the gods—the Asgardian gods—are dead. They should be happy, then, right?"

"Some mixed-blood descendants of both Asgard and Jotunheim have survived," Reginn said. "Those who fell at Ragnarok—gods, humans, elves, trolls, and other monsters of all sorts—still lie on the battlefield at Vigrid. You must have crossed it on your way to the rift."

Eiric nodded. "I could tell that I was walking over graves, but it looked like the killing happened long ago. Most were buried by time and not by survivors."

"Asgardian tradition says the gods will rise again on Ithavoll. The wyrdspinners intend to make sure that does not happen. Tyra was born in the Archipelago and nurses a serious grudge against the people there. They intend to cleanse the Archipelago of their enemies and fuel their power with Asgardian blood."

Somehow, this was as surprising to Reginn as it must have been to Eiric. She'd had a growing awareness of a framework for future calamity, but had never articulated it this clearly until now.

"Everything you've said convinces me that I need to stay here and fight," Eiric said. "We need to talk to Liv and figure out how to put a stop to this."

Reginn cleared her throat, at a loss for how to frame this. "Are you sure that she wants to put a stop to it?"

Eiric stiffened, then turned his head to look at her, the glow from the lamp highlighting the planes and shadows of his face. "You're suggesting that my systir's planning a slaughter?"

Reginn shrugged. "You would know better than I do. Tell me–what was Liv's life like in Muckleholm? What does she have to go back to? Who would she want to save?"

"Well," Eiric said, "our brodir is waiting for us at Sundgard." After a pause, he added, "As for the rest, she'd just as soon drop them into the rift."

Reginn took hold of his calloused hands and faced him squarely. "My advice to you is to leave Eimyrja while you still can, cross to Ithavoll, find your ship, and sail back home. Tell anyone who will listen to prepare for an invasion."

"That's what the matrona told me to do," Eiric said, pain and regret tracking across his face.

"The matrona is–was–a wise woman," Reginn said. "It's not that I want the jarls to win. I hope that if the Jotun are met with strength, they will content themselves with paradise and go back home."

"How do you propose I cross the boundary without the sunstone?" Eiric said.

"That shouldn't be a problem," Reginn said.

"Oh, really?" Eiric lifted a skeptical eyebrow. "I just went through it *with* the sunstone. My crew was washed overboard, and we all but foundered. I'm not looking forward to doing it again."

"I believe the boundary is down."

"You believe?"

"The matrona was responsible for maintaining the boundary. Now she's dead. It stands to reason that the boundary is down."

"That's reassuring," Eiric said with a bitter smile. "What about you?

Will you run away to the Archipelago with me?" She could tell by his expression that he already knew the answer.

Reginn shook her head. "There are good people here. I owe it to them to stay and try to convince Liv that a war between the gods is always a bad idea–especially a war of extermination."

"You believe you'd have more success convincing my systir than I would."

"I believe so," Reginn said. "And I'm less likely to be killed in the meantime. The important thing is that you survive."

"My survival is not the important thing," Eiric said grimly.

"Maybe not, but you can't *do* the important thing if you're dead."

Maybe Eiric had the sense that he was losing this argument, because he changed the subject. "Do you consider yourself to be Jotun, then? Wouldn't that make us enemies?" Eiric was a person who'd come across a suspicious-looking snake and begin poking it with a stick to see if it would bite.

"Are you worried that maybe you're in bed with a monster?"

Eiric flushed and shifted his gaze away. "I didn't say that. I'm just trying to–"

"I don't know where I fit," Reginn said bluntly. "Look, Heidin and Tyra return from Ithavoll tomorrow. It would be best if you left tonight. There's just too much chance that Heidin will be followed and give your location away.

"We'll have the guards to deal with, but I think I can manage them without drawing attention to–" She broke off because Eiric was shaking his head, his jaw set stubbornly. "What?" she said, though she already knew what he would say.

"I will speak with my systir before I go anywhere," Eiric said. "All I know about what is going on here in Eimyrja is what Tyra has told me, and the keeper, and you. I have more reason to trust Liv than anyone else."

Reginn knew when she was beaten. “All right,” she said. “I'll ask Heidin to come see you. I'll warn you, though, that she will not willingly allow you to return to the Archipelago. She has no desire to meet you on the battlefield.”

“Who knows?” Eiric said. “If it comes down to a fight, maybe I'll be fighting on her side.”

8

LIV

THE NEXT MORNING, BEFORE EIRIC had even rolled from his sleeping bench, he heard a commotion in the corridor, followed by the rattle of metal as each door in turn was unlocked.

Eiric sat up, blinking the sleep from his eyes, raking his hand through his sleep-tumbled hair. What now? Had the day of his execution finally arrived?

The door opened and Liv swept in, impatiently waving away the guards who tried to follow her. "Leave us," she said, and they retreated, stumbling over themselves in their hurry.

"Heil, systir," Eiric said, pushing to his feet. He crossed the room to her and opened his arms to embrace her, but she took a quick step back, planting her staff between them. There was something new—something distant and untouchable about her.

"Heil, brodir," she said warily.

He dropped his arms to his sides. "It is good to see you," he said, making no further claim.

Liv gazed at him, cradling her staff in the crook of her arm. She looked spectacular. Her hair had been done up in braids and coils, and she wore a gold tiara set with amber along with her amulet. Her dress was of fine white linen shot through with gold silk threads, and she wore a cloak embroidered with crimson and gold feathers.

Firebird. Tyra had called her that.

"Elder Reginn says that you are much improved." There was a question in the statement.

"Aye," he said. "My mind is much clearer than before." After an awkward pause, he added, "You look . . . well. And prosperous. Eimyrja must agree with you."

She scowled, as if that observation irritated her. "I'm sorry I haven't been to visit," she said. "It's been busy. So much to do."

"Until a few days ago, it would have been a wasted visit," Eiric said.

She looked around his cell, crossed to the window, and took in the view. Then nodded and turned, resting her hip on the sill of the window.

"Are you well-fed? Comfortably housed?" As if those were her primary concerns.

"I am," Eiric said. "Thank you for asking."

Silence rose between them like a stagnant sea, its murky surface hiding history and secrets. He knew if he waited long enough, she would speak.

Liv had never been good with silence.

"So," she said, "the clothes seem to fit. They do good work here."

"Yes," Eiric said.

"I'll have some more sent over," Liv said. "And new socks and shoes."

"That seems like a waste," Eiric said. "It's unlikely I'll live long enough to wear these out."

"Stop feeling sorry for yourself!" Liv snapped. "You're lucky to be alive."

"I'm not complaining," Eiric said. "I'm just being practical. I've never had more than one set of clothes before."

"Those days are over, brodir."

"So it seems," Eiric said. "I am sorry about ruining your return to Eimyrja with a massacre."

"Quit apologizing," Liv snapped again. "Once is enough."

"For ruining a shirt, maybe, or breaking your favorite spindle, but–"

"Just stop it!"

Eiric gestured to one of the benches against the wall, as if he were the host of this hall. "Please. Sit. Can I get you anything?" He scooped up the bowl of fruit from the night before and peered into it. "I believe there are apples and–apples. I seem to have eaten all the cherries."

"I don't need anything," Liv said. "I ate less than an hour ago."

She sat. Reluctantly. She seemed unaccountably nervous, plucking at her overdress, settling her skirt around her knees.

Eiric pulled up another bench and sat opposite her. "Now. Tell me the news."

He knew it would remind her of Sundgard. Whenever she returned from one of her many forays into town, she would share the latest gossip with her less-than-sociable brodir.

Liv sighed, then looked him in the eyes. "We're preparing to fight back against the jarls," she said. "We plan to end their war against the gifted once and for all."

"What war?"

"Have you forgotten Emi? They burned her alive."

"That wasn't the jarls. That was our stepfadir's short-witted relatives who would set their own house on fire just to spite us."

"The gifted are suffering in the Archipelago."

"*Everyone* is suffering in the Archipelago," Eiric said.

Liv pressed her lips together but didn't reply.

"Despite what Tyra said, the jarls didn't send me here to assassinate people. Any killing I did, I did on my own." Eiric tossed out that spear, to see how it would land.

"I know that," Liv said.

"I didn't know anything about the place before I sailed, except that you were born here, and our fadir thought it was so dangerous that he brought you home with him to Muckleholm."

Liv said nothing.

"I told you what Rikhard wanted," Eiric said. "I was to find the Temple at the Grove, verify if the stories about Eimyrja were true, and find out what was happening to the children taken from the Archipelago."

"They were *saving* gifted children from the Archipelago," Liv said.

"Are you sure about that, Liv?"

"Heidin!" Liv said. "My name is Heidin."

"*Heidin,*" Eiric said. "I'm trying, but it's hard to unlearn the name I've used all my life."

"Work on it," Liv/Heidin said through gritted teeth.

"*Systir,* I am hearing that even the children here are disappearing."

Heidin frowned. "Disappearing? What are you talking about? Who told you that?"

Relief washed over him. *She doesn't know.*

And then panic. Who could he say had told him?

"I was speaking with the prisoner next door. Naima Bondi."

"No doubt a reliable source," Heidin said. "I do know that the council has done some despicable things these past few years. With the new council, and Modir Tyra as directress of the academy and the temple, we have put all that behind us."

"That's good to hear," Eiric said. "Still—is it really necessary to invade the Archipelago? It's not like this place is vulnerable to attacks. It would be impossible to get here without the sunstone. Even with the sunstone, it wasn't easy. It's unlikely that any other helmsman could have made it through." He threw out that little boast to see if she would dispute it.

"Oh, stop it, brodir. Counting Bjorn and Leif, you're the third. More will come."

"Not without cooperation from someone here. You told me yourself that no one would ever find Eimyrja without a sunstone."

"Stop arguing!" Liv practically shouted. "And call me Heidin."

"I did," Eiric said.

"You call me Liv in your head," she snarled. She stalked to the window and gazed out to the sea.

Eiric sighed. At Sundgard, he and his systir often disagreed, wielding their wits against one another. Their verbal sparring occasionally drew blood, but their common war against Sten had made them allies.

He knew from long experience that he was wasting his time. Liv had made up her mind, and prolonging the argument only irritated her.

After a moment, he came up beside her. "What do you want from me?"

"I want your support."

"You have it," Eiric said. "Always. You know that." He knew that there was an ask coming.

"I want you to fight for us," she said.

"Fight for you? Against who?" Eiric already knew, but he was going to make her say it.

"We are building a fleet of ships–the finest I've ever seen. I can't wait for you to see them. I want you to help train our crews in blue water sailing, and lead them to the Archipelago."

For a moment, Eiric allowed himself to savor that image. Eiric Halvorsen, at the tiller of a great ship, punching through ocean swells, spray flying, the sound of the oarsmen's chant.

He remembered lecturing Rikhard on the nature of leadership, that power was earned, not given by anyone other than those who chose to follow.

He'd been naive.

"Well, brodir?" Liv broke into his thoughts, impatient as always.

"You want me to fight Jarl Karlsen and his bannermen from Muckleholm."

"And anyone else who threatens our people."

"I am not one of your 'people.' Why would I fight for New Jotunheim? I'm usually not one to criticize the hospitality of strangers, but

I haven't felt particularly welcome here."

"You'd be fighting for me."

"I'd be surrounded by soldiers who call me a barbarian, who blame me for the death of hundreds of their comrades and a beloved old woman."

"They'll forget all that when they see what you can do."

"If I live that long. I think I'd be safer running off yonder cliff."

"Are you afraid, brodir?" Heidin stared out the window, the wind from the sea teasing her hair out of its bindings. "I've never known you to be afraid of a fight."

Eiric wasn't falling for that. "There is a difference between courage and foolhardiness. I'm not used to fighting in a crowd, and I'm not a sell-sword who fights for whoever offers the highest price."

"I will arrange for you to fight in whatever setting you prefer, with a hird of your choosing or none at all," Heidin said. Her voice dropped to a whisper. "But I need you with me. I am surrounded by enemies. You're the only one I can trust."

Eiric gripped her elbow, turned her to face him. "Then let's leave together. There is no reason we need to stay here. We'll fetch the sunstone, my sword and amulet. We can gather enough treasure to satisfy Rikhard on our way back to the ship. Or, if you like, we'll say nothing to Rikhard. We'll sail back to Sundgard, collect Ivar, and leave the farm behind. There's no reason to wait around for an invasion."

Maybe Reginn will come with us, he thought. *It's a big world.*

But Heidin was already shaking her head. "I can't leave. This is my destiny–the future the fates wove for me. This is what I was born for, to lead New Jotunheim into a new era."

"Is this what Tyra is telling you?" Eiric said, trying to keep his tone neutral.

"It's what I know. But–" She looked down at her amulet, ran her fingertips over the engraving, her expression mingled fear and fascination.

"Sometimes I feel like she's taking over. I need you to help me remember who I am."

"Who's taking over? Tyra?"

"Forget Tyra," Heidin snarled in a stranger's voice, glaring at him through a stranger's eyes. *"She is a useful tool, nothing more."*

Eiric took two steps back, raised his hands, palms out. "Systir?" he whispered, unsure what other name to call her.

And just like that, the stranger was gone. Liv stood, trembling, looking as frightened as he'd ever seen her.

He cleared his throat. "What was that?" he said.

"I'm just . . . really tired," she said. "Too tired to argue with you."

"Liv–Heidin–you are one of the strongest people I know," Eiric said. "If you really want an ally, then release me. Return my weapons so I can defend myself. Let me loose in New Jotunheim so I can ask questions, take a closer look at your military facilities, talk to faculty and students at the academy, and find out what goes on at the temple. I'll have a better idea if there are grounds for worry."

"There's no time for that," Heidin said. "Anyway, how would I know that you won't be collecting information for Rikhard?"

"Is my word not good enough?"

Heidin bit her lip, knowing that admitting that would be a mistake. So she changed the subject.

"You can't go back to the Archipelago."

"I have to. Our brodir is there–or have you forgotten? What will happen to him in an invasion?"

"I can't have you fighting for Rikhard."

"Who says I'll fight for Rikhard? Maybe I'll just go fishing."

"If there's a fight, you'll be in it," Liv/Heidin said. "The blood of the Aesir gods runs in your veins. It's your fate."

Eiric rolled his eyes. "So you're saying Odin Allfadir stopped by the farm when Leif was out coasting?"

He'd hoped to make his systir laugh, but she was serious as death. "Your blood heritage comes from Leif," she said. "That is why he was able to reach this island when no one else succeeded."

"What about you?" he said. "Whose blood do you carry?"

She looked at him with an expression of both pity and disbelief. "Do you really not know who I am?"

Eiric's patience had run out. "I'm sorry, but I really don't. You can't keep me locked up here forever. Either execute me or let me go."

"Don't force that choice, brodir," Heidin said, stalking toward the door. "I'll give you more time to think on it."

Eiric didn't know how much later it was that he awoke, startled, to find a tall figure standing over him–a silhouette in the light of the lamp.

He blinked, squinted. It was Tyra. She did not look happy.

"Is there nothing that can break that bond between you and my headstrong dottir?" she murmured with something like jealousy in her eyes.

Eiric said nothing.

"You remind me of your fadir, who was useful, until he wasn't."

Eiric said nothing.

Tyra shook her head as if dismissing that memory. "It doesn't matter. Heidin may have custody of your living body, as long as it lasts, but there's no coming back from where I'll send you."

She slammed the butt of her staff into the floor and set it spinning, catching the tattered threads of Eiric's consciousness, pulling them tighter and tighter until they snapped.

9
HONOREE

THE NEW COUNCIL MET FOR the first time in what had been Founder's Hall. It was an evening meeting, with food provided, so as not to interfere with the busy workday.

Reginn would have preferred to meet anywhere else. The hall swarmed with ghosts. Creepy Skarde, who wanted to provide "supervision" to the barbarian child from Muckleholm; Margareta, who'd treated her as an object of pity; and condescending Gisli, who'd made it clear that a performer from an alehall was unlikely to make any substantial contribution on Eimyrja.

Frodi, of course, who was never satisfied with being just a scholar, but hungered after more power and found a way to get it.

All of them, seeking to use her for their own ends, with no interest in who she was or what she could do.

And finally Amma Inger, who'd spoken up for Reginn when it was least expected and direly needed.

All of them dead now.

The room had been transformed since Reginn's interviews when she'd first arrived on Eimyrja. Gone were the massive oak table and burnished chairs that had looked down on petitioners from their high seat. Gone were the small tables around the perimeter where scribes took notes on the proceedings.

The dais was empty save for two thronelike chairs, neither one occupied.

On the floor of the hall stood a small, round table surrounded by comfortable chairs. The perimeter was lined with sideboards, piled high with platters and bowls of cheese, smoked fish, bread, and pastry.

When Reginn arrived, the other council members were helping themselves to food and drink, milling about, exchanging greetings, admiring each other's council garb. Like the old council, they'd shed their uniform temple clothing for finer, more creative regalia. It was unnerving.

Shelby wore blue silks that fit perfectly, accentuating his lithe body and contrasting with the green in his eyes. The wispy vaettir who fluttered around Katia's shoulders reflected back the jewel tones from her tunic and trousers. Even Bryn had stepped up with a change from his usual Brenna's House blues. He wore a navy blue coat with black fur trim.

She looked for Grima, but she wasn't there. Nor was Tyra.

Reginn brushed at her new coat–black, edged with sapphire wool, with blue glass buttons. She wore narrow black trousers underneath and black leather boots. They were beautifully made, well-fitted, but not fancy. She was dressed for work, not for showing off.

That's when Stian noticed her. "Look who's here," he said loudly. "Counselor Reginn."

Multiple conversations died as they all turned to look at her.

Heidin walked out onto the dais, finely dressed, the familiar staff in hand. Asger ghosted in behind her, keeping to the shadows, his glowing eyes the only sign that he was there.

"Reginn Lund, come forward," Heidin commanded.

Reginn's first impulse was to turn and flee, but the council members had formed a semicircle around Reginn, as if to prevent escape.

Why should your audience believe in you if you don't believe in yourself?

Reginn threw back her shoulders, lifted her chin, and strode down the aisle like any queen until she stood at the foot of the dais, facing Heidin. She tried to read her face, but she wore a solemn, stonelike expression.

Reginn dipped into a graceful curtsy. "Lady Heidin. I am sorry to keep you waiting." She saw movement out of the corner of her eye. It was Grima, slipping in late. Now the executioner stood to one side, dressed head to toe in black silk, with a black catskin hood and gloves.

Is this how it's done? Reginn thought, failure sitting like lead in the pit of her stomach. Would she be dismissed in front of everyone?

Or worse. Had Heidin discovered that she was encouraging Eiric to escape?

She thought of all the ribbons fluttering on the Memory Tree. Lives taken, not given.

"Reginn of the Oak Grove," Heidin said. "When I was under attack in the catacombs, I was a stranger, and yet you came to my aid, saving my life. Not only that, you tended my wounds and brought me to a place of safety so that I could reunite with my modir and assume my rightful place in New Jotunheim. I will never forget what you did for me."

Reginn stole a look at Asger, to see how he was reacting to the praise being heaped on his former thrall. He appeared to be bored. He was absently tossing a ball of flame from hand to hand.

"Finally," Heidin said, "you have been working hard to heal my brodir, and free him from the demons who now possess him."

That caused a bit of a stir. Reginn would have preferred that went unsaid. She glanced at Grima, who pretended indifference.

"And so," Heidin said, "Reginn Lund, for your service to me, and to New Jotunheim, now and in the future, we thank you. If the fates allow, we will write a new history together."

Reginn's eyes stung with tears, her heart full. The contrast between her expectations and reality was almost too much to take in.

"And, finally," Heidin said, "in gratitude for your service to me, I would grant you a boon."

"A boon?"

"What is your heart's desire? If it is within my power, I will grant it."

Reginn had no idea what might be appropriate. "Could you–could you give me an example?"

Heidin shrugged. "A favor, a privilege, a pardon, a horse, a keg of wine every Solstice, a home in the mountains? What would make you happy?"

Reginn was momentarily speechless. She wished she'd had some warning. Her head was still spinning, having whiplashed from worry about being expelled or executed to the relief of being praised and promoted.

She didn't want to be like one of those characters in stories who squander the wishes they're given and are out of luck when they're in a real fix.

Reginn raised her hand, palm out. "Just give me a moment. I–need a little time."

"It is wise to give this some thought," Heidin said, smiling. "A gift from the gods is not to be chosen lightly."

A gift from the gods? Reginn wasn't going to let this opportunity slide by and be forgotten.

Her first thought was to ask for freedom for the coaster Eiric Halvorsen and safe passage back home. But she knew that was a gift Heidin would not grant. She hoped to have her brodir fighting beside her in the coming war.

Failing that, she wouldn't want him fighting on the other side.

Besides, Tyra would do everything in her power to make sure that Eiric never got out alive.

It would help to have some parameters, Reginn thought. There was a lot of distance between asking for an armband to match your gold brooch and, say, the ability to shoot flames from her eyes. But if she aimed too high, she might be laughed out of the room.

All at once, Reginn knew what to ask for. Something she knew she wouldn't get any other way.

"Highest," she said. "I ask for the gift of mercy–a pardon and freedom for Naima Bondi."

A murmur ran through the crowded room. The servants replenishing the refreshments paused in their work to turn and look at her.

"Who is this Naima Bondi, and what was her crime?" Heidin said.

"She killed Elder Skarde, the chair of the Council of Elders," Reginn said.

"Skarde," Heidin said. She closed her eyes, brushing her fingertips over the puckered leavings of the flame. Collecting herself, she turned back to Reginn. "Why would you have us pardon someone who murdered an elder?" she said.

"Because he deserved to be killed," Reginn found herself saying.

"Why? What did he do?"

"He seized a child, and killed her fadir when he tried to stop him."

A murmur rose again, like the sound of the wind through aspen trees. Or a flight of arrows arcing toward her.

Whatever happened to "keep your head down" and "find a way to succeed"? Reginn thought, mortified.

Heidin laughed, a low, bitter sound. "Knowing Skarde, I'm not surprised."

Reginn wondered how, if Heidin had left as an eight-year-old, she would remember anything about Skarde. Obviously, she did, and it was nothing good.

Heidin wavered, cleared her throat. "Still," she said. "It would set a dangerous precedent. What if someone attacked members of the new council? We cannot allow individuals to take justice into their own hands."

There is no justice for the bondi! Reginn wanted to say, but some vestige of common sense or instinct for self-preservation prevented it.

"That is why I am requesting a pardon," Reginn said. "Skarde was despicable, and Naima's is a life well worth saving."

Then Erland stepped forward, his fingers laced around the head of his staff, his face shadowed by his hat. "Highest, Naima is . . ." He stopped, groped for words. "A very good friend of mine. Music is what brought us together. She has been . . . a great influence on my music." Erland was usually good with words, but he was stumbling around, focused on avoiding the great secret at the center of it all.

Reginn was worried that he would say more, but he stopped at that.

Then, to her astonishment, Bryn moved up alongside Erland. "Naima has been a great help to me at Brenna's House. If I had a patient who needed a particular form of nourishment, or food prepared a certain way, she would find a way to provide it. I believe that her work has saved many lives. As a member of the new council, I recommend mercy."

Katia knelt before Heidin, while the vaettir dove and swirled around her, agitated by her distress. "When you think about it, even if Naima had not killed Elder Skarde, the–ah–Halvorsen murdered the entire council not long after. So." She took in a deep breath. "It doesn't matter so much that she killed him, because he'd be dead, either way."

Which made a certain kind of sense.

Still, Reginn was beginning to fidget, concerned that this chorus of support might arouse suspicions that this was planned.

Especially when even Grima joined in. "It seems to me," she said, "that if the barbarian is to be spared after slaughtering the entire council, that Naima could be forgiven for killing the worst of the lot."

It was an astonishingly bold thing to say, critical of Heidin's intervention on behalf of her brodir. Reginn could tell from the firebird's expression that she felt the bite of it. Reginn half expected to see Grima explode into flame or otherwise meet the brutal ending she deserved.

Then Heidin smiled. It was a good argument, after all.

She turned to Reginn. "Your wish is granted," she said, "but you'll be responsible for Naima's actions from this point on. She will serve as your assistant in all things."

"Thank you, Highest," Reginn murmured, hoping that she was not making a fatal mistake. In her experience, Naima was not particularly governable nor especially interested in staying alive.

During the reception that followed, Reginn was surprised at how many of her fellow council members thanked her for her intervention on behalf of Naima and expressed the opinion that Skarde deserved whatever he got.

As the crowd thinned out, she managed to draw Heidin aside. "You spoke with your brodir?"

Heidin scowled. "I did speak with him," she said. "You are right–his mind was clear."

"His time away from–away–seems to have done him good."

Heidin closed her eyes and breathed out slowly. "Yes," she said.

This was not the reaction Reginn was expecting. "Is something wrong?"

"I had forgotten how stubborn he could be," Heidin said. Seeing Reginn's expression, her eyes narrowed. "What?"

"Stubbornness is a trait that he shares with you, Highest," Reginn said.

Heidin laughed. "I can always count on you to be blunt. I asked Eiric to fight with us, but he refused."

"Ah," Reginn said. "Did he say why?"

"He said that he had too many questions about New Jotunheim that need answers before he could agree. He wants me to let him out to do his own investigation first."

"And . . . is that a possibility?"

Heidin shook her head. "I don't see how. There are some in Eimyrja that would slaughter him on sight–"

"Perhaps easier said than done," Reginn said.

"Perhaps," Heidin said, "but it's the last thing we need as we prepare for war. And there's always the chance that he'd sail for the Archipelago at the first chance. Our brodir is there."

"Do you blame him? With war coming?"

She shook her head. "You always make me admit things that I don't want to admit," she said. "A trait *you* share with my brodir."

"He can't sail away without the sunstone," Reginn said. "Would it do any harm to allow him to explore a little, maybe with an escort? Would he agree to sail with us if he could sail his own ship, and land first at your farm to retrieve your brodir?"

"Maybe," Heidin said thoughtfully. "I can understand why my modir named you counselor."

"Just a suggestion," Reginn said. "Maybe tomorrow we could–"

Heidin seized her hand. "Thank you, Reginn. We'll go and see him first thing tomorrow morning. We'll make arrangements for Naima at the same time."

10
RELAPSE

REGINN AND HEIDIN MET IN the entryway of the House of Elders at first light the following day. It *should* have been first light, but it was gloomy and dark, pouring down rain.

"Well," Reginn said when she saw Heidin's scowl, "it has to rain sometime. Even in Eimyrja." She raised the hood of her cloak and splashed out into the wet, glad she'd worn boots and trousers instead of a dress. Heidin followed, grumbling.

"Come on," Reginn said, laughing, stomping in a puddle, spattering the hem of Heidin's cloak. "You spent years in Muckleholm. You're used to weather."

"I may be used to it," Heidin said, "but I don't have to like it."

Reginn found herself wishing that she had known Heidin–Liv–back in the Archipelago. What a difference it would have made to have had a friend.

She looked over her shoulder at Asger's ember eyes, his form a deeper sort of dark. That would have been impossible, of course.

Reginn faced forward again. She wasn't going to let Asger ruin what promised to be a good day. Eiric was improving, and Naima would be freed.

The light from their staffs rippled out ahead of them, illuminating the forest path. As they walked, Reginn dithered over a number of questions.

Reginn recalled what the guard had said. *The prisoner has been undergoing intense interrogation. That takes a toll. Otherwise she'll have no problem making it to the block.*

Reginn had brought her remedy bags along, including the pouchful of runestones. What if she needed more than that? Maybe Sibba would be willing to look after both Eiric and Naima. Maybe Reginn could open a healing hall on the fifth floor of the academy building.

If Naima asked why she'd intervened, what should she say? That she was trying to make up for doing nothing when she should have done something?

Should she offer to have Naima stay in her rooms in the council house, or might she prefer the privacy of her own quarters?

Reginn was more worried about the interview with Naima than the meetup with Eiric. If she could just convince Eiric to promise his systir that he would fight for New Jotunheim, that didn't mean that he actually had to do it. And that way, he might regain his weapons and his freedom. Then he would have more options.

As they emerged from the forest and the building on the cliff came into view, Reginn saw that, despite the rain, it was surrounded by a crowd, many carrying torches.

Now what? Reginn thought, heart sinking. Who were they here for? Most people gave the building–and its courtyard–a wide berth.

As they got closer, Reginn saw that it was more of a mob than a celebration. She heard chanting, shouting, saw people shaking their fists at the wall of the building. She saw Modir Tyra's tall form at the edge of the crowd, a sapphire against a sea of dun. And beside her, Grima, like a shard of obsidian.

As they approached, Tyra strode out to meet them, Grima following like a shadow. Tyra's hair peeked from the hood of her cloak in damp metallic ringlets.

"What's going on, Kennari?" Reginn said, gesturing at the crowd.

"They seem to believe that the barbarian is being held inside," Tyra said, looking from Reginn to Heidin as if they were two guilty children. "They are definitely out for blood."

Well, that didn't take long, Reginn thought. She knew it was just a matter of time, but–

"Is it true that he's being held here?" Tyra said.

"Yes, Modir, he is here," Heidin said, chin up, unapologetic. "Too many people had access to the prison under the council house. I wanted to minimize his contact with others while he heals, for everyone's safety."

By "too many people" Heidin meant Tyra, and they both knew it.

Tyra had more to say about that, Reginn could tell, but she saved it for another time. She had other axes to grind. "I also hear that the cook, Naima Bondi, has been pardoned."

Someone who attended the reception must have rushed off to make sure Tyra was informed of everything she missed.

"Yes," Heidin said. "Elder Reginn asked for mercy, and I have granted it."

Tyra looked at Reginn and Heidin in turn. "I wish that you would have discussed that with me first," the kennari said.

Modir and dottir glared at each other for a long, charged moment.

Then Heidin reached out and took Tyra's hand. "Let's not fight, Modir. I am new to Eimyrja, and I have strong opinions, and so it's no wonder I step on toes. The good news is that my brodir seems to be improving." She smiled. "Come and see."

"As you wish," Modir Tyra said. "I am eager to see how the barbarian is faring." Something in the kennari's expression set off alarm bells in Reginn's head.

"Heidin," Reginn murmured, overtaken by a sense of grim foreboding. "Maybe we should go and see how Eiric is doing this morning before we–"

But Heidin and Tyra were already walking away. Asger waited until Reginn followed, then trailed after.

The four of them walked toward the academy building, buffered by a wedge of soldiers. Silently, the crowd parted to let them through, then closed again behind them. They were nearly to the double doors when somebody shouted, "Free Naima Bondi!"

The crowd took up the chant.

Others shouted, "Where's Sibba?"

Something's going on here, Reginn thought, and it's nothing good. She scanned the crowd, hoping to spot someone she knew so that she could find out. But she saw no familiar faces.

Heidin leaned toward Reginn. "Do you know what you are getting into?"

"Not at all," Reginn said with a tight smile. "But no doubt I'll regret it."

They left the guards outside the building and entered, accompanied only by Asger. Right away, they could hear shouting and banging and crashing from the upper floors.

It sounded like a fight.

More of a battle.

Tyra spun around to face Heidin. "Who else is being held here?"

Heidin shrugged and looked at Reginn.

"The only two I know of are Naima and Halvorsen," Reginn said. What if someone was trying to preempt any freeing or forgiving?

She ran for the stairs, the others calling after her, then following behind as best they could. As she climbed, the sound got louder and louder until she exited on the fifth floor, where both Naima and Eiric were being held. It was easy to tell that the noise was coming from Eiric's cell. Chairs and tables and massive storage chests had been dragged in front of the door, as if to contain a dangerous beast. Four guards were standing in the corridor, swords in hand, seeming to be at a loss for what to do.

"What's going on?" Reginn said. She nodded toward the door. "Who is in there?"

"The barbarian's gone berserk," one of the soldiers said. A little extra braid on his collar said that he was the one in charge. "He started screaming and carrying on last night. We let him be, figuring he'd wear himself out."

"Had you considered that he might be hurt and needed help?" Heidin snapped.

The soldiers looked at each other. It was obvious they hadn't.

Licking his lips, the officer continued. "He started battering his way through the inner door. When we saw he was coming through, we barricaded the outer door. Since then, it sounds like he's been breaking apart every piece of furniture that's in there. He doesn't seem to be slowing down."

Reginn swore silently. It would have been reasonable to assume that the outer door would hold against any prisoner, but Reginn knew better, and so, apparently, did the guards on duty.

"Where's Sibba?" Reginn said. "Is she in there?"

"I don't know, Highest," the officer said. "I haven't seen her." After a moment's hesitation, he added a little sheepishly, "We went to the kitchen to get some supper. We were gone a little longer than we planned on, but–"

"You left my brodir unprotected?" Heidin said in a stinging voice.

"Well, Highest–my lady–we were put here to keep watch on Naima Bondi. We didn't even know the barbarian was here until–ah–you came to see him yesterday."

The other soldier spoke up. "Naima's never given us a bit of trouble. She was locked in, and as far as we knew, she was asleep. So we didn't see any harm in having a bite. We haven't had anything since the dagmal."

Tyra put her hand on Heidin's shoulder. "I thought you said that he was improving."

"He was," Heidin said. "Just yesterday he–"

The sound of voices prompted a renewed frenzy of pounding on the door. "Let me out!" Eiric shouted, his voice hoarse from hours of raging.

"Open the door," Heidin commanded. "I will see my brodir."

"No!" Tyra cried, stepping between Heidin and the door. "It's too dangerous."

"I am not afraid of him," Heidin snapped.

"Then you are a fool," Tyra said. "I will not allow you to put yourself at risk."

"This is my fault," Heidin said. "I should have listened to him. I know that he cannot abide being locked up." And then, to the guards, "Did you not hear me? Open the door."

The guards looked from Tyra to Heidin, unsure which way to jump.

"I will subdue the barbarian," Grima said. The assassin stood relaxed, confident, what appeared to be a blowgun in her hand. "I have done it before."

Reginn read her expression as *This time he won't get up again.*

Heidin must have seen something herself because she said "No!" and stepped between Grima and the door.

"Let Elder Reginn try first," Tyra said. "Perhaps she can calm him."

Heidin glanced at Reginn. "Do you really believe that Reginn can calm him when I cannot?"

It reminded Reginn of Eiric's response when she'd urged him to leave Eimyrja without seeing his systir.

You believe you'd have more success convincing my systir than I would.

"Sometimes it is difficult for close family members to do what is required of a healer," Reginn said diplomatically. "I will do what I can, if you wish."

Tyra nodded approval, almost imperceptibly, not wanting to set off her mercurial dottir.

"All right," Heidin said. "You can try. But please–be careful."

Reginn turned to the guards, not wanting to leave any thread unsecured in case things went wrong. "It might be prudent to free the prisoner next door, and escort her out of harm's way. After all, she has been pardoned."

The soldiers looked at each other, then back at Reginn, trying to hide their surprise. Then they turned to Tyra. "Is this true, Highest?"

Tyra sighed, making it clear that it was not her idea. Then nodded. "It is true."

One produced a key to unlock the cell next door. They tried to push the door open, but it would not budge. Then one of the guards put his shoulder to the door, trying to force it. No luck. He pounded the door. "Open up!" he shouted. "Good news! You've been pardoned."

"Go away!" Naima shouted back.

"What's wrong with you? We're trying to let you out."

"I don't believe you."

The guard turned to Reginn, raising both hands, palms up. "Highest? What do you suggest?"

Well, Reginn thought, at least Naima is alive and clearheaded. For now.

"Leave her be," Reginn said. "Clear Halvorsen's door."

Faces shrouded in doubt, the soldiers proceeded to dismantle the temporary barrier they had erected. When a narrow path had been cleared to the door, Reginn waved the soldiers back.

Reginn turned to Tyra and Heidin. "I'm not sure what will happen when I open the door, but I don't want any distractions. I want him to focus on me alone. I would like all of you to go downstairs, out of sight, while I talk with him."

The soldiers needed no further encouragement. They loped down the hallway, the sound of their footsteps fading as they descended the stairs.

"Reginn," Heidin said. "You don't have to do this on your own. Asger can stay."

The demon stood ready, eyes fixed on Reginn, hands relaxed at his sides, expressing no objection to being volunteered.

Grima, however, looked furious at being overlooked.

"No," Reginn said. "I cannot think of any way a demon's presence would improve things. If you want me to help, then we need to do it my way. But if anything happens to me, Lady Heidin, I hope you will see to it that Naima is freed and well-treated."

"Of course," Heidin said. She held her ground for a moment, as if debating whether to stay or go, then embraced her, her cheeks wet with tears. "I will never forget how you put yourself at risk to help my brodir," she said.

"As he put himself at risk for me," Reginn said. "Before you thank me, let's see how it comes out. Whatever you do, don't come looking for me. Wait for me to come get you."

"But what if you–?" Heidin stopped midsentence.

"If I am dead, I can lie there a little longer," Reginn said. "Better that than your sudden arrival ending in bloodshed."

Heidin gestured to Asger, and they turned toward the stairs. Grima, however, leaned in close to Reginn's ear, as if to add her own blessing. "You would do well to remember that the barbarian is mine."

Somehow Asger was between them, sending Grima stumbling backward into the wall. "You would do well to keep your distance from the counselor," he said in his edged silken voice. He pointed toward the stairs, waited for her to start walking, and then followed her.

Tyra stayed until her dottir and the demon were out of earshot, then took Reginn's arm, leaned in, and whispered, "Do you still have the bottle I gave you?"

"Yes," Reginn said, knowing what was coming.

"Now is the time to use it." Tyra gazed into her eyes for a long moment, then kissed her on the top of her head and followed after Heidin.

11

TAMING THE WOLF

AND JUST LIKE THAT, THE stage was set and the play was in motion. Reginn had to admit, it was a clever move on Tyra's part. Heidin had told her modir that if anything happened to Eiric, Tyra would get the blame. This way, she would be rid of her barbarian problem with no whiff of suspicion attaching to her. Tyra was willing to risk Reginn's life to accomplish this, though she probably preferred that her "counselor" survived. Reginn liked to think that, anyway.

The noise from inside Eiric's cell had stopped. It was not an easy quiet. It was the breath-holding kind. Reginn's beating heart sounded loud in her ears. Was there any way the two of them could come out alive on the other side of this?

She rolled Brenna's staff between her hands. More than ever, she wished she were skilled in its use. She'd gone to the crypt, hoping to persuade Brenna to teach her, but Tyra had interrupted that visit. Reginn had never followed up.

With a sigh, Reginn dragged one of the casks that had been used to block the door back into position and climbed on top of it so that she could peer through the grate in the metal door.

She could see where the inside door had been splintered, the leather hinges snapped, smashed through in places so that light leaked in from the room beyond. It would not have held him much longer.

"Eiric?" she called. "It's Reginn. Can you hear me?"

There was no answer.

"I hear you had a bad night," she said. "How are you doing now?"

There was no answer.

Was he passed out? Asleep? Too overcome with personal demons to respond? Lying in wait?

"Liv is worried about you," she said, hoping the familiar name would spark a response.

It didn't.

"I may be able to help, but I need to know that you–that it's all right if I come in."

He didn't respond. She was not going to extract any promises from him.

With a sigh, Reginn climbed down from her perch and pushed it aside. She unlocked the metal door and pulled it open, the hinges protesting loudly. The room that had been Sibba's quarters appeared to be undisturbed.

She advanced to the other door and peered through the broken places. Eiric's cell was a muddle of destroyed furniture and shredded bedlinens and clothing tossed every which way. She didn't see the coaster.

Gingerly, she opened the door from the hinge side, leaning it against the wall to prevent it from falling on her.

"Eiric?" she said, taking one step forward, then another. Then she saw the body sprawled on the floor, blood spattered over her bondi buff, her tow-colored hair a halo on the stone floor.

Reginn's heart lurched, leaving her breathless. "Sibba?" she whispered.

A slight sound behind her was her only warning. Without turning to look, Reginn launched herself forward and to the side. She planted her staff, which was all that saved her from landing flat on her face.

She turned to find Eiric Halvorsen advancing on her, a bloody knife in his right hand, his blue-green eyes as icy and turbulent as the winter sea. There was no hint of recognition on his face.

And now he was between her and the door.

She backed away, testing each step, knowing that if she stumbled over the debris on the floor it would be over.

Had Tyra gotten to him despite all their precautions? And where would he get such a knife?

"What's happened?" she said, trying not to look at Sibba's body. "Was someone here? Did someone . . . hurt you?"

"Be quiet, witch," Eiric growled. "Always talking, spinning a web of lies, tying knots that can't be picked apart. Every day. Every night. Spinning, spinning, spinning . . . talking, talking." He pressed the heels of his hands against his skull, as if he could squeeze the clamor out. "I am done with you, done with this place, done with this."

"Eiric, it's Reginn. Remember? We met in an alehouse in Langvik? You stopped Asger from hurting me." She paused. "We kissed."

Eiric didn't seem to hear her. Maybe the voices in his head drowned her out. Finally, he dropped his hands, broadened his stance, and stood lightly balanced on the balls of his feet. "Now I know what I have to do."

His voice was icy, calm, and the expression on his face sent a rivulet of fear through her middle.

"What do you mean?" Reginn said.

"It's right that we meet on the field of battle. The fates will decide who wins. That will clear my mind of sorcery."

"I am not a warrior," Reginn said.

"We are all warriors," Eiric said, as if glad to have joined a fight he knew how to win, relieved that he finally had a familiar way forward. He mopped his face with the hem of his shirt, revealing a glimpse of his flat stomach, a dusting of golden hair down the center.

"I did not bewitch you, and I did not come to fight."

"Fight or die." He lunged at her, attempting to grab her staff. She swung it at him, hard, hitting him mid-thigh in a blow that might have crippled anyone else. Then spun away, guessing that it would scarcely slow him down.

She was right. She felt his fingers graze her ankle before she kicked free.

Again, they stood facing each other. She was breathing hard.

"What's the matter?" he said. "Is there no sorcery in your little stick? Is that why you are using it like a club?"

"This is a staff," Reginn said. "There's nothing evil about it. It's just a tool. You've seen Liv use one."

"Who is Liv?" Eiric said. "Another witch?"

Reginn's heart sank. Clearly, Eiric had no pole of memory and connection to guide him, no way to distinguish truth from lies. The only truth he knew had been put there by someone else–someone who wanted him dead.

"I'm not here to hurt you. I have been trying to heal you."

"Still talking," Eiric said. "Still spinning lies into truth."

"Please," she said. "Put down your weapon, and let's talk." She gestured toward the knife in his hand.

He looked down at it, then back at her. Showed his teeth in a predator's smile. "I will put down my weapon if you'll put down yours, but I'll give you fair warning–I don't plan on talking." He opened his hand and the knife fell, pinging off to one side. "Now you," he said. "Drop the witch stick."

Reginn released a long breath. He'd called her bluff. An Asgardian warrior had no need of a knife. In the scheme of things, it was a minor enhancement. In her case, a staff should have been central to her power–if she knew how to wield it.

She looked left, right, but there was no escape unless she could get around him to the door. And if she escaped–then what? She hadn't come here only to escape again. She'd come here–foolishly, perhaps–on a mission.

She opened her hand, and the staff clattered to the floor. They both jumped, as if neither one had expected it.

Eiric recovered first. He gazed at her, eyes narrowed, as if trying to ferret out her game. "You still have a belt dagger," he said, pointing.

The Eiric she knew would have been embarrassed to ask her to give that up.

Reginn drew the dagger. Without taking her eyes off Eiric, she scratched the familiar symbols into her skin, working by touch and memory. *Isa* for focus and concentration. *Uruz* for stamina. *Algiz* for protection.

"What are you doing?" Eiric said suspiciously.

"Taking first blood," Reginn said. She extended her hand and let the dagger slip from her fingers. And with it, any obvious means of fighting back.

In the sagas, when an enemy made such a gesture of faith, the warrior would be shamed into standing down.

Tove always warned her that sagas and stories are not always faithful to real life.

"Now it's just us, Asgard against Jotunheim," Eiric said.

"Listen to yourself," Reginn said, backing away as he came forward. "Those aren't your words."

For such a large person, he moved quickly. What saved her was rune magic and her considerable experience at avoiding Asger's grasp. Unlike Asger, who could change directions in a heartbeat, Eiric had considerable momentum, so it took him longer to adjust to her moves. Her brief stints as an acrobat also served her well. They spent the next few minutes playing cat and mouse around the room, with Eiric lunging and pouncing, catching nothing but air.

The entire time, Reginn tried to talk reason to him, tried to soothe him, but it is nearly impossible to soothe someone who is trying to kill you.

To be honest, he didn't need soothing. He went about the work in a relentless, businesslike way, as something that needed to be completed before he could move on.

It was exhausting. And Reginn knew she couldn't keep it up for long. Sooner or later, she would falter and he would catch her, unless she could figure out how to run up the wall and cling to the ceiling like a bat. Once he got a hand on her, it would be over quickly.

She needed to make him angry. It was a technique she sometimes used with hecklers in alehouses, to get them thrown from the hall.

It was dangerous, but no more dangerous than the game they were playing now. She needed to shatter that icy calm. Reginn groped in her runestone bag, found the one she wanted by feel, and palmed it.

He was stalking her again, smooth and silent, like an issvargr hunting down prey. She allowed him to get fairly close, then pulled a pouch from her remedy bag, opened the neck, and flung the contents in his face.

It was glitter powder that she used in some of her illusions, but she knew from experience that it was irritating to the eyes. Eiric swore, crossed to the basin on the bedside table, and dunked his face into it. He straightened, flinging water in all directions, then again mopped his face with his shirttail.

Now he had wet, spiky, glittery hair. And glittery eyebrows, too.

"What is this?" he growled. "Some kind of poison?"

"Just trying to put a little shine on you."

He stared at her, trying to make sense of the words.

"Do you think I'm not serious?" he said, his voice low and furious. "Do you think this is a game?"

"Yes," Reginn said. "It's a deadly game, and I'll likely be dead at the end of this. If I could bewitch you, do you think I would have let this go on so long?"

Eiric massaged his forehead. "Why don't you run?"

"I might have a chance to outrun you on horseback with a tailwind. Otherwise . . ." She shrugged. "Why don't *you* run, if you're so afraid of sorcery?"

Reginn was used to baiting drunks in alehouses, who could not match their rage with physical action. That was not true of Eiric Halvorsen. So although she fully expected Eiric to charge–was counting on it, in fact–he still managed to take her by surprise. He hit her like a runaway cart, and she landed flat on her back, her head bouncing on the stone floor. She was lucky she wasn't knocked unconscious or that would have been the end. As it was, it took a precious moment to collect herself. She was dazed, conscious of his weight on top of her, his hands wrapped around her throat, squeezing. She opened her eyes to see his beautiful face inches away, feel his hot breath on her face. She looked into his desperately empty eyes, as frozen as sea ice.

She was running out of time, starving for air, black spots swarming through her vision. She managed to free one arm enough to slide it under his shirt and press the runestone against his bare skin, right over his thudding heart.

And, just like that, the pressure on her windpipe was gone and she was dragging in desperate, ragged breaths. Eiric Halvorsen lay still, a dead weight on top of her, his hair spilling over her face, his hands still loosely wrapped around her throat.

Bracing her feet against the wall, she squirmed out from under him. Then sat up, her back against the wall, still hungry for air. In the sudden silence, she could hear the crowd outside shouting, "Sibba!" and "Free Naima!"

She had no time to lose. Eventually, despite her instructions, someone would show up to see if anyone was still alive.

She pulled Tyra's bottle out of her remedy bag, uncorked it, and sprinkled a few drops of mourner's tears over Eiric's shirt, the floor, and her own clothing, carefully smearing it into the corners of his mouth. Then she wiped most of it away with a rag, leaving traces for anyone who looked closely. The scent of cherries all but gagged her now.

Lifting his shirt, she bound a length of linen around his waist, folding the thorn of sleep inside, but making sure that it still pressed against his skin.

Tyra had seen Reginn's resurrection of Thurston in the alehouse in Langvik, but that had been real. Reginn had never shown her the runestone or explained the gambit. She hoped that it would not strike a chord of memory.

Reginn stood, swaying a little, scanned the room until she located Eiric's knife. She used it to slice into the skin on her hands and arms, inflicting cuts consistent with fighting off an attacker with a knife.

Her experience as a healer, as always, served her well.

Since nobody had yet come to see who had died and who survived, Reginn took the opportunity to examine Sibba's body. She rolled her assistant over and found that her throat had been cut from ear to ear in a very tidy fashion. Too tidy for the raging Eiric she had just put down.

There wasn't much blood around the body, either, which Reginn would have expected if Sibba had been killed here. She returned to Sibba's quarters and did a more thorough search, finding nothing amiss. Until she looked under her sleeping bench and found a pile of bloody rags that had been shoved out of sight.

Had Sibba been killed by someone who didn't want to leave any witnesses to the intrusion? Had Sibba been killed elsewhere and her body left here so that it would be blamed on Eiric? Why not do for both of them at once and save time?

But Tyra wouldn't do that, because she knew that Heidin would blame her.

Reginn still needed answers, and there was one other possible witness to what had happened. But first she needed to finish the play in Eiric's cell.

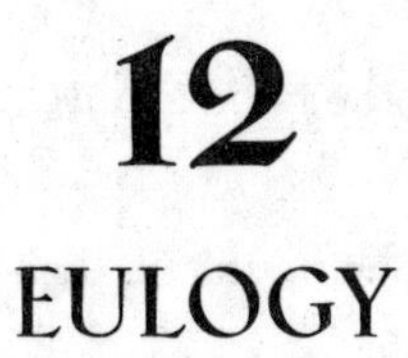

12

EULOGY

REGINN CLOSED WHAT WAS LEFT of the interior door and the outside metal door to Eiric's cell. Taking a deep breath, she squared her shoulders and began to descend the stairs.

Two floors down, Tyra, Heidin, Asger, and Grima waited on the landing in various states of worry and anticipation.

When Reginn reached the foot of the stairs, Heidin rushed forward and gripped her hands. "Is he–?"

"I'm sorry," Reginn said. "There was nothing I could do."

"No," Heidin said, backing away, her expression a mask of denial.

"Both Halvorsen and Sibba are dead," Reginn said. She opened her arms, but Heidin spun away, as if by accepting solace from Reginn, she was admitting it was true.

Now Reginn spoke to Heidin's back. "I don't think he felt any pain," she said. "One moment he was storming around the room while I tried to calm him, and the next–he fell to his knees. . . ."

Heidin turned and strode toward Reginn, gripping her shoulders with bruising force. "What kind of healer are you?" she practically shouted, although they were face-to-face.

"Today, it seems, I am an unsuccessful one," Reginn said.

She'd contended with the grief and anger of mourning family members many times before. Some just needed to shout at someone, and Reginn was the obvious target. Others raged at whatever gods might be listening, or tried to make bargains on behalf of their loved ones. Some were weighed down by guilt, deserved or not.

"Dottir," Tyra murmured, "it is not Reginn's fault."

Grima stared down at the floor, a muscle in her jaw working, like a geysir of rage building.

"Come," Reginn said. She hesitated, then took Heidin's hand. "Let's go see your brodir."

The two of them climbed the steps, side by side, while the others followed. When they reached the fifth floor, they exited into the hallway. As they passed Naima's door, Heidin missed a step. "The prisoner . . . that you wanted pardoned . . . did you–?"

"I'll talk to her after we make arrangements for–for Eiric."

Reginn was watching Grima, and saw the assassin's head come up when she said that. Reginn turned to Asger. "With Lady Heidin's permission, could you and Grima keep watch here in the hallway so that we are not disturbed?"

Asger looked to Heidin, who nodded.

"Delighted," he said, and took up his position between the two hallway doors. Grima sat, leaning her back against the wall on the other side, glaring her displeasure.

When they reached Eiric's door, Reginn opened the unlocked metal door, crossed Sibba's chamber, and eased the inner door out of the way.

Sibba was closest to the door. Reginn had arranged her on her back, hair spilling over stone, hands folded over her heart.

Heidin stood looking down at her. "Do you think Eiric–"

"She was already dead when I arrived. I don't know for sure if Eiric killed her," Reginn said, "though it's likely people will assume that he did."

Heidin met this with a narrow-eyed look, then stepped around Sibba to where Eiric lay, nearly against the wall. She fell to her knees beside him, tears pooling in her eyes and dropping onto his shirt. She looked him over, head to toe, picked up his right hand, and held it between her two.

Tyra stood at Eiric's feet, taking her own long look. She remained expressionless, but Reginn had no doubt that she'd noticed the "evidence" Reginn had left for her.

"There doesn't seem to be a mark on him," Heidin said. She looked up at Reginn, at her cuts and bruises and abrasions, some earned in the fight for her life, and some of which she had applied herself. "But you–you should see a healer."

Reginn knew that this was Heidin's way of saying sorry for her harsh words downstairs.

"It's nothing," Reginn said. "I'll clean up later, when I return to my rooms."

Now Heidin was blaming herself. "Oh, brodir," she whispered, blotting at her eyes with Eiric's shirt, "this is my fault. I am so sorry."

"Dottir," Tyra murmured, kneeling beside her, "don't be so hard on yourself. It was always going to be difficult for an Asgardian warrior to thrive here."

"He is here because of me–and you," Heidin said. "Our fadir came here because of you, and Eiric came because of me. I knew he was miserable being locked up. I should have sent him back home."

"But, dottir, he murdered scores of our soldiers, and our beloved amma."

But Heidin didn't seem to hear. She was focused on her brodir, straightening his clothing, putting his hair to rights. "He told me to execute him or release him. I did neither. I selfishly wanted him beside me."

Tyra bit her lip, no doubt to keep from reminding her dottir that if she'd had her way, Halvorsen would have been long since dead and buried.

Still, she couldn't seem to shut up and accept the win. She had to justify herself.

"Our people are demanding blood. What would they have thought if we let him go?"

Heidin sat back on her heels. Her amulet kindled, underlighting the angry landscape of her face. "I am the firebird. Gullveig, now Heidin. Twice burned. I don't care what people think."

Tyra's eyes widened a little, and she took a step back.

"Heidin," Reginn said, kneeling beside her, "would you do me the honor of allowing me to handle your brodir's memorial arrangements? Because of public sentiment, I suggest that he lie in state in the crypt under the Memory Tree rather than in the open. We'll post a guard at the entrance, and I will attend him at all times. That will forestall any . . . unfortunate incidents."

"Anyone who brings dishonor to my brodir will answer to me," Heidin said fiercely.

"Of course," Reginn said. "I can prevent any–I can maintain the body for ten days to two weeks, if you like, to allow you time to say a proper goodbye."

Now Heidin's tears spilled over and ran down her cheeks. "You would do that for me?"

"Of course," Reginn said. "I have a favor to ask, however."

"Name it," Heidin said.

"If at all possible, I would ask that your fadir's bequest to him be included in his grave goods."

Heidin shook her head. "I don't know what you–"

"Several times, he's asked about his sword and amulet," Reginn said. "They seem to be precious to him. Having them back might help his spirit rest in peace."

Reginn was counting on the fact that Heidin would not want to keep her fadir's Asgardian sword and amulet herself. She was right.

"That's perfect," Heidin said, as if having back his belongings would make being dead more tolerable. "That's exactly what we'll do." Impulsively, she turned and embraced Reginn. "Thank you, Reginn. You are a better friend than I deserve."

Reginn returned the embrace. "I was not able to save your brodir's life, but I can make sure that he goes forward with all honor."

Reginn could no longer hear shouting from outside. Maybe the crowd surrounding the academy building had dissipated by now, given the relentless rain and hours without news from within the building. Reginn hoped so, because, in her current mood there was a good chance that Heidin would react badly to any challenges along the way.

It was decided that Heidin, Asger, and a squad of soldiers would escort Halvorsen's body to the crypt under the Memory Tree and post a guard. Reginn would get Naima sorted, make arrangements for Sibba, and begin her vigil in the crypt the following morning.

Reginn was physically and mentally exhausted and just wanted everyone else to leave. After the others walked out, Tyra remained behind.

"Dottir," she said. "I just want you to know that your performance was masterful. You have been kind to my dottir and loyal to me. You've proven that you are capable of doing what's necessary, even if it is difficult. I owe you a great debt, and hope that I can repay it one day."

"Thank you, Kennari," Reginn murmured, thinking, I've been a performer all my life. I cannot seem to get out of the business.

"There is much to do in these days before we sail," Tyra said. "I will need your help now more than ever. I know you promised Heidin you would stand watch over the barbarian's body, but that seems a poor use of your time. I can easily detail a guard of soldiers to–"

"I made your dottir a promise, Kennari," Reginn said, "and I will keep it."

Their eyes met, held. "Of course," Tyra said with a rueful smile. "I know that will bring her great comfort."

Reginn watched the headmistress walk away, then heard her steps on the stairs.

Now she needed to speak with Naima.

13
NAIMA

WHEN SHE WAS SURE TYRA was gone, Reginn went to Eiric's window, hoisted herself up, and leaned out the opening, the wind-driven rain stinging her face.

"Naima!" she shouted, hoping that her voice was powerful enough to reach the next window. "It's Reginn. I wanted to make sure that you're all right."

There was no answer, but her sixth sense could feel the hard push-back of Naima's mistrust.

"I came to tell you that Lady Heidin has granted you a pardon on the condition that you come to work for me."

Finally, Naima poked her head out her window. Her face was green and purple with bruises, with one eye nearly swollen shut. Her fair hair had been shorn close to the scalp.

Rage and sympathy warred within Reginn, but she knew that the last thing Naima would welcome was pity.

Naima's open eye narrowed. "Who's Lady Heidin?" she demanded.

Naima had been locked up since before Heidin arrived. She was behind on the news. "She's Modir Tyra's long-lost dottir. And systir to Halvorsen."

"Tyra's dottir is systir to a barbarian? But that means Tyra–"

"Love is love, they say."

Naima snorted, close to a laugh. "Why would somebody I don't even know–especially Tyra's dottir–pardon me?"

"Because I asked her to," Reginn said. Hurriedly, she added, "Others spoke up for you, too. Erland, and Katia, and Bryn and . . . even Grima. Sort of."

After a long pause, Naima said, "You miss my cooking, do you?"

Reginn laughed. "Well, in truth I do, but if you come work for me you won't be cooking." She worried Naima might ask what it was she *would* be doing, if not cooking, and Reginn wasn't quite sure she was ready to answer that question.

She hurried on. "Do you think we could talk face-to-face? Out of the rain?" When Naima didn't answer right away, Reginn said, "You could come here. Or I could come over there, if you'll let me in."

"Who else is with you?"

"Nobody," Reginn said, and never had it seemed more true. "I'm alone."

"All right," Naima said, as if finally deciding that a meetup was unavoidable. "I'll come to you. Give me a minute."

Speaking of cooking, Reginn realized that she was hungry. Starving, in fact. What had happened to the day? She returned to Sibba's room and searched it thoroughly, coming up with a jug of cider and some oat cakes. She set them out on the table there, deciding that Naima deserved a warning before she encountered the scene beyond. Reginn sat down at the table and poured two cups of cider.

Naima appeared in the doorway, visibly wary, scanning the room for an ambush. Then said, "Are we having a tea party?"

"Just having a bite. Please. Sit and have a drink with me. I think we can both use one."

Naima came into the room. When she saw the half-demolished door leading to Eiric's cell, she stopped, staring. Finally, she collapsed into the other chair and downed half a cup of cider at a go, then sat back, resting her elbows on the table and lacing her fingers so that she could study Reginn's battered face.

"Well," she said, "you've looked better."

"I could say the same about you," Reginn said. "I left my healing supplies in the other room. I'd be glad to–"

"It's fine," Naima said, waving the offer away. "It's better than it was." That was the end of the pleasantries. "What's happened to the barbarian? He kept me up all night, screaming and raving, and now, all of a sudden, it's quiet."

"He and Sibba are both dead," Reginn said. Sometimes simple was best.

"Dead," Naima said, as if this confirmed a truth she already knew. "Who killed them?"

"I killed Halvorsen," Reginn said.

Naima took another long look at her. "*You* . . . killed an Asgardian warrior three times your size?"

"I had no choice. It was him or me."

One corner of Naima's mouth curved up. "Of course," she said. "And Sibba?"

"Sibba was already dead when I arrived."

"Do you think he killed her?"

"You tell me. I believe you might know more about it than I do."

Naima went quiet for what seemed like an eternity, then chose to ignore the gauntlet Reginn had thrown down. "I guess we'll never know," she said, blotting at her eyes. "Sibba and I . . . we were good friends. I only spoke to the–to Halvorsen once."

"He said that you told him about the children."

"Did he?" Naima selected an oat cake, took a bite.

Reginn nodded. "He was outraged. He demanded to know whether I knew about it, and why I hadn't done anything about it."

"Typical hero type," Naima said. "They think there is no problem that cannot be solved with a strong arm and a sword. Still, I thought–well–he didn't sound like a barbarian. Or a madman." She held up the half-eaten oat cake. "These are pretty good."

"Not as good as yours," Reginn said, having thirds. "Eiric's not–he wasn't a madman. Something happened last night. I saw him two days ago, and he was greatly improved, talking, making perfect sense. Lady Heidin saw him yesterday, same thing. This morning he was raging, incoherent, doing his best to tear this building down, right?"

"Right," Naima said, not meeting Reginn's eyes. Neither of them said what they both knew–that Tyra must have had a hand in it.

"So. I need the truth. What did you hear last night?" Reginn said. "Why was your cell barricaded from the inside?" She rested her hands on the table and sat back, waiting.

Naima ran both hands over her head and poured herself another cup of cider. "I've underestimated you," she said, a new note of respect in her voice.

"Good," Reginn said. "Around here, being underestimated is the way to stay alive. If you plan on telling me the truth, do it now, because I suspect there are some who'd prefer to shut you up permanently."

"It all went wrong," Naima said, her voice hitching. "Sibba never meant all this to happen. I'm so sorry."

"Sibba was a good person," Reginn said. "If it helps, I know that she was upset because you were facing the axe for killing one council member, while it seemed like Eiric wouldn't be punished even though he'd killed the rest. And Amma Inger. She didn't think it was fair."

Naima nodded. "So. You may have heard that there was a plan to break me out of the House of Elders. The council or somebody caught wind of it and had me moved over here–next door to Halvorsen. Sibba knew that nobody was supposed to know where Halvorsen was being kept. But–but the kennari–Tyra knew that Sibba had been taking care of him, and so she hauled her in to try to find out where he was.

"Sibba–she tried to strike a deal. She agreed to tell Tyra where Halvorsen was, in exchange for a pardon for me. Tyra agreed."

"Did Sibba know what Tyra intended to do?" Reginn said softly.

"No," Naima said quickly. Then backtracked. "Look, she's not–wasn't–stupid. Sibba knew that Tyra tried to execute Halvorsen and this–this Lady Heidin got in the way of it. She knew that it was a bone of contention between them. She knew the barbarian had killed Amma Inger. So. Frankly, my life was worth more to her than his."

"That's understandable."

Naima blinked at Reginn, as if surprised at this opinion. "So. When she told me about the plan, I told her it was a mistake, that she absolutely couldn't trust Tyra. But by then she was in too deep.

"Word got out about the plan, somehow–at least, about my whereabouts. I think Sibba might have hoped that public pressure might convince Tyra to keep her word. I don't think it gave her a moment's pause. I asked Sibba to leave Halvorsen's rain shutters open so that I could hear how things were going down next door. Sibba, Tyra, and–that little nightmare elder, Grima–came in the night. The guards were gone to–wherever guards go when they are not where they are supposed to be. The dining hall, most likely.

"If I leaned out the window, I could hear some of what was being said next door. Sibba did not want to stay for the–for whatever Tyra meant to do. She kept asking for the keys to my cell so that we could leave." Naima gulped down more cider for courage and blotted her eyes with her sleeve.

"Tyra must have finished tormenting poor Halvorsen, because he began screaming and shouting and crashing around." Naima shuddered. "I don't know why she didn't just kill him outright."

"She had her reasons," Reginn murmured.

"Right after that, Sibba went silent. I knew in my bones she was dead.

"So. I guessed that they'd want to tidy up, and I would likely be next. So I blocked the door with everything I could lay my hands on.

I would have pried stone from the walls if I could have. Fortunately, this building having been a school and not a gaol, the door opened in.

"I heard them at the door, at first quiet, hoping to be in and out and done. When they realized the door was blocked, they knocked politely, called my name, and said Sibba was waiting for me downstairs. I didn't respond. Meanwhile, I guess the crowd was growing outside, demanding to see me and Sibba.

"They left then. A little while later, I heard a guard pounding on the door, again telling me to open up, I was pardoned. I assume that was you?"

Reginn nodded.

"I knew I'd have to open up eventually, or starve, but tomorrow seemed less risky than today. I could hear bits and pieces of what went on after that. Those assholes sent you in there alone?"

"I volunteered," Reginn said. "Sort of. Heidin hoped that I could calm her brodir, and so save his life. I failed." She stood. "Let's go see Sibba."

By the time Naima and Reginn left the academy building, the rain had stopped, and the sky in the east was already growing light with the promise of dawn. Naima carried Sibba's body, and Reginn carried Naima's talharpa, the only thing she owned that she wanted to keep. They resembled battle-marked soldiers leaving the field, limping, their clothing filthy and torn.

When they stepped outside, a small crowd of bondi still waited for them. When they saw Naima, they cheered, though it died to a murmur when they saw Sibba's limp body.

"Why don't you speak to them?" Reginn said. "You're the one they're here to see."

"I wouldn't know what to say."

Reginn leaned in closer. "Tell them justice is done, that Halvorsen is dead, and you are pardoned. Don't mention the deal Sibba made with Tyra."

Naima frowned. "But they should know that you stuck your neck out for me, too," she said.

"You and I know it, and that's enough. Sibba risked more, and paid a blood price. I want her to be remembered for the hero that she was."

"And if they ask how she died?"

"Tell them the truth–that you're not sure. Or tell them it might have been Halvorsen–which it might have been. He's dead, so he won't mind."

"But you don't believe that's true!"

"No, I don't, but you don't start a fire when you don't know which way the wind blows. It might overtake everyone and everything you love. You have to be ready to follow it through to the end."

Even as she said it, Reginn thought, Where did that come from?

"I can't figure you out," Naima said softly. "What are you after? What is it that you want? Whose side are you on?"

"I'm the rift, the middle, where the two sides meet," Reginn said. "I just want to save someone." *Maybe the world.*

She felt the weight of it on her shoulders as Naima walked forward, cradling Sibba in her arms.

Naima planted her feet, took a deep breath, and said, "I would like to introduce you to Sibba Bondi–a hero."

14

TALES FROM THE CRYPT

AFTER BEING UP ALL NIGHT, Reginn found it nearly impossible to roll out of bed the next day. Every muscle in her body hurt—muscles she hadn't known existed up to now. Several times, she opened her eyes, aware the day was wasting, then closed them again, thinking she would get up when she quit hurting. If that ever happened.

As was often the case, it was the smell of food that roused her. When she rolled onto her side on the sleeping bench, she saw that Naima was seated at the small table in the chambers they now shared, eating.

It was more a midday than a dagmal, Reginn guessed. Clearly, her friend had been up for hours. She was freshly bathed, wearing clean clothes, her wounds attended to.

Reginn propped up on one elbow. "I can see that I'm already way behind," she said. "Maybe I'll just try again tomorrow." She flopped onto her stomach and pulled the bedclothes over her head.

"I brought enough for both of us," Naima said through a mouthful of food. "It's getting cold, so if you don't get up, I'll eat it all."

"You are heartless." Groaning, Reginn sat up, putting her feet on the floor. "Is that bacon?"

It *was* bacon, and porridge, and oat cakes with bilberry jam. Reginn sat down in the chair opposite Naima, crumbled bacon over her porridge and added a little honey from the pitcher.

"There's hot water on the hearth, if you want to clean up," Naima said, pointing to a pot at the edge of the mealfire. "It's fresh. I went to the baths at Brenna's House, and they cleaned up my wounds."

"So what are your plans for today?" Reginn asked, finishing off the bilberries.

"My plans?" Naima cocked her head. "I thought you would tell me what you want done."

"I will," Reginn said, "but I know you've been locked up for a while, and I'm sure that you have friends and family you want to catch up with. After that, I need eyes and ears. I'll be spending the next ten days or so in the crypt under the Memory Tree. I promised Lady Heidin that I would keep vigil over her brodir's body for that time so that she could come and go, yet have time to mourn him properly before he goes to the flames."

Reginn could see that Naima was biting back questions. "Go ahead," she said. "Ask."

"I just wondered why you, of all people–counselor to the kennari, member of the elder council–why you would be assigned to tend the body."

"I offered to do it," Reginn said. "Lady Heidin had asked me to try to heal him. For a while, I seemed to be succeeding. And then–at the end, I failed. I was the one who killed him."

Naima bristled. "She can't blame you for that!"

"She doesn't–not really–but you and I both know that she could. The killing Halvorsen did wasn't his fault, either, but he's blamed for it still." Their eyes met, held. Reginn looked away, then, making it plain that was all she planned to say on that subject.

"So, now the work begins. For the next few days, I'd ask you to bring my meals–and the news–several times a day. Heidin promised to set a guard outside the crypt. Make sure they are doing their jobs, and I'm not surprised down there. I'll ask you to spell me if I need to leave for a while."

"All right," Naima said. "What else?"

"That's it for now. I need to put together a bedroll and clothing for several days."

"I can help with that," Naima said.

It was after the midday by the time Reginn and Naima made their way through the old forest toward the crypt. As they stepped into the dense shade of the canopy, the heady scent of the flowers washed over them. Heidin had been true to her word. Two guards were posted under the canopy. One was Svend.

"Highest!" he said, coming to attention when he saw Reginn and Naima approaching. The other soldier followed suit.

Reginn waved away that formality, but, still–they were both gaping at her with something like awe.

"Afternoon, Svend, and–?"

"Lars, Highest," the second soldier said, a sheen of sweat blossoming on his face.

"Good to meet you, Lars," Reginn said. After a pause, she said, "Is everything all right?"

"We're just–we heard that you single-handedly killed the barbarian," Svend said.

"Ah," Reginn said, shooting a look at Naima. "Things tend to get exaggerated with time. It makes for a better story."

"I was at the rift the day he arrived," Lars said. "I saw him kill fifty men with one sweep of his giant sword."

Well, Reginn thought, to be fair, this time he didn't have a sword.

"And he killed every single member of the Council of Elders," Svend said. "Except, of course, for Elder Skarde." He nodded at Naima in recognition of her contribution.

"Our captain told us that we could learn a lot about courage from you," Svend said.

"I was just lucky I caught him on a bad day," Reginn said.

They both laughed.

"Has Lady Heidin been here today?" Reginn asked the two guards.

"She oversaw his laying out when he was brought here," Lars said. "She came back at the midday and brought in some grave goods."

"Grave goods?" Reginn said.

"His sword and a pendant," Svend said. "I've never seen a finer sword. It's a shame to bury it."

"That kind of sword finds a way to return to the world," Reginn said. She motioned to Naima, and they walked on to the entrance to the crypt cradled amid the roots of the tree.

Reginn opened the door that led to the stairway down. "I'll be fine until the nattmal," she said to Naima. "Bring me supper then, and plan to spell me for an hour so that I can take care of a few things. When I come back, you can leave for the night. If I need anything, I can ask the guards on duty."

Reginn turned and began her descent into the cool dark. By now, every twist and turn and hazard of the steep narrow staircase had become second nature.

Eiric was laid out in the main chamber on an elaborate table spread with pristine linen. Oil lamps burned at his head and at his feet. The blood and dirt had been washed from his hair and skin so that his hair glowed like spun gold in the lamplight. His clothes were finer than any she'd seen him wear before (although, to be fair, their previous meetings had been in an alehouse and in prison). His amulet had been returned to its usual place on the chain next to the runestick. His hands had been arranged around the hilt of his sword, which lay lengthwise down his body from his breastbone past his knees. His axe lay at his side.

Reginn made a quick check to make sure the thorn of sleep was still in place. It was.

She was at a loss for what to do next. If she woke Eiric now, it seemed likely that he would go straight back to trying to kill her. And now he would do it with a legendary sword while she fended him off with a "witch stick" she didn't know how to use.

She hoped that being away from Tyra would, once again, heal him. But there wasn't much time. Reginn needed a "hurry up" rune. An emergency healing rune. Sorting through the runes in her head, she could think of none suitable.

Reginn knew where to find more runes. And, possibly, advice on how to use them. And how to use her staff from the person who made it.

It seemed unlikely that she would get any of those things. And, yet, when Reginn had chosen her staff, Brenna had said, "I only hope it will help you find your way."

Leaving the main chamber that housed Eiric's body, Reginn walked into the side chamber that held the oldest of the crypts.

Lamps still burned in front of Brenna's tomb, and fresh vases of elderflowers stood to either side. Amma Inger was dead, but someone was still tending this grave.

Other than that, the chamber appeared undisturbed since the day Reginn entered Brenna's tomb and found Asger and Heidin in the tunnels beyond. If she looked closely, she could see a trail of brown spots that led from the door of Brenna's tomb to the steps. It was Heidin's blood, still undisturbed, like a remnant of a nightmare Reginn had no desire to revisit.

Reginn did not enter Brenna's tomb uninvited, this time, but sat on the small stone bench facing the door, cradling her staff in the crook of one arm like a spinner with a distaff.

Reginn cleared her throat, suddenly reluctant to speak.

"Brenna Half-Foot, it is your dottir, Reginn Eiklund, seeking your wise counsel."

There was no response.

"You told me that a staff might allow me to use my power safely. I have your staff, but I need guidance."

There was no response.

"War is coming. I want to prevent the carnage that will result when the armies of New Jotunheim invade the Archipelago, but I need your help."

Again, the silence pressed in on Reginn like a suffocating shroud. Reginn could feel Brenna's exasperation building, like a massive wall of "No." But she soldiered on.

"I am sorry that I entered your tomb against your express wishes, but I felt I had no choice."

Finally, Brenna spoke, in a voice like steel against stone. "There is always a choice, Aldrnari, and you chose wrongly. Haven't you done enough damage? I told you before–I am done with the Midlands. Now more than ever. You have destroyed and misused every gift I gave you. Inger was the last remaining treasure in New Jotunheim."

"Please forgive me, Highest," Reginn said, trying to tamp down her annoyance. "If I have made a mess, then I will do everything in my power to clean it up. The bigger the mess, the more important it will be for me to have a staff that I know how to use."

This was met with stony silence.

"None of this is of my choosing. I want to find a way to keep the people I love alive and to rein in the evil that has taken root in New Jotunheim, fueled by the blood of the innocent. In a matter of days or weeks they will set sail for the Archipelago to conquer and enslave the people there."

"A pretty speech, when you have done more to start this war than anyone. You have unleashed a great power into this world that, if left unchecked, can end life as we know it."

Reginn waited for Brenna to elaborate, but she didn't.

Reginn had been accused of many things in her life, most of them with at least a seed of truth, but this left her baffled.

"How so?"

"We've devoted centuries to making sure that the gods–Jotun or Asgardian–never returned to Ithavoll. The tunnels between Eimyrja and Ithavoll have been blocked and guarded for years. Gullveig should never have set foot on Eimyrja. She should have been stopped by the weather wall. Then she should have been stopped in the tunnels. I never expected you to counter with a herd of aurochs and a demon."

"Not my demon," Reginn muttered. "The aurochs were an accident and an example of why I need to learn how to use this staff. Besides, that was Heidin, Tyra's dottir, who–"

"Tyra's dottir, I know," Brenna said. "Inger realized what Tyra was up to and arranged to send the child away. Gullveig the volva becomes Heidin the goddess. And then she will lead the armies of New Jotunheim against the remnants of Asgard. You saved her life, and so set her loose in the Midlands."

Reginn couldn't conjure any kind of logical framework to explain this, but she hoped that if she kept asking questions, one would emerge.

"But–isn't that a good thing? It makes New Jotunheim a harder target."

"It *was* a hard target until Tyra came along. If I had wanted to start a war, I would have done so hundreds of years ago. My goal was separation and sanctuary, not engagement."

"And yet you've left a mess behind," Reginn said. "Aren't you going to clean it up?"

"The Archipelago was a disaster," Brenna said.

"It's still a disaster, so I'll take your word for it. So you rounded up the gifted and brought them here–which by your own account was *not* a disaster–until you arrived."

"Why would you say that? We turned Eimyrja into a garden."

"Your garden–not theirs. And then put the bondi to work in it.

They had a life, before–one that suited them. You set up a system of winners and losers, powerful and powerless. You turned them into servants."

"If you've read my journal, you know that was not my intention."

"We are not judged by our intentions. Else you wouldn't be judging me so harshly."

Brenna said nothing. Reginn figured that must mean that, as far as she was concerned, the conversation was over.

But Reginn was stuffed full of words that needed releasing, so she plowed on.

"You suggested that I ask Tyra to help with my staff. If I do that, I'll end up as just another one of her game pieces on the board. So I'm not going to do that. I'm going to copy down the runes and try them out. I'll practice with my staff and hope the world doesn't end before I learn how to use it."

As she reached for the face of the granite tomb, Brenna said, "You're right."

Reginn froze, waiting.

"Inger has kindly pointed out that you may be our one last hope of saving this world that birthed her, that she has loved and protected for so long. If the Midlands are destroyed, then that means her life's work was wasted.

"The help you need will come through the staff you have chosen."

Her voice strengthened, echoing against stone. "Reginn Eiklund Aldrnari, I release my staff to you, invested with all the power and wisdom and knowledge I have gained over centuries."

Reginn heard another voice, familiar. The keeper. "Brenna, is it wise to–?"

"Dearest, I must release this burden to someone else," Brenna said, "someone who may succeed where I have failed."

The shank of the distaff heated under Reginn's hands, the metal becoming malleable under her fingers, fitting itself to the size of her hands and her stature. The raw amber at its head kindled, warming the entire chamber and gilding Reginn's skin. Tendrils of magic connected to muscle and bone, lifting and supporting her in a way no walking stick ever had.

"And so it is done, child," Brenna said.

"Have you used this staff for healing? I know you founded the healing halls, and so–"

"No," Brenna said. "A staff is best suited for large magic over distances, or magic directed at more than one person. I see healing as close work. Personal. I wanted to apply techniques that local healers could use themselves. They taught me a lot, too."

"What about runes?"

"Runes are more useful for healing, but your knowledge of them goes beyond mine. Nor can I teach you how to use this staff to extend and enhance your elemental gifts. In that realm, you will need to tread carefully and find your own way. My advice is if you intend to persist in calling up the dead, that you hone your aim and precision and choose carefully. It may be that, with a staff, you can direct your magic in order to choose which of the dead you want to rouse and who you choose to leave in peace."

15
HEALER

WHEN REGINN RETURNED TO THE entrance chamber housing Eiric's body, she found Heidin sitting on a bench next to the dais, holding his hand.

"Reginn!" she said. "Where were you?"

Good question, Reginn thought. Where was I? She'd told Tyra she hadn't been able to access the tunnels since the night she rescued Heidin.

"I'm sorry," she said. "I was around the corner at the–around the corner."

"I wanted to let you know that I'll be over on Ithavoll for a few days, inspecting our ships and loading gear and weapons." Heidin sighed, blotting at her eyes with her sleeve. "Eiric would have been so much help if he were here. I wish–" She laughed ruefully. "Our modir Sylvi had a saying–if wishes were fishes, our nets would be full."

"It sounds like she was a wise woman."

Heidin nodded. "I miss her, too." She cleared her throat. "Anyway. Tyra is keen to set a date for sailing."

A fist of dread formed in Reginn's gut. "Any idea when that will be?"

"Soon," Heidin said, "and so I would like to plan my brodir's sending for when I return from the boatyard."

How long are you willing to wait?

"Perhaps, in a week?" Reginn found herself saying.

"Let's say four days." Heidin stood. "Could you have everything prepared for when I return?"

"Of course," Reginn said, seeing no other option. "I thought we could send him from the clifftop so that he would have a view of the sea. Thank you for returning his sword, axe, and amulet. Are there other belongings or supplies you would want to have included?"

"I'll think on that," Heidin said, and stood. "Eiric is fortunate to have you looking after him in life, and in death."

"It is my honor," Reginn murmured.

Four days may seem to be a long time to say goodbye, but it's a short time in which to perform a miracle. Reginn was accustomed to healing physical wounds–broken limbs, cuts and contusions, poxes, plagues, and wasting sickness. In her experience, diseases of the mind got better on their own, or they didn't. She had no knowledge of how to hurry things along.

If she awakened the warrior in his present state, she would pay with her life. If she didn't wake him before the sending, he would be burned alive.

Tyra used her staff to tangle the threads of mind and memory. It stood to reason that a staff might be key to untangling them.

That evening, Naima brought the nattmal and the news. "Tyra is happier than I've ever seen her. Almost giddy.

"Well, I'm glad somebody is happy," Reginn said, rolling her eyes. "How are you feeling?"

"Well, I wouldn't describe myself as 'giddy,'" Naima said. "Can a person be enraged and grateful at the same time?" She looked Reginn in the eyes. "Have I told you how grateful I am?"

Reginn laughed. "You might want to wait a while before you thank me."

"No, really. I feel like a noose has been removed from around my neck."

"There are worse things than dying," Reginn said. She gestured toward Eiric's bier. "You said that you spoke to Eiric once. Would you like to see him?" When Naima hesitated, Reginn said, "Go ahead. He won't mind."

Naima looked down at Eiric's body, seeming a little awestruck. "I spoke to him that one night in gaol, but I never got a good look at him. Everyone said how big he was, and it's true. But nobody mentioned how young he was."

"The only time most people saw him was at the executioner's block, and that wasn't his best day."

"Now there's hardly a mark on him," Naima murmured. "It's like he's asleep."

Sometimes Naima was a little *too* observant.

"What are people saying, now that he's dead?"

"What do you expect?" Seeing Reginn's expression, Naima laughed. "I know it's hard to lose a patient, but your barbarian is just not that popular in New Jotunheim. Yes, he rid us of the council, which is a mark in his favor, but he also killed Amma Inger and dozens of soldiers on Ithavoll and here. Swapping out a council doesn't change our lives much, to be honest."

Reginn nodded. "I understand."

"There's one thing he said, though, about Amma Inger." Naima closed her eyes, as if to focus. "He said Tyra told him to kill her, that she was the worst of the lot. He claimed that he went to her rooms, but when it came down to it, he couldn't do it."

"She's dead."

"That's what I said, too. He says she drank poison so he wouldn't have her murder on his conscience. And I thought, that sounds like something the keeper would do." Naima reached out and gingerly straightened an errant lock of Eiric's hair.

"She just happened to have some poison handy?"

Naima shrugged. "That's what he said. When I told him she'd been stabbed, he seemed stunned. He said that if he'd done it, he wouldn't have left his sword behind."

Hmm, Reginn thought. I need to find out the truth of the matter.

Naima turned away and began unpacking food and drink from her carry bags. "Do you want to eat now?"

"Have I ever said no to that question?" Reginn chose out an apple and took a big bite, juice running down her chin. "Please–join me if you haven't eaten."

Naima patted her middle. "People have been feeding me all day, but . . . I'm thirsty from all this talking." She pulled the cork on a jug of wine with her teeth and poured herself a cup. Naima was fond of wine.

"What are people saying about . . . all of this?"

Naima sat back on her heels. "You can probably guess. They're mourning Sibba. They're grateful I've been pardoned."

"Where is Sibba?"

"We took her to her home village, on Ithavoll. She'll have a sending worthy of a hero."

"Good. Speaking of sendings, I promised Lady Heidin that I would make arrangements for her brodir, but I'll need your help."

"What do you want me to do?"

"I suggested that we build his spirit ship on the cliff overlooking the sea. Could you do that for me?"

Naima cocked her head. "Why me?"

"Because I trust you to do a good job. Also, I don't have anyone else."

Naima laughed.

"Before you say yes, Heidin wants to have it when she returns in four days."

Naima thought for a moment. "That should be doable, but I've never planned a showy sending for a–a high-up. I wouldn't know what's expected."

"Heidin will want something simple and meaningful. He was her brodir, after all, and she loved him. I want something that burns quick and hot. After, we'll slide the remains over the cliff and return him to the sea."

After Naima left, Reginn sat on the stone floor next to Eiric's bier with a cup of cider, unrolled a sheet of vellum, and wrote down every rune she could remember, those she'd used, and those she'd never tried.

Eiric already wore Thurisaz from his fadir and Yngvi from his modir. They might already be working on him—she wouldn't know until she removed the thorn of sleep.

What else? Kenaz, the rune of clarity, light, and knowledge? That would make sense. She circled it again.

Here was one she'd never used. Wunjo, the rune of love, connection, harmony, trust. Said to counteract hate.

Tove had never used runes in dealing with love, romance, or affairs of the heart. *Runes are too powerful,* she'd said. *People should be free to make and break connections on their own and not be ensnared by sorcery.* That said, she was not above providing love potions, charms, or posies to put under a lover's pillow. Which probably spoke to how ineffective they were.

Reginn knew it must be getting late. She found herself yawning and rubbing her eyes.

But there wasn't much time. She needed to act.

Carefully, she lifted Eiric's sword away, turned, and propped it in the mourner's chair. She followed with the axe. She was taking no chances with a legendary blade.

She sat on the bier next to Eiric and unsheathed her blade. She lifted away his shirt, rolling it up from the hem, exposing his torso.

With the speed of long practice, she carved Kenaz into his skin in two quick strokes.

ᚲ

The wound kindled, flamed blue, and then faded to a raised scar. Clarity, light, and knowledge.

Forging on, she bound it with Uruz, for health and strength.

ᚢ

And finished with Wunjo. For love and joy.

She sat back, all but holding her breath, awaiting some response. There was none, of course, and there wouldn't be until she removed the thorn.

What if the bindrune was too much?

What if it was too little?

Maybe she should wait a day or two before she woke him.

She discarded that idea almost as soon as it surfaced. The runes of healing generally began to work more or less immediately. To wait might mean she was only losing time that she couldn't get back.

Reginn took a deep breath, then released it. She climbed onto the bier and knelt next to Eiric. Carefully, she slid her fingers into the pouch in the waist of his trousers that contained the thorn of sleep. She pulled it free and palmed it in case she needed it again in a hurry. Sitting back on her heels, she waited.

Nothing happened.

Leaning forward, she ran her fingers over the runes and rechecked her vellum list. Some of these were ones she'd been using for years, so she was sure of them. The others she reviewed to make sure they were right. They were, as far as she could tell.

She picked up his hand and massaged his palm. His hand hadn't the dead-fish feel that Thurston's had, but it seemed to be unchanged from before. His skin was cool and dry. She lightly slapped his cheeks, then slapped him harder. She rolled back an eyelid to see if he reacted. He did not. She pressed her fingertips into the pulse pockets at his neck and felt no reassuring drumbeat of life.

Panic welled up inside her. What had possessed her to combine so many powerful runes together, to use runes she'd never used before? It would have made more sense to apply them one at time, to see how he reacted before she added more.

What else? Ansuz? Odin's rune? An Asgardian rune for an Asgardian warrior?

Laguz? The water rune? Coasters had an affinity for water, after all.

And then came that voice of doubt in her head.

Haven't you done enough damage?

Runes go deep. They cannot be erased.

Then another voice. Kinder.

Use the tools you know, young one.

So she fetched her flute, raised it to her lips, then lowered it again.

They'd never shared a song together.

Truth be told, she knew too little about Eiric to choose. So she began with shore-songs, calling-the-coaster-home songs, warnings about krakens and other sea monsters.

She sang the vardlokkur, as she had so many times in an effort to rouse Brenna. Sang to exhaustion, until her throat was so sore that she could not push out another sound.

Nothing. It seemed that the only person who didn't know Eiric was dead was Reginn herself.

By now, the lamps were burning low, so it was either replenish them or allow them to burn out.

Finally, hoarse, worn out, grieving, and guilty, Reginn climbed onto the bier and lay down beside Eiric. She removed the layers of cloth between them so that they were skin to skin, and snuggled in under his chin.

There was one more option to try. She felt a little jolt as the connection was made between the blodkyn runes. She opened a channel between them, and let the energy flow. From her and into him.

Eventually, she slept.

16

THE WARRIOR REBORN

EIRIC OPENED HIS EYES TO a tangle of thick, fleshy vines overhead, peppered with red berries like spots of fresh blood. Though the light was dim, it was still too bright, and he threw his arm across his eyes to shade them.

At first, he thought he must be in a forest, but the air was moist and smelled more like a cave—of stone and decay, and lamp oil. Roots dangled all around him, as if the trees above had lost their way.

He swallowed, and felt something metallic against the skin of his neck, demanding his attention. He reached for it and found that his fadir's amulet had been returned to him.

He tried to roll over onto his side, but encountered something warm and yielding, a tangle of hair in his face, the curve of a bare shoulder. He couldn't see her face.

Had there been a girl in his bed when he went to sleep? It seemed like something a man would remember.

Something a man would want to remember. There were holes in his memory that needed filling.

This was not a bed suited to sharing, especially for a person of his size. He shifted and squirmed, trying to get comfortable without waking her, and finally managed to accidentally plant an elbow in her ribs.

That drew a response. She yelped and rolled off the bed, landing hard from the sound of it.

"I'm sorry," he said, peering over the edge of the bed. And then, "Reginn?"

She looked up at him, her eyes like blue glacial ice set in copper.

"Eiric," she whispered. "Are you–well?"

"I don't know," he said. "Have I slaughtered anyone lately?"

She launched from the floor like an arrow from a crossbow, but faltered halfway and leaned on the edge of the bed to keep from falling.

"Are you all right?" he said, alarmed. "What's wrong?"

"I'm . . . good," she said, breathing deeply. "Just . . . fine."

Eiric stood, lifted her, and sat her on the edge of the bed, standing in front of her so as to catch her if she fell. Her face was as pale as he'd ever seen it, sweat beading her skin. "Convince me," he growled.

"I'm just a little . . . drained," she said. "A little dizzy. I must have gotten up too quick."

"It would help if this bed wasn't so–" His voice trailed off as he took in their surroundings. Cool, damp, stone walls, lit only by the dying flames of lanterns. Like a cave, but for the engraved slabs set into the walls. An old fear writhed, like a snake in his middle.

"Where are we?" he said, though he already knew.

"We're in the Hall of Memory–the crypt, where the high-ups in Eimyrja are buried," Reginn said. Her eyes narrowed, and she rested her hands on his shoulders. "What's wrong?"

When he was a child, he'd had regular nightmares about being buried alive. Or burned alive. Or both. Those fears had only faded when Sylvi had convinced him it was out of his hands.

If that's what the fates decree, then go forward.

Why he found that soothing, he couldn't say.

He still didn't like tight spaces.

"Why are we here?"

"Because you're dead," Reginn said, shifting her gaze away.

Dead? That made no sense. Eiric wasn't dead–in fact, he felt better than he had for a long time. And yet–he wore only a fine, long-sleeved, silk-and-linen tunic that barely reached his knees.

"I'm not dead," he said, ready to argue the point.

"Everyone else thinks you're dead," she amended.

"Everyone? Including Liv?"

Reginn nodded, plucking at the fine linen covering the bier.

Eiric reached out and tilted her chin up so that she had to meet his eyes. "Where would 'everyone' get the idea that I am dead?"

"Well, you looked dead," Reginn said. "And I told everyone you were dead." She must have seen that he wasn't happy with that answer, because she hurried on with a question. "What's the last thing you remember?"

"I was being attacked by witches," Eiric said. "You were the worst of the lot." He knew that couldn't be right, but it was the first thing that popped into his head.

She didn't question it, though. "Before that?"

This was happening too often—waking up bumble-minded, like after a night in the alehouse. With no memory of the alehouse to console him.

"Liv and I had a fight," he said. "She wanted me to join her army, and I said that I needed to know more before signing on. Things really went sideways after that. She accused me of spying for Rikhard, of being her enemy because I 'have the blood of the Aesir gods in my veins,' or some such. I couldn't name an Aesir god if my life depended on it. She said she'd keep me locked up until I changed my mind. Then she left."

"The floggings will continue until morale improves," Reginn murmured.

Eiric laughed. "I think I went to sleep then. I woke up, and there were three people in the room—Tyra, that executioner—"

"Grima," Reginn said.

"—and Sibba, I think. Tyra was furious, ranting about breaking the bond between Liv and me. Then she did her spinning thing. That's the last thing I remember." He paused, afraid to ask the question. "I hope I didn't—it wasn't—"

"You should know that Sibba is dead, but I'm not sure that you're the one who killed her."

A sick despair welled up inside him. "You're not *sure*?" It was as if she was doling out small bites of misery so that he wouldn't choke on them.

"She was found dead in your cell with her throat cut. You weren't in any condition to question. We can't assume that–"

"Seems pretty clear to me," Eiric said bitterly.

"Naima doesn't think so."

"Naima?" It took a moment to connect the name to the musician in the cell next door. "What does she have to do with this?"

Reginn sighed. "Sibba was the one who gave you up to Tyra. She was trying to make a deal for Naima. I don't hold it against her and I hope you won't, either."

Eiric scrubbed a hand over his face. "She paid a blood price for it. What's happened to Naima?" Eiric felt like he needed to complete the tally of the dead.

Reginn brightened a little, as if glad to finally deliver some good news. "Naima is fine. She's been pardoned. She's working with me."

Eiric eyed her suspiciously. He wasn't sure whether to believe her. The spinners didn't seem to be the forgiving sort.

"I don't understand why Tyra doesn't just kill me. That's the play that nobody can answer."

"Because Heidin–Liv–would never forgive her if she did. She told her that to her face."

"She did?" Despite everything, Eiric couldn't help feeling a flicker of hope that he would get his systir back somehow.

"Tyra has been trying to change her mind, telling her that your time in the deadlands drove you mad, that you will never be the brodir she remembers. Liv asked me to try and heal you. Tyra gave me a bottle of poison and told me to put you out of your misery."

Eiric knew Tyra wanted him out of the way, but to hear it put into such stark terms was unsettling.

"So," he said, clearing his throat. "What happened? It didn't work?"

"Sure it did," Reginn said with a sly smile. "You're dead, aren't you?"

"Everyone *thinks* I'm dead."

"For now." She changed the subject. "Speaking of murder, could I ask you a question?"

He shrugged. "If I say no, I know you're going to ask it anyway."

"Tell me about what happened with the keeper. Amma Inger. At your execution, you said you never stabbed her."

"That's right, I didn't." He licked his lips, not meaning to make himself out as a hero. "That's what I came to do, but in the end, I couldn't."

"So what happened, then?"

Eiric couldn't figure out where she was going with this. "She had a jug of wine on a shelf above the hearth. The cask was dusty, as if it had been there awhile. She took it down and asked if it was all right if she drank a cup of wine to settle her nerves. She drank a cup, and then another. She said Tyra had given her the wine in Langvik, the last time she tried to kill her. That's when I realized the wine was poisoned, but it was too late. Before she died, she told me to leave New Jotunheim and return to the Archipelago.

"So I left, but they were waiting for me when I went to fetch my belongings. Someone must have brought my sword back there and stabbed her in order to hang it on me." Seeing Reginn's face, he said, "What's the matter?"

Reginn was staring at him as if she'd seen a ghost. "I was there when Tyra gave the keeper the wine in the alehouse where I was performing. The keeper didn't drink it, but my friend Thurston did, and it killed him." Reginn's expression said that she was the loneliest, guiltiest person in the world. "Those are the people I took up with to get away from Asger. I think I jumped from the cauldron into the flame."

"It's not your fault," Eiric said. "We can't control what the fates hand us. All we can do is navigate the best we can, given the weather in the moment. And be ready to change course if we run into a storm."

Gods, he thought. I'm turning into my grandfadir.

"I don't want to wait for good weather," Reginn snapped. "I want to make my own." She paused, then continued in a soft voice, "It's just–it would be a blessing to see some good weather, for a change."

With that, her tears spilled over. Eiric leaned in, pulled her close, and kissed her, twining his fingers into her hair. He felt her tears, wet against his skin, and kissed them away.

Then it was just the two of them, kissing, exploring, eliminating whatever barriers remained between them. At some point, Eiric scooped her up and carried her to the makeshift pile of blankets she must have been using for a bed.

"Do you want to–?"

"Yes," she said.

It was desperate and dangerous, frantic and foolish, rowdy and risky. It was poorly timed. It somehow seemed fitting for their odd pairing–making love in a charnel house. Apt to be interrupted at any time by the living or the restless dead.

There were times, with this girl, that Eiric felt like a novice, a poser–awkward and untried. Other times, her frank desire inflamed him.

In the end, he thought–whatever happens, whatever price I pay for this–it was worth it.

The fires banked, but still smoldering, they lay entwined. Eiric would have slept, but Reginn eventually disentangled herself. She scrambled to her feet and began gathering clothing, her body gilded by lamplight.

He squinted up at her. "Going somewhere?"

"We've got to stop kissing and get moving. You're lying in state until your sending four days from now, when Heidin and Tyra return from

Ithavoll. I've given orders that no one is to enter the Hall of Memory until then. That will give us some lead time. You need to leave before they get back, if you don't want to be the guest of honor at your own funeral."

Leave and go where? If he returned to the Archipelago, no doubt he would end up going to war against his systir, something he didn't want to do.

If he stayed here, he knew Reginn was right when she said that he wouldn't last long. With one or two exceptions, everyone on Eimyrja hated him. And Tyra wouldn't miss again.

What he wanted to do was sail away with Reginn on his karvi and leave all this behind. Assuming they made it through the weather wall, they could stop at Sundgard, pick up Ivar, and find friendlier waters.

"Come with me," he said.

"I can't," she said, offering no further explanation. She pulled her shirt over her head, linen whispering over skin, and stepped into the loose breeches some women wore in Eimyrja.

"I . . . just don't want to leave you behind, knowing I may never see you again. I did that once–in Langvik–and I thought I'd lost you."

"I'm not yours to lose."

Never in his life had he been so flat-footed with a girl.

Do better, Halvorsen.

She began to pace back and forth. "For so many years, that's what I prayed for–to be able to sail away from my problems to a place where nobody knew me and I could start over. I had this idea that I could settle in a little town somewhere, and be the local healer and spakona." She sighed and blotted at her eyes with her forearm. "From what you've said about Rikhard, I'm not sure Muckleholm is that place anymore, even in Asger's absence. I'm not sure it ever was."

"It's a big world," Eiric said. "There are other places beyond Muckleholm."

It was hard to make a case when he had his own doubts about what he could offer this girl. It was one thing to invite a sweetheart from two villages over for a summer of fishing, sailing, coasting, making love, and tracking the stars across the night sky.

Reginn was a counselor, elder, healer, and seer, and all he could offer was bad weather, rough seas, random food, hard work, and calloused hands.

"You have to understand," she said. "I have work to do here. I've come to care about the people here. I'm not giving up paradise without a fight."

"I do understand," he said. "Yet if anything happens to you, I'll blame myself."

"Every place is dangerous," Reginn said. "The Archipelago, New Jotunheim, and the ocean between. The weavers at the well will decide what happens to me. My business is here, for now."

She paused, and the air thickened between them. She wavered. Then spoke. "I want to come with you, more than I should. All I can do is show you the way," she said. "And then I'll have to turn back."

17

RAIDING THE BONEYARD

NAIMA WASTED NO TIME IN preparing the funeral site for Eiric. The very next night, she led Reginn up the point to the frowning cliffs behind the academy building.

A ring of small standing stones formed the outline of a longship. Within it, a shallow pit had been dug and lined with tar-soaked tree bark. A folded linen cloth lay ready nearby, next to a large pile of wood and a stoppered cask of tar.

"This is perfect, Naima," Reginn said. "Thank you."

Hands on hips, Naima eyed it critically. "I'm going to add some standard grave goods–bread and skyr, a cask of ale, and a fire-steel. Is there anything else you want the barbarian to have in the afterlife? Want me to sacrifice a sheep or something?"

Reginn laughed. "I'm sure that won't be necessary. He'll get wherever he's going without any help from me. There are some personal items and weapons that will go with him. I'll have the body and belongings sewn up in a shroud, inside the crypt, on a litter for easy carrying. I would like to have Halvorsen in place on the pyre and ready to go when Lady Heidin returns. If there's anything you need, you can requisition it at the House of Elders using my name.

"After the body is moved to the sending site, cover it with plenty of fuel and pitch so that it burns cleanly and completely. I want a blaze big enough to be seen in Vesthavn."

Naima's expression required more of an explanation.

"Lady Heidin is having trouble with–with all of this. She'll want to see her brodir celebrated with all honor. I think it might be easier if she doesn't have to see the body before it burns."

"Should we requisition some of that fine elders' wine to ease the pain?" Naima suggested.

"Please do," Reginn said. "If I'm not back when Lady Heidin returns, can I count on you to meet her at the sending site to assist?"

"Are you going somewhere?"

"I have every intention of being back. But if I'm delayed, I want to keep my promise to Lady Heidin."

Naima continued to study her. "You like her, don't you?" she said finally.

Reginn took a moment to think about it. "Yes," she said finally. "I suppose I do."

"Why?" Naima said, blunt as always.

"She's a survivor. She's been through a lot, none of it by choice, but it only seems to make her stronger, like quality metal being honed. I would have thought that, coming into Eiric's family the way she did, she might resent him. But she is–was–loyal to her brodir, as he was to her. They seemed to care about each other." Reginn shrugged. "I never had that."

"Me neither," Naima said. "My parents decided that they would not have more children to give to the temple."

"I don't know why anyone would have children in this godsforsaken place," Reginn said.

"So says the barbarian." Naima held her gaze for a long moment. "You have my word that I will do everything in my power to assure a successful sending. Just . . . whatever you're doing, be careful. If anything happens to you, Grima will be sharpening her axe in no time."

"Oh, she keeps it plenty sharp as it is," Reginn said. "You be careful, too, whether I'm here or not. I'm not confident that my presence or absence makes that much difference."

With that gloomy summary, they parted. Reginn had been slowly accumulating supplies for the coming journey so as not to draw suspicion. Now she headed for the kitchen and filled a sack with bread, barley, hard cheese, and salted meat and fish. She then stopped at the armory and, over the armorer's objections, chose the largest sword and axe she could carry.

"But, Elder Reginn," he said, "even in a baldric this blade will drag on the ground. You'll be plowing up the fields of Barbaria with this. Let me guide you. It's not the size of the sword, it's the–"

"I intend to be much taller by the time I return to Barbaria," Reginn said.

He looked her up and down, shaking his head. "Highest, at least take this seax." He extended it toward her hilt-first. "It's a great choice for close-in fighting, especially in a shield wall situation."

"All right," Reginn said, in too much of a hurry to argue. "Pile it on top."

The armorer was right, of course. Reginn had to carry the weapons back to the crypt horizontally across her body so that they would not drag on the ground.

By the time she reached the Memory Tree, her arms ached, her fingers were numb, and she was exhausted.

How could soldiers wield these all day on the battlefield?

Svend stood guard at the door of the crypt. Always circumspect, he said nothing about her armload of gear.

"Has anyone tried to enter the hall?"

Svend shook his head. "No, Elder Reginn, but someone dropped this off for you."

Reginn accepted the bundle of linen cloth, piling it on top of her new weapons. Then made her way blindly down the steps, hoping she wouldn't tumble head over heels and break her neck. Or cut herself in half.

Happily, she reached the bottom in one piece. Then dropped her burden with a clatter as she caught a flicker of movement out of the corner of her eye.

Eiric looked from her face to the dagger in her hand. "Impressive," he said.

"How can someone as big as you move so quietly?" Reginn muttered, returning her blade to its hidden sheath.

"It comes from hunting issvargr in the deep forest, where a snapping twig can give you away," Eiric said. After a pause, he added, "And slipping into the longhouse late at night, bloody from a fight, stinking of ale, without waking my modir."

Reginn was never sure whether the coaster was being serious or not.

"What's all this?" he said, squatting next to the pile of steel and fabric, the lamplight gilding his hair and casting his face into shadow. He slid the seax from its scabbard and weighed it in his hands. "Are you planning on getting into a fight?"

"I brought you some weapons to take to Helgafjell. And a shroud for your corpse."

He stood and tried out the seax, moving from stance to stance, thrusting, parrying, the blade a blur.

I could watch him move all day long, Reginn thought, mesmerized, desire rising in her like a full-moon tide.

Where had it come from, this inconvenient itch for coupling?

Finally, he slowed, then stopped, a sheen of sweat on his upper lip, cheeks flushed from the exertion. "It's a good blade," he said, testing the edge with his thumb. "I always wanted one of these."

"Take it," Reginn said. "It will be of more use to you alive than in the grave. Oh. I almost forgot." She groped inside her neckline and came up with a pendant on a chain that she lifted over her head. "Here, take this. It may come in handy."

He put the chain around his neck and tucked the pendant under his shirt. It glowed red-purple. It was still warm from Reginn's body.

"What's this?" he said. "A token of your everlasting love?"

"It's a kynstone," Reginn said. "It's an indicator of magical inheritance. I am guessing it's glowing red right now because you have Asgardian blood. In the presence of the Jotun, it stays blue."

"Why is all this necessary?" He waved his hand. "If you know a secret way out, why don't I just go and let people sort it out on their own?"

Reginn had to tread carefully here. "I want the funeral to proceed as planned. If Tyra believes you are dead, she won't be looking for you. And I won't get the blame for helping you escape."

Eiric frowned. "Liv will know this is not my sword."

"Not if she doesn't see it," Reginn said. She held up the linen shroud. "We're going to rig up something that will pass a cursory inspection. If all goes well, a cursory inspection will be all she gets." When he still looked skeptical, she said, "Just trust me, all right? We need to fill this with bones. A corpse would be better, but bones will have to do." She paused. "Better bring your axe."

Eiric stared at her, lips twitching with mischief. "Reginn, truly that's the most romantic thing a girl has ever said to me."

He followed her into the chamber that housed Brenna's tomb. He stood a moment in front of the stone monument, running his fingertips across the engraving. "Whose is this?" he said.

She realized with a twinge that he could not read it.

"Brenna Half-Foot," Reginn said, tracing the rune letters with her fingers. "She was the founder of New Jotunheim, remember?"

She pointed him toward a pile of bones in a dark corner–bones she had carried out of the tunnels.

Eiric examined the bones with the same interest he had given the jewelry. "These are human bones," he said, holding up a skull with one side caved in. "Where did they come from?"

"This is a crypt," Reginn said vaguely. "There are plenty of bones around here."

"Aren't you worried about disturbing the dead?"

You have no idea how worried I am, Reginn thought.

She dumped a few small bones into the shroud to weight the bottom, then stood and spread the mouth of it open. "Bones, please," she said.

With both of them working, it didn't take long to fill the shroud with bones and pack all the empty spaces with scraps of clothing. They ended up with a bulky, bumpy linen sausage.

Reginn eyed it critically. Could anyone possibly mistake this for a corpse?

"Hold it up to yourself," she said.

Obediently, Eiric held it up, arms extended. The length was right, but–

"It really needs to be broader in the shoulders and narrower in the waist," Eiric said, looking down at it. "It would be more realistic if it had a very large–"

"I think it'll do," Reginn said, "unless you want to attach a bigger head. Help me carry it back out into the main room."

They set it atop the dais that Eiric's "dead" body had recently occupied, added more bones, poking and prodding it into shape. Reginn set the sword and axe beside it and covered it all with a fine linen cloth.

They stood back to assess their work.

"Now imagine it covered with tar and buried under kindling," Reginn said.

"I'm trying not to," Eiric said, seeming a little spooked by the notion of planning his own funeral. "They can't do a sending from here. Let me help you take this to the cliffside before I leave."

Reginn shook her head. She could tell that Eiric wanted to make this as easy as possible on his systir. But Reginn didn't want to take any chances that someone would see Eiric Halvorsen, alive and well, tending to his own funeral pyre. "Naima promised to handle that. I don't want anyone to tamper with this before Heidin returns. Or examine it too closely."

She took a last look at the dais, assured herself that the room had been cleared of incriminating evidence, picked up her staff and flute, and hoisted a bulging carry bag onto her shoulder. "Are you ready, coaster?"

Eiric looked up, startled. "We're leaving now? Wouldn't it be better to wait until after dark?"

"On the road you're taking, it won't matter."

18

STAY ALIVE

EIRIC SLID HIS SWORD INTO its scabbard, enjoying the hiss of steel against leather. He threaded Bjorn's axe through the loop on his belt and found a place for the seax beside it. It was good to have weapons close at hand again. There were times when he'd feared that would never happen. He slung a heavy carry bag over each shoulder for balance.

Assuming he actually made it to Ithavoll, it seemed likely that his ship was still hidden in the inlet where he'd left it, since nobody on Ithavoll seemed willing to risk the old battleground.

He eyed Reginn, who resembled a snappish, cranky peddler with her pouches and bags.

Eiric was by no means a sensitive reader of people, but even he could tell that she was hiding something. Would he ever find out what it was? Was she worried that neither one of them would survive the day?

He knew his chances of making it all the way to Muckleholm were slim to none, but he preferred actual death to playing dead.

But Reginn stood to lose a lot—power, respect, and a life of ease in a land of forever summer. Servants at her beck and call. Beauty that would never fade. More books than a person could read in a lifetime. Would want to read, anyway.

Yes, this hall was founded on the blood of the vulnerable, but people found ways to scab over the truth when convenient.

Was it selfish to want her to come with him, when even his escape attempt was putting Reginn at risk?

"If we see anyone, pretend that you're my prisoner," he suggested.

"Pretend that I forced you to lead me out of Eimyrja."

"Good idea," Reginn said, "if you'll explain how I got kidnapped by a dead person."

She waited, but he had no answer for that, so Reginn said, "This way."

Instead of climbing the steps to the door under the Memory Tree, Reginn led the way back into the room housing Brenna's tomb.

This time, she crossed to the tomb and pressed her palm against the face of it, and it slid open silently, revealing a narrow doorway into darkness.

How did you do that? he thought, followed by, Why did you do that?

He had no opportunity to ask, because Reginn had already stepped through the opening and into the tomb.

"This is the way out?" Eiric said, his voice echoing against stone. "Your secret path is through a *tomb*?"

His voice echoed against stone. *Tomb . . . tomb . . . tomb . . .*

She did not answer. Suspicion flickered through him. What if the spinners had decided to bury him alive, to sacrifice him to their mysterious Jotun gods? What if they were toying with him, amused at his spirited attempt at escape?

The old panic rose inside him.

No. He'd be dead already if not for Reginn.

Besides, if that were the game, he had no choice but to play it.

Taking a deep breath, he unslung his carry bags, pushed them through the narrow opening, then followed with his sword. It took considerable twisting and turning, swearing and sweating, to maneuver his broad shoulders through.

By the time he was back on his feet, Reginn had already kindled the end of her staff, throwing light and shadow across the burial chamber. When she saw his face, she said, "What's the matter?"

"I don't like being underground," he said.

"Is that why warriors always want to go to Valhalla?" she said. "Hel isn't good enough?"

"Hel holds too many people I don't want to see again."

Then Eiric was distracted from his discomfort by the grave goods on display.

A stone burial ship took up much of the space in the room. At the center of the stones was an ornate gold casket, studded with jewels. More treasure was piled all around it–loose gemstones and coins, gold and silver armbands, casks and bottles that likely contained food and drink for the journey, and glass beads. There were other, more modest gifts as well–knitted mittens and shawls, and baskets that must have contained food that had long since been eaten by vermin or disintegrated to dust after hundreds of years underground.

Eiric knelt beside the casket, picked up a gold torc, and weighed it in his hands. It was fine work, unlike anything he'd seen before.

Something brushed against his cheek. Startled, he dropped the neckpiece with a clatter.

He looked around and saw nothing to explain it. Was it a bat? A gravewight?

A cobweb?

He raked his fingers through his hair but found nothing.

You are jumpy as a skogkatt, he thought. He reached for the torc again. As soon as his fingers closed around it, the light shifted as Reginn flinched and looked around the room. She seemed as jumpy as he was.

"What is it?" he said. "Did you hear something?"

Reginn waved away the question. "Just–leave that be," she said. "It's never wise to steal from the gods."

He looked up. "Brenna was a god? Are you saying that she was a *Jotun* god?"

"Not a god, but close. It's all getting kind of murky."

"Still. God or not, what good does it do anyone to have these things hidden away down here?" Eiric said, thinking this hoard could be put to a better purpose aboveground. Still, he returned the jewelry to its place and reluctantly turned away.

Reginn now stood before an armored door on the far side of the crypt. She had her back turned to him, but she appeared to be arguing with someone. Someone who wasn't there.

Or, maybe, someone on the other side of the door.

She turned around, putting her back to the door as if to prevent it from opening, her ice-blue eyes vivid against her sun-burnished skin.

"The way out is through here," Reginn said, nodding toward the door behind her. "But there are things you should know before you go."

"All right," Eiric said, thinking, Here it comes. The catch.

"Beyond this door is a network of tunnels that lead to Ithavoll," Reginn said. "At least, I'm pretty sure they do, because that's where I found Heidin, and she said that she came that way from where she and Asger landed. I've never been all the way through them, so I don't exactly know the way."

"I see," Eiric said.

"I don't know what or who you'll encounter in there," Reginn said. "Heidin was attacked in these tunnels by wild boars. Then some aurochs showed up and drove them away." Eiric had the sense that she was skirting around the important part.

"If I run into them, I'll deal with it," Eiric said, shrugging. "I don't have a choice."

"There's something else," she said. "The tunnels are filled with the remains of those who fought in the Last Battle–on both sides. Men and women and monsters of all kinds. Brenna warned me not to go into the tunnels."

"Brenna?" Eiric said. "You mean Brenna the founder, who's been dead for centuries?" He pointed at the casket. "That Brenna?"

Reginn nodded.

"How do you know what Brenna is thinking?" Eiric said.

"She told me."

Eiric waited for more information. When it didn't come, he said, "Did she come to you in a dream, or–?"

"I summoned her. There was information Brenna had that Tyra wanted. In Landvik, Tyra saw my act, when I raised my friend Thurston from the dead. I think that she specifically recruited me because she wanted to try to get information from Brenna–secrets the founder took to the grave. The keeper did not want me to come. I think she suspected what Tyra had in mind.

"Now Tyra knows about the tunnels and wants me to lead her in. I've told her that I haven't been able to get into the tomb since the day Heidin arrived. I told her Brenna knew your systir was in danger and that's why I was able to get in."

Something was happening. The air crackled with tension and magic. It pressed against his skin and stuffed his nostrils, making it difficult to breathe.

He suspected that Reginn felt it, too, because she hunched her shoulders and drew her head in like a turtle. But she returned to her story without mentioning it.

"It took a while, but Brenna finally spoke to me, here in the crypt. She told me my magic was dangerous and unstable–that if I entered the tunnels, there was a risk that I would raise the dead–even if I didn't mean to."

That left Eiric so full of questions he didn't know where to start. It reminded him of the time Liv offered to summon his grandfadir back from the grave to testify at the Thing.

"Do you think it was really her?" he said. "Could Tyra–or someone–be using mind magic on you?"

Reginn shook her head. "I don't see how it could have been Tyra. The person I spoke with knew things that only Brenna would know. She knew things that Tyra wants to know–but doesn't." She fingered the cage at the head of her staff. "This is Brenna's staff. I found it in the tunnels."

"So . . . you've been in the tunnels already," Eiric said.

She nodded, seeming in no hurry to answer the obvious next question.

"And so?"

"Both times, in the tunnels, I heard a clamor of voices, asking me to raise them or lead them."

"You're saying an army of the dead was asking you to take command?"

"That's the way I heard it," Reginn said. "I don't know if it was real, but after Brenna's warning, and my experience in the tunnels, and what happened to Heidin, I can't go with you. I can't afford to take that chance. I worry that I was the one who stirred them up."

"These–vaettir–did they touch you, or grab you or try to stop you?" Eiric said.

Reginn thought for a moment, then shook her head. "I could see them, and hear them, but I don't remember ever being touched by them or hurt by them." She shivered. "The boars and aurochs were real enough."

"If they wanted you to lead, could you have ordered them to stand down?"

"I don't know," she said with a wry smile. "I never thought of that. "So. What I'm saying is that I don't know what might be waiting on the other side of this door."

"I'm not afraid of ghosts," Eiric said, which wasn't entirely true.

The tremors were getting worse. The floor quivered under his feet, and small stones spattered down from overhead, stinging his skin when they hit. The tremor dislodged white berries from the vines that covered the walls and ceiling, and they pelted down all around him.

Reginn looked up, shaking the debris from her hair, protecting her face with her arm. Then she stood. "You need to go," she said. "Now. Get your things."

He stood also, strapped on his scabbard, and scooped up the carry bags. "What's going on?"

There came a rumbling from under their feet. A fissure opened in the stone floor, snaking toward them from the far wall.

"Brenna doesn't want you in the tunnels, either. She's afraid you will launch a repeat of the Last Battle." Reginn grabbed his arm, tugging him toward the door. As she had with the tomb, she pressed her palm against the door and pushed.

It didn't budge.

Dirt and sand sifted down from overhead. A fist-sized rock slammed into Eiric's shoulder, and he hissed out an oath. Between his feet, the fissure was widening, threatening to swallow them both.

"Get back!" he shouted, lifting her away from the widening chasm. He slammed his shoulder against the door and it gave way, sending him staggering into the room beyond, all but stumbling over the heaps of bones all around.

He turned to see her framed in the doorway, a small figure with a staff, a halo of hair escaping from its braid, silhouetted against the growing chaos behind her.

"Raidho," she whispered. Or something like that. Light poured through the doorway, illuminating the way forward.

He reached toward her, knowing there was no way to cross the distance between them. "Stay alive, Reginn," he said. "Stay alive and I will find you."

"Stay alive, Halvorsen," she said, making no further promises.

19
DOUBLE CROSSING

WHEN THE DOOR TO BRENNA'S tomb slammed shut, Eiric retreated a few steps, half expecting it to splinter under the founder's assault. But, gradually, the earth quieted under his feet, and the sounds of falling rock and shattered stone from beyond the door dwindled and died. Warily, he moved closer. Eager for reassurance, he called, "Reginn?"

There was no answer.

He tried the door. It was locked again.

She risked her life to help you escape. The least you can do is take advantage of it.

He pulled a torch from his carry bag and lit it with his fire-steel, even though the light from Reginn's rune showed the way forward.

He began to walk, away from Eimyrja, away from the witches' temples, away from the dead he'd left behind. Away from the systir he no longer knew and the girl who'd left an aching hole in his heart.

All around him lay the remains of the dead and whatever they'd brought with them as they tried to escape the Last Battle. Ragnarok–the end of the world. Bones, of course. Some remains were hard to identify. He assumed they must be creatures he'd never seen before. Creatures of legend, from Bjorn's stories. Creatures he had no desire to meet alive and in person.

Also weapons and armor, ranging from fine swords to battle-axes, mail shirts and helmets to makeshift weapons, such as spears fashioned from sharpened sticks.

There was treasure–enough to set up a coaster for the rest of his life. Gold, silver, and copper coins, arm rings and torcs, pendants and precious stones, rings set with jewels, protected for centuries in this stone graveyard.

What would he take with him if he were fleeing for his life?

He stowed a precious few items in his carry bag. He knew he had to be selective, or be foundered by greed. He collected a few more of the game pieces that Rikhard was so fond of. Always the gold, never the silver.

A little farther along, Eiric's nostrils flared as he caught the stench of decay. It grew stronger and stronger until he rounded a corner and reached a point where the tunnel opened into a wider chamber.

The bodies of dead boars were scattered around the cave, swarming with blind, white, many-legged insects that were feasting on the remaining flesh. This must be the place where Liv was attacked, and Reginn came to her rescue.

There were scorch marks on the walls, from Asger's lash or Reginn's staff or both. Boar bristles on some of the bodies were charred.

Behind a heap of rocks, he found Liv's carry bag that she'd brought with her from Sundgard. It contained her share of the coins he had divided between them, and Sylvi's jewelry, which he'd given to Liv after his modir's death. An amber necklace, two dress brooches, and her silver armband.

They were Liv's last connections to her life at Sundgard.

In the end, he took the bag and all its contents.

He would see her again. He would return them to her.

He left everything else in the stone chamber as it was.

He might have walked for days, or weeks, measuring time by the limitations of his body. He might have walked to Muckleholm and back. He walked until he could walk no more, then slept, the haft of his axe under his hand. Then rose and walked some more. He ate and drank sparingly from his stores, hoping they would last until he died or found the surface.

Reginn's ribbon of light never failed him. He finally extinguished his torch, thinking to save it for a time when the light–and his luck–ran out.

He hadn't heard the voices Reginn had warned him about, or encountered any walking dead. Though he kept his axe ready by his side, he was not troubled by boars or aurochs, though now he was seeing more signs of habitation.

If he hadn't been in such a hurry, he might have paid more attention to the piles of bones swarming with flies that signified more recent kills than those he'd found deeper in the tunnels.

When he rounded a turn, he saw brighter light up ahead and breathed in fresh air. His heart leaped. This must mean this long ordeal was nearly over. He hurried forward.

Until, all at once, the light was blotted out.

Eiric skidded to a stop as his nose was filled with a musky, mildewed stench. He peered ahead along the dimly lit path, and saw a large–no, immense–shape, a silhouette against the light in the doorway.

They stood motionless, looking at each other for what seemed an interminable stretch of time. Eiric knew no more at the end of it than he did at the beginning. Maybe it was some sort of benign cave dweller, though none came to mind in the moment.

Now he saw movement. It was walking toward him, the silhouette growing larger, unexpectedly quiet save for its heavy, wet breathing. The closer it came, the stronger the musky scent, until Eiric's eyes were watering, his stomach turning.

Eiric resisted the temptation to draw his sword, knowing that was the quickest path to a fight he uncharacteristically hoped to avoid. But he rested his hand on Gramr's hilt, signaling his willingness to defend himself.

When the creature drew close enough that Eiric could make out its features in the dim light, his heart sank.

It was some sort of troll, likely a cave troll, given their surroundings. He'd heard that there were trolls in the Archipelago, though they were rumored to be much reduced in size due to interbreeding and lack of adequate food.

Eiric had never seen one close up, and could've gone happily to his grave never having had the pleasure. Its skin hung in sagging gray folds over its heavily muscled body, as if, big as it was, it still had growing to do. Tufts of coarse brown hair sprouted all over its body, everywhere but the top of its head. Slitted nostrils, red-flecked eyes, and a gaping mouth filled with teeth the size of broadswords completed the picture. It carried a massive club that, wielded properly, would prevent Eiric from coming anywhere near it.

He tried to remember what he'd been told about trolls. When he was very small, he used to listen, breathless, to Bjorn's stories.

Were trolls the ones that feared iron and steel? Or were they the ones that asked three riddles?

He sighed and drew his sword, guessing that, once again, this was a fight he could not avoid. Suspecting that it might also be a fight he could not win.

"I am Adulphus," the troll said, "guardian of these tunnels."

"Stand aside," Eiric said. "I would pass in peace."

"The sword in your hand does not speak of peace," the troll said.

"It doesn't bite unless provoked," Eiric said.

"I think you are a thief," the troll said. "Drop your sword and toss your bags to me."

Eiric sighed, rolled his eyes, and fished the runestick from under his shirt. He extended it toward the troll. "Satisfied?"

Adulphus squinted at him. "What is that?"

"A writ of safe passage," Eiric said.

The troll thrust out a hand the size of a side of beef. "Let's see it," it said.

"You can see it well enough from there, if you lean down," Eiric said.

Planting its hands on its thighs, the troll leaned down, its foul breath all but wilting Eiric where he stood. Gripping Gramr's hilt with both hands, Eiric drove the blade into the belly of the troll.

It should have been a killing blow. It *would* have been a killing blow for anyone else, but the troll's skin was so tough that it blunted the power of the thrust.

Adulphus let out a howl so loud it could likely be heard at Sundgard. Steaming black blood poured over Eiric, fouling him head to toe.

He hoped it was blood.

At least it could be argued that he no longer carried the stink of Asgard.

Eiric dove to one side to avoid being drowned or crushed, slamming hard into the stone wall of the tunnel. He lay, stunned, for a moment, while Adulphus staggered around, still bellowing in pain, its club smashing against stone, sending shards of rock and larger boulders flying.

Eiric scrambled to his feet and slid Gramr into its scabbard. His seax and his axe would serve him better in close quarters. A weapon in each hand, he flattened himself against the wall of the tunnel and sidled toward the light.

"There you are!" the troll shouted. It swung the club at Eiric with both hands, striking the wall of the cave with such force that it all but opened a new side tunnel. But Eiric was no longer there.

He charged forward, inside its reach, and buried his axe in the flesh of its thigh. Ripping the blade free, Eiric sprinted toward what he hoped was the way out.

"Stand and fight, coward!" the troll cried. Eiric could feel its hot breath on the back of his neck. Twice, the club whistled past his ear, uncomfortably close. One lucky hit, and Eiric would be done for good.

Eiric breathed in the sea air and squinted against the sunlight, feeling a flicker of hope. He was nearly there. He was crossing the threshold when something slammed into him, sending him tumbling head over heels through a mass of shrubbery and down a slight incline, his weapons flying from his hands.

Eiric crab-scrambled to one side, into the underbrush, half expecting Adulphus to land on top of him, but it didn't. He crouched there, listening, but heard only birdsong and the crash of the sea onto rocks nearby.

It seemed that every part of him hurt. He was covered in scratches, scrapes, and bruises, and he was sure he would discover more by the end of the day.

The troll blood was almost worse. He felt as if he'd fallen into his uncles' tar pits.

But he was still alive, for now.

Scanning the area around him, he retrieved Bjorn's axe. Again, he waited. Finally, still hearing nothing, he stood and peered back toward the mouth of the cave.

It was now half obscured by a massive stone that hadn't been there before. Had Adulphus dislodged an outcropping with a blow of its club that had ended at the entrance to the tunnels? Was it still possible to get in and out?

More important, had it crushed the troll?

Eiric searched and found his seax, keeping an eye on the cave mouth, but there was no sign of life. He moved out of the line of sight of the cave and climbed to a position on the hill above so that he would have the high ground and time to react if the troll reappeared.

He stood on a point of land, with a clear view in three directions.

His heart sank. He'd come out on the wrong side of the rift, and about as far from his ship as he could be. In order to reach it, he would need to thread his way through the military complex, successfully cross the rift without being seen, and travel across the battlefield of Vigrid.

And hope that the karvi was still there, and sailable.

At that rate, he might set sail in time to meet the storms of the winter solstice.

Would the troll sound the alarm in the meantime?

He circled around until he could approach the mouth of the cave from the side. Every few steps, he stopped and listened. Scanning the hill above, he couldn't see a gash where the stone had broken free and tumbled down into place.

Finally, he reached a spot where he could take a good look at the boulder. The stone glittered where the sunlight hit it. It was bulky, unweathered, the shape resembling a crouching bear, or some other—

Abruptly, Eiric collapsed against the stone, sliding down until his buttocks hit the ground, helpless with laughter and relief.

It didn't just resemble a crouching creature. That's exactly what it was. It was the troll, its club beside it, with a level of detail that would gladden the heart of a master stone-carver.

Now Eiric remembered what Bjorn had told him about trolls. They lived in caves and traveled by night because sunlight turned them to stone.

20

THE SENDING

THE FOUR WOMEN STOOD ON the cliff top, clutching cloaks that might otherwise have been ripped from their shoulders in the rising gale.

Tyra gazed out at the churning ocean. "I've never seen the seas so turbulent here in Eimyrja," she said.

"My brodir's grandfadir Bjorn always claimed to descend from Njord, the Vanir god of the sea," Heidin said. "Maybe that explains it." She turned back toward Eiric's bier, and rearranged some of the kindling stacked on top. It did not need rearranging, but Heidin seemed driven to provide care to her brodir at his sending.

Naima stood nearby, next to a small table that held a cask of wine and four cups. Fine elders' wine, as she had promised. Reginn had already gulped down far too much of it.

Tyra and Heidin had returned from Ithavoll the night before to news that Eiric's sending was scheduled for the following morning.

"That's good," Tyra had said, "since we intend to sail for the Archipelago as soon as everything is in readiness." The kennari was trying hard to appear somber, to match Heidin's mood.

Naima handed Heidin a bag of flower petals, and she scattered them over the pyre. The wind instantly snatched them up and swirled them away and out to sea until they were swallowed by the gloom.

"It's a good sign," Tyra said, smiling, "that the barbarian has returned to the sea."

Yes, Reginn thought, he has, if the fates allow.

Stay alive.

Staff in hand, Reginn strode to the foot of the pyre. "Lady Heidin," she said. "Would you like to speak for your brodir?"

Heidin nodded and took her place at the head of the bier. "Brodir," she said. "We've had our differences over the years, but the bond between us has only strengthened. We have always looked out for each other. The fates have decreed that we part ways–for now, at least. I am glad that we will never take up arms against each other, but I regret that we will never again stand back to back against our enemies. If the time comes that I must leave the Midlands, I would join you, wherever you are, so that we can be together again."

Tyra was still smiling, but only because it seemed to be frozen to her face.

Heidin tilted her staff down and touched the flaming tip of it to the bier. She took a quick step back as the pyre erupted in flame. Reginn exchanged glances with Naima, nodded her approval, and set her end of the pyre aflame.

Reginn, too, was forced back as the heat of the fire scorched her skin. The offshore winds whipped the blaze higher until she guessed it could be seen for miles out to sea.

She liked to think that Eiric might see it, from wherever he was.

Maybe he could, if the barrier was down, which she prayed it was.

Reginn helped herself to more wine.

21

ANY PORT IN A STORM

EIRIC BATHED IN A ROCKY pool just inside the mouth of a narrow, deep fjord that extended south from the north shore of Ithavoll. Happily, it turned out that troll blood is easier to wash off than tar. He rinsed his stinking clothes and laid them in the sun to dry, then put on the one pair of reasonably clean breeches and a shirt left in his carry bag.

He followed the fjord south, reasoning that there would be settlements along the water, hoping to find food and a horse to steal.

That was easier said than done. The stone walls of the fjord rose so steeply from the water that in most places, there was no alternative to swimming.

So he climbed up a rocky gorge, navigating around multiple waterfalls, until he came upon a faint wildlife trail far enough below the rim that he wouldn't be silhouetted against the sky.

He continued on, with the setting sun over his right shoulder and a stomach-turning drop-off to his right. There were places where the trail was cut by ravines, rockfalls, and streams. These were likely not a problem for the mountain goats that had made the trail, but they presented a challenge to any two-legged traveler. Still, it was good to test his strength again, after so much idleness.

Eiric walked until the waning light made it too dangerous to go on, ate hunks of barley bread, cheese, and a handful of dried fruit, then curled up and slept like the dead.

The next morning, while shadow still cloaked the narrow valley, Eiric took up his trek again. By the end of that second day, he was weary and a little footsore, but encouraged that the terrain was changing, softening, the walls of the fjord becoming less steep. Now and then he saw a fishing cottage or other small dwelling near the water's edge. None of them looked prosperous enough to offer an opportunity for a horse, but he suspected they meant that he was nearing the southern end.

And finally, it came into sight, a horseshoe of stone enclosing the landward end of the fjord. A river entered the fjord here, its delta forming a wide, flattened valley.

Buildings clustered at the water's edge, with long wharves poking out into the deep water.

More important, several ships were at anchor in this natural harbor.

Ships! Horses of a sort.

Maybe better than horses.

Eiric stowed his gear, scrambled a short distance down from the trail, and flopped onto his belly so he could peer over the edge.

The tide was coming in, swelling the river. The anchored ships strained at their leashes. He counted three longships, each with thirty sections–ships that could carry upward of two hundred crew. With a full crew, these ships would fly–assuming they were properly built. There were also two knarrs, with fewer oars and more stowage. And, finally, a sleek, half-size karvi, a pretty little dragon that reminded him of the one that he hoped still lay hidden on the south shore.

He saw people aboard some of the ships, strapping down supplies, getting ready to sail soon.

This must be the fleet his systir wanted him to lead to Muckleholm.

Well then. He'd just leave a little ahead of everyone else.

Eiric climbed back up to where his gear was hidden, settled in, and ate his nattmal of more cheese, dried fruit, and hard bread. He rolled up in his blanket and lay down, meaning to wait for a favorable tide during the night watch, when the ships would be lightly crewed.

Somehow, he slept. In fact, he slept longer than he anticipated, because the moon had already set by the time he roused himself. That meant he had to navigate the descent to the water's edge in the dead dark, which might have ended the adventure right then. Happily, he made it down in one piece. Even better, he saw a small oarboat dragged up on the shore, no doubt used to carry supplies and crew to and from the ships in the harbor.

When he looked up and down the wharf, he saw no sign that they'd set a watch. The ships were dark, with no lights showing. That didn't mean a lot. It was risky to leave lamps unattended on a wooden ship.

Once again, he surveyed his systir's fleet, weighing his prospects. His gaze lingered on the great ships, his heart filled with longing. They were bigger than any of the ships he'd crewed on before, bigger than Leif's longship, even.

But there was no way he could sail such a ship by himself. The knarrs were a better bet, since they relied more on wind than rowing. He might be able to manage, once underway, but right now, the ships' banners hung limply on the masts. Not much wind found its way between these high walls, so, even with the tide in his favor, he knew it would take a good deal of rowing to find the wind.

The only ship he could possibly sail on his own was the half-size dragon. Even then, if he was seen, he was sure to be overtaken by a ship with a full complement of rowers.

To the east, the sky was lightening along the top of the cliff. There was no time for dithering.

Eiric shrugged. He would do his best, and the fates would determine the outcome. He was beginning to understand why Bjorn was so fond of the fates—they made it easier to make decisions.

Now decided, he crossed to the oarboat and dropped his gear

between the thwarts. Gripping the prow, he shoved it off the gravel shore and leaped aboard.

His momentum carried the boat forward, into deeper water. Eiric loosed the oars from their clips under the gunwales and took a seat. Though his muscles complained, it felt good to have oars in his hands again.

Eiric threaded the oarboat between the ships, careful not to splash. Once he caught the river current, his major task was to avoid being driven into the side of one of the ships.

The little dragon was, of course, farthest from the wharf, which made for more rowing now, but perhaps less risk of discovery later.

Eiric came up alongside the ship without incident. Seeing no activity on board, he tethered the lines to the shield rack and dropped his belongings over the gunwale. Taking another quick look around, he boarded.

It was easy to tell that this ship was brand-new–the smell of tar and green wood was thick in his nose. The sail was neatly rolled and tied along the yard, unfaded, still smelling of lanolin. The sea had not yet marked it as its own.

He liked what he saw. It had been designed and built by an expert, using techniques familiar from the time he'd spent in Bjorn's boathouse.

Liv, he thought. Liv had a hand in this. Though some claimed it was bad luck to allow a woman to build a boat, Bjorn never subscribed to that. When Liv first arrived at Sundgard, Bjorn enlisted her help in building a small fishing boat while Eiric looked on jealously. It was through those long winter hours in the boathouse that Bjorn had finally earned Liv's trust and forgiveness.

This theory was reinforced when Eiric saw the figurehead on the bow stem. A bird emerging, flaming, from an egg. The firebird. Liv's signia.

"Who are you?"

Eiric spun around, startled, his axe in one hand and the seax in the other.

There were two of them, blinking like owls, as if they'd just awakened. Young–a couple of years younger than Eiric, a boy and a girl. And behind them, two more, peering out from under the tarp they'd been sleeping under.

They were clad in what appeared to be bondi buff, but it had been repeatedly stamped with a blue wavelet symbol. The same emblem was burned into their upper arms.

By now they all stood together, eyes fixed on his weapons like a grove of saplings ready to be cut down.

Eiric was not getting the reaction he'd come to expect in New Jotunheim–virulent hatred, revulsion, or fear.

"Do you know who I am?" Eiric said.

They all looked at each other, as if embarrassed.

Finally, the girl spoke up. "Are you the navigator? Knut said that they would send an experienced styrman or ship's master to command our ship."

"He told us to stay on the ship until the styrman came," added a boy with a shaved head and a scalp lock. "He didn't mention a name."

Their accents were a little different from others Eiric had heard on Eimyrja and Ithavoll. Their light eyes and sculpted faces reminded him of some he'd seen from the far north and east.

"They never told us you would be so big," one of the boys said.

Scalp Lock elbowed him and said, "Shut up, Levi." He was heads taller than the other boys, barrel-chested, with muscled arms. Cocky.

"What's your name?" Eiric said.

"Rorik," the boy said.

Eiric had a decision to make, and quickly. He couldn't allow these ones to return to shore and report the big, fair-haired stranger who'd stolen their ship. He'd have a longship up his ass in no time. Maybe two. There was no way he'd outrun them or fight them off alone.

And then they would know that Reginn had betrayed them. He couldn't let that happen.

He tightened his grip on his seax. The safest thing would be to cut their throats and toss them overboard once he was in the open ocean.

Welcome to the war. How was it for you?

In stories, these problems were easy to solve.

Not in his life. Never in his life.

"My name is Bjorn Eiricsen, your new commander," Eiric said. "Can someone explain to me why I was able to board this ship with nobody raising an alarm?"

"They never said to set a guard," Rorik said.

"Ah. So you were waiting for somebody to tell you what to do."

"Well, the enemy is in Barbaria," Rorik said, his confidence flagging a little. "The boundary is in the way."

"Is it? Do you know that for certain?"

"Well, nobody else has set a guard," the girl said.

"What if you're wrong?" Eiric said. "What if I am your enemy? You are all dead."

"Maybe," Rorik said, flushing, fists clenched. "Maybe not."

"Maybe not," Eiric conceded. "Where are your weapons?"

"Weapons?" The girl hesitated, as if momentarily confused, then pointed over her shoulder. "Midships."

"Are they doing you any good there? Do you think your enemy will wait while you fetch them?"

Again, that brief hesitation, the tell for a lie. She glanced at the others, then shook her head. "No."

"If you are midway between here and Muckleholm, and your captain falls overboard, do you drop your sail and hope somebody comes by with orders?"

"No," the girl said, glowering. "We divvy up the captain's tasks and sail on."

"Good," Eiric said. "Even if the captain is on board, it can be hard to hear orders in a storm, or in a battle. My point is that in a small crew, everyone has to be able to read the situation and make decisions, in the absence of orders from somebody else." He paused. "What's your name?"

"Reyna Fisker," she said, planting herself and lifting her chin as if she expected to be challenged.

"Are there provisions on board?"

They nodded.

"How much and what kind?"

"Smoked fish and pork, barley, dried fruit, honey, and hazelnuts, fresh water, enough for a week," said a slender, green-eyed boy. He looked Eiric up and down. "Though if you're coming aboard, we might need to recalculate. I'm Levi, by the way."

"The tide's in our favor," Eiric said. "How long will it take you to get this ship ready to go to sea?"

Not long at all, it turned out, which was a good thing, because the rising sun had set the rim of the fjord aflame and light was leaking into the valley.

In no time, they had the decks cleared, their bedding stowed away, the sail unstrapped and ready to raise, and oars deployed, two on each side. The ship could accommodate six to a side, but two would do. From the looks of things, they'd done this many times before. Together.

His little crew was good. Very good, in fact. Not warriors, perhaps, but good sailors.

"We're ready, Styrman," Rorik said. He looked shoreward. "When will the others be here?"

"There are no others," Eiric said. "It's just us this time."

Eiric took his place by the styrboard. He would have been happy to join in on the oars, but that would make an odd number. As soon as they found the wind, there would be plenty to do.

He saw movement onshore now, workers arriving at the boat-houses, throwing open the doors. Visitors on horseback, greeted by officials. It was past time to be gone.

Eiric lowered his voice in order to avoid the sound carrying over the water. "The best way for me to get to know you and our ship is to take her out and see what you can do. We're going to allow the tide to carry us, correcting our course as needed with the oars and styrboard. When we're well away, we'll raise the sail."

"And go where?" Reyna said.

"That depends on how this goes," Eiric said, thinking, Maybe nowhere.

22

THE SHIPYARD

WHEN THE ASHES OF EIRIC'S bonefires had cooled, Reginn quickly scooped them into an ornate silver casket and sealed it up to prevent anyone taking a closer look.

Rather than entomb the remains of her controversial brodir in the Hall of Memory, Heidin elected to construct a small shrine at the edge of the cliff.

"That way my brodir will always be able to hear the sound of the sea," she said, blotting her eyes with the back of her hand.

Within days, the shrine was covered with ribbons, each in memory of someone the barbarian had slain. Reginn took them down before Heidin could see them.

In the somber days following Eiric's sending, Heidin often sought Reginn's company, possibly seeing her as her one ally in the attempt to save her brodir's life. Or, at least, one of the few who regretted his death.

Reginn had expected to get the blame for failing. But Heidin was blaming herself.

A few days after the sending, Heidin invited Reginn to ride to Ithavoll with her to visit the new shipyard and see the fledgling Jotunheim fleet.

Since her return to New Jotunheim, Heidin had used her experiences coasting with her fadir and brodir to design longships suitable for war, though still broad enough in the beam to carry soldiers.

Reginn and Heidin set out in the middle of the night to take advantage of low tide at the crossing and to avoid the hird that Tyra insisted should accompany Heidin everywhere.

"If I can't protect myself, I have no business leading an attack on Muckleholm," Heidin said dryly. Reginn suspected that Tyra also wanted to keep tabs on her strong-willed dottir.

Only Svend came along as escort, having won Heidin over with his quiet competence.

The light from their staffs gilded the ripples of the incoming tide as they made the crossing. Even then, there was still a distance to ride. The shipyard was at the north end of Ithavoll, within the shelter of a fjord that bit into the island between the iron furnace and the foundry.

Even though it was too dark to see anything but a few scattered lamps in the villages, Reginn kept looking back over her shoulder toward the rift and the sea crossing. Had Eiric made it to Ithavoll? If the cave exit was on the wrong side of the river, could he have made it across the rift without being seen?

"You're awfully quiet," Heidin said, reining in at an overlook. "Is something wrong?"

"No," Reginn said. Then shook her head. "That's really not true. It's just–so much has happened, and so much will happen, most of which I can't control."

Heidin nodded. "I know what you mean. I feel like a small ship, driven by the storm, toward a destination I never chose."

"You don't have to go," Reginn said. "Tove always said, if you don't know where you're going, slow down."

"Who's Tove?"

"My foster modir." After a pause, she added, "She had her own agenda, so I'm not sure you should rely on her advice."

Heidin laughed. "Beware of modirs and their agendas." She heeled her horse and they rode on.

As they topped a low rise, the fjord finally came into view, a dark blue-green finger poking in from the sea. Now a river appeared on their right-hand side, a narrow, swift stream that funneled down from even higher ground to the east. Reginn became aware of a low roaring sound that grew gradually louder as they rode on.

Heidin pointed forward, to where a cloud of mist all but obscured the trail ahead. "That's Nordfoss," she said. "That's where we're going."

Finally, they reached an overlook, a relatively flat platform of rock. On one side, Nordfoss–where the river tumbled hundreds of feet into the fjord below, so loud that it was difficult to make conversation. On the other, a guard post, confirmed when two soldiers in buff stormed out to challenge them.

When they saw who it was, they all but fell on their faces. "Highest!" they croaked. "We did not expect you."

"Calamity is always unexpected," Heidin said. "Be at ease." Then turned to Reginn. "This is the best place to get a good view of the ships before we ride down to the shipyard." She slid to the ground, and Reginn followed suit. In tandem, they advanced to a low wall along the cliff's edge and looked down into the fjord.

At the near end, buildings and docks clustered on the banks of a river that entered the fjord at the near end. Six ships studded the harbor. Three were longships, similar to ones Reginn had seen in Muckleholm every spring, preparing to go vikingr. Two others were shorter, with a broader beam, more like the knarr that had carried Reginn to Eimyrja in the first place. And, finally, there was a small ship that appeared to be modeled after the warships, but was about half the length. Its gilded vane caught the first rays of the sun.

Though it was still early, she could see figures moving on board.

"Do you like my little *Firebird*?" Heidin said, following her gaze. "We've been using her for training. We begin here in the fjord, which presents its own challenges due to the high cliffs on all sides that block the wind. Here, we focus on working with the oars. Then, when they're ready, we raise the sail and go out to the open sea."

"It's beautiful," Reginn murmured. "Will it be going to war as well?"

Heidin nodded. "It's going to help us with the problem of the sunstones. As you know, we have only three, which means that only three ships can cross the weather boundary at a time. Our plan is to position the fleet just inside the boundary and send three across at a time, using the *Firebird* to ferry stones back to the remaining ships."

"Good idea," Reginn said. "How are you doing for crew?"

"Pretty well, now," Heidin said. "Our master shipbuilder, Knut, comes from Vestholm, where most people used to make their living fishing. He has been helpful in recruiting skilled sailors from there and other nearby islands. They've been sailing these waters for centuries. The challenge is to turn skilled sailors into warriors. For that, we need helmsmen who can do both." She paused and then, her voice roughened, said, "I had planned to give Eiric his choice of ships."

A silence fell heavy between them.

What if I told her? Would she be grateful or enraged? Or both?

The moment passed. "Here they are," Heidin said, pointing to two mounted figures climbing the rocky trail from the harbor. "I asked Knut and Elder Eira to meet us up here. They can answer your questions better than I can."

When the newcomers reached the top, they dismounted and handed off their horses to the waiting guards.

One was Elder Eira, the maker. No elder finery for her–she was clad in faded coveralls, a tool belt around her waist. Even after the ride to the top, her raven's-wing hair was powdered with sawdust and studded with wood chips.

The other was a man of middle age, similarly attired, but in bondi buff. His arms were covered with blue wavelets and his seamed face said that he had spent a lifetime working in the weather.

"Welcome, Highest," Eira said, bowing to Heidin. Turning to

Reginn, she embraced her. "Reginn! I can't believe you've never been here!"

"We keep her busy in the Hall of Memory," Heidin said.

I spend my time with dead people, Reginn thought, not the living.

"Elder Reginn, this is Knut," Eira said, nodding toward the man. "He is our master shipbuilder. He is the one responsible for"–she gestured toward the harbor–"all of this."

"You give me too much credit," Knut said. "I could not have done it without the help of our lady." He bowed to Heidin. "I've built knarrs and fishing boats only. There are so many details that I didn't know about warships."

"It's amazing, what you've done in so short a time," Reginn said.

"We're still finishing up the sails for some of them," Eira said. "That's the most time-consuming part, but we have a whole team of weavers working on it."

"Have you taken these ships out of the fjord?"

"Some, to test for balance and seaworthiness," Eira said. "We won't be able to take the entire fleet to sea until we can recruit some more navigators and helmsmen."

"Could some of Durinn's commanders be repurposed?"

"It's not that easy, even with the kennari's help," Eira said. "There are so few here in New Jotunheim who have that combination of skills–warrior and sailor."

They're all waiting for you in Barbaria, Reginn thought. A flicker of movement drew her gaze to the harbor. It was the *Firebird*, expertly threading her way down the fjord toward the open sea, her oars rising and falling as one.

She traveled impossibly fast, practically skimming across the water. Then Reginn realized that the styrman was taking advantage of the river current and the outflowing tide.

The tall helmsman stood next to the styrboard, his fair hair glittering in the first rays of the sun. Something about his shoulders and the way he moved stole her breath in a familiar way and set her heart to pounding.

It was Eiric Halvorsen. It could be no one else. But how did that make sense? She tried to conjure a sequence of events that would bring all of them together in this place. Panic boiled into her throat. If Reginn recognized him at this distance, then surely his systir would.

She knew she should do something, cause some kind of distraction, but she could not tear her eyes away.

Now a light breeze stirred his hair. He glanced up at the vane, then moved forward to the mast. He bent, unfastened the straps binding the sail, then hauled on the lines, head back, his bound hair swinging out behind him. Slowly, the red-and-white sail climbed the mast, then bellied out as it caught the wind. The *Firebird* lunged, moving faster and faster until she was flying.

Soon, Reginn hoped, they would fly out of sight.

Not soon enough.

Reginn looked over her shoulder to find Heidin deep in conversation with Knut, something about what supplies were needed to repair damage to ships at sea.

But Eira was staring down the fjord, a perplexed frown on her face.

"Knut," she said. "Who's taking *Firebird* out? I gave orders that all the ships were to remain in port until Her Highness and Elder Reginn completed their review."

"*Especially* the *Firebird*," Heidin said. "I intended to invite Reginn aboard to show her off."

Now Knut and Heidin joined Eira along the wall.

"I don't understand," Knut said. "She has a good young crew aboard, but no helmsman. Their orders were to wait until we sent one."

"Then who's that?" Eira said, pointing at the tall figure at the helm.

Heidin's face displayed no sign of recognition. "Well now," she said, her eyes still fixed on the ship, "they must have found a helmsman somewhere."

"It might be one of the pilots from Fiskeholm," Knut said. "They're still not accustomed to following orders."

"Is there any chance of catching them now?" Heidin said as the *Firebird* merged with the horizon, then disappeared.

Knut shook his head. "No, ma'am, not with the tide behind them. Now they're out of sight, there'll be no way of knowing which way they'll turn when they reach the open sea. I'm sorry, Highest. They'll be in real trouble when they return."

"*If* they return," Heidin murmured. "Tell me, Eira, are the sunstones secure?"

"Yes, Highest," Eira said.

"I'd like to verify that," Heidin said. "Let's go down to the wharfside and see if anything else is missing."

"Highest," Knut said, "though young, they are an honest crew. I chose them for your ship because they are skilled and trustworthy. I hope that you will take that into account if they–when they return."

"We'll see, won't we?" Heidin said. And then, turning to Reginn, said, "Given what's happened, Counselor, we're not going to be able to complete your review of the fleet and tour of our facilities today." Reginn could tell that she was embarrassed that this had happened so close to their departure.

Heidin turned to Svend. "As soon as the tide allows, please escort Elder Reginn back to her quarters at the House of Elders. We will speak when I return to Eimyrja."

23
THIRD BURNING

WHEN HEIDIN FINALLY RETURNED TO the Grove, Reginn waited to be summoned, then reached out, twice, and got no response.

What had Heidin seen? What had she learned at the shipyard? Had they tracked down the rogue ship and its helmsman?

Every time Reginn crossed the quad, she felt like a mouse under the eye of a hawk, scurrying for cover, back hunched in anticipation of claws shredding her flesh to ribbons.

She'd all but given up hope that Trude, the library mouse, would reconnect. Every time she returned to the library, she checked the message niche, finding only her own note, growing more brittle with time.

Reginn continued to hunt for books and manuscripts that might provide her some means of preventing the coming war. The likelihood that she would come up empty-handed after days or hours or months of work made her want to go back to her quarters and take a nap.

One night, as she emerged from the library, she found Asger waiting outside, flaming.

"*There* you are," he said.

"Here I am," Reginn said, surprised to find him there. It seemed weeks since she had last seen him. Today he was looking unusually fine–his black silk coat embroidered with Heidin's firebird, his hair less tumbled than usual, his leather boots freshly shined. "Why–were you looking for me?"

"Did you not get the kennari's message?"

"No," Reginn said, her mouth going dry. *This is it–the reckoning.* "I've been holed up in the library."

"You were supposed to be at the House of Elders half an hour ago."

"I was? Why?"

Asger took her arm, pulling her toward the center of the campus. "You know, it would help if you at least made an effort. The kennari's patience is wearing thin, and the Jotun queen becomes more dangerous by the day."

"I *am* making an effort," Reginn said, wrenching free. "You seem to have forgotten that you are not my master anymore."

"I am well aware of that," Asger said. "If I were, you would be better served." He reached for her again, then dropped his hand. "Please," he said. "I am trying to keep you alive."

Please? Reginn stared at him for a long moment, dumbfounded. Then nodded briskly, and turned toward the quad. "If you tell me what is going on."

"I don't exactly know," he said, his long legs covering ground at a remarkable pace, "but it seems to be important."

When they came in sight of the House of Elders, Reginn saw that the wide steps and dais fronting the building were crowded with people, lit with blazing torches. Large tents were set up on the grassy quad, flying pennants with Heidin's firebird emblem.

"Good," Asger said. "It hasn't started yet."

Reginn's skin prickled. It reminded her too much of the day the Council of Elders had been murdered. The day that was supposed to be Eiric Halvorsen's "execution" day.

Unlike on that day, the crowd parted to let them through, bowing and murmuring, "Highest."

At the base of the steps, a phalanx of guards awaited them, six deep. One of them was Svend, who ushered them to the right and up the steps.

"What's going on?" Reginn whispered to Svend.

"Some kind of big announcement, Highest," Svend whispered back. "A ceremony, followed by a feast. I hope it is good news. We need some good news."

The other members of the new council comprised two blue wings on either side of the dais. Reginn took her place between Shelby and Katia, while Asger removed himself to a position just behind a roped-off area.

That's when Reginn saw it: a huge pile of wood and kindling intertwined with sage and lavender, studded with sweet resins and poppies, centered by the trunk of an oak tree stripped of bark.

For one stricken moment, Reginn thought it must be a preparation for an execution by burning. She immediately thought of Eiric Halvorsen. Had he been intercepted? Had this one great risk she'd taken ended in failure?

Perhaps the pyre was meant for her.

The kennari's patience is wearing thin.

But the scene had a festive air, with canopies mounted over the crowd to either side, and festooned with greens and flowers, as for a wedding.

Or a sacrifice.

And there was music—a lyre, expertly played, the notes winging over the crowd like birds. Familiar. Reginn scanned Founder's Square until she found him. Erland was seated atop a platform overlooking the square.

The music rose to a crescendo and died away. The crowd stilled as a tall figure walked to center stage, staff in hand.

Tyra wore her usual sapphire blue, the bone carving of Heidin on a cord at her neck alongside the kynstone. The amma's blood-red garnet ring glittered on her left hand.

Modir Tyra's voice rang out over the square. "Welcome, everyone. We face many challenges in the days ahead—challenges that will test our courage and resolve. As we prepare for war, it is important to remember that the foe we face is ruthless. Thousands of jotnar are still held captive in the Archipelago, stigmatized by their gift of magic. No longer satisfied with extinguishing the spark of magic at home, they are coming after us. The barbarians have taken aim at the very heart of our sanctuary. No doubt they will return in force and lay waste to our paradise–unless we strike first.

"The good news is that we have a weapon they have never seen, and could never imagine."

Reginn leaned toward Katia. "Any idea what she's talking about?" she whispered.

She shrugged. "It's probably something Eira and the others are working on over on Ithavoll."

"Shhh!" someone behind them said, because Tyra was speaking again.

"Many of you know the story of the Jotun goddess Gullveig, who traveled to Asgard as an emissary from the Utangard. We were tired of Asgardian incursions into our lands, stealing our treasures, carrying us off as thralls, spilling their seed everywhere. On the advice of the Vanir gods, Gullveig offered the secrets of sorcery to the warriors of the Innangard. They responded by trying to kill her. Three times they burned her. And at the end, she was reborn as Heidin, more powerful than before. From that day forward, she defended the Utangard until she was struck down during the Last Battle at Ragnarok.

"For centuries, she has slept, biding her time, regaining strength, awaiting the arrival of those who could raise her once more." She paused. "That time has come." She turned back toward the House of Elders just as the great double doors slammed open, and Heidin emerged.

She was barefoot, clad in a long linen underdress, her hair done up in a crown of braids. Her scarred and twisted skin contrasted starkly with the bleached white linen. Her only ornaments were the familiar gold-and-silver pendant set with the amber figure of the goddess and the elaborate staff she carried.

Slowly, she walked from the rear of the dais toward the front, as if unaware of the crowds lining the platform and the square. They, in turn, fell silent, breathless as she came, the hem of her dress stirred by her movement, revealing, then concealing, bare toes on stone.

Scanning the crowd, Reginn saw an ashy gray figure pass through it, like mist through a forest at dawn.

Trude. It was the first time Reginn had ever seen her outside of the library.

She hadn't noticed Reginn. She took her place at the front and stood, fists clenched, fixed on Heidin as if unable to turn away.

Reginn wanted to leap from the dais and confront this erstwhile ally who had abandoned her. But Tyra's voice broke into her thoughts.

"Behold Heidin, warrior goddess of the Jotun, twice burned," Modir Tyra proclaimed. Heidin walked past the kennari, chin up, without acknowledging her presence. She continued until she came abreast of the prepared pyre. Turning, she walked into the center of the ring of firewood, positioning herself with her back to the oak tree.

"Heidin," Reginn whispered, horrified. "Heidin, no!"

Four adepts rushed forward with burning torches to set the pyre alight, but Heidin said, "No!" in a voice that could have carried all the way to Ithavoll. The adepts backed away.

Reginn's momentary relief gave way to horror as Heidin said, "This time, I claim my own destiny." The distaff end of her staff kindled and she spun it round, so that the fuel piled high around her caught and exploded into flame.

"Behold!" Heidin cried, spreading her arms wide like wings. "I rise!"

Some in the crowd below screamed and fled the square, but others cheered and cried, "Firebird! Rise!"

Reginn tried to rush forward, but someone seized hold of her arms and dragged her back. She spun, her staff whistling through the air. She barely missed Shelby, who threw himself backward, landing flat on his back. He rolled to his feet, both hands raised, as if to fend her off.

"Don't you . . . ever . . . do that again," Reginn gasped. "Don't you ever take hold of me uninvited."

"I'm just trying to prevent you from throwing your life away," Shelby said. "I don't know why you're different, but you are, and it's putting you at risk."

Reginn turned back to the roaring flames, but it was already too late to intervene. It had been too late from the start. The smoke rolled over her. She expected to breathe in the stench of burning flesh, but all she smelled was lavender, sage, and myrrh.

Heidin never made a sound.

"Reginn," Shelby said softly. "Don't you believe in the fates? This is her destiny."

"No!" Reginn growled. She pointed to where the kennari stood, firelight bloodying the contours of her face, watching as the blaze showered sparks over the rapt onlookers. "Tyra did this. She sacrificed her own daughter. Her desire for revenge has driven her mad."

"Shhh," Shelby said, looking around for eavesdroppers. "You don't understand. Heidin has prepared for this all her life. She was born for this."

Now it was Reginn's turn to get up in Shelby's face. "What do you mean?" she demanded. "What are you saying?"

"Well, she–you know–she's the firebird. Thrice burned. The one weapon Asgard cannot counter."

Everyone knew about this but me, Reginn realized. *Everyone approves of this but me.*

What will Eiric Halvorsen do when he finds out that his systir was burned to death while everyone stood and watched?

While *I* stood and watched.

The flames rose, the heat driving adepts, dedicates, and soldiers back to the edge of the dais, until some were forced to leap from the platform to avoid being pushed off.

Reginn and Shelby stood with the rest of the council, nobody moving or speaking, as embers spiraled into the sky. Finally, Reginn tore her gaze away from the dwindling flames and looked down at her toes, eyes filling with tears of remorse. "I'm sorry, Heidin," she whispered. "I'm sorry, Eiric. I should have gone with you, so I wouldn't have to see this."

Minutes passed, during which Reginn wondered if she should stay or go. Then a murmur of excitement rose from those who still remained on the platform.

"Reginn," Shelby whispered, his breath warm against her ear. "Look."

Reginn looked up to see movement amid the flames and smoke. A form seemed to coalesce before their eyes, gathering itself as it emerged from the pyre. A woman with golden skin, hair, and eyes, as if she'd been dipped into a crucible of molten metal. And, yet, light shone through, as if her skin was translucent, or the light held within it was too brilliant to contain.

When Reginn looked into those golden eyes, she saw a stranger.

Heidin was entirely naked except for the familiar pendant. The amber had burned away, and the engraved metal was married to her–embedded into the skin of her chest.

"Behold," Tyra said, "our queen, the goddess, Heidin reborn."

All around her, people fell to their knees like trees going down under the axe, leaving only three still standing–Tyra, Reginn, and Trude–like so many snags amid stumps. Shelby and Katia gripped Reginn's arm and pulled her down beside them. This time, she was too stunned to protest.

Two adepts rushed forward with a cloak of brilliant feathers and draped it around Heidin's shoulders. Heidin extended her arms, and the effect was that of a bird spreading its wings.

"Now," she said. "I fly."

With that, Trude faded back into the crowd. Reginn scrambled to her feet and chased after her, not caring who noticed.

24

SUDDENLY AT SEA

WHEN EIRIC'S SHIP LEFT THE shelter of the fjord, he was at sea in more ways than one–on an unfamiliar ship with an unfamiliar crew in unfamiliar waters. His mind careened from one worry to another like a karvi in a gale.

Reginn had said that the weather boundary was down–but what if she was wrong? This could be a very short and unsuccessful voyage without the sunstone.

Until he made the crossing to Muckleholm, he wanted to stay close to the coast, both to put off any possible encounter with a boundary and to avoid arousing suspicion among the crew. In clear weather and quiet seas, their sail would be visible at a distance. He watched their wake for signs of pursuit, but saw nobody. Maybe they'd gotten away clean–nobody had questioned their sudden departure.

He didn't know the currents or this coastline or what kind of reefs and other obstacles might be in their way. Fortunately, they carried some provisions and fresh water, but soon they would need more. He'd have to hug the shoreline with all its hazards until that could be handled.

He needed to go far enough north to clear Ithavoll, and then sail east. Once they turned toward Muckleholm, he'd be fighting the westerlies all the way unless he could find some friendlier trade winds.

He couldn't complain about his new crew. Though they were young, they were hardworking, experienced sailors that needed little direction. To be honest, they knew more about their ship than he did. He could feel their eyes on him, weighing and measuring, while they conversed in a language he didn't understand. Still, he didn't expect to be challenged until later on, when they realized they weren't returning to the boathouse.

Ahead, Eiric could see the rippled surface that signified shallow water funneling over a reef. There appeared to be a channel through on the shoreward side, so he turned toward it. This was met with a clamor of alarm from his crew.

"Styrman!" Nils called. At least, Eiric thought that was his name. "I wouldn't go that way."

"No? Why not?"

"They call that–" He paused a moment, seemingly translating in his head, "Fisker's Folly. Or sometimes Witch's Fingers. It's a dead-end channel too narrow to turn around in with enough wave action to smash you against the rocks."

"Which way, then?" Eiric said, already shifting the styrboard.

Nils stared at him for a long moment, as if surprised at Eiric's easy acceptance of this advice. "Out and around," he said. "It's the long way, but better than swimming or drowning."

"Let's do it." The fiskers took up their oars, back-paddling until they could turn seaward.

That night, they made camp in a small cove along the north shore of Ithavoll. *Camp* was probably too generous a word. Eiric wanted to make sure that they could get away quickly if they were seen.

"Leave everything on board that you won't be using," he said. "We'll be having no fires. I'll stay with the ship while you wash up. Come straight back here when you're finished, and we'll do some weapons work before the nattmal."

They looked at each other.

"Styrman," Reyna said. "I have a question."

"Go on."

"This is still Ithavoll, right?"

"Yes," Eiric said.

"So it should be friendly territory."

"Yes," he said, his gaze meeting hers, making it clear there would be no more explanation than that.

After a long moment, she smiled quizzically. "Just making sure."

Nobody dawdled returning to the ship. It seemed that the notion of working with weapons was highly popular. In no time, his crew was lined up along the shore, their weapons laid out in front of them like identical game pieces. Each member of the crew had one sword, one short-handled axe, a shield, a longbow, and a quiver of iron-tipped arrows. Weapons Eiric could only dream of as a boy. Weapons his fadir and grandfadir would say should be earned.

They must have been made in the same smithy, or by the same hand, so that they were identical in size and construction. Reyna's was the same as Rorik's. None were tailored to the size and strength of the warrior who would wield it.

But that was true of most weapons in the Midlands. Warriors did not dig their weapons from the barrows of heroes or pull them from the trunks of trees. Odin did not appear at their weddings with gifts of edged steel. They repurposed wood axes, or bought spear points and arrowheads from the local blacksmith and found shafts in the nearby forest. When they went to war, they chose the weapons that served them best from the limited supply on hand.

Bjorn and Leif often brought weapons back from their summer raids, some taken directly from their previous owners, others scavenged from ancient battlefields. There was always a market for weapons in the Midlands. With everyone fighting, there were never enough to go around.

"Choose your best weapon," Eiric said.

After side-eying their colleagues, everyone but Reyna chose a sword. She chose her axe and shield. Eiric paired them up–Nils and

Levi, Rorik and Reyna.

"I'm fighting *Reyna*?" Rorik said. "Why can't I have a go with you?"

"Rorik's afraid of me," Reyna confided in a loud whisper.

"It's not that," Rorik growled. "I just don't see any point in–"

"In a battle, you don't get to choose your opponent or your weapon," Eiric said. "We'll be switching off. Don't worry–you'll have your chance.

"Now. These are edged weapons, not sparring sticks. You are getting the feel of them. We're a small crew as it is–we can't afford to lose anyone. A warrior in control of his weapon uses it intentionally–he doesn't kill or wound unless he means to." He paused. "Most of the time he means to."

That drew scattered laughter. It was an old joke, and the exchange brought back memories of countless summer evenings, camped on some nameless island, the sun still high in the sky after a full day of raiding. Grappling with some much older opponent amid shouted advice and catcalls from warriors deep in their cups.

Better watch yourself, Galo. One day that boy will have a brain to match those shoulders.

His fadir's calloused hands on his, demonstrating the best way to use his growing strength to draw back the bowstring, how to anchor it on his cheek before the release.

Bjorn demonstrating how to disarm an axeman with a shield.

"Styrman?"

Eiric came back to Ithavoll to find his crew watching him anxiously.

"So, hear this: the first man–or woman–who draws blood will be cleaning fish for the rest of the trip. Understood? Good. Then go to," he said.

It wasn't pretty. Eiric didn't let it go for long before he raised both hands.

"That's enough!" he said. "Good bouts, everyone."

Actually, terrible.

"Now, let's eat and talk about it."

In no time, they were seated in a circle just above the waterline, an array of the ship's provisions in the center. Eiric sat on the seaward side, closest to the ship, so that he could keep an eye on the surrounding woods. He set his axe on one side and seax on the other, his carry bag behind him to serve as a backrest.

"I'm curious," he said, biting off a hunk of hard cheese on flatbread. "Three of you chose swords. Why?"

"Well, everybody wants one," Nils said, brushing crumbs from his sleeve, "and nobody has one."

"That must mean that swords are the best weapons," Levi said.

"Does it?" Eiric said.

"Swords are expensive," Rorik said. "Harder to make, and they have a lot more steel in them than an axe. It has to be good steel, too, so it holds an edge."

Eiric nodded. "Right," he said. "It sounds like you know something about swords."

"The making of them, yes," Rorik said. He looked around at the others, then faced Eiric and added, with a hint of defiance, "but we've had no practice *fighting* with them."

"Shut up, Rorik," Nils hissed.

"That's not unusual," Eiric said, looking from one to the other. "When a jarl calls up his liegemen, most will have axes, or spears, and not–"

"We are not liegemen!" Reyna all but shouted. "Or bondi or fodder for barbarians. We. Are. *Fiskers.*"

It seemed that he had hit a nerve.

They hunched their shoulders then and looked around, as if expecting Thor's hammer to come down on them.

When Eiric reached into the carry bag behind him, they all faded back a little, no doubt expecting him to come up with a weapon. Instead, he pulled out a large, leather-wrapped bottle he'd somehow carried all the way from the Grove. Yanking out the stopper with his teeth, he raised the bottle to his lips and drank deeply.

"Will you drink with me?" he said, extending it toward Nils.

The crewman accepted the bottle but eyed it skeptically. "What is it?"

"Mead of the gods," Eiric said. "Drink too little, and live a life of regret. Drink too much, and it will turn you into a barbarian. The key is to drink just enough."

Nils took an experimental sip. Then two fully committed swallows.

"Hey," Rorik said, reaching for the bottle. "Leave some for the rest of us."

The bottle went around twice before it was empty.

With that, Levi produced a flask from his carry bag. It contained a clear, head-spinning liquor. It made it around once.

"Now," Eiric said as a warm blaze kindled in his middle, "let's talk about weapons. The best weapons are the ones you are skilled at using." He paused, but it was in his nature to speak bluntly. "I'm surprised you'd be given swords and the like with no training on how to use them."

"That's because we're not the ones who are supposed to be using them," Nils blurted.

This was met by mead-blurred glares from the others.

"Shut up, Nils," Rorik growled.

"Don't you think he's already figured it out?" Nils said. "He probably knew before he came aboard. He's just playing games with us."

"I'm not playing games," Eiric said, feeling a little guilty because that wasn't exactly true. "This ship is too small and I don't have the time. Now, why doesn't somebody tell me where you are from, and how you ended up crewing on a spinner ship headed for a war you're not supposed to fight in?"

"We're from Fiskeholm, an island to the west of the island you call Eimyrja," Reyna said. "Our clans have lived there since before the dawn of memory."

Eiric frowned. "I don't recall hearing about an island called Fiskeholm," he said. Though he had to admit, he hadn't seen much of New Jotunheim.

"The spinners call it Vestholm," Reyna said, her contempt plain to see. "After they founded the Temple at the Grove, they tried to get us to give up our boats and submit, but that didn't go well. Eventually, they put up the windwall to keep us from sailing across the blue ocean and pretty much left us alone. That is the story the speakers have handed down."

"I think they had their hands full on Eimyrja and Ithavoll," Nils said, upending Eiric's bottle to see if there might be a friendly drop left. There wasn't. "Until recently. They seem to have found a way to tame the bondi and are in need of a place to put them. So they came to Fiskeholm."

"The spinners cut down the forests and turned the whole island into a farm," Reyna said. "I think they thought that they were going to turn us into farmers."

"We are not farmers," Levi said, rolling his eyes. "They've discovered that we are not very tameable."

"They tried to tame you?" Eiric said, apprehension like a fist in his gut. "What did they do?"

"They sent a spinner over," Reyna said. "She carried a big stick." She grabbed up a stick and rolled it between her palms. "It looked like she was trying to start a fire without a strike-spark. It didn't work." The others laughed. Eiric did not.

They must be resistant to mind magic, he thought. *That's the best of all weapons.*

"What did you do before?" Eiric said. "Just fishing?"

"We were hunters and trappers," Rorik said. "Gathered nuts and berries, roots and fruit and greens. Collected crabs and shellfish in the marshes. We built fine boats. And we fished."

"We still fish," Reyna said. "They haven't figured out how to fence off the ocean. Now they're suddenly finding that they need boatbuilders and sailors to launch an invasion in Barbaria to the east."

"So you volunteered?" Eiric said, knowing the answer to the question before he asked it.

Reyna's face hardened. "No," she said, and clamped her mouth shut.

Eiric waited for someone to speak up, but no one did. It was as if a cold wind had driven off the last vestiges of mead-fueled fellowship.

"What happened?" he said finally.

"You should know," Nils said.

Eiric shook his head. "I–I'm new here," he said.

In the end, Rorik broke the silence. "They sent some soldiers over to convince us that, after seizing our lands and plowing them up, and putting bondi to work on them, we should serve them as pilots and boatbuilders. When we refused, they rounded up our families and threatened to kill them if we did not cooperate."

When all else fails, take hostages, Eiric thought. "I'm sorry," he said. "Where are they now?"

"We think they are still on Fiskeholm, but we aren't sure," Reyna said. She fondled her axe, no doubt dreaming of necks to chop. "We don't even know for sure if they're still alive. We've been on Ithavoll, building boats."

"We thought of putting a hole in each and every one of them," Levi said. "We'd fill them with tallow so it would dissolve away on the blue ocean and they could make their case to Njord."

Eiric laughed, thinking that he wouldn't want these ones as enemies. "Now, what about the weapons?"

"The weapons were intended for the queen's guard," Reyna said. "As you know, this was supposed to be her flagship." She gestured toward *Firebird*.

"The queen?" Eiric said. "Oh. Ah, you mean Lady Heidin."

Reyna eyed him as if he might not be the brightest ember on the hearth. "Whatever her name is. We were supposed to crew her ship during the war and ferry her wherever she wanted to go."

"A great honor," Levi murmured.

"We had a different plan," Nils said.

"Shut up, Nils," Rorik said.

But Nils was not shutting up. He stood, swaying a little. "Our plan was to wait until their queen came aboard with her guard, kill the guard, and sail off with their queen." He smiled benignly at Eiric and raised an imaginary cup. "Two can play the hostage game."

25
USES FOR DEAD PEOPLE

SOMETIMES ANIMALS FLEE BACK INTO a burning forest, if it is the only place of refuge they've ever known. Going up in flames seems preferable to surviving in an unrecognizable world.

So when Trude fled the pavilion at the House of Elders, Reginn knew where the library mouse had gone.

When Reginn burst through the great double doors, she found everything as she'd left it–books and manuscripts spread out on the tables–the ones she'd already reviewed set aside so she wouldn't go through them again.

"Trude!" she shouted. And again, "Trude! I need to talk to you."

There was no answer.

Reginn stood, mind seething, at a loss for how to summon a spirit that had no desire to be called to account. Then she remembered something Brenna had said. *It may be that, with a staff, you can direct your magic in order to choose which of the dead you want to rouse and who you choose to leave in peace.*

If Tyra could use her staff to gather and control the consciousness of the living, was it possible that Reginn could do the same with the dead? Especially in a place where trauma and unfinished business tethered them to the living world.

Instead of being hounded by the restless dead, was it possible that she could control them?

Raise us. Lead us.

Reginn climbed onto a table near the foot of the staircase and anchored Brenna's staff in front of her. She spun it between her palms, faster and faster, channeling power into it. Then flung threads of power out from the battered metal distaff into every corner and crevice.

Reginn began to sing the old songs, the vardlokkur, as had been taught to her by Tove.

"Spirits," she sang. "Come to me now."

Nothing.

She kept on singing.

Nothing.

"I am the space between fire and ice, between the living and the dead," Reginn sang. "Come to me."

Reginn felt the threads catch like a sticky spiderweb, then go taut as she pulled back against sudden resistance. She'd seen fishermen struggling to haul in nets heavy with fish. This must be what it feels like, she thought.

Then, all at once, the net went slack and somebody tumbled into view. Two somebodies.

It was Trude and Frodi, both looking a little rumpled. Instead of his usual soiled linen shirt or court finery, the archivist was dressed in baggy gray linen, similar to Trude's ashy garb. Even his shock of red hair had gone gray in places, resembling dying coals on the hearth.

Skita, Reginn thought. She hadn't counted on having uninvited guests.

Trude recovered first. "Well," she said, "look what the cat dragged in." With that, she launched herself at Frodi, their collision oddly silent, achieving nothing.

Reginn was in no mood for drama. "Stop it!" she said, and then repeated "Stop it!" louder, yanking on the nearly invisible tether. Trude and Frodi came upright, shocked expressions on their faces.

"You two have been lying to me, and that stops now," Reginn said. "I just witnessed a ceremony in which the kennari's daughter was burned alive and emerged as the goddess Heidin. I need an explanation."

"He's the liar," Trude said, pointing at Frodi. "You know that."

Frodi looked from Reginn to Trude and back again. Reginn could all but see the wheels turning in the archivist's head, trying to match what was happening with an explanation that made sense.

Finally, he nodded briskly, as if he'd sorted it out. He'd apparently decided to try to ignore this inconvenient haunt, and focus on Reginn.

"Please forgive me for the recent unpleasantness, dottir," he said, turning on the charm. "As a scholar yourself, no doubt you understand my desire to finally solve some of the mysteries that have plagued us for centuries."

"It's too late, Frodi," Trude murmured.

Frodi said, "Systir Reginn, could you please dismiss this tedious bit of conjury and speak to me directly?"

"I think you'd better listen to her," Reginn said. "And it's Elder Reginn now. Or Counselor."

"A lot has happened," Trude said. "The goddess Heidin is reborn and ready to go to war against the barbarians. Amma Inger is dead, as is the entire Elder Council. Including you." She paused, then repeated it. "You're dead, Frodi. Better get used to it."

"That's preposterous," Frodi growled. He stalked toward the door, but was yanked back by Reginn's tether.

He spun around and glared at Reginn. "Set. Me. Loose," he said.

"I'm not your student anymore, and I'm not interested in your squabbling," Reginn said. "What I need from both of you is the truth. All of it." She sat on the edge of the library table, her staff resting in the crook of her arm. She pointed at Trude. "You start."

The library mouse shrank a little, as if to disappear. "I'm sorry I wasn't straight with you," she said. "I was afraid that if I told you everything, you wouldn't come see me anymore.

"At first, I didn't know whether to trust you. I thought that you might be a spy for . . . someone. Of course, I had no idea how much time had passed since I died. And when I found out that my former partners were still alive, even thriving, I knew something was up."

"You were hardly a partner," Frodi said dismissively.

"Neither were you," Trude shot back. "Tyra played the two of us for fools." She shifted back to Reginn. "Once I shared the blodkyn rune, I think Frodi suspected that I knew more than I was saying. He kept pestering me to figure out how to get into the founder's tomb. It occurred to me that I was being played, that when Frodi had what he wanted, I would end up dead.

"So I went to Tyra."

Frodi muttered an oath.

"Tyra was reassuring. She told me that she doubted that Frodi intended me harm, but in any case she would protect me. She was excited about the blodkyn rune in particular, and told me it would be helpful to students who needed just a little more megin to succeed. I would be a hero to my peers, who had always considered me to be a little peculiar.

"She encouraged me to come to her directly with any new information so that she could identify possible risks and make sure I was credited with new discoveries. She was obviously interested in finding a way into the tomb and the tunnels beyond.

"Brenna should never have trusted me. She told me to tell no one, and now I had told two people. The wrong people."

"There was no need to tell Tyra, because I was keeping her informed," Frodi snapped.

"And yet *you* never told me that, and you never mentioned me to Tyra, either."

"You wouldn't have understood. Tyra and I had so much in common. We were young and ambitious, and hoped to reshape New Jotunheim into a major power. You would have shared in our success."

"You were in love with her, weren't you?" Trude said.

The words fell like so many millstones into a shallow pool.

"That's–that's–"

"Preposterous?" Trude suggested. "She never gave you a second look, until you came to her with the blodkyn rune and stories about speaking to the dead. I'm guessing that then she took a sudden interest in you."

"It was not that she took a sudden interest in me," Frodi said stiffly. "It was that we now shared a common research project that all but consumed us."

"Just like you and me," Trude said dryly. "All those late nights in the library. But Tyra was growing impatient with entertaining your fantasies. So she decided to cut you out."

Trude faced off with Frodi, planted her feet, and drove the blade home, her words dripping like venom from the serpent's tooth. "She said it was best that you didn't know. You wouldn't have understood. Tyra and I had so much in common. She didn't want to hurt you."

Now Frodi's shade was shrinking like an empty wineskin.

"I never told Tyra I'd been into the tomb," Trude said. "That was the only smart move I made."

"I knew it!" Frodi said. "I knew you were holding out on me."

"I always claimed that the goddess came to me in dreams, dropping the odd rune and bits of information here and there. That way I could control the flow of information. Tyra always asked about the runes, but I soon realized that she was looking for something else–an object. I think she suspected that it was in the tomb or the tunnels beyond. That was why she was so keen to get in.

"I asked her what she was looking for, and if I could help, and she said, 'I have to do this on my own.' When we'd circled for months with no success, she finally gave in, saying, 'Maybe if the goddess knows what we are looking for, she will tell you where to find it.'

"She showed me an old manuscript, barely readable, written in the earliest alphabet runes I'd ever seen. Tyra claimed that it had been written by Heidin herself, in the final days, when the gods were all scrambling to devise the best way to position and preserve themselves so that they would have the upper hand when the world was reborn, as predicted by the volva's prophecy."

"If it was from the library," Frodi said, "I probably gave it to her."

Trude ignored this belated claim to ownership. "The Jotun were determined to stay close to Ithavoll, because that was to be the gathering place of the surviving gods."

Frodi shifted impatiently, but for once had nothing to say.

"Heidin commissioned a dwarven metalsmith to make an amulet in her image that would capture her essence at the point of death. The manuscript included a sketch of the amulet and directions for how to rekindle the spark of life.

"As soon as I saw the sketch, I knew exactly where it was."

Frodi looked up, suddenly attentive.

"There's a large chamber in the tunnels beyond Brenna's tomb that was apparently used as a meeting place for the Jotun and their allies during the war. The walls are decorated with frescoes, paintings, statuary, and carvings. I remembered that there was a statue of Heidin in a niche overlooking the room. It looked to be solid gold, or gilded silver. The pendant described in the manuscript hung from a chain around her neck."

I know where that is, Reginn thought. That was where she'd found Asger and Heidin and driven off the boars.

"The first time I entered the chamber, I noticed the statue right away. It was as if it was calling me. As if it wanted to be found.

"So I returned to the tunnels to find it. The goddess spoke to me, reassured me, encouraged me until I could finally lay my hands on the pendant.

"When I touched it, it stung like needles penetrating my skin, sending tendrils of magic deep into my flesh. I tried to yank my hand away, but I could not. It was firmly attached, like a leech. I climbed back down again in a panic, wondering if I would have to see a healer to have it cut from my hand."

Reginn shivered, recalling how the pendant had embedded itself in Heidin's flesh.

"I bolted for the door. I was out of the tomb before the founder realized what I had. She was not happy. She was screaming in my ears as I climbed the steps from the Hall of Memory. I went to Tyra. When she touched the pendant, it dropped into her hand, but it didn't stick to her like it did to me. I made up a story about a spirit coming to me in a dream, leading me to a spot between the roots of the Memory Tree, and telling me to start digging.

"Maybe she believed me–maybe not, but it didn't seem to matter. I remember we were on the gallery outside her office. Tyra held the amulet up by the chain and set it spinning in the sunlight, the reflection casting light and shadow over her face. I thought she might claim the pendant for herself, but instead, she put it in a velvet bag and locked it away.

"She seemed as taken with me as she was with the pendant. 'Here you were, right under my nose, and I did not see you. *I did not see you.* You are descended from the gods, and so destined for greatness, if you so choose.'

"I had no idea what she meant by that, but I basked in her approval. All at once, it was as if we were peers–true partners. She told me that we had to take our time, and keep our secret, so that no one could get in our way.

"I didn't really know what secret I was keeping, but figured that she would tell me when the time was right.

"From then on, she denied me nothing. She still pressed me about the runes, but not like before. Some of the other students began to resent me because they saw me as her favorite."

Reginn turned to Frodi. "Now you. You told us about what happened the night Trude was killed, but what led up to it?"

Reginn didn't expect the arrogant archivist to offer up any explanation. But maybe being dead made a difference because he raked his hands through his hair and said, "I began to notice that my partnership with Tyra had changed . . . dwindled into nothing at all. She could no longer spare time to meet with me, and seemed uninterested in my discoveries and insights. I finally confronted Tyra about it, and she basically told me that she had found it much more efficient to work with Trude directly than to channel everything through me. She was curt and dismissive."

Ouch, Reginn thought, with a rush of unexpected sympathy.

"I decided to go and see Trude. My intent was to convince her that our arrangement had been working well, and that my role as a go-between offered her some protection. I found her in the library, and–" The archivist paused, as if he'd lost his way. "I don't really remember what happened after that. I must have lost my temper. And in the process, discovered the other secret of the blodkyn rune.

"Afterward, I think Tyra knew that I was the guilty party, but she must have had her own reasons for not wanting to raise questions or draw attention. So we never spoke of it again."

"She did have her own reasons," Trude said.

"Go on," Reginn said into the sudden silence.

"Tyra was growing weary of dealing with Frodi and worried about what information he might take to the Elder Council. She did not want to lose control of me. Frodi was useful–until he wasn't. She asked me to handle the problem."

"She asked *you* to handle *me*?" Frodi said, looking baffled. "Handle me how?"

"She said to make it look like an accident," Trude said.

Neither Reginn nor Frodi could muster a response. Reginn felt like she'd been upended, over and over again, each new revelation rolling in like a giant breaker knocking her off her feet.

"She . . . told you to *kill* me?" Frodi said. His tone was mingled hurt and disbelief.

"Poor Elder Frodi," Trude said. "You continually underestimate people–especially women." She paused, but Frodi, still shaken, didn't argue.

"I think it was meant to be a test of whether I had what it took–the ruthlessness and ambition required to host Heidin's return. Rekindling the heart required a host who carried a spark of divinity. Someone with the bloodlines of a god. Someone who could rise from the flames."

"And so–?" Reginn said, feeling as if she'd lost control of this conversation.

"Even then, Frodi drank too much. So I told him to meet me in the library after curfew and we'd discuss a way forward. I waited for him at the top of the staircase with a bottle of elder wine. I'd cut through the anchors on one of the railings. When he joined me at the top, I figured it would be an easy matter to tip him over."

Frodi shook his head. "I don't remember any of this."

Trude ignored the interruption. "Obviously, it didn't go as planned. You showed up relatively sober, no doubt hoping to win me over with your scholarly charm. We passed the bottle back and forth, but the wine affected me much more than it did you. You were flattering me, attempting to kiss me. When I tried to pitch you over, you grabbed onto the platform for support, and I was the one who went over the rail.

"So it was no surprise that Tyra didn't ask many questions, because she knew exactly what had happened since she had a role in it. She did, however, manipulate your memory of the event, leaving you convinced that you had killed me in a drunken rage."

"So Tyra's plan fell apart," Reginn said. "Why would she wait several hundred years to try again?"

"Tyra was left with Heidin's heart and no candidate to host it," Trude said. "With the weather boundary in place, that wouldn't change for a good long time. She might never have pulled it off, but Frodi's discovery of the transfer of power at the point of death extended her timeline indefinitely. At the same time, it strengthened the elders and made them resistant to her mind magic.

"After the founder's death, Tyra began traveling to the Archipelago to recruit students," Frodi said. "Her power grew, over time, as she substituted mind magic for traditional schooling. Each new class of dedicates became her disciples, loyal only to her. Eventually, it became obvious that she was expecting a child."

"That must have been disappointing," Trude said.

"By then, I'd launched my love affair with the bottle," Frodi said. "It never disappoints. One advantage–or disadvantage–of being immortal is that it is all but impossible to drink yourself into the grave.

"Tyra was closemouthed about the father, but people speculated that she had met him in Barbaria. Some say she even gave him a sunstone so that he could visit her here. If he did, I never saw him.

"After her baby was born, Tyra was obsessed with her. It was a good thing she'd discovered a shortcut to teaching, because she had little time for her students. It was about that time that her relationship with the matrona began to sour. I think Inger suspected what Tyra was up to and was trying to discourage it.

"The final straw was the burning. I don't know how old the girl was–eight years, perhaps? Tyra took her into the Grove, tied her to a stake, and set her on fire."

Reginn must have known this, or at least suspected it, but it still struck her with the force of a physical blow. "*Tyra* did it?"

Frodi nodded. "I wasn't there, but I was told that the girl stood stoically, as if in a trance, until a group of adepts intervened, cut her loose, and smothered the flames. They said that she was wearing a pendant–one they hadn't seen before.

"By then, I was on the Council of Elders. We convened to determine what to do. Everyone agreed that Tyra's ability to recruit new candidates for the academy and the temple was invaluable, along with her gift that pacified the bondi and streamlined the training process. But it wouldn't do to have her setting fire to children on a regular basis–not in public. We took a vote and determined that we needed to get rid of the girl in a way that would not be traced back to us."

"So you were so worried about Heidin's safety that you decided that the best way to protect her was to kill her," Reginn said.

"An interesting approach, don't you agree?" Frodi said. "Yet I was certain that, sooner or later, someone on the council would be willing to take the risk in view of the payoff. So I went to the keeper and explained the situation."

Reginn's head came up in surprise. "You did?"

"I am–was–not the monster you think I am," Frodi said. "I seriously thought that perhaps Tyra was mentally ill. Whatever the explanation, I knew that if Tyra discovered that the council was behind the murder of Heidin, there would be hell to pay. She would never, ever forget it, and she would find a way to destroy us." He paused. "From what you tell me, she found a way to do it anyway.

"The keeper told me that she would arrange for Tyra's dottir to disappear, in a way that we would not be blamed, but it would take a little while to arrange. She was as good as her word. I don't know exactly what happened, but Heidin disappeared and Tyra blamed Inger. I was surprised the old woman survived as long as she did."

Reginn thought of that night in Landvik, the night Tyra and Inger came into the alehouse. Arguing. And then the keeper leaving the table and taking the wine up the stairs.

Tyra had tried to poison her that night.

Reginn took a breath and let it out slowly. It struck her that she was the only person breathing in the room.

"Well, however it happened, Heidin's transformation is now complete," Reginn said. "I expect they will launch an invasion of the Archipelago as soon as possible."

With that, she cut the tethers holding Frodi and Trude in the world, and they disappeared.

26

SHORELINE SAILORS

AFTER HEARING THE STORY ABOUT the fiskers' captive families on Fiskeholm, Eiric was wary of his crew—not a good thing on a long sea voyage on a small ship. A styrman who sleeps with one eye open doesn't get much rest.

The fiskers knew the northern coastline, the natural harbors and inlets, villages and military facilities. Eiric honored their judgment in choosing where to put in for the night. He would have liked to replenish their stores before they left New Jotunheim behind, but decided that it was more important to get away clean.

They cleared the northernmost coast of Ithavoll and turned southeast. They camped that night near the mouth of a small creek. Levi returned from foraging with a basket of apples, large and crisp and sweet.

"I have to admit," Levi said, "the bondi are great farmers."

"Where did these come from?" Eiric said. He took a bite, and the juice ran down his chin.

Levi jerked his thumb toward the forest beyond the beach. "There's a huge orchard over there," he said, "with different kinds of apples. They won't miss this lot."

"Next time, find us a mead hall," Rorik said.

After supper, the sparring began. One night, it was swords, the next, axe throwing, then lausatok. And, always, words.

"Are you planning to sail clear around the island?" Reyna wanted to know. "If so, we might need more than a handful of apples."

"Do you have any suggestions?" Eiric said, ignoring the real question.

"Eat less and sail faster?" Nils said, dumping a pouch of hazelnuts into his mouth.

"Speak for yourself," Reyna said.

"Go fishing?" Levi said. Anyone could tell he wasn't serious. Anyone but Rorik.

"You know the fishing isn't that good on this side of the island," Rorik said. "Besides, that would take too long."

"Besides, *you* would have to clean the fish," Reyna said. "No. There's a bondi village not too far south of the old temple, just above the rift. There are several army storehouses there, right on the coast. They should have anything we'd need."

"I don't want to have to answer a bunch of questions," Eiric said, painfully aware of the fact that he was supposed to be a member of that army and so entitled to requisition supplies.

"If you leave it to me and Reyna, we'll get what we need, no questions asked," Levi said.

"No," Eiric said. "We'll get by with what we have."

"Porridge," Reyna said, rolling her eyes.

Eiric could tell from the way they looked at him that they knew their new captain wasn't being straight with them.

Eiric *was* worried about their supplies lasting through the crossing. There was no telling how long it would take, given the prevailing winds. That said, a raiding party from a friendly ship would be hard to explain. Better to live hungry than die well-fed. Said no coaster he ever knew.

They continued south, keeping the coastline in sight, until a ribbon of steam and the faint scent of sulfur told him they were passing the rift. A few miles south of there, he angled the ship toward a landing spot in a shallow bay. They'd camp here overnight, then strike due east in the morning. He hoped they'd find a fair easterly. Otherwise they would have a job sailing against the wind.

The story of your life–sailing against the wind.

"Styrman," Rorik said, staring shoreward, squinting against the declining sun, "we can't stop here."

"Why not?"

"Those are the deadlands. No one goes there. It's forbidden."

"It's only one night," Eiric said. "Besides, you never struck me as someone who's afraid of breaking the rules."

"I don't fear the living," Rorik said, folding his arms. "I fear the dead."

"And yet, any successful warrior ends the day surrounded by the dead. I would rather face a thousand dead enemies than a handful of the living."

If he thought this would draw a laugh, he was mistaken. Instead, the others left off what they were doing and watched the exchange, a silent shield wall of resistance.

In the meantime, their momentum had carried them closer to shore.

"Levi," Eiric said, judging him the most likely to follow orders, "drop the sail and tie it down."

"Aye," Levi said, and scrambled to the mast.

"Rorik, take a sounding, and drop anchor when you can."

Firebird found the end of the anchor chain and shivered to a stop, turning slightly abeam to the shoreline before she straightened, pointed into the rolling swells, just outside the first breakers. Eiric judged she'd be relatively stable in the quieter waters of the bay.

"I've been to the deadlands," Eiric said. "It is an ancient battleground and holds the remains of countless dead. That's it. I would not return there otherwise." He paused. "Trust me on that."

"You are asking us to trust you," Nils said. "Why should we trust you when you don't trust us enough to tell us the truth?"

"We all admit that you are big, and strong, a skilled fighter, and a fair styrman," Reyna said, shrugging as if that was less than impressive. "But we fiskers hunt the great whales."

The fiskers' hands strayed to hidden weapons. Nils was one to watch, he decided. Rorik was blustery, Reyna was smart, Levi was crafty, but Nils would do whatever it took to survive.

As if reading his thoughts, Nils said, "If you keep disrespecting *us*, you will end up hugging a rock at the bottom of the sea. That seems less risky to us than sailing under your command."

Eiric stood, speechless, for a long moment, stung by the realization that they were right. He was disrespecting them, using them as a means to an end, relying on his size and strength to force compliance. In so doing, he'd achieved the impossible. He'd united this squabbling crew of sailors.

He recalled something Bjorn had said to him, years ago, when they were assembling a crew in spring.

A crew signs on with a coaster because that coaster is known to have hamingja*–good fortune. He has been successful in the past and provides a fair split of the takings. Good crewmen are always in demand, so they will choose to sail with a chief skilled in seamanship who respects his crew enough not to risk their lives for little reward. If they survive that kind of styrman, they won't be back the next spring.*

Eiric had lectured Rikhard on this very topic.

"You're right," Eiric said. "I'm sorry. What do you want to know? I may not answer every question, but you have my word that I will tell you the truth."

It took a moment for the crew to recover from their surprise.

"Who are you, really, and whose side are you on?" Reyna said.

"My name is Eiric Halvorsen, and I'm from Selvagr, on Muckleholm," he said. When they stared at him blankly, he added, "In Barbaria."

"You're lying," Rorik said. "Barbarians are covered in hair and carry clubs."

"Some of us, maybe," Eiric said, not wanting to get into it. "We have monsters of all kinds back home. You have monsters here, too, but they speak pretty words and dress up in fancy clothes. I'm here because I stand to lose my farm and my only brodir if I don't find out what the spinners are doing with children from the Archipelago."

Nils studied him through narrowed eyes. "*You*—are a farmer." These fiskers seemingly had little use for farmers.

"Aye," Eiric said.

"They sent a farmer to fight the witches," Nils said. "What must your warriors be like, then?"

"No farmer in the Archipelago will hold on to what's his for long if he can't fight for it." Eiric paused. "I'm a coaster as well as a farmer. Most men do both."

"How did you get to Ithavoll?" Levi waved vaguely landward.

"I told you. I sailed here."

"From Barbaria."

Eiric nodded. "From Barbaria."

"Through the spinners' shield wall."

"Through the windwall, yes. To be fair, I had a sunstone. A spinner's key."

"Let's see it, then," Reyna said.

"I *had* a sunstone," Eiric said. "The spinners took it from me."

"Where's your ship, then?" Rorik said. "Why did you have to take ours?"

"I left my ship on the southern coast of Ithavoll, in what you call the deadlands. It may still be there." He shrugged. "Your ship was more convenient. I was in a hurry. I got into some trouble at the spinners' grove."

Rorik looked him up and down, reassessing. "Is there a price on your head? A reward we could collect?" It was more a taunt than a real threat.

"No reward," Eiric said. "The spinners have been trying to kill me ever since I arrived. At the moment, they believe that they have succeeded."

"You're the barbarian that slaughtered the spinners' council," Levi said, the light of understanding kindling in his eyes.

"And half the soldiers at the rift," Reyna added. "And yet you say that you did not come to fight?"

"I found their lack of hospitality . . . off-putting," Eiric said. He chose not to share the fact that he had brought the new queen back to New Jotunheim. Or the fact that she was his systir. There was a chance they'd already heard about the connection, but if they hadn't, he wasn't going to tell them.

"Is that where we're going? To fetch your ship, then?" Nils said.

"No," Eiric said. "There's not enough time. War is coming, my younger brodir is at risk, and I need to go home. I mean to set a course due east–straight for the Archipelago."

"*All* of us?" Levi's voice rose.

"All of us," Eiric said. "I can't risk leaving you behind to be questioned by the spinners. They can be very persuasive."

They stared at him, wordless, faces gone pale. "We are coastal sailors," Reyna said. "We always keep the shoreland in sight. Away from landmarks, in the featureless ocean, we could be sailing in circles and we would never know it."

"The ocean has its own landmarks if you know what to look for," Eiric said. "Winds, currents, the stars, the position of the sun, where it rises and sets, the presence and absence of birds . . ." He trailed off. Spoken out loud, it didn't sound like much.

They still scowled at him, the distrust plain on their faces.

He tried a different tack. "As the crew of Liv–the queen's–flagship, where did you think you'd be sailing?" Eiric said.

"We never intended to sail to Barbaria, remember," Reyna said. "*Our* plan was to take the queen to Fiskeholm, where we would make a trade for our families."

"But *you* got in the way," Levi said. "It could still work if we can get back to the boathouse in time."

"If your plan is successful, then what?"

"And then we will take our island back," Nils said. "The witches can go live or die in Barbaria if they want."

Eiric shook his head. "This queen is more powerful than you know. You've seen the armies they are assembling, the weapons they are building. Any victory would be temporary. They will not tolerate an independent Fiskeholm so close to their shores.

"If they conquer the Archipelago, the power they draw from the slain will render them unstoppable. Driving the witches out of Fiskeholm will buy you a little time, that's all, at great cost."

"And yet, it seems like a better bet than sailing headlong into a magical barrier that has confounded us for centuries," Nils said.

"I am told that the barrier is down," Eiric said.

"Who told you?"

"Someone in a position to know," Eiric said.

"Knut and the elders seem to believe that it's still up," Rorik said. "They are busy making plans for getting the fleet through the barrier with only three sunstones."

"If they don't know it's down, they will, soon," Eiric said. "That's why it's important to get a head start."

"Give us a moment," Reyna said. "Let us talk."

The fiskers clustered midships, arguing. It was probably just as well that Eiric didn't understand the language. Now and then Rorik or Levi would jerk a thumb at Eiric and then lean in to make a point.

It was an impasse. Eiric couldn't let his crew return to Ithavoll, but if they refused to sail to the Archipelago, he would have no choice but to carry out the plan that he had discarded when he first came aboard. It would be a bloodbath, with him the only survivor.

He'd already done a great deal of killing out of necessity. No doubt there would be more to do. His world seemed to be filled with people who needed killing. He had no desire to shed the blood of innocents who happened to get in his way.

After, he'd be faced with his least favorite question: Then what? He'd face the difficulty of sailing the blue water ocean by himself in a ship larger than his karvi. Improvisation only goes so far.

The discussion was over. Apparently Reyna had either been appointed the spokesperson or claimed the job for herself.

"Styrman," Reyna said. "We have a proposition for you."

"Go on. I'm listening."

Reyna ran her fingers lovingly over *Firebird*'s gunwale. "The fates have decreed that we share a common enemy. We will sail as your crew across the blue ocean to Barbaria. You will continue our weapons training as time permits. Once there, we will face your enemies alongside you."

"Do that, and you'll likely end up dead," Eiric said.

"Maybe," Reyna said. "The fates will decide. When that work is done, you will return with us to New Jotunheim and fight beside us to reclaim our homes, our families, and our freedom."

Eiric cleared his throat. "You must know that it is possible that your families are already dead. The spinners don't hold prisoners for very long, and the ship you built and crewed has gone missing. They will assume that you took it."

"We know that, Styrman. If that is the case, then you will assist in our revenge."

27
REGINN'S ARMY

IN THE DAYS FOLLOWING HEIDIN'S third burning and the revelations in the library, Reginn bobbed like a cork in a sea of apprehension.

She still hadn't spoken to Heidin since their visit to the boathouse on Ithavoll. And now, since the third burning, would the queen even remember her?

The other elders were nowhere to be found. Likely they were on Ithavoll, preparing for battle. Unlike them, Reginn had never been given a specific role on the battlefield.

There was a time, back in the Archipelago, when she would have been eager to make a list of deserving targets. Not anymore. No one deserved what was coming.

If Reginn set sail with the others, was there anything she could do to prevent a slaughter? Or would she be forced to witness a bloodbath?

She knew the sailing date must be close, so she wasn't surprised when all the elders and adepts and military officers were called to a meeting in Ithavoll, at the temple at the rift. They were instructed to bring weapons, clothing, and gear for a cold-weather campaign.

Like everyone else, Reginn had been issued a uniform of sorts—heavy boots and tan breeches paired with linen shirts and heavy, structured coats in blue wool. Clothing that was much too warm for New Jotunheim, but which they hoped would be suitable for Barbaria.

You said you'd never go back there.

She'd promptly stuffed it all under her sleeping bench.

Now she dug it out, sat down on her bed, and yanked on the breeches and the boots, which fit perfectly (of course). She followed with the linen overshirt, then strapped on her belt dagger and remedy belt, more from habit than from hope. She fingered the baldric carrying her flute. Music? She didn't know any marches, but she did know some laments.

Reginn wrapped it carefully in a linen shirt and added it to her carry bag along with her coat and everything else. Shrugging it onto her shoulders, she picked up her staff and left the House of Elders for possibly the last time.

The grounds in front of the barracks at Ithavoll seethed with activity—soldiers hurrying here and there, bondi loading wagons, and teamsters calming wild-eyed horses. Once loaded, the wagons took the road north—toward the boatyard.

It was really happening. They were moving supplies and preparing to sail.

Elders and adepts were gathered in a puddle of blue around the entrance of the temple. As if driven by the invisible hand of fate, Reginn joined them.

They'd been looking for her, it seemed. Her fellow elders greeted her with warm embraces and thinly veiled relief.

"We're glad you're here, Reginn," Shelby said. "You'll be great."

"Gyllir is already on her way to the boatyard," Stian said, referring to Reginn's horse.

Reginn could have sworn he said *boneyard.*

We're all on our way to the boneyard.

Speaking of. "Where's Grima?" Reginn said. That was a person Reginn tried to keep track of.

"Grima?" Katia looked lost for a moment. "Oh. She left weeks ago on some mission for Tyra."

Looking past the temple to the rift, Reginn saw that there was something new—an iron bridge extended across the rift from the temple to the far bank, the underlayment already discolored by the fumes from the river below. It seemed like a frail protection against certain death.

Soldiers clustered around the temple, bristling with weapons, some grim-faced, others seemingly scared to death. Durinn and several of their officers sat their horses in a rough ring around the soldiers as if to prevent escape.

Did they mean to force their army to march across the bridge? Clearly, the soldiers thought so. After all, why would they build a bridge if they did not intend to use it?

"Come on," Katia said. "Let's go in."

The other adepts were streaming into the temple. Reginn was glad to turn away from the bridge and join them.

Inside, a party mood prevailed. Servants threaded their way through a sea of blue, carrying refreshments. Some appeared to have been celebrating for some time.

Reginn's skin pebbled up when she recalled Eiric's story about the ceremony at this temple when he first arrived in New Jotunheim.

Did they plan a sacrifice, perhaps, to assure a successful venture?

No.

Reginn backed toward the doors. Maybe she couldn't prevent this, but she did not have to be a party to it. She didn't have to be a witness.

A voice in her head said, *You never confront the evil around you. You always turn away.*

Not this time. The way was blocked by bodies crowding in behind her. Then the temple doors slammed shut with a bang, silencing the clamor of voices.

Tyra and Heidin walked onto the dais from opposite sides of the temple, meeting up in the middle as the crowd around the dais rolled back from the stage.

Tyra was striking, as always–this time in a black silk robe edged in red. As sleek and poisonous as a spider. Yet she appeared small, even diminished, next to Heidin. The queen was absolutely dazzling, her hair shot through with gold and silver. The scars from three burnings shone like copper runes against the burnished gold of her skin.

As Heidin turned to face the crowd, her firebird feather cape swished across the stones, the jewels in her staff and in the crown on her head glittering in the light from the torches.

"I have awaited this day for centuries," she said, her voice ringing through the hall like a bell. "After Ragnarok, my physical body moldered under the cold earth of Vigrid, dissolving to dust as mortal bodies do. But my flame burned on, seeking a new host, a new body to inhabit in which to finish the work I began so long ago.

"This is the saga of the thrice-burned goddess reborn. Some of you know parts of it, but it will be new to most of you. The long road to this day began when my modir, the scholar Tyra Lund, came to New Jotunheim. Her treatment at the hands of the barbarians left her determined that she would never again fall victim to them. She realized that the Jotun would never be safe until the flames of Asgard were extinguished and the barbarians disarmed.

"She exhumed the secrets of the past in the lost texts in the library. She read the true histories of the conflict between the gods of Asgard and Jotunheim. Though she was just a young girl, she vowed to do whatever was necessary to restore the realm of Jotunheim and avenge the indiscriminate slaughter of the Jotun at the hands of Asgard.

"To that end, she explored the tunnels that lay between Vigrid and Eimyrja, courageous in the face of scenes of carnage that would have frightened a seasoned warrior. After all, she had encountered much worse at the hands of the barbarians. Using knowledge gained from the old texts, Tyra found my mortal remains and recognized my amulet for what it was–the key to the final defeat of Asgard and the establishment of a free Jotunheim."

Heidin turned toward Tyra, inclining her head in acknowledgment, and the assembled spinners cheered and clapped.

Reginn thought of those who'd been cut from the story–Frodi and Trude.

"Thank you, Your Highness," Tyra said, radiant with pride. "I was proud to serve as the maternal vessel, and I found a man in Barbaria who carried the necessary spark of divinity.

"I began preparing Heidin for her destiny from birth. She wore the firebird's amulet from the time she was old enough to understand the importance of concealing it.

"As time went on, Amma Inger became suspicious of my intentions, but by then my power was growing. The elders were finding that my ability to efficiently instruct dedicates and bondi suited their agenda very well."

Indoctrinate, you mean, Reginn thought, growing restless with the endless self-praise. Yes, you are clever. Yes, it appears that you are on your way to a win. Can we leave now?

"It was after the first ritual burning that the keeper decided to take drastic action. She must have reached out to the barbarians and told them to come get Heidin before she grew further in power."

Or, maybe, Reginn thought, she told them to come get her before you set her on fire again.

"And so they came, and carried her away. For years, I believed that she was dead. I never forgave the keeper for that betrayal."

Even Heidin was becoming visibly impatient with this recitation of history. Now she spoke up. "That's all behind us, Kennari. Let us focus on our future. I call forward Reginn Eiklund, elder, counselor, and now commander of our legacy army."

Reginn's mind had been wandering, but that last phrase pierced her consciousness like a shiv to the heart.

Commander of our legacy army.

And like a shiv to the heart, it was already too late to react. She was being pushed forward toward the dais, hands gripping her elbows, lifting her from her feet and setting her on the stone dais next to Heidin.

The firebird gripped her shoulders, with hands as cold and hard as hammered gold. "I have allies and enemies. The time has come to decide–which will you be?"

"I–I'm an ally, of course," Reginn said.

"Then prove it." Heidin turned her to face the rift, then raised her staff high, flooding the deadlands with light. "Your army lies over there, Counselor. The Asgardians that died at Ragnarok went to Valhalla or Folkvangr. The Jotun dead have lain on the battlefield, waiting centuries for their revenge."

"You want me to lead an army of the dead," Reginn said, the words sticking in her throat like a tough piece of meat.

"They are motivated, and they are trained. They have been waiting for you for centuries."

"You're the goddess," Reginn said. "Why don't you raise them?"

"You are the aldrnari," Heidin said. "You are the flame that connects the living and the dead. If you call them, they will rise."

"And if they don't?"

"If they don't answer, there is always an alternative." Light flooded the far end of the temple, and Reginn saw what she hadn't before. The area closest to the rift was crowded with people. Many were children, hiding their eyes against the sudden brilliance. Others were old–their faces seamed from long hours spent working outside in the yearlong summers. Here and there, Reginn saw dots of blue–perhaps acolytes from the academy at Vesthavn, called to serve early.

Everyone has a role to play in New Jotunheim.

Heidin waved her hand, taking in the assembly. "Commander, behold your other option."

"I don't understand," Reginn said, though she did.

"You will lead an army in the assault on Barbaria," Heidin said.

"This one or that one." She pointed across the rift.

Reginn took a deep breath, gathering her thoughts. *This is not Liv, Eiric's systir. This is not the girl you rescued from the tunnels. This is the goddess Gullveig reborn.*

"I am no commander, Your Highness. These are not soldiers. They'll be slaughtered."

"And if they are, they'll be remembered as heroes," Heidin said. "Their blood will strengthen us as we remake the world. Their sacrifice will save the lives of countless of our soldiers."

"No," Reginn said, drawing herself up, feeling the pressure of her colleagues' eyes. "I will not play in your game. I will not have their blood on my hands."

"If you refuse, Counselor, this army goes into the rift today," Heidin said. "They will still contribute to our cause via the blodkyn rune. Your obstinance will not save them. Your gifts and your leadership might."

Reginn shifted her gaze to Tyra, who wore the expression of a host at a table ready to carve a succulent piece of meat. She knew in that instant that this was Tyra's plan all along–the reason she had plucked Reginn from the obscurity of an alehouse in Langvik and carried her across the sea to Eimyrja. She had seen Reginn raise Thurston from the dead and intended that she do the same for the dead warriors of Jotunheim.

It wasn't a fair choice. It wasn't a choice at all. If she spared the bondi now, there was no guarantee that they wouldn't be sent to war anyway. Or held hostage indefinitely, forcing one evil choice after another.

Don't take the bait, Reginn thought. This is a false choice. When you fail, you will blame yourself.

Some in the crowd of unwilling conscripts understood the queen's meaning and began shouting in protest.

One voice rose above the others.

"Now is the time to stand for those who have stood for you," she said, her voice ringing through the temple like a bell. "Do not go willingly into the void. Make them pay for every life they take. If they want an army, we will give them one."

Naima.

The crowd began pushing at the soldiers around them, trying to force a way through to the door.

Reginn charged toward the near end of the bridge, thrusting aside anyone who didn't get out of her path quickly enough. Where the bridge met the dais, she turned, planted herself, and raised her staff.

"If you mean to throw anyone into the Elivagar, you'll have to start with me."

"Reginn, no!" someone shouted. Maybe Katia. Several of the elders moved toward her.

"Please," Shelby said, pressing his sleeve over his mouth and nose. "Save the living, raise the dead."

The goddess strode toward her, glittering in the torchlight, reminding Reginn of the source of her original name. Gullveig–gold-drunk.

Out of the corner of her eye, she saw Asger edging in from the side. As they advanced, Reginn backed out onto the bridge.

When the full force of the fumes hit, Reginn's head swam and she swayed, all but overcome by the vapors boiling up from below. Alarm flickered across Heidin's face. Then she knew–the firebird needed her. For all the good that did her.

There was no guarantee except that if Reginn refused to do as Heidin commanded, they would die for sure, and now. She had no doubt that they were marked with the blodkyn rune, and so their deaths would only serve to strengthen the Jotun forces.

Yet–what evil would be unleashed if it was true–if she really was able to awaken the dead of Ragnarok?

Raise us, Aldrnari.

Lead us.

Maybe she would be lucky and be struck dead as soon as she set foot on the deadlands of Vigrid.

And so, in that moment, she made her decision.

Save the living, raise the dead.

Swinging her staff in an arc, once again, she swept the poisonous fumes away from the fragile bridge and strode forward. As she left the cliffside behind, the wind grew stronger, howling through the rift from sea to sea. It ripped her hair from its careful braid, nearly knocked her down, but thankfully brought a bit of fresh sea air with it, clearing her head.

As she reached the middle of the bridge, it swayed, all but toppling her. She grabbed onto the railing as the bridge twisted and writhed like a serpent in its death throes.

Help us, Aldrnari.

Save us.

Raise us.

When she looked over the railing, she saw them, breaking the surface of the river of poison, reaching toward the bridge with fleshless fingers, mouths gaping in hollow-eyed skulls. The rift seethed with bodies and echoed with the voices of all who had died in the Elivagar since the dawn of time. Bone rattled against metal as they leaped and clung onto the underside of the bridge. Long tentacles looped over the bridge surface, with suckers like so many questing mouths. More and more, forming a fleshy cage around her.

Reginn sank to her knees. Her staff slipped from her nerveless fingers and clattered on the deck of the bridge.

The spectators on the cliffside had fallen silent.

All at once, the tentacles disappeared.

And then he was there, without warning, as he had been so many times before, the fumes from below obliterating his usual telltale scent of flame and ash. She felt the heat of his hands through leather gloves as he gathered her up, cradling her against his chest. He bent once more to retrieve her staff, then covered the distance to the far end of the bridge with his long-legged stride as the crowd at the temple cheered.

On the other side, he set her down on her feet, keeping one arm around her until he was sure she wouldn't topple over, then handed her the staff.

"Lean on this," Asger said. "Breathe."

She did both of those things, then looked up at him and said, "Why does it matter what happens to me? Why can't you just let me go?"

He stood looking at her for a long moment, his spare figure haloed in vapor. Some emotion flickered over his face, but she couldn't sort out what it was. Finally, he said, "You are better than this. Stronger than this. You are the bravest creature I know. It would be out of character for you to throw it all away."

"You don't know me," Reginn growled. "You know nothing about me."

"You are wrong, Reginn Eiklund," he said. "I know you better than you know yourself. I have known you since before you were born."

Amid all the clamor around them, his words still struck her ear.

Reginn Eiklund. Not Meyla.

She had left the clamor of the dead under the bridge only to meet the plaintive voices rising from the old battlefield.

Raise us, Aldrnari.

Lead us.

Save us.

Asger looked back at the crowd in the temple, his face a landscape of memory and grief. "They would wield you as a weapon, Aldrnari," he said. "They would use all of us, as they have before. But never forget, you are the one holding the sword. Only you can decide what to do with it."

He turned, the fumes rippling about him like a cape, and walked past her, into the deadlands, disappearing into the ruins of the ancient battlefield.

Reginn drew a long breath, let it out slowly, then tightened her grip on her staff, and called to the legions under earth and stone. "If you choose to join this fight, rise, and come to me."

So they came. Some appeared to rise up out of the earth, while others flooded in from all sides. Jotun warriors of all genders, some so large that they towered over her, others short and stocky, with varied dress and armaments. Though she assumed that some of them must have suffered grievous wounds in the battle at Ragnarok, they appeared intact to her eyes. Perhaps their spirit bodies were built of memory and self-perception.

Their leader approached Reginn and bowed. "Aldrnari," he said. "I am Hrym, commander of the Jotun army."

"Why are you here?" Reginn said.

"I am here to serve, Lady," Hrym said. "I am hoping for a second chance to leave this field with honor."

"Thank you, Hrym," Reginn said.

The Alfar came as well–dark and light elves of all ages. At least Reginn guessed they were elves, based on their physical beauty and the quality of their armor and weapons. They moved silently, so light of foot that they left no mark on the earth.

It surprised Reginn to see them, since she'd always understood that the elves were more akin to the Vanir gods than to the Jotun. Hadn't the Aesir gifted Freyr the realm of Alfheim when they joined forces?

The gods were always giving away things that didn't belong to them.

A tall, spare elf with hair as black and shining as a raven's wing and quicksilver eyes turned off to greet Reginn.

"I am Dainn, of the Alfar," he said, "elven runemaker."

"Welcome," Reginn said. "Why would you volunteer to fight in yet another war?"

"We elves have learned that it is best to be at the table when decisions are made and the spoils are handed out," Dainn said. With that, he rejoined the elven army.

The acrid scent of flame and ash caught Reginn's attention, bringing with it a familiar rush of panic.

It was an army of thursen–demons of all kinds. The lords of chaos. Eldrjotun with their flaming swords; issjotun, whose touch froze any living creature until it was brittle enough to break; vatnjotun, who could lift the water from a lake or sea and set it spinning, destroying everything in its path.

There were Dvergar–the dwarves, who mined the riches of the Midlands and Jotunheim, cunning crafters who forged the weapons and adornments that Asgard treasured, and often stole. Their leader stopped and paid her respects to Reginn. "The name is Stonebiter," she said. "Dori Stonebiter. The dwarves will do our part."

There came elaborate carriages pulled by wild boars, the passengers hidden by thick, embroidered draperies to keep out the sun. Reginn guessed that these must be trolls–fierce fighters who labored under a major handicap–when exposed to sunlight they turned to stone. They did their best fighting at night, and underground.

Orcs lumbered along in the wake of the carriages, slow on two feet, lightning quick on all fours. They were a cross between trolls and ogres, combining the charm and good looks of the trolls with the ogres' sun tolerance. Their commander, Raghat, introduced himself.

And, finally, the beasts, and their commander, Ursinus, one of the bjorn–huge brown bears with saber teeth and a near-human intelligence. The vargr–the wolves–bigger than any Reginn had ever seen before, yet still raw-boned and hungry. And, there–the largest of all. Fenrir, who'd killed Odin and, in turn, was killed by Vithar, Odin's son. It was amazing how the old stories flooded back, prompted by the sight of the risen heroes of Jotunheim. It was more like the uncovering of buried memories than the recollection of stories.

I know them, Reginn thought. And then: Why do I know them? Why do I feel a kinship with them?

By the time the flood of warriors slowed to a trickle, the assembly seemed to stretch across the plateau to the hills beyond. When she turned to look back across the bridge to the temple, she saw that the officials gathered there had fallen silent, staring at Reginn's army, looking unsettled and alarmed. A few fell to their knees, while others fled.

Even Tyra and Heidin displayed a measure of apprehension. After hundreds of years, it was easy to forget just who was fighting on your side.

For a moment, Reginn allowed herself to savor the notion of sending her army across that fragile bridge to introduce themselves.

"Here's the army you requested, Your Majesty," Reginn said, sweeping low in a sardonic bow. "And it will stay where it is until you let the others go."

28

ACROSS THE BLUE OCEAN

AND SO THE *FIREBIRD* SAILED east, into the burn of the rising sun, her crew grim, stoic, ready to meet the deaths they fully expected. The one possible exception was Reyna, who climbed the mast several times a day to scan the horizon with a glass.

"What are you looking for?" Nils asked finally.

"The witchwall or the end of the world, whichever comes first," Reyna said. "I just don't want to be surprised."

As days passed and they encountered neither, she left off climbing. "It's true," Reyna said. "The witchwall is down."

"Looks that way," Eiric said.

"So we could have escaped a long time ago," Levi said.

Eiric shook his head. "This is new."

Besides, he thought, you can never be sure if where you're going is any better than the place you're escaping from.

Fortunately, the skies were clear for much of the journey, so Eiric was reasonably confident that they were going the right way. Also, the days were growing shorter, and it was noticeably colder.

More and more, Eiric found his grandfadir's words tumbling out of his own mouth.

Only a fool sails into a storm if he has a choice. Plenty of gales will find you even so. Save your strength for those. Have a plan for when your mast breaks, because it will, sooner or later. You can't row home from mid-ocean.

Landmarks are hard to come by after days at sea. The ocean changes day to day, and hour to hour. Sometimes a styrman loses the stars he's come to count on, and even the winds are no longer reliable. He goes forward on faith, and the memory of having found his way before.

Eiric's thoughts turned to home. What might have happened while he was gone? He hoped that those he'd left at Sundgard were safe. He'd found and lost enough treasure in New Jotunheim to ransom a king. Still, he hoped he'd come away with enough to satisfy Rikhard that Eiric's debt was paid.

That would be the sweetener before Eiric told him there was an invading army on the way.

Eiric recalled what Rikhard had said about his plans for the wyrd-spinners.

It may be that their motives are pure and their practice innocent. They may indeed be training healers, weather workers, seers, harvest witches, artisans, and scholars, in which case I hope to persuade them to return to the Archipelago–under proper supervision, of course.

Good luck with that, Lord, Eiric thought. It would be amusing to watch were the stakes not so high.

So many questions.

Was there any way to reclaim his systir from the fate the spinners had spun up for her? A fate she seemed to embrace?

Did he have any right to intervene, after everything she'd endured on Muckleholm? If this was what she wanted?

Would the jarl believe him when he told him what was coming? Or would he be brushed off and laughed at?

If so, should he collect his brodir, recruit a crew, and sail his long-ship back to Vestholm to keep his promise to the fiskers?

Would Reginn sail with his systir's fleet or remain behind in New Jotunheim? If the latter, would there be any way to reconnect with her there?

If such a meeting took place, would it feed the flames that had erupted between them?

And after that? There was no point in planning that far out.

The day came when Eiric saw shorebirds circling overhead. Bits of vegetation appeared, floating on the surface, and the character of the waves changed, signaling that they had crossed into the shallower water over the shelf that surrounded the western shore of Muckleholm. That night, a sounding confirmed it.

When they took their places around the ship for the nattmal, Eiric noticed that they had all put on heavier clothing and pulled knit hats down over their ears to cut the wind. "We're close. We'll likely make landfall tomorrow."

"Skol!" Rorik said, raising his cup and then draining it.

"Are we going straight to the farm?" Nils said. "Will you teach us how to milk a cow?" This was met with snorts of laughter and hoots of derision.

"Any fool can milk a cow," Reyna said. "It takes a barbarian farmer to milk a bull."

"I hear that barbarian farmers sleep with their cows to stay warm," Rorik said with an exaggerated shiver.

Eiric the barbarian farmer had become a running joke.

"Better be careful, or he'll put you to work, shoveling out the barn," Levi said.

"That would be you," Rorik shot back. "Nobody is better at shoveling skita."

"I suspect," Nils observed, "that a barbarian farmer could kick your ass."

"You are no farmer, Eiric," his modir had said. "You are too much like your fadir and grandfadir to stay home for long. You have always been more interested in what's over the horizon than what's behind you."

"We're coming up on Muckleholm from the west," Eiric said. "My farm is on the other side of the island. There are several major ports on the west side, but I don't know yet which we're closest to. I plan to go into town first and catch up on the news before I show my face at Sundgard."

There were questions he needed answered. Had Rikhard kept his promise to protect Sundgard and the people living there? Did Sten's family still have a price on Eiric's head?

Finally, in Muckleholm, the question always had to be asked: How many of my friends and enemies are still alive?

"Can we come with you?" Rorik said, not bothering to hide his eagerness. No true sailor appreciates dry land until he's been at sea for a while. Then nobody appreciates it more.

Eiric shook his head. "Not this time. I've been away six months, and a lot can change, even from solstice to solstice. I don't want you to have sailed all this way only to walk into a slaughter."

The next day, as the sun cleared the eastern horizon, Muckleholm came into view. At first, it was a thin gray line where the water met the sky that grew thicker as they closed the distance. Eiric had sailed up and down this coast more times than he could count, but it was not until he saw the long spine of coastal mountains curving off to the left and a series of conical volcanic islands extending off to the right that he knew for sure where they were. These were the seaward barriers that protected the ports of Sweinhavn and Langvik from the winter storms that roared out of the northwest.

Good, Eiric thought. He'd hoped for Langvik or Vandrgardr, places he knew well, but where he was less likely to be recognized than in Selvagr.

Best of all, he had a coaster's knowledge of the area, how to get in and out quickly, and where a person could hide a ship so that no one else would find it.

Eiric made for the channel between the spine of mountains and the first island to the south. He used the sail as long as he could, then dropped it and managed the tiller while the rest of the crew took to the oars. In places, the passage was so narrow that his crew could touch stone to either side with their oars. It was fortunate that Eiric had become so well acquainted with *Firebird* on the wide ocean.

Finally, they were through and the force of the sea behind them spat them out into the broad sound.

"Good work," Eiric said as his crew shipped their oars and congratulated each other. "That's not a passage you'd want to make in heavy weather."

Eiric was surprised at the busy ship traffic in the sound. The days were growing shorter, but it was still early for most coasters and fishermen to be returning to their home ports. It could be the haustblot–the first harvest–though that was a festival celebrated mostly at the home hearth.

There seemed to be an unusual number of longships–impressive vessels with full crews, with shields racked along the sides–rather than the smaller family boats typically used for coasting and fishing.

The fiskers were unusually quiet as they maneuvered their little *Firebird* through the crowded roads. It was as if reality was setting in.

"You were right," Levi said finally. "They do have lots of ships here. Big ones, too."

"To be honest," Eiric said, "this is more ships than I've ever seen before."

"Do you think word is out that war is coming?" Reyna said.

Eiric shrugged. "Could be, but you've been working on the fleet in New Jotunheim for more than a year, with many hands to do that work. How could they have produced so many, so fast?"

Having built ships himself, Eiric had a clear idea of how long it took, not to mention the time to spin, weave, and stitch the woolen sails.

"Maybe I'll learn more in Langvik," Eiric said.

They took shelter in a small cove Eiric knew, just south of the city. They sailed a short distance up an estuary and landed on a rocky beach that had served a small farm, now abandoned. Working together, they hauled their ship up into the edge of a drowned forest so that it could not be seen from the water.

Eiric moved some of Liv's money into a small pouch inside the waist of his breeches. Then strapped on his belt and slid Gramr into its scabbard, finishing with Bjorn's axe.

The fiskers watched these preparations with interest. "You look like you're going to war," Levi observed.

"We are in Barbaria, after all," Eiric said. He looked them up and down. Some were still shivering. "Are those the warmest clothes you have?" When they nodded, he said, "There's a coasters' market in town. If it's open, I'll see what I can find."

"Bring us a bucket of ale," Levi suggested. "That will keep us warm."

"While I'm gone, go over the ship for damage and make any repairs you can. Take note of any needed repairs that have to wait for lack of tools and supplies. Replenish the fresh water. Then practice your forms some more."

"So, in other words, relax, have a bite, raise your cup, you've earned it?" Nils said.

Eiric laughed. "Exactly. Just–whatever you do–do it close to the ship, and do it quietly. I know it's cold, but don't build a fire. The road between Langvik and Sweinhavn is just east of us." He pointed.

"When will you be back?" Rorik said.

Eiric judged the angle of the autumn sun. "I shouldn't be too long. It's not that far. I'll find an alehouse and get the news, visit the market, and be back before the nattmal. I still mean to set sail for Sundgard tomorrow morning."

As Eiric began his climb to the road, the fiskers were already testing the rigging and bailing out seawater.

29

THE TOUCH OF THE VALKYRIE

WHEN EIRIC REACHED THE EDGE of the road, he stopped within the cover of the trees and scanned it for traffic.

The road was wider than he remembered, with a surface of packed-down gravel and stone. When had that happened? When was the last time he'd been on the road?

As he watched, a half-dozen riders thundered by, all wearing the same red coats with a familiar signia–Rikhard's fossegrim.

What were they doing so far afield?

Shrugging, Eiric turned onto the road, walking north, keeping close to the margin in case of more traffic. Several wagons rumbled by, heavily loaded, going his way, but none offered him a ride.

He looked down at himself, scraping salt from his clothing with his fingernails. After a week at sea, heavily armed as he was, he might be mistaken for an outlaw or a sell-sword down on his luck.

He walked on, picking up the pace a little, assuming he was on his own to get to Langvik. As he'd said, it wasn't that far.

Eiric was nearly there, when a wagon drawn by a team of spavined horses passed him, then slowed to a stop, allowing him to catch up.

The driver was barrel-chested and unsavory-looking with a stubble of beard and a crop of boils on his neck. He gave Eiric a long, appraising look, then said, "Get in."

Eiric climbed up and sat on the bench seat beside him, laying Gramr across his lap so it wouldn't get in his way. So the driver could get a good look at it.

"Thank you," Eiric said.

The driver grunted, deployed his whip, and his team shuffled into motion. Eiric looked over his shoulder and saw that the wagon bed was empty, but oddly configured, with benches to either side, as if it was intended to carry people instead of goods. Heavy iron rings were set into the benches at intervals.

Was this some sort of transport for farmworkers or ship's crew who needed to travel overland?

It was probably for the best that the wagon was empty, considering the condition of the horses. Eiric worried that his weight in the wagon might push them past the tipping point.

"I'm Alverus," the wagon master said.

"Eiric."

"You're a big one."

"Big enough."

"You have some fine weapons there," Alverus said.

"Family heirlooms," Eiric said.

"Looks to me like you know how to use them."

"I get by," Eiric said. "I'm actually a farmer." He had never before been so eager to claim that title.

"Are you now?" The driver raised a skeptical eyebrow. "Farm life must suit you. What brings you to Langvik? Do you have family here?"

"Just passing through," Eiric said, already sorry that he'd accepted a ride. But he'd found that one way to stop a flood of questions was to ask questions of his own. He gestured at the wagon bed. "What business are you in? What do you haul?"

"I haul people, mostly," Alverus said. "Workers, soldiers, thralls, prisoners."

Eiric counted himself lucky to be sitting up front.

Fortunately, by then, they had entered the outskirts of the town, passing the last of the small farms that surrounded every town and village.

Langvik had changed considerably from what Eiric remembered. Before, it had consisted of a few shabby alehouses and bordels, warehouses, a stable, and a small central market. Its best feature was a fine harbor within the protection of the sound.

Now the town stretched around the harbor in both directions, and also farther inland, straddling the road. Across the water, Eiric could see what appeared to be a boatyard, with piles of split oak and several ships in varying stages of completion.

That would explain the swarm of ships they'd seen on the way in.

How could all this have happened so quickly?

"There seems to be a lot of building going on," Eiric observed.

"Aye," Alverus said. "Some say that Karlsen must be made of chop silver and gold."

"Karlsen? *Rikhard* built all this?" Eiric said.

"Not all of it, no. But, look–you'll see some of the buildings have his signia over the door." He pointed at several warehouses, an alehouse, and the land gate to the boatyard.

They all bore Rikhard's fossegrim.

"That's Karlsen's mark," the driver said. "It's a hardanger fiddle like the ones the fossegrim play to lure young ladies into the river. Or young men, as it were." He chuckled. "They say the king can charm the balls off a badger. Rikhard the Great, they call him, first of his name."

Eiric's thoughts stumbled to a halt, then retreated. *Hang on. What?*

"The . . . king? Rikhard is king?"

"Where have you been?" the driver said. "You must have just woke up from a long sleep."

Eiric scrambled to recover. "I'm from one of the out islands," he said. "We don't get much news. I mean, I knew Rikhard was king, but I didn't know he was king of *everything*."

Not a great recovery. He soldiered on. "When did that happen?"

"Five, six years ago," the driver said. The horses had ambled to a stop while he was distracted. Now he slapped the reins to urge them forward. "I mean, that's when he took over Muckleholm. Since then, he's been taking the out islands, one by one."

Eiric felt ambushed. He recalled his conversation with Karlsen at the compound the new jarl was building on the road to Selvagr.

"You're saying we need a king," Eiric had said, and Rikhard had denied it. That was less than a year ago. Wasn't it?

If Alverus had noticed Eiric's baffled reaction, he didn't show it. "What's the name of your island?" he said.

"Ithavoll."

"*Hmpf.* Never heard of it. But no worries. Might be he'll be paying you a visit real soon." Alverus slapped his thigh, which startled the horses, so they shambled forward with new enthusiasm.

"It's only–it seems like just yesterday that Harald died and Rikhard became jarl of the eastlands."

"That's been at least ten or twelve years ago now, I'd say," the driver said. "Time passes, whether we're paying attention or not."

Eiric had promised to return with the information Rikhard wanted within a year, or the farm would be forfeit. If it had really been ten or twelve years, then he was late. Very late. He recalled Rikhard's warning.

If you fail to keep your word, at the end of a year I will seize Sundgard, sell your family into the slave markets, and hunt you down with every resource at my command.

"I may not find your temple," Eiric had said, "but I will keep my word."

He'd been so confident, then. What would have happened to his brodir, Ivar, and the Stevensons? And the farm?

Eiric looked up and saw that the teamster was staring at him, eyes narrowed. "What's the matter?"

Eiric floundered for something to say that would keep the teamster talking so he wouldn't have to. "Does Rikhard have much support, from jarls and landowners? Are people glad to have him as king?"

Alverus shrugged. "I'd say so, for the most part. Don't get me wrong–there's lots of things that haven't changed, and people always complain about higher taxes. At least, with Rikhard, there's something to show for it. He's dug out some of the harbors that've silted up, and turned marshland into farmland. He's cleared out the trolls and outlaws in the north."

Maybe we did need a king.

"He's got foundries making weapons, boathouses making ships. I'll be honest–people are excited."

Sounds like he's getting ready for war, Eiric thought. Will people be excited then?

"Did he mention where all the ships would be sailing to?"

"I suppose we'll find out. He's not the type to be satisfied with the Archipelago for long. He's building the biggest army I've ever seen, plucking likely lads off farms and out of fisheries." He said this with the confidence of a man who knew that he was unlikely to be plucked.

"Will men fight for him?" *And pour his wine?*

"Maybe. Probably. People want to believe in him, and believe in themselves. For so long, we've felt like the dregs in the bottom of an ale barrel–the part that's left over, that nobody wants. He uses words like *honor* and *courage* and *destiny* that we haven't heard for a while. It's just–he makes folks feel hopeful, for the first time in a long time." He rubbed his thumb and first two fingers together. "And like I said, he's got plenty of money and he isn't afraid to spread it around."

Maybe Rikhard's inheritance from Harald was more generous than Eiric had thought.

Alverus gave Eiric another appraising look. "Young man like you, you'd have lots of opportunities at the king's court. Or you could go for a soldier. If the enemy laid eyes on you, they'd turn tail and run."

"Where is King Rikhard's hall?" Eiric said, ignoring the fact that Alverus seemed to think that he was in need of a job.

"'Halls,' you mean," Alverus said. "He has several. His main holding is on the east coast, near Selvagr. It's quite a place, I hear."

Eiric thought of Rikhard's "guesthouse" overlooking the sound. Was that what Alverus meant?

By now, they were traveling down the main street, the one that ran parallel to the harbor. Eiric looked for the alehall where he'd met Reginn for the first time. Then he remembered that Asger had burned it down that same night.

By now, no doubt, something else must have been built in its place. Eiric felt as if who he was and where he'd been had been rubbed out by the calloused thumb of time.

The wagon rolled to a stop in front of what appeared to be one of the finer establishments in town. Larger than the rest, sturdily built, with smoke spiraling up from what must be a generous central hearth. Two of Rikhard's red-coated soldiers lingered on the porch, and his signia was carved over the door, though at some point a crown had been added.

"This is as far as I go," Alverus said. "It's called King Harald's Hall. If you're looking for a bite and a cup, this is a good place. Cheap, too. There's even a couple of beds in the loft if you can put up with the noise from below."

Eiric grunted in response. What he wanted to do was to steal a horse and ride hard to Sundgard. He fought the impulse down, successfully stowing it in his growing stash of bad ideas. Not only would he be leaving his crew stranded with no information, he'd be breaking one of his personal rules–a coaster never roams too far from his ship. He'd broken that rule in New Jotunheim, and it had nearly cost him his life.

Eiric climbed down out of the wagon and slung his carry bag over his shoulder, resheathing his weapons. "Thank you for the ride," he said.

"Don't mention it," Alverus said. "You were going my way." He jumped down from the wagon, looping the reins around a post. "Come on in, I'll buy you a drink and introduce you around."

Eiric felt the prickle on the back of his neck that told him trouble was in the offing.

Bjorn always called it the touch of the Valkyrie, choosing for Valhalla.

As Sylvi always said, *If you're looking for trouble, you can always find it in an alehouse.*

It was strange. When his modir was alive, she couldn't tell him a thing. Now that she was dead, she had his ear every day.

"Maybe I'll stop in later," Eiric said. "Is there still a market down by the waterfront?"

"Aye," Alverus said, then added quickly, "They've likely already closed up for the day. You'd best come with me."

Eiric shook his head. "Sorry, but no. That's the whole reason I'm here–shopping." He trotted back down the street in the opposite direction as the wagon was aimed, and turned down an alleyway that led toward the waterfront. He resisted the temptation to break into a run, afraid he'd take a tumble and break his neck on the uneven pavers.

Besides, no one draws attention more quickly than someone running for no apparent reason. He compromised with a long-legged lope, all the while suspecting that he was making a fool of himself. Alverus was likely telling the other patrons about the country farmer who fled from the offer of a drink as if there were demons after him.

30

A DAY AT THE MARKET

THE MARKET AT LANGVIK WAS a collage of bright colors against the harbor. Some vendors sat on stools and benches under boiled wool canopies and rough bark roofs, while others sat on the ground, their wares spread before them on blankets.

Some of the more prosperous vendors had semipermanent buildings, with three walls and an open front. This market had more on offer than he'd ever seen at any market on Muckleholm.

Eiric slowed his pace and cut between two stalls so that he was on the harbor side of the market and less visible from the street above. Then he hustled along, picking up an item now and then, setting it back down, always moving toward the south edge of town, and his ship.

Yet, still, people stared at him as if he were an issvargr trying to blend in with a flock of sheep. When he smiled, they faded back, avoiding eye contact, as if he'd shown his teeth. If he expressed a special interest in something, they would hurry forward, press it into his hands, and say, "It's yours, Lord. A gift."

Then it was his turn to drop it and back away, saying, "Thank you, just looking."

It was a contrast with the market at home, where he'd haggle for half an hour over a pound of salt and later find out that it was short-weighted.

People are afraid of soldiers here, he thought. Or anyone who looks like a soldier. He did manage to buy a wheel of cheese, a bag of nuts and dried fruit, and a block of smoked fish, which was all he could stow in his carry bag.

As the fishmonger wrapped up his purchase, Eiric asked, "Is there a shop here that sells used clothing?" He wasn't particularly hopeful. In his experience, most people wore their clothes until mending would no longer serve them, and then cut them up for rags.

To his surprise, the shopkeeper pointed farther down the market. "Try at the sign of the spider, down the way."

At the sign of the spider?

At the far end of the market, a little removed from the others, he found the shop. The banner outside bore the image of a spider on its web. Not exactly enticing.

Still, the shop looked to be more prosperous than most, with two fine entry-posts with carvings of gods and heroes, a roof of bark and thatch, and a counter to divide shopkeeper from customer.

Inside, the air carried a faint whiff of sulfur. Eiric looked for some type of lamp or burner to explain it, but saw none.

No one stood behind the counter.

Shrugging, Eiric took a look around. There were several bins of clothing in different sizes. To his surprise, some looked to be quite fine, in velvets and silk, and scarcely worn. He set those aside and kept looking. He was going for warmth, not looks.

Almost immediately, then, he pulled out two likely-looking heavy wool coats and a cloak.

The coats were all right, but the cloak had a definite sword cut down the front that had been carefully mended. He took a cautious sniff. It smelled like the wood-ash soap Sylvi made every year. So, recently washed. No sign of blood.

His crew would probably like wearing the evidence of past battles, even those they hadn't fought in. Eiric had been wearing that look all his life. He added it to the keeper pile.

He found one more heavy coat, smaller than the others, that might fit Reyna.

"My apologies, Lord, I had to step out for a moment."

The voice came from behind him.

He swung around to find the shopkeeper standing in the doorway. She was young and pretty, with mahogany skin, eyes like tannin pools, and close-cropped hair. She was finely dressed, in a long crimson gown with a short hooded cloak trimmed in white fur overtop. The baubles and pouches at her waist reminded Eiric of the ones Reginn wore.

When she got a good look at Eiric, she stopped short, eyes widening. Her gaze touched on the axe at his waist, his sword in its baldric.

"No," she said, taking a step back, shaking her head as if to deny his presence. "Impossible."

Eiric was getting used to people reacting to his size and, admittedly, he was unshorn and stubble-faced after a week at sea.

"I'm sorry if I startled you, my lady," Eiric said. "My appearance is rough, but I mean no harm."

"I knew the bitch was lying."

If Eiric thought she might turn and run out the door, he was mistaken. Instead, she groped at her waist and came up with something that glittered in the light slanting through the doorway behind her. A throwing knife. Her aim was spot-on. She would have hit her mark had he not dodged aside.

The problem with a throwing knife is that, once thrown, it's gone.

No problem after all. She had another. And another. He took shelter behind the counter, hearing more blades thud into the wood.

Sooner or later she had to run out of knives. Surely, she would.

Eiric was at a loss. Could this be an enemy he'd made in Langvik before he sailed for the Grove? He usually made a point of remembering his enemies. A former sweetheart holding a grudge?

"Ma'am," he called. "If you want me gone from your shop, I'll leave. But you'll need to stop trying to kill me and get out of my way."

In answer, a small object arced over the counter and landed next to him. A tightly wrapped package with a burning fuse. He grabbed it up and threw it back. Seconds later, he heard an explosion and the patter of debris falling all around him.

He peeked over the counter to find the front of the shop blown out, and the shopkeeper picking herself up from the floor, the front of her fine dress spattered with soot. If it was a bomb, it had been a small one, but even a small blast would draw unwanted attention.

He vaulted over the counter and made a run for the door. She stepped into his path, and he thrust her aside. Just as he crossed the ruined threshold, he ran smack into a brace of the king's guardsmen. His momentum was such that he nearly knocked them over. But there were more crowding in behind the first two.

They maneuvered him back into the shop and slammed him to the floor, delivering a few rib-cracking kicks for good measure. He felt the slither of metal on leather as they relieved him of his sword and axe.

Once they'd bound Eiric's hands behind his back, they sat him up, leaned him against the counter, and formed a rough circle around him. There were five altogether. They stared at him, mouths all but hanging open. None seemed eager to get within arm's length.

From her expression, the shopkeeper wasn't any happier to see them than Eiric himself.

The Valkyrie was no longer tapping Eiric's shoulder. She was yanking his arm.

One of the soldiers, who seemed to be in charge, turned to face the shopkeeper. "So, Lady Agata, what have we here? Did one of your cauldrons explode? Did you use too heavy a hand with the lizard skins and baby eyes?"

Eiric flinched. It was the kind of derisive comment that Liv had to put up with on a daily basis back home in Selvagr. The sort he hadn't heard since he sailed for the Grove.

He shifted uncomfortably, feeling something hard on the floor under him. He groped with his bound hands.

It was one of Agata's knives.

Eiric turned it around, braced the hilt on the floor, and set to sawing away at the ropes that bound him, all the while feigning deep interest in the conversation going on over his head.

"What did you give this one, to grow him so big?" another soldier said. "We could all use some of that."

"I'm afraid there's been a misunderstanding, stallari," Agata said. "This is my cousin, Haki. It's been years since I've seen him. I was showing him one of the–projects–I've been working on for the king. There was an accident. I apologize for the noise and your trouble. Now, could you please cut him loose? None of this is his fault."

Eiric felt like he had so often in New Jotunheim–like someone was stirring his thoughts with a stick. Moments ago, Agata had been doing her best to kill him. Now they were cousins?

"Tell me this, witch–why are you building dangerous weapons in the middle of town?" the officer persisted, as if determined to come away with evidence of a crime.

"That wasn't a dangerous weapon," Agata said. "If it was a dangerous weapon, the whole town would be gone."

The stallari didn't like the implied threat. "Cousin or not, he's just what we're looking for." He nodded to two of his men, and they hauled Eiric to his feet so that he lost hold of the knife. "Haki, is it? How would you like to join the king's army?"

"He cannot," Agata protested. "He's the only one who can work their farm. That's why he hasn't visited here before now. He has a little systir and brodir–"

"They'll get by," the stallari said with no trace of sympathy. "Children grow up quick in the Archipelago." He dug inside his tunic and tossed a small bag to Agata that jangled as she caught it. "Thank you for the tip, witch. Well done."

She flung it back at him, barely missing his head. "You cannot put my cousin in your army. He is not right in the head."

"He can carry a sword, can't he? Looks to me like he has everything we're looking for in a soldier."

It wasn't as if she was worried that Eiric would be killed in the fighting. It was more like she just wanted to do the killing herself.

He continued to strain against the ropes binding him, scraping flesh from his wrists. He'd made progress; he could feel that the rope was frayed. But it wouldn't help if he was already in the army by the time he freed himself.

"We'll let the king have a look at him and see what he says," the officer said. "Who knows? Maybe he'll send him back."

"Do you ever wonder why Rikhard needs such a large army?" Agata said.

"That's the king's business," one of the soldiers snapped. "What does a shop girl know about–?"

"Shut up, Rune!" the officer said. "Remember who you're talking to."

"I'm just saying that it doesn't sit well with me to hear this witch criticize King Rikhard–"

"She didn't criticize him. She asked a question. She may be a witch–but she's the king's witch, and under the king's protection. So leave off before you get into real trouble."

The king's witch?

"The king should burn the lot of them is what he should do." Rune seemed to be a man who didn't know how to shut up. "He's cleaned out the trolls and outlaws in the north. He should do the same with the witches, once and for all."

"You wait and see," the stallari said. "These witches are treacherous, all right, but under the king's control they have been valuable assets. You've seen how one island after another has fallen under Rikhard's sword."

Eiric sensed resentment rising in Agata like a full-moon tide as the soldiers debated the pros and cons of witches as if she weren't even there. So many times, he'd seen Liv seething under the same treatment. Had he spoken up enough? Had he appreciated what it was like to be belittled and humiliated day after day?

Now, if anything, it was worse than before.

"Let's go," the stallari said. "We'll take this one back to the barracks and get him settled so we can have ourselves a cup and a bite to celebrate."

Eiric all but dragged his feet as they turned him toward the doorway. That's when he saw a flicker of movement just outside, then heard a voice.

"Are you still open for business?" The voice was familiar.

It was Rorik, with Levi just behind him. They didn't wait for an answer, but charged forward through the rubble with swords drawn.

Eiric made one last desperate effort and broke the bonds between his wrists with such force that the two soldiers pinioning his arms flew into each other.

"Styrman." Reyna extended Gramr toward him, hilt-first. Eiric pivoted and drove his sword between Rune's ribs and up, all but lifting him from the floor. Eiric planted his foot on the body and wrenched his weapon free. When he spun around, the fiskers had two men down, but Levi was hard-pressed by the stallari until Rorik took the officer from behind with his shiny new axe.

Four men down, but where was the fifth? And where was Agata?

Hearing sounds of a struggle from the back room, he grabbed his axe and plunged between the curtains to find Reyna standing on a table, apparently weaponless and bleeding, nimbly avoiding the fifth man's efforts to cut her in half. Hearing Eiric behind him, the man turned toward him, brandishing his axe. Reyna leaped onto his back and cut the soldier's throat with her wicked-looking knife, spraying

Eiric with blood head to toe.

Reyna leaped free as the soldier crashed to the floor, twitched a little, then went still, surrounded by a growing puddle of blood.

"Reyna," Eiric said, looking anxiously into her face. "Are you all right?"

"I'll live," she said. "But–" She broke off at the squeal of hinges from the back of the room. Eiric sprinted toward the sound and found Agata halfway through a hatch in the floor behind the sleeping bench.

He lunged forward, slid his hands under her arms, and hauled her back out as she twisted and struggled to get free, swearing like a first-year coaster.

"Shut up, will you?" he growled. "I'm in a bad mood as it is, and that's not helping."

To his surprise, she shut up.

Eiric turned to Reyna. "See if you can find a way to barricade or block the front entrance. It doesn't have to be perfect–just enough to suggest we're closed. Is it just the three of you in town?"

"Just us," Reyna said.

"Tell Rorik and Levi to stash the dead bodies out of sight and straighten up as best you can. When you're finished, you'll find some coats piled up next to the bins in front. I thought they might suit you. Have a look outside and see if the guard is still swarming the streets. I need a few minutes with Agata."

Reyna's gaze flicked from Eiric to Agata and back again. "Yes, Styrman," she said, and went out front.

Eiric was just turning back toward Agata when some small sound alerted him. He shifted just in time, so that the dagger missed his throat and sliced into his coat instead. The miss put her off-balance enough that, by the time she recovered and came at him again, his longer reach allowed him to grip both her wrists and slam her against the wall.

He pinned her there and growled, "Drop it, or I'll break both your wrists for a start."

After a moment's defiance, she complied. Eiric kicked it aside, then, pinioning both her hands with one of his, he performed the most thorough search he'd ever done on a woman. In all, he surfaced three more knives, an empty sheath for the dagger, what appeared to be a garrote, and a long needle hidden in the hem of her skirt.

How many knives does one woman need?

To save time, he used one of her knives to cut away her remedy belts and pouches and set them out of reach.

There was something else. She wore a pendant, a rough-hewn stone similar to the one Reginn had given him in the crypt. It glowed deep blue against Agata's skin, but when he cradled it in his hand, it turned a sullen red.

What was it she'd called it? A kynstone. Useful for identifying and sorting the gifted. He broke the chain and took it from her.

"You're a thief now?"

He ignored her and retrieved the dagger, meaning to return it to its sheath. He noticed a substance painted on the blade, both sides, all the way to the tip. Not blood. Poison.

"What's this?" he said, displaying it to Agata. "Playing for keeps, are we?" He slid it into its sheath.

"Styrman?" It was Levi, from the doorway. "We've cleaned things up the best we could. The streets are still full of soldiers. A couple have poked their heads in, asking if we'd seen a tall, unsavory-looking stranger with a big sword and an axe. We told them he tried to come in here, but the witch blew up the doorway and scared him off."

Eiric laughed, even weighed down by worries as he was. "Well done," he said. "Did they buy it?"

"They did–for now."

"Good. Give me another few minutes, and then we'll go."

Eiric waited until Levi was gone before he turned back to Agata. "You're still alive because I need you to help me solve a problem. We didn't come looking for trouble, but now five of Rikhard's men are dead, and the king is not the forgiving kind."

Her eyes narrowed. "You know him, then?"

He ignored the question. "If we leave you alive, you'll sound the alarm and we'll never make it out of town."

"Why would I do that? I tried to help you before, it ended in a bloodbath, and now I'll get the blame."

"Did you really? Try to help me? I came in here to buy some clothes. You tried to kill me. Why?"

"Maybe I didn't like your looks. Have you ever looked in a mirror?"

"I got the impression that you recognized me–or thought you did, and that's why you came after me. But when the king's soldiers showed up, you tried to persuade them to let me go. Why? You could have sent me off to the king's army and collected your finder's fee and never have to think of me again."

She studied on this, as if surprised he'd noticed in the heat of the moment. "Look," she said. "You saw how the king's soldiers treated me. They are despicable bastards. If they brought in a prize like you, they wouldn't have to buy a drink for a week. Why should I help them?"

"You're helping the king."

Agata sighed, out of answers. "So–what's your point? I know you're going to kill me–how could you not?" Her gaze never wavered. "Just go ahead and be done with it. I can't take the suspense."

"I'm asking you to give me another option–a way out. You were trying to escape through the cellar. Where does it go?"

She eyed him, head cocked, as if wondering if he would believe her if she denied it. Or keep his word if she agreed to help.

"All right, you win." Meaning that despite what she'd said, she wanted to live, and had run out of options for the moment.

"As you may know, the Muckleholm Neck is honeycombed with limestone caves and tunnels. The cellar connects to a tunnel that leads to a sea cave on the sound. You should find some small boats there that will take you where you want to go."

"You're being straight with me."

"Yes."

"Why should I believe you?"

"Why ask me questions if you don't believe the answers?"

She had a point.

"How far to the sea cave?"

"A half an hour, maybe more," Agata said. "The terrain is rough. That limits how fast you can go."

"You've been through it, then."

She nodded. "Many times."

"Good," Eiric said. "That's what we'll do, then. I'll call the others in."

"So—you're going to let me go?" From her expression, Eiric suspected that he was fulfilling her low expectations.

"I'll make that decision when we get to the cave."

"At the—wait! I'm not going with you."

"Yes. You are, as far as the cave. If all goes well, we'll release you there."

She raised both hands. Clearly, this was not in the plan. "No. I'll give you directions, but I'm not coming."

If she wanted sympathy, she wasn't getting it from him. "I came here to shop. What happened from there is on you. You're coming with us. I want to make sure that, if we make a wrong turn, or run into any nasty surprises, you're there to explain."

Something flickered across her face, something that told him that blade had struck true.

"Can I bring my staff, at least, to light the way?"

"Leave the staff here," Eiric said, wrung out of trust. "We'll use torches, like regular people."

Levi poked his head around the curtain. "Time to go?"

"Yes," Eiric said. "Don't forget the clothes. We've paid a high price for them."

31

GHOST SHIP

Naglfar is loose.

O'er the sea from the north there sails a ship

With the people of Hel, at the helm stands Loki;

After the wolf do wild men follow,

And with them the brother of Byleist goes.

–The Poetic Edda, *stanzas 50-51*

REGINN'S ALLIES SEEMED TO PREFER to keep the rift between them and the risen veterans of Ragnarok. Either that, or they still feared the consequences of setting foot in the deadlands. From the temple end of the bridge, Durinn directed Reginn to lead the dead brigade along the south edge of the rift to the eastern shore. The commander followed along on the north side with a small band of mounted soldiers.

Reginn chose her path carefully. There was no wall on this side of the rift, since no living creature should be walking the deadlands. When she peered over the edge, the river below boiled as the backs of sea creatures broke the surface again and again. Shadows swarmed along the cliff edge. When she looked up, eagles circled like carrion crows.

At the coast, the Elivagar poured into the sea, shrouding the shoreline with a stinging mist that set Reginn's eyes to watering. Just offshore, a massive ship sat at anchor. A small ship's boat was drawn up on the shore just south of the rift.

As Reginn's soldiers crowded around her at the edge of the sea cliff, she tried not to flinch away from their yawning need. It was like being in the presence of a thousand Asgers, all nipping away bits of her power and consciousness, leaving in their place unfathomable pain.

They are yours. They are your creations, and your responsibility.

Focus! She eyed the little oarboat skeptically. There was no way she could transport this army in that–even one at a time. The impossibility of it all paralyzed her.

Dainn and Hrym found their way to her side. "What are your orders, ma'am?"

She pointed. "There's our ship," she said. "Somehow, we need to get aboard."

The draugr did not wait for clarification. They swarmed down the cliff and across the sand to the water's edge. Without hesitation, they plunged in, wading, swimming–whatever suited them to cross the expanse of water to the ship. The elves simply trod upon the surface like water striders. The sea boiled around the eldrjotun, and cracked and hardened around the issjotun.

As they clambered up the near side of the ship, they came close to foundering it before they split their forces to either side and set the ship straight on its keel.

The kraken, serpents, and other sea creatures poured from the mouth of the river and reappeared in the waters surrounding the ship of the dead.

Seeing this, Reginn scrambled down the cliff, all but tumbling head over heels once or twice. She landed on the soft sand with both feet, then crossed to the oarboat to find Naima Bondi and Asger Eldr waiting for her. Asger carried an unsheathed flaming sword, much larger than before.

Reginn stared at her former master. There was something different about Asger, an aspect she hadn't seen before.

It was joy.

Having shown it off, Asger slid the sword into its scabbard, which seemed like a good idea when boarding a wooden boat. Naima and

Reginn waded out and vaulted into the boat. Asger cast off, leaping nimbly aboard without getting his feet wet. A frightened-looking young soldier took to the oars.

"Your ship is named *Naglfar,*" Asger said, with a certain pride of ownership. "It's the largest ship in the entire fleet. That's a good thing, since you will be leading the largest force in the queen's army. Hopefully it will allow enough space to prevent fights from breaking out due to crowding."

"*Naglfar,*" Reginn said, frowning. "That sounds familiar."

"That was Loki's ship at Ragnarok, made from the nail-parings of the dead," Asger said.

Reginn squinted at the ship.

"This one, I believe, is built of oak," Asger said. "Your crew boarded at Austhavn. Durinn was afraid that some might desert when they got a look at the passengers."

Reginn was watching the oarsman. She saw his back stiffen and his head draw into his shoulders like a turtle's.

Don't worry, she wanted to say. *We're all going to die anyway.*

Naima spoke up for the first time, seeming to sense Reginn's discomfort. "You'll have some help from people you know. Katia and the vaettir will be fighting alongside you. Stian thought that he might be able to help with the–with the non-human soldiers. Svend asked to serve under your command, too. A number of my friends will be on board, in the crew and among the guards."

Reginn knew that Naima intended to make her feel better, but in some ways, it made her feel worse. For one thing, it seemed that everyone–even some of those she considered friends–had known about this plan for a while. For another, this meant that her lack of training and experience in warfare would put those she cared about at risk.

She remembered the day she had spent with Katia and Durinn,

watching war games involving Katia's dragons. At least she didn't have to try to manage *them*.

"But . . . I don't know why anyone would put me in charge of an army," Reginn said. "I don't know the first thing about how to manage a battlefield, or weapons, or strategy. I did my part–I called them out. Now somebody else should command them."

"You don't understand," Asger said. "You are the only one they will follow." He paused. "The only one. Without your guidance, there is no telling what they will do. You cannot step away."

When they came alongside the ship, she saw that, once again, the draugr were crowded along the rail, watching her approach. The ship listed toward them again, so close that Reginn could count the planks along the hull.

"Get back!" she shouted, standing, waving them off, setting the oarboat to rocking dangerously.

"My lady," Asger said. "Please sit down, unless you really have learned to swim."

My lady?

The crowd thinned, the ship righted itself, and disaster was once again averted. A short rope ladder tumbled over the gunwale and they climbed aboard.

Once again, Reginn was in the midst of a crowd of revenants, pressing in from all sides so that her head swam. That was the problem with these open-decked, agile longships–there was no refuge, no privacy to be had anywhere.

"Take her to her quarters," Asger said to Naima, while he ran interference, using a combination of his sharp-edged lash and intimidation to clear a path through to midships. There, just ahead of the mast, a small tent had been erected.

Naima lifted the flap so Reginn could crawl inside, then followed after, allowing the flap to drop back into place.

Instantly, the cacophony of sound ceased.

Reginn sat very still, gripping her staff with both hands. "Are they gone?" she whispered.

Naima shook her head. "They're still out there. This tent is a gift from Eira. She thought you would need a sanctuary from–from all this." She lifted the flap an inch or two, and noise poured in. Then she closed it. Blessed silence.

"Aaaah," Reginn said, diving headfirst into a muddle of pillows and silk blankets. "If I live long enough to have children, I'll have twin girls, and I'm going to name them Naima and Eira."

"And they'll fight like wolverines," Naima said. "You'll have to send them into the forest and see who comes back alive."

"That's another thing," Reginn said. "You're the warrior. You're the one who should be commanding this army. Not me."

Naima laughed. "I don't think the kennari wants me anywhere near her with an army under my command. I can't believe I'm still alive."

"Tyra defers to Heidin," Reginn said. "So far, at least." She reached out and touched the fabric of the tent. "Does it block sound both ways? Can someone outside hear what we're saying?"

"It works both ways," Naima said. "I already checked. Besides, I don't think anyone is going to get close enough to hear anything. Lord Asger is right outside and nobody's getting past him."

"Isn't he supposed to be serving Lady Heidin?" Reginn snapped, suddenly irritable. She always felt that way when she was being corralled into doing something she didn't want to do. Which seemed to be most of the time.

"He says that Lady Heidin can take care of herself."

"I guess that's true," Reginn said. *He probably wants to make sure I don't jump overboard again.*

"You'd be welcome to stay here, too–if you want," Reginn said. "There's plenty of room."

"Gods, Reginn, I was hoping you would ask. If I had to listen to that noise all day long, I'd cut my own throat. And look." She dug under a pile of belongings at the rear of the tent and produced the talharpa.

That's when Reginn realized that Naima had already moved in.

"It's been a while," she said. "Don't armies play music around the campfire?" She paused. "No worries. I won't be here all the time. I have a few other options."

Reginn raised an eyebrow, wondering what those might be. "I see. Well, there's a place for you here whenever." She paused. "Have you–has anyone said anything about food?"

Naima laughed. "I knew that topic would come up, sooner or later. I brought a basket of food along, and a jar of wine. We'll start with that. But first–"

Reginn caught a flicker of movement as someone fumbled with the tent flap. Naima drew her knife and said, "Who is it?"

"Svend."

Naima looked to Reginn, who nodded. "Come," Naima said, as if inviting a guest into the queen's hall.

The tent flaps parted, and the noise poured in, along with Svend, who crawled forward on his hands and knees, folding his long body until everything was inside.

He faced Reginn and bowed his head even lower. "Counselor," he said. "I trust that you are reasonably comfortable?"

"This is much finer than I ever expected," Reginn said. Which was true.

Svend nodded. "Good. I wanted to explain the chain of command aboard ship."

"Please," Reginn said, gesturing for him to go on.

"You have overall command of the ship, and direct command of the–of the Risen army. The human soldiers and the ship's crew report directly to me."

You can have the whole lot, Reginn wanted to say. But quashed the impulse.

"Most of the ship's crew are seasoned sailors," Svend said, "which is a good thing, because I am not."

"Where did you find seasoned sailors?"

"They are fiskers from Vestholm," Svend said. "They grew up building and sailing ships. They helped us get the shipyard started. They're still getting used to blue water sailing.

"We view these ships primarily as a means of transportation, since we're untried in naval battles. We hope to make landfall before we encounter any enemy forces. Then we can regroup and Durinn will assume overall command of the battle plan. Likely we'll use our ships for coastal travel and raiding."

"That makes sense," Reginn said, nodding.

"I have something else for you." Svend handed her a parcel wrapped in chamois.

"What's this?"

"Eira sent it."

Reginn carefully unwrapped it. It was a mail shirt, obviously made to Reginn's measure, and a helmet, both exquisitely crafted. Also an axe, smaller than standard, with a razor-sharp bit and motifs lightly engraved over the butt and cheeks of the blade–fire, ice, a spreading oak. All the touch points of her life.

"Eira said to tell you to take care of it, or you'll answer to her," Svend said. "Don't let anybody get close enough to land a blow, because you don't want dings in it or blood all over it." It was a warrior's blessing.

Uninvited tears stung Reginn's eyes, driven by double-edged emotion. It was a stunning gift, crafted and given in love, but it represented a future she would not have chosen on her own.

Naima must have noticed, because she charged ahead, revealing that she was in on it, too. "I told her that you had a dagger–remember, you threatened me with it once–but I'd never seen you with an axe.

We guessed that you would favor your staff over a sword, and there's only so much weaponry you can reasonably carry, but Eira said she could forge a sword for you if–"

Reginn reached out and put her hand over Naima's mouth, stoppering the flow. "It's okay. You can stop now. Thank you. It's just–nobody's ever done anything like this for me before."

"We want to keep you safe," Naima said. "That's all."

Reginn took a shaky breath. "I know. I'll try not to get dings in it–or anything else."

"You swear?"

"I swear."

"Try it on," Naima said. "See if it fits before you have to use it."

Reginn would have rather hung it on the wall to admire than to wear it. But Naima had a point.

Reginn came up on her knees and slid the shirt over her head and down over her body, all the way to her knees, where it puddled a little on the floor.

The metal warmed, the rings shifting, tightening, loosening, molding to her body like a second skin.

Her warrior skin.

She turned, to find Naima eyeing her critically.

"How does it feel?" she said.

"It's not as heavy as I expected," Reginn said. She picked up the axe, swung it in a little arc. "It doesn't feel stiff at all."

"It's magicked to change with you, to fit you even if you grow, or–or shrink."

"May it please the gods, not that," Reginn said, rolling her eyes.

Naima thrust the helmet at her. "Now the helmet."

That, too, fit perfectly. Her head was covered in steel from nape to the bridge of her nose, and riveted nose and eye pieces protected the upper half of her face, while not interfering with her vision.

She felt oddly at home in it. Had she been a warrior in a past life? Was she keeping secrets from herself?

Reginn removed the helmet and armor, a little relieved to find that it was not permanently attached.

"Tell Eira it's perfect, if you see her before I do," she said.

Svend came as close as he ever did to a smile. "I will, my lady."

After Svend took his leave, Naima produced the promised basket of food. "Now," she said. "Let's eat."

It was easy, within the sanctuary of Eira's magic tent, eating and drinking with her friend, to ignore what was happening outside of it.

Reginn was just washing down the last of a piece of honey-soaked bread when she felt a vibration through the deck beneath her. It took her a moment to realize what it was–they were raising the anchor. Not long after, the ship lurched as the sail was raised and they got underway.

Like it or not, she was on her way home.

32

LEAVING LANGVIK

ONE BY ONE, EIRIC AND his crew dropped through the hatch and into the cellar below. Agata went second-to-last, and Eiric brought up the rear, pulling the hatch cover back into place behind him.

The chamber was larger than he would have guessed. The ceiling wasn't high enough for him to stand upright, but that was nothing new. As Eiric's eyes adjusted, he saw that it had a dry stone floor, unlit oil lamps in the corners, a pallet on the floor, benches and a small table piled with cloth.

A workspace, maybe, though this light wouldn't be the best. Or a hiding place. Tunnels led off to either side.

"Where do these go?" Eiric said, pointing to the two tunnels.

He watched as Agata considered a lie, discarded it.

Pointing left, she said, "This goes to the king's prison." Pointing right, she said, "This goes to the sea cave."

The king's prison?

"Let's go. Agata, you lead the way so we don't make a wrong turn."

They'd gone only a short distance, when a side tunnel veered off to the left, this time blocked by a heavy oak door.

"What's this?" Eiric said, trying the door, which was locked.

"Nothing," Agata said. "Just my workroom." She took a step forward, to go past it.

"I'd like to see it," Eiric said. "Could you open the door?"

He sensed the restlessness of his crew, but Eiric's years of coasting had taught him that the biggest prizes and the best secrets were often kept behind locked doors, in the places they wanted to keep you out of.

Agata clenched her jaw and sorted through a set of keys hanging from a chain at her neck until she found the one she wanted. She inserted it into the heavy iron lock and Eiric heard the smooth click as the lock released. She gave the door a push, and it swung open.

This room is well-used, he thought.

"Show me around," Eiric said, motioning her in ahead of him. His crew followed after, no doubt thinking that their styrman had gone mad.

At first glance, the room looked to be a workroom, just as she'd said. To the left was an area that resembled a kitchen or an herbalist's hearth, with bunches of herbs hanging to dry and shelves with rows of casks and bottles. A large pot sat next to the cold hearth, its contents reeking. In another corner stood a loom, similar to Liv's at home, surrounded by bins of weaving swords, distaffs, and unspun fiber that smelled of sheep. On one of the side walls, a sleeping bench, piled high with blankets, with furs across the foot.

It was a typical domestic scene, except for a few key details. Fumes leaked from a niche in the wall, staining the surrounding stone a sulfurous yellow. This must be where the sulfur smell was coming from.

Eiric crossed the room to take a closer look. Most of the heat and fumes appeared to go up a chimney hewn into the rock, but some escaped into the room. He peeked into the niche and drew back quickly as the heat seared his face. Molten rock seethed far below.

Two small cells were bolted into the wall, each furnished with a pallet, a chamber pot, and a pair of manacles mounted into the stone wall behind.

"What goes on here?" he said, adding, "This time, start with the truth. It will save time."

"This is where we tend the dead from the king's prisons," Agata said. "We remove clothes and any other valuables. Any valuables go to the king. You already know about the clothes."

“And then what?” Eiric said. He pointed to the cells. “Do you lock up the dead so they can’t get away?”

She flushed. “Of course not. They go into the furnace, there.” She pointed to the niche in the wall. “We usually include some personal item to take to the next world.”

“If the cells aren’t for the dead, then who are they for?” Eiric persisted.

“I am the king’s examiner,” Agata said, seeing no way around it. “King Rikhard is especially keen to identify others with the gift of seidr. I help with that.”

“Is that what the kynstone is for?”

After so many ambushes, Eiric took pleasure in seeing Agata broadsided.

“Yes,” she said stiffly. “It is helpful.”

“Where did you get it?”

“I can’t remember,” Agata said.

I need a stone to tell truths from lies, Eiric thought.

“And what does the king do when he has identified such people?” Eiric asked.

“He recruits them to serve the crown,” Agata said. Something about the way she said it implied a joke she didn’t share.

He didn’t have time to get to the root of it now.

“Let’s go on to the water gate, then.”

As Agata had promised, the way was hard going. After another half hour of walking, they came upon an apparent dead end–a smooth rock face with no obvious path over, under, or around.

And yet–Eiric could still feel the brush of air against his cheek, air that carried the scent of the sea. He reached out his hand, and felt cool, hard stone.

He turned to Agata. “Now what?”

“We need the key,” she said. Reaching into a crevice in the stone, she retrieved a distaff. It was shorter than the ones the volur used, and plain, much like the ones he'd seen Sylvi and Liv use for spinning.

With some effort, Eiric kept his hands at his sides, resisting the urge to snatch it away and break it over his knee. Fighting the temptation to draw a weapon of his own. Instead, he stood and waited for the next play.

"No one passes through this barrier save the gifted–and those with permission from me. As far as the king knows, the tunnel ends here."

When she pointed her staff at the stone, it appeared to dissolve away, revealing a corridor beyond. Agata ushered them forward. As Eiric passed over the threshold, he half expected to be incinerated. But they all made it safely to the other side.

The scent of the sea was even stronger now. Eiric could taste it on his tongue, and even imagined that he could hear the crash of water on stone.

"The rest of you, keep walking," Agata said. "I need to speak to your styrman in private."

"They can hear whatever you have to say," Eiric said.

"Then I have nothing to say."

When Eiric shrugged and went to turn away, she added, "It's about your brodir."

He spun back around. "What about him?"

She nodded toward the crew.

Eiric waved them off. "Stay within sight," he said, squaring off with her and freeing his axe.

"I'm done playing games, Agata," Eiric said. "Tell me what you know."

Agata stood with her back to the gate, her finery somewhat worse for wear, her hem torn and soiled, her expression one of grudging respect.

"Halvorsen, I underestimated you. I was convinced that you died in Eimyrja. I heard it from the aldrnari's own lips. It makes me wonder what else she was lying about."

Once again, she'd thrown him off-balance. "Who are you?" Eiric whispered. "How do you know all about me?"

"I've been coming and going from Muckleholm since before Rikhard became king."

"Coming and going to Muckleholm from–New Jotunheim?"

She nodded. "You can imagine how surprised I was to see you walk in, but some jobs you have to do yourself. I was just happy to get a second chance to claim the kill. I would have succeeded had the king's guard not interfered. That was a problem. The last thing I wanted was to see you recruited into the king's army. Fortunately, your crew showed up. Fiskers, right?"

"Who *are* you?" Eiric repeated.

"I'm a spy, of course. A saboteur–a successful one, at that. I've put a lot of time into this setup, and now I'm going to have to abandon it because of you."

"I'm all out of sad songs," Eiric said. "What setup?"

"The king sends me anyone he suspects of being gifted for testing. When I do find a volva, I smuggle her away to New Jotunheim. I kill the Asgardians. The rest, I send back to Rikhard. It's one reason he's been having so much trouble establishing his magical brigade. I seem to be the only spinner left in the Archipelago.

"Now, I suppose, I'll have to shut it down. Nothing lasts forever. The queen will be here before long, and I'll have plenty to do.

"A little farther on, you'll begin to hear the sound of the sea. It will be dark by then, but you will find a small oarboat moored within the cave. Take that boat wherever you want to go, but I would caution you to do it quietly until you put some distance between you and the gate."

"You mentioned my brodir," Eiric said through gritted teeth. "What about him?"

"Since I've been unsuccessful in killing you, I'm going to give you some advice. Don't try to stop this. Don't go to the king and tell him what you know. Considerable blood and sweat and countless lives have been spent preparing for this invasion. The queen hoped to have you with her, but I knew from the start that was a fool's errand. She has a weakness for you that endangers all our plans.

"The king will ask you to join the fight against the Jotun. He plans to use your brodir as bait, to ensnare you. Do not let that happen, or the next time we meet, I will finally claim that kill."

"You can try," Eiric said.

"Oh, I have," Agata said. "Your Asgardian luck cannot last forever." With that, her face grew fuzzy, indistinct, the features rippling away. Then sharpened, revealing a new face, finely sculpted. Familiar roughly shorn black hair peeking from within a hood.

It was Grima.

"You should sail for Rikhard's hall at Kingshavn, collect your brodir, and go. Find some place far from here and become a sell-sword for somebody else. Or be a farmer or a fisherman–I don't care. Just don't dawdle. If necessary, we will kill the boy to take that game piece out of his hands."

Eiric lunged at her, his axe whistling through the air. But Grima stepped back through the stone and was gone.

Eiric slammed his shoulder against the stone and ended up with a bruised shoulder.

He turned to find the fiskers staring at him.

"I'm glad to be done with her," he said. "Let's find that boat."

They reached their camp as the moon was rising. Nils walked out of the woods, axe in hand, to greet them. Then stopped and stared at their disheveled appearance and visible wounds and bruises. "The shopkeepers in Barbaria must drive a hard bargain," he said. "Where'd you get the little boat?"

"We paid a blood price," Reyna said. She tossed him a bundle of clothing, then flopped down in her usual spot by the fire and was instantly asleep.

"Well, that was fun," Levi said. "What are we going to do tomorrow?"

"Tomorrow," Eiric said, "I'm going home."

33
MUTINY

DURING THE CROSSING, REGINN SPENT most of her time huddled in her tent, relying on Naima for food, water, and news. The neediness of her army gutted her. There were times that she wished she could tell them to jump overboard and swim to Barbaria and she'd meet them there.

The other ships were never far away. Heidin had planted her banner on one of the larger longships, now that her little dragon was gone. Sometimes Reginn would see her standing in the bow like a second gilded figurehead, eyes fixed on the horizon, straining forward like a horse at the gate.

A few times a day, Reginn would emerge to get some fresh air under the pressure of what felt like a thousand eyes, all but foundering in an ocean of need. Asger drove off anyone who came too close.

So far, the ship's crew had nothing to say to Reginn. They would turn away when she came near, and they wouldn't even meet her eyes. But now and then, she'd catch one or another of them glaring at her. That needed to be sorted. So she asked Svend for an introduction.

Svend introduced her to the styrman, Rollo, and a few of the crew, both men and women, and all with the surname Fisker. They were lean and wiry, with muscled arms inked with Brimrunar, the wave runes that protect ships. They all had stick-straight hair, light eyes, and sculpted faces.

"The fiskers are keen shipbuilders," Svend said, "and skilled sailors. We'd have no fleet without them."

"It's a beautiful ship, Rollo," Reginn said. "I would like to learn more about it. Perhaps you could show me around one day."

Rollo stared up at the rigging as if he found it fascinating. "Sorry," he said. "That would not be possible." His voice carried a trace of an accent, and an element of disdain.

Svend stared at him. "Surely you could spare a few moments to–"

"Never mind," Reginn said, raising a hand. "I understand that this is a small crew, and our styrman has more important things to do." She turned back to Rollo. "I can tell that we are in good hands. I see that you are wearing Brimrunar."

If she thought that might be a point of connection, she was dead wrong. Rollo's eyes widened, and he slapped his hand over his inked bicep as if to hide it. "No," he said. "This is not for your eyes."

Svend was looking from Rollo to Reginn, eyes narrowed in puzzlement.

"Carry on," Reginn said. She motioned for Svend to follow her back to midships.

"What was that all about?" he said when they were out of earshot.

"Magical tactics," Reginn said. "They all have the same surname, and they resemble each other. Are they siblings?"

Svend shook his head. "Not that I know of. Everyone from Vestholm looks like that. They all marry within the clan. They are closemouthed and standoffish, but not usually rude."

"Tell me," Reginn said. "Do the fiskers hold some sort of a grudge against the spinners?"

"I don't really–" He stopped, decided to tell the truth. "Yes. The fiskers were pretty much left alone on their home island until recently. The temple decided to develop their island for farming, which caused some ill feeling."

Now, why would that be?

"Their home island is Vestholm?" Reginn recalled that Shelby had been posted there, to establish an agricultural program.

"It is Vestholm now," Svend said. "It was formerly called Fiskeholm."

Days passed, and Reginn still hid in her tent, unwilling to confront the hostility of the fisker crew and the pressure of the needy Risen.

Asger grew increasingly impatient. He seemed to have something to say, but was weighing his words. That was unusual. He always assumed that she needed to hear what he had to say, no matter what it was.

"Counselor," the demon said finally. "They can smell your fear."

Reginn bristled, grateful for a familiar target. "Oh, really? They can smell my fear? That's so helpful," she spat. "Perhaps I should have splashed on some courage before I dressed."

"Good," the demon said, nodding. "Anger is better."

Asger was right, of course. The armor of Reginn's anger had shattered, leaving the vulnerability of fear of failure. Who did she think she was, leading an army of monsters against the Archipelago? Her previous experience with soldiers amounted to fending them off in countless alehalls.

"We are not subtle creatures, except, perhaps, for the wood elves, I suppose," Asger said. "We are not masters of nuance and we don't read the meaning behind words. We are not vulnerable to persuasion, nor do we respond to flattery. We require plain speech, clear rules, and strong leadership."

Reginn eyed him. "By 'we' you mean—?"

"The Jotun—whether demons, trolls, issvargr, the draugr. We are agents of chaos and we respect power. That is why we are drawn to you."

"I don't feel so much respected as besieged," Reginn said.

Asger nodded. "They don't know what to make of you, because someone as powerful as you are shouldn't radiate fear."

"Don't radiate fear," Reginn said. "Got it."

The thin autumn sun was setting, gilding the tips of the waves, when Reginn emerged from her tent for her evening walk around. As usual, the army of Ragnarok surged toward her, each member fighting to be at the front of the pack. The issvargr crept forward, ears pasted to their heads, lips drawn back to reveal teeth resembling razor-like shards of ice. Serpents dangled from the rigging, arcing toward her.

Reginn froze, fighting the urge to dive back into her tent, to cover her head with her arms.

They smell your fear.

No, she thought. I am not going to be intimidated by my own army.

So, instead, she planted her staff and spun it, sending a wall of energy to meet them.

They all but bounced off it. Some scrambled to their feet and made another go, with the same result.

"Now," Reginn said, pounding her staff against the deck for emphasis. "All of you–stand down and listen." She looked forward and aft, and saw that the ship's crew had collected at either end, putting as much distance as they could between themselves and Reginn's army. There was no help there.

It was up to her.

This is an audience. You know how to command an audience. You will have all the power you need if you claim it.

You need to make eye contact, establish a connection.

Can you do that without showing fear?

"Stay where you are," she said. "Let me have a look at you."

Taking a deep breath, Reginn dropped the barrier.

Nobody moved. To her relief, there was no rush forward. They seemed to be waiting for what more she might have to say.

She allowed her gaze to travel from face to face–or whatever appeared to be face-ish. She looked every soldier in the eyes, plumbing the flaming portals of the eldrjotun, diving into the bone-shattering cold of the issvargr. Elven eyes, full of sorrow, as unfathomable as forest pools. The intelligent brown eyes of the bjorn, housed in an intimidating body. The pitiless yellow eyes of wolves, impenetrable. The eyes of dwarves, all but hidden between the foam of bristled beards and bristling brows. The angry eyes of trolls, like torches in the shadow of their hoods. Eyes that were windows on a darkness so chaotic that Reginn couldn't hold that gaze for long.

You need to see them as individuals and not as a faceless mob. That will help you understand where the danger is.

"I am Elder Reginn Eiklund, who called you," Reginn said. "I see you. Do you see me?"

A murmur of affirmation rolled over her. So, it seemed that they'd understood what she said, though they'd never shown any sign of it before.

"I am your commander because I am an aldrnari. I live between fire and ice, life and death, and for that reason I was able to reach you and raise you."

Gaah! She sounded too much like one of the traveling skalds she encountered sometimes–the ones not good enough to win a patron.

"You are the Risen army of the jotnar. Though you fought bravely at Ragnarok, you never received the honor you deserved. This is your opportunity to finally claim it. If you choose.

"You came when I summoned you, so I assume that you all chose to be here. If there is anyone having second thoughts, speak now, and I will arrange to send you back to the deadlands."

How that could be accomplished, she didn't know.

Fortunately no one spoke up.

"If you stay, you will need to follow some basic rules."

She paused, desperately trying to think of some. The only army she'd seen in action was the army of New Jotunheim, under Durinn's command. She wished she'd spent more time on Ithavoll, observing Durinn.

Where that time would have come from, she couldn't say.

Reginn ticked each one off on her fingers as she thought of it. "You must give me the courtesy of space. You are not allowed to hound me wherever I go, aboard ship or anywhere else. Do not touch me or anyone else without permission."

Taking a quick breath, she continued. "Right now we're on a ship, and so we follow ship's rules. Your orders are to remain at midships for the most part, and not to–to swarm around the ship in a crowd. That frightens people, and risks putting all of us in the water. Let the sailors do their jobs, and try to stay out of their way."

She meant to continue but hesitated, distracted by the sight of one of the issvargr creeping toward her, ears flat, hackles raised, tongue dropping ice pellets on the deck.

"That's close enough," Reginn said. "Did you need something?"

The wolf's forward progress stopped, though his threatening stance didn't change. "We are hungry, Aldrnari," the wolf said, his voice as brittle and icy as midwinter. "It has been so very long since we've eaten."

"Shut up, Finnulf," an orc said. "She's hardly more than a mouthful anyway."

"Stand down," Ursinus said. He was the bjorn who commanded the beasts.

"We choose our own alphas," Finnulf said.

"Why, are you putting in a bid for the job?" The orc laughed. "Do you think we would take orders from a flea-bitten slinker? We use the pelts of issvargr to keep our privates warm."

After years of performing in alehouses, Reginn knew how to anticipate trouble. She knew better than to be distracted by the verbal sparring.

Watch their eyes, Tove said. *That will tell you where they're going next.*

"Why should we follow this scrap of a girl?" Finnulf's yellow eyes shifted to Reginn as he sprang. She snapped the head of her staff forward, spooling out power, catching the issvargr in midair.

For a moment, the issvargr hung there, wrapped in a golden cocoon of magic. Then fell to the deck with a clatter, as a pile of bleached bones.

"That's why," Reginn said into the sudden silence. "Does anyone else have any questions?"

There were none. One of the other issvargr nosed at the bones, then nudged them with her paw.

New rule: soldiers are not allowed to eat each other or their commanders.

"Asger, Dainn, Ursinus, and Hrym, come forward."

Dainn, Ursinus, and Hrym forced their way through the crowd and joined her. Asger, of course, was already there.

"These are your officers," Reginn said. "Asger Eldr commands the thursen of every kind; Dainn, the elven forces; Ursinus, the beasts; and Hrym—ah—everyone else. Go through your officers if there is something you need. Please do not bring everything to me.

"I don't know what we'll find when we land in the Archipelago. We may wade into a fight right away. I hope that we don't. I hope that we'll have the chance to train together first, but we can't always get what we want.

"Are there any questions?"

Again, there were none. Reginn didn't know whether the lack of questions was because she'd done such a good job explaining, or if they hadn't understood a thing she said.

"All right, then. Ah—dismissed. And remember, stay midships, and no traveling in a pack."

Reginn had to admit, it wasn't a terribly inspirational speech, but now, at least, she could walk across the deck unmolested.

As Asger walked past, he said, "That's a start."

"The bones thing was a nice touch," Naima said. "Very convincing." She squeezed her shoulder and said, "Good job with the mutiny."

"It wasn't exactly a mutiny–" Reginn began, but Naima had already turned away.

34

HOMECOMING

HAD EIRIC NOT KNOWN THAT ten years had passed since he'd left Muckleholm, he would have been bewildered by the changes along the east coast, the part of the island that he knew the best.

South of Thornby, the coastline had once been absolutely barren of settlement. It was all sand until it ran into the ocean and so became a beach.

Now there were hamlets here and there, what appeared to be nascent fishing villages.

As they continued north toward Selvagr, the sea lanes became even more congested. Many of the ships were long, sleek dragons with shields racked on both sides and little room for cargo. Warships.

Eiric swiped sleet from the back of his neck before it could melt and run down inside his neckline.

"Is it always like this?" Reyna said, making her way aft. She looked to be encased in ice, down to a coating on her lashes.

At least the weather hadn't changed.

"Of course not," Eiric said. "It's usually much worse."

She eyed him, head cocked, trying to assess whether he was joking.

That was what passed for humor in the Archipelago.

Selvagr would be coming up before long. He wondered what he might learn if he dropped in on his uncles. They hadn't any legal claim on him anymore–Rikhard had paid Sten's blood price. The issue was now between Eiric and Rikhard.

It might be worth it to see the look on their faces.

No. That was the kind of impulse that always landed him in the middle of a fight. What his modir called “poking the wolverine.” He should have learned his lesson in Langvik. He suspected that the temptation to detour to Selvagr was just one more way to borrow trouble–and to put off facing what he might find at the farm.

He remembered what Liv had said after Rikhard’s intervention at the Thing.

Oh, brodir. Sten was a pig. This man is a snake. There’s no way you can outwit him.

Rikhard had made him a promise.

If you fail to keep your word, at the end of a year I will seize Sundgard, sell your family into the slave markets, and hunt you down with every resource at my command.

Well, Eiric thought, I might come see you and save you some trouble.

Sailing was busy work that day.

“I don’t think I’ve ever seen so many ships,” Nils muttered. “How are the spinners going to match up with this?”

“It’s not just the ships,” Eiric said. “There are lots of good sailors in the Archipelago, too. Unlike in New Jotunheim, sailors here have always been free to sail wherever they want.” He paused. “Then again, we all know that the spinners have their own advantages.”

He had no taste for either side–his systir and her flock of bloodthirsty crows, or Rikhard, packed full of arrogance and ambition, a man who would slay his own fadir in the pursuit of power.

Ironic, coming from a man who’d been convicted of killing his stepfadir.

He would warn Rikhard what was coming, collect his brodir, and do his best to keep his promise to the fiskers. He owed more to them than he did his would-be king.

Another possibility kept surfacing, despite his efforts to drown it. What if Rikhard had made good on his threat and sold his little brodir into slavery?

If so, his mission had changed. He needed to find Ivar, if he still lived, and then they would take their revenge together.

After that? In his last words to Reginn, he'd made a promise. *Stay alive and I will find you.*

She'd made no promises back to him.

They rowed past Selvagr as the sun was setting, dying behind the uplands west of the city.

His hometown had grown, too—swelling like a boil on the tip of the peninsula. They traveled slowly, oars only, since the risk of collision was high in the congested waters. The fiskers avidly watched the darkening city slip by as the lamps kindled up the hill.

How many times had Eiric sailed this sound, crewing a longship with his fadir and grandfadir, setting out in springtime to raid the far islands, returning in the fall, sitting low in the water with a full hold? And, later, alone in the little karvi, an unwilling fisherman.

"We're not going to stop in town?" Nils said.

"No," Eiric said. "We'll camp somewhere along the shore past the town and head on to the farm in the morning."

Eiric was beginning to wonder if the town had expanded all the way to Sundgard. But eventually the lights thinned out and vanished, and the shoreline became a dark smudge on the horizon. Eiric angled the *Firebird* in toward shore, where a shallow curve in the shoreline provided some protection from heavy seas. Working together, they hauled her onto the beach.

They faced another freezing night on a beach with no fire, eating cold food in company that had been together all day, so there was little to say.

"What's your farm like?" Rorik said, breaking a long silence.

"When I left, it was the most prosperous farm on Muckleholm."

"Why did you leave, then?"

"I was convicted of killing my stepfadir and declared an outlaw,"

Eiric said, figuring that they were going to find out sooner or later. "Rikhard paid the blood price in exchange for a year of service. He sent me to find the Temple at the Grove."

After a heartbeat of silence, Nils said, "You're working for the *king*?"

Eiric thought it interesting that nobody asked if he was guilty of the crime he'd been convicted of. "He wasn't the king then," Eiric said. "I told you. He sent me to see what was happening to children taken from Muckleholm."

No ship's crew likes surprises. Their expressions said they'd just discovered that they'd been sailing with a viper on board.

"Look," Eiric said. "I don't know what we'll find tomorrow, or what my reception might be. I'm vargr in the king's eyes–an outlaw. I'm nine years late keeping a promise. The farm no longer belongs to me. I hope to meet up with the king and let him know what's coming, but I don't know if I'll stay alive long enough. So. I would like to offer better hospitality but it's best if I go in alone and see what's what. That way, you won't be putting the ship at risk and you can be on your way if the worst happens."

That idea got a cold reception.

"You promised to sail back with us and help free our families on Fiskeholm," Reyna said. "Don't think you're getting out of that."

Rorik yawned. "Me, I don't have any plans for tomorrow. I would like to see your old place."

"Besides," Nils said. "I missed the market at Langvik. I am hoping to make up for it at Sundgard."

"I didn't come here for a fight I can't win," Eiric said. "I'm hoping to avoid one."

In his head, he heard Liv. *Who are you, and what have you done with my brodir?*

"Who knows?" Reyna said. "I've never met a king before. Maybe he'll invite us all for a cup and a bite."

* * *

And so it was that, despite Eiric's misgivings, the *Firebird* sailed for Sundgard with her full complement of crew.

It wasn't long before Eiric realized that this coastline that had played such a large role in his childhood–this coast that he could navigate in his sleep–this, too, had dramatically changed.

He'd kept an eye to port as they sailed north along the eastern shore of Muckleholm, careful not to sail too close. It was along here, between Selvagr and the sound, that Rikhard had begun to build his hall.

When it finally came up, to Eiric's surprise, it wasn't much changed from ten years ago. The guesthouse where they'd stayed the day he met the king was still there, and the longhouse had been finished, but there was no sign of progress beyond that.

He didn't want to tell his crew that this was the king's keep, because, after the temple at Eimyrja, it looked pretty piss-poor. Maybe Rikhard had been too busy conquering the Archipelago to finish his house.

Or maybe he'd moved to Sundgard full time.

As they sailed more deeply into the shelter of the sound, buildings reappeared along the shore–not houses, but manufactories, often clustered around a central burn pit. Though the sun had barely cleared the horizon to the west, the foundries were already ablaze, plumes of heat and smoke rising in the cold air. Maybe they burned all night. The furnaces gave off so much heat that many of the men working the bellows and feeding the flames were shirtless and steaming despite the cold day, dancing like demons at the gates of Hel.

Was it possible that Ulff Stevenson had expanded his blacksmithing business into something more elaborate?

Reyna squinted, peering through the haze. "Can you tell what they're making?"

Eiric shook his head.

Just past the casting yard was a series of open-fronted buildings centered by stone anvils, their chimneys pouring out ripples of heat and vapor into the frosty air. Smithies–a dozen or more. When Eiric had left, there had been one lone forge at Sundgard, the one a hopeful Ulf Stevenson had installed when he was wooing Sylvi.

Not too much farther, the longhouse and outbuildings should be coming into view. But there were more buildings lining the shore, some of them up on pillars out over the tideline. A long pier extended into the sound, and several ships were moored there. Some appeared to be unfinished, while others had visible damage. Workers swarmed over the ships, putting them to rights. There was an urgency about the work that said they were eager to get them back in service.

"It's a shipyard," Eiric murmured, almost to himself.

"I'm guessing that's new, too," Rorik said, reading his expression. "How long did you say you've been gone?"

"Less than a year in New Jotunheim," Eiric said. "Ten years here."

Rorik cocked his head skeptically. "How does that work?"

"I have no idea," Eiric said.

As they passed the shipyard, several workers stopped what they were doing and looked their way, shading their eyes against the rising sun.

"Is this it?" Nils said, pointing north.

Eiric looked forward as the longhouse came into view, and the summer barn and the family boathouse. They seemed to be relatively intact, but somehow stripped, standing vulnerable on the peninsula. Two more outbuildings had been added, their purpose unclear.

"I thought you said this was a farm," Reyna said. "So where are the fields?"

Good question. Distracted by the iron works and the shipyard, Eiric hadn't noticed the other big change–nothing was growing as far as the eye could see.

The barley, rye, and oat fields that had been the bane of Eiric's existence would lie fallow this time of year, but Sylvi's kitchen garden should still offer cabbage, onions, and other greens until the ground froze. It lay barren, not even weeds surviving where the garden used to be. All but two of Sylvi's precious apple trees were gone, too.

Also missing was the woods behind the house that had once extended up the mountain, providing firewood, pitch, walnuts, hazelnuts, and oaks that could be split into planks for shipbuilding.

The woods where Sylvi died. Where, as far as he knew, Sten still lay at the bottom of a crevasse.

There were other changes. The trees that had clothed the slopes of the mountains to the northwest had been scraped away, like algae from a ship's hull, leaving bare rock behind. Those trees had provided timber for countless ships, and broke the winds that roared down out of the mountains in the winter dark.

Had it all been turned to ships, fuel, and charcoal?

If so, it appeared that no attempt had been made to replant what had been taken. Was this Rikhard's revenge–turning a fertile farm into a desert?

"It *was* a farm," Eiric said, releasing a long breath. "Not anymore."

They were coming up on the farmstead now, so Eiric angled their boat in toward shore, until it scraped bottom in the shallow water. He dropped anchor while the rudder was still free, in case they needed to make a quick getaway.

"The rest of you, stay with the ship," Eiric said, vaulting over the gunwale and landing knee-deep in the shallow water. "If the worst happens, take the ship and go."

As he waded the short distance to shore, he heard a series of splashes that told him that the rest were coming, too.

It appeared that the longhouse was occupied. Someone was keeping it in good repair, and the dirt yard in front had been trampled down by many feet. Eiric expected a challenge, but none came.

When he reached the door, Eiric turned and motioned to his crew to stay back. Nobody is eager to open the door to a pack of heavily armed coasters.

This time, they obeyed.

He knocked. There was no answer. He knocked louder. He heard someone coming from around the back of the longhouse. "The dagmal is over, if that's what you're looking for," she said.

A woman came into view, her arms loaded with firewood higher than her head. "There's a couple of oat cakes left, if you want them, but I won't be cooking again until tonight."

Eiric hurried forward to meet her. "Let me help with that," he said, sliding his arms under the load to take the weight. As the pile shifted, her face came into view.

"Hilde?" he said.

She rolled her eyes. "Don't think you can sweet-talk me into making a second meal when you–"

She stopped, her eyes widening in recognition. Then stepped back, dropping her arms, allowing the firewood to roll off and land on the ground between them.

They knelt, facing each other, with Eiric scooping up the entire load this time.

"Has anyone seen you?" Hilde whispered, looking both ways for witnesses. "Does anyone know you're here?"

"No. Not that I know of," Eiric said, taking a look around himself.

"Who are they?" She pointed at the fiskers.

"They're with me," Eiric said.

"Do you trust them?"

"Yes," he said, a little surprised to find that he did.

"Then, all of you, come in." Eiric motioned to the fiskers, then followed Hilde into the longhouse with his arms full of wood. He heard the crew close on his heels. Once everyone was inside, Hilde threw the bar across the door.

Walking into the longhouse after being away so long was an emotional fist to the gut. The first thing Eiric noticed was that it smelled the same–of woodsmoke and straw.

Maybe, he thought, all longhouses smell alike.

The only thing missing was the winter barn. That appeared to have been converted to living quarters.

Eiric set the load of wood next to the central hearth and added a fresh log to the fire. Then tended the mealfire as well, falling into these chores like he had never left.

When he stood and turned back toward Hilde, he noticed what he hadn't before–she was with child.

It was all he could do not to stand and gape. Speaking of a fist to the gut.

A lot can happen in ten years.

He could hear his modir's sarcastic voice in his ear. Had he expected Hilde to sit quietly by the hearth, hoping Eiric would return and make her life complete? When he hadn't made her any promises at all?

Sylvi had no tolerance for arrogant men. And yet, somehow, she'd married Sten.

Eiric scanned the hall with fresh eyes, looking for evidence of a male presence–whatever that might be.

Most of the sleeping benches were gone, replaced by bins and shelves of kitchen goods. Two long tables took up nearly all the space at the center of the hall, one on either side of the hearths.

He caught a flicker of movement in the shadows at the rear of the hall, next to the winter barn, then the sound of hushed voices. Had he been led into a trap?

His hand on the hilt of his seax, he called, "Who's there? Show yourself." He heard the whisper of steel behind him as the fiskers bared their own weapons.

"Put your weapons away or take them outside," Hilde said, her voice as sharp as any blade. "Bare steel is not allowed in my hall."

"Do as she says," Eiric ordered, letting go of his knife but keeping it in easy reach.

"Dottirs, come forward and be introduced," Hilde said.

Two young girls emerged from the shadows, hand in hand, obviously systirs. Their hair was the color of wet sand, done up in long braids. Eiric wasn't good at estimating ages, but the older of the two might have been fourteen, so of marriageable age, the younger maybe ten years old. They stared at Eiric, eyes wide, faces pale save for spots of color on their cheeks.

"These are my dottirs, Frida and Gudrun," Hilde said, standing between them, her hands on their shoulders. "Their parents were killed in the war for the islands. They help me out here in the hall.

"Girls, this is a–an old friend. He used to live here, long ago."

There was no mistaking that Hilde had very definitely put him in the past.

Eiric squatted, hoping that would make him seem less intimidating. "Good to meet you," he said.

"Where do you live now?" Frida, the older one, said.

That turned out to be a hard question to answer.

"I haven't decided yet," Eiric said. "Right now I live on a boat."

"That must be fun," Gudrun said.

Frida wasn't so impressed. "I hope that it's a big boat."

Hilde addressed Eiric's crew. "Welcome to Sundgard. If you're hungry, we've got oat cakes, apples, and cheese. Maybe some cider if the hungry hordes haven't drunk it all. Gudrun and Frida will help you with that. You can eat down at that end of the table, but clean up after yourselves because it won't be long before I'll be setting up for the nattmal."

Hilde issued orders like a natural lord, one accustomed to being obeyed. And Eiric's crew did, with the promise of food as an incentive.

"Let's go sit," she said, leading the way to the other end of the hall, where they would be unlikely to be overheard. She had created a small, curtained-off area where sleeping benches used to be. She pulled a cask and a pair of cups from a shelf, set them on a small table, and poured.

They sat facing each other.

"So," Hilde said, "why are you here?"

35
NEW ALLIANCES

"WHY ARE YOU HERE?" HILDE had said.

There was a challenge in the question that Eiric didn't know how to meet. So he proceeded cautiously.

"I promised that I would return," he said. "It wasn't until I landed in Muckleholm that I realized how much time had passed."

Hilde resettled her skirts over her knees. "I suppose it would be easy to lose track of time in paradise."

Eiric reared back, stung. "I didn't–it wasn't–" He stopped, took a breath. Paradise? He recalled the pitched battle at the edge of the rift, the slaughter of the elders in the Lundhof, the keeper's murder, his interrupted execution, and the fits of madness that had plagued him until Reginn somehow ended them.

He hadn't come back expecting forgiveness or redemption.

Well, maybe he had. Understanding, anyway.

He planned to say little about what he'd learned until he spoke with Rikhard. But he owed Hilde an explanation, at least.

"I found the Temple at the Grove, in a place called New Jotunheim," Eiric said. "It *is* a paradise, fueled by magic and the blood of innocents." He looked down at his hands. "They plan to invade the Archipelago. They may already be on their way."

Hilde emptied her cup, then filled it again. "And so you . . . hurried back to warn us?" She cocked her head. "So glad you didn't dawdle."

She didn't seem particularly worried, as if he was just making up excuses for why he was late. Was this the reaction he could expect from the king?

"Time works differently there," Eiric said. "One year there apparently translates to ten years here."

"Ah," she said. "I see. Where's Liv? She didn't come back with you?"

Eiric debated how much to share. Hilde and Liv had grown closer during Hilde's time as a wet nurse to Ivar.

But, again, he didn't want stories circulating before he had the chance to speak with the king.

If he had that chance.

He shook his head. "She stayed behind."

"I don't blame her," Hilde said. "She never had an easy time of it here."

"She may be sailing with the Jotun forces when they come."

"Jotun? Is that what they call themselves?"

"That's what they are," Eiric said. Then plunged ahead. "Where is Ivar?"

As if on cue, Frida called out. "Modir! I know I baked five fresh loaves this morning. Do you know where they got to?"

Hilde pushed to her feet and strode over to where the fiskers were flirting with the servers and enjoying a meal they didn't cook themselves.

While she got that sorted, Eiric drained his own cup, then turned it between his hands, debating how to make his case.

Hilde had changed, and it wasn't just the new lines on her face and the strands of silver in her hair. There was a no-nonsense self-assurance that hadn't been there before.

He recalled what she'd said before he set sail.

You're a good man, Eiric Halvorsen, and you won't convince me otherwise.

Did she still believe that, after ten years? The fact that she hadn't mentioned Ivar was telling.

Telling what?

When she reclaimed her seat, Eiric said, "What's happened here? I wouldn't have recognized Sundgard if I hadn't sailed from here and back hundreds of times since I was little." He paused, summoned his courage, and pushed on. "Where are Ulff and Ivar? What happened to the livestock, the forests, and the fields?"

He did his best not to sound accusing. Maybe he succeeded, because Hilde didn't seem to take it that way.

"The land began to fail not long after you and Liv set sail for the witches' temple. The king's shipyards needed wood, so the forests fell, since that was the one cash crop that we had a lot of. Yields dwindled from fields that had been fertile year after year. We broke up fallow fields and rotated the plantings, but the result was the same. Still, my fadir was bound and determined that you would return home to a thriving farm. He literally worked himself to death."

"He's crossed the borderlands, then," Eiric said.

Hilde nodded. "About five years ago."

"I'm sorry." Somehow, he'd already known. Ulff was the kind of man who leaves a gaping hole behind that lesser men can only nibble at.

"I'm surprised that the king has allowed you to stay this long," Eiric said. "Rikhard was clear about what would happen if I did not return within a year."

He'd threatened to sell Eiric's family into slavery and claim the farm for himself.

"Rikhard has been occupied elsewhere. Perhaps you've heard that he's been consolidating his hold on Muckleholm and seizing control of the surrounding islands. He's been on the march ever since you left.

"Since the king had made no move to seize the farm, your uncles assumed that he'd forgotten about it. They seemed to believe that it was time to take custody of Ivar and claim the property for themselves."

The old anger rose up in Eiric, that feeling of being constantly disrespected and besieged. "They came after Sundgard, even now?"

Hilde laughed. "I think it was more about the win than anything else. They were confident that, in the right hands, it could be restored to its former glory. They moved in here and started ordering me around."

"What happened?"

"I took Ivar and went to Rikhard," Hilde said. Something in Eiric's expression must have prompted her to add, "Look, I know you have your reasons–good reasons–for mistrusting Rikhard," she said. "Yet he has been more than fair with us. I think–I think he waited to seize the farm because he still hoped you would return with news from the temple."

"So what did Rikhard do?" Eiric tried to keep a neutral tone.

"He took custody of Ivar," Hilde said. "Your brodir is under the king's protection."

"He . . . took custody . . . of my brodir?" Eiric said, throwing neutrality out the door. "How can he do that?"

"He's the king," Hilde said, shrugging, as if that was explanation enough. "As far as anyone knew, the only blood relatives Ivar had left were the Knudsens. I told Rikhard that if Ivar went with his uncles, he would meet with some kind of accident within the year, leaving them with clear title to the farm. Rickard could offer the kind of protection that I could not."

"Protection?" Eiric snorted. "That's one way to put it. Where is Ivar being held?"

"He's usually with the king, wherever he is," Hilde said. "He's been fighting alongside him for a year or two now."

"Fighting? But he's only–"

"How old were you when you began crewing for your fadir?"

Eiric raised both hands, his cheeks heating. "I yield the point." Hilde had developed a talent for getting to the heart of the matter. Or maybe it had been there all along.

"Ivar is tall for his age," Hilde said. "Not like you, but still. He lives much older than his years. Men stand aside for him."

Eiric grappled with the notion of this new and different Ivar. "Does he–does he still have shake spells?"

Hilde nodded. "Now and then, when he's really tired, or under stress. Rikhard says they are due to the rising of Ivar's Asgardian blood. He has brought in the best spinners to tend to him in the hopes of channeling that power."

Such a different response than from Sten, Ivar's own fadir, who'd left him in the forest to die.

"So Rikhard took control of the farm and put up a foundry?"

"Actually," Hilde said, "he gave the farm to me."

"To you? You own Sundgard now?" This conversation was like a series of unanswered punches to the head that left him reeling.

Hilde nodded. "I was already living here, making the best use of it I could after my fadir died. Ivar owns estates in the out islands, but this way he has a place to call home here on Muckleholm."

It was the move of a man who has a full view of the battlefield. Eiric might fight the king for Sundgard. He most certainly would fight his uncles. The one person he would not fight was Hilde.

Also. *Ivar owns estates.*

Eiric decided that it was time for another pour. He refilled both their glasses. "So *you* built the foundries?"

Hilde laughed. "Not exactly. I lease land to your uncles, and they run that business. I operate this hall as an inn, providing housing and board to workers, and the king buys everything they can produce." She paused. "A lot can happen in ten years."

"So I see." Eiric had never wanted to be a farmer, but a farm was a good place to return to after a season of raiding. "You haven't remarried?" It was an awkward question, since Hilde's fadir had hoped for a match between the two of them.

Hilde shook her head. "I never saw a need to marry. While we were farming, my fadir did the heavy work that I could not. By the time he passed, I was moving on from farming. No one dares bother me, since I'm under the king's protection. And I've grown used to doing things my own way." She laughed. "Not that I haven't had offers."

"It's not my business, but–"

"Your uncles. I could have my pick. They're always eager to get in bed with a woman with property." She stopped, her cheeks reddening. "I'm sorry. I know that your modir–"

"I would not wish my uncles on my worst enemy," Eiric said.

"I am content. Ivar is like a son to me, and I have two dottirs, and a baby on the way." She rested her hands on her swollen middle. When she looked up at Eiric, she laughed at his expression. "You do know that it's not necessary to marry to have a baby. The world is full of willing would-be fadirs."

"I see," Eiric said. "I'll take your word for it." An ocean of silence grew until he was all but drowning in it. He grasped for words, a shipwreck survivor clinging to debris in order to stay afloat. "When is your baby due?"

"I don't know for certain," Hilde said. "He may be a winter solstice baby, like Ivar."

Eiric was happy to change the subject. "Do you know where Rikhard is now?"

"I believe he might be in residence at his hall near here. I saw his banner flying when I passed by on my way back from town." She paused. "He knows you're here–in Muckleholm, at least. You made quite an impression in Langvik. People can't stop speculating about the giant warrior. It wasn't difficult to figure out who it was–even after ten years."

"And yet he hasn't come after me."

"He's waiting for you to come to him."

Eiric blew out a long breath. "I need to see Ivar. I have reason to believe he may be in danger. If I visit Rikhard's hall, what do you think my reception would be?"

"He wants you with him," Hilde said bluntly. "And I don't mean as a foot soldier in his army. You are the image of what he dreams of—Asgard aligning with kings and kingdoms as they did before Ragnarok. Magic under the control of the gods and their human allies. He's willing to forgive a lot in order to achieve that."

He might be more wary of aligning with Asgard if he knew what's coming, Eiric thought.

"Are you . . . close to the king?" Eiric said, knowing that he was dancing along the edge of danger. Subtlety had never been among his strengths.

"What do you mean?"

"You seem to know quite a lot about what the king is thinking, planning, and dreaming."

To Eiric's relief, Hilde seemed more amused than angry. "Rikhard is finding that a king has no peers to advise him—only rivals. Men confide in women because they don't see us as threats. Men often prefer talking to listening. You don't learn much that way."

Hilde looked over at the table where the fiskers were making her point by dominating the conversation with Hilde's dottirs. "Before long, this hall will be full of hungry men and women looking for the nattmal. What are your plans from here?"

"Would there be room for us to stay here tonight?" Eiric said, careful not to claim more than his due. "I'd be happy to pay for bed and board."

Hilde shook her head. "This hall is always full. But I have another place that might suit, that's warm and dry, at least. Tell your men—and women—to bring whatever gear they'll need."

Reluctantly, the fiskers parted ways with Hilde's dottirs, fetched their gear from the ship, and followed Eiric and Hilde across the home yard to the boathouse, Eiric's old sanctuary. Hilde chose one of the keys from the lot on her breast chain and unlocked the smaller side door.

Eiric half expected the boat shed to be filled with sleeping platforms and dining tables, too. But it looked to be unchanged from the day he'd sailed off with Liv and Asger Eldr, seeking the spinners' temple. Here was the empty spot where the karvi should be, this time of year. And, next to it, the dragon ship they'd sailed every summer of his childhood. How had it remained unspoiled for so long?

"My fadir knew how much this meant to you," Hilde said behind him. "We kept it safe for you and Ivar."

Oak planks stood in the far corner–planks Eiric had split from trees that grew at Sundgard. They must be thoroughly seasoned by now.

His tools still lay on the worktable, some rusting in the sea air, others wrapped in chamois to protect them. His adze, two awls, that draw knife that wouldn't keep an edge, a gouge. A pile of wood shavings still lay on the floor from a long-ago project.

Beside the tools, he found a carved wooden horse, nearly finished. It looked tiny between his hands. A little polishing, a bit of finish work, and it would be ready for–Ivar. He'd been making it for the new baby before his brodir was born, and never picked it up again after the series of catastrophes that had turned his life upside down.

"Styrman. Who built this?"

Levi's voice close at hand startled him. Eiric turned and found his crew gathered around the ship.

"My family," Eiric said. "My grandfadir, my fadir, my systir, and me."

"What's her name?"

"Sylvi."

"Have you sailed her?" Reyna's voice was muffled because she had slid under the ship to examine the keel.

"Every summer of my childhood," Eiric said, memory pounding him like a summer squall. "I haven't sailed her since my grandfadir died."

Levi ran his fingers over the lapstrake hull, layered as tightly as a pine cone at midsummer. "Is it possible that some of your forebears were fiskers?"

Eiric recognized it for the compliment it was. "Anything is possible," he said. "I would be honored to claim fisker blood."

While Eiric and his crew had been admiring each other and the ship, Hilde had laid the fire in the central hearth and lit it with a firesteel. It blazed up, sending shadows dancing across the walls.

"I've got work to do," she said. "I'll leave you to get settled. You'll find blankets and ticking in the chest against the wall. I know you're used to sleeping rough, but let me know if there's anything else you need. I'll have the girls bring more food when the nattmal is over. Do *not*, under any circumstances, invite them in." She ran her gaze over the lot of them to bind them, and then left through the side door.

That night, long after Eiric's crew had crossed into slumber, sleep eluded him. The boat shed had been a refuge for Eiric as long as he could remember. Days spent working alongside his fadir and grandfadir, learning how to build magic into ships. Looking on, while Leif and Bjorn met with their holumenn, or longship crews, taking their measure.

It was here, and everywhere, that Bjorn tried to instill in his grandson a respect for the old gods.

Later, this was the sanctuary, the threshold Sten did not dare cross.

It was here that Sylvi had told him that he had to leave the farm, that his stepfadir intended to kill him.

He was humbler now than he had been then.

As always, he petitioned the gods on Reginn's behalf. She'd taken a grave risk in setting him free, and remained in extraordinary danger.

Keep her safe. Bring her victory.

But what victory might look like, he couldn't have said.

36
FIRST BLOOD

THE SECOND HALF OF THE journey from New Jotunheim to Muckleholm should have been less stressful than the first. Once Reginn's legacy soldiers had realized that she couldn't escape from the ship and leave them behind, they kept a respectful distance. Reginn could now walk the length of the ship without being swarmed.

The ship's crew relaxed when it became clear that there was no magical boundary to navigate. Rumors spread that there had never been a wall, that it had been a ploy by the former council to discourage escape by sea.

The new understanding between Reginn and her army should have brought with it some peace of mind. But as they neared their destination, her misery grew.

What would she do with this army she'd raised? The queen expected Reginn to use it to help New Jotunheim conquer the Archipelago, slaughter everyone who carried the taint of Asgard, conscript the gifted, and enslave the population.

Then what? Would the new council turn into the old council, consolidating power and growing fat on the labors of others?

The weather worsened as Heidin's fleet escaped the influence of New Jotunheim. The winds blew harder and colder, whipping sleet that coated the rigging with ice. Each day, the passengers emerged from their beds with additional layers of clothing.

Throughout the journey, they had kept at least some of the other ships within sight–until they ran into a squall that was worse than all the others. When the weather cleared, they found themselves alone on the foam-speckled sea.

The fiskers seemed a little unsettled, but Rollo said that it was never easy to keep a fleet together in a storm, that they'd meet up again when they made landfall.

Reginn stood at the gunwale, staring out at the seething ocean, squinting against the wind as ice collected on her eyelashes.

Naima joined her there. "You were right," she said, shivering. "The weather here is terrible. I wish the keeper was still with us. We could use a weatherspinner right about now."

"It's not this bad all year," Reginn said, a little amazed to find herself defending her homeland. "There are some very fine days in summer. It's just that this is not the best time to start a war in the Archipelago. Especially with an army that's never seen winter. Before long the harbors will ice up, which means that we'll be trapped here until spring."

Heidin would know that, Reginn thought. Had she chosen this season in order to render Muckleholm's superiority at sea useless?

To prevent escape by those she meant to conquer?

To prevent her own army from fleeing?

Or was she just so intent on her goal that she didn't care?

"Tell me about the Archipelago," Naima said.

Reginn was at a loss. What should she say? Could she scuffle up some good memories to share?

Or should she tell the truth?

That's not fair, she thought. There are good people in Muckleholm. Granted, most of them are dead, but–

"Reginn?" Naima was frowning at her, head cocked. "If you'd rather not talk about it, I'm–"

"No, it's not that, I'm just trying to decide where to begin. Eimyrja is pretty much populated or under the plow, but there are parts of the Archipelago where almost nobody lives, because they're overrun by beasts and monsters. The only people who live there are outlaws, because they don't have a choice."

"What are outlaws?" Naima said.

Right. "Well, in the Archipelago, they don't have lockups or jail guards, or mind magic to reform wrongdoers. So when people break the law, there are basically two choices. The guilty can compensate the victim or the family if they agree on a price, or the offender can be outlawed or banished. That can amount to a death sentence, especially if the victim's family decides to deliver justice themselves. That's what happened to Halvorsen, until the local jarl stepped in and paid the fine."

It all seemed so long ago.

Naima pivoted to a more cheerful topic. "Is the food different than in Eimyrja?"

"It's similar," Reginn said, "though less variety. Because of the weather–and the soil–often there isn't enough food for everyone. Or maybe there is, but it doesn't get fairly distributed. The clothing is similar to what we wear in New Jotunheim–linen and wool, most made at home, with heavier layers this time of year."

"What about magic? Are there spinners here, too?"

"It's rare to find anyone admitting to it because they've been hunted and mistreated in the past. I think it's likely that there are more than we think."

There were signs that they would make landfall soon. Shorebirds soared overhead as *Naglfar* threaded its way through a group of small, seemingly uninhabited islands. This was new territory. Reginn had never had reason to go to the out islands–no alehouses there.

They slipped between two small islands and into another swarm of islands beyond.

Naima gripped Reginn's arm and pointed, back toward the islands they had just cleared. It took a moment for Reginn to register what she was seeing. A ship had emerged from the shadow of one of the islands and was plowing toward them, her sail bellied out with the northwest wind behind them.

She was coming on fast, and Reginn squinted to make out the mark on the ship's red banner.

The fossegrim. Jarl Rikhard's signia.

She looked for Svend. The tall guardsman was deep in conversation with Rollo at the tiller. He hadn't seen the ship.

"Svend!" Reginn shouted. "Enemy ship aft, closing fast."

It took Svend a moment to sort that out, but Rollo swung around, spotted the other ship, and began calling orders to his crew in a language Reginn didn't understand.

Happily, the crew did, and leaped to obey. Meanwhile Svend ordered his handful of soldiers to collect their weapons and stand ready. As Reginn worked her way aft, she was met by her commanders, Hrym, Ursinus, Dainn, and Asger, his sword sheathed in a baldric, the hilt visible over his shoulder.

"What are your orders, Lady?" Hrym said.

"Ah . . . stand by until I speak with the . . . other commanders. It may be that we can bluff our way out of this, but that won't work if we start rattling weapons."

Naima appeared beside her with her mail shirt and helmet. "Put this on, in case the bluff doesn't work."

"Nobody looks peaceable in a mail shirt," Reginn said.

"Put it on under your coat," Naima said. "Maybe it'll keep you warm."

But Reginn still refused. "We're not fighting," she said. "When we're fighting, I'll put it on."

When Reginn joined Svend and Rollo in the stern, Rollo glanced down at her, frowning, then turned back to Svend.

"They mean to pin us against the island yonder," Rollo said. "There's a strong incoming tide, plus the onshore wind. Whatever happens, we've got to stay out of that trap so we have room to maneuver."

Whatever happens, we've got to prevent them from coming close enough to see who's on board.

"What do you suggest?" Reginn said.

Again, that flicker of annoyance. "We'll have to come about and sail with the wind abeam and hope we can get around the tip of the island and into the passage before they catch up with us."

"Let's do it, then," Reginn said. "How can we help?"

"You can stay out of the way and keep quiet."

Svend stared at him, his expression shifting from astonishment to fury. "Do you know who you're talking to? I'd suggest you–"

"Svend," Reginn said. "Let's not distract the man. We'll discuss this later." Back straight, she walked forward and took a position midships where she could keep a close eye on events. Turning to her troops, she motioned for them to keep still and lay low.

Rollo called out orders, and his crew leaped to obey, turning the sail to meet the wind at an angle. The ship stalled a moment, then surged ahead, departing from its original course. A few more adjustments, and *Naglfar* was sailing nearly parallel to the shoreline. The turn had slowed them down, though, and by now the other ship was nearly on top of them.

Naglfar was bigger, and broader in beam, so it could carry more warriors, but that did them no good on the water unless it came down to hand-to-hand fighting. The jarl's ship was narrow as a blade–a true dragon ship–nimbler and easier to maneuver.

It came abreast of them, sailing a hundred yards to seaward. Within shouting distance.

An officer in a red storm coat shouted across the choppy waves. "Heave to, in the name of the king, and identify yourselves."

Instead, Rollo gestured to two of his crew and they took their places at the oars, sliding them through the ports and pulling hard. He sent a third sailor forward to Reginn.

"Styrman wants to know can any of your monsters handle an oar," the fisker said.

Reginn turned to her army. "Does anyone know how to row?"

A dozen stepped forward, a mixture of humans, elves, dwarves, and orcs. Silently, they took the empty places at the oars and joined in.

The ship leaped forward at such speed that Reginn nearly toppled over. Even Rollo staggered before he broadened his stance, looking over his shoulder at his new rowing crew.

They rounded the tip of the island, then turned east again, the sail filling. They seemed on course to outrun the warship.

A shout came from the lookout in the bow–first in the fisker language, and then in the common speech. "Broken water ahead! Hard to port."

The sail swung around, and Rollo laid on the styrboard, and the rowers back-paddled to slow the ship, but it was too late. Reginn felt a vibration under her feet and heard a grinding crunch as the ship finally came to a stop.

Water began boiling up from between two of the burden boards. Reginn picked up a pail and began bailing out water. Two of her soldiers saw what she was doing and followed suit, but it was a losing battle.

"See if this helps."

Reginn looked up from bailing to find Naima beside her with a length of oilcloth used as a tarp. She and Naima spread it across the hole, anchoring it on all sides. It didn't entirely prevent the water from coming in, but longships were leaky under the best of circumstances.

They appeared to have run aground on either a large reef or underwater outcropping, hitting with such force that the hull was damaged. When Reginn looked down through the clear water, the rocks appeared to be inches beneath the surface.

The whispers rose, all around her, causing the hairs to stand up on the back of her neck. The voices of all the seafarers lost on these rocks.

Raise us, Aldrnari. Lead us.

The fiskers were trying various tactics to free up their ship. They dropped the sail and had the rowers gently back-paddle, hoping that would be enough to back off the reef. When that didn't work, they used a spare spar to try to shove off.

Finally, most of the ship's crew jumped into the freezing water, reducing the weight, then stood on the reef, attempting to lift the ship free. Several times, a crew member nearly lost his footing, which would have meant being pounded to death on the rocks. Finally, they boosted themselves back onto the deck, shivering, their feet bleeding from being cut on the rocks.

"They don't give up, do they?" Naima murmured.

Reginn nodded. She was coming to admire their stubborn tenacity.

"Should I round up some dry clothes, or blankets or . . . something?"

"Please do," Reginn said. "I should have thought of that. See if you can find something to wrap their feet until they can be tended properly."

Meanwhile, the jarl's ship had caught up with them, though they kept a safe distance seaward. Reginn saw several crew members at the gunwales, watching their marooned ship with some amusement.

Eventually, the officer reappeared and shooed the others away from the rail. "Now that you are stationary," he said, "identify yourselves."

Svend looked to Reginn.

"We are fishers from an island far to the north," Reginn said. "We were blown off course in that squall yesterday."

"What island? Nordreyjar?"

"I don't know that name," Reginn said, afraid that the officer's question was some kind of trick. "Our island is so small, it has no name."

"That doesn't look like any fishing boat I've ever seen," the officer said.

"She's a beauty, isn't she?" Reginn said. "She sailed through that storm like she was built by Ivaldi's sons. Can you tell me where we are?"

"You are within the realm of King Rikhard of the Archipelago, first of his name."

"Rikhard? Isn't he down in Muckleholm?" Reginn said. "What are you doing way up . . . wherever we are?"

"It appears that you need to get out a little more often," the officer said. "Rikhard now rules the entire Archipelago. Including, I assume, your nameless island."

"We just want to get back to our families," Reginn said. "They're likely worried sick."

"Perhaps you could explain why you fled when we asked you to identify yourselves," the officer said.

"We've had problems with pirates in the past," Reginn said. "We did not recognize the emblem on your flag. That seemed to be the safest course." She gestured at the stranded ship. "I guess we were wrong."

"Now that you know who we are, I assume that you will have no objection to our boarding your ship and having a look around. Perhaps you can show us your catch."

"I wish we could," Reginn said. "But we had to dump our catch to avoid being swamped during the storm."

By now, Svend was staring at her in amazement as she came up with one story after another. She could tell, though, that the officer was becoming more and more annoyed, apparently unimpressed by her creativity.

"Nevertheless, we will board and search your vessel. We've been having a problem with smugglers in this area."

"If you board us, the additional weight might destabilize us and cause us to break apart," Reginn said. "We're hoping we can float off in the next high tide."

"My dear, the only way you're getting off that reef is if we take you aboard our ship. And bear in mind, there isn't room for all of you. It would be in your best interest to cooperate."

"Ahh–let me speak to my offi–mates," Reginn said. It wasn't easy to stay in the role of fisher.

Asger and the other commanders had ghosted up beside her.

"Let them come aboard," Asger said with a feral smile. "We can thin them out a little."

"And when they see what's happening, they'll hit us with everything they've got," Svend said. "Or sail away and bring back reinforcements. Either way, the barbarians will have a heads-up that they have something more than smugglers on their hands."

Naima appeared with Reginn's staff. She handed it off to Reginn and said, "Couldn't you–" She mimicked rolling the staff between her hands. "Couldn't you just . . . blow them up or something?"

"I was hoping that we could get through this without any bloodshed," Reginn said.

They all stared at her, as if each hoped that someone else would state the obvious.

Naturally, Asger broke the impasse. "It would be most unusual, Counselor, to have a war without bloodshed."

Who says I want a war? Reginn thought.

They were right, of course. Her squeamishness was putting their lives in danger. She planted the butt of the staff on the decking and sorted through the spellwork the founder had taught her.

Something was happening. Reginn heard shouted orders from the other ship, and warning cries from her own. She turned to look in time to see a volley of arrows like deadly birds arcing up, up, and then down toward the deck of the *Naglfar*.

It was too late. Apparently, the king's men had run out of patience.

Something pounded into her upper chest, just below the collarbone and above her left breast. She went down on her back in the water sloshing between the ribs. The salt water was shockingly cold, soaking into her storm coat and burning wherever the skin was broken. The clamor of battle rose all around her, roaring rage and cries of pain.

Whether she liked it or not, the war had begun, though it might be over for her.

37
LEGACY

EVERYONE HAD AN OPINION ABOUT how best to manage Eiric's meeting with the king.

Hilde discouraged any notion of dropping in on Rikhard unannounced. "Rikhard's hird is exceedingly loyal and tends to err on the side of shooting intruders and unexpected guests," she said.

The fiskers insisted that the only proper way to travel to the king's hall would be aboard the *Firebird*. It would be a poor show for a famous styrman and coaster to show up on horseback or, even worse, on foot.

"First impressions are important," Reyna said. "You've gone a-viking, and you need to look the part. You sail in to the king's landing bold as can be, and approach the king's hall with your own hird by your side."

"That being us," Levi added, in case it wasn't clear.

"Too bad we don't have matching coats," Nils said, straightening his hand-me-down.

The fiskers were fearless—Eiric had to give them that, though he suspected that part of it was a desire to show off their ship and get a look at a king and his hall.

"And if he slaughters all of you and takes your ship, would that suit you?" Eiric said. "If I go on my own, and the worst happens, you'll still be free to sail your ship wherever you please."

"Don't try to get out of coming back with us and helping us free our families," Nils said. "We're sticking with you until you keep your word."

"Is that so?" Eiric said. "What I'm trying to do is free my brodir, so how I do it is my decision."

That shut them up.

In the end, Hilde sent Frida to Rikhard's court to announce that Eiric Halvorsen requested an audience at the king's earliest convenience. That evening, she returned with a message.

"His Majesty King Rikhard requests the favor of your attendance on him tomorrow for the nattmal. Accommodations will be made for your personal guard and for our mutual friend, Hilde Stevenson."

Eiric had to assume that Frida had brought Rikhard up to date. That night, he sorted through the artifacts he had brought back from New Jotunheim. Nearly all of it, he'd collected in the tunnels that led from the founder's tomb to Ithavoll. A cloth bag filled with gold game pieces. Another filled with jewelry in gold and silver, set with precious gems. A pouch filled with gold and silver coins engraved with unfamiliar symbols.

They were all small items. Eiric's many near misses and narrow escapes in New Jotunheim had not allowed him to carry away anything big and showy. He had nothing that would adequately communicate the threat heading this way.

He would do his best to demonstrate that he'd completed the task Rikhard had handed him. And do whatever was necessary to free his brodir.

And then what? Would Reginn be with Liv's army? Would there be any way to redeem them both?

He'd also made a promise to the fiskers, and he meant to keep it, if he was still alive at the end of this.

The next morning dawned clear and very cold. Eiric woke early and raked the banked fire on the central hearth. Familiar from a thousand mornings of his childhood, he snatched up an axe by the door, went out to the woodpile, and began splitting logs. He wondered where they had come from, now that the old forest was gone.

It seemed so long ago, and yet it might have been yesterday. So familiar, and yet he noticed that the once-heavy axe was now light in his hands.

How would he do, in a rematch with Sten? The notion charmed him for a moment before he let it go.

It didn't matter anymore. His modir was dead, his systir no longer recognizable, his brodir a stranger, and Sundgard was no longer his.

Fueled by these many losses, he made short work of the cut timber, carried in an armload of firewood, and built up the fire. He was restoring the edge on the axe when the fiskers stirred and emerged, blinking, from their pallets. By the time they had visited the privy, Frida appeared with a bucket of porridge and apples from the fall harvest.

The apples were smaller than he remembered, but the flavor was the same–sweet and tart, exploding with juice. Sundgard apples had once been famous throughout the region.

After the dagmal, the crew put on their heavy barbarian coats and went down to the waterside to prepare the *Firebird* for showing off. Meanwhile, Eiric heated water in the iron cauldron Bjorn had used to steam-shape the wood for the ship's stem and stern.

"Bending and shaping wood is like raising children," his grandfadir had said. "Wood will bend without breaking if you take your time and treat it with respect, apply heat when needed, and show it where you want it to go."

When the water was hot enough, Eiric stripped and washed his hair and body with soap Hilde provided. It must have been made with hardwood ash and tallow, like the soap Sylvi made every summer–always outside, to disperse the fumes. But this was gentler, and had a pleasant fragrance to it.

Fortunately, he'd dried off and pulled his breeches back on when the door swung open and Hilde entered, carrying an armload of clothing.

She stopped just inside the door, looking him up and down. "By the goddess, Eiric, the only man I've ever seen who could rival you in looks was your fadir. Maybe my memory is fading, but you might be the handsomer of the two of you."

Eiric had nothing useful to say to that. He was nearly overcome by the desire to grab up his shirt and put it on, as if it were protective armor.

But Hilde wasn't finished. "Now, please tell me that you are *not* wearing dirty breeches to an audience with the king."

Eiric looked down at himself and realized that he'd been wearing the same trousers since Langvik–for good reason. They were the only ones he had. With his thumbnail, he scraped at a spot of mud. Or was it blood?

He glanced at his shirt, wadded up on the floor. He suspected that it wasn't much better. Probably worse.

"Here," Hilde said, spreading out her armload of clothing on a table. "I found these in a trunk in the summer barn. Based on the size, I believe they must have belonged to your fadir."

Eiric fingered the fabrics, some of it rich and finely made. "I'm surprised Liv or Sylvi never remade these for someone else in the family."

"Maybe she kept them for sentimental reasons," Hilde said. "My fadir always said Sylvi was crazy in love with Leif."

"Ulff told me that, too," Eiric said. A memory came back to him, from soon after Leif died. Sylvi wearing one of his fadir's shirts, all but lost in it, pressing the sleeve against her nose to breathe in his scent once more.

"Try these on and see if any of them suit you. But before then, sit and let me trim your hair and beard." She gestured toward one of the benches.

"Do you really think the king notices grooming?"

"You would be surprised at what the king notices–and remembers," Hilde said.

"Should I bat my eyes at him, too? Offer to clean his boots?"

"Sit, Halvorsen," Hilde said. "Your pride will be the end of you. I just want to hone some of your rough edges."

Eiric sat. I like my rough edges, he thought, but didn't say it aloud, knowing he would sound like a sulking child, with Hilde as the grown-up. She was only a few years older than him, but now it seemed like a chasm.

The real problem was that Eiric did not like to be in the position of petitioner. He'd made a promise, and despite all his efforts, he hadn't kept it.

If you fail to keep your word, at the end of a year I will seize Sundgard, sell your family into the slave markets, and hunt you down with every resource at my command.

The only family within reach was Eiric and Ivar. He might be required to pay the king's price, but would not accept the consequences for Ivar. His brodir had made no promises to the king.

Hilde combed the tangles from his hair, collected the top lock, and braided it close to his scalp, catching it in a thong at the back of his head. A memory intruded, of the night he'd met Reginn at an alehouse, and she'd cleaned him up and tended his wounds.

Hilde moved on to his beard. He didn't have a lot, yet, more of a reddish stubble. She eyed him critically, then reached for a small pot. "Close your eyes."

"What's that?" he said, though he already knew.

"War paint." Using her fingertips, she applied it all around his eyes.

Kohl. His fadir's warbands often applied it before they waded ashore. He would never forget the day Leif himself smeared the black around his eyes, signaling that Eiric was ready to join in with the others.

Hilde finally set her tools aside and stood, surveying his imperfections. "That's as much as I have time to do. Try these on, choose what you like best, and we can be on our way."

"Hilde," Eiric said as she turned away.

She turned back. "What is it?"

"Why do you care how this turns out?"

"I have children to look out for, a business to protect, and I care about all three of you–you and Ivar and the king. If what you say is true about the coming invasion, everything I care about will be at risk. In my opinion, you are most likely to survive if all three of you work together."

After Hilde had gone, Eiric tried on garments, one after another. Most fit passably well, though the linen tunics were a little tight over the shoulders and short in the sleeves, and some of the breeches were a bit short, but nothing leg wrapping couldn't address. He chose blue trousers–a color he'd rarely seen in clothing–a rust-red tunic of fine linen, and a richly embroidered wool cloak in the same rust red. He added two arm rings–one in gold and one in silver with carnelian set into it.

He owned one pair of boots, and those would have to do.

It was getting late, and Eiric heard raised voices outside. Sliding Gramr into its scabbard, he walked out into the cold, slanted light of afternoon.

The fiskers were standing in a rough semicircle on the beach where *Firebird* was drawn up on the sand. They faced off with three men, tall and broad-backed.

Stomach-turningly familiar.

Eiric knew who it was before Garth spoke.

"We want to know who you are and whose ship that is," his uncle said.

"We are guests here at Sundgard," Rorik replied. "Who are you?"

"We manage this property and so are responsible for ensuring the safety of everyone here." That was his stepgrandfadir, Gustav. "The inn doesn't accept outside guests."

"Perhaps you should speak to the innkeeper," Levi said, "so you don't make a fool of yourself."

By now, Eiric's entire crew was staring past the Knudsens at him, so he stepped around Sten's family to join them. "Good evening, Grandfadir, Uncles," he said. "This is my ship, and my crew. Is there a problem?"

The Knudsens were not nimble-witted at the best of times. Now, when they fished for words, none broke the surface. They just stared at him, mouths hanging open.

The past ten years had not been kind to them. Garth and Finni had grown thicker in the middle, and more repulsive, something that he would have guessed was impossible. Somewhere along the line, Finni had lost an eye.

Gustav was shrinking. Little remained of the muscle he'd earned in the tar pits.

"These are your *relatives*?" Nils blurted, obviously comparing them to Eiric in his finery and finding them wanting.

"Only by marriage," Eiric said, "and that connection was broken a while back."

"When *you* murdered Sten," Gustav said, being the first to recover.

Eiric sighed. "How many times do I have to tell you? That wasn't me, that was Liv."

Good news—she's coming back to finish the job.

Finni finally found his voice. "Nobody believes that story, Halvorsen. You were found guilty of our brodir's murder."

"And the murder of his own modir, don't forget that," Garth said. "And then he took the king's gold and sailed off, abandoning his brodir and breaking his promises to King Rikhard."

"You are mistaken, Uncle," Eiric said. "You were the ones who took the king's gold. As for Sylvi, you should look closer to home for the killer."

The fiskers were watching this exchange with mingled admiration and delight, Eiric's notoriety growing by the minute. They'd set sail with a styrman who'd turned out to be a murderous pirate with a sordid past.

It was happening again—a few minutes with Sten's family was like a serious case of the itches: seemingly endless. They were cheering each other on, like a pack of hunters confronting a bear, each trying to get somebody else to go in for the kill.

But something had changed—in him and in them. They kept sneaking looks at him as if making sure he didn't make a move, keeping a close watch on his hands.

That was when he realized—*they're afraid of me*. It was a revelation after years of abuse at Sten's hands.

He recalled what his modir had said when she begged him not to confront Sten.

"I'm big enough," Eiric had said. "I'll kill him."

"No," Sylvi had said. "Promise me that you will not try. That's what he wants. He is still stronger than you, and a more experienced fighter. He will find a way to kill you."

Things had changed. Well then. He stared down all three of them in turn. "If there's nothing else," he said, "we need to be on our way."

And then, very deliberately, he turned his back on the Knudsens and faced his crew. "Is everything loaded, then?"

"Aye, except for your seabag, Lord," Reyna said. "Shall I fetch it?"

When Eiric nodded, she sprinted toward the boathouse.

Lord?

"You'd better run hard, boy," Finni said. "When the king finds out you're here, he'll be up your ass in no time."

"Where'd you get this crew, anyway?" Garth joined in, gaining confidence. "Did you scrape them off the floor of a horhouse?"

Eiric looked for Nils. The fisker had been hungry for blood since Langvik. Now he was eyeing the brodirs, heavy-lidded as a lynx choosing its prey from a herd.

"Nils," Eiric said, startling the fisker. "Could you go up to the longhouse and see if Hilde is ready?"

Nils took one last hungry look at the Knudsens, then made for the longhouse.

"You're taking Hilde with you?" Gustav blurted.

Eiric shrugged. "She is always welcome aboard my ship," he said, intentionally vague. "She's an old friend."

Suddenly, the Knudsens had something else to worry about.

"No," Garth said. "Absolutely not. Hilde is–is under the protection of the king. When he finds out that you've carried her off, there will be hell to pay."

Looking over Garth's shoulder, Eiric saw Hilde, Nils, and Reyna emerge from the longhouse and stride toward them, Hilde wearing a storm coat and carrying a seabag. The Knudsens hadn't seen her yet.

"You're just like your fadir," Gustav said. "Leif could talk any woman into anything, whether good for her or not."

"Don't think that you can use Hilde as a bargaining chip to win a pardon from Rikhard," Finni said. "He won't play those games."

By now, Hilde and Nils had come close enough to overhear the conversation.

"What's going on?" Hilde said, reading the mood of the group.

The Knudsens, startled, turned to face her.

"This boy–Halvorsen–tells us you're sailing off with him," Garth said. "But we know you're smarter than that." No doubt Eiric's uncle believed that was a deft play–working a compliment into an insult.

Hilde frowned as if puzzled. "Whatever I mean to do, what business is it of yours?"

"We worry about you," Finni said. "You have those two dottirs to think of, and a–" His eyes strayed to Hilde's middle, and he clamped his mouth shut. Obviously this was not a topic that he had permission to talk about.

"Your fadir was a close friend of mine," Gustav said.

Hilde shrugged, as if to say, *Not that close.*

"I like to think that he would be glad if we took an interest in the welfare of his dottir. You work hard here, I know that. No doubt the idea of running off with a coaster seems tempting–"

Hilde's confusion cleared, crowded out by irritation. "You think that I am boarding Halvorsen's ship and going straight to his bed?"

"Well, ah, that *is* his reputation," Gustav said. "I mean, look at him, all tricked out in his fancy coat he probably stole, his hair done up like a hor's."

"You say that's *his* reputation," Hilde said. "What about mine? Do you think I need advice from you about coupling?" She pointed at his bachelor sons. "Maybe you should begin with *them.*"

The Knudsens deflated like a sail in the doldrums. They looked to be men who'd just realized they were knee-deep in skita and getting in deeper.

"People will talk," Gustav said, his quiver all but empty.

"No doubt," Hilde said. "Your lot are the worst gossips on Muckleholm."

"Halvorsen!" Finni said. "Don't you have anything to say?"

"I have nothing to add," Eiric said, holding the boat steady with one hand and giving Hilde an assist with the other.

Bjorn always said, *If your enemy is gutting himself, don't get in his way.*

Eiric took his usual seat by the styrboard, with Reyna as bow lookout. Rorik and Levi pushed them off the sand and leaped aboard themselves.

The water in the sound was already deep beneath their keel, and crystal clear, as cold as it could get before turning to ice. He looked back at Sundgard, as he had so many times before, wondering if he would ever make it back there.

Wondering if it mattered if he did.

"Hilde!" It was Gustav, making one last effort. "Use your head. Halvorsen's a wanted man, and he's just trying to get his farm back. When King Rikhard comes after him, it'll put you in danger."

"No worries!" Hilde called back. "We're dining with the king tonight. I'll give him your regards."

There's something about Sundgard, Eiric thought. It grows strong women.

38
KRAKEN

AND THEN NAIMA WAS THERE, lifting Reginn's head and shoulders out of the water, alternately swearing at her and shouting for help.

Who knew there were so many ways to say *stupid*?

Reginn reached up and found the shaft of the arrow protruding from her chest. She measured the length of it with her fingers, from the sticky mouth of the wound to the fletching.

"Naima."

"What is it? What do you need?"

"Go find cover or you're going to get shot."

"They're not shooting at us anymore," Naima said.

It was true. They were no longer taking fire from the other ship. Maybe the enemy commander was waiting for a flag of surrender before they pressed on. Arrows don't grow on trees, after all. Well, they sort of do. . . .

"Reginn!" Naima shouted, unnecessarily loud, as if Reginn might already be crossing the borderlands. "Don't you die on me."

"It's unlikely I am dying," Reginn said, always more comfortable in the role of healer than as a patient. "The arrow didn't go that deep."

"Let me get some help and we'll carry you into your tent, so–"

"I can't fight a war from inside my tent," Reginn said. *All right, fine–it's a war.* "Now, please, fetch my remedy bag."

"That's the first thing you've said that makes sense." Naima disappeared.

When Naima reappeared with the remedy bag, Reginn dug around to find the right runestone. When she found what she was looking for, she slid her hand under her tunic and tucked the stone into an inside pocket.

At once, the pain eased. She took another long breath, released it. It would do for now.

"Help me sit up so I can see what's going on. Drag over that sea chest, and I'll sit on that and lean on the gunwale."

"We've got to get that arrow out of you," Naima said stubbornly.

Reginn shook her head. "It's not bleeding now, but if we start fooling with it, it will. We need to wait until we have time to deal with it properly."

Naima glared at her, frustrated, but Reginn stood her ground. She knew it was likely she'd be dead or a captive before the day was out, so they might not have to deal with it at all.

It might be a very short war for *Naglfar* and her crew.

Grumbling, Naima helped Reginn sit up on the sea chest so that she was out of the water. Wet and shivering, but out of the water.

Propping herself against the gunwale, Reginn looked for her army midships. It wasn't there. She scanned the entire deck and saw only Svend's soldiers and some of the fisker crew.

Had they abandoned ship when they saw her go down?

"Where'd everybody go?" Reginn said. "The Risen, I mean. I told them to stay put."

Naima hesitated, then pointed at the enemy ship. "They're over there."

Reginn looked again and saw what she hadn't before. The other ship's deck was a battlefield, swarming with soldiers, most of them hers, though soldiers in red uniform tunics carpeted the deck. As she watched, one of the issvargr tore a man in half.

Which explained why they were no longer shooting.

"How did they get over there?" Reginn said.

"They swam, walked, flew," Naima said. "You remember how they–"

"Yes," Reginn said. "But I didn't order them to attack."

"When they saw you go down, they took matters into their own, uh, hands," Naima said.

"When the survivors tell Rikhard what happened, he'll–"

"Counselor," Naima said gently. "Based on what I'm seeing, there won't be any survivors."

Indeed, the fighting on the longship was diminishing as Reginn's dead brigade found fewer and fewer living soldiers. The sun was setting, turning the ocean between the two ships the color of blood.

At last, she saw no redcoats moving on the deck of the longship. But to her amazement, the ship rose a little in the water and began sliding toward them, as if it were moved by an invisible hand.

"What sorcery is this?" Svend muttered. He called orders to his remaining warriors, and they lined up, arrows nocked, along the rail.

As they got nearer, Reginn could see movement around the king's ship, some great shape underwater. Now and then a tentacle broke the surface, wet and covered with suckers. Familiar.

A kraken.

Her soldier. One of the creatures of the Elivagar that had followed along through the rift and out to sea.

All around her, soldiers were whispering whatever charms they knew, calling on dead gods, just in case any were listening. On Svend's signal, they raised their bows and took aim.

"No!" Reginn shouted. "Don't shoot! That's not the enemy," she added. "They're with us."

The archers looked back at her, and then to Svend, who raised his hand to signal *Hold.*

The ship came to a stop a short distance away. Now Reginn could make out her commanders standing on deck–Asger, Hrym, Ursinus, and Dainn.

"Help me up," Reginn said. Naima supported her as she rose to her feet.

"Aldrnari," Dainn said. "Shouldn't you be under the care of a healer?"

"Soon," Reginn said. "What's this?" She gestured at the longship.

"We brought you a new ship," Hrym said. "It will require some cleanup," he added apologetically.

"Thank you, Commander," Reginn said. "That's a fine gift. What shall we name her?"

"How about the *Kraken*?" Hrym said with a trace of a smile, the first Reginn had seen on the hard-bitten commander.

There wasn't enough room on the new ship to carry everyone who had sailed aboard the *Naglfar*, so the *Kraken* made several trips to ferry the crew and supplies from the stricken ship to the shore.

Over Naima's strenuous objections, Reginn insisted on staying on board until the last of the crew disembarked, though the ship was rapidly disintegrating around them.

Finally, Svend made his way midships to Reginn. "These last four are refusing to leave," he said, pointing.

It was Rollo and three other fiskers.

"Tell them it's an order," Reginn said.

"I already did," Svend said. "They insist on staying and attempting to salvage the *Naglfar*."

"Fine," Naima said. "Let them. Let's go ashore." She stood carefully and extended her hand.

"No," Reginn said. "Send Rollo to me." The throbbing wound in her shoulder was sucking all the patience out of her.

Rollo came and stood before her, stance broad, arms folded, the picture of resistance. Yet when he spoke, he said, "I hope that your wounds are not too painful, and wish you a quick recovery."

"Explain to me why you are refusing a direct order," Reginn said. "If you stay here, you'll die."

Rollo blinked, as if she'd slapped his well-wishes down. "If I die, it is my business, Counselor."

"When it leaves us down a styrman and three crew, it is our business, too," Reginn said.

"I built this ship," he said, spreading his hands to capture the wreckage all around them. "It is the finest ship I have ever built." His voice shook a little. "I had something to prove to the spinners, who have mistreated us.

"So, earlier today, when I saw the other ship, I was eager to demonstrate what we can do–to show off our seamanship and save the day. Instead, I made a childish mistake."

"You had no way of knowing about the rocks," Reginn said. "This coastline is new to all of us."

"That is my point. Only a fool would sail at top speed into unknown coastal waters. My pride and my anger turned me into a fool. For that, I apologize."

"Your apology is accepted, Styrman," Reginn said. "We all make mistakes. That is how we learn."

Rollo stared at her, his pale green eyes wide with surprise. He seemed unmoored by her forgiveness. He swallowed hard, then went on.

"Even so," he said, "I am submitting my resignation as styrman."

"So that you can do what?" Reginn said. "Die on this reef?"

"I plan to salvage *Naglfar.* Three of my crew have agreed to join me."

"If you are successful in salvaging it, do you intend to return it to New Jotunheim?"

"If we save our ship, we would have salvage rights," Rollo said through gritted teeth.

"So. You would salvage *my* ship with *my* crew, and then claim it yourself? That doesn't seem fair."

Rollo was beginning to look as if he wished that Rikhard's archer had taken better aim. "The ship does you no good, breaking apart on the rocks."

"Where you put it," Reginn said.

"Never mind," Rollo said, his sculpted features hardening. "I can tell that I am wasting my time."

"What I am saying is that we're all taking a big risk, and there's no reward in it for us. Whether you succeed or not, we lose our ship *and* four valuable crew members that we might need down the road. Not a good bargain."

Rollo didn't respond but stood, lips pressed together, staring at nothing, waiting for dismissal.

"Before I agree to any plan, let me see if I can make the salvage process safer and more likely to succeed. If I can, I will give you what you need to repair *Naglfar*. In return, you agree to sail for me for a year, or until the war is over. After that, win or lose, the ship is yours."

Rollo thought this over. "It'll have to be soon. If a squall comes in, it'll break up in no time."

"Is later today soon enough?" Reginn said. "I have an idea, but we all have to go ashore first. You have work to do, and I need to ask some help from one of our allies." When Rollo still looked doubtful, she said, "If it's a trick, you can swim back out here and dash your head against the rocks for all I care."

The first thing Naima did was pitch Reginn's tent and hustle her inside so that her shoulder could be tended. As Reginn had suspected, the arrow had passed nearly clean through her shoulder, the point cracking her shoulder blade. Reginn talked a reluctant Naima through the process of cutting away the fletching, freeing the point, and then drawing the shaft of the arrow all the way through.

The entire time, Naima kept muttering, "I'm not a healer, you know I'm not a healer, and if this goes wrong, I just want you to remember I . . ."

This went on until an impatient Reginn said, "Either bring in the real healer, or shut up and do what I say. You can blame me if it goes wrong."

Eventually, the wound was clean and bandaged, with runes painted around it to speed healing and ease the pain. After a meal and an hour's nap, Reginn roused herself from her bed to see how salvage preparations were going.

Rollo led them to the place he'd prepared for their shipyard. It was a few hundred yards into a small inlet, behind high dunes that hid it from view from the water.

They'd felled and split two large trees and created a track on which to roll a ship from the water's edge to the frame that would lift the ship off the sand so they could get at the keel.

Reginn was stunned. "How could you have done all this so quickly?"

"The sea waits for no one," Rollo said, looking pleased. "Everyone helped."

They boarded an oarboat and rowed out of the inlet, around the tip of the island to where they could see the wreck of their ship marooned atop the reef. It was high tide, but they could still see the waves breaking over the rocks near the surface, slamming into the sides of the ship, carrying bits of it away.

"Don't get too close," Reginn said. "If this works, it will be safer to watch from a distance." She nodded to Asger.

He rose up, looming taller and taller, reaching an impossible height without even rocking their small boat. The oarsmen huddled low while constantly rowing to keep the vessel from foundering on the rocks.

"Hafgufa," he called. "Sea Mist–the aldrnari would speak with you, to thank you for your service and to ask another favor."

The demon repeated the call twice before a disturbance on the surface of the water signaled a response. First, long, sinewy tentacles scribbled over the surface of the water, sending ripples in all directions. Finally, the kraken's head broke the surface. Its head was round, eyes set midway down beneath a high forehead. A voice, then, like spring water that flows from the deepest parts of the earth, so ancient that Reginn could taste it on the back of her tongue.

"Modir of sorrows, breaker of bonds, builder of bridges, Reginn of the Oak Grove, what would you have of me?"

"Old One, I would have my ship back," Reginn said.

"I gave you a ship," the kraken said.

"Aye," Reginn said, "and it's a fine ship. But the ship yonder was built with the blood and sweat and hearts of men who love the sea, who intended to sail it all over this world and into the next. It is not its time."

She couldn't claim that she would be fighting in a noble cause, because it wasn't true.

When she looked into the kraken's eyes, she could see that he already knew.

"Your ship is breaking in the space between land and sea," the kraken said. "It is not my doing, and not for me the undoing."

"Do you remember how you carried the enemy ship to us? If you and your brethren could lift *Naglfar* off the rocks and convey her to shore, we'll take it from there."

"It will take more than one of us," Hafgufa said. "If we are successful, may I ask a favor of you?"

Reginn couldn't fathom what she could offer. "What would you ask of me?"

"To be remembered, Aldrnari."

Reginn bit her lip. "I'm not sure I understand."

"Right now, we are forgotten casualties of a long-ago war, mere shades, violence enclosed in nightmare skins of your creation. Those who die in war live on as long as they are remembered, loved, mourned–as long as their true stories are told. To be remembered is to be immortal.

"I ask you to have the courage to recognize our kinship, to see me as a peer and not a monster. I want to be more than a cautionary tale. I want a place in the sagas in a different role."

Reginn looked into the kraken's eyes and found no subterfuge there, only keen intelligence and limitless sorrow.

"If you help us, I will remember you, and claim you, and honor you as you deserve," Reginn said. Bracing her hands on the gunwale, she leaned down and kissed him between the eyes.

Reginn heard a murmur of surprise and alarm from the shore.

And so the bargain was made.

Rollo and his crew took their places on the shore of the inlet, ready to play their part. The oarboat crew dropped anchor in the shallows a short distance from the reef, where they could watch the proceedings.

The tide was going out again, so time was limited. A dark shape circled the reef, visible just beneath the surface, sending water slopping over the rocks so that the ship shivered under the assault.

Then another took up its position on the other side.

A long tentacle slid over the rocks, questing until it encountered the keel of the ship. Carefully, it snaked around it as far as it could reach. The other kraken followed suit from the opposite side. They alternated, forming a web of fleshy arms encasing the ship from bow to stern, from keel to deck, like a cradle. By now, the krakens were halfway out of the water, sprawled across the reef so they nearly met in the middle, the outgoing tide boiling around them.

"They–they won't dry out, will they?" Reginn said, watching

anxiously. She scooped up one of the many bailing buckets. "If we could get closer, we could pour water over them."

"Please sit down, my lady, before you get us all killed," Asger said. "Let's assume that they know when they need to get back in the water."

Slowly, slowly, the foundered ship began to move, the stressed wood shrieking in protest as it slid across the reef, but held together by the krakens' arms, lifted a bit to reduce damage from the rocky underlayment. When Reginn looked back at Rollo and his crew waiting onshore, they flinched and shifted, as if they could feel every creak and crack in their own bones.

Their way was smoother once the ship slid from the reef and into the deeper water between the reef and the island. The water grew shallower again as they rounded the tip of the island and approached the inlet. The fiskers waded out to meet the ship, spreading a large, weighted rope web underneath, replacing the krakens' embrace as they withdrew. Once again, Reginn was grateful that *Naglfar,* even as big as she was, had a shallow draft.

Others from the crew of *Naglfar*–Svend's soldiers and the rest of the fiskers–everyone able-bodied enough to do so, joined the fiskers as they hauled their ship up the slope of the beach and onto the rollers they had prepared. As they labored on, Reginn and Asger brought the oarboat closer to shore.

The kraken resurfaced on the seaward side of their boat. "I hope that the ship of the dead can be made seaworthy again," he said.

"If it can be, it's thanks to you," Reginn said. "You may also have saved the lives of some of my crew who were determined to find a way to get it off the rocks at the risk of their own lives." She paused. "Is there another name we should honor?"

"Hafgufa suits us both," the kraken said, and disappeared into the deep.

* * *

As their boat crunched onto the sand, Reginn waded through the shallows, eager to see if their gambit had worked.

When she reached the newborn boatyard, *Naglfar* had already been lashed to a wooden framework, still held together by a net of thick ropes, and Rollo was calling out orders to his men to stabilize her.

When Rollo saw Reginn and Asger approaching, he dropped to one knee. "My lady," he said. "Once again, I find myself apologizing to you for my lack of faith. Generations will tell the story of how a tiny witch charmed a sea monster with a kiss."

That was *not* the story she wanted told.

"Thank you, Rollo, but all credit goes to Hafgufa and his brethren."

"Hafgufa? The sea monster?"

"Hafgufa is not a monster, but an ally and friend who has done us a great service. I hope you will remember him in that way." She paused. "It's still a good story, you know."

He laughed. "It is, and I'll never tire of telling it."

"We will leave here by the midday tomorrow and try to put some distance between us and where the king's ship went missing. You've only had a quick look, but do you have everything you need to put *Naglfar* in sailable condition?"

"We carry tools and extra masts with us, but most of the damage appears to be to her skin. If we don't need a lot of new timber, we might be able to put her into sailing condition quickly. I hope we don't need much timber, because this place has a lack of trees."

"I know," Reginn said. "Do the best you can, and when she's sailable, come find us. We are meeting the rest of the fleet on the near coast of Muckleholm near Vandrgardr to evaluate what we have and what we've lost."

When had it become her war?

"Of the six of your crew who are staying, who would you recommend as styrman in your place?"

Rollo thought for a moment. "I would choose Gyda. She is the best styrman after me, but her size makes her more useful as a styrman than in salvage."

"Good. Please send her to see me before we sail."

Rollo nodded. "We will come to you at Vandrgardr."

39
KINGSHAVN

THE CREW OF *FIREBIRD* REVIEWED and replayed the confrontation with the Knudsens as they had the "battle" in the market, reenacting the best bits.

Reyna, as Hilde, struck a pose. "You think that I am boarding Halvorsen's ship and going straight to his bed?" She glared around the deck, then shrugged. "Yes, it's true. I cannot resist a man with a *very big sword*." She froze, then stared at Hilde, wide-eyed, as if she'd only just remembered that the new mistress of Sundgard was on board. Eiric had seen enough fisker drama to know that it was part of the act.

Hilde just laughed. She'd been hosting foundrymen and ironworkers for years. That was no business for the faint of heart.

She had taken a seat on the sea chest just forward of Eiric at the styrboard. Now she leaned in and said, "I've never seen a crew like yours. Where are they from?"

"An island called Fiskeholm, near Eimyrja, where the spinners' temple is." Eiric had resolved to call their homeland by the name given it by those who knew it best. "They have been fishers and boatbuilders for generations."

When they reached the mouth of the sound, to Eiric's surprise, Hilde directed them to turn north instead of south.

"I thought Rikhard lived between Sundgard and Selvagr," Eiric said. "He was building a hall when–when I left."

"He outgrew that place in a hurry," Hilde said. "It wasn't defensible, either–just a shallow bay along a well-traveled shoreline. That became apparent when some of the other jarls built some ships and began fighting back. So he moved north, around the next headland, deep into Ulfness Fjord, where he could control traffic. You'll see."

It had been years since Eiric had reason to sail into Ulfness Fjord. Not that it would have mattered. Nothing was the same. Nothing would ever be the same.

Ulfness Fjord had long been regarded as a place of mystery and magic, with its steep, forested sides and water so deep, it was rumored to be bottomless. If there were sea monsters swimming around Muckleholm, this was the place.

The fjord was shallow at its mouth, but grew deeper until it met the twin rivers that flowed out of the mountains at its head. Eiric had heard that there was a decent pass through the mountains to the plains beyond. From there, it was several days' ride across the plains to Vandrgardr, if you evaded the beasts and outlaws that prowled there.

Eiric had never been through there. He'd never spent that much time inland.

The first thing he noticed were the watchtowers atop the headlands where the fjord met the open sea. They were fortified with stone and so high above the water that it would be difficult to target them from a ship in the strait.

Shooting down would be another matter. Any ship coming through there would be an easy target, although it might be possible to stay out of range by keeping to the center of the strait.

It had been years since Eiric sailed with his fadir, but he still saw the world through the eyes of a coaster.

As the *Firebird* passed between the towers, Eiric saw movement, the glitter of the dying sun on steel. They had been seen. Moments later, a bird winged its way from the watchtower, heading west. It wouldn't take long for coasters to learn to give Ulfness Fjord a wide berth.

Along the shore to either side, small farms and villages had sprouted on the flat ground between the fjord and the slope, where streams had deposited enough soil to plow, or graze sheep. All of them had boathouses or docks, since the residents would have to take the water roads wherever they went.

"This is all new," Eiric said, pointing to a snug longhouse with a kitchen garden, a boathouse, and a barn.

Hilde nodded. "In the past, these would have been vulnerable to hit-and-run raids, strung out as they are along the water's edge. Now the presence of the king discourages mischief and provides a market for the goods they produce."

Hilde made the Archipelago sound like a paradise under the rule of a wise and benevolent king. Eiric tried to match that with what he'd heard in Langvik.

"Are there people who don't approve of Rikhard as king?" Eiric said. "Who opposed him when he came to power, and still do?"

Hilde laughed. "I suppose I have painted a rather one-sided picture. Rikhard is not perfect–not by a long shot. He can be thin-skinned and vengeful–I think you know that already. He's proud and stubborn–a lot like you in that way. And yes, there are plenty of jarls who look at Rikhard and think, Why him? Why not me?"

"He sent me to find the spinners' temple," Eiric said. "How is he getting along with the gifted now?"

"He's still fixed on control of magic and its practitioners, from healers to augurers, to spinners of curses. He sees magic as a threat that he cannot counter. I've encouraged him to engage with them, to treat them with respect and win them over as allies. He's made some moves in that direction, but the gifted are harder and harder to find."

He's going to find a whole lot of them before long, Eiric thought. Or they're going to find him.

The fjord was growing narrower, the walls higher, so that it was already twilight here, with lights kindling on the shore. When Rikhard's longhouse came into view, lamps were burning on the docks and illuminating the path from the shore to the front door.

The longhouse was as large as any he'd seen, and finely built, though it looked small and rustic compared to some of the buildings he'd seen in New Jotunheim. It was surrounded by outbuildings, which provided a better sense of his wealth. Boathouses and stables and barns and barracks large enough to house hundreds of liegemen. Several longships were anchored in the surrounding waters, while others were moored to an elaborate dock.

"That's the king's house?" Levi said, looking a little disappointed. "I thought it would be a castle, built of stone. Or more of a palace."

"It has towers," Reyna pointed out, and it did, at either end. "It reminds me of the old temples."

"When did you ever see an old temple?" Rorik said. "They were destroyed long before you were born."

"Isn't the king afraid that someone will burn it down?" Nils said. "Being made of wood and all?"

"Your house was made of wood," Levi said.

"And it got burned down," Nils said, winning the tournament of words.

"Everything in Muckleholm is made of wood," Eiric said. "The trick is to make sure your enemy never gets close enough to burn it. And to let everybody know they'll pay a blood price if they do."

Eiric had already decided to tie up at the royal docks rather than drop anchor in the fjord and take an oarboat to shore. It was just the tiniest claim of privilege.

It also made it less likely he'd have to wade to shore in his fancy clothes, which were already becoming a burden.

A hundred yards out, he gave orders to drop and secure the sail, maintaining position with the oars.

"All of you, I want you to stay close to the ship. Make sure nobody gets near it. I don't want any surprises later tonight."

"You're going in there alone?" Nils said. "Wouldn't it be better to bring us in with you? Some of us, at least?"

Eiric shook his head. "His guard won't let you bring your weapons in. Besides, if our meeting goes wrong, your presence won't help me, and you'll just end up dead."

Now they were all scowling.

"If things go obviously wrong, then cast off and save the ship and yourselves."

He didn't mention the fact that it would be difficult to get out of the fjord if the king moved to prevent it.

"That's not what a hird does," Rorik said. "We don't leave our styrman in the lurch."

"Someone needs to go back and free your families," Eiric said. "Now might be a good time, since the spinner army is sailing this way." He paused. "And no, Levi, this is not just a trick to get out of my promise."

When they came alongside the dock, Eiric himself vaulted onto the pier and secured the mooring lines, then gave Hilde a hand up and hefted the sack of spoils from New Jotunheim. They left the unhappy crew on the pier and walked together toward shore.

"You really don't trust him, do you?" Hilde said, glancing over her shoulder at the fiskers. "Even though I told you—he wants you as an ally, not an enemy."

"I don't have any reason to trust him," Eiric said. "I tried to leave my hird at Sundgard for that reason. We'll see what happens."

By the time they'd reached the shore, a welcoming party of servants and soldiers had assembled in the courtyard.

Rikhard cut through the crowd like a dragon ship through a fleet of oarboats at anchor.

The former jarl was little changed from ten years ago. Still stiletto-thin, though, if Eiric was any judge, he'd put on muscle in the last ten years. The breeze off the fjord ruffled his rough-cut blond hair, and his sun-bronzed skin set off his intense blue eyes.

Rikhard's clothes were even finer than Eiric remembered, and he wore a fortune in gold. The difference was that now, apparently, the finery was earned.

"Hilde," Rikhard said, taking her hands and kissing her on the cheek. "It is always a pleasure to see you."

He turned to Eiric, scowling. "Halvorsen," he said. "You're late." He stopped short, took a second look, then laughed and said, "Gods, look at you! I always heard that the gods left their chance-children at Sundgard for raising, and now I believe that it's true." He paused, growing serious. "It's good to see you, Halvorsen. I'm glad you came."

All in all, Eiric was glad that he had changed his breeches.

"I understand that congratulations are in order, Your Majesty," Eiric said.

"Ah, yes, I suppose," Rikhard said. "Be careful what you wish for, Halvorsen. Some days it seems that a kingdom is more trouble than it's worth."

Good news! Eiric thought. Someone is coming who wants to take it off your hands.

"Let's have a look at your ship," Rikhard said, striding toward the dock, motioning for his hird to remain behind.

"I'll be inside," Hilde said, begging off a return to the pier.

When the fiskers saw the king coming toward them, with Eiric right behind, they all but stood at attention.

"This is not the ship you sailed away on," the king said, "unless the witches have learned to grow ships as well as men."

"*Firebird* is a new ship," Eiric said. "This is her first sailing."

"She's a beauty," Rikhard said, squatting to take a closer look. "Is this what you've been doing for ten years–building boats?"

"All credit for the building goes to her crew," Eiric said. "She was already perfect the day I first set foot on deck."

Rikhard stood, shifting his attention to the fiskers. "Well done," he said. "Where did you learn to do such fine work?"

"From my fadir," Rorik said. "And he learned from his fadir. When you make your living at sea, the quality of your ship can be the difference between life and death."

"I agree," Rikhard said. "Where are you from?"

"We are from Fiskeholm, in New Jotunheim, across the blue water sea," Nils said.

Rikhard's eyes narrowed, as if he was startled, but he recovered quickly. "We can always use skilled shipbuilders here," Rikhard said. "You would never lack for work in the Archipelago."

"No, thank you," Reyna said, pulling her hat down over her ears. "It's too cold here."

Rikhard laughed. "Come back in the spring, when it's warmer. Are you staying with your ship?"

Reyna nodded, sliding a resentful look at Eiric.

"Then I'll have some food and drink brought down here to you," Rikhard said.

The fiskers shrugged and mumbled, but Eiric could tell the king had charmed them just the same.

"Now, let's go back, and see how the nattmal is coming along," Rikhard said, leading the way back to the house. His hird followed them inside, but nobody demanded that Eiric give up his weapons.

The longhouse was much larger and more elaborate than Rikhard's guesthouse near Selvagr. Eiric guessed that three hundred people could gather in the hall without crowding. Nothing barnlike here–the support posts were carved with ornate designs, and ladders led up to loft space above.

As in the guesthouse, Rikhard had built a private chamber at one end of the longhouse, where a winter barn might be in a lesser dwelling.

In most longhouses in the Archipelago, especially in winter, the smoke from the central hearth never quite found the smoke hole. As a result, everything was covered in a thin layer of soot, and the hall smelled of woodsmoke, even in midsummer.

Here, instead of a central hearth with a smoke hole, there were hearths at either end, with stone chimneys to collect the smoke.

He's seen that somewhere else, Eiric thought, and copied it.

The hearth at the far end served as the mealfire, with several servants clustered around it. This hall was permeated with the delicious smell of roasting pork.

Rikhard breathed it in with deep appreciation. "It seems that Faregildis is making good progress on dinner. Do you remember Faregildis?"

Eiric nodded. "Thrall from Frankia. You were hoping to make wine."

"That's right," Rikhard said, obviously surprised that Eiric had remembered.

"Alas, the wine-making has had to be deferred, but I still have hopes. In the meantime, there are great wines in the market. Speaking of–come with me to my solar. Ivar will meet us there shortly. Hilde and Faregildis are allowing us some time to talk before dinner."

40

TRUTH-TELLING

EIRIC FOLLOWED THE KING TOWARD his private quarters at the rear of the hall, head spinning, unaccountably nervous.

Ivar will meet us there.

To Eiric, it seemed that this meeting was barreling toward him like a runaway cart. Ivar had been an infant when he and Liv left for the temple. What would Hilde have told him about his brodir and systir? And Rikhard—he'd spent much more time with Ivar than his blood family ever had.

As a child, Eiric had been left behind while his fadir and grandfadir went coasting for months at a time. He'd felt left out, but he knew they would be back for the harvest. Besides, Sylvi was always there, keeping him busy with chores, and he always knew his turn would come.

He had no doubt that while Ivar had been at Sundgard with Hilde, he had felt loved, and secure. But how would he have been treated by a king who might believe he'd been played by Ivar's siblings?

Eiric had brought the carved horse along as a peace offering—and now he felt foolish. *Here's a toy. How has your life been?*

The king's quarters were sumptuously appointed, a definite step up from the guesthouse Eiric had visited before. Several adjoining rooms surrounded a central courtyard with a few winter-sered plants and a fountain that had been drained for the winter.

"This is much prettier in the summer, when I'm not around," Rikhard said with a laugh. "With winter coming on, the fire is more appealing."

A small table with three chairs was set up next to the hearth. On a sideboard, there were two carafes of wine–one a lush red, the other honey-gold–and what looked to be Frankian crystal glasses.

There were also little plates, and bowls of hazelnuts and fruits, so a person wouldn't starve while visiting the king.

"You are fond of wine, as I recall," Rikhard said, no doubt referring to their one previous meeting during which they had nearly come to blows. "What's your pleasure?"

Eiric chose the red, and the king poured for both of them.

"You see?" Rikhard said. "I no longer require my liegemen to pour my wine. They have more important things to do." He paused. "When you have power, you don't have to constantly prove it."

It was Eiric's turn to be surprised. The king obviously remembered Eiric's reaction to that practice at the guesthouse. Ten years ago.

Which brought to mind what Hilde had said.

You would be surprised at what the king notices–and remembers.

They sat down at the table. Eiric was tempted by the wine, but wanted to remain clearheaded.

Remember who controls the game board, he thought. Remember what's at stake.

So he helped himself to hazelnuts.

"So," Rikhard said, "since your crew and your ship came from across the ocean, I'm assuming that you found the spinners' temple."

"I did," Eiric said.

"And you found a reservoir of magic there?"

"I did," Eiric said.

Rikhard waited, obviously expecting Eiric to elaborate. "So–were the streets paved with gold?"

Eiric shook his head. "No, but the weather is pleasant year-round, the harbors never freeze up, and crops of all kinds thrive there. Nobody goes hungry."

Rikhard leaned forward, his face alight with interest. "Even the poor?"

"I didn't actually see any poor people," Eiric said.

Everyone has a role to play in New Jotunheim. It's just that you don't get to choose how to serve.

Eiric wasn't trying to be clever or evasive, but this story was like a bomb that, once detonated, would obliterate everything around it.

Rikhard gestured toward Eiric's carry bag. "Did you bring back artifacts as I requested?"

"Your Majesty, this is just a sampling of what I found." Untying the neck, he dumped the contents out on the table: jewelry in gold and silver, inset with precious stones, gold arm rings so heavy they might weigh a man down. There were small carvings in stone, castings in precious metals, swatches of elaborate fabrics, gold tablets inscribed with runes.

The king sorted through them, murmuring in amazement. "These are—I've never seen anything like this."

Eiric held out one of the heavy gold arm rings to Rikhard. "This alone should be worth enough to reimburse you for your payment to my stepfadir's family."

The king took it, admired it, and slipped it onto his arm. "A fine gift," Rikhard said. "What did you find out about the spinners' temple?"

Eiric knew the king would not allow him to get off so easily.

"You asked me to investigate what the spinners wanted with the children of the Archipelago. They do not choose at random. They choose children who carry a spark of magic. Children they suspect of having descended from the gods."

Rikhard slapped the table with both hands, nearly spilling the wine. "I knew it! Our heritage is being stolen from us. No wonder the weather worsens all the time, crops are failing, and prosperity slips through our fingers. No wonder magic is disappearing, and the gods are nowhere to be found in the Archipelago."

"If I may speak frankly, Your Majesty, practitioners of magic have been poorly treated here. Why wouldn't they leave, given the chance?"

"You know very well that is something I am trying to change," Rikhard said, scowling. "I've been trying to recruit the wyrdspinners into my service."

"And if they choose not to serve?" Eiric said. Then quickly changed tacks. "How is that going?"

Rikhard leaned back, resting the heels of his hands on the table. "Not well," he admitted. "I have an agent in Langvik, a spinner, but–" His voice trailed away. "She's worked for me for years, but she hasn't been that successful in finding any. In fact, she was the one who gave me the idea to try to find the Grove."

Interesting. "How does your agent identify the gifted?"

"She uses magic," Rikhard said. "She has some kind of a pendant that tells her."

"Like this?" Eiric pulled the chain with the kynstone out of his shirt. It glowed red against his hand.

"Yes," the king said. "Just like that. And the red means–"

"It means that I have an Asgardian bloodline."

"I didn't know it could be used to identify the gods. I thought it was just–witches." Rikhard eyed the kynstone jealously.

"Would you like to try?" Eiric handed the kynstone to Rikhard. The red drained away, leaving a clear, cold light.

"Well," Rikhard said with a sigh. "I suppose I will have to be satisfied with being a king among men." He handed the kynstone back. "So the spinners take our children with the spark of divinity and train them up in magic–"

"Not all of them," Eiric said. "All the children they take descend from the gods, but when they are young, they can't sort out which are Asgardian and which ones descend from the Jotun."

"The Jotun? You mean, beasts and monsters? Demons?"

"The Jotun were gods, just like the Aesir and Vanir gods of Asgard. Well, not 'just like.' The Asgardians were warriors. The Jotun were masters of magic and defenders of the natural world, some in the form of creatures that we consider monsters, like the issvargr, kraken, trolls, and demons. Others, like the dwarves and elves, we feel more kinship with. The wyrdspinners come from Jotun bloodlines."

Rikhard stared at Eiric as if baffled that his Asgardian warrior had turned scholar and defender of monsters. "You're saying the spinners are monsters?"

"Not at all. I'm saying that the spinners descend from a rival pantheon of gods. Ragnarok was a battle between the gods of Asgard and the rival Jotun. Asgard had been attacking Jotunheim for centuries—stealing everything they could lay their hands on."

"Your ancestors."

Eiric selected an especially fine arm ring and slid it onto his arm. "Still stealing."

The king laughed, shaking his head and blotting tears from his eyes. He had a good laugh. "Fair enough. That's how you become king—stealing. So why do people worship the Asgardian gods, but the Jotun are despised?"

"I suppose you could say that, when it comes to the sagas, at least, the Asgardians and their supporters wrote the histories."

"And the Jotun still hold a grudge."

"They have reason to."

Eiric himself was surprised so much knowledge and conviction had seeped into him during his time in New Jotunheim. Had Tyra put it there? Could he trust it?

But the conversation was getting off course with this complicated discussion of gods and monsters. Even though it was key to the threat that faced the Archipelago.

"Your Majesty, you are in more danger than you realize," Eiric said. "There is something you should know about your agent in Langvik, and what happens to the children from the Archipelago."

Rikhard raised his hand. "Wait," he said. "I believe Ivar has arrived."

Eiric heard footsteps, a murmured conversation with the guards outside.

"Ivar!" Rikhard called. "Come in and meet your brodir."

Eiric stood, palms sweating, as his brodir walked in.

Hilde had said that Ivar was tall, and he was, and slender, though that might change when he'd gotten his growth. His flaming hair might have come from Sten, but the rest was all Sylvi–her gray eyes and fine features.

Ivar was well dressed, everything made to measure. When Eiric was that age, he was lucky to have more than one shirt at a time, because he grew faster than Sylvi and Liv could spin, weave, and sew a replacement.

Ivar inclined his head to the king. "Lord," he said. He turned to Eiric. "And you must be Eiric Halvorsen. I trust you had a safe and pleasant journey back to the Archipelago?" His expression was neutral, unreadable, careful, wary. The very last words a person would assign to Eiric.

Eiric embraced his brodir and said, "Heil, Ivar. It does me good to see you."

Ivar stiffened a bit at the uninvited contact, and Eiric quickly released him.

It's no wonder he's careful, Eiric thought. He's been a guest all his life, always dependent on the favor of others for everything that comes to him. Hilde had said that Ivar had estates somewhere, but for that he was probably beholden to the king.

Life in the Archipelago had always been family- and clan-oriented. Betrothals were contracts between families. Your family had your back, upheld your honor, and provided sanctuary when you needed it.

He'd failed his brodir on that account.

"I brought you this," Eiric said, holding out the horse carving. "I made it for you before you were born, but I never had a chance to give it to you." He paused. "It's late, I'm afraid."

Ivar took it and examined it from all sides, running his long fingers over the gouged wood. "Thank you for thinking of me, brodir," he said. "This is fine work."

"Ivar, please help yourself to a drink and sit down," Rikhard said. "Eiric has been telling me about his adventures at the witches' grove. And look what he's brought back to us."

While you were being shunted from household to household, Eiric was out adventuring.

Setting the horse on the table, Ivar moved to the sideboard, poured himself some wine, filled a plate, and occupied the empty chair. Then immediately set to examining Eiric's golden hoard.

Ivar was as enthralled as Rikhard had been. He picked up one, and then another, tracing the engravings with his fingertips, exclaiming over a particularly fine piece, pointing out its virtues to the king.

Eiric had the sense that Ivar looked beyond each piece's weight in gold and silver to its meaning, its place in history.

"Ivar is something of a scholar," Rikhard said. "His tutors have nothing but good things to say about him, and I myself have learned a lot from him."

"Is that so, Ivar?" Eiric said, feeling like an unwashed ruffian next to his brodir. "What are you studying?"

"History," Ivar said. "Science and mathematics. Poetry."

Eiric had never thought to be outshone by his little brodir. *Look, Ivar! Look at my shiny loot! Look at this little horse!*

Children grew up quickly in the Midlands, but still–Ivar seemed decades older than his years.

"Halvorsen, show Ivar the kynstone," Rikhard said. "Let him try it." As if it were a trick he'd seen in a traveling show.

Reluctantly, Eiric passed it over. It glowed in Ivar's hands, a deep purple light, like a bruise. A kynstone color he'd never seen before.

"What does that mean?" Ivar said, passing the pendant back to Eiric.

A good question. Eiric thought fast.

"It means that you carry the spark of the divine," he said. "But we won't know whether it's Asgardian or Jotun until you are older. Likely Asgard, through our modir, but it's possible your fadir had–ah–hidden gifts."

That was as diplomatic as Eiric could make it.

"Tell me–where did you find these items?" Rikhard said. "Were they in the temple, or–?"

"Many of these came from Vigrid–the battlefield on Ithavoll," Eiric said. "Some from the tunnels the survivors used to escape."

Now both Ivar and Rikhard sat forward.

"You saw the site of the Last Battle?" Ivar said. "What was it like?" He took another look at the contents of the carry bag, as if he might have overlooked Thor's hammer, Mjolnir, amid the artifacts. He came up with a runestone and weighed it in his palm.

"It's been centuries since the battle," Eiric said. "The forces of weather and time have swallowed the bones of the dead and healed the scars of war."

"The volur–do they recognize the battlefield for what it is?" Rikhard said.

"Yes," Eiric said. "That's why they are there. They've read the same texts as you. When the gods gather at Ithavoll, they mean to make sure they are Jotun gods."

"Jotun gods," Rikhard said, glancing at Ivar. "I'm still grappling with that idea. Eiric was just telling me that the Jotun were rivals to Asgard–that they were gods themselves."

"Really?" Ivar said. "I haven't seen that in any of the old texts." He paused. "Could we go there–to the Grove? To Vigrid? I would love to walk that battlefield, read the texts, perhaps meet with their scholars–"

"Perhaps we can," Rikhard said, "with Eiric's help."

Eiric had the feeling that he was at the center of a tightening web. He just wasn't sure who the spider was.

"That knowledge might be the beating heart our kingdom needs," Ivar said. "The common history and sense of purpose you speak of."

It sounded like they were planning to make a pilgrimage to a shrine.

"Yes, Ivar, you may be right," Rikhard said, smiling. "Let's drink to that." He stood, and raised his glass. Ivar followed suit, and Eiric, reluctantly, joined in. Making a point in Rikhard's company was like sailing against the wind.

As soon as Eiric raised his glass, the scent filled his nose. Cherries.

He recalled something the keeper had said, the night she died.

Considering the enemies you have already made, I recommend that you avoid drinking anything that smells like cherries.

"Don't drink that!"

Eiric lunged across the table and knocked the glass from Ivar's hand. It smashed on the floor, splashing wine on his brodir's fine trousers, sending shards of glass flying and rivulets of red trickling between the stones.

Rikhard, who had frozen, his glass halfway to his mouth, set it down with a clunk. "It's really very good wine," he said. "But would you prefer the white?"

"It's poisoned," Eiric said. "The poison is called mourner's tears."

"What makes you think so?"

"It smells of cherries."

Rikhard took a cautious sniff. "It does," he said. "Could it be from the fruit used to make the wine?"

By now, the whole room smelled of cherries.

"The scent does seem awfully strong," Ivar said. He crossed to the sidebar, unstoppered the honey wine, took a sniff, and wrinkled his nose. "This smells the same," he said, frowning. "And it shouldn't. There are no cherries in it."

"I've never heard of mourner's tears," Rikhard said.

"It's favored by assassins in New Jotunheim," Eiric said.

"I cannot believe that anyone here would have tampered with the wine," Rikhard said. "My hird has been with me for years."

"Your Majesty, may I speak frankly?" Eiric said.

"Of course," Rikhard said.

"You are sailing straight into disaster and you can't see it. The spinners are not naive villagers or hedge witches. They are powerful, smart, and ruthless, and they have a major grudge against the Archipelago.

"Before I left New Jotunheim, I saw the Jotun fleet preparing to sail for the Archipelago. No doubt they are on their way by now, if they are not here already. They already have a queen, and I don't imagine they'll have much use for a king. They are coming here in force, and they're coming to conquer, not to serve."

"They told you this?" Rikhard said. "Weren't they worried that you would give the game away?"

"As far as they know, I'm dead. I was executed for the crime of killing their elder council–and for being a son of Asgard."

"But you escaped?" Ivar said.

"I had help," Eiric said. He paused. "Have you heard from your agent in Langvik?"

"Not–not lately," Rikhard said, looking puzzled at the change in subject. "I usually only see her when I visit my hall in town."

"I met her in Langvik–Agata, right? Her real name is Grima. She is an assassin and spy for New Jotunheim. When you refer suspected spinners to her, she tests them. If they descend from Asgard, she kills them. If they are Jotun, she smuggles them out of the Archipelago. It's no wonder your recruitment program is a failure."

Eiric's words must have carried the conviction of truth, because Rikhard didn't argue.

"How–how did you find this out so quickly?"

"I walked into her shop, hoping to find some cold-weather clothes for my crew. She recognized me from Eimyrja."

"You didn't recognize her?"

Eiric shook his head. "She has the gift of magical disguise. What tipped me off was the fact that, as soon as I walked in the door, she tried to kill me. But that drew the attention of your guardsmen, who decided that I was a good fit for your army."

Rikhard smiled faintly. "I'm not surprised."

"My crew came looking for me then." Eiric paused, not eager to get into specifics. "It ended with five guardsmen dead. Have you had any reports of dead soldiers in Langvik?"

Rikhard shook his head. "That doesn't mean it didn't happen. I wouldn't necessarily hear about it right away."

"Grima warned me not to tell you what I know. She told me to come collect my brodir and sail away and not look back. Otherwise, we would all end up dead." Eiric paused. "She mentioned Ivar in particular."

Rikhard glanced at Ivar, who stood, serious as death, taking it all in. Then looked back at Eiric, a muscle working in his jaw. "You let her go?"

"Not exactly. Between *your* agent and *your* soldiers, we were lucky to get out of town alive."

The king scowled, feeling the hit. "I will send a bird to Langvik immediately and have Agata taken into custody for questioning."

"Tell them to be careful–she's more dangerous than she appears–but I don't think they'll find her. She complained that I had ruined a perfect setup, so I had the feeling that she wasn't planning to stick around–in that role, anyway. She can change her appearance completely, so she is all but impossible to defend against. I suspect she found out I was coming here, and thought to do for three at once."

"You think she poisoned the wine."

"It's a Jotun poison. If she did it, she might still be here. If she is, she won't look anything like the Agata you know."

Reflexively, Rikhard looked around. All at once, sitting down to dinner seemed less appealing. "It seems that I have need of a taster," he said with a wry smile.

"Your Majesty."

A red-jacketed guard had appeared in the doorway to the solar.

"Yes, what is it?" Rikhard snapped.

"You said you were not to be interrupted, but I thought you should know this. Trygve is dead. We found him in the horse barn. One of the horses is missing, too."

Rikhard shot a look at Eiric. "Trygve is dead? How?"

The guard shrugged. "No obvious wound that would kill a man. Only this was stuck in the back of his neck." He unfolded a square of leather. On it was a tiny, feathered dart. Eiric recognized it from the night he killed the council in the Lundhof. A hooded figure with a blowgun had been waiting for him when he returned to his rooms.

Grima.

Rikhard looked to Eiric. "Well?"

"The blowgun is one of Grima's weapons of choice," Eiric said. "That doesn't mean it was her, but–"

"If she's a witch, why wouldn't she just use magic?"

Eiric shrugged. "I've only ever seen her use magic to shapeshift and disguise herself. Maybe that's her gift. Or maybe she believes that the use of magic in other ways would draw suspicion."

Rikhard sighed and ran a hand over his face as if suddenly tired. "See to the body, Captain. Have the healers examine the dart and report any findings to you. See if anyone else is missing. Double the watch tonight."

"Yes, my lord," the captain said, and backed from the room.

41

VANDRGARDR

REGINN HAD BEEN TO THE town of Vandrgardr several times before, with Asger, but had seen little beyond the insides of alehouses near the docks. In most harbor towns, it wasn't safe to go exploring without an escort. Or so Asger said.

They gave the town a wide berth, not wanting to give away their presence. Their target was an inlet just south of town, surrounded by a vast marshland infested by venomous snakes, trolls, and wolves that should discourage casual traffic. As they entered the inlet, large birds rose from the bluffs on either side and set off small flares to signal their arrival.

Not birds. Dragons.

That's when it occurred to Reginn that they were sailing a barbarian ship into the face of the queen's fleet. "Run the firebird banner up the mast," she called.

Three ships had arrived ahead of them. Two were drawn up on the shore, while the third remained at anchor–Heidin's flagship. The crew of the *Kraken* hurriedly dropped the sail and anchored in the shallows, her prow resting on the sandy muck. The Risen remained on board, while Reginn, Naima, Asger, Svend, and their soldiers and crew disembarked.

Vegetation had been cleared back from the shoreline to provide room to erect tents and picket horses. Despite the cold, no fires had been laid.

By the time Reginn and the others set foot onshore, a small crowd had gathered. Among the others, she saw Durinn, Tyra, and Heidin.

Plus Katia, Eira, and Bryn.

Reginn was glad to see those last three. They weren't exactly confidantes, but, aside from Naima, they were among the few people in New Jotunheim that didn't make her feel besieged.

"Counselor," Durinn said, raising an eyebrow, "you left New Jotunheim in the largest ship in the fleet and arrived in a karvi. Whoever made that trade got the best of you."

"Maybe not," Svend said. "They are all dead, and we're still alive."

The commander's smile faded. "What happened?"

"We encountered an enemy ship as we entered the Archipelago," Reginn said. "When we wouldn't allow them to board us, they attacked."

"The counselor took an arrow in the shoulder," Naima said, in her new role as Reginn's court skald, "and yet she fought on until the last of the enemy fell."

On cue, Svend's soldiers shouted, "All hail, Reginn of the Oak Grove!"

Also Naima's work, no doubt, given the smirk on her face.

The crowd parted as Heidin swept forward, trailing flame, with Tyra right behind. The queen looked taller, brighter, and more intimidating than Reginn remembered, glittering in her golden armor. Tyra looked small, even diminished next to her firebird dottir.

"Reginn–you're hurt!" Heidin looked her up and down. "You're covered in blood."

"It's old blood," Reginn said, brushing at the crusted wool of her storm jacket. "I only had the one coat."

"Come rest in my tent until yours is ready. I'll ask my healers to have a look."

"Thank you, Your Majesty, but there's no need," Reginn said. "I'm better every day. You and I–we're hard to kill."

"I'm grateful for that," Heidin said. "But does this mean that the barbarians know we are here?"

"I don't believe so," Reginn said. "I think this was a chance encounter. After they attacked us, the Risen boarded the enemy ship and . . . cleared it of the living. *Naglfar* was badly damaged, and so we brought her ashore for repairs and sailed here in the ship we took from them. Once our ship is seaworthy, she'll join us here."

"It sounds as if your army fought well," Tyra said, speaking up for the first time. "Congratulations, Counselor."

Between the lines, Reginn heard, *Now, see? Forcing you to raise an army of the dead by threatening the lives of living children was worth it.*

That afternoon, Katia brought an armload of new clothes and led Reginn to a secluded marsh pool to bathe. The water was numbingly cold–so cold that Reginn had to break through a skin of ice to get in. So cold that the pain in her shoulder was quickly muted.

"I've missed this," Reginn said through chattering teeth, raking crusted salt from her hair.

"Liar," Katia said.

Reginn laughed. "You're right. I don't miss this. Give me the hot spring at Brenna's House."

Katia hesitated, unsure whether to believe her or not. "Barbarians are in the habit of bathing in the woods?"

"My foster modir and I lived rough during hunting season."

"What were you hunting?"

"We weren't hunting anything," Reginn said. "We were the ones being hunted." That was in the desperate time before Asger. As opposed to the desperate time after he arrived.

After a moment of shocked silence, Katia said, "This place must bring back a lot of bad memories."

"Mixed memories," Reginn said. "Like anywhere."

Katia stood guard, handing Reginn the clean clothes the quartermaster had provided. One item was a needle-knit vest unlike anything she'd ever seen. Once she pulled it on over her head, a delicious warmth flooded through her.

She looked up at Naima. "What magic is this?"

"Another innovation from Eira's shop," Katia said, lifting the hem of her tunic to display her own. "If you're going to invade a country where the weather is abysmal, this is good to have. In hot weather, it's cooling."

Good to have, even if you're not invading another country, If you're going fishing, for instance.

"Who else is here?" Reginn said. "Shelby? Grima?"

"Shelby is establishing an agricultural outpost to the south, in a place called the Sand Barrens." Katia wrinkled her nose. "Doesn't sound too promising, but he's all confidence. He and Grima are supposed to join us here before long. Grima has been a valuable resource. She has been coming to Barbaria for–"

"Not Barbaria," Reginn said. "Muckleholm."

"Muckleholm," Katia said, as if Reginn was splitting hairs. "Anyway. It turns out that Grima's been coming here for years, gathering information, recruiting agents, identifying key targets, and eliminating threats to the gifted."

Eliminating threats to the gifted.

"As in assassinating people?"

Katia stared at Reginn as if she'd started singing alehouse songs in the temple. "If necessary, yes," she said. "To protect New Jotunheim and our mission."

"What's our mission?" Reginn said.

"To–to raise up the jotnar and–honestly, what is *wrong* with you, Reginn?"

Reginn had a feeling that Katia was not referring to the hole in her shoulder.

"What do you mean?"

"You're just–different. Full of doubt. We'll be having a simple conversation, and then, all at once, you go sideways. You start asking questions that nobody has ever asked before, questioning truths we've all known for ages."

Really? When I arrived in Eimyrja, you all thought Grima was creepy. Now she's the savior of the realm.

"Shelby pretty much said the same thing–that I'm different."

"He did?" Katia cocked her head, as if surprised. "Well then. He's really interested in you, Reginn, trying to get something going, but he feels like you just slam the door in his face."

"He's not used to anyone saying no," Reginn murmured.

She rolled her eyes. "No, he is not. He says it's like you're always trying to start a fight."

"So you've been talking about me."

"We're your friends," Katia said, blushing. "Of course we would talk about you."

We can be friends, as long as we never talk about anything important.

"To start a fight is the last thing I want," Reginn said, running a hand over her face. "Maybe it's not a good idea to recruit older dedicates. We're more set in our ways. It's difficult to leave past experiences behind."

Katia sighed. "I'm sorry. We're all under stress." She gestured toward a nearby stump. "Here, sit. Let me dry and braid your hair before you catch your death."

"Thank you," Reginn said. "It's hard for me to reach."

"I figured that." Katia made short work of the braid, pulling her hair tightly against her scalp, scraping away the ice that was forming. "Anyway, if you have questions about what Grima has been up to, you can ask her yourself. We expect her here any day now."

Well, there's something to look forward to.

Durinn had scheduled a strategy meeting for that evening. But first, Naima, who had been circulating, asking questions all day long, met with Reginn in her tent for a debriefing.

Naima studied Reginn critically. "You look much better," she said. "You're going to have to work harder at playing the wounded hero I made you out to be."

"I never asked to be a hero."

"Anyway. Here are some things you should know, if you don't already. First thing–and don't ask me to explain it–but there's some kind of time hitch between here and New Jotunheim. You've spent a year in Eimyrja, but it's been ten years here."

Reginn eyed her. "Seriously?"

Naima nodded. "So don't be surprised that so much has happened. The king's been on a military campaign ever since–"

"Wait–what king?"

"King Rikhard. Anyway, he's built up his fleet and his army and he's conquered the rest of the Archipelago. So fighting the barbarians–I mean, Muckleholmians–may not be as easy as some expect."

Rikhard Karlsen had been a jarl when Reginn left Muckleholm for the temple. He was the man Asger thought to partner with. He'd sent her to the jarl's ship in the harbor at Langvik, but instead, she'd jumped overboard and swum to the spinners' ship.

She'd leaped from the cooking pot and into the flame.

And now Rikhard was more powerful than ever.

The command tent was scarcely large enough to hold all the officers and commanders. Tyra and Heidin sat in, on the periphery, but they signaled their intention to allow Durinn to run the show.

Durinn introduced their field officers–Hersir Torsten for the infantry, Hersir Caitilin, commander of the ships, Hersir Stian, for the cavalry. Bryn was in charge of healing services, Katia of vaettir of all kinds, and a man named Randolfr for logistics and supplies. Then, finally, Counselor Reginn Eiklund, commander of the Risen.

Reginn introduced her section leaders–Hrym for the Jotun and Dainn for the elven forces, Asger for the thursen, and Svend, who would lead the human dead and his own living soldiers. This was met with uneasy murmuring.

"Speak up, Torsten," Durinn said. "Tell us what's on your mind."

The infantry commander was thickset, completely bald, with a long and highly styled black beard.

"Some of us were wondering if–if we'd be fighting alongside the dead, or in front of them, or if they'd be, you know, fighting somewhere else."

"Why do you ask, Commander?"

Torsten shot a look at Reginn and her soldiers. "Being as this is our first big battle, it might be distracting to feel like we have to watch our backs all the time."

Dainn bristled. The elves had the reputation of being proud and thin-skinned. "The implication being that those of us who fought and died for Jotunheim at Ragnarok are somehow . . . untrustworthy?"

"We thursen have our own reservations about fighting alongside humans, given that they are fragile and apparently easily frightened," Asger said, creating a cat's cradle out of flame. It evolved into a catapult that flung tiny balls of fire that flamed out before they reached anyone.

"I don't know about your backs," Svend said, "but the Risen saved our asses and our ship yesterday. It's good to have tested warriors, living or dead, fighting alongside new recruits."

"That is exactly what they are–tested warriors," Reginn said. "This is New Jotunheim, where we pride ourselves in honoring nature and all of those living in it. Some of the factors that make the Risen frightening to you make them frightening–and deadly–to the enemy. Fight alongside them before you make a judgment."

Then Heidin spoke up. "As your queen and one of the architects of this alliance, I want to remind you that in wartime, we don't always get to choose our allies and their roles in the fighting. Instead, we welcome their assistance. Trust me—we are going to need it."

Durinn waited a moment to make sure that debate was over, then unrolled a large map of the Archipelago. It was incredibly detailed—better than any Reginn had seen before. Pressing a calloused forefinger into the map, they said, "We're here, south of Vandrgardr, in a position that should afford us easy access to the entire west coast of Muckleholm. There are several important ports along here, but the king's base of operations is on the opposite coast, at Ulfness, due east from here through the mountains. In addition, there are major weapons manufactories and shipyards at Sundgard, south of the king's seat of power."

Sundgard? Reginn thought. Wasn't that the name of Eiric's family's farm?

Raise us, Aldrnari. Lead us.

She pressed her hands against the sides of her head, covering her ears to shut out the voices. That didn't work, because the voices were coming from inside her head.

Muckleholm seemed to have an oversupply of the restless dead. Reginn tried to focus on the commander's words.

"The Archipelago has many more ships and skilled sailors than we do, and they know these waters. It is likely that we have the advantage when it comes to the size of our army and the magical assets at our disposal. We could stick to the land. There's a good road from here to Langvik and on to Sweinhavn, then due west to Thornby, on the east coast. From there, we march due north up the coast to Sundgard and Ulfness."

"Just in time to greet the king's great-great-grandson in his dotage," Heidin said, to general laughter.

"Aye, Your Majesty, it's a long march through unfamiliar territory," Durinn said, rubbing their chin, "and no telling what we'll find along the way. It's unlikely such an operation would go unnoticed. The king would have plenty of time to prepare a welcome."

Randolfr, the logistics man, raised his hand. "I'm concerned about provisions and supplies over such a long route. From what we know, there is very little to be gleaned in the countryside. Once we reach the far coast, we can be resupplied by ship."

"Unless the king uses his ships to his advantage to blockade the ports," Hersir Caitilin, the naval commander, said. "You'll not find an inlet or a fjord without a warship lurking in it."

"Well," Svend said, "this invasion seemed like a good idea back on Ithavoll, but maybe we'd better go home." He made as if to get up.

"Sit," Heidin said. He sat.

"So we have a choice," the queen said, "and there are risks, whichever we choose. We've discussed the disadvantages of a long land march, leaving our ships behind. Coming from a family of coasters, I don't like to stray too far from our ships.

"We can take a sea passage all the way south along the coast and around the southernmost cape. I know from experience that the currents and winds are difficult to navigate at the tip, so there's a risk we'll lose ships, something we can ill afford.

"Or we combine the two. We sail south, then through the Sudreyjar Islands into the sound. From there, we can target Langvik or sail farther south to Sweinhavn, where we know for a fact there's a road to the east coast.

"I favor Langvik. Grima says the king is sometimes in residence there. That would be convenient, but we can't count on it. We'll learn more when she arrives. An attack on Langvik might draw Rikhard overland to us."

She traced the route with her forefinger. "When I lived here, no one would dare make that crossing, as the grasslands were infested with outlaws, vargr, saber-toothed cats, and poisonous snakes. That may have changed, as I understand the king has cleared the Archipelago of vermin like us." She smiled a sharklike smile.

A disturbance at the entrance to the tent signaled that someone new had arrived. One of the officers hurried forward and murmured something to Heidin and Tyra.

"Ah," Heidin said. "Grima is finally here."

The assassin swept into the tent like a plume of gray smoke. She wore narrow gray breeches, a sleek gray tunic, and a rough wool cloak that absorbed light instead of reflecting it.

Katia, who had ended up sitting next to Reginn, leaned in and whispered, "Eira made her that ghost cloak. It makes her very difficult to see."

Behind her came nine women, similarly clad, carrying identical staffs. They all wore identical gold torcs around their necks.

Grima stopped just inside the entrance and swept her gaze over the assembly. It lingered on Reginn a little too long. Reginn read her expression as triumph. That signified nothing good.

Dread rose in Reginn's throat, making it difficult to breathe.

Grima approached the queen and bowed low. "Welcome back to Barbaria, Your Majesty. I cannot tell you how much it means to me to see our plans finally coming to fruition."

Reginn couldn't put her finger on it, but there was something in her attitude, in the way she said it, that suggested that she viewed the queen as an equal, not a superior.

What's that about?

"Elder Grima," Tyra said. "Who are your companions?"

"These are my wraiths–spinners I've recruited in the Archipelago to join my personal guard," Grima said. "I've provided them with intensive training over the past several years."

"We require that all spinners identified in Barbaria be sent to New Jotunheim for evaluation and training," Tyra said.

"Most have been, Kennari," Grima said. "Except for these. These ones have displayed exceptional talents that I wanted to nurture myself."

"So you kept the best and sent us your leavings?" Heidin said, the flames coming up in her eyes.

Grima didn't flinch, didn't apologize. "They have enabled me to extend my reach throughout the islands and accomplish much more than I would have otherwise."

"Good for you, Grima," Heidin said. "Now send your guard outside and deliver your report."

"As you wish," Grima said. She gestured to her hird, and they filed back outside. She seemed unworried that her report to the queen was getting off on the wrong foot.

Grima and Tyra had always seemed tight, but Heidin and Grima were like oil and water. They'd clashed in the past over the assassin's eagerness to execute Eiric Halvorsen. Possibly, the third burning had changed things. Reginn was never sure which Heidin she would encounter on any given day.

"Now. What's the news?" Heidin said with a trace of impatience.

"We have eliminated more than one hundred fifty Asgardians throughout the Archipelago in the past month," Grima said. "So many that our activity has drawn some attention from the king's guard. More important, we have learned that the Asgardian warrior Eiric Halvorsen is here on Muckleholm."

42

RECONNAISSANCE

IT SEEMED THAT GRIMA HAD succeeded where Eiric had failed–to create a sense of urgency in the king. In the days following the assassination attempt, Rikhard was an army of one. As promised, he sent word to the garrison at Langvik to take Agata into custody, but she was nowhere to be found. The boarded-up shop was still there, the bins full of clothing, and a used plate and cup on the table in the back room, as if the shopkeeper had just stepped out for a moment.

The garrison commander reported that five soldiers had gone missing, but no bodies had been found. Agata must have tidied up before she left.

They searched the tunnels as well and broke into Agata's "workroom." She hadn't cleared that out entirely. That might mean that she intended to return. Or maybe she had left in a hurry.

She must have another bolt hole somewhere nearby, Eiric thought. A place to go when she didn't want to be under the nose of the king.

The king messaged his eyes and ears throughout the Archipelago, knowing it was possible the enemy fleet had landed on one of the smaller islands and planned to launch an attack from there.

No sightings had been reported, but one of Rikhard's smaller longships had gone missing off the northwest shore of Muckleholm. There had been a series of storms, however, and it wasn't uncommon for a ship to be driven off course–sometimes for weeks. That area was sparsely populated, so it was conceivable that no one would have noticed a shipwreck.

"It's possible the Jotun haven't left the boatyard," Eiric said. "When

I left New Jotunheim, I had the impression that departure was imminent. But something could have happened."

Rikhard shrugged. "If they are not here, I expect they will be soon." He was a man who seemed glad to have a problem to solve. For ten years, he'd been busy conquering the other realms in the Archipelago. Now he needed something else to do.

Rikhard asked Eiric to stay on at Kingshavn for a time to meet with his commanders and prepare for the coming war, although he'd not yet asked him to commit to a particular role in the fighting. It suited Eiric because he felt like an awkward interloper at Sundgard now.

During his time at Rikhard's hall, Eiric hoped to get to know Ivar, who was a stranger to him. His brodir was tight-lipped and wary–for good reason. Had he been well-treated? Ivar and Hilde were close. It seemed that when Ivar wasn't with Rikhard, he was with Hilde. Eiric often saw them with their heads together. Although modirless almost from birth, at least Hilde had filled that role for him.

The king provided a ship and a detachment of soldiers to transport Hilde back to Sundgard and protect the manufactories there. Before she left, she pulled Eiric aside.

"Do not let your enemies get to Ivar," she said. "Protect him. He's been through too much already."

Eiric studied her for a long moment, trying to read her meaning. "*My* enemies?" he said finally.

She flushed. "I know that's unfair, but Ivar's connection with you–and the king–puts him at risk. It's brought him to the notice of Agata and others."

"Have you considered that you–and your baby–are at risk yourselves?" Eiric said.

"Yes. But I won't be armoring up and picking up a sword and shield in order to impress the king. Rikhard is the closest to a fadir Ivar's ever had. Whatever is asked of him, Ivar never says no."

That bolt hit home. "You have my word that I'll do everything I can to keep him out of this war," Eiric said. "It might help if you spoke to the king as well."

"I have," Hilde said, "but I'm not sure I'm getting through."

As she turned toward the ship, Eiric said, "Hilde."

She swung around to face him.

"Thank you for providing a sanctuary for my brodir when his family did not. Thank you for teaching him the value of love and compassion when we failed him."

Hilde smiled. "As you get to know your brodir, you'll find that Ivar gives more than he receives."

Some days later, Ivar joined Eiric and his crew aboard *Firebird* to patrol the coastline between Ulfness and Selvagr. Ivar wore scaled-down chain mail and weapons that were finer than any Eiric had owned before the ones he inherited from his fadir and grandfadir.

Late in the afternoon, as they rounded the headland and entered the fjord, Eiric gave over the styrboard to his brodir and sat close by to supervise. Ivar needed little supervision. He had a sure hand, quick reflexes, and a natural grace. Though he couldn't match Eiric's size at the same age, he, too, had been crewing since early childhood.

He impressed the fiskers, not an easy thing. They took to calling him Smal Eiric until Ivar put a stop to it. "I am not 'smal' anyone," he said. "I am myself." So they took to calling him Ivar Himself, which he seemed to find acceptable.

When they arrived back at Kingshavn, Eiric said to Ivar, "Sit with me for a moment," as the rest of the crew disembarked and walked up toward the longhouse, some looking over their shoulders at the two of them.

Ivar sat on his sea chest, his hands on his knees, his gray eyes fixed on Eiric.

"You are a skilled styrman," Eiric said. "Who taught you? The king?"

"King Rikhard has many skilled styrmen, though he is not one himself. They have taught me."

"I'm told that you have already seen your share of battles," Eiric said.

"I have not embarrassed myself," Ivar said. "I will contribute more when I've gained my full height and reach."

If you live that long, Eiric thought.

"Have you thought about what you would like to do when you are grown?" Eiric said.

"That will depend on what paths are open to me when the time comes," Ivar said, displaying his ability to talk around any question.

"There are a few things you should know–some you might already know as well or better than me. It seems you are able to read?"

Ivar nodded. "The king has brought in western tutors to instruct me in reading and writing."

"The old texts describe the final battle between the Asgardian gods and the Jotun–the agents of chaos."

Ivar nodded. "Ragnarok."

"I've not read them, but I've heard the stories, and it's not very clear what happens after the battle. It's implied that all the Jotun are dead, and a handful of Asgardian gods usher in a new golden age. Right?"

Ivar nodded. "Basically, yes."

"New Jotunheim has become a haven for descendants of the Jotun and their allies, who are unhappy with the outcome of the war. They've been building ships and raising an army. One of their primary weapons is magic."

"Magic? You mean like the spinners the king is trying to recruit?"

"I saw magic in New Jotunheim that was much more dangerous than anything I've seen on Muckleholm."

Ivar shifted uncomfortably. "Why are you telling me this, and not the king?"

Eiric took a deep breath. "The Jotun are ruled by our half systir, Liv. She is their queen. You might have heard her name."

Ivar stared at him, eyes wide. "Hilde has spoken well of her. They were friends. She said Liv was fearless."

Eiric nodded. "She was your fiercest protector, Ivar, after our modir died. She loved you very much."

"So–I don't understand. Why would she fight against us?"

"She was born across the sea, in Eimyrja, to a spinner. We shared a fadir. She seemed to be at the center of a plot to bring back Heidin, a Jotun volva who died at Ragnarok. My fadir and our grandfadir brought her here to Muckleholm because she was in danger in New Jotunheim. Liv found a home with us, but was often a target because of her interest in and use of magic.

"Her modir had given her an amulet bearing an image of Heidin. Our modir, Sylvi, locked it away, but Liv found it after Sylvi died and has worn it ever since. It's as if she's under some kind of evil spell."

The wind stirred Ivar's hair so that it spilled over his eyes. Absently, he raked it back, tucking it behind his ears.

"Does the king know about Liv?"

"He met her before we left for the temple. But he doesn't know that she is leading the Jotun."

"Why haven't you told him?"

"I wasn't sure how he would react," Eiric said. "Whether he would lose trust in us–in me, anyway. Whether he might try to use us against Liv somehow, though I don't know how well that piece would play. Whatever happens, it is going to be a dangerous time.

"For Rikhard, we represent the connection to Asgard that he's always wanted–that would make him a king among men. For the Jotun, we represent a competing claim on their queen."

Eiric stopped, cleared his throat. He hadn't meant to say so much. It must seem like an impenetrable tangle to a ten-year-old. And yet he had the sense that Ivar was teasing apart the various threads like a fisherman with a net.

"My point is, we'll be targeted–by both sides, probably. I don't know how to keep you safe."

Ivar looked up, surprised. "Is that your job?"

"I suppose I haven't done very well so far," Eiric said, feeling his face heat as the blood came up. He'd thought he could protect his modir from Sten–and he'd failed.

"Here's the thing–we don't have to stay here as proxies for the gods. We have a good ship and a willing crew. We can be gone before the armies arrive. Though it's been ten years, I know the Archipelago better than anyone. And I promised to help my crew right a wrong back in New Jotunheim."

"You would run *away*?" Ivar shook his head, disbelieving.

"I'm not known as someone who turns his back on a fight," Eiric said, "even when I should. The question is whether this is our fight. When the king offered to pay my blood price in exchange for a year of service, Liv didn't want me to make that bargain. She proposed that the three of us (or maybe four of us, if Hilde agreed)–that we leave the farm, sail away, and find a new home, coasting and fishing until we had a stake.

"Maybe I should have taken that advice. It might have saved us a world of trouble. But I didn't. So now I'm making that offer to you."

Ivar tilted his chin up. "Thank you, brodir. But this is my home. I'm a good styrman, but I prefer to be on land. Rikhard is my king. He gave me a place when I had none. And I know Hilde won't leave Sundgard–she's invested too much in her business there. I will stay and provide what help I can."

It was as simple as that. They had been here for him, and Eiric had not. Now Ivar would return the favor.

"Then I will stay, also," Eiric said. "I'll provide what help I can, and let the fates decide the outcome."

43
VERBAL DUEL

MORE IMPORTANT, WE HAVE LEARNED that the Asgardian warrior Eiric Halvorsen is here on Muckleholm.

Grima's words fell like a stone into a bucket. For a long moment, the only sound was the crackling of the hearth fire.

"Eiric?" Heidin whispered. "Here?"

Relief washed over Reginn. *He's alive! He made it!* But panic followed in its wake. How could she possibly explain this?

"That can't be true," Reginn said. "Halvorsen is dead. You were there, Grima. We all saw him dead. The queen held vigil for him in the crypts. We were all at his sending."

"And, yet–he came into my shop in Langvik looking as alive as you or me."

"What was he doing there?" Asger said.

"Shopping," Grima said. "Looking for warm clothes for his crew."

"What happened?" Tyra said. "Did he recognize you?"

"Not at first," Grima said, "but I was so startled that I gave myself away."

"How?" Tyra said.

Grima rolled her eyes. "I tried to kill him. I should have known that it wouldn't be easy, that it required advance planning. My efforts caught the attention of the king's guard, and they barged in and took him prisoner, intending to gang him into the king's army."

"Eiric is fighting for Rikhard?" Heidin all but shouted.

"Let me finish," Grima said. "Then Halvorsen's crew showed up, there was a brawl, and they escaped."

"Who did?" Reginn was getting lost in the verbal tangle.

"Halvorsen and his crew," Grima said.

"What about the king's soldiers?" Durinn said. "Did they give chase?"

"They're all dead," Grima said. "Killed in the brawl."

"And yet, both you and Halvorsen are alive," Asger said. "Curious."

Grima glared at him. "Maybe Halvorsen is immortal, given his multiple Asgardian bloodlines. Or maybe he wasn't really alive to start with. Maybe the aldrnari raised him, like she did the other demons and monsters in this army."

"Careful, Grima," Asger said. The sword across his knees glowed a sullen red. "You don't want to hurt my feelings."

Grima wasn't making any friends among the Risen.

"Highest," Durinn said, shifting uncomfortably. "Perhaps this discussion should be reserved for a more private meeting."

"Enough!" Heidin said. "Did my brodir give you any indication of why he was there, and what he planned to do?"

"He did not," Grima said. "I warned him to leave the Archipelago and not to have any contact with the king."

"He would not leave without seeing Ivar," Heidin said, unfurling the map again. "And Sundgard is close to Rikhard's new hold at Kingshavn."

"There is no need to speculate," Grima said. "The boy is at Kingshavn and so is Halvorsen, and they both recently dined with the king. I tried to do for all three of them then and there, but I did not succeed. It would be helpful if Modir Tyra could develop a poison that does not stink of cherries." She scowled at Tyra.

"Elder Grima," Heidin said, each word a shard of ice, "if you are saying that you attempted to poison both of my brodirs, then you are fortunate that you did not succeed."

"Dottir," Tyra began, "consider what could have been accomplished if Elder Grima had succeeded. It would have all but eliminated organized resistance to the rise of the Jotun."

"It would have delivered justice to those responsible for a cowardly strike against New Jotunheim," Grima said. "Rikhard sent Halvorsen, an Asgardian warrior, to New Jotunheim, where he slaughtered hundreds of our soldiers, the entire Council of Elders, and our beloved keeper. He should have gone to the block for his crimes, but . . . he was spared."

Reginn recalled Grima's expression as she stood on the dais, axe in hand, only to be disappointed when Heidin intervened. No doubt Heidin felt the prick of that blade. Reginn sensed the rage building in the firebird, like a storm rolling toward them.

"While in prison, Halvorsen lost his mind, killed his caretaker, and mysteriously died under Elder Reginn's care."

Grima had blades to spare.

"Ask her if she wants to meet your army," Naima whispered to Reginn. "Does she know you have one?"

"Shh."

"You speak from a place of ignorance," Heidin said. Flames ran over her skin, and her fiery hair writhed around her head. Her eyes burned like sunset through smoke. "Eiric came to New Jotunheim because he had no choice. He was wrongfully convicted of murder and stood to lose his life, as well as the title to our farm. Rikhard agreed to pay his blood price in exchange for a year of service."

"A convicted murderer would seem to have been a good choice for the job," Grima said. "Whatever the price, the king certainly got his money's worth."

Why is she doing this? Reginn thought. Why is she tangling with Heidin? Or was she merely trying to divide the queen from her dangerous and inconvenient brodir?

If so, she wasn't very good at it. Grima had a transactional view of the world. The kind of bond that existed between Heidin and her brodir was beyond her experience. It was the kind of connection that Reginn had longed for all her life.

Reginn stole a look at Tyra, who was listening, tight-lipped. She and Grima had been allies in their attempts to dispose of Eiric Halvorsen, and now they each knew secrets about the other.

Better be careful, Grima, Reginn thought. If Tyra has to choose between you and Heidin, my money is on Heidin.

Grima hadn't struck her final blow. "After a hurried funeral, Halvorsen miraculously reappears in the Archipelago, none the worse for wear, his escape facilitated by the fact that the weather wall is down after hundreds of years.

"He obviously had help. The question is, who was it?" Now Grima looked directly at Reginn. "Who had the skills of trickery, sleight of hand, and subterfuge to pull this off? Who had been traveling the Archipelago, taking money from fools for telling fortunes, healing the sick and raising the dead? Who might have met a handsome coaster in an alehouse and agreed to an alliance?"

"She's taking no prisoners," Naima muttered in Reginn's ear.

"She rarely does, unless there's an opportunity for torture. Help me up." With Naima's help, Reginn came to her feet and pulled her flute from its case.

"Gods," Grima said, rolling her eyes when she saw the flute.

"Your Majesty, may I respond?"

"Go to," Heidin said.

Reginn bowed to the queen, to the crowd, and, mockingly, to the assassin. "Grima, forgive me. I have truly underestimated you. I assumed your skills were limited to back-alley stabbings, ambushes, poisoning, and torture, and now I find that you are a talented spinner of tales. You have taken a series of events and stitched them together into an extravagant fantasy that implicates everyone but you.

"Let's take the same facts, and write a new story." Reginn played a few notes on her flute, signaling that her story was about to begin. "In my story, an underpowered temple dedicate with specialized skills has been coming and going from Muckleholm for years, doing whatever tasks are demanded of her by her superiors–murder, espionage, kidnapping, or theft. All along, she understood this to be preparation for an eventual invasion. A war would provide an abundant opportunity to collect blood magic–perhaps enough to allow our ambitious dedicate to take the power she believes she deserves." Reginn played another cascade of notes, this time a lively marching tune.

"But it is becoming increasingly clear that the ruling council at home is satisfied with the status quo. They live an easy life in paradise, servants at their beck and call. There is no room for advancement, because it seems the council members intend to live forever.

"But there are a hundred ways to start a war. She finds allies at home who view the council as an obstacle to power. She begins building a secret guard of spinners in the Archipelago. She encourages an ambitious jarl to send a ship to New Jotunheim in search of treasure, well aware of the reception such a visit is likely to receive.

"Her gambit pays off in ways she never dreamed of. In one move, she is free of the old council, the keeper–everyone who stood in her way. New Jotunheim prepares to launch a war against the Archipelago. Only one task remains–to eliminate the enemy warrior who opened the path to her ascendance. That proves to be more difficult than she expected.

"Even more unexpected was the arrival of a competitor–the risen queen of the Jotun, who happens to have a connection to both the Asgardian warrior and the beloved kennari–director of the academy. If she cannot find a way to break these attachments, her plans are in ashes."

A few more sad notes signaled the end of the story.

Reginn got off a bit of a curtsy to the crowd and returned her flute to its sheath. There was something for everyone to like and to worry about in that narrative. Her fellow elders were staring at her with mingled astonishment and apprehension. Asger was looking from Reginn to Heidin as if unsure which way to jump.

"How do you like my story, Grima? It fits the facts as well as yours, and implicates only one person." Indeed, she had carefully crafted this story to leave out any implication of Modir Tyra. Heidin's relationship with her long-lost modir was as complicated as that with her brodir. Better to make one enemy instead of two, although Tyra was looking at her, narrow-eyed, no doubt wondering just how much she'd figured out. Reginn met her gaze straight on. Nothing to hide here.

"The elders have given us much to think about," Tyra said. "Perhaps we should reconvene this meeting tomorrow afternoon, when we are rested and our heads are clear. We will try to sort some of this out in the meantime." She extended her hand to Heidin. "Come, Your Majesty."

"No!" Heidin said. "You–and everyone–get out."

For a split second, nobody moved. Tyra froze, her hand still extended. Grima opened her mouth, then closed it again, even though she obviously had something more to say.

"DID YOU HEAR ME? Go!" Flame jetted from the head of Heidin's staff, and the gathered officers scattered like crows from a carcass. Though it wasn't the queen's tent, nobody asked any questions. The crowd flooded out, even Grima, but when Reginn and Naima made as if to follow, Heidin said, "No! You stay."

They both turned around to face the queen.

Behind them, Asger said, "Your Majesty–"

"I would speak with the counselor alone," Heidin said, waving him off. Then, glaring at Naima, she said, "Are you deaf? GO!"

Reginn knew that Naima had no intention of leaving, but she saw no reason her friend should pay the blood price for her own mistakes.

"Naima, please go," Reginn said. When Naima planted herself, folding her arms, Reginn repeated, "Please."

"As you wish," Naima said with the brisk formality of anger. She turned toward the entrance, then swung back and embraced Reginn, her tears spotting Reginn's tunic. She took a long look at Heidin over Reginn's shoulder. Then she was gone.

44

CHANGE OF MISSION

THEY LEFT REGINN AND HEIDIN alone in the massive tent, two splashes of light against military drab. As soon as the others left, Heidin began pacing, making tight turns in a swirl of her feathered cape, pivoting with her staff centering the axis, shedding sparks.

It reminded Reginn of the night Eiric Halvorsen tried to kill her—like being penned up with a lion. But where Eiric wielded raw physical power, Heidin's untethered magic buffeted her like breakers on a beach so that she staggered back and forth, scarcely able to keep her feet. The air crackled and sparked, lifting Reginn's hair away from her head and stinging her skin like a thousand nettles.

"You lied to me," Heidin said, her voice clamoring like a bell. "I knew the Asgardian was alive."

"I didn't exactly—"

"You helped him escape, and now he's dining with the king of Asgard, and they're laughing at me."

"I doubt he's laughing," Reginn said, her voice a whisper against the goddess.

"And now my own brodir will be fighting against me—against ME. And he's probably turned my brodir Ivar against me, calling me a monster and worse."

"Isn't Ivar an Asgardian, too? What did you intend to do about him?"

A particularly strong blow lifted her up and slammed her against the wall of the tent so that she hit one of the iron supports. She dropped like a stone, her arm twisted under her, and remained there, gasping for air, seeing no point in getting back up.

At once, Heidin was kneeling at her side. "Reginn," she said. "Reginn, I'm sorry. Are you hurt? Is anything broken?"

The voice of the goddess was gone for the moment, replaced by the voice of the person Reginn once thought might be a friend.

"I think–I wrenched my shoulder," Reginn whispered. "Let me roll a little this way–" At this slight movement, pain rocketed all the way down her arm, and tears leaked from under her lashes.

Heidin was weeping, too. "You saved my life, and this is how I repay you. I don't know what I–what came over me." She paused, then shook her head. "No. That's a lie. I do know what came over me." She touched the amulet embedded in her skin. "Sometimes I feel like I'm losing my mind."

Reginn cleared her throat. "Have you–would you consider removing it, maybe for just a little while, and see how you feel?"

"You're trying to trick me," Heidin said, covering the emblem with both hands. "You want it for yourself."

"Heidin, please believe me when I tell you–I don't want that. It's just that it seems to be making you miserable, so I thought–"

"I can't take it off. It's everywhere now–in every part of my body, burning away my old self. I don't know how much of me is left, and when I'll be gone for good. As it is, I feel like if I remove it, I'll die."

The tent flap moved, then opened a crack. "Reginn?"

"It's all right, Naima," Reginn said. "We're just talking–sorting things out. We won't be much longer."

The flap fell back into place.

"I'll be straight with you," Reginn said. "Yes, I lied to you. I knew that, even if Eiric survived the night, sooner or later, his luck would run out. I also knew that if he died as your prisoner, it would cut your last ties to Liv–the human girl you used to be. There is no way that Liv could go forward with that memory."

"You don't know Liv. You've never even met her."

"But I have. When you first arrived on Eimyrja and through your brodir's eyes. I didn't want to lose you. I didn't want to lose him. It was the only thing I could think of to do to try and save you both."

"Gods, you are arrogant," Heidin said, rolling her eyes.

"It's a common flaw among healers," Reginn said. "Otherwise, we'd take up a new trade." She reached a tentative hand toward Heidin's amulet. "Would you mind if I–"

The blow slammed her backward, sending her sliding across the pebbled beach on her butt and shoulders. She struggled to sit up, using only her good arm. Once again, the goddess had flamed up in Heidin's eyes. Even her face changed, the golden planes hardening, all traces of humor and humanity sliding away.

"HOW. DARE. YOU?" the goddess said.

"You are not in this conversation," Reginn said. "I'm speaking with Liv."

"GET OUT," the goddess said, "or your friend Liv will squash you like a bug."

"I don't think so," Reginn said. "Not yet. But why don't you give it a go?" Where that confidence came from, she didn't know. Maybe it was because she knew that if Heidin had full control, Reginn would be dead already.

Maybe it was because Liv's expression had shifted, softened, so that now she looked confused and distressed. She pressed her fingers to her temples, as if to rearrange her thoughts, then came up on her knees, her eyes wide and frightened. "Reginn! You have to go–now. Find Eiric and Ivar. Warn them. Protect them. She knows that the three of you are a threat, and she means to kill you all."

"I can't just leave you here to–I want to help you," Reginn said. "Why don't we–"

"Reginn!" Heidin rose, and kept rising, until she resembled a pillar of flame that reached nearly to the roof of the tent. "Don't talk! Run for your life!!"

Reginn bolted from the tent, racing past Naima and Asger, who were waiting by the door. They called after her as she sprinted through the rows of tents that had sprouted on the rocky shoreline. Soon she heard footsteps pounding along behind her.

Heidin had told her to run, but she hadn't said how far. Reginn wanted to get beyond the camp so that if the worst happened (whatever that was) she would be the only casualty.

She heard an explosion behind her and took a quick look over her shoulder. It appeared that the tent where the commanders had assembled was on fire. Shooting out flames, anyway. Soldiers poured from their tents, milling around, waiting for orders. Was Heidin still inside?

"Run!" Heidin had said. Should she be running away or trying to do something to help?

By now, she was within the fringe of trees along the shoreline and so hopefully screened from sight. The various ships of the Jotun army were anchored just offshore, but the *Kraken* was moored on the far side of the camp. As she looked out over the harbor, she heard someone approaching on foot. She faded into the trees until she saw it was Naima.

"Naima!" she hissed.

"What are you–you're hurt!" Naima said, gently touching her elbow. "What happened? Did you fall or–?"

"Something's happening with Heidin," Reginn said. "She's being possessed by a malevolent spirit tied to that amulet she wears. She knocked me down and I hurt my arm, and then she told me to run–she was afraid she would hurt me. So I ran."

"I didn't see what all was happening, because I was chasing after you. The demon went the other way down the beach. We need to find some–ow!" She turned up her collar and waved her arms around. "I wouldn't think biting flies would be out in this cold."

"I'm getting bit, too," Reginn said

Biting flies. That struck a chord of memory. What? Reginn shook her head.

"Could you find Svend and the rest of the *Kraken* crew and tell them to be ready to sail with the next tide?"

"Only if you promise you can go five minutes without getting shot or–" She stopped, eyes narrowed, swayed, and crumpled to the ground.

Reginn was turning, raising her arm to ward off attack, when she went down herself.

ASGER

ASGER ELDR WAS IN A dangerous mood. Truth be told, he was always dangerous, but just now he was in the mood to burn down the world.

He cut through the camp like a fast-moving flame through a dry forest, leaving a trail of ash and smoke behind him. His sword, Laevateinn, flamed across his back, hungry to be put to use.

The other commanders of the Risen were waiting for him outside of Durinn's new tent–Hrym, commander of the humans who fell at Ragnarok; Ursinus, leader of the beasts; and Dainn, the elven commander. With them were Svend Bondi, the commander of the living human forces that had sailed with Reginn on *Naglfar*, and Gyda Fisker, the *Kraken*'s styrman.

"Anything?" Asger said, knowing the answer before he asked the question.

Svend shook his head. "We've swept the entire camp–twice–and she's nowhere to be found. Naima is missing as well."

"I last saw Naima after Reginn . . . abruptly . . . left her meeting with the queen," Asger said. "We were waiting for her outside, but she got past us and took off running. We both went after her. I went one way and Naima went the other."

"We have searched every one of our ships moored along this coastline," Gyda said. "The–ah–kraken, Hafgufa, has searched the waters and beaches. Nobody has seen her."

"I would know if she were nearby," Asger said. "She is not." He gestured toward the tent entrance. "Let's go see what the queen knows."

The guards at the door stepped aside quickly when they saw who was coming.

The Jotun queen, Heidin, was huddled over breakfast with Durinn, Tyra, and the new elders. They looked up, visibly annoyed, at the unannounced visit.

Tyra, of course, was the one who spoke up. The spinner had become Heidin's self-appointed personal valet, spokesperson, and secretary.

"Lord Asger, and . . . colleagues . . . this is not a good time. We'll be meeting until sometime this afternoon or this evening. At that time, we will be ready to announce our strategy for our campaign against the barbarian army."

"Is that so?" Asger said. "It sounds like important decisions are being made at this meeting. I find it curious that there are no representatives of your Risen allies here."

Tyra and Heidin looked at each other. "Ah–I believe that Reginn Eiklund was invited but has not come," Tyra said.

"That is because she has disappeared," Asger said.

"Disappeared?" Tyra said, rolling her eyes. "We assumed that she had overslept. She has always kept alehouse hours. Did you check her tent?"

"She is nowhere near here," Asger said, "if she still lives. Any and all planning should be suspended until she is located."

That finally got everyone's attention. He watched the faces of the assembly closely. Most of these had been present while Grima and Reginn traded accusations and the queen ordered everyone out but the aldrnari. Although he had little interest in reading human emotions, he'd become skilled at detecting tells for guilt, lies, and evasion.

Some had seen Reginn fleeing the command tent in the face of the queen's displeasure. So, while all of them kept their mouths closed, theories and suspicions tracked across their faces. The young elders in particular appeared stricken. Asger noticed that one face was missing.

"Where is Grima?" Asger said, taking another look around.

"Grima?" Durinn said. "She is not a part of the command team, so she was not invited to this meeting."

"Has anyone seen her this morning? Or did she oversleep as well?"

Nobody admitted to it.

Asger stole a glance at the queen, surprised that she hadn't contributed. That was highly unusual for the girl he knew as Liv, who had an opinion on everything and did not hesitate to share it.

How long had it been since he'd taken a good look at her? He was surprised at the changes in her, at how little remained that was human. She sat, fists clenched, taut as a bowstring, as if barely under control. If there was any human who could stand fast against a goddess, Liv would be the one.

Gods, he thought. We are in real trouble. But he had to ask.

"Your Majesty?" he said. "I know you met privately with Reginn after the–ah–meeting last night. Did she share any plans with you?"

Heidin pressed her lips together and said nothing, drawing in deep breaths as if in physical pain.

"Perhaps she doesn't consider this to be her fight," Tyra said. "She has never been an enthusiastic supporter of our cause."

"What, exactly, is our cause?" Dainn said, speaking up for the first time. "Or is it possibly *your* cause?"

"Should we be successful in this war," Hrym said, "what outcome are you seeking?"

"Outcome?"

"Do you intend to slaughter everyone in the Archipelago, or would it be enough to persuade them to stay on the other side of the ocean and leave us alone?" Hrym paused. "Keep in mind that the Asgardians and their allies are no threat to the Risen, as we have already paid the ultimate price."

"Why would we slaughter everyone in the Archipelago?" Tyra said.

"What purpose would that serve?"

"For one thing, it would produce an all but inexhaustible supply of blood magic," Asger said. "Who knows? It might provide an opportunity to those Jotun who desire to form a new pantheon of gods."

"How dare you?" Tyra hissed, looking to her council and receiving a muted mumble of outrage and support in return. She was learning that an obedient council is not much trouble, but not much help, either. It looks to its leader to solve problems. "How hypocritical is it for a demon to preach to the rest of us?"

"I never claimed to be innocent," Asger said, shrugging. "If I were innocent, I would not be asking these questions."

"Even if that was the plan–and I am not saying that it is–isn't it a kind of justice that those who stole our legacy would help us win it back?"

"It *might* be justice, if the millers, the fiskers, the farmers and coasters of the Archipelago had stood against you at Ragnarok."

Tyra scowled. She'd always managed to dampen controversy with mind magic. She wasn't used to being asked hard or challenging questions.

At that point, Heidin stood, startling everyone. "I grow weary of this endless and pointless debate." She directed her withering goddess gaze at Asger. "If you seek the traitor, Reginn Eiklund, I told her to leave, or face the consequences for treason."

With that, she swept out of the tent, leaving shocked silence in her wake.

That is likely the first true thing we've heard today, Asger thought. It fit with what he'd seen the night before, when Reginn fled the command tent and disappeared.

"Well then," Tyra said briskly. "As you can tell, the queen is not herself this morning. I should have known better than to convene this meeting under the circumstances."

"She's accusing the aldrnari of *treason*?" Hrym said.

"A misunderstanding that we will no doubt sort out as soon as we get the parties together. Let's take a short recess and make another thorough search of the entire area. If she cannot be found, it may be that Elder Eiklund is gone for good. In that case, perhaps you, Lord Eldr, would be willing to take command of the Risen army."

Tyra obviously saw that command as a prize a power-hungry demon might covet.

"That is not possible," Asger said. "Reginn Eiklund raised this army, as you ordered her to do. She is the only one they will follow. If she cannot be found, you will lose them all. Worse, having no leader, no doubt they will find other, more destructive pursuits. They may blame you for her disappearance."

"Is that a threat, Lord Eldr?"

"I simply suggest that you do everything in your power to locate the aldrnari. Otherwise, you will have a disaster on your hands."

46
COLLARED

REGINN AWOKE TO THE FAMILIAR sound of a sailing ship underway—the creaking of strakes against the pressure of the ocean, the flap of the sail overhead until it found the wind, the sting of cold salt air against her cheeks, and the scent of tar.

Ships take you to places you do not want to go.

Her hands were heavy—manacled together—and a collar chafed against the skin of her neck.

A collar?

Disbelieving, she reached up with both hands and closed her fingers around metal that thrummed with magic. Smooth, jointless—not like the jewel-encrusted thrall collar Asger had forced on her.

But a collar nonetheless. She grasped her staff, reached for magic, and found none. She had a raging headache, a churning stomach, and a sense of hopelessness she could not shake.

She pressed her fingertips against her scalp, willing the pain in her head to either go away or kill her quick.

A memory came back to her—in Eira's shop on Ithavoll. The maker displaying a weapon she'd made at Grima's request—a collar that would suck magic out of a person.

Her past stampeded toward her like a runaway cart, while she stood frozen, unable to outrun it or dodge out of the way.

Your modir sold you for a thrall, and the only escape from thralldom is death. You knew that, and yet you dared hope for something different.

"Reginn!" Someone was shaking her, hard. "Wake up! You're having a nightmare."

Reginn opened her eyes to find Naima leaning over her and was pierced by a shard of hope. Was it only a dream? But when she reached up, the collar was still there, and her wrists still heavy with iron.

"I'm awake," Reginn growled. "Just . . . put me out of my misery. Or give me your knife and I'll do it myself."

"If I still had my knife, I'd consider it," Naima said. "I feel like I woke up on the floor of an alehouse privy."

She seemed to think Reginn was joking.

Naima wore no collar, but her hands were chained together as well. And yes, they were in the bow of a longship, chained to the stem post, beneath a tarp and a pile of blankets that stank of sick.

"Sorry about the smell," Naima said, wrinkling her nose. "I aimed to heave over the side, but I couldn't get that far."

Reginn closed her eyes. "It doesn't matter."

She would not live as a thrall again. There was always a choice–a way out.

They'd taken her access to magic. But not her remedy bag. She could still feel its weight at her waist. Surely, they'd searched it for weapons. But Reginn carried weapons they might not recognize. She wormed her way forward to put some slack into the chain, then bent nearly in half until she could reach the pouch at her waist. Forcing her fingers into the opening, she groped through the contents, finally closing on a smaller, rough-spun pouch.

"What are you doing?" Naima said.

"I think I left some biscuits in my bag." Working by feel, she extracted the smaller pouch from her belt bag, pinching the mouth of it so it wouldn't spill. She wasn't sure how much she had, but she guessed it was enough, if she took it all.

"Oh!" Naima said. "Are you hungry? I nearly forgot. They left us some cheese and kefir and dried fruit." Naima turned away and began rummaging through the stinking blankets.

"I don't need anything else. This will do."

That was a mistake. Reginn never turned down food. Naima swung back around in time to see her upend the pouch, meaning to pour the contents into her mouth.

Naima slapped it out of her hand, sending the contents spraying across the both of them. Reginn tried to save some, but it was a lost cause.

"What are you doing?" Reginn glared at Naima.

"I think that's a better question for you," Naima said. She brushed some of the powder off her sleeve into her palm and took a cautious sniff. "Did you think I wouldn't recognize henbane seeds?"

"What about it? It's not your business."

"You're going to leave me here on my own? I never thought of you as a quitter."

Reginn bit back the response that first came to mind. Then said, "I'm sorry, Naima. I just can't do this anymore."

Naima said nothing, only waited for Reginn to go on.

"It was bad enough coming back here to Muckleholm. And now, within days, I'm locked into a thrall collar again." She closed her eyes, feeling the burn of tears behind her lids.

"Nearly a year ago, I gambled everything to escape thralldom. I ran away from Asger, set fire to a boat, and jumped into deep water even though I couldn't swim. From the time I set foot in New Jotunheim, it's been a constant battle. And for what? Nothing's changed."

"If it *is* a thrall collar, then why don't I have one?"

"Why, are you jealous?"

Naima glared at her.

Reginn tapped the collar with her fingertips. "This collar is especially made to drain or block magic. I saw a sample in Elder Eira's workshop on Ithavoll. She was making them for Grima." She nudged her staff with her knee. "This might as well be a fence post."

Comprehension dawned on Naima's face. "So this is Grima's ship."

"I think so."

"Then why am I here?"

"Well, I assume it was because we were together when–"

"No," Naima said impatiently. "If you're the prize, then I'm the witness nobody needs. If they were worried about leaving a body behind, they could have dumped me overboard once they were out to sea."

"What's your point?"

"My point is, neither of us knows what's ahead. It's probably terrible, but maybe not. Maybe it's a fantastic surprise. Maybe Grima is going to crown us systir queens of the Archipelago."

Reginn rolled her eyes. "Maybe."

It was hard to feel sorry for yourself with Naima around.

"Just promise me you won't give up before we have more information. If the news is bad, I'm sure you'll find a way to escape one way or another."

"Fine," Reginn said, rubbing her aching head. "I promise. I'm out of henbane anyway."

Reginn was awakened by the sound of voices and movement all around them. The tarp was abruptly stripped away, leaving Reginn and Naima shivering in the clammy air. A sailor unlocked the chain binding them to the stem post. Reginn had just enough time to grab her remedy bag, her flute, and her useless staff before she was hauled to her feet. The boat rocked beneath them so that Reginn nearly fell, her limbs made awkward by lack of use. Two crew members helped them across a plank-and-rope bridge to the rocky shore, where they were handed off to four soldiers. By their dress, Reginn guessed that they were members of Grima's personal guard.

What was it she'd called them? Wraiths. One man, three women. All four of them wore narrow gold torcs similar to Reginn's.

Where were they? The air was cool, though not as cold as it had been at sea. When she looked up, she saw no stars overhead–only an impenetrable blackness. The water sloshed against unseen walls all around. Sounds echoed before they died away.

Behind them, the light was a little brighter, revealing an opening. The way in, and maybe the way out.

Was this some sort of boathouse? A cavern?

"Where are we?" Reginn said, her voice unnaturally loud, clamoring against stone.

"Shut up," one of the wraiths hissed.

Apparently, they had shown too much interest in their surroundings, because they were immediately blindfolded. Not that it made much difference in the inky dark. They were led through a series of tunnels and stopped by several sets of guards before they climbed a flight of stairs. Reginn guessed they were aboveground now, since the air was fresher and drier. They took a few more turns, crossed a threshold, and then their blindfolds were stripped away.

They were in a chamber with a wall hearth, a small table and chairs, and a sideboard with a pitcher and basin. Sleeping benches were lined up against another wall, clothing piled on top. Double doors apparently led to the outside, because the room was cold, and the wind howled and leaked between the doors.

Their escorts unlocked their manacles and removed them, but left Reginn's collar in place.

"What about this?" Reginn said, touching her collar. It was worth a shot.

"That doesn't come off," the wraith said, touching her own collar. "You'll get used to it after a while and forget it's there."

No, Reginn thought. I won't.

"We'll come back for you in an hour or so." She wrinkled her nose. "I suggest you wash up and change clothes before then if you don't want to stink up the place."

The four wraiths backed from the room, and Reginn heard the click of a lock.

To be honest, Reginn and Naima didn't want to share a room with themselves in their current state. So by the time their escorts returned, they'd scrubbed off and dressed in the poorly fitting, nondescript but clean gray linen clothes that had been provided. Naima had lost a shoe somewhere, so she went without. When Reginn picked up her staff, one of their escorts said, "Leave that here. It won't do you any good anyway."

They were led down a short hallway and to a door, where they were handed off to a more finely dressed pair that took them inside.

They were met by a wall of laughter, conversation, and calls for more food and drink.

The hall might have belonged to a prosperous jarl in a previous life. It was centered by a large dining table. Every seat was filled by men and women clad in gray linen, as if a winter mist had rolled in off the sea and settled in.

When she looked closely, she saw that they all wore collars, too. Why?

The answer came as quickly as the question. *Grima doesn't trust anyone.*

Conversation stuttered, then died away as the diners noticed the intruders. They then sat silently as the newcomers threaded their way through the gallery that ran along the side of the room. They were nearly at the front when their escorts turned aside, ushering them into a small, private dining room with one occupant–Grima, sitting at the head of the table.

She raised a glass at their entrance. "Welcome to the court of wraiths," she said. "Please–sit down. We have much to talk about."

47

TROUBLE IN THE RANKS

AND SO THE HUNT FOR the missing Reginn Eiklund began.

Officers of the army of New Jotunheim searched the peninsula around Vandrgardr, following the river all the way to the mountains in the east, traveling south into impenetrable swampland, and all the way to Grimsby in the north. Hrym even sent his Risen soldiers into the town, since the dead have no fear of dying and Grimsby was always full of scoundrels of all sorts.

Most of the searchers weren't entirely clear on who they were searching for. Was it Reginn Eiklund, aldrnari, member of the Council of Elders and counselor to the queen, or was it Reginn Eiklund, traitor, who'd helped the notorious Asgardian murderer, Eiric Halvorsen, escape justice?

Only Asger and his commanders were clear on their mission–find Reginn Eiklund and protect her at all costs. They went about their search differently, too. Instead of ranging far and wide, they focused on the footprint surrounding the camp and went over it with a close eye. Asger brought in Garm, the Risen hellhound, to pick up the scent from Reginn's belongings. Since the area around the command tent had been thoroughly over-trampled, Asger led the hound in ever-expanding circles around the camp until he set off, his nose to the ground, in a straight line, away from camp and toward the shore.

The trail ended just within the fringe of trees in a beaten-down patch of undergrowth. There, Garm appeared to lose the scent, trotting back and forth in frustration. Asger oversaw an inch-by-inch search of the area that surfaced a tiny feathered dart, and one of Naima's shoes.

Flanked by the other commanders of the Risen army, he took this evidence to the queen.

At least, he intended to take it to the queen, but when the delegation arrived at her tent, they were told that she was ill and could not see anyone.

"Send Tyra, then," Asger commanded, dripping flames from his fingertips.

"She is looking after the queen," the guard said, backing away and stomping several sparks that came too close.

"Tell Tyra that if she does not appear within the half hour, we will send the Risen army into the countryside to conduct the search ourselves."

"One moment, please," the guard said, and disappeared. He returned in a few minutes and motioned for them to come inside.

The tent was divided into two parts–a reception area just inside, and a curtained-off area in the rear that Asger assumed was the queen's sleeping quarters. From behind the curtain, they could hear screaming and cursing mingled with Tyra's soothing voice.

Heidin's words came clearly. "Modir, back off. Do not try to use your puny mind magic on me. It's time to embrace what we have created."

The commanders looked at each other but had nothing to say.

Finally, the noise died down, and Tyra emerged from the back room. She looked to have aged ten years, her skin drawn taut over bones Asger had never noticed before. Wisps of hair haloed her face, and she gripped her staff as if she needed it for support.

"As you can see, this is not a good time," she said, her voice hoarse from cajoling.

Asger might have been sympathetic, if he were a sympathetic sort of person. Instead, his gut response was annoyance. "It appears that there are no good times coming in the near future, and this matter cannot wait."

Tyra sighed wearily. "If this is about the aldrnari, I don't know what else you want me to do. I wish she had stayed, but she is gone, and so we must make a new plan. The queen is eager to march. You would be the obvious choice to lead the Risen, but if you will not, perhaps you can nominate someone else."

Asger held up the dart by its feathers. "Does this look familiar to you?"

"It appears to be one of our blow darts," Tyra said, as if wary of a trap. "Eira's team developed them for use in clandestine operations when it is important to take down the enemy silently."

"When you say 'take down the enemy,' are we speaking of assassination or incapacitation?"

"Either or both, depending on the agent used," Tyra said. "Eira can tell you more about it. Shall I arrange for–?"

Asger shook his head. "Is anyone using them now?"

"Well, we're not actually–" Tyra paused, thinking. "I believe that Grima was the one who requested them in the first place. She's been using them in her work for several years." Tyra was regaining her imperious footing. "Why was it so urgent to have these questions answered that you would call me from the queen's bedside to–?"

"We tracked Reginn's scent from the command tent into the woods. The trail ended in a spot where there appeared to have been a scuffle. We found this dart on the ground. Also this." He turned to Svend, who dangled Naima's shoe from the tips of his fingers. "The shoe belongs to Naima."

"I assume that you have a theory underpinning all this?"

"As you'll recall, Grima came into our meeting with her private guard and began launching accusations at everyone, including Reginn Eiklund, the queen, and the queen's brodir–Halvorsen. This was not well received, and Heidin ordered everyone out except for the aldrnari. That interview did not go well, either, because Reginn left the tent as if she was being chased by a pack of hellhounds. She fled into the woods, and Naima went after her. I believe they were intercepted by Grima and her hird and either killed or carried off."

"All this based on a lost shoe and a blow dart?" Tyra said wearily. "Why is Grima suddenly a suspect? She has always been loyal to me."

"Has she?" Asger said. "You just found out that she has been keeping secrets from you. She's been building her own hird of spinners here in the Archipelago. She and Heidin have been at odds since Heidin arrived and prevented Halvorsen's execution. She's been trying to get to Halvorsen ever since."

Tyra rubbed her chin, glancing around at the other commanders as if wishing she could make them disappear. "Some of that may have been my influence. Halvorsen wreaks havoc wherever he goes, and I have worried that he is a weakness that my dottir can ill afford."

"Have you told Heidin that?"

"I have tried, but she won't hear it."

"Consider the theory that Reginn Eiklund shared on the night she disappeared."

"That was an impressive bit of storytelling," Tyra said, "but hardly believable."

"No? Well then, let's talk to Grima. I'm sure that she can quickly sort this out."

"Grima," Tyra said, brow furrowed. "That's a problem."

"How so?"

"She's disappeared. I don't know where she is."

"So Grima disappeared the same night as Reginn and Naima, and you don't think that was suspicious?" It seemed that Svend Bondi, normally slow to speak up, could not hold his peace any longer.

Tyra turned an odd, ashy rose color. "Who is this man, Lord Eldr, and why is he privy to this discussion?"

"This is Captain Svend Bondi, who commands the soldiers who

serve alongside the Risen," Asger said. "He is not Risen, but we consider him an honorary officer in the Dead Brigade."

Tyra let it go. "I have always taught my students that the simplest explanation is generally the correct answer. Isn't it more likely that the counselor, being on her home ground and perhaps worried about her future in New Jotunheim, has simply taken her talents elsewhere?"

A new voice entered the discussion. "I think you should listen to Lord Eldr, Modir. What he says makes a lot of sense."

They all spun around, startled.

Heidin had pulled aside the curtain dividing the tent and was standing in her underdress, barefoot. To Asger's eyes, she more closely resembled the woman he'd sailed across the ocean with. How much of their conversation had she heard?

"Dottir, it is not seemly to appear before your subjects in this state of–"

"Listen to me, Modir," Heidin said. "I don't know how much longer I will be clearheaded. Where does Grima stay when she is here in the Archipelago?"

"I really don't–"

"Does she have a headquarters, a hideout, a longhouse here? Where might we find her?"

"Well . . . I know she has a shop in Langvik. . . ."

"We already know that, Modir. Where else? Where might she be training her own spinners and cooking up schemes?"

Tyra hesitated, and Asger guessed that it was in that moment she decided to pitch the assassin overboard. "I don't know for sure, but I have the impression she has a more extensive holding not far from Langvik, accessible by ship. That way she can transport candidates without answering questions. There's a chain of islands south of here that protects the sound at Langvik. Maybe there somewhere."

That would be a lot of territory to cover.

"We'll assemble a team to look for her," Asger said. "We'll take the *Kraken* and her crew and begin a search of Langvik Sound."

"We need to speak with Commander Durinn first," Tyra said. "We'll most likely launch our attack at Kingshavn, which is the seat of Rikhard's power. There's a risk that if you are spotted near Langvik, it will alert the king to our presence."

"I'll speak to Durinn," Asger said. "The *Kraken* is one of the king's ships, and we'll fly the enemy banner. That should allow us to pass anything but a close inspection.

"The Risen army will stay here for now, with orders to wait for our return. You'll want to consider what you'll do if they get tired of waiting."

He could tell that Tyra was furious at this presumption, but he did not care. He would not allow the queen's meddlesome modir to ruin something that had been years in the making.

Asger inclined his head to the queen. "Your Majesty. I hope that, when we meet again, you will be on the mend."

"Thank you, Lord Eldr," Heidin whispered. But when he looked into her eyes, he saw someone who knew she was dying.

One of the elders–Katia, was it?–approached Asger as he and his fisker crew were preparing the *Kraken* for sailing.

"I wondered if I might come along when you search for Reginn and Naima," she said. She looked over her shoulder, as if worried that someone might be watching.

Asger turned away from his work and studied her, surprised. In the past, she'd always given him a wide berth, which was satisfactory, as far as he was concerned.

"I doubt that General Durinn and the kennari will give you permission," Asger said.

"I am not asking permission," Katia said. "I haven't always been as good a friend to Reginn as I should have been. I knew that Grima was a vicious, cruel person, and yet I did nothing." She paused. "It occurs to me that the vaettir, especially the dragons, might be helpful in your search."

Asger had been preparing to say no, but that caught his interest. He'd always had a great respect and affinity for dragons. But a flaming creature on a wooden boat seemed to be a bad idea.

Flaming demons were bad enough.

"I'm worried there is not room for them on our ship," he said.

Katia smiled. "Don't worry. They can fly to me from anywhere in the Archipelago. They won't need a ride."

"Then you–and the vaettir–would be most welcome."

48

NEW STAKES

"PLEASE, SIT DOWN," GRIMA SAID, motioning to two other chairs at the table.

Reginn sat, and Naima followed suit. The table was spread with an array of cold foods–cheese, smoked meats, nuts, and dried fruit.

As usual, the assassin appeared as sleek as a ferret, her hair streaked with color and gathered into braids, collected into a knot on the back of her head. Her tunic and trousers were black and made to measure of the finest wool, but bore the same spider emblem as the wraiths. Reginn and Naima resembled stable hands in comparison. No doubt that was intentional.

Whatever fate awaited them, it was best to meet it with a full stomach. Reginn began to fill a plate.

"Poor little waif," Grima said. "Always hungry. Would you like some wine? Or, perhaps, something stronger?" Seeing their expressions, she laughed. "Come, now. Why would I go to all the trouble to carry you off alive if I meant to turn around and poison you?"

"Maybe you left your best poisons at home," Naima said. "Or maybe you're just not very smart."

Kill me quick, Naima seemed to be saying. *I can't stand the suspense.*

"What shall we do with Naima?" Grima said, speaking to Reginn. "I would have thought she'd have learned some manners by now. She aspires to greatness, but, alas, she does her best work in the kitchen."

"In other words, I nourish people, while you feed on them."

That drew Grima's attention. "Keep telling yourself that, if it makes you feel better." Grima turned back to Reginn. "Forgive me for not hosting you in our large hall, but I have reasons to keep this conversation private."

"I assume that you also have reasons for drugging and abducting two people who are, ostensibly, your allies."

Grima laughed. "I hope that your journey here was not too arduous. Had I more time to plan, I would have arranged much better accommodations. I simply saw an opportunity, and I took it."

"The problem was not the accommodations," Reginn said. "It was the treachery."

"Oh, please." Grima rolled her eyes. "You've been scheming and double-dealing ever since you came to New Jotunheim. Charming everyone with your flute and your stage patter. Claiming to be the aldrnari, the flame, the nourisher of life, speaker to the dead."

"I did not claim that name," Reginn said. "It was forced on me."

Grima waved that away. "Whatever. What matters is that they believe it. I tried to warn them, but Tyra was obsessed with her new pet, and even the old bag, Brenna, was dazzled."

"Jealous, were you?"

Grima ignored that. "It's no coincidence that Halvorsen showed up so soon after you arrived. Did you leave a trail of breadcrumbs across the ocean so that he could find his way there?"

"That's an old story," Reginn said, "and it wasn't believable the first time you told it." She tapped the collar with her fingertips. "Tell me about this."

"Ah," Grima said. "Do you like it? Eira made those for me, to assist in my work finding and recruiting the gifted in the Archipelago. It prevents them from accessing and using their magic without permission. These are particularly useful for children who are too young to be sorted."

"You collar children," Reginn said, struggling to keep her voice matter-of-fact.

"Yes–or we will, once we are able to ramp up production. Eira has a lot on her hands right now."

"Clever," Reginn said. "How do I take it off?"

"You don't," Grima said. "I do, when it suits me. Right now, it doesn't suit me, because it prevents you from accessing magic, and it keeps your pet demon and your dead army from finding you."

"I don't understand," Reginn said. "What's the point of locking me up? Who are you working for?"

"I'm working for myself," Grima said. "Why would I use my talents to elevate someone else? I chose the position of assassin, executioner, and spy because I knew it would open the door to unlimited access to power. The beauty of blood magic is that it allows anyone to aspire to be a god."

"Anyone who is willing to slaughter the innocent," Reginn said.

"The beauty of it is that the guilty count, too. Who is innocent–your murderous cook here, who killed a member of the Council of Elders? The beloved kennari, who coupled with a barbarian and had a nightmare of a child? The kiss of flame and a wash of gold does not change her basic nature. Your Asgardian lover who killed hundreds of our soldiers, the rest of the elders, and the keeper? Your demon familiar, who leaves a trail of dead behind him wherever he goes?

"I'm not passing judgment–far from it. I rather admire the splash you've made. The point is, there are no innocents in this story, and innocence and guilt have nothing to do with alliances. It's all about strength and weakness. An alliance with the weak is like dragging a boulder behind you wherever you go. It slows you down, wears you out, and makes you less nimble. You cannot protect them, and in the end, you both lose."

"Are you saying that you'll align with anyone, no matter how despicable, if it strengthens your hand? And break that alliance when it suits you?"

Grima nodded. "That's fair, I suppose."

"You still haven't answered my question—why am I here?"

"You are the first of the academy recruits whose talents complement mine."

"How so?" Reginn said, thinking, I really don't want to share any talents with you.

"I send people to the deadlands and so collect blood magic. You bring them back compliant and ready to serve—the perfect soldiers."

"You're making a lot of assumptions," Reginn said, recalling the "mutiny" aboard ship. "We don't know much about the Risen or how they will fare in battle, and how long their loyalty and compliance might persist. They might just go rogue."

"What I've seen has impressed me so far," Grima said. "So much that I propose an alliance—you, me, and Halvorsen."

It was so preposterous that it was all Reginn could do not to burst out laughing. Instead, it came out as a snort. "Halvorsen? The man you tried so hard to kill in Langvik?"

"That I was unsuccessful is impressive," Grima said.

"I'm not sure he'll see it that way," Reginn said, rolling her eyes. "I cannot imagine anything that would convince Halvorsen to partner with you."

"You are the key," Grima said. "Once he knows that you're in, he'll sign on right away." As if unable to contain herself, she rose and began pacing back and forth. "Think of it! With the three of us, and your army—no one will be able to stand against us."

"You might be right," Reginn said. "Remove this collar, and I'll call my army here. Then we can discuss a partnership on a more equal footing. Otherwise, I'm just another thrall."

I've done that.

"As you may have noticed, nearly all of my wraiths wear collars."

"Seems to me your collared wraiths are servants, not partners or peers. If I am mistaken, why not give them a choice?"

How stupid do you think I am?

Grima shrugged as if she didn't care, but Reginn could tell she was irritated. "Have it your way," she said. "Be a game piece, not a player. But make no mistake, we will make Halvorsen an offer he will not refuse."

"Release my assistant, at least," Reginn said. "Naima has nothing to do with any arrangement between us."

"No," Grima said. "I have a feeling that the cook may prove useful after all." She gestured to her guard. "Return them to their quarters to think about it. Find the barefoot cook some shoes."

Later, when they were alone, Reginn said, "Naima, please listen to me."

Naima was sitting cross-legged on the bed, trying to master a sailor's knot. She looked up. "Listening," she said.

"Grima is not interested in partnering with anybody," Reginn said. "She doesn't play well with others. She's been betraying Tyra and the council for years, and I have no reason to believe she would play it straight with me, let alone Eiric. She hates both of us. I've been trying to figure out why they didn't dump you in the ocean between here and Vandrgardr, and I think I may have figured it out."

Naima's hands stopped moving. "Really? Tell me more."

"I believe she plans to use you somehow. Eiric knows you, and if you bring him terms of a deal, he may trust it, coming from you."

"I think you're giving me too much credit. I met the man only once, and then gave him a send-off to the deadlands."

"Still–will you promise me something?"

"Such as?" Naima said, frowning at a tangle that would not yield.

"Promise me you won't play emissary. If she sends you out as a messenger, find yourself a safe place and wait this thing out. If you give him her message, it will be a trap."

"Mmm," Naima said. "And then what happens to you?"

"I'll be fine," Reginn said. When Naima looked skeptical, she added, "I have a secret plan. Trust me."

"I don't trust you and I won't promise you," Naima said. "I'll make my own decision if and when the time comes."

"At least wear this." Reginn dropped a silver chain and pendant into Naima's hand.

Naima examined both sides of the pendant. "What are these–runes? You know I don't know anything about runes. They're useless to me."

"Just wear it–please, in memory of me," Reginn said. "It may help."

They came for Naima two days later. In the early morning they woke her from a sound sleep and told her to gather her belongings.

"Will I be coming back here?" Naima said.

The guard rocked his hand. "Doubtful," he said. "Better say your goodbyes now."

Still blinking away sleep, Naima and Reginn embraced.

"That's long enough," the guard said. "Hurry up, or we're going to miss the tide."

"Where are we going?" Naima said.

"You'll find out."

"Remember what I said." Reginn blotted her eyes with the backs of her hands.

"Remember what *I* said," Naima shot back. And then she was gone.

49

THE KING'S STYRMAN

AS IT BECAME CLEAR THAT Eiric intended to stay in the Archipelago and fight alongside his brodir, the king did everything he could to reinforce that decision. He housed both of them in his finest guest lodging, sought Eiric's advice on matters large and small, offered the services of his armorer, and made it clear that all his needs would be met, from food and drink to custom clothes to music and someone to share his bed if he liked. He sent the fiskers to the armorer to evaluate their weapons and suggest changes that would make their stolen weapons more suitable to their size and skills.

Eiric was familiar with basic battlefield strategies such as the shield wall, but he knew little about war tactics in a larger army, having mostly fought with smaller, hit-and-run raiding parties. To him, a battle was a collection of one-on-one contests between individual warriors, and the side with the most left standing at the end was the winner.

Even in a naval battle, the object was to board the enemy ship and kill their crew before they killed yours.

Rikhard, on the other hand, had ten years of war behind him with a large, experienced army, a fleet of ships, and better weaponry than Eiric had ever seen in the Archipelago. How important, really, was any individual soldier in winning this sort of war? Yet Rikhard introduced Eiric to all his officers and showed him off in every possible way.

"Why?" Eiric asked the king after he was trotted out for the fifth or sixth time. "I'm probably less use to you than most of your experienced battlefield commanders."

"Armies fight with their hearts as well as their bodies," Rikhard said. "They need to believe that the gods are on their side."

"I'm not a god," Eiric said.

Rikhard laughed. "Close enough."

Eiric spent time sparring with Ivar, who'd had considerable training in swordsmanship and archery, but had never heard of lausatok, the hand-to-hand grappling Leif and Bjorn had taught Eiric as a prelude to weapons work.

Ivar's natural agility, speed, and grace were all but otherworldly. Where had that come from? Not from Sten.

This is what I should have been doing these ten years, Eiric thought—teaching my brodir how to stay alive.

Ever since Eiric's arrival, the king had been urging him to return to Sundgard, to survey the work in the boathouses and choose a larger ship to command.

Eiric was not keen on the idea. A brand-new ship always required some work to address flaws that were overlooked during the building. And it seemed unlikely that the king kept any of his best ships idle at Sundgard, in case a styrman happened by.

"*Firebird* suits me," he said, "and I've got a crew that suits me, too. We work well together. Why would I want to make a change?"

"A bigger ship means that you can carry more warriors, giving you a larger footprint in any battle," Rikhard said. "You will become a target once it's known that you are here. I have a ship in mind that I think will suit you." Rikhard paused and, when Eiric didn't answer right away, said, "Besides, it's past time for Hilde's lying in, and we haven't heard anything from Sundgard for a week."

Eiric reluctantly agreed to have a look at this ship Rikhard was recommending. They set sail in *Firebird*, crewed by the fiskers, because he wanted their opinions on this new ship as well.

A bit of sunshine had returned to Muckleholm, taking the edge off the cold, and it was always good to get out on the water for any reason. Rikhard sat midships, with two of his hird near at hand, while Eiric and his crew took their turns at the styrboard and the sails.

"Isn't it confusing to have your crew members shifting from task to task?" Rikhard said. "Wouldn't a little more focus enhance their skills in a given position?"

He addressed this to Eiric, but received answers from every direction.

"On a small ship, the crew is often called to pitch in on a variety of jobs," Rorik said.

"It would be boring to do the same thing every day on a long voyage," Levi said. "Especially if it's digging latrines." He slid a look at Eiric.

"If we had only one styrman," Reyna said, "and Halvorsen got drunk and fell overboard, we'd be lost."

Rikhard looked somewhat alarmed at Eiric's unfiltered, outspoken crew, but didn't say so out loud.

That's the difference between you and me, remember? Kings inherit their thrones as a birthright. Styrmen choose their crews, and crews choose a styrman.

Eventually, they turned west, into Eiric's home sound. Between a fair wind and the incoming tide, they flew across the surface of the water like a skimmer.

Eiric was surprised he didn't see more traffic in the sound. Between the foundries, the smithies, and the boatyard, he would expect a lot of coming and going. The plumes of smoke that usually rose over the shoulder of the hill, marking the manufactories, were missing, too.

Is there a blot or a festival that I don't know about?

They rounded the headland and the foundry came into view. It appeared to be deserted, the furnaces cold, though, oddly, the air was thick with the scent of woodsmoke.

Something's *burning,* he thought. Or has burned.

There was no activity at the boatyard or the smithies, either. Tools, equipment, and materials were all there, as far as he could see. Just no people.

"Where is everybody?" Ivar muttered.

When the farmstead came into view, they saw the source of the woodsmoke–the longhouse was a smoldering ruin. The roof was gone completely, and even the great pillars were scorched, with some nearly burned through.

"Hilde," Ivar whispered. He planted his hands, meaning to vault over the gunwale and into the shallows, but for the king's hand holding him in place.

"Wait," Rikhard said, scanning the shoreline and the ruins of the buildings beyond. "It might be a trap."

"I–don't–care–if it's a trap," Ivar said, trying to twist away from the king's grip. "Let me go."

"Stay, brodir," Eiric said. "The best time to care about traps is before you're in one." He rolled over the side, planted his feet in the shoreward muck, and steadied the rocking ship with one hand. "Rorik, Levi, come with me. Ivar, whoever did this might be long gone, or they may be waiting to ambush us on our way out of the sound. We don't have enough crew to fight off a force of any size, so we don't take that fight.

"You know this sound as well or better than anyone. Will you serve as styrman and help the rest of the crew get the king safely back to Kingshavn?"

Ivar glowered at him, his lips pressed together as if to keep words from spilling out. Something he must have done all his life.

"Then you can return with the larger army, if the king approves," Eiric said.

"And what, exactly, will you be doing in the meantime?" Ivar said, keeping his eyes fixed on the thwarts beneath his feet.

"Look at me, Ivar," Eiric said.

Ivar looked up at Eiric, his eyes so much like Sylvi's that Eiric's breath caught in his throat.

"I'm not here for the fight," Eiric said, "though I'll fight if I have to. I'm here for any possible survivors. Something happened here, and I need to find out what it was. Understand?"

Ivar nodded.

"Some things, once seen, cannot be unseen, Ivar. You will see terrible things soon enough. You don't need to see them right now."

"What about you?" Ivar said. "What if it's an ambush?"

"Ivar's right, Halvorsen," Rikhard said. "There is no reason that you need to take this risk. We can go back to Kingshavn, gather a substantial force, and return in strength."

Eiric shook his head. "Though it no longer belongs to me, I still consider this my home. I grew up here, and much of what I've learned, for better or worse, I learned here. My modir burned on yonder headland, and it was here that my grandfadir and I built our first ship.

"There may be survivors I can help, or property that can be saved. I'll try to put things in order before you return." He met Rikhard's eyes, and the king nodded his understanding. Ivar did not remember Sylvi, who had died to save his life. Hilde had been like a modir to Ivar, and that was what Eiric wanted him to remember.

50
SUNDGARD

EIRIC, LEVI, AND RORIK WADED to shore, their weapons in hand, but they saw no movement at the docks or amid the ruins. Eiric turned around in time to see *Firebird*'s sail climbing the mast, fluttering a little until it filled with the northwest winds that blew into the landward end of the sound in winter. He saw the red smudge of Ivar's hair as he took his place at the styrboard.

Eiric surveyed the home place. The house and the summer barn were charred ruins, although the boathouse appeared intact. That would be the most likely place for survivors–or the enemy–to take shelter. There were no signs of fighting in the home yard–no bodies or weapons or dropped belongings.

"Spread out a little," Eiric said to Levi and Rorik. "It looks like a hit-and-run, but we can't be sure. Give me a shout if you see anyone moving. I'm going to take a look in the house first."

Rorik and Levi nodded, grim-faced.

Oddly, the heavily carved posts on either side of the door were intact, as was the door, providing the illusion of normalcy, though it was a door to nowhere.

Slabs of wood had been nailed over the door from top to bottom, a hasty, sloppy job, but effective. It was a jarring reminder of the day that he and Liv had barricaded those same doors from the inside, to keep Sten out.

This was not intended to keep danger out, but to keep something or someone inside.

A symbol had been carved into the door, the raw wood contrasting with the weathered oak surrounding it. Eiric looked more closely, then recoiled, recognition gutting him.

It was the blodkyn rune.

Eiric took a deep breath, let it out. Turned to look at the *Firebird*, growing smaller and smaller in the distance. He was glad he'd sent them away. He felt responsible for leading this curse to their door.

He stepped back from the threshold and circled around the ruined longhouse to where the side door had been, between the main hall and what he'd known as the winter barn but was now space that Hilde had claimed for her own. That part of the building was almost completely destroyed, but here, too, he saw evidence that the door had been barricaded from the outside using split logs from the woodpile.

He drew Gramr, holding the blade vertical as he peered through what had been the doorway. A blackened body lay at his feet, as if someone had nearly escaped the flames, but died before making it out. The smell of charred flesh mingled with woodsmoke.

Eiric was no stranger to violence and death, but it was different when it was visited on a place that had housed so much of his own history.

With the roof gone, sunlight slanted in from above, casting shadows so that everything looked unfamiliar and sinister.

"Hello!" Eiric shouted into echoing silence. "Is anyone here?"

Is anyone alive?

There was no answer.

He stepped over the body that lay across the threshold and kicked aside some fallen debris blocking the dog run. As he entered the hall, a flock of ravens rose into the air, complaining bitterly about the interruption.

Most of the dead were in the main hall, perhaps a hundred people. There were a few children, but mainly working-age adults. Some still wore leather aprons and other work clothes from the smithies, the foundries, the boatyard.

A few were charred beyond recognition, but most seemed to have died from the smoke, leaving even their clothing intact. Eiric took a quick walk around the main hall, but did not see Hilde or her dottirs.

In one corner, huddled against the wall, were the bodies of his stepuncles and grandfadir. Finni, Garth, and Gustav. He'd had plenty of cause to wish them dead, but he found no pleasure in it now.

Finni appeared the most intact, so Eiric took a moment to examine him more closely. When he rolled him over, he found that his hands were bound, and the blodkyn rune was carved into the back of his head. Given the amount of blood, he was probably still alive when it was done.

Eiric sat back on his heels, swallowing down the bitterness that rose in his throat. It was, in a way, a kind of justice for all the crimes, known and unknown, that the Knudsens had committed, beginning with Sylvi's death, Sten's attempt to murder Eiric and Liv, their disinheritance, Eiric's exile, and, finally, Emi's burning.

He did not question that they deserved it. What haunted him was the suspicion that it had been his systir who did it. Liv. Or, rather, the creature that had possessed her.

Would Liv return to Sundgard, where they had become brodir and systir, where they had developed the fierce bond that had sustained them through all kinds of trouble? Would she return here now and burn it to the ground, with innocent people inside, boarding up the doors so that they could not escape?

He would not, could not allow himself to believe that.

Eiric examined several more bodies, and found that all of them were marked with the blodkyn rune. He gave up trying to keep a count, simply looking for anyone else he recognized. He had no way to inventory any takings, since he didn't know what was there to take. In truth, he was stalling, putting off entering Hilde's quarters in the former winter barn.

Liv would not kill Hilde. That, he knew.

He was not so sure about Heidin.

When he could put it off no longer, he returned to the rear of the hall and ducked through the doorway into Hilde's private quarters, hoping to find nobody there.

In that, as in so many things, he was disappointed.

As soon as he entered Hilde's quarters, Eiric's attention was drawn to light leaking through a hole that had been hacked into the far wall. It illuminated three bodies, arranged like spokes around the opening.

Frida and Gudrun were nestled together on the earthen floor. Hilde lay face up next to them, one arm flung over her two dottirs, as if she were still protecting them in the deadlands. An axe lay by her other hand, and an arrow transfixed her throat. Her swollen belly was rimed by the light from the window.

Hilde, a warrior in her own way, had been chopping through a wall in order to save those she loved. Just another hero in a sad story that he was duty-bound to live.

"Styrman?"

Eiric looked up to see Levi silhouetted in the ruined doorway.

"Everything is quiet outside."

"Good," Eiric said.

"Can you tell what happened?"

"They forced everyone into the longhouse, boarded up the doors, and then set it on fire."

"Hilde? The girls?"

Eiric shook his head, unable to speak, and gestured toward the bodies on the floor.

Levi squatted next to him, then reached out and straightened

Gudrun's sleeve. He seemed visibly shaken. "Who would do this?"

"Have a look at this arrow and tell me what you think."

Levi fingered the shaft, the fletching. "I would say that it was made in the fletcheries on Ithavoll," he said.

Eiric nodded. "That's what I thought, too." He scrubbed his hands over his face.

"So it must have been the Jotun army," Levi said.

"Seems that way."

"May I ask a question?"

"Of course."

"Why would they come here?" When Eiric didn't answer right away, Levi hurried on. "They must have arrived on the east side of the island, like we did, where there are rich cities for the taking. Instead, they circled around and attacked this place when right up the shoreline is Kingshavn."

"They might have guessed that Kingshavn would be a harder target. Or maybe they wanted to send a message."

"What message? To whom?"

The fisker's questions were taking Eiric to places that he did not want to go. "Levi, I know you have questions, but I'm all out of answers. Let's search the rest of the property and then maybe we'll have a better idea about what to report to the king."

The boathouse was next, given that it was the only building still standing. He was surprised, because it seemed like an obvious target. Then again, they'd left the foundries, the smithies, and the boatyard intact. They'd just removed the people. Perhaps that meant they planned to move new people in.

As far as he knew, there were no spinners there.

Rorik met them on their way to the boathouse. The three of them approached the wide doors that faced the sea, but then thought better of it. Instead, they circled around to the back door.

The interior was chilly and dark, the hearth cold, the oil lamps unlit, but Eiric could see the silhouette of the dragon ship, apparently unmoved from where they'd last seen it.

"I can't believe they left this ship behind," Rorik muttered.

"Maybe they plan to come back for it," Levi said. "There's always a need for good ships."

Rorik lit lamps with his strike-steel, and Eiric and Levi followed on with a superficial search of the building. They found no survivors—or dead bodies. The tools and supplies appeared to be right where they'd left them.

Just as they were finishing searching the boathouse, Levi called out, "I see four ships in the sound, flying the king's banner."

51
THE RELUCTANT GUEST

Don't mourn what you've lost, use what you have.

–Tove

REGINN KEPT THINKING ABOUT TOVE'S lesson while sitting alone in her cell in the days after Naima was taken away. It seemed that she had lost everything–her friend, her freedom, her access to magic. The coaster who never failed to steal her breath away and set her heart to hammering.

What was left? Her wits, her patter, her flute, the magic of her own mind. Her memory of the lessons Tove had taught her.

The runes. Would they still work with the collar on? That was a magic so old that neither Grima nor Eira would have heard of it.

The dead. The voices of the dead still came through, though faintly. Local voices.

Bodi? Where are you?

I'm cold.

I want something to eat.

There might be a lot of dead people wandering Grima's keep, but it seemed to have been emptied of the living. Reginn no longer heard scraps of conversation from servants hurrying down the halls. Someone was cooking, because her meals kept coming, but they were all delivered by two of the same four wraiths. Where was everyone else?

When the nattmal was brought in, Reginn said, "Could you let–" She stopped, at a loss for a title. "Could you let Elder Grima know that I am ready to discuss our alliance?"

"Lady Grima won't be back for several more days," one of the wraiths said. She was young and fresh-faced.

The other wraith glared at her companion. "Keila! Lady Grima's comings and goings are not ours to share."

"That's disappointing," Reginn said. "I had understood that we would be meeting today or tomorrow. This is wasted time that we cannot get back. My commanders will not wait forever."

The wraith shifted her weight, as if put off-balance by Reginn's patter. "I will let Lady Grima know of your interest in speaking with her when she returns."

"The sooner the better," Reginn said. "What is your name?"

"Atla," the wraith said reluctantly.

"I don't mean to add to your burden, Atla. I know you're probably busy, being short-staffed and all."

"Who said we were short-staffed?"

Reginn lifted an eyebrow. "Fortunately, my needs are simple, and easily met. I love the terrace, but it is quite cold and windy. In order to make use of it, I require a warm coat, a hat, a lap blanket, and gloves–"

Atla rolled her eyes. "You *require*–"

"It's freezing out," the friendly wraith–Keila–said. "Why would you want to go out there? My hands get so chapped this time of year."

"Really? Let me see."

The wraith extended her hands, which were cracked and bleeding.

"I have something that would help that," Reginn said. "Let me fetch my–"

"Keila!" Atla said. "Let's go. We have too much work to do."

Keila jerked her hands back. "I just mentioned that my hands–"

"It will just take a moment," Reginn said. She rooted in her remedy bag and came up with a small, stoppered jar. "Here," she said, handing it to Keila. "It's lanolin cream, for your hands. Use it morning and night. At night, rub it in and then wrap your hands with linen strips so it doesn't get all over your bedclothes. Otherwise, you'll smell like you're sleeping in a sheep shed."

"Th-thank you," Keila said, cradling the jar in her hands. "I'll give it a try."

"Now, come on," Atla said. In the doorway, she turned back to Reginn. "I will see what I can do about the clothes."

The warm clothes came quickly, as if Reginn had put Atla off-balance, and so she was hedging her bets.

Use what you have. Reginn had a lifetime of experience at gathering information in casual conversation that could be used in foretelling.

The next time Keila brought a meal, Reginn asked her to bring it out onto the terrace and set it on the small table.

"Look at this view," Reginn said, sweeping her arm in a wide arc.

"Beautiful," Keila said, teeth chattering, chafing her arms to warm them. She pointed at the bowl of stew. "You should probably eat that before it gets cold." She turned to go back inside.

"Stay a minute," Reginn said. "I had a couple of questions about the view." She handed Keila the lap blanket. "Wrap up in this."

Keila did. Reginn picked up the bowl and began to eat standing up.

They were looking east across a narrow sound to what appeared to be a much larger island. Reginn could see the lights of a town across the water, kindling as the sun set behind them.

"Where are we, exactly?"

"We always called it Klettrholm–island of cliffs. It's one of the Sudreyjars–maybe the smallest, and farthest east."

Reginn tried to conjure up the maps she'd seen. So that was Muckleholm they were looking at. They hadn't traveled that far after all.

"I'm all turned around," Reginn said. She pointed to the lights across the water. "Is that Langvik?"

Keila shook her head. "Sweinhavn."

"Have you been there?"

"That's where I was born," Keila said.

"Really? Do you still have family there?

Keila nodded, gazing across the ruffled gray water to the far shore. "Everyone–my modir, fadir, a little brodir."

Having finished the stew, Reginn set the bowl down and picked up an apple. "Good thing you're close enough to go back for visits."

"Not really," Keila said wistfully. "We're not allowed to leave Klettrholm without permission. I haven't seen my family for four years."

"Are there no boats?" Reginn said. "Grima doesn't need to know."

"But that's just it–she would know." Keila touched her collar. "She can track us with this."

Reginn frowned. "Really? Is that what she told you, or have you seen this for yourself?"

"Several wraiths who left were brought back and executed," Keila said. "I suppose she could have found them some other way, but . . ."

"What else does the collar do?"

Keila glanced back at the veranda doors, then leaned in close so she could be heard over the wind. "I don't know for sure, but people say it collects magic."

"I don't understand," Reginn said.

"It collects power–potency," Keila said.

"Do you mean megin?" Reginn said.

Keila shrugged. "I don't know what it's called. We cannot perform spinner magic while wearing the collar without Grima's permission. But the collar stores it, so that later, it can be used, by the wraith it came from or it can be transferred to someone else. So it's not wasted."

"But–how is the collar controlled? How is it turned off and on? How is the power transferred?"

"I don't know," Keila said, raising both hands to ward off questions. "Atla knows all about it. Ask her."

There it was–the perfect solution for rebellious and insubordinate spinners, and one that did not require killing them in order to gain access to blood magic. Grima could have an entire hird of uncooperative spinners and still put them to use, milking them of magic.

Maybe that was what Grima had in mind for the Archipelago. That thought pierced Reginn like shards of ice. Did Eira have any idea how her creation was being used?

Eira would know how it worked–how to beat it. If Reginn lived long enough to ask her about it.

"Are there any spinners who are not required to wear collars?"

Keila shrugged. "Everyone wears a collar," she said. "But I suspect that the spinners in her personal guard–like Atla–their collars might be inactivated."

So it would be difficult to tell who could access magic and who could not. "When will Grima be back?" Reginn was pushing her luck, but Keila seemed to enjoy talking to someone who wasn't Atla.

Keila glanced back toward the terrace doors. "Atla said it might be three more days."

"Where did she go?"

"I heard that they were sailing around to the other side of the island, to raid a farm over there."

"A farm? They couldn't choose a farm on this side of Muckleholm?"

"It had to be this farm in particular. I think it belongs to the king, and she wanted to poke him in the nose."

At least it isn't Sundgard. Assuming it still exists.

A bell sounded somewhere above. Keila jumped, as if startled. "Um . . . Reginn? I'm going to need to get back." She slipped the wrap from her shoulders, folded it, and laid it on the chair.

"One more question," Reginn said as Keila scooped up the tray. "How are your hands feeling?"

"Much better, thank you," Keila said, and shouldered her way through the terrace doors.

Reginn stared out at the waves, the northwest wind teasing her hair out from under her cap. She'd learned a lot in this brief conversation.

Now, how to use it.

52
THE ARRANGEMENT

EIRIC HAD SEEN HIS SHARE of violent death—maybe more than his share—but not so many massacres of innocents. During their summer raids, Bjorn sanctioned a hard hand to put down resistance, but he discouraged needless killing and even the taking of thralls and concubines.

Some coasters complained about it—but not to Bjorn. It was safer to complain to his grandson at the market or the alehouse.

Eiric asked Bjorn about it once, one winter evening when they were plying rope in the boathouse.

"Some say the takings aren't as good," Eiric said. "They say they might sign on with somebody else."

"That's their choice," Bjorn said, shrugging. "I've never had trouble filling out a crew. My ship, my rules."

"Why do you have different rules?"

Bjorn tied off the end of the rope and began coiling it over his shoulder. "We go vikingr because the fates have dealt us a difficult hand. The weather grows harsher every year. Here at Sundgard, we're more fortunate than most, but, still—it is harder than ever to support a household on farming and fishing alone.

"The people we raid are not our enemies—they're our rivals. If we're strong enough, and smart enough, we take what they have. If they're stronger, they take what we have. It's the way the world works.

"Why would we slaughter everyone, carry off the able-bodied, burn down their houses, and salt the fields? That turns rivals into enemies. No. Instead, we leave them the means to rebuild."

He grinned. "And that means there'll be something to steal when we come back in a year or two."

Whoever raided Sundgard had a different philosophy. This was a fist to the belly. A blade to the gut from someone holding a grudge.

Liv?

Eiric met the king and his retinue on the shore. He put his hand on his brodir's shoulder, but Ivar flinched away. "It's bad news, Ivar. The worst news. I'm sorry."

"Are there any survivors?" Rikhard scanned the yard. The only ones moving were Eiric's crew, collecting bodies. "Any witnesses?"

"No survivors," Eiric said. "No witnesses."

Ivar took a deep breath, then released it in a rush of sorrow. "Where is she?"

Eiric led Rikhard and Ivar and the others to the dog run door.

"I told my crew to leave this be until you came," Eiric said. "It's your choice, brodir. You don't need to see this if you don't want to carry this memory with you. No one will think badly of you."

"I will see her," Ivar said through gritted teeth.

Eiric nodded and led the way.

The autumn sun was nearing the horizon. It was growing late, shadows deepening in the corners. The light through the gash in the wall had shifted away from Hilde and her dottirs so that they now rested in twilight. Ivar knelt next to Hilde's body and brushed his fingers over her cheek.

To Eiric's surprise, Rikhard knelt on her other side, his expression grim and grieving and furious all at once. The three of them seemed to be bound together by tragedy, leaving Eiric on the outside.

"Be at peace, Hilde Stevenson," the king said. He rested his hand lightly on her swollen belly. "Be at peace, Little Prince."

Little Prince?

Speaking of a blade to the gut—this revelation took his breath, and all but sent him reeling. He took another look at Rikhard's grief-stricken expression. He knew that Hilde and the king liked and respected each other. Rikhard had given her the farm, after all. He remembered that she had defended Rikhard when Eiric first returned from Eimyrja. But he'd never seen any obvious displays of affection between them.

He'd missed it, like he'd missed so many other things.

Liv had often accused Eiric of blundering through relationships like a bull in the temple, oblivious of the damage left in his wake. She never hesitated to point out his shortcomings.

One day she returned from town and came to find him where he was busy chopping wood for the coming winter. Always, always chopping wood.

Liv went straight to the point. "I know you're not stupid, brodir, so you must be blind and deaf. Your summer girl is in love with you, and you broke her heart."

He'd looked up, mopping sweat from his face with his sleeve. "What girl? Shelba?"

Liv nodded.

"That doesn't make any sense," Eiric said. "We spent the Disting together and then she sailed with me for part of the summer. She told me she wasn't interested in anything more than that. So we parted as friends."

"Just because she said that, brodir, doesn't mean it's true." Rolling her eyes, Liv walked away, leaving him shaking his head.

Still. He wanted that eye-rolling Liv back again.

Eventually, Ivar moved on to pay his respects to his foster systirs, Gudrun and Frida. After a few minutes, he sat back on his heels and looked up at Eiric. "What are these markings? Most of the dead seem to have them." He pointed to the blood-encrusted scratches on Frida's upper arm.

"It's also painted on some of the doors," the king said.

Eiric's heart sank. This was not a burden he wanted his brodir to carry. But he'd made himself a promise that he would tell the truth to Ivar.

"It's called the blodkyn rune. It channels power to the slayer from the slain."

Ivar shook his head. "I'm not sure I understand."

"It means that if I kill an enemy on the battlefield–"

"Or in their beds, or by the hearth," Rikhard interjected.

"–their power is added to mine."

Understanding dawned in Ivar's eyes. "So. All those people who died in the longhouse–"

"Serve to strengthen the enemy," Eiric said. "It's called blood magic."

Abruptly, Rikhard stood. "It's been several days, so we had better see to the bodies." He turned to his hird. "I want the royal consort and her dottirs prepared for their sending with all honors. We'd best do that tonight."

It seemed that Rikhard's hird was practiced at arranging sendings on short notice. By nightfall, two pyres were burning on the headland–one devoted to Hilde and her dottirs, the other for the rest of the dead. It was a clear night, unusual for the time of year, and sparks rose and mingled with the stars overhead.

As chief mourners, Rikhard and Ivar sat together, the king's arm around Ivar's shoulders. Eiric and his crew sat nearby, passing a jar of mead back and forth, as gloomy as Fimbulwinter.

"I'm sorry about your farm–and everything," Reyna said.

"Not my farm," Eiric murmured.

"It should be," Rorik said loyally.

"I don't want it," Eiric said. "I'm not a farmer." He pointed to the flames rising over the dark sound. "My modir and grandfadir burned there, too."

There was nothing to say for a long time.

"Frida and Gudrun were kind," Levi said, "even when we came stinking off our ship."

"Frida kissed me once," Nils said.

"Who cares?" Reyna said.

After a long silence, Rorik said, "So. Hilde and the king. How about that?"

"No," Eiric said, quelling him with a look.

"Eiric," Levi said, pointing toward where the king and Ivar were sitting.

Ivar was lying on his side, Rikhard on his knees beside him.

"Ivar!" Rikhard was saying, his voice low and urgent.

Eiric's first thought was that Grima had somehow gotten to him.

In a few long steps, he was beside them. As soon as he got a closer look, he knew. Tremors rolled through Ivar's body like the earth-shakes that sometimes happened along the rifts where the land broke apart.

Two members of Rikhard's hird stood by, looking as useless as Eiric felt.

"Is there anything you need?" Eiric said. "Anything I can do?"

"The worst is over," Rikhard said, his face drawn. "This hasn't happened in a long time."

Gradually, the tremors eased, and Ivar's rigid muscles relaxed. Rikhard stroked his hair with what appeared to be real affection.

Ivar's eyes fluttered open in a face clouded with confusion.

"Your private gods are at war again," Rikhard said.

Ivar swore softly, a stream of invective too powerful for any ten-year-old to know.

Eiric offered him a few swallows from his flask, and then he and the king together helped him to his feet.

Rikhard motioned to the two warriors. "Could you take Lord Ivar back to his quarters?" he said. "He's done for the night."

"Your Majesty?" one of the guards said. "Where are his quarters?"

The question neatly captured Ivar's losses.

"Take him back to my ship, and put him to bed in my cabin," Rikhard said.

"I'll come with you," Eiric said, in case he could offer help ten years late.

As they walked toward the beach, Eiric supporting Ivar with an arm around his waist, he heard the two guards' muttered conversation.

"It isn't right," one of them said. "The boy's bewitched."

"The king's in danger, and he just won't see it. And when something happens, we'll get the blame."

It took considerable effort for Eiric to keep his mouth shut until Ivar was settled on the sleeping bench in Rikhard's cabin.

By the time Eiric returned to the vigil, the bonefires had burned to embers, and the conversation had long since died away, too. It was deathly cold, and growing colder, the slaughter moon rising in the crystalline air. Rorik and Levi were asleep, and Nils and Reyna sat in a mead-fueled stupor. Rikhard still sat alone.

Eiric shook the sleepers awake. "Go back to the boathouse, and try to get some sleep. I'll take the watch aboard *Firebird*. Tomorrow we'll decide what we're going to do."

"Will we go after the ones that did this?" Nils said.

"We'll talk about it tomorrow," Eiric said.

When the fiskers had gone, Eiric crossed the headland to where Rikhard sat, staring out to sea. Eiric sensed new pain, new tension, new hostility in the king. He sat down beside him, and for a long while neither said anything.

"Your Majesty," Eiric began, the words unfamiliar in his mouth.

"You're wondering about Hilde–and the baby," Rikhard snapped.

"Yes," Eiric said.

"Hilde was carrying my heir," Rikhard said.

"I see," Eiric said. He picked up a stick and stirred the ashes.

After another brief silence, Rikhard said, "Speak, Halvorsen. What's on your mind?"

"Why has she not been recognized as consort . . . until now?" Eiric said.

"Now she–and my son–are beyond the reach of my enemies," Rikhard said.

"So they are . . . now," Eiric said. "It's a shame that no one was here to–"

"Blood and bone, Halvorsen! You have the dubious gift of making your opinion plain even when you say nothing at all." The king snapped a stick of kindling over his knee and hurled the pieces into the sea.

"I am not skilled at courtly–"

"You are *not* skilled at deferring judgment until you know all the facts." Rikhard said. "You are *not* skilled at knowing that you are walking a knife's edge."

Eiric said nothing, thus demonstrating good judgment.

"It has been a long and bloody ten years," Rikhard said. "When I set out to conquer the Archipelago, jarls and chieftains who had never displayed any talent or interest in governance objected."

Imagine that.

"It is human nature that when one man sees another's successes, his first instinct is to say, 'Why not me?'"

"I've noticed," Eiric said.

"I have scores of enemies who are waiting for any vulnerability, any display of weakness. A king without an heir is always at risk.

"So. I got to know Hilde through our dealings around Sundgard. I came to admire and respect her resilience and capability."

Not the first thing most men look for in a woman.

Perhaps they should.

"I was not eager to marry, and neither was she. She wanted another child, and I needed one. So we made an arrangement."

"Why did you never acknowledge it publicly?" Eiric said.

"Hilde insisted on that until after the baby was born. She knew that she would be a target as soon as the . . . arrangement became known. She had no intention of holing up in my keep for protection. She had a business to run. The plan was that she would care for my son–"

"Or dottir?"

"–until he was weaned. Then he would be named as my heir and come under my protection."

"I'm sorry for your loss," Eiric said. Then the demon within him added, "Hopefully, there's still time, and another arrangement can be made."

That was the spark that ignited the king. Eiric was a virtual firesteel where Rikhard was concerned. The king came to his feet and stood, looking down at him. Moonlight gilded his fair hair like a crown.

This time, he did not reach for his sword. He didn't have to. His words cut well enough.

"Halvorsen, I set you a task with the understanding that it would be completed within a year. Instead, you sailed off with your systir and I heard nothing for ten years. Now you return, practically in the van of an army led by that same systir intent on conquering the Archipelago."

A river of ice ran down Eiric's spine. "My . . . systir?"

"Ivar told me. Did you really think that you could keep it a secret? Especially after what's happened? Ivar lost the only modir he's ever known, and I lost my partner and advisor and my unborn son."

"My lord–" Eiric began, but the king cut him off.

"A more prudent man would see that it might be in his best interest to guard his tongue. I have half a mind to throw you into the gaol at

Kingshavn and send word to your systir to come get you if she dares." The king turned away, toward the tents that had been erected on the grounds where horses used to graze.

"You're right," Eiric called, in a voice that couldn't help but reach the king's ears. The king stopped walking but did not turn around. "I'm the last person who should be passing judgment on others, especially when it comes to relationships."

The king swung around to face him now.

"It's unlikely that Liv would attempt a rescue even if you put it out that I was imprisoned. We did not part on the best of terms. As I told you before, with any luck, she still thinks that I am dead."

"If your systir is here, no doubt Agata has shared the news of your presence here in the Archipelago." He paused and, when Eiric didn't respond, added, "Ivar said she . . . she's possessed by an evil queen?"

"Something like that," Eiric said. "It has to do with a pendant Liv was given as a little girl at the temple grove. It connects her to a Jotun volva named Gullveig. The gods of Asgard tried to kill her, but each time she rose more powerful than before. She's known as Heidin now."

"Why did they try to kill her?"

"She was a powerful sorceress, and the gods mistrusted her use of magic. There's been bad blood between Asgard and the Jotun ever since."

"And now your systir is a god?" Rikhard said skeptically.

"I think Liv is still there, somewhere, but it may not be enough."

"It is not enough," the king said. "It will never be enough, not now. I promised Ivar that we would hunt the witch to the ends of the earth if need be.

"You'll need to decide whose side you are on."

With that, the king turned and strode away.

53

THE RESTLESS DEAD

AFTER KEILA LEFT, REGINN SAT by the warm hearth and mulled over what she had learned. Keila said that she couldn't use spinner magic without permission with the collar on, and that Grima could trace her movements using the collar. No doubt that was why they had allowed her to keep her staff. She tapped the collar with her fingertips, trying to recall the kinds of locks, fasteners, and clasps Eira had used before. But Reginn had spent most of her time in the crypts on Eimyrja. She'd never seen most of the devices the magical fabricator had built.

What about other kinds of magic? Grima had claimed that the collar would prevent Asger and her Risen army from finding her. Was that true? If so, how would Grima know?

Yet she had heard the voices of the dead.

Reginn sat on the edge of the bed. She took a deep breath, knowing she was taking a risk. The keep appeared to be hundreds of years old. Considerable history could have happened here, with lots and lots of dying.

"I speak to the fallen in this house, to those who died unwilling, before their time," Reginn said. "Rise, if you would be heard."

Even to Reginn's ears, it sounded like alehouse patter.

For what seemed like a long time, nothing happened. Then she thought she saw movement in a shadowy corner. When she lifted her lamp high, it reflected off a pair of eyes, too close to the floor to be anything but a–rat!

No, two rats. Now three.

Shuddering, Reginn drew her feet up onto the bed. It wasn't as if she'd led a sheltered life, but she didn't like sharing a room with uninvited . . .

Wait.

She took a closer look. Even in the light from the lamp, the rodents appeared vaporous, not quite solid. As she watched, one passed through a wall. Moments later, it burst back into view, with a monster on its heels.

Not a monster. A cadaverous cat with a torn ear.

These were not intruders after all. They were the restless dead–risen from hidden graves–in the walls, under the floors, wherever death caught them unawares.

"Who are you?"

The voice came from behind Reginn, startling her so that she rolled to the floor. She crouched next to the bed, groping for her belt knife, which, of course, was not there. Reginn peered over the edge of the mattress like a child in hiding.

The girl was tall, sturdily built, but retained the slightly mismatched awkwardness of childhood. Her hands and feet were large enough to suggest she would have grown still taller, given more time. Her gauzy, diaphanous quality said that would never happen.

"I *said*, who are you?" The girl's voice had sharpened, strengthened.

"My name is Reginn. What is your name?"

"Bodil. What are you doing in my room?"

The shadow cat had given up chasing rats and was rubbing against Bodil's legs, purring.

"It's been assigned to me," Reginn said gently.

Bodil shook her head. "You are mistaken. I chose this room specifically because of the–" Her eyes lit on Reginn's collar. She reached for her own, and seemed surprised to find it missing.

"Finally," she whispered. "I'm finally free."

"Yes," Reginn said.

There was no easy way to explain to someone that they were dead. Reginn was used to telling family members that their loved one had died. She'd never had to explain it to the deceased.

"What is the last thing you remember?"

Bodil frowned, doubt rolling in like a bank of clouds. She sank down onto the bed, and the cat leaped up and settled in next to her.

"I remember that we escaped," she said.

"From who?"

"From the Spider." She pointed at the emblem on Reginn's gray linen tunic.

"Grima?"

Bodil eyed her warily. "Maybe I shouldn't be telling you this."

"I'm no threat to you," Reginn said. "Nor is Grima–not anymore."

Bodil brightened. "She's dead?"

"Not yet. But she can't reach you now."

"Good."

"How many of you escaped?" Reginn said.

"There were four of us," Bodil said. She pushed out with both hands as if to make more space. As if the world was too tight for comfort.

"Why did you run away?"

She shifted. "Grima promised to protect us from the people who blamed us for every bad thing that happened. They didn't tell us we were trading one kind of prison for another."

"How did you get off the island?"

"We stole a boat." She laughed. "You should have seen us. None of us had ever rowed a boat before. We're lucky we didn't sink."

"But they found you."

"They found us in Grimsby," she whispered. "I don't know how–nobody ever goes to Grimsby."

"It's the collar," Reginn said, tapping it with her fingertips. "I'm told they can track you with the collar."

"Ah," Bodil said, nodding. "Of course."

"What happened then?"

"They brought us back here, and . . . and . . ." Her voice trailed off. "No, that doesn't make sense. I must have dreamed it. Or am I dreaming now?" She looked up at Reginn, stricken.

"You're not dreaming," Reginn said. "You are dead."

"Dead?" Bodil's shade was a frail screen that displayed every storm and shower that passed behind it.

Shame sluiced over Reginn like a rogue wave. Who was she to criticize Tyra and Heidin for using the dead to further their own aims when she'd called them up herself with no real purpose in mind other than to see if she could still do it.

"I am sorry," Reginn said. "This is my fault. I hope you can forgive me. I should leave you in peace."

But Bodil was having none of that. "That's just it–I was not at peace. I was angry, and bitter, and restless, and resentful. Plagued with dreams." She paused, then rushed ahead. "I'm really dead?"

"Yes," Reginn said, realizing that she had no remedies to offer the dead.

"Are *you* dead?"

Reginn shook her head. "Not yet."

"Then why is this happening?"

"I'm alive, but my gift is that I speak to the dead," Reginn said. "I'm a prisoner, and I need to find a way out of here before Grima gets back. I thought maybe one of you could help me."

Bodil snorted. "I'm not sure you want to take advice from me." She stood, extended her arms, and twirled like a dancer. There was something childlike in her fascination with her shape and form.

"How old were you when . . . you ran away?" Reginn said.

"I'm not a child, if that's what you're asking," Bodil said. "I was–am–twelve. Nearly thirteen." She looked around. "Where are the others?"

"Others?"

"Like I said, there were four of us. There was Odger and Hjordis and"–her voice caught–"Eva–my little systir."

"You were the only one who answered," Reginn said.

"Could you try again?"

Reginn sighed. "I hate to disturb them–if they are truly at peace."

"They probably blame me. It was all my fault."

"What do you mean?"

"I convinced the others to run away with me." Her shade dwindled and dimmed. "Grima made me watch. She made me watch Eva die. Eva kept looking at me, expecting me to do something to stop it." Bodil shuddered. "I was the last to be executed."

"I can't even imagine what that must have been like." In fact, Reginn *could* imagine, knowing Grima. "But it was not your fault. Put the blame where it belongs–on the Spider."

No wonder you have nightmares.

Bodil settled herself, shed her memories like an old cloak, and got down to business. "So. You speak to the dead. Then go ahead, speak. What can I do for you?"

"I had a question about these collars," Reginn said. "Do you know how to open them? How do they come off?"

"Grima had a key. I never got a close look at it. Do you want me to try and find it?"

Reginn shook her head. "This place is too big and time is too short. Besides, she may have it with her."

"Who is still here?"

"Keila and Atla, for two," Reginn said.

Bodil nodded. "I remember them. They were at our execution."

"They mentioned that," Reginn said. "There might be a handful of others. The rest went with Grima."

Bodil raised a hand for quiet. "Did you hear that?"

Now Reginn heard it, too—a voice calling, "Bodie?"

Bodil turned toward the sound, slid through the wall, and was gone, leaving Reginn with two risen rats and a raggedy cat for company.

After what seemed like a long time, Bodil was back, towing a weeping little girl by the hand. The resemblance between the two of them was striking—strong chins, fawny hair, gray eyes.

"You see?" Bodil said. "This is Reginn. She woke us up."

Eva shrank back, trying to hide behind her systir.

Reginn squatted so she was at eye level with Eva. "You must be Eva. I'm sorry I disturbed you."

"I don't like sleeping anyway," Eva said.

"You can hear us and see us," Bodil said. "Can other people see us, too?"

"Yes," Reginn said, "they should be able to."

"Can they hit us or hurt us or trap us?" Bodil said.

"No," Reginn said. "Not anymore."

"Eva, I'm going to go get Atla and Keila and make them let Reginn go," Bodil said. "Can you stay here with Reginn until I come back?"

"No!" Eva clung to Bodil's side like a cold-water barnacle. "I'm coming with you."

"It might be dangerous, sweetling," Bodil said.

"If it's dangerous, then *you* shouldn't go," Eva said. "Anyway, Reginn says it isn't dangerous."

"Let's try this," Reginn said hastily. "The first thing I need to do is to get out of this room. Could you go out in the hallway and see if you can unlock the door from the outside? That would be a big help."

The two systirs passed like vapors through the stone wall of the room. A few moments later, Reginn heard fumbling at her door, then metal against metal as a bolt was shoved back. The door opened a crack, and then all the way to reveal Bodil and Eva, giddy with success.

54
THE MESSENGER

WHEN EIRIC ENTERED THE BOATHOUSE, he'd expected to find his crew fast asleep, given their condition when they'd left the bonefires. Instead, he found them lined up on the scaffolding supporting the dragon ship, peering over the gunwale.

Eiric was in no mood to talk to anyone after his conversation with the king. But there was no way to slip past them to his sleeping bench without being seen.

"Styrman," Nils said, looking down at him, "we found another body. Someone from New Jotunheim. Could you have a look and tell us if it's anyone you know?"

The last thing Eiric needed was more bad news. *Can't it wait until tomorrow?* He wanted to say, but the damage was done. All he could do was get it over with.

Eiric scrambled up the scaffolding and sidled toward where the fiskers were huddled midships. When he looked over the gunwale, he saw that it was a woman dressed in bondi buff, her fair hair gathered into a fat braid, her hands clasped around the shaft of an arrow that had gone in just under her rib cage.

She was familiar in a way that made no sense.

It was Naima.

"Skita," he muttered.

"Someone you know?" Reyna said.

Eiric nodded. "Not well, but–" He stopped. Something wasn't right. If she'd been lying here dead for five days, her body would tell the tale. He unlaced her fingers from around the arrow shaft. It was not one of the black-fletched arrows made on Ithavoll. It appeared to be local to Muckleholm. Her hands were supple, not stiff. To Eiric's eyes, the arrow tip hadn't penetrated deeply enough to hit anything vital.

"Styrman?" Levi said. "Are you all right? Do you want us to take care of the body?"

Eiric shook his head. Gripping the shaft of the arrow just behind the head, Eiric carefully pulled the arrow out. Blood leaked from the wound–something else that shouldn't happen in a person dead for very long. He pressed his fingers into the side of her neck, then sat back. "She's alive," he said, scarcely able to believe it himself.

"Do you want me to go find a healer?" Levi said.

"No," Eiric said quickly. Then added, "Not just yet. But could two of you carry her down? The rest of you, make up a pallet on one of the benches and fetch me some water and clean rags."

Fortunately, they managed to lift her down from the scaffolding without dropping her and deposited her on an unoccupied bench in the farthest corner. Meanwhile, Eiric walked the length of the ship, doing a cursory search. He found ten years' worth of dust, along with the oars, ropes, buckets, a spare mast, and other supplies he would expect. There were no weapons or other gear to suggest that Naima had taken refuge here, or used it as an ambush point.

Eiric cleaned the wound with a wet rag, pressing a little to encourage the flow of blood. He used another rag to carefully clean the tip of the arrow of blood. It was difficult to tell, but he thought he detected a bluish staining above where the tip had penetrated.

"The arrow didn't go deep–it must've hit a rib–but I think the tip was poisoned," he said, thinking, I wish Reginn was here. She would know what to do.

"Could I see that?" Nils said. "I know something about poisons."

That was somehow not surprising. Eiric handed it over.

"Who is she, exactly?" Rorik said.

"Her name is Naima Bondi," Eiric said. "She had the cell next to mine when we were imprisoned on Eimyrja."

"*That's* Naima Bondi?" Rorik sounded awestruck. The rest of the crew edged forward so they could get a better look.

"I take it you've heard of her?" Eiric said, bemused.

"She's a hero," Nils said. "She was–is–a leader of the resistance on the main island. She killed the head of the Elders' Council to save a little girl."

I killed the rest, Eiric thought of saying, but resisted it.

"How did she get here?" Reyna said.

"She must have come with the Jotun army," Eiric said.

Levi scowled. "Why would she do that?"

"Why did *you* come here?" Eiric fired back.

"A barbarian coaster needed a ride and wouldn't take no for an answer," Levi said.

"Exactly," Eiric said. "Maybe she didn't have a choice. Or maybe she had her own reasons."

Eiric tried to remember what happened to Naima after he left prison. "Naima is fine," Reginn had said. "She's been pardoned. She's working with me." She'd even said something about Naima helping with his "sending."

How had she ended up in a dragon ship at Sundgard with an arrow in her?

He took a closer look. The clothes she was wearing were ill-fitting, as if they belonged to somebody else. Methodically, he began to search her. She wore a silver pendant around her neck, each side inscribed with a rune. When he fingered it, the magic in it vibrated under his touch. It looked like Reginn's work, with each symbol one of her healing or protective runes.

That might be why Naima was still alive.

When he continued his search, he surfaced a leather packet with pages inside it. The outside was inscribed with a name.

EIRIC

"It's for you," Reyna breathed, reading over his shoulder. "Naima Bondi brought a message for you." Eiric's status was rising by the minute.

He unfolded the pages. On the first page, he could read *EIRIC* at the top and *REGINN* at the bottom. And that was it. He could not read the text in between.

"Who is Reginn?" Reyna said, having caught sight of the signature.

"She is counselor to the Jotun queen," Eiric said, turning the page to prevent further peeking.

He examined the second sheet. It was a map of the western coast of Muckleholm, of the sound that divided the main island from the Sudreyjar chain of islands. The smallest, northernmost island in the chain was marked with an *X*.

His first impulse was to take the note to Ivar, and they could read it together. But he didn't want to risk it, without knowing what it said. He was in trouble with the king as it was. Rikhard had made it clear that he would be ruthless in avenging the death of his consort and heir, and the attack on Sundgard. He would do what he saw as best for his fledgling kingdom.

Eiric looked up at his crew. There was no getting around it. "Could somebody read this to me?"

He saw the realization kindle in their eyes. Their styrman could not read.

Then everyone clamored for the honor. "Stop it!" Eiric said. "I only need one person. Nils, it's you." He handed Nils the page with Reginn's note. He kept the other one to himself.

He thought about asking Nils to move out of earshot, but knew it wouldn't matter–everyone would know about it before the day was over.

Nils struck a stance like an alehouse skald and began to read.

EIRIC

We are preparing to set sail from Sundgard, and I am leaving this with Naima in the hopes that you'll both stay alive long enough for her to pass it on. First, let me say that I am so very sorry about what happened here. Heidin has a major grudge against everyone and everything on Muckleholm, and seems determined to destroy as much of it as she can. I have tried to tell her that the people who died here had nothing to do with what happened in the past.

Naima can tell you more about your poor systir. She has markedly deteriorated.

I have managed to convince Heidin to leave the east coast behind and return to Langvik Sound before launching an attack on Kingshavn. We established a small outpost on Klettrholm, in the Sudreyjar Islands, when we first arrived. I'm hoping that time away from the scene of so much heartache might heal her spirit and strengthen her so that she can fight off the demon that threatens to possess her. I will use all the tools and skills at my command to heal her. I'm convinced that your systir is still there if we can free her.

Heidin has always responded to you. I believe it would help if she could see you–and your brodir as well, if he is willing. It's a huge risk, with an uncertain payoff. If you decide to come, please come sooner rather than later. I'm not sure how long I'll be able to hold her here. Most important of all, whatever you decide, say nothing to the king. He will not be in a forgiving mood.

REGINN

Nils looked up. "You never said you had a systir. And she's ill?"

"What's wrong with her?" Reyna said. "And what does the queen have to do with it?"

They all waited, then, while Eiric tried to sieve out an answer from the flotsam in his head. He should have told them sooner. In fact, he'd actually forgotten that they didn't know. Now events had elbowed out ahead of him.

"My systir Liv is under a—a kind of curse from a dead Jotun goddess, and I don't know if I'll ever get her back."

His crew stared at him with mingled awe and sympathy.

"Gods," Reyna said. "I didn't even know that was something a person had to worry about."

Eiric took a deep breath. "There's more. She is the person you know as Heidin, queen of New Jotunheim."

This was met by a silence that lived like ten years.

"The queen is your systir?" Rorik said. "And you forgot to tell us?"

"I needed a good crew, and you're among the best I've ever sailed with," Eiric said. "After you told me you'd intended to take the queen hostage, it seemed like it would be awkward."

"Awkward? *Awkward?*" Nils said. "*Awkward* is finding out that you and your brodir are courting the same girl."

"Our styrman is the brodir to the queen that is holding our families hostage," Reyna said. "The same styrman who's agreed to help us free them. There's a different word for that."

"Betrayal?" Rorik said. "Deceit?"

Eiric blew his breath out in frustration. "Do any of you have a systir? Or a brodir?"

"I have a younger brodir," Levi said. "He's being held hostage by your systir."

Don't ask questions you don't know the answer to. Eiric was sure somebody said that sometime.

"My systir did not choose this," Eiric said. "This was forced on her by her modir, Tyra, when she was a lytling. Our fadir tried to save her from it by carrying her off to the Archipelago. She's only recently returned to New Jotunheim, so she was not the agent of much of the harm that's been done to you.

"All my life, she has been the strongest voice for justice that I know.

I may not be able to help her, but I will if I can. You want to save your families. So do I."

An annoying voice in the back of his head said, *Didn't you just tell Ivar you would stay and fight with him?*

"I'm not asking you to join me in this. I am asking you to keep this information to yourselves and help me protect Naima. She needs better care than I can provide, but if the king finds out she came with the Jotun, she'll be blamed, interrogated, maybe imprisoned. Do it for her, if not for me."

"What would you have us do?" Reyna said warily.

"I'm hoping to pass her off as a survivor of the attack," Eiric said. "Someone from Sundgard who survived by hiding in the boat shed. She'll need a new set of clothes–something a person here would wear."

Reyna took a good look at Naima, measuring with her eyes. "I'll find something," she said.

"What are *you* going to do?" Levi said, unable to stand the suspense anymore.

"I don't know yet," Eiric said.

"He can't go," Levi said. "Anyone can see that it's a trap."

"Naima Bondi would not lead him into a trap," Rorik said.

"How do you know?" Nils said. "Don't forget–our styrman killed hundreds of soldiers on Ithavoll. Why would she look out for him?"

Generally, when his crew's conversations got blown off course, Eiric let it go. But this time, he put a stop to it.

"Look," Eiric said. "This is not a group decision, it's mine. My systir, my life on the line. I do not expect you to help me. I'll have more information if we can revive Naima, but it had better be soon. She can't last much longer without food or water.

"In the meantime, keep this quiet. I don't want to have to deal with interference from the king–or anyone else."

55
ON THE LOOSE

BODIL AND EVA WATCHED IMPATIENTLY as Reginn packed up her few belongings and slid into her warm coat.

Finally, she soft-footed it out into the deserted corridor, closing the door behind her. The Risen took a more direct route through the wall.

No one was more eager to leave than Reginn. But where should she go? Keila had said that Reginn's collar would enable Grima to follow her, wherever she went. That meant she would have to move quickly, and keep moving. She needed to find a way off this island.

That would require a boat.

"Do you know where they keep the boats?"

That turned out to be a hard question. Bodil and Eva looked at each other.

"If there are boats in the water, they would be at the docks in the sea cave," Bodil said finally. "Let's head down there."

Reginn's next question would be even harder–where can I find a crew?

They were nearing the top of the stairs just as Keila and Atla emerged from the stairwell, Atla with her staff, and Keila carrying a tray with what must be Reginn's nattmal. They stopped in their tracks, staring. "You!" Atla said when she saw Reginn. "How did you–?"

Then both Keila and Atla spotted Reginn's companions and turned as white as shades themselves. Keila dropped the tray and it careened back down the stairwell and out of sight.

"Bodil," Keila whispered, and fell to her knees, hands clasped together. "Forgive me."

Atla just kept shaking her head, her eyes fixed on Reginn as if she could ignore her companions out of existence. "Lady Reginn, I'm going to have to insist that you return to your . . . room and wait until the–until Lady Grima returns. We will say nothing about this if you return to your quarters right now."

"Atla, look at me," Bodil said, raising her hand, waggling her fingers. Eva laughed.

"I really need to go," Reginn said. "Tell Grima to get in touch if she wants to talk further." She paused. "I will need transportation back to the mainland, the sooner the better."

"Did you not hear me?" Atla said. "This bit of conjury is impressive, but if Grima returns and finds you gone, there'll be hell to pay." She smacked the butt of her staff against the floor, and the head ignited.

Bodil walked toward Atla until she stood directly in front of her face so that she couldn't be overlooked.

"Atla," she said. "We're done with that. One advantage of being dead is that Grima can't hurt me. *You* can't hurt me. On the other hand–" She ripped Atla's staff out of her hands, broke it across her knee, and tossed the pieces toward the stairwell. "*You* have to worry about *me*."

"Bodil, easy, Atla wants to help us, she just doesn't know it yet." Reginn turned back to Atla. "I don't want to hurt anyone. Give me a ship and a crew, and we'll be fine."

"That's just it," Keila blurted. "There are no ships."

"What do you mean, there are no ships?" Bodil said, looking from Atla to Keila.

"Grima took them," Atla said, gazing longingly at the stairwell as if dreaming of escape. "There were only two to begin with. She did not know what kind of resistance she would meet, so she gave it everything she had."

"To attack a *farm*?" Reginn rolled her eyes. "How many people are left here?"

"More than enough, if that's what you're thinking," Atla said gamely.

"You are able to use your magic even though you are wearing a collar," Reginn said. "Why is that?"

Atla flushed. "It's because I am a part of Grima's personal guard. Her inner web. That's what she calls it. This collar is–is temporarily disabled."

"She trusts you," Reginn said. She raised her hand to forestall any protest. "She trusts you as much as she trusts anyone. She needs people who can perform magic unsupervised."

"Your point is–?"

"Perhaps she needs people who can apply and remove collars, and turn them off and on," Reginn said.

"No," Atla said warily. "Only Grima does that. Now, do as I say or I'll call in the guard." She looked at Keila for support and received none.

"Do it," Reginn said. "Call the guard. I'll wait."

"I'll go get them," Keila said, and was gone before anyone could object.

"While we're waiting, Atla–I'm curious–what is your gift?" Reginn said.

"My . . . gift?"

"What is a special ability you have that sets you apart? Something you can do that most people can't." When Atla did not volunteer anything, Reginn persisted.

Atla still seemed baffled by this line of questioning. "Maybe not something Grima values," Reginn said. "Something–anything–a small thing—that *you* value. For instance—I play the flute. It's not the flashiest gift I have, but it's the one that makes me the happiest."

"Well," Atla said, glancing at Bodil as if she wished she didn't have an audience, "I talk to birds."

"Really?" Reginn said. "Do they answer?"

"Some do. Others don't see the point in it."

"All kinds of birds, or just certain ones?"

"All of them, though some are more interesting than others. Siskins are hopeless gossips. If you can persuade a raven to speak to you, it's always worthwhile. Eagles, on the other hand, are showy, but they are dumb as a box of rocks."

"So you can understand what they are saying."

"Pretty much. I think most people would understand more, if they just paid attention."

"That truth goes beyond birds," Reginn said. "You have a unique and useful gift. Grima is fortunate to have you."

"Grima?" Atla said, obviously confused. "Oh. Um . . . She hasn't really . . . Grima is more interested in—in—"

"In your ability to shoot flame out of a stick?"

Atla scowled. "Why do you care about any of this?"

"Because I used to be enslaved to a demon who decided which of my gifts were useful and which were not. Who stole my magic to use himself. I'm not doing that anymore."

Just then, Keila arrived with a score of soldiers, a mix of men and women, all collared. Most carried staffs, but some carried more conventional weapons. A few of them obviously recognized Bodil and Eva, because they nearly stumbled and then stood staring at them.

The rest saluted Atla. "Ma'am? You wanted to see us?"

"Actually," Reginn said, "I asked Keila to go get you because I was hoping you could help settle an argument. We've been discussing these collars"—she reached up and touched the circlet around her neck—"I've been saying that we would all be happier with the collars off, so we could make our own decisions and control our own magic, but Atla isn't so sure. What do you think?"

"I think you should stop putting words in my mouth," Atla said.

"I think if Atla loves collars so much, she's more than welcome to mine." This came from a weathered old man who would have been more at home at the helm of a fishing boat.

This was met with a rush of shushing from his companions. They shifted, armor creaking, leaned on their staffs, and scanned the ceilings and walls, trying to avoid making eye contact with anyone.

"We all know how you feel, Njal," Atla said. "How could we not? You'll live longer if you just shut up."

"Did I ever say I wanted to live longer?"

Reginn cleared her throat. "Some of you might recognize Bodil and Eva here. I thought they could offer a different perspective since, you know, they're dead."

It was obvious that the soldiers suspected that this was one of Grima's traps, and so were reluctant to speak.

"Viggo?" Bodil said. "Cat got your tongue?"

One of the younger guards turned even paler than he was already. He closed his eyes as if that would make the apparitions disappear. "Bodil," he whispered. "Maybe I backed out on running away with you, but I'm not the one who told on you."

"I know that, Viggo," Bodil said. "In hindsight, you were the smart one." She addressed the assembled guards. "I'm told that we were traced through our collars, hunted down and executed. So you can put me down as anti-collar."

"I hoped maybe one of you might have the key, or the tool, or the trick for turning them off," Reginn said. She looked around hopefully, but was met with glum silence.

"Has anyone tried heat? Is there a smithy here someplace that might get hot enough to melt them?"

"I was an apprentice blacksmith before I was collared," Viggo said. "The collars are made of some kind of magicked gold that doesn't melt at typical forge temperatures."

"I take it you've tried?"

Viggo hesitated, glancing at Atla, then nodded. "They're made to be resistant to spinner magic."

"Why are we even having this conversation?" another wraith said. "It's not like we have a choice."

"There's always a choice," a woman drawled. "These collars'll come right off after the beheadings."

"Grima won't behead you," Atla said. "She'll send the lot of us to the Deeps."

This was met with shocked silence. "Why would she do that?" Njal said. "We're Jotun, not Asgardians."

"Never mind," Atla said. "I misspoke."

"Wait," Reginn said. "What do you mean? What are you talking about when you say 'the Deeps'?"

"There's a dungeon beneath the Cliff House where they–they keep Asgardian spinners," Atla said.

"*Asgardian* spinners?" Bodil said. "That doesn't make any sense."

The guard muttered their agreement.

"You need to take us there–right now," Reginn said.

Atla backed away, shaking her head. "That's not a good idea, when we–"

Bodil gave her a shove that nearly knocked her off her feet. "Did you hear the lady? Right. Now."

"If you insist," Atla said. "But you're not going to like it, and I want you to know that I don't have anything–"

"Move!" Bodil said. "The rest of you, come with us if you want to see this with your own eyes."

56
REQUIEM

THE KING AND HIS HIRD remained at Sundgard a few more days, cleaning up the buildings and facilities that had been destroyed and securing what was left. Ivar stuck to Rikhard like a burr to woolen breeches as if he was afraid that Eiric might be catching if he got too close.

He blames me for the attack, Eiric thought, though he probably knows it's unfair.

It was easier than he'd expected to sell the story that Naima was the sole survivor from Sundgard. People wanted to believe it, needed a symbol of survival amid the carnage. Besides, no one else was left alive to contradict it. Rikhard called in his own healer to tend her. Eiric asked that the runestone pendant around her neck be left in place.

"I think there must be magic in it," he said. "It may explain why she survived, when so many died."

Naima made some progress under the care of the healer, reviving enough to take food and drink—at least when fed. But on the rare occasions that she spoke, she would fly into a panic, grab hold of whomever was closest, and cry out a warning that no one could understand.

To Eiric's surprise, Nils volunteered to assist the king's healer. When Eiric asked about it, he shrugged. "I've always been interested in the borderlands between life and death, the relationship between the taking and the saving of lives. Besides, you'll want someone there if she wakes and begins talking in order to match and manage stories."

If you decide to come, please come sooner rather than later.

Reginn knew he couldn't read. She would not write him a note to ask him to come.

Of course it was a trap.

Of course he had to go.

He was already making a plan.

It was not a very good plan.

He needed a boat he could sail on his own, though he knew it meant that he would be sailing a very long way in a very small boat.

Was there a better option?

He might manage the *Firebird*—that had been the plan when he left Ithavoll, but he'd promised her to his crew. He could keep that promise even if he didn't live long enough to help rescue their families.

He looked through Hilde's papers until he found a recent map of Muckleholm. It was much better, more detailed, than any he'd seen before. He stowed the map inside his coat and walked down to the boat manufactory.

It still surprised him that the attackers had left most of the facilities intact. He was no expert on large-scale warfare, but wouldn't it make sense to cripple your enemy's ability to build more ships, forge more weapons, and the like? If you were in it to win?

In the shipbuilding hall, there were several ships in progress—some not much more than a keel, a stem, and a stern. Others were in varying stages of completion, some nearly ready to sail. Eiric had never seen so many ships in progress at once. A man on his home farm might be lucky to complete a ship in a year's time, and that with help and a ready supply of timber and other supplies. The other holdup was usually the making of the sail.

One small part of the hall seemed to be devoted to repairs rather than new builds. The only ship on the rack was startlingly familiar.

Ship was a generous term. It was the little fishing boat Liv and Bjorn had built together that first winter. The following summer, Bjorn had taken Liv out fishing in the quiet waters at the head of the sound. She'd learned to handle the oars, and then the sail, traveling all the way down the sound to where it met the open sea.

They called her *Thistle* because she skimmed the water as light as a thistle seed. All their ships had a shallow draft, but this one barely broke the surface.

Another man might have worried that Liv would use her newfound skills to try to sail back to Eimyrja. His grandfadir was wise enough to know that it was this time together that made her want to stay.

In the summers before Eiric was old enough to sail with his fadir, Liv took Eiric out in the *Thistle*, exploring the sound and the tidal river and salt marsh at its head, penetrating ever deeper into the wilderness, risking attack by outlaws and wolves. That was their playground, the scene of a hundred ambushes and skirmishes that Liv always won. At first.

He couldn't remember the last time he'd seen the little boat. The mock battles with his systir had been crowded out when he took to the longships. Where had it been all this time?

It was obvious that the little boat had been completely rebuilt. New wood stood out against the old. Who had done that?

"It was supposed to be a surprise for the new baby."

Eiric turned to find Ivar in the doorway.

"I found it in the scrap lumber pile. It was in dismal shape, but the keel was intact, and it's not easy to find quality timber these days. Some of the master builders helped me work on it after hours. I was going to carve a figurehead."

"You did fine work, brodir," Eiric said.

Ivar waved the praise away. "It would have been a while before he could enjoy it, but I thought I could teach him to fish, and to sail, and to handle a boat." He hunched his shoulders. "Guess it will go back on the scrap heap now."

"Your systir taught me to fish, and to sail in this very boat," Eiric said. "Wait a bit before you decide to discard it."

"You take it, then," Ivar said, his carefully neutral expression slipping a little. "I don't have a systir." He let that sit for a beat, then said, "I'm here because the king wants to see you." He turned away without looking back to see if Eiric was following.

Rikhard had set up a makeshift court in a refurbished warehouse. It still resembled a warehouse, with barrels of tar, grains, ships nails and roves, spools of rope and other cordage. A small area was set aside for dining. In lieu of a throne, the king sat behind a heavy oak table piled with papers, Ivar by his side. Four armed guardsmen formed a half circle around them–members of the king's hird. Others lined the walls. Eiric was glad to see that, after the assassination attempt, the king was taking reasonable precautions.

"Lord," Eiric said, inclining his head a reasonable amount.

"Halvorsen," Rikhard said without looking up from his paperwork. "Thank you for coming. Please. Sit."

Eiric sat in one of two chairs facing the king.

Rikhard finally put his paperwork aside and looked up at Eiric, studying him. The king's usually meticulous appearance had frayed a bit, as if he'd aged a decade in a week.

That's when Eiric realized that the blade of loss had struck bone.

This was not just a matter of wounded pride. Rikhard had loved Hilde, or as close as a man like him could come to it. Which made what Liv had done unforgivable.

"It seems like years since we sailed from Kingshavn," Rikhard said.

"Aye, Lord. It does."

"As I recall, we were coming here to look at a ship for you to command."

"I remember."

"The longship in the boat shed is the one I had in mind," Rikhard said.

Eiric looked up, startled. "*Sylvi?*"

Ivar came to attention, looking from Eiric to Rikhard. "Is that her name?"

"Yes," Eiric said. "Built by my fadir and grandfadir, named after my modir. But she has seventeen sections. My crew is not large enough to sail her."

"If you sail for me, I can fill in with as many additional oarsmen as you need. Experienced sailors, not scrubs."

Eiric knew that the fiskers would not welcome having barbarian sailors looking over their shoulders. That said, they *were* eager to put *Sylvi* back in the water.

When Eiric didn't answer right away, Rikhard said, "We are planning to return to Kingshavn tomorrow. I will leave some of my best soldiers to protect Sundgard and continue the cleanup."

And to keep an eye on me, Eiric thought.

"I would ask you and your crew to inspect the longship—*Sylvi*—make any repairs necessary, and get her into the water. If she turns out to be seaworthy, you can sail her to Kingshavn and we'll discuss next steps.

"If you decide not to sail for me, then I would ask for your word that you will not fight for the witches. You and your crew should leave the Archipelago and sail your ship back to New Jotunheim or some other harbor to wait out the war. There can be no neutral parties in this. You have made a name for yourself, and you will be a target for both sides."

"You have my word that I will not fight for New Jotunheim," Eiric said. "My refusal to do so landed me in trouble with the queen and nearly cost me my life. If I wanted them to win, I would not have warned you that they were coming."

The king chewed his lower lip, frowning. It was as if he was poking at Eiric's words from all sides, looking for a catch. Eiric could feel the pressure of Ivar's gaze.

"I will, however, do whatever I can to save my systir."

"What about your brodir?" Rikhard said.

"I hope it won't come down to that sort of choice," Eiric said. "I offered to take Ivar to a place of safety before the fighting began. He declined. He said that his place is at your side."

"I appreciate that loyalty," Rikhard said, in a way that made sure Eiric felt the sting.

Ivar said nothing.

"Halvorsen, it seems to me that you are walking the most dangerous road of all. I fear that you will end up dead before this is over."

"That's up to the weavers at the well," Eiric said.

"Sometimes the Norns need a little nudge," Rikhard said.

"I hope that, one day, you can teach me the trick of that." Eiric could tell that he'd made the king angry again. He hadn't lost his touch.

"Take a few days," Rikhard said. "Feel free to use the ships hall, tools, and materials there. When the ship is ready, sail her to Kingshavn and we'll talk."

Eiric liked the sound of that. He could use some time out from under the eye of the king.

As if Rikhard had overheard his thoughts, the king said, "Don't wait too long. I've called in my liege lords to a thing at Ulfness. Hopefully by then, we'll have pinpointed the location of the Jotun army. We won't wait for another attack."

"I understand."

As Eiric made as if to turn away, Rikhard said, "There's one more thing."

"Lord?"

"It is always important, especially in wartime, to have a clear line of succession. I had hoped to be introducing my son and heir by year's end. That won't happen now."

"That was a great loss, Lord. For all of us, but for you and for Ivar most of all."

Rikhard nodded. "I do not want to go to war with the issue of succession unresolved. Therefore, at Ulfness, I will introduce my adopted son, Ivar Karlsen, as prince of the realm and heir to the Fossegrim throne."

Eiric was generally quick off the mark, but it seemed to take forever for him to process what he'd just heard. He was just getting used to the idea of a king, and now–

"Ivar–your adopted son? A prince?" That was the best he could do.

Rikhard nodded. "I became his guardian at a time when his only living relatives were members of his fadir's family–your stepfamily. In Hilde's estimation, they were totally unsuitable."

"Hilde was right," Eiric said. "But he *has* family–I am his brodir."

"Where have you been these past ten years?"

"You know very well where I've been," Eiric said.

"And where will you be next year? Or the year after that?"

"I take your point," Eiric said. "But–"

"In so many ways, Ivar is the perfect heir to my legacy. He brings a divine lineage, experience in battle on land and sea, and a hunger for knowledge even greater than my own. He is not the warrior that you are, but I hope that, one day, men will not have to fight their way to the throne."

Says the man who murdered his own fadir and took his place.

"I chose this, brodir," Ivar said, his face as calm and unfathomable as a glacial lake. "It seemed the best way to serve my country and my king." After a brief pause, he added, "I thought you might be happy for me."

Eiric gathered his thoughts, discarding the first three things he might have said. "Forgive me, Ivar. This is a great honor, for you and for our entire family. I wish our modir and grandfadir could be here to see it."

"But–?"

"I'm afraid it will make you a target."

"I'm not a target now?"

"As the heir to the throne, it won't just be the jotnar who are targeting you. Every ambitious thane and chieftain in the Archipelago will look at you and say, 'Why not me?'"

"I am young, and have not yet got my growth," Ivar said. "I am not battle-hardened, but I will be. Until then, I am hoping I will have you at my side."

57
RESTORATION

ATLA LED THE WAY TO the stairwell, looked over her shoulder to see who was coming along, and saw that it was nearly everybody. She sighed heavily, then clattered down the stairs. Flight after flight after flight, until it seemed like they must have penetrated all the way through the earth to the other side.

Reginn knew they were getting close when she began to smell the sea.

Finally, they emerged into the cavern that housed the docks. As Keila had said, the slips were empty, the ships gone. Atla paid little attention to that, but crossed the floor of the cave to a fortified door on the other side. Atla chose a key from among several that hung from a chain around her neck and unlocked the door.

Immediately, their path was blocked by two massive wraiths with shaved heads and metal-strapped staffs. When they recognized Atla, they inclined their heads. "Ma'am," the bigger one said, looking past her at the others. "What is this?"

"These ones would like to see the Deeps."

"Why?" the wraith blurted, as if baffled as to why anyone would request a tour.

Atla looked to Reginn, who said, "I'm building a dungeon and I wanted to get some ideas."

The guard looked from Reginn to Atla. "Why were we not notified that you were coming? If you'd given us a little more time to prepare—"

"It was not my call," Atla said.

"It's too many," the other guard said. "There's not room."

"We have no choice," Atla said. "Make it happen."

"They'll all want to leave, soon enough," the other guard muttered.

They stood aside, allowing the visitors to file past and through a second doorway into the room where the prisoners were being held. As Reginn passed the two guards, she motioned to the nearest one. "You–come with us."

The guard scowled. "I don't take orders from you."

"Do as she says, Kåre," Atla said, glancing at Bodil. "Trust me, it's easier."

The door opened onto a gallery that ran around the perimeter of a high-ceilinged room. As soon as Reginn stepped inside, she was met with the stench of unwashed bodies, ripe chamber pots, and festering wounds.

They were looking down on maybe thirty prisoners, chained to the wall, fifteen to a side. Their ages ranged from older children to the elderly, their hair roughly shorn so that it was difficult to distinguish the genders. They wore shapeless linen tunics, like acolytes in a strict religion, or sacrifices at a blot. They all wore the familiar collars, linked to the wall, and to a thick cable that disappeared into the far wall.

One or two of the children pointed and whispered, but most of the prisoners didn't seem to notice their entrance. They slumped, heads lolling, as if asleep.

At one end of the room was a hearth fire that had been recently replenished. Beside each person was a chamber pot, a plate of food, and a stoppered jar. The plates appeared to be untouched, though several rats huddled just out of reach, awaiting an opportunity. She saw one man pick up his jar, pull the cork with his teeth, take a long swallow, then restopper it and carefully set it aside.

The crowd of wraiths around Reginn stood in stunned silence, finally broken by the sound of someone vomiting.

Not even Reginn could have summoned an appetite under the circumstances.

Reginn had worked as a healer in the most desperate corners of the Archipelago, including some lockups, but this had to be among the worst. Black spots swam in front of her eyes and she had to cling to the metal railing to keep from toppling. It was sheer determination that kept her from spewing over the railing. She breathed deeply, sucking in the scent of the sea.

Between the two rows of prisoners, a grate covered an opening to the sea below. Reginn could hear the ebb and flow of the sea, whispering against the rocky shore, sucking on wooden piers. They might have been thralls being ferried to market by coasters after a successful raid.

It was horrible, but, more than that, there was something about the setup that struck a nerve, that kindled a disproportionate dread. The cable, the collars, the lolling heads–there was a meaning there she wasn't teasing out.

Behind her, Bodil and Eva whispered together, seemingly having some kind of debate.

"Why does it stink so bad?" Eva said.

The gaoler reddened, cleared his throat. "It's usually not this bad," he said. "It's just we're temporarily shorthanded and it's hard to keep up. As I said, if we'd had a little notice . . ."

"This is an unusual arrangement," Reginn said, licking dry lips. "What's the purpose? How does it work?"

"The collars, I believe, you know about," Kåre said. "The megin is collected by the collars and shunted through the cable to a storage device. It ensures delivery of power to the system consistently, while providing support and care to the–to the–contributors." He seemed to be having trouble coming up with the appropriate word.

The truth hit Reginn like a runaway horse, and it took her a moment to spit out a question. "So . . . so . . . so . . . you are stripping them of megin? Milking them, so to speak?"

Kåre seemed to catch a discordant note in what Reginn said. "W-we prefer to call it harvesting. Fortunately, up to a point, it's a renewable crop."

Up to a point? Then what?

"What's that they're drinking?" Reginn said.

"Ah, an excellent question," Kåre said, showing his first trace of enthusiasm. "We are constantly improving it. It is a mixture of opium, herbs, and tinctures, in a base of the very best mead we can source."

Kåre was obviously proud of his little fiefdom, but it reminded Reginn of an opium market that she and Asger had visited years ago to replenish her remedy bag. The colorful merchant tents rippled like sails on a sea of need, with people drowning all around.

"Look closely, Meyla," Asger had said. "This is why you never, ever eat the poppy."

"Ma'am?" Atla said hopefully. "Are you all right? Have you seen enough?"

"What sorts of crimes might bring them here?" Reginn said.

"They are all Asgardians, seditious to the bone."

"Imagine that," Reginn said. "Even the children are seditious."

Kåre flushed. "Some of the younglings came with their parents because they had no place else to go. We used to just kill them outright, but that was barbaric."

"And also a serious waste of megin," Reginn said.

"Well, of course, but that's not the–"

"How long has this been going on?"

"You mean the younglings? I–"

"This whole . . . thing."

"In this location, maybe two years. The Spider began with a small operation on the main island, but that seemed too vulnerable to discovery. That's when we moved here."

"The . . . Spider." That was it—the arrangement reminded Reginn of a spiderweb, the unfortunate victims held fast while the spider sucked the life out of them.

"Reginn." Bodil touched her arm, then pointed down at the prisoners. "They're not all Asgardians."

"How do you know?"

"That's Odger," she whispered, pointing to an emaciated man at the far end.

"Who's Odger?" Reginn whispered back, lost.

"He escaped with us. They told us he was executed. So why is he here? He's no Asgardian."

Reginn nodded to signify that she understood. Then turned back to the commander.

"Kåre—what's the plan for this—long-term?"

"Eventually, as the conquest of the Archipelago continues, there are plans to greatly expand this facility, using what we've learned here. The entire island will become a sanctuary for relocated Asgardians and serious offenders who can continue to contribute to the public good while remaining safely confined. It will be an engine of power for the new realm." He paused, smiled modestly. "I've been told that I'll be in charge."

Reginn pulled her kynstone out from under her tunic and palmed it. Gingerly, she stepped out onto the stairs leading down from the gallery.

"Stop!" Atla said. "What are you doing?"

"Just taking a closer look."

Once at the bottom, she continued onto the grate and began walking down the line of prisoners, feeling the pressure of Kåre's anxious gaze. "Be careful, ma'am, that you don't trip. The footing's uneven out there."

Reginn kept walking, glancing down at the kynstone now and then.

The dishonest terminology Kåre used was setting Reginn's nerves aflame. It reminded her of the language used in Eimyrja to pretty up terrible things.

Everyone belongs. Everyone has a role to play, even if it's not of their choosing.

Reginn continued walking down the line of captives, none of whom acknowledged her. "Hello," Reginn said, several times. "My name is Reginn. How are you feeling?"

She received no answer. But when she touched their shoulders, she could feel the bones just under the skin, with little flesh and fat between. It reminded her of the addicts she'd seen in port towns throughout the Archipelago.

Finally, at the end of the line of prisoners, a younger woman sat in a stupor, her empty jar lying on its side a short distance away. A little girl was tucked in next to her, one skeletal arm flung over the woman's waist. She was dead.

Something in Reginn snapped.

"Kåre!" she shouted in a voice that could possibly be heard on the mainland.

"Ma'am?" he said.

"This girl is dead, commander," Reginn said, raking the little one's lank hair away from her face. "How many have died here?"

Kåre frowned. "Well, as for an exact number, I–I–"

"How long do people stay here, on average?"

"That's hard to say. Some last longer than others, depending on how healthy they were to begin with."

Reginn swiveled around. "You're saying that they stay chained to the wall in this dungeon until they die? That it's a death sentence?"

"In effect, yes," Kåre said. "It would be cruel to send them away without support." He gestured to the nodding prisoners. "Most seem content."

"You said that this facility is used to house Asgardian prisoners,"

Reginn said. "But nearly half the people in this lockup are Jotun."

"That's not true," Kåre said unconvincingly.

"Liar!" somebody shouted from above.

Reginn held up the kynstone. It shone a bright blue, reflecting the status of the prisoner closest to her. "This is a kynstone. Blue means Jotun, red means Asgardian."

Kåre licked his lips. "I wouldn't know about that, ma'am. I just go by what Lady Grima tells me."

"Then you are a fool."

The unhappy clamor on the gallery was growing louder.

"Where is the power stored after it is stolen from them?"

Kåre flinched at the word *stolen*. "There's a stone," he said. "A–a jewel."

"Show me," Reginn said.

After a longing look at the exit door, the dungeon-master said, "It's off the gallery. You'll have to come back up here."

By the time she reached the gallery, Kåre was standing in front of a reinforced door at the far end. Reginn motioned for the other observers on the gallery to stay where they were and joined him. He fished a key from under his tunic, unlocked it, and pulled it open, spilling purple light over them.

He stood aside, gesturing for her to enter first.

Reginn shook her head. "After you."

It was a small, octagonal room empty save for a table against the near wall and connected to it by the cable. On the table was an elaborate stand cradling the source of the light–a black gemstone the size of a raven's egg. It pulsed with energy, swirled with color. Blue and red flame flickered over the surface, responding to their presence like something alive, charging the air so that Reginn's hair haloed out.

It's reacting like a kynstone, Reginn thought. It's a mixture of red and blue. Jotun and Asgardian.

It commanded her attention like an infected wound–impossible to ignore. Attracting and repelling her in equal measure.

"How does Grima use the stone?" Reginn said. "How does she get the power back out?"

Kåre looked stumped. "I don't know that I've seen that." He paused. "She wears it sometimes, like a pendant."

Grima was jealous of Heidin and her pendant, and what it meant for her future. Maybe she thought she'd found her own path to divinity.

The beauty of blood magic is that it allows anyone to aspire to be a god.

"How many of your prisoners have died here since you took charge of this . . . program?"

Kåre looked away. "I haven't really kept count, ma'am. Not so very many."

"Just take a rough guess," Reginn said. "It doesn't need to be exact."

"I really couldn't say."

"Let's take a head count, then."

"What do you mean?"

"I have the ability to raise the dead—especially the restless dead. Would you like to meet them all? Reminisce, perhaps?"

Kåre's expression said that he would not. "What is it you want from me?"

"Grima comes and goes a lot," Reginn said. "She's often not here. You and I both know that Grima wouldn't leave you in charge of this many prisoners without giving you the ability to unlock them if you need to. This dead child, for instance. Please don't tell me that you would leave her chained to her modir for months until Grima returns?"

"It won't be that long," Kåre said.

"Even an hour is too long. I need the key to unlock these collars."

"She'll kill me," Kåre said. "Or lock me down there with the others,"

"You have a choice, then. You give me the key, or I will raise every person who died in this prison to tell their stories."

"No," Kåre whispered, his face gleaming with sweat.

"If it's not so very many, you have nothing to worry about."

He sighed. "All right. You win."

I don't know that I would call it winning.

Using the same key he'd used to unlock the chamber with the gemstone, Kåre unlocked a small iron door set into the stone wall and retrieved a tiny key on a silver chain. He dangled it so it swung a little. "Here's the key you were asking about."

"Show me how it works."

"What would you like me to–"

"Remove my collar," Reginn said.

Kåre came forward until he stood a foot away. Biting his lower lip, he took hold of Reginn's collar with one hand and inserted the key with the other.

He pushed hard, then turned it to the left. With a soft click, the collar opened and fell to the floor with a clatter, leaving Reginn dizzy with relief and hungry for air. She hadn't realized she'd been holding her breath.

Reginn scooped up the collar, examining the hinge and how it went together. "Where's the keyhole?"

"It appears when the key comes close. Here. Try it." He handed her the key.

It was true. There was no sign of a keyhole or a joint until she brought the key close.

"How do you turn it off?"

"You turn the key the other way," Kåre said.

"And how do I get the magic back out?"

"That I don't know. I've never tried."

Someone tapped on the door. "Is everything all right?"

"Give us another minute," Reginn said.

Kåre was massaging his forehead with the heel of his hand, muttering to himself.

"What is it?"

"She's going to kill me. You're looking at a dead man."

"Ah, well," Reginn said. "Death finds all of us sooner or later. If Grima returns, I'll be sooner and you'll be later."

Kåre didn't seem to find this reassuring. "What now?"

"Now we're going to free everyone. Beginning with you."

For days, the *Kraken* had prowled up and down the western coast of the Sudreyjar Islands, looking for activity on one or another of the islands that would signal the need to take a closer look. When they saw smoke rising from one of the southernmost islands, they stormed ashore to frighten an old man tending a tar pit.

Katia's dragons flew high in the sky, barely visible to Asger and his crew, but Katia claimed they could find a mouse in a thicket at that distance.

When they'd rounded the southernmost island, they sailed north along the sound side of the islands. Asger was beginning to lose hope. If the aldrnari were anywhere nearby, he ought to be able to sense her presence.

She could be dead, though that possibility was not acceptable.

His kind was not prone to worries or regret, but he couldn't shake the notion that they were running out of time.

And then, one morning, Reginn's presence awakened him, slamming into him like a rogue wave. He sat up, gasping, drowning in her scent, like magic boiling off a forest witch's cauldron. Levering to his feet, he sprinted aft, his footfalls scarcely registering, to where Gyda Fisker had just taken over the styrboard.

She looked up, startled, dropping the apple she was eating.

"Lord Eldr," she said, "what's the matter?"

"Raise the sail," he said. "Hurry. I know where she is."

Weighed down by worry, Durinn couldn't sleep. They commanded the best-equipped, best-trained army they'd ever seen, and the spinners were wasting it. Frittering it away.

Armies don't keep. You can't just park an army somewhere and keep it waiting until you decide what you're going to do with it. Not a living army, anyway. If you don't give it something to do, it will find something to do on its own.

Durinn had explained this to the new council in interminable meetings. Discipline was breaking down. Supplies were dwindling. It was only their isolated location that kept this army from terrorizing the countryside. Good officers can only do so much. They needed to fight or go home.

Everyone was sympathetic. Nobody argued. Nobody took action.

The queen was fighting her own demons. The kennari was focused on the queen. The council was useless without direction. Their best officers were sailing around the southern islands, looking for their missing counselor.

Durinn was beginning to appreciate the advantages of a dead army.

The sun was coming up when they heard a commotion outside. The captain of the night watch burst into the command tent.

"They're leaving!" Lars said.

"Who's leaving?"

"The Risen army."

"Where are their officers?"

"They're going, too."

Strapping on their sword, Durinn pushed outside.

It was true. The Risen swarmed the shoreline, more and more of them sliding into the waves as the breakers sluiced over them. Three of Durinn's living officers were flanking them, shouting at them, trying to drag them back, but Durinn could tell that was a lost cause. After watching an orc fling one of the officers back onto the sand, Durinn shouted, "Stand down. Leave them go. You won't stop them."

So they stood on the beach and watched them go until the beach was empty and the ocean aboil with dead warriors as far as the eye could see.

"Good riddance," Torsten, the infantry commander, said. He'd been against them from the beginning.

"Me, I'm sorry to see them go," Lars said. "They were the least troublesome of any of our soldiers."

"What is happening, Commander?" It was Tyra's voice.

Durinn turned to see Tyra and Heidin standing outside their tent, fully dressed and apparently ready for action.

"The Risen are leaving, my lady," Durinn said.

Now Heidin spoke. "And you did not try to stop them?"

Durinn glanced at their officers. "We tried, but it was not possible."

"Did you? Did you really try?" Heidin looked around. "Find Katia. No doubt her dragons could force them to turn back."

"Your... Grace," Durinn said. And stopped, unsure how to proceed, having no experience dealing with royalty. "Katia left with Lord Eldr to look for the counselor. They've not yet returned."

Heidin's face hardened. "Why is it that no one is where they should be? Why am I obstructed at every turn? I understood that I had an army at my disposal."

"And you do, Your Grace," Tyra said. "Perhaps we should catch up with the Risen. They may lead us to the others. And then we can–"

"No!" Heidin said. "We have dithered long enough. I am tired of being led around by Midlanders who are supposed to serve me. We will find the king wherever he is hiding and bring the war to him."

58
PARTINGS

WHEN THE KING AND HIS retinue sailed for Kingshavn, Ivar was aboard, and so was Naima, who remained under the care of the king's healer. Eiric was reluctant to see her go, but couldn't think of any argument he could make to keep her at Sundgard. At least Nils went with them. He'd been assisting the healer since she'd begun tending Naima.

"Send word if she wakes," Eiric said.

"Don't start any wars without me," Nils said.

Rikhard also left thirty heavily armed soldiers to keep an eye on the place and, Eiric suspected, also on him.

"I'll leave lookouts at the mouth of the sound," the king said. "If they see trouble coming, they'll light bonfires on top of the bluffs and send a bird to me."

Eiric inclined his head. "Thank you, Lord."

"See you soon." The king leaped nimbly aboard his flagship. They watched as she sailed out of sight.

They spent the rest of the day crawling all over the *Sylvi*, looking for any obvious damage. She was in remarkably good shape to have sat in the boat shed through ten winters and ten summers.

Much of the cording needed replacing, having rotted or been nibbled away by rats. The sail, too, was in ruins–moth-eaten and raided by rodents. Happily, the boatworks had spare cording, fittings, rope, and, yes, even some sails, which were often the pinch point.

Bjorn had been a stickler for proper ship stowage. Eiric was usually the one assigned to tar the ships at the haustblot so they would have the winter to dry. It was hard to do after a long summer of coasting and fishing when Eiric would have preferred to sit by the fire, tell stories, and taste the fruits of the new harvest.

Take care of your ship in the fall, and she'll reward you in the spring, his grandfadir would say from his seat by the fire, in between stories.

The scent of tar, fresh-sawn pine, bast, and lanolin took Eiric back. But the light was wrong–slanted sun, shorter days. This was not the season for putting ships into the water. This was the season for taking them out.

Now and then, the fiskers would stop to study a particularly fine bit of joinery or suggest a better way to redo it.

Finally, it was time to reintroduce her to the sea.

Working together, using the remains of an early snowfall to ease their path, they slid *Sylvi* out of the boat shed and down the shallow slope to the water's edge. Eiric waited for the rest of them to climb aboard, then seized the sternpost and launched her off the beach, swinging up and over the gunwale.

"She floats!" Rorik said, which drew a bit of cheering and the raising of invisible cups.

Eiric let *Sylvi* coast a bit, walking the length of her, looking for trouble spots. There was a little water coming in–there always was–but nothing worrisome. Nothing a little bailing couldn't handle.

"We're going to sail to the end of the sound and back," Eiric said. "One purpose is to test the sail and lines. I also want to see what a minimum crew would be. How many hands would it take to handle her under sail and oars?"

He returned to the styrboard and set a seaward course, feeling the touch of his grandfadir's hands on his own.

It was bitter cold, the air sharp and fresh as if it had never been breathed. Eiric was glad of the warm clothes the king had provided. He pulled the good wool hat down over his ears as sleet stung his face.

Kings were good for something after all.

Eventually, he handed over the styrboard to Reyna and took over the sheets for the sail. It was a larger sail than he'd managed in a long time, but he was bigger and stronger than he used to be, and the sound more sheltered than the open sea.

Gods, he'd missed this. Though he'd been unaware of ten years passing, his spirit felt the loss.

By the time they reached the mouth of the sound, Eiric knew two things—*Sylvi* was seaworthy, and, with a few adjustments, four crew could manage her for short distances. Though it was by no means a battle crew, it might be enough to get her to Kingshavn. But they really needed to get Nils back.

Before they turned around, he pulled out a spotting glass Bjorn had brought back from somewhere and scanned the bluffs to either side of the sound. He saw movement, and light reflecting off metal.

"Heads up," he said, pointing. "The king promised to post lookouts, and maybe he has. Be aware that someone is watching our comings and goings."

"You're sure it's the king?"

Eiric shrugged. "Probably. Could be spies from Jotunheim, though. Whoever they are, they're not here to kill us, at least not yet, or we'd be dead already. This pinch point is a double-edged sword. Properly monitored, it can prevent surprise attacks. But if an enemy gains control of the bluffs, it turns into a trap. Post some talented bowmen up there, and nobody's getting in or out.

"Now, let's go back home while there's still daylight, and I'll show you how to rework the lines."

Despite the excitement of the day, the nattmal was more somber than some. They all knew change was coming, but they didn't know what kind.

There was still plenty of food and drink—the raiders had been focused on killing, not stealing. Though most of the stores in the main hall were burned, some of the outbuildings remained intact, including the smokehouse and the springhouse.

It made for a simple meal–smoked chicken, barley, Sundgard apples, and plenty of ale and wine.

Eiric found himself giving them counsel–none too subtly–like a fadir leaving for a season of coasting and unsure whether he would survive the summer.

"Hopefully, it will take the king's soldiers a while to discover that I am gone. Use that time to make the adjustments to *Sylvi*'s rigging. When they ask, tell them you don't know where I am, but I promised to return. And I give you my word that I will return, if I can."

"You're really leaving," Rorik said.

Eiric lifted his hands, palms up. "I said I was."

"But how will you manage a ship on your own?" Levi said.

"I have a plan," Eiric said. "Now, if I'm not back and Rikhard gets impatient, you'll have a decision to make. The king has a temper and you don't want to be the target. You can take *Firebird* and whatever weapons seem useful, sail back to Fiskeholm and find your families. This might be a good time, with the Jotun army focused elsewhere.

"Or you can sign on with Rikhard, and fight the Jotun here. You've met him, he's impressed with you, he knows you are good sailors. If Rikhard wins this thing, he's likely to be generous with you."

As Eiric was speaking, the fiskers had become increasingly restless. Finally, Rorik spoke up. "Listen," he said, looking around at the others before he continued. "We've talked, and we've never met a better styrman. We've learned so much. You've always been honest with us, and–"

"No, he hasn't," Reyna said. "Not always."

Rorik took a breath, began again. "You haven't always been honest with us, but you've done only necessary lying."

Reyna rolled her eyes. "What Rorik is trying to say is, we understand the pull of kinship. We trust your judgment. We'll sail with you, and help you save your systir if we can."

Tears stung Eiric's eyes, and he was unable to speak for a moment. Instead, he stood, and walked around the table, embracing each of them.

"Thank you," he said. "Whatever I decide, please know that I've never sailed with a better crew."

59
KLETTRHOLM

IN THE DAYS FOLLOWING REGINN'S visit to the Deeps, she worked harder than she ever had—even during her time with Asger Eldr. In the space of an hour, she could be healer, counselor, military commander, and quartermaster.

All of the collared spinners were given the choice whether to keep their collars and their allegiance to Grima or to have their collars removed. All elected to lose the collars.

Reginn's first priority was to move the prisoners from the Deeps to a large, sunny room on the first floor of the Cliff House. Hearths at each end kept the room pleasantly warm, and windows and a terrace could be used for fresh air if the weather ever improved. She sent foragers out to scour the island for herbs, willow bark, and other remedies.

Reginn had some experience treating opium eaters. Healthier users came directly to her, hoping that she might have opium in her remedy bag. Those didn't stay long, if Asger was around. Later, she would be called in by families seeking a cure. She had no way of knowing if what she did was helpful in the long term. Most she never saw again.

Some of those rescued from the Deeps were too far gone to save—by Reginn, anyway. The runes were helpful, as always, and, for some, it was a matter of carefully refeeding them and so restoring their strength.

Fortunately, the Cliff House had been built as a fortress, a refuge and hideout for Grima and her spider spinners. She had been collecting tools, weapons, foodstuffs, and supplies for a long time. A strong freshwater spring provided a reliable source of water, and Reginn took steps to protect it.

Unfortunately, Grima knew the fortress's strengths and weaknesses better than anyone.

The presence of the Spider's gemstone weighed on Reginn. She hated the Deeps, but, still, she returned to the locked room to make sure that it was still there. She knew that if Grima still lived, she would come for it.

She was tempted to throw it into the churning waves at the base of the cliffs. Or to bury it, or lock it away where no one would find it.

All things hidden will be found, Tove used to say. *All doors locked will be opened.*

Even if Reginn Eiklund wore the key on a chain around her neck.

Other times, she fingered the gold webbing that encased the stone, tempted to take it for herself. Why not? She would need all the power she could get.

No. She would not feed on power stolen from others.

Indecision led to inertia. She let it be.

Her rogue mind went to dark places. Had Heidin turned into a monster? Had Eiric Halvorsen sailed into a trap? Was Naima still alive? Had Reginn escaped Asger Eldr only to be locked up tight in a fortress? Could it be that, outside these walls, everything she loved was being destroyed?

The residents of Klettrholm were tentative and wary in celebrating their new freedom. They knew everything could change in a heartbeat if Grima returned. Reginn suspected that, had boats been available, they all would have fled. Herself included.

Reginn could have used more hands. Grima had taken most of the gifted with her and left only a small force of soldiers to protect the island. When Reginn did a head count, she had thirty healthy spinners and one hundred or so soldiers, along with a dozen servants and other workers.

All the healthy spinners had staffs. She met with them, one by one, to ask about their individual gifts. Most had no idea. Grima had never shown any interest in that. They were all trained to use their staffs as weapons and channel their megin there.

After persistent questioning, Reginn determined that two were weather witches, one was a seer. Atla, of course, spoke to birds. One was a diviner who could sieve truths from lies. One was a master of light and dark, another a moodcaster who could strip one emotion from an attacker and replace it with another.

Reginn just wished she had more time to get to know them in order to make the best use of their talents. It would be months before they could turn away an army of any size. She hoped that the fortress would help even the odds.

When she'd left the Archipelago, there were no real armies that she knew of. Now there were at least three–King Rikhard's, Queen Heidin's, and Grima's.

Kåre, all but giddy at the fact that he was still alive, became one of Reginn's best sources. He seemed to realize that his future prospects rested on her success, and, fortunately, he knew a lot about the island's fortifications, strengths, and weaknesses.

The seaward face of the Cliff House was all but invisible, resembling a sheer cliff with numerous ledges that concealed terraces, doorways, and vantage points for archers.

The landward side had high walls built of the native stone, which made it appear to be more a feature of a craggy landscape than a castle. Only at a close distance could the entry be seen. Attackers would never get that close, if the sentries were doing their job.

"If you're defending this island, what keeps you up at night?" Reginn said.

"The sea caves," Kåre said promptly, as if he'd been thinking about this for some time. "They're all over this island, hidden in the cliffs and underwater. Attackers who know where they are could be in the middle of us before we even know they're here."

"Does Grima know where they are?"

Kåre rocked his hand. "Some of them. She asked me to figure out a way to block them.

"And have you?"

He shook his head. "Nothing stops the sea forever. It will find its way in."

"We don't have to stop the sea forever," Reginn said thoughtfully. "Just long enough. Is there a map of the caves?"

Kåre nodded. "Some of them. The ones we know of. I'll get it to you."

60

THROUGH THE MUCKLANDS

EIRIC FELT GUILTY ABOUT LEAVING Sundgard without a real goodbye, but he knew from experience how obstinate the fiskers could be. His only hope of survival on the path he'd chosen was by stealth. He would take the little fishing boat Bjorn and Liv had built, and Ivar restored, and hopefully skim across land Bjorn described as "too thin to farm and too thick to drink."

The channels he and Liv had made would be long gone. But water continued to flow from the river, through the marsh and into the sound, until pushed back by the tide. So he hoped he could still find a channel of some sort. If all else failed, he could portage his boat over short distances.

There was no good cover on the marsh or the river beyond. The best he could hope for was darkness, fog, and rain to keep everyone else inside, by the fire.

He never asked for sleet, but that's what he got.

Thistle nosed into the marshes at the head of the sound, the mast and sail lashed down so that they wouldn't poke up against the flat horizon. Sound carried across the marshes, too, so he wielded the oars with care to avoid splashing. Frozen grasses whispered against the gunwales as they brushed past and clattered when the Gormanudur winds caught them.

There is no cold like Gormanudur, a damp cold that sinks into the bone. The prospect of a long winter ahead makes it worse.

Ice crusted Eiric's coat, stung his cheeks, and rimed his hair and lashes. He must resemble the issvargr–the ice monsters–of Bjorn's stories. Yet, still, his undergarments were soaked in sweat.

Once, he got hung up in a tangle of dead snags and rushes, but he reversed his oars and managed to push off with them. When he looked back, his track was rapidly icing over. When he looked forward, the trees seemed just as far away as ever.

His goal was to make it through the marsh and into the cover of trees by the river before the sun rose. Fortunately, nights were long this time of year.

The relentless bad weather began clearing a little before dawn. A few stars came out before the brightening sky washed them out. It was good that he was getting closer to the river and its welcome fringe of trees. Eiric raked the ice from his hair and brushed it from his clothing before the rising sun could melt it.

He heard a cry from overhead, faint and far away. He looked up, and saw two specks, too high up to identify. They passed over him, making a huge circle, then returned, at a lower altitude, as if they were searching for something. Whatever they were, they must be huge. He'd never seen birds that large fly over Muckleholm—or anywhere else in the Archipelago.

When they came around a third time, he realized they were dragons.

Dragons? Of all the tales he'd heard about the beasts of the interior, he'd never heard dragons mentioned. He slid down and lay flat in the freezing water atop the burden boards and pulled the sleeping tarp over himself.

Just in case they were looking for him.

Apparently, they weren't, because after that third pass, they flew off.

With the light growing, Eiric, wet and half-frozen, knew he had better find cover quickly. Happily, the marsh's many channels were finally flowing together, narrowing into one deep one—the river. The mountains loomed up high on his right side and he finally found himself within a fringe of trees. When he was well in, he dragged *Thistle* far up into the trees to where the shoulder of the mountain began. He pitched his tarp in the shelter of a ravine and used his fire-steel to light a small, hot fire that hopefully wouldn't show up in the daylight. He stripped, hung his clothes over a small tree to dry, and lay down next to the fire with Gramr by his side. He pulled his wolfskin throw over himself and slept like the dead.

61

IVAR

IVAR HAD RETURNED TO KINGSHAVN from Sundgard with the king to prepare to go to war against those who had carried out the massacre at Sundgard. The days were growing shorter in the run-up to the winter solstice, so he rose when the first streaks of light brightened the horizon across the eastern sea and often worked by lamplight long after the sun had disappeared behind the western mountains. Much of what he'd been doing was inspecting ships, inventorying stores, and seeing that all of Rikhard's soldiers were properly kitted out after a relatively quiet summer.

Rikhard didn't quite know what to do with a prince on his hands. When he saw Ivar handling logistics, he said, "Ivar! You're not a clerk or a quartermaster." More and more, he had Ivar sit in on his meetings with his commanders, his business factors, and nobility from all over the Archipelago.

And yet, Rikhard was reluctant to allow Ivar to go to war with him. "Your Grace," Ivar said. "I've been sailing with you since I was six years old."

"You were not my heir when you were six years old," Rikhard said. "The realm was much smaller. There was less at stake."

"Even more reason I should fight for my legacy," Ivar said. "Why should your liege lords bend the knee to someone who isn't willing to fight alongside them?"

"I have named you my heir," Rikhard said, jaw hard, eyes glittering. "It is not a matter of their choice."

"Soldiers always have a choice," Ivar said. "As do the jarls. It might be an unpleasant choice, but the notion of a king is still new to them."

Rikhard rolled his eyes. "What was I thinking when I hired all those tutors and teachers and logicians? Did I hope that, one day, I would lose more arguments?"

Ivar laughed. "You probably hoped that, in the end, you would have a very good clerk."

Then one morning, Sif, the healer tending the sole survivor of the Sundgard massacre, came to Ivar and told him that her patient was finally awake and talking. Ivar dropped what he was doing and followed her.

He hoped to learn more about the attack, as if knowledge could be the answer to pain. Most raiders would smash any resistance, steal valuables, and carry off prospects for the slave markets. This was different. He'd never seen such wholesale slaughter, down to children and livestock. Why would Liv attack her home farm so viciously? What message was she sending?

When he and Sif arrived at the bedside, he was disappointed to find that someone else was already there. Familiar. Ivar groped for a name.

"Nils, Your Grace," the interloper said, standing, trying out a little bow. "I've been helping Sif with Naima's care. I was the one who found her at Sundgard."

Right. Nils was one of his brodir's crew members. The fiskers, he called them. "Has she said anything?"

"My name is Naima," the patient said, "and it's rude to talk about me as if I'm not here."

Ivar blinked at her. "My apologies, Naima. You're right."

"Who are you?" she said. "Where am I? Apparently nobody is allowed to tell me anything but you." She studied him. "How old are you, anyway?"

"Ten," Ivar said. "Eleven, just after the Solstice. My name is Ivar."

Naima's eyes narrowed, so he could tell she'd heard the name.

So he continued. "You're at Kingshavn, the seat of King Rikhard of the Archipelago."

"Not at Sundgard."

"No," he said, and cleared his throat. "Not at Sundgard." He claimed the bedside chair. "How are you feeling?"

"I've been better," she said, fingering the etched pendant.

"If you're from Sundgard, I'm surprised we haven't met," Ivar said. "I was born there, and I know–knew–almost everyone there." He was mortified to find his vision blurring with tears.

Naima didn't seem to notice the tears or the implied question. "I can see the resemblance," she said, studying him.

"Resemblance?"

"Between you and your brodir. Halvorsen."

"You know my brodir?" Ivar said.

"Not well," Naima said. "I had the cell next door to him in prison, and then I helped with his sending."

"His . . . sending?" Ivar said. They all looked at each other. Was it possible she was still dreaming?

"I need to talk to Halvorsen right away," Naima said, brushing past obvious questions. "There was a note." She patted herself down and scanned the bedclothes. "Did you find a note?"

"I didn't see a note," Ivar said. He looked up at Nils and Sif, and they shook their heads, though Nils shifted his gaze away.

Ivar wondered if their sole witness was still addled by the poison.

Sif thought the same, apparently. "Look, you've been quite ill, and sleeping for days, so it will take some time to–"

"Days?" Naima said, eyes wide. "I've been sleeping for *days*?" She sat up and swung her legs over the side of the bench. "Where's Halvorsen? Did he see the note?"

Naima tried to get to her feet, and it was only Sif's arm around her that kept her from falling. "Halvorsen's still at Sundgard," Sif said. "He'll be here in a few days."

"Naima," Nils said. The fisker had gone pale as mare's milk. "What about a note? Why is that important?"

"It's a trap," Naima said. "The note is a trap. She tried to get me to lie to Halvorsen, to get him to sail into a trap. When I refused, she decided to plant a note on my dead body so he'd be convinced that it was real."

"Liv is trying to trap her own brodir?" Ivar said, lost.

"Who's Liv?" Naima said. "I'm talking about Grima. She was the one who attacked Sundgard."

62

OUT THE BACK DOOR

THE MORNING AFTER THE RESTORED *Sylvi*'s maiden voyage, Levi awoke from a dead sleep to Reyna shaking him. "He's gone," she whispered.

"What?" Levi said groggily, feeling the effects of too much drink the night before. "Who's gone?"

"Halvorsen."

"Are you sure?"

"Pretty sure. His bed is empty, and his armor and weapons are gone."

Levi had to look for himself. Halvorsen's coat and carry bags and the wolf pelt he slept under were gone, too. The bed looked as if it hadn't been slept in. But atop the bedclothes was a folded packet made of chamois, tied with a string. The word *IVAR* was scratched into the surface with an awkward hand.

"What's that?" Levi said. "Maybe it's a note. Did you open it?"

"It says *I-V-A-R*. Not *R-E-Y-N-A*."

Filled with foreboding, Levi said, "Are there any boats missing?"

"*Firebird* and *Sylvi* are still anchored in the shallows."

"What's he planning to do?" Levi muttered, massaging his aching head. "Walk all the way? Swim?"

"Rorik went to the shipbuilding hall to have a look," Reyna said. "Let's go see if he's found anything."

Levi gestured toward the packet on Eiric's bed. "What about this?"

"Leave it for now," Reyna said.

Rorik met them at the door.

"Anything?" Reyna said.

Rorik shook his head. "I've walked around a couple of times, but nothing seems to be missing. Most of the ships in here weren't much more than a keel and a pair of stems–not nearly ready to meet the water. They must have finished up everything they had that was close and stopped there."

Levi had been to the shipbuilding hall several times in the past few days to find fittings and parts for ship repair. So he took a walk around himself. It was harder to look for something that was missing than for something that was there.

Next, he tried the repair shop.

"Here's something," he said. "I don't know if it's important."

They all gathered around him. He pointed to the empty rack. "There was a little boat there a few days ago."

Reyna stamped her feet and tucked her hands under her arms. "I don't remember a boat."

"I only noticed it because Halvorsen was giving it a good going-over, as if seeing if the repair was sound. I made fun of it–told him it wasn't much of a boat, but maybe we could use it for the harbor boat on *Sylvi*. He said his grandfadir and systir built it years ago. Ivar was restoring it, and he wanted to make sure it was safe."

"Could Ivar have taken it back to Kingshavn with him?" Rorik said.

Levi shook his head. "I've seen it since the king and his party left. Yesterday, in fact."

"Remember the rough water around the southern tip of Muckleholm? Do you think he's planning to sail that toy boat through there?"

"It would take forever, hugging the coast," Levi said. "By the time he gets there, the war will be over, one way or another. His systir will be queen of the world, or she'll be dead."

"That can't be his plan," Reyna said. "He's smarter than that."

"Maybe he has no plan," Levi said. "Maybe he wants to go down in battle and get to Valhalla as quick as he can."

Reyna shook her head. "We're overlooking something. I wish Nils was here. He's clever at puzzles."

Levi was stung by the notion that Reyna thought Nils was cleverer than he was. He racked his brain.

There was a map nailed up on the boathouse wall—a detailed map of the entire island of Muckleholm. Levi went to take a closer look.

"Come here and look at this," he called to the others. "There was something else that Halvorsen said. He said that before he was old enough to go vikingr, he and his systir would sail that little boat up into the tidal river and the marshes at the head of the sound."

"That's touching," Rorik said. "So?"

Levi traced the course of the river alongside the mountains and into the marsh near Vandrgardr. "I wonder if Halvorsen knows of a back door through the middle of the island to the other side. One that might be navigable with a boat with an unusually shallow draft."

They looked at each other, stunned.

"Let's go look," Reyna said, and they boiled out the door. They stopped short when they saw a boat approaching the beach under full sail. It was a small, bladelike longboat that reminded Levi of *Firebird*. Rikhard's pennant flew from the mast. At the last minute, they dropped the sail, and the styrman ran the boat straight up onto the shingle beach and leaped out to anchor the bowline.

That's when Levi realized that the styrman was Ivar Himself, Halvorsen's man-child of a brodir.

Besides Ivar, the ship carried four soldiers and two passengers—Nils and Naima.

By the time the passengers disembarked, the king's guardsmen had formed a rough half circle around the landing spot.

Naima! Levi studied her. She looked paler than before, weaker than before—but she was alive, her expression grim and determined.

Matching everybody else's. When she saw the charred longhouse, she shuddered and swayed, on her way to a fall, until Nils steadied her.

The king's guard, of course, was focused on Ivar.

"Your . . . Grace," Captain Larssen said, as if unsure what title to choose. He bowed low, and the rest of the guard rippled down like a stand of saplings under the blade. "To what do we owe the pleasure of your visit?"

Right, Levi thought. Ivar was a prince now. He had a gold circlet pinned into his flaming hair to prove it.

But something else had caught the prince's eye. "Is that the *Sylvi*?" Ivar said, staring. "I never thought to see her on the water again."

"The king asked us to get her ready to sail," Rorik said. "We've been working on her all week."

"You should be proud of the work you've done," Ivar said. Then turned to Larssen. "I would speak with my brodir, Captain. Where is he?"

"Should you be traveling without an escort, Your Grace?" Larssen said. "As we've seen, these are dangerous times."

"Your prince has asked a question," one of Ivar's guards said. "Should you be answering it?"

Ivar's lips twitched, a trace of a smile.

Getting used to the prince thing, are you? Levi thought.

Captain Larssen cleared his throat, then turned to the fiskers. "Has anyone seen Halvorsen? Is he in the boat shed?"

"He's not in the boat shed," Rorik said. "We just came from there."

"Then where is he?"

"He must have gone out very early this morning," Rorik said. "He was gone before we woke up."

"But none of the ships are missing," Larssen persisted. "Would he have taken one of the horses, or–"

"*I need to speak with Halvorsen,*" Naima said, her voice like a punch to the gut. "Where is he?"

"This is Naima's first day out of bed," Nils said. "Let's not make her stand here while we catch up on the news. Let's go into the boat shed, where we can sit."

As they walked back toward the boat shed, Larssen called, "Your Highness, shall I attend you–"

"Find my brodir, Captain," Ivar said without turning around. "Search every inch of this property, both the home farm and the manufactories while we talk."

With the *Sylvi* gone, the boat shed seemed cavernous. Ivar felt the absence keenly. When he was little, he used to climb up the scaffolding, take the styrman's seat, and sail her to all the places he'd never been and might not get to. His uncles had wanted to sell her, no doubt eager to be rid of the history she represented, but Hilde had stepped in. As she always had. As she never would again.

Every child needs one person to have his back.

They gathered in the living area Hilde had set up for them when Eiric and his crew had first arrived. Where the fiskers had continued to sleep and take their meals.

Naima was given the best chair–a charred armchair rescued from the ruins of the longhouse. The fiskers buzzed around, offering food and drink, blankets and pillows. They acted as if they were in the presence of royalty–not Ivar, but Naima.

Ivar rested his palms on his knees. Calloused palms. Bony knees. "Naima has told this story once. She has asked me to help in the retelling, though I know she will speak up if I make a mistake–which I probably will."

That drew a few strained smiles.

"First, and most important, Naima says that it was not Liv Halvorsen–or Heidin, as she calls herself now–who was behind the attack on Sundgard, but Grima Lund. I believe some of you met her in Langvik?" He looked up at Eiric's crew, and they nodded. Then he looked to Naima.

"Grima's been playing her own game for years," Naima said. "Here in the Archipelago, she is out from under the eye of the academy and the council, building her own hird of spinners she calls wraiths. She calls herself the Spider. Your king thinks she's working for him, the Jotun queen thinks she's working for them, when in reality, she's working for herself.

"Heidin's armies are camped on the western shore of Muckleholm, near Vandrgardr," Naima continued. "I was there when Grima brought her wraiths to camp. There was a big row and Heidin threw everyone out. In the confusion, Grima kidnapped me and my . . . friend . . . Reginn Eiklund."

"But why would she target Sundgard?" Rorik said. "Why not have a go at Kingshavn? And why would she be so–so–" He took a breath. "Why would she slaughter everyone?"

"I think it was a message to Eiric Halvorsen. Grima's obsessed with him. She was set to execute him in New Jotunheim until Heidin–Liv–intervened. So she felt cheated. That's why she laid this trap for him."

"What trap?" Levi said.

"She wanted me to deliver a message to Halvorsen, supposedly from Reginn, inviting Halvorsen to a meetup with Liv so they could sort things out. If I handed her Halvorsen, she would free me and Reginn. I refused, so they brought me along to Sundgard and left me on the battlefield with the rest of the dead and a note."

"But you weren't dead," Nils said.

"I wasn't dead. Maybe it was this." Naima pulled out a silver pendant inscribed with runes and held it up for everyone to see. "Reginn gave me this before I was taken away, for protection, she said. Or maybe it was good care." She nodded at Nils. "Or maybe I was just too pissed to die."

That drew a smattering of laughter.

"Naima says there was a note," Ivar said, "but she doesn't have it now. Does anyone know anything about that?"

"There *was* a note," Levi said. "And a map. Halvorsen must have it with him. But we can show you where he's going."

"And we can tell you what the note said." Nils glanced at Naima. "It's pretty much as Naima described."

"So he's gone," Ivar said with a sigh. "He's gone to have this meeting."

"We believe so, yes," Reyna said. "We think he left last night or early this morning while we were sleeping. He took his weapons and belongings with him. He said that he would come back as soon as he could." She handed a leather packet to Ivar. "He left this."

IVAR. He traced the letters with his forefinger, then unfolded the leather.

He held it up, dangling from its chain. It was Eiric's amulet—the one that had belonged to his fadir, Leif.

They stared at it in silence. Ivar knew what they were thinking. It felt too much like a legacy.

"He probably wanted you to keep it safe for him until he returns," Levi said. "Or maybe he hoped it would keep you safe."

Everyone nodded in agreement.

Yes. That was it.

Ivar dropped the chain over his head and tucked the tarnished silver pendant out of sight. "But why would he go?" Ivar said. "It's obviously a trap."

"He knows it's a trap," Reyna said. "But he still hopes to find a way to save his systir."

"But how would he get there, without a ship?" Ivar said.

"There is a ship missing," Levi said. "Not from here, from the main boathouse. It was the little one that you were restoring."

"*Thistle,*" Ivar whispered. A memory struck Ivar to the bone—that last conversation with Eiric, when Eiric reminisced about sailing with Liv when he was small, and Ivar had said, "I don't have a systir."

"I told him to take it," Ivar said. "I told him I didn't want it." He paused, allowing that to ripple through the fiskers. "But why would he choose that one? It's scarcely big enough to hold two people."

"He wanted a ship that he could manage by himself," Levi said.

"We wanted to go with him," Reyna said, "but he didn't want to put anyone else at risk. He told us we should either sail back to our home island or join Rikhard at Kingshavn and fight for him. Then he slipped away last night."

"He also might have chosen *Thistle* for another reason," Levi said. He took the map down off the wall and spread it on the table. "Here is where he's going." He pointed to a small island off the west coast of Muckleholm. "We thought he might be planning to go by way of the river." He traced the route with his finger. "Is it possible? Have you ever sailed up that way?"

Ivar smiled ruefully and shook his head. "We were always too busy, you know, conquering the Archipelago to explore the sound. It wasn't a priority. And *Thistle* was in ruins."

It struck Ivar that Eiric's crew knew him much better than he did. Perhaps much better than he ever would.

"Whichever way he's gone, at least we know what his destination is," Nils said.

"So," Ivar said. "What have you decided to do?" When they looked at him, puzzled, he said, "Are you going to sail back home or come to Kingshavn?"

They looked at one another.

"We haven't discussed it," Rorik said, "but I'm thinking we'll go look for our styrman."

Ivar laughed, for the first time in a long time. "Do you only follow the orders you like?"

Reyna snorted. "We're not very good at following orders at all."

"If you go to Klettrholm," Naima said, "could I come with you?"

They all turned, startled. It had been so long since she'd spoken that they had nearly forgotten she was there.

"I grow stronger every day," she said. "I'm not a deft hand with a sail, but I'm a hard worker and a quick learner. I'll pull my weight. If I don't, you can leave me off somewhere."

"I don't doubt that you'll pull your weight," Nils said, "but you've been through a lot already. Wouldn't it be better to rest and heal before you launch into a new–?"

"If I wait, I may be too late," Naima said. "Reginn Eiklund saved my life in New Jotunheim. She didn't have to, and she stuck her neck out to do it. I hadn't even been that nice to her."

The fiskers looked at each other. Finally, Levi said, "I–we didn't know that the queen's counselor had saved your life."

"We didn't noise it around," Naima said. "She was always one step away from trouble as it was. Ever since, I've been trying to return the favor, and let me tell you, it hasn't been easy to keep her alive. Now she's in Grima's hands, if she's not dead already. You've seen what Grima did here in Sundgard."

The fiskers looked at each other, came to a silent agreement.

"We would be honored to have you with us," Levi said.

"You could come with us, too," Reyna said to Ivar. "That would bring us up to a point where we could properly crew *Sylvi*. Not for battle, but for speed. She's a much faster ship than *Firebird*."

Levi could tell that Ivar was tempted. But then the new prince sighed and shook his head. "When I left Kingshavn, Rikhard was preparing to sail. He needs to hear this news before then. I didn't exactly ask permission to come here." He drummed his fingers on the tabletop. "What if we all sailed *Sylvi* back to Kingshavn, updated the king, and then set sail for Klettrholm?"

Rorik shook his head. "We're going the long way as it is. A stop in Kingshavn will mean days of delay, if the king allows us to sail at all. He has other priorities. He may have received word that the Jotun army is on the move. We don't want Eiric sailing into Klettrholm Harbor thinking to find his systir and finding Grima instead."

"Understood," Ivar said. "I'll return to Kingshavn, update the king, and hope he'll allow me to bring at least a handful of ships to your aid." He paused. "I would suggest that you be on your way as soon as possible. King Rikhard may very well decide that he has other plans for you."

Ivar turned toward his ship, then turned back. "Take *Sylvi*, if you can crew her. I believe she wants to go to sea again."

63

INTERCEPTION

IVAR PULLED HIS WOOL CAP down over his ears and turned up the collar of his storm coat. His longboat lunged forward as the sail caught the wind, until they were flying. "We'll drop the sail when we reach the narrows," he called, keeping a firm grip on the styrboard. On the water, he issued orders like a lord, and not a ten-year-old orphan with a hole in his heart.

His crew was good—or at least good enough for him to take some time mulling over the story that Naima had told. In the dark days after the attack at Sundgard, he was faced with bottomless grief and no satisfactory way to address it.

All lines of connection had been cut away, setting him adrift. Even his uncles and grandfadir were gone.

Taking vengeance on his own systir seemed unlikely to bring the redemption he hoped for, even though the sagas were peppered with such stories. Eiric's obvious love and respect for Liv were hard to ignore.

Slow down, he thought. Remember—Eiric had said that Liv was possessed by a dead goddess, and so was not herself.

Still. For the first time in a long time, he felt like he was facing an enemy worth having. He'd never liked or trusted Agata/Grima. She'd always struck him as a predator, and he felt like prey.

Rikhard would not be happy to learn that his Asgardian warrior had gone off on a mission of his own. It would not help that the fisker crew had commandeered the dragon ship that the king had planned to use as a flagship. Ivar needed to present this story to the king in a way that would cool the flames of his temper.

A skill he'd developed over years at Kingshavn.

"Coming up on the narrows, Styrman," Drifa called.

"Drop sail and let's go to the oars."

Drifa was already on it, of course. She was the most experienced member of his growing hird. Rikhard had assigned her to him at an age when he was more in need of a nanny than a guard. And yet she'd thwarted more than one attempt on his life.

His immediate challenge was to navigate the narrows and round the headland into Ulfness Sound. He'd been through this way a hundred times, but the tide was running seaward. Between that and the westerly wind, they had put on speed. Too much speed, for safety.

A voice from some past ship's master whispered in his ear.

Always slow through the narrows, boy, even though you've passed through a hundred times before. The sea never stands still. In the narrows, when something goes wrong, there's no place to go.

They were nearly through, when the bowman shouted, "Ship dead ahead."

Another ship had appeared from beyond the headland, crossing directly in front of them, so that a collision appeared inevitable.

Were they doing it on purpose?

Ivar wrenched the styrboard over, making a hard turn, knowing he was putting them at risk for foundering, given their current rate of speed.

He preferred foundering to a collision, so he all but put the gunwale in the water and hoped for the best.

Hoping for the best–not usually a winning strategy. In this case they skinned past the other ship by inches, only to slam into the rocky outcropping that framed the narrows.

The bow lookout died instantly, thrown from the ship into the rock face, then sliding down and disappearing into the sea. Two other crew were tossed from the ship into the water boiling against the rocks. Only Ivar and Drifa were left aboard a ship that was rapidly disintegrating against the rocks.

That was how quickly disaster could strike in the narrows.

The wreckage was temporarily trapped behind a rocky outcropping. That prevented it from being carried out to sea, but he knew that wouldn't last long.

All at once, Drifa was beside him. "Highness," she said. "Get ready to climb."

She waited until the ship's gunwale was temporarily lodged against the rocks, then gave Ivar a boost up and over, onto an icy ledge. He sat up, teeth chattering, and saw that the movement had pushed the ship away from the edge temporarily. Drifa clutched a coil of rope under her arm, and when the ship slammed into the rocks again, she threw it to Ivar.

He looked for an anchor. Great fingers of rock thrust upward from a rocky base, and Ivar looped the rope around one of them, secured it with a good knot, then knotted a loop into the free end and dropped it into Drifa's waiting hands. Looping the rope around herself, Drifa walked up the sheer rocks until she could join Ivar on his ledge.

They both turned and scanned the waters below, looking for any other survivors. They saw only their broken ship, shivering into pieces. Ivar knew that no one could survive for long in that freezing water.

No one could survive for long, soaking wet, clinging to the icy rocks as they were, with no dry clothes, not even a fire-steel.

Worse, the strange ship had reappeared, and was now making slow progress toward them under oar power, fighting the tide and the winds. A banner flew from the mast, a brilliant bird taking flight from the flames. Familiar. It was the same one that Eiric's ship had carried when he'd arrived in Muckleholm.

The Firebird of New Jotunheim.

"Skita," Ivar muttered. "Let's climb."

With any luck, the jotnar would be too wary of coming close enough to the rocks to come ashore and pursue them.

And so they climbed, up and away from the churning sea, sometimes scrambling, sometimes using the rope. It was a dangerous business. Ivar's hands were so numb that it was difficult to tell when he had a good handhold or not. The same was true of his feet, which felt like clumsy blocks of ice. They did their best to stay out of view of the channel, but that meant that they could not see what the enemy was up to, either.

It would not matter what the enemy was up to if they did not find shelter soon. Ivar racked his brain, trying to remember if there was anything atop the headland–a shepherd's cottage, a lookout shelter–something.

Nothing came to mind.

When they finally crested the bluff, the wind hit them like Thor's hammer, sending Ivar staggering back, nearly to the edge of the drop-off, before Drifa gripped his shoulder.

When they turned landward, they found a squadron of soldiers waiting for them.

Most were clad in unfamiliar buff-colored uniforms and heavy storm coats emblazoned with the same emblem as was displayed on the ship's banner. A handful wore finely made coats in a brilliant blue, silk sashes with emblems on them, and carried staffs. They were younger than the others, close to Eiric's age, and finely made themselves. Spinners of all genders–unheard of in the Archipelago.

Two women stood out. One was slightly older, with strong features and hair streaked with copper, silver, and gold, as if metals were woven into it.

The other was unlike anyone Ivar had ever seen before–spectacular in every way. Taller than most men, she wore what resembled a coat of flames that seethed around her body and gave off a heat of its own.

Her hair also writhed and snapped, shedding sparks all around. Her skin was a coppery gold, engraved by flame, and an amulet bearing the image of a firebird was embedded in the skin of her chest.

Was this, then, Liv–the systir who had been hammered and flamed and forged into a goddess?

That question was answered when an officer cried, "On your knees before the divine queen Heidin of the Jotun, thrice burned, thrice raised."

Drifa pulled Ivar down beside her and whispered, "I'm going to try to persuade them to let you go."

Ivar nodded once, his eyes fixed on the ground. He was shivering, teeth chattering. He could not help it.

He heard the swish and hiss of the queen's skirts as she approached.

"What have we here?" she said. "A soldier and . . . a drowned rat?" Her voice was low and husky, like that of the opium smokers Ivar had encountered in the port cities of the Archipelago. "On your feet, both of you."

Ivar and Drifa stood, Drifa pulling Ivar close to her side.

"Shame about your little ship," Heidin said. "You should watch where you're going."

"That was my fault, ma'am," Ivar said, ignoring Drifa's glare. "I was styrman. I should have slowed down when we entered the narrows. When I saw your ship, I panicked."

"Please, ma'am, I'm hoping you might consider letting the boy go," Drifa said quickly. "He's my son, you see. We've been to Sundgard many times, and I brought him along today so he could–so he could see the damage."

"Well," the queen said, sounding amused. "That was poor timing." She paused. "What *did* happen here? Who did this?"

Ivar could tell that Drifa was groping for a safe answer. "Sundgard is destroyed, the longhouse burned, everyone killed. It was invaders from New Jotunheim, across the sea," he said. "Spinners."

Heidin was close now, so close that Ivar could feel her heat roll over him. In his present half-frozen state, it was all he could do not to purr like a cat and bask in it.

"Who commanded these spinners?" Heidin said.

Ivar and Drifa looked at each other.

"We are told that a witch named Grima led the attack," Drifa said.

"Grima." Heidin's expression was unreadable. "I am not surprised."

"We assumed that she attacked on your orders," Ivar said.

"Don't make assumptions, and you'll make fewer mistakes," Heidin snapped.

"We're wasting time here," the older spinner said. "Dispose of them, and let's go on to Sundgard and see for ourselves."

"Shut up, Modir," Heidin said.

Yes, Ivar thought. Shut up, Modir. His own interests aside, he didn't want the fiskers intercepted, either.

"Does the king still live?"

"Yes," Drifa said. "It is a blessing that he was not here."

"There's also an Asgardian warrior that I have heard of," Heidin said. "Fair-haired, blue-green eyes, a fierce fighter. His name is Eiric Halvorsen. I know that Grima has a special grudge against him. Did he die at Sundgard?" The edge to her voice said that her interest was more than casual.

"No," Ivar said. "He was not there." His cheeks burned, so he knew he was blushing.

"Are you sure?" Cupping his chin in her hot hand, she lifted it until she could look him in the eyes. After a moment's study, she drew back, frowning.

"Have we met?" she said.

"No, ma'am," he said. He felt as if his neck was in a noose that was constantly tightening. That the volva was toying with him. That she already knew the answers to all the questions she was asking.

"Tell me, are you shivering because you are frightened, or cold?"

"Mostly cold," Ivar said, "but maybe some of both."

"An honest answer," Heidin said. "How . . . singular." Handing off her staff to the blue-jacketed spinner beside her, she pulled Ivar into her arms.

He was too stunned to resist. It was like hugging an iron furnace, with molten metal flowing into every part of him, until everything that was Ivar was crowded into a small corner. Distilled. Though they shared no blood, it was as if there was a linkage between them.

Heidin must have sensed something, too, because she held him out at arm's length as if to reassess him.

All the ice and water had been driven from his clothing and he was warm to the core.

"Thank you," Ivar said.

"This is not the first time that I have saved you from the cold. Has anyone ever told you that you have your modir's eyes?"

Ivar took a breath. "I have been told that, yes."

"And yet, in a way, you favor your brodir."

Ivar said nothing, acutely aware of the weight of Eiric's pendant against his chest. Alongside one other–that Hilde had given him.

"Where is your brodir now?"

"I don't know," Ivar said. "He's disappeared."

"I also hear that the king has named a new heir–an adopted son," Heidin said. "Is that true?"

In the past, whenever Ivar was caught in a lie, Hilde always said, *Tell the truth, Ivar. It's much easier than finding your way out of a maze of lies.*

"It is," Ivar said, meeting her eyes.

"He chose you."

"Yes," Ivar said.

"He is just a child, Highest," Drifa said, seeing where this was going.

"He is no threat to anyone."

"On the contrary," Heidin's modir said. "He is a great threat as long as he is alive. Even if the king is defeated, this boy will always be a rival for the throne. You will save yourself considerable grief later if you dispose of him now."

"Do not tell me what to do, Tyra," Heidin said. "I am no longer a child."

After a beat, Tyra said, "I know that you are no longer a child. You remind me of it, daily. I only think to look out for your best interest, based on my experience."

"Sometimes a live hostage is worth more than a dead rival," Heidin said. She turned to Drifa. "We will find you some dry clothing so that you don't perish from the cold before you take my message to King Rikhard."

"Your message, ma'am?" Drifa said, shooting a helpless look at Ivar.

"Tell the king that his princeling is my prisoner. Tell him to come find me at Vandrgardr when he is ready to surrender."

64

INTO THE SOUND

FORTUNATELY FOR EIRIC, MOST OF the tidal river was navigable for a shallow-draft boat like *Thistle*. When it wasn't, he simply lifted *Thistle* onto his shoulders and portaged around.

He wasn't sure what he would find when he reached the headwaters. The river was fed by snowmelt–streams that roared down off the mountains, in spring and summer. This time of year, snow already cloaked the heights, and the flow of water would be throttled until after the Disting.

He reached a place where the river flowing down from the mountains divided. One fork was the tributary he'd been following, and the other fork flowed southwest. He beached his boat and climbed to get a better view.

He was at the narrow waist of Muckleholm. To the southwest, the rocky spine of the Sudreyjar Islands divided the sound from the sea. If he kept to the river, he would sail due west, to where the river met the sea at Vandrgardr. From there, he could follow the coast down until he reached the islands.

But that would expose *Thistle* to the storms that roared in from the west this time of year, storms that much larger ships avoided. Also, his systir's army was camped somewhere near Vandrgardr, and there wouldn't be much cover on the marshy peninsula.

If you decide to come, please come sooner rather than later.

Eiric climbed down from his viewpoint, boarded *Thistle,* and sailed southwest. That meant more time in the swamp, and less on the open sea. Fortunately, he encountered no one along the way.

When he reached the wetlands along the shore, he climbed out and waded, sometimes waist-deep, towing his ship through the drowned trees, marsh thistle, and seagrasses until the brackish water was deep enough to use the oars. Once free of the salt marsh, he sailed south, hugging the coast, taking cautious advantage of the sail. His back and shoulders thanked him for the respite, but he kept a weather eye to the west, where dark clouds were piling up, driven by a freshening wind. There was a danger of being driven into the shore before he reached the passage south of Klettrholm and could take refuge in the quieter waters of the sound.

This is why we don't go vikingr this time of year.

It was midday by the time he saw the cliffs of Klettrholm rising to the southeast, wind-driven waves lashing against them. And, there, the mouth of the passage to the sound. He made sure that he was well clear of the headland before he made the turn. The tide was coming in, so he dropped the sail and allowed the tide and his momentum to carry him through.

Eiric was half-frozen and exhausted, and the visibility so poor that he could be on top of a cargo ship before he knew it was there. So he turned away from Klettrholm and landed his ship on the island across the passage. He dragged *Thistle* into cover, lashed an oilskin between two sturdy trees to keep it from flying away, and crawled underneath, wondering if he would ever be warm again. He unrolled his strike-steel and dry kindling from their oilskin wrappings and managed to get a small fire going. He was beyond caring if he might be spotted by someone foolish enough to be out in this weather.

Tomorrow, he would be faced with the challenge of finding Liv and Reginn–if they were even there. Klettrholm was a large island, faced with sheer cliffs on all sides. It would be difficult to spot someone from the water even if they wanted to be found.

It would be even harder to climb up there unobserved and avoid whatever trap had been set for him.

65

A KNIFE TO THE HEART

DRIFA KNEW SHE WAS IN trouble. She'd accompanied the king's son and heir on an unauthorized trip to Sundgard. It wasn't as if there was an official rule against doing that, but that didn't mean that the king would see it that way. Thanes and kings were not required to be fair or reasonable–not like other people.

She was also the bearer of bad news. First, that the attack on Sundgard that had taken his consort and their unborn child had been carried out by Grima Lund, an agent who had been betraying him for years and even attempted to assassinate him in his own hall. Next, Eiric Halvorsen, the warrior and styrman that he'd hoped would help him fight against an invasion of witches, had disappeared. Third, Halvorsen's crew planned to take one of the king's finest longships to go looking for their missing styrman. They were probably already gone.

None of that mattered against the news that Rikhard's adopted son and heir had been taken hostage by the witch queen of the Jotun and carried off to the other side of Muckleholm.

Drifa would be better off if she'd died fighting for the prince.

She should have stayed with the clothes she'd nearly drowned in. She looked far too presentable to be delivering such bad news. She ought to be covered in a thousand wounds, to match those on the inside.

When Drifa reached Kingshavn, she was told that the king was in the great hall, sharing the nattmal with his commanders. The last thing Drifa wanted was an audience, but she had to get it over with. She'd learned that bad news, like fish, doesn't improve with age.

She walked the long dock, where the king's fleet was preparing to sail. Knarrs sat low in the water, loaded with provisions for hundreds of soldiers. Sleek longboats strained at their tethers like racehorses at the gate.

The king's hall was bright and cheerful against the dark winter's night. Rikhard could afford plenty of wood to feed the great hearths at either end, and the mealfire at the center. All three were ablaze, and oil lamps created pools of light. Rikhard shared his table with a dozen thanes and chieftains, though it appeared that they had moved beyond the feasting stage and into the drinking and toasting and bragging stage.

After so much time at war, the king kept an informal hall, though his hird had grown to include a taster.

When Drifa was announced, Rikhard motioned her over. "Drifa! Welcome. The main service is over, but no doubt the cooks can find something for you. Is Ivar with you?"

Drifa shook her head. "No, Lord," she said. "I bring urgent news." She paused, took a breath, and said, in a rush, "It may be something you'll want to hear in private."

Rikhard studied her face, then signaled for everyone else to leave. Just like that.

"What is it?" he said when it was just the two of them.

Drifa stumbled at first, but gained confidence as her story spilled out. Rikhard listened, grim-faced, blue eyes deepening to stormy gray. Now and then, he snapped out a question. Many, she could not answer. Everything she knew, she'd heard from someone else. If she wasn't such an alert and curious person, she would know nothing at all.

"So the sole survivor at Sundgard was carrying a note, and nobody told me?"

"Her name is Naima, and she is not from Sundgard. She arrived with the Jotun army. Halvorsen knew her from before, and the note was for him, so he kept it to himself."

"So we don't know what it said?"

"I know something of it, because he shared it with his crew. It was to arrange a meeting with his systir, the Jotun queen."

"Where is this meeting?"

"I don't know," Drifa said. "But he told his crew he was going to meet up with her, and left."

"So Halvorsen was conspiring with the spinners all along."

"I don't know that, either. But after he left, Naima recovered enough to tell Prince Ivar that Grima was the one who attacked Sundgard and that the note was a trick and a trap."

"She told *Ivar*?"

Drifa nodded. "He had been looking in on her, because he hoped she would be able to tell him more about the attack on Sundgard."

"The attack hit all of us hard," Rikhard murmured. "Ivar has always answered pain with knowledge."

"Ah, I see," Drifa said, not really seeing. "When the prince found out the truth, we immediately sailed back to Sundgard to warn Halvorsen, but he was already gone. His crew planned to go after him to try to warn him, while we sailed for Kingshavn, to let you know what was going on. But we were attacked where the sound meets the open sea."

The king went still. "Attacked? By whom?"

"The Jotun queen. Our ship was destroyed, all of us killed except me and the young prince. When Heidin realized who it was she held, she took Prince Ivar prisoner and sent me back here with a message."

"What was the message?" Rikhard said.

Drifa had practiced until she got it right. "The queen said, 'Tell the king that his princeling is my prisoner. Tell him to come find me at Vandrgardr when he is ready to surrender.' That was it."

She braced herself. Now was the time that the king might choose to visit his rage on her.

But he didn't. His face appeared as hard as granite, and yet brittle–fissured with grief, as if the slightest blow would break it into pieces. For what seemed like a lifetime, he said nothing at all.

Drifa wasn't sure whether she should stay or go or further explain or say nothing at all. Finally, she said, "Your Majesty. Should I–?"

"So," Rikhard said. "My every attempt to form an alliance with the witches has resulted in losses too grievous to bear. While I've been distracted, focused on constructing an empire strong enough to survive–one in which all parties could thrive, the spinners have been undermining me and betraying me every step of the way.

"No more. I will not sail to Vandrgardr to surrender. I will marshal all the warriors and weapons available to me, and sail west in the hopes of rescuing my son and bringing him home alive. Whether I succeed in that or not, I will do everything in my power to eradicate the spinners and their allies from the Midlands."

66

REINFORCEMENTS

REGINN AWOKE FROM A SOUND sleep to a persistent pounding. Instantly, Bodil and Eva were on their feet. They seemed to have appointed themselves Reginn's personal wraiths.

"Someone's at the door," Bodil whispered.

"See who it is."

Bodil poked her head through the wall, which Reginn still found unnerving. "It's Kåre," she said, her voice muffled. "He says he needs to talk to you right away. Something about an army."

Reginn resisted the urge to pull her covers over her head. Instead, she pulled them up to her chin. "Show him in, then."

Kåre seemed startled to find Reginn still in bed.

"Ma'am," he said. "Your . . . Grace. I apologize for waking you, but I thought you should know. There's an army outside."

I could have waited for that news, Reginn thought.

"Tell them to come back at a decent hour."

"Your pardon?"

"Is it Grima?"

"No, ma'am."

"Who is it, then? Did you see a banner?"

Kåre licked his lips. He was literally shaking. "They carry no banners. They wear no colors. They're unlike any army I've seen before."

"When you say they're 'outside,' do you mean they are out in the hallway, outside the gate, or are they aboard ships in the sound?"

"Some are swimming," Kåre said, which was enough to persuade

Reginn to put her boots on, pick up her staff, and follow him down the hall.

"Did they say what they want?"

"They are demanding to see you."

The best vantage point for a view of the rest of the island as well as the harbor was a gallery that overlooked both the harbor and the outer ward.

The plain beyond the castle walls was crowded with soldiers. Immediately, she understood the reason for Kåre's distress. There were battle-hardened men and women, but also orcs, light and dark elves, giants, ice wolves, and demons of all sorts. The water in the cove churned and boiled with life.

A ship was hauled up into the shallows, its bow resting on the rocky beach. Reginn recognized it as the *Kraken*.

So Heidin's army had made it here ahead of everyone else. Reginn understood why Kåre was rattled.

"Perhaps you should stay out of sight, ma'am," he said. "Who knows what kinds of weapons they have at their disposal?"

Bodil and Eva joined Reginn and Kåre at the wall.

A tall, spare figure broke away from the others and walked forward. The flaming sword on his back drove away the predawn darkness and reddened the entire field.

It was Asger Eldr. Other officers came a step behind him—Hrym of the Jotun, Dainn of the elves, Stonebiter of the dwarves, Ursinus of the allies among the beasts. Svend Bondi and Katia Lund just because.

Reginn finally realized that it was not Heidin's army they were facing. It was her own.

"We are not here to negotiate," Asger said, his voice ringing out across the keep. "When you've released the prisoners Reginn Eiklund and Naima Bondi, alive and in good health, we will outline the terms of your surrender."

He drew his sword and swept it in a broad arc, sending torrents of flame into the small cluster of wooden buildings at the edge of the parade ground. A stable and some equipment sheds exploded into flame. Reginn was glad that she'd brought everyone living inside the walls.

Asger looked to Katia. She gestured, and two dragons shot like flaming bolts across the sky. They came in low over the cliff house, raking the rooftops with their fiery breath. The thatching burst into flame. The implication was clear. Stone walls would not protect them.

Meanwhile, Reginn had a fire on her hands. She turned to where a number of spinners had gathered. "Where's Haki?"

The weatherspinner stepped forward. "Ma'am?"

"Could we have a little rain, please?" Reginn said. "Enough to wet everything down?"

"Yes, ma'am," Haki said. She swept her staff in an arc, spinning clouds into position overhead. Rain clouds, fat with moisture, piled high until they dumped a torrent of water and ice across the keep. The fires hissed and snapped and fizzled out.

"Perfect! Thank you," Reginn said, even though she'd been drenched along with the others.

Haki smiled. It was the first time Reginn had seen the wraith smile.

Reginn walked out to the edge of the parapet. "Asger Eldr! Stop setting things on fire!"

The noise from the assembled army subsided. "Aldrnari?" Asger said. "Are you well? Where is Grima?"

"She's out there, somewhere," Reginn said, gesturing toward the sea. "Better watch your back."

Several of the soldiers looked over their shoulders.

"In the meantime, the fortress has changed hands. The wraiths are in charge."

"The . . . wraiths," Asger said, cautiously.

"In case you're wondering, that is good news," Reginn said. "They are spinners, once Grima's unwilling servants, and now they are our willing allies. They have no love for Grima."

"Where's Naima?" Svend said, his voice sharpened by worry.

"Grima took her with her when she sailed." Reginn cleared her throat, wishing she could offer better news. "I don't know where they are, or if she's still alive."

There was some discussion among the commanders of the Risen that Reginn couldn't hear. Then Asger turned back toward her. "Seeing that you are not in need of rescuing or avenging, what are your orders?"

"Where is the queen, and her forces?" Reginn said.

"We left her at the camp at Vandrgardr," Asger said. "I would be surprised if she's still there. Armies need feeding, idle or not."

Yet another example of the advantages of an army of the dead.

"It's nasty weather," Reginn said, swiping ice from her lashes. "Would you like to come in and we can sort it out over supper?"

67
A COMMON CAUSE

THE STORM RAGED ALONG THE western coast of Muckleholm all that night and the next day. Eiric found himself thanking whatever gods he had not yet offended that he was through the passage and into the sound before the worst of it hit. But after three days sleeping on the cold ground, he was ready for a change.

On the second night, the winds diminished, so that branches no longer clattered together overhead. By morning, Eiric woke, sweating under the oilskins in his heavy clothing. He slid free of the tarp and stripped off his storm coat, the clothing underneath steaming.

Shafts of sunlight slid through the tree canopy and set the ice-glazed forest ablaze. Eiric was hungry–ravenous, in fact. He'd brought limited supplies, having no room, but there was dried fruit, salted fish, flatbread, and honey still in his ship, unless it had floated away.

He took a step toward the water and froze, hearing voices, dangerously close. He scooped his sword and axe from under the tarp and eased his way through the fringe of trees until he could survey the shore.

There were four of them, standing in a circle around *Thistle*, speaking in the fisker tongue. But they were strangers to him.

Beyond them, a ship was moored in the shallows. It was one of the largest longships Eiric had ever seen. Several of the strakes stood out against the weathered oak surrounding them, suggesting the ship had been recently repaired. It carried no banner, but it reminded him of the ships he'd seen in the boatyard at Ithavoll.

It soon become obvious that the newcomers were making fun of his ship, posing with it and seeing how many of them could pile on board.

Eiric stepped out from the shelter of the trees. "Good morning," he said, having mastered that much in the fisker tongue. "Do you have questions about my ship?"

The fiskers scrambled out of his boat like rats fleeing a house fire, then formed a rough circle, bristling with whatever weapons they had to hand. They seemed more seasoned than the crew he'd left at Sundgard.

When they saw there was just one of him, they visibly relaxed.

"That's not a ship," one of them said. He was muscled and handsome, with the fisker wavelet runes covering his exposed skin. "That's a wad of spit. You must take a dump in the morning before you set sail so you don't founder."

"Better that than a wallowing scow," Eiric said. "That looks like you put a styrboard and a mast on a barn and went to sea."

This was familiar ground, the kind of dockside skita that occurred in every port in the Archipelago.

"You're far from Fiskeholm," Eiric said. "What brings you to Muckleholm this time of year?"

Their spokesman seemed startled by his use of the fisker name for their homeland.

"What do you know about Fiskeholm?" he said.

"I haven't been there," Eiric admitted, "but I sailed here from Ithavoll on a fisker ship with a fisker crew. A fine ship and a fine crew."

"Not that ship." The fisker pointed.

"Not that ship," Eiric said.

"What happened to your fine fisker ship and crew? Did you misplace them?"

Eiric shook his head. "I'm here on my own business. My name is Eiric Halvorsen."

His name caused a bit of a stir–the rubbing of chins, exchanges of glances, the fingering of weapons–which happened a lot lately.

"You're the barbarian who stole the queen's flagship," the spokesman said, broadening his stance, narrowing his eyes. "One of the crew was my niece."

"You must mean Reyna," Eiric said. "She's with the rest of the crew and their ship at Sundgard."

"She's still alive?"

Eiric nodded. "I was sorry to leave her behind. She's showing real promise as a styrman."

"Reyna?"

"Her sword work is improving, too, though we haven't been able to find a blade the right size. She was already a skilled street fighter."

The styrman's face darkened as he took Eiric's measure. "If you've trifled with her, coaster, I'll–"

"If you think Reyna can be trifled with, you don't know her very well," Eiric said. "Any crew would be lucky to have her." After a beat, he added, "You still haven't told me your name."

"My name is Rollo," the fisker styrman said grudgingly, then introduced the other three–Harri, Leina, Aksel. "We were sailing with the–with the Jotun fleet when we came under attack by one of the king's longships." He paused, as if he wanted to skip the next part. "While trying to outrun them, we ran aground and seriously damaged our ship. It was my fault, as styrman. We seized the enemy ship, moved our soldiers onto it, and they sailed on. The four of us stayed behind to salvage *Naglfar.*"

"*Naglfar*?" A faint memory came back to him, from one of Bjorn's stories. "Wasn't that the ship of monsters Loki helmed at Ragnarok?"

Rollo snorted. "Fiskers don't believe in any of that. We were carrying the aldrnari's Risen army."

"Wait," Eiric said. "*Whose* army?"

"Reginn Eiklund. Called the aldrnari. She raised the dead from the battlefield at Ithavoll to join the army of New Jotunheim."

"What?"

Rollo smiled, as if pleased by Eiric's reaction. "She commands thousands of monsters and men–trolls and orcs and giants and–"

"Krakens," someone else said.

"–and krakens," Rollo said.

Eiric remembered that last desperate day in the tunnels under the crypts, when Reginn was trying to unload a cargo of warnings in just a few minutes.

Brenna . . . told me my magic was dangerous and unstable–that if I entered the tunnels, there was a risk that I would raise the dead–even if I didn't mean to.

Rollo continued his story. "The kraken–"

"Hafgufa," one of the crew said.

"–*Hafgufa* helped us move our ship onshore so it wouldn't break apart on the reef. The aldrnari told us that when we'd finished the ship repair, we should meet her at Vandrgardr. But when we went there, her army was still there, but she and Naima had apparently gone missing. Nobody would say much. They wanted to hand us off to a new commander, but we declined. We made no promises to *them*. We've been searching ever since."

"Was the queen at Vandrgardr when you were there?"

The fiskers looked at each other.

"If she was," Rollo said with a feral smile, "she did not offer us an audience."

"I'm looking for Reginn, too," Eiric said.

This was met with rolled eyes and skepticism.

"Tell me, Eiric Halvorsen," Rollo said. "Is there any stinking pile of skita in the Midlands that you haven't stepped in?"

"Skita finds me," Eiric said, shrugging. "Anyway. I might know where Reginn is." He pulled out the crinkled map and the note that came with it and handed them to Rollo.

The fisker scanned the map first, then looked up. "That's right across the channel," he said, pointing.

"I know," Eiric said. "That's why I'm here."

Rollo read the other page, twice, then shook his head. "If I'm reading this right, the aldrnari is attempting to arrange a meeting between you and your systir, who happens to be the witch queen of the Jotun."

Eiric nodded. "Basically. That's why I asked if the queen was at Vandrgardr." He waved toward Klettrholm. "This is probably a trap, but if Reginn disappeared from Vandrgardr, she might be here."

Rollo didn't disagree. "Where did you get this?"

"Naima Bondi was left for dead at Sundgard. The note was found on her person. She was too ill to question directly."

Rollo nodded grudgingly. "Naima was with the aldrnari aboard *Naglfar.*" He thrust the page back at Eiric and began pacing. "I can't figure you out. You are barbarian by birth. You sail to New Jotunheim, slaughter hundreds of soldiers, the entire Council of Elders, and Modir Inger. At the executioner's block, the witch queen intervenes and throws you in jail instead, claiming you're her brodir. Amid rumors of your death, you escape, steal a ship, and sail back here to the barbarian king. Then I find out that resistance hero Naima Bondi is carrying messages to you from Reginn Eiklund, counselor to the queen and commander of her Risen army."

He stopped for breath, and Eiric said, "You seem to know a lot about me."

"More than I want to, except—whose side are you on?"

"What do you mean?"

"Who are you fighting for? Or are you just a sell-sword who changes allegiances whenever it suits you?"

A good question.

Eiric took his time answering it. "We're not so different. Reyna and the others told me that New Jotunheim took your homes and is holding your families hostage to force you to sail for them."

"She told you that?" Rollo said, as if surprised Reyna would spill so much fisker business.

"She did. This started for me when I was convicted of murder and stood to lose my farm and family. Rikhard offered to pay the blood price if I would sail for him and find the witches' temple. My systir came with me, because she's a skilled hand and she had business there herself. The rest played out from there. I guess you could say I'm not fighting for a side, I'm fighting to protect the people I care about." He paused. "It's not going well so far."

"So," Rollo said, rubbing his chin, "where does the aldrnari come in?"

Eiric had already said too much, but there was no choice but to go on.

"She is one of the people I care about," he said. "She and my systir may or may not be on Klettrholm, and this may or may not be a trap. Still, I need to go. I have no quarrel with you. We can part ways here."

"You left Reyna and the others on the far side of the island?"

Eiric nodded. "I don't know if they're still there. I promised that if they waited for me, I'd return with them to New Jotunheim to help free their families. But they might have gone home on their own."

Rollo snorted. "And how would they get home? Swim?"

"I told them to take the ship we brought from Ithavoll," Eiric said. "They built it, after all. They have more claim to it than I do."

"Why would you do that?" Rollo said.

"We made a bargain," Eiric said. "I needed a crew. They did their part."

This was met with astonished silence that was broken when Rollo said, "Give us a moment." And he and his crew stepped away.

It reminded Eiric of when the fisker crew of *Firebird* held a council to decide whether to continue on to Barbaria under his command.

Eiric methodically packed up his gear while they talked. It was still wet, and it would stay wet, unless it froze.

Muckleholm—where only a fool goes to war during the bonefires of autumn.

When they returned, Rollo said, "We made a promise as well—to return this ship to the aldrnari, and to sail for her for one year.

"So. We propose that we sail to Klettrholm together and find out for ourselves whether the aldrnari is there and what she's done with her Risen army. There's one condition—we take our ship, not yours."

68

FISSURES

DURING THE FIRST PART OF the long voyage south along the coast of Muckleholm, Ivar tried his usual tactic of fading into the background, where he could watch and listen and sort allies from enemies.

It wasn't working. Here, on his systir's ship, he seemed to have lost his ability to become invisible.

Instead, he was just another captive from a successful raid, to be gloated over, humiliated, and threatened. There was no escape from drama on a longboat. The ship was just too small.

He had not forgotten the dustup between Heidin and her modir, Tyra, about whether to kill him or take him prisoner.

How strong was Heidin?

How persuasive was Tyra?

Or would she act on her own and seek forgiveness after?

He felt the pressure of many eyes upon him, not all of them friendly.

It wasn't as if Heidin ignored him. Each evening, as the early winter darkness fell, she would make her way aft with a bowl of porridge, ship's biscuits, and smoked pork. These, she would put between them so they could both eat from the same vessel. He didn't know whether this was for convenience, or to reassure him that this, at least, was not poisoned.

He was never sure which Heidin was coming for the nattmal. Sometimes it was the goddess–cold, arrogant, filled with grievance, her eyes hard and flaming, like yarkastein opal.

He knew the legend–that yarkastein was forged from the eyes of children.

Sometimes knowledge was a burden, not a gift.

The goddess Heidin dogged him about what would happen when they reached Vandrgardr.

"Will Rikhard come, do you think?" she said. "Or will he hole up at Kingshavn, licking his wounds while I conquer the rest of the Archipelago?"

"I cannot predict what he'll do," Ivar said, "but I suspect that he won't surrender and he won't stay home."

The goddess reached out and gripped his chin, forcing him to look at her. "If the king refuses to redeem you, then what should I do? Should I send him your head in a basket? Should I burn you at the stake three times and deliver your ashes in an urn?"

"Three times seems excessive," Ivar said. "Once would probably be enough."

Somehow, this bit of dark humor broke through. "Ah," she said, a smile twitching at her lips, the ice in her eyes softening. "Very well, then. Once. Three times is for goddesses."

"I know what they did to you at Asgard," Ivar said.

"Your ancestors," Heidin said, the rage rising in her like a full-moon tide.

"Yours, too, as my systir."

Heidin spat over the gunwale. "Your systir is simply the carcass I inhabit."

"Yet Hilde told me that she saved my life when I was just a baby. Eiric told me that she was my fiercest defender."

Heidin looked lost, and Ivar was afraid he'd misstepped. Then she said, "Ah, yes. She was stronger then. From the very beginning, there was something about you. You were a very appealing . . . mongrel. That's no doubt why you've lived so long." She shook her head. "Never mind. That was a long time ago." Then, after a pause, "Whatever happened to Hilde?"

"She's dead," Ivar said. "Grima killed her."

"That's too bad," Heidin said. "Hilde tried to take care of everyone, but in the end, it wasn't enough."

Ivar's thinking was getting more and more muddled, and he knew from experience that he shouldn't be having a conversation when a shake spell was coming on. Still, he pushed on.

"Or maybe it was just enough," Ivar said. "Maybe Hilde gave me what Sylvi gave to you–a safe harbor in a storm."

Heidin eyed him. "Did she give you wisdom, too? I know you didn't get that from Sten."

"I didn't get anything from Sten."

The words were out before he could stop them. Heidin was a battleground between a goddess and his strong-willed systir. Ivar was at war with himself.

He shouldn't have ignored the knot in his stomach, the burning in his fingertips, and the flickers of light at the edges of his vision that meant a headstorm was coming on.

Heidin was saying something, asking a question, but he couldn't make sense of it. She called his name. That was all he heard for a long time.

Ivar awoke dead tired, as usual after one of his shake spells. It was only the raised voices that roused him, both practically in his ear. Heidin and Tyra. So nothing had changed.

Or had it?

"Modir, don't you see? This changes everything," Heidin was saying.

"It changes nothing," Tyra said. "I cannot believe I'm hearing this from you at a time when victory is within our grasp. We hold the king's heart in our hands. Why would we give it up?"

"We are not giving it up," Heidin all but shouted. "Don't you see? Ivar is Jotun. He's one of us."

Ivar peered out through his lashes. He was still in the bow of the longship on his way to a place not of his choosing. Now both Heidin and Tyra were packed in there with him, one on either side, arguing above him.

"Ivar is not one of us," Tyra said. "His value to us is in his relationship with Rikhard. That is our leverage. Rikhard believes that the Jotun are witches, and that all witches are females who should serve under the supervision of men. He wants to be king of the Midlands, and thinks that having the backing of the gods would give him more legitimacy. When he speaks of gods, he means the Asgardian pantheon, because those are the only gods he knows."

"That doesn't matter," Heidin said. "If Rikhard dies in the war, then Ivar ascends the throne. All we need to do is make sure that happens."

"The boy's allegiance is to the king. Putting him on the throne would be like installing a younger and savvier Rikhard with an unpredictable gift of magic."

"If Ivar's allegiance is to the king, then we need to change that. You're the queen of mind magic, right? Make yourself useful, for a change."

Tyra sighed. "That will need to wait until we are back onshore."

Ivar wanted nothing more than to shut his ears to the conversation around him and go back to sleep, but he decided that he had better find out what was going on. He stirred, stretched, rubbed his eyes.

Heidin was holding his hand. Tyra was looking at him with murder eyes.

"What happened?" he mumbled. "Did I have a shake spell?"

"It seems that way," Heidin said. "While we were examining you, something odd happened with my kynstone." She pointed. It was then that he realized that Heidin's kynstone was resting on top of his coat, the chain around his own neck. Ivar lifted it by the chain and stared at it.

It was not red for Asgard or blue for Jotun. It was not the odd, purplish color that Eiric's kynstone had turned. Instead, each end of the crystal was its own, distinctive color, one end cherry red, the other a clear, vivid blue. The two colors bled into each other in the middle. He shook it, but each color kept to itself.

"That's strange," Ivar said. "I've never seen a kynstone do that before. Maybe it has something to do with the shake spell, and it will shift back eventually."

"I agree," Tyra said. "Or maybe it was influenced by being close to both of you. It doesn't mean anything."

"Oh, I think it might," Heidin said. "It raises a question." She looked into Ivar's face as if she could drink his thoughts. "Was Sten Knudsen really your fadir?"

Ivar frowned, as if puzzled. "Who else could it have been?"

"It's safe," Heidin said. "He's dead now. You can tell the truth."

Ivar felt anything but safe. "I am telling the truth as it was told to me, though I wouldn't mourn the loss of Sten as a fadir. I'm told that he left me in the woods to die, and my modir died trying to save me."

Too quick an answer. A plan made too long ago.

"Don't lie to me, Ivar."

"It's not a lie," Ivar said. "That's what I was told."

Heidin's expression said that she was not finished with this topic. But she said only, "We should make landfall sometime tomorrow. Get some sleep."

That was easier said than done. For five years, Ivar had navigated the twisty politics at Rikhard's court, aware of his tenuous position there. He'd been careful to follow Hilde's advice and keep his secrets close.

Now he was in a situation where keeping his secrets might cost him his life. And so might telling the truth.

69

INTO THE BREACH

EIRIC AND THE FISKERS SET sail aboard *Naglfar,* though Eiric insisted on towing *Thistle* behind them. When they asked him why, he said, "*Naglfar* is a fine ship, and you won't want to put her at risk."

"So we'll use your dinghy to soften them up before we go in for the kill?" Rollo said.

"Something like that," Eiric said. "Or maybe, if we don't look too threatening, they'll simply open the doors and invite us in."

Nobody believed that. But Eiric still hadn't figured out what the play would be. Would they face friends or enemies? If they were enemies, then which ones?

Fiskers were skilled sailors and boatbuilders, and these ones had weapons skills, but they were not coasters. Eiric knew from experience that it made no sense to assault a fortress from a longship on the water, especially with a crew as lean as theirs. The best archers would be lucky to lob a few shafts over the walls from below, while defenders of the keep could drop rocks on them if they came too close, or shoot flaming arrows down until the ships caught fire, or, if adequately provisioned, could sit tight and simply wait for them to go away.

Eiric had been to Klettrholm a few times with his grandfadir. It was a popular hideout for coasters, where they could stow their takings and deal them out, a little at a time, at the markets. The crinkled shoreline was riddled with sea caves, if a person could find them.

The entire coast of the island was lined with cliffs, and so it would be a hard go wherever they landed. But it seemed likely that other parts of the island would be less well guarded. They debated whether to simply sail north across the channel and attempt a landing on Klettrholm's southern coast, but decided to circle the island at a safe distance to assess its defenses and to see who else might be on the water.

As they entered the main sound, Eiric saw a ship approaching Klettrholm under oar power, making for what appeared to be a solid wall of rock. Another ship hovered offshore. Both flew the Firebird banner. The same one that fluttered from *Naglfar*'s rigging.

"Who is that?" Rollo muttered. "And what are they doing?"

Eiric's heart sank. "Maybe they've already come to retrieve the queen and her counselor. Maybe we've run out of time."

"Look." Harri, one of Rollo's crew, pointed. Soldiers lined the tops of the cliffs, behind a low wall. The slanting light of morning glittered off steel. "Who are they? Did the aldrnari bring her army?"

Eiric was still having trouble getting his head around the notion of Reginn leading an army of dead creatures of legend. Dead creatures that looked less than welcoming.

As the longship neared the rocky face of the cliff, the defenders above launched a volley of rocks that landed all around the approaching ship without hitting it. It seemed to be a warning shot. At least the ship's crew took it that way, because after a moment of confusion, they hastily back-paddled, putting distance between their ship and the wall of the fortress.

"There must be an entrance there they're heading for," Eiric murmured.

As they watched, the Firebird banner came down, and a new one rose in its place–a stylized spider in a web. Cautiously, the ship approached the cliffside again.

"Whose signia is that?" Rollo said. "Could it be the king's?"

Eiric shook his head. "Rikhard's is the fossegrim."

The symbol was familiar, though. Why?

A spark of memory kindled, flamed up. Now he remembered where he'd seen that mark before: it was outside Grima's used clothing shop in Langvik.

"Skita," he said, almost to himself. "It's Grima. Or Grima's ship, at least."

"Who's Grima?" Leina said.

"The witches' executioner on New Jotunheim," Rollo said. "Haven't heard much of her lately, though."

"She's been around," Eiric said, thinking of the attack in Langvik and the attempted poisoning at Kingshavn. "She's been busy."

The new banner received no better welcome. As the ship neared land, the rocks came down again, thicker and harder than before. This time, one of them smashed through the decking of the ship. Water spouted up as the crew scrambled to contain the leak.

Two of the ship's passengers stood then, bracing themselves against the motion of the ship, staffs in hand. A blaze of light from the heads of the staffs illuminated the faces of the spinners as they launched a river of flame toward the parapet. The soldiers lined up along the wall took cover, so the flames scorched the stone but seemed to do little other damage.

The spider-flagged ship sought to take advantage of the break in defense by using sail and oars to speed toward the seawall.

Something caught Eiric's eye. On any other night, he might have taken it for a shooting star. It came from the east, from the direction of the mainland, a bolt of flame streaking through the sky overhead. It crossed the sound in a matter of seconds, turned north, flying nearly all the way to Langvik before it turned again and came straight at the spider-flagged ship.

The crew was so intent on making it to the battlements before the defenders responded that they didn't even see what was coming.

It was a dragon, trailing sparks, painting the waters of the sound a lurid orange, like molten metal. Its translucent skin seemed barely strong enough to contain the inferno within as it swooped low over the longship and flamed it from stern stem to masthead.

One pass was all it took. The dragon flew back east, leaving behind a smoldering ruin with no sign of survivors. Steam rose from the wreck as seawater rushed in to claim it. All around him, the fiskers' voices rose in a chant. Not a celebration, but a eulogy.

Everything is born of the sea, and so returns to her embrace.

Understandably, the other spider ship beat a hasty retreat, putting considerable distance between itself and Klettrholm before turning north and disappearing into the weather.

Were they retreating for good, or planning an attack from a different direction?

"Now what?" Harri said, speaking for everyone. "Should we approach?"

Eiric shook his head. "We're flying the same flag as Grima's ships did at the start, so the defenders aren't likely to welcome us. We're too thinly crewed to engage in more than a skirmish, and we don't want to risk our ship. We'll have to find a different way in."

"Who's that?" Leina said, pointing.

They all turned to see another ship approaching from the south under full sail. She was a fine warship that sliced through the water like a honed blade. Though she displayed no colors, Eiric recognized her immediately.

"It's the *Sylvi*," Eiric said. "Last I saw her, she was at Sundgard."

It had been a crime to allow her to sit idle for so long.

"Who's crewing her?" Rollo asked.

Eiric pulled out his glass and scanned the deck. "It's the fisker crew that sailed with me from New Jotunheim."

"Who's the styrman?"

He took another look. "I believe it's Reyna." Their ship was already past them and turning west. That was when he realized where they were heading.

"They are on a course for Klettrholm. Unless they know something we don't, we've got to stop them before they get too close."

As he adjusted the styrboard, his crew was already changing the angle of sail. *Naglfar* was too large to be nimble, but was fast once underway.

Shouts of alarm rose as the crew of *Sylvi* spotted them. They immediately changed course, moving upwind to evade pursuit, but with a large ship and a skeleton crew, it was difficult to pull off a sudden change in direction.

"They don't recognize us," Rollo muttered.

"If I saw an unflagged ship on a course to intercept, I'd try to prevent a meetup, too," Eiric said.

"Reyna!" Rollo bellowed, but the wind snatched his words away.

There began a crude dance in which the two ships circled and maneuvered across the sound, with *Sylvi* attempting to make a run for Klettrholm and *Naglfar* blocking the way.

Without a word, Aksel dug into his seabag and came up with a fistful of cloth, smoothing it as best he could. It was white linen with black scrawls over it. Threading cordage through an eyelet in the corner, he ran it up to the top of the mast.

It was a banner bearing the fisker wavelets. Crude, but identifiable. The only colors that might be reassuring to a ship commanded by Reyna Fisker.

It took a while for their signal to register. By now they'd maneuvered close enough that Eiric could make out who was who. He saw Levi shade his eyes, studying the banner, and then the crew, then shouted something to Reyna, who looked for herself.

Rollo shouted "Reyna!" again, and this time, she heard it.

"Rollo?" she said.

"We need to talk."

* * *

An hour later, *Sylvi* and *Naglfar* were beached, side by side, on the eastern coast of the island where they'd camped the night before. They were no closer to their goal than they had been then, but the arrival of Naima with the fiskers from Sundgard brought Eiric more information about the challenge before him.

They had also brought provisions, so they moved into the shelter of the trees, built a fire, and put some smoked meat on to boil.

"So, it's definitely a trap," Eiric said, for probably the second or third time, as if hoping for a different answer. He hadn't realized how hopeful he'd been that, with Reginn's help, he could somehow get his systir back.

Naima nodded wearily. She was thinner than he remembered, her face drawn, with dark circles under her eyes. "It was Grima's plan all along. Reginn had no input at all. Heidin is not on Klettrholm. The last we saw her was at Vandrgardr."

It fit with Eiric's theory that Grima had a stronghold not far from Langvik, a place she could do as she pleased out from under the king's eye. But it didn't explain why Grima's soldiers would attack a ship flying the spider flag. And where the dragon had come from.

"If Grima and Heidin have had a falling-out, could the ships have been from Heidin's fleet?" he said. "Maybe Grima didn't trust the change in colors. That still doesn't explain the dragons."

"The spinners have dragons," Rorik said. "I've seen them flying over Ithavoll."

Eiric could appreciate what a major advantage that would be, not only for warfare, but for surveillance of the field. He felt as if he were playing a high-stakes game of hnefatafl blindfolded. And he still didn't know for sure who held the cliff fortress on Klettrholm. Or who had incinerated the spider ship. Or where the king might be.

"Do you know what Rikhard's plans were?" Eiric asked the crew who had sailed from Sundgard.

Reyna spoke up. "Ivar brought Naima to Sundgard to try to stop you from falling into Grima's trap, but you were already gone. He said he was in a hurry to get back to Kingshavn because the king was about to set sail. He didn't plan to be left behind."

Stay safe, brodir, Eiric thought. Get bigger and stronger before you go back to war.

It seemed like all the players would be here in the sound before long, if they weren't already. Eiric had two good-sized ships and a little wisp of a boat. How could he best use those?

Naima was sitting, leaning against a tree, wrapped in a dry blanket, eating smoked pork on flatbread.

Eiric sat down beside her and handed her a cup of mead. "Naima," he said, "what can you tell me about the fortress on the cliff?"

70

FIELD OF BATTLE

AFTER THE ARRIVAL OF THE Risen army on Klettrholm, Reginn convened her commanders each morning to discuss events overnight and plans for the coming day. On the morning after the immolation of Grima's ship, the meeting commenced with considerable crowing, backslapping, and revisiting of the details for those who did not witness it firsthand.

Reginn understood the need for celebration, especially among those who had suffered under Grima's hard hand on Klettrholm, and who had lost loved ones to the Deeps. But she couldn't join in. Reginn was the one who had ordered the attack. The same Reginn who had suggested that they try and get through the war without anyone getting hurt.

Reginn was the only one who heard the cries of souls leaving behind the world they knew without knowing where they were going.

Worse, she wasn't as confident as some of the others that Grima had been aboard the ship that had been destroyed. One of her ships was still out there.

Katia seemed embarrassed to find herself at the center of a mixed-species circle of admirers who wanted to bask in reflected glory. More than once, Reginn heard her trying to explain the nature of the vaettir and her affinity to them.

"They are not dragons," she would say. "A better term would be eldrvaettir, fire spirits. They are prickly and hard to win over, but intensely loyal with a voracious appetite for–"

Before long, the intended audience would raise both hands, step back, and find someone else to talk to.

War is not all that appealing when you get into the weeds. Katia viewed the vaettir as friends, even kindred. Some of her allies viewed them as little more than weapons.

"So," Reginn said when they finally sat down together, "first of all, I would like to thank the eldrvaettir who warned us of the approach of Grima's ships and forced their retreat."

"That's one way to put it," someone said, to general laughter. It was Stonebiter, commander of the dwarves. "They should have done for both and saved us some time."

"You trolls should remember that Grima is the enemy," Keila said. "Her crews are captive wraiths, serving against their will."

"I am no troll, witch," Stonebiter said, her hand on her war hammer.

"Something for which all trolls everywhere are grateful," Asger said. "Shut up and listen." The thursen signified their agreement with jeers and catcalls that eventually died away, though there continued a constant undercurrent of muttering.

This is hopeless, Reginn thought. How in the world could anyone as inexperienced as she was command such an army?

"Since the burning of Grima's ship, the eldrvaettir have been patrolling the sound," Reginn said. "Katia, what are you hearing from them?"

"As you know, after the—ah—destruction of the enemy ship, Grima's other ship sailed north at speed and the vaettir lost it. They must have found a hole to hide in, because we haven't seen them since."

"I worry that they might have landed somewhere on Klettrholm," Reginn said.

"We've begun shore patrols around the island," Hrym said. "We'll make sure no one—whether Grima or someone else—surprises us again."

Reginn did not share his confidence.

"What about other ships and other armies? The king? The queen of

New Jotunheim?" She paused. "Are we truly alone in the Midlands?"

Some people laughed.

"We left Queen Heidin and the rest of her army at Vandrgardr on the main island," Asger said. "There has been more activity there of late, ships coming and going and the like, but no one has come this way."

"So if we keep our heads down," Reginn said, "no one needs to know we're here."

This was met with awkward silence, shifting bodies, and shifting eyes.

Katia cleared her throat. "During the assault on Klettrholm, two other ships were spotted to the south, in the channel between this island and the next. They were unflagged, and of different sizes, so we don't know if they were Grima's or someone else's. They, too, waited until the fighting was over, and then left in a hurry, sailing south.

"More important, a fleet of ships flying the king's banner was seen this morning rounding the southern cape. We'll need to fly another sortie to find out if they've entered the sound or are keeping to the ocean side of the Sudreyjar." She paused. "Either way, time is running out for us to rejoin Heidin's forces at Vandrgardr."

"Exactly," Hrym said. "Or should we plan a rearguard action that would trap the king's forces between our ships and the queen's army on the shore?"

"Ship," Reginn said.

"I beg your pardon?"

"We have one ship, Commander, the one you sailed in on. So a naval operation would be difficult at present. Instead of burning Grima's ship, perhaps we should have seized it."

"Good point," Hrym said. "Perhaps our–" He shot a look at Katia. "Perhaps our eldrvaettir allies could be persuaded to carry a message to Vandrgardr, alerting them to the approach of the king's fleet, and requesting transport to the field of battle."

"We could," Reginn said. "What I don't understand is why you would want to do that."

With that, all the murmured squabbling ceased.

"Ma'am?" Hrym said.

"We have an army of the dead with a handful of the living," Reginn said. "The dead have nothing to gain by being here. I raised you in order to spare the lives of the innocent, but wars by their nature do the opposite."

"We would fight on the side of justice, my lady," Dainn said.

"Which side is that?" Reginn said. "If New Jotunheim wins, they intend to sacrifice the children of Asgard, enslave the Jotun, and install a goddess with a grudge as ruler over all.

"If King Rikhard wins, which seems unlikely, he'll suffer considerable losses and no doubt expand and extend discrimination against the gifted, if he doesn't slaughter us outright.

"Involvement of the Risen army will mean greater casualties among the living on both sides, and no obvious benefit to the dead."

"What would you have us do, Aldrnari?" Hrym said, his expression stricken.

"I haven't a clue," Reginn said, and walked out.

Reginn should know by now that if you are going to do something stupid, it's best not to do that on an island packed with people who disapprove and will let you know it, one way or another.

She could pretend to ignore the conversations that stopped when she walked by, the scowling dwarves, mournful soldiers, and narrow-eyed demons. The one person she could not ignore was Asger Eldr.

After an entire day of skulking from hidey-hole to back corridor, filching food from the kitchen to avoid appearing for meals, Reginn returned to her room late at night, having successfully evaded an entire day of possible conversations.

As soon as she opened the door, she smelled the familiar scent of flame and smoke. Someone had lit the hearth, of course, but that wasn't it.

Asger Eldr was sprawled in a chair next to the fire, his eyes glowing like embers spit from the hearth.

"Get out," Reginn said, stepping aside to clear the doorway. "I have nothing to say to you."

"Good," Asger said. "That gives me more time to talk." He threw something at her, and she caught it reflexively. It was a roll with a hunk of smoked meat stuffed into it. "Eat that," he said. "You are impossible to reason with when you are hungry."

Something else flew toward her. It was an apple, the skin slightly charred from the heat of his fingers. A warm cup of cider waited for her on the table next to her sleeping bench.

She *was* hungry. "I don't want to hear a lecture from you, of all people." She sat down on the bed and took a bite of bread and meat. "You were the one who got me into this."

Asger rolled his eyes. "*You,* in fact, got *me* into this. You are the reason I am here–to keep you alive so that you would be here when the time came."

"When the time came for what? Another Ragnarok?"

"Maybe. Maybe not. That's up to you. This is all about fate. You were born for this, Aldrnari."

"Really? I thought I was born to be hauled from town to town, performing in alehouses to support you and donating power whenever you were running low."

Lacing his fingers, Asger looked away.

With the bread and meat gone, Reginn crunched into the apple. Juice ran down her chin.

Asger sat, silently watching. Finally, he stood. "I cannot say much more than this: You raised this army. You are the only one who can decide how to use it. Not me, not the Jotun queen, and not Rikhard. Choose."

She stood, facing him, fists clenched. "Why is it you can never give me a straight answer?"

Asger smiled, something rarely seen. "If you wanted clarity, if you wanted kindness or charm, you should never have raised a demon." With that, he left, closing the door behind him.

Raised a demon? What was he talking about?

Reginn resisted the temptation to kick the door. Instead, she collapsed back onto the bed.

It really didn't matter which side she chose.

Of the Nine Worlds that existed prior to Ragnarok, there was only one left.

In her heart, Reginn knew that if the two sides came to blows, it would destroy the only world left to them.

71
ORIGIN STORY

WHEN IVAR WAS JUST FIVE years old, his foster modir, Hilde, sat him down for a Serious Discussion. He could always tell when one of those was going to happen because she would take him into her private office at the back of the longhouse and clear the other rooms to make sure that no one could listen in.

"Ivar," she said, "you are a very unusual boy."

"I know," he said. "I have shake spells."

"You are not unusual because you have shake spells; you have shake spells because you are unusual."

"Explain," Ivar said.

"If I close my eyes when I'm talking to you, I could easily believe that I'm speaking with a grown-up. But when I open my eyes, you are just this tall." She demonstrated with her hand.

"Am I a dwarf, then?" Ivar said. "Short and savvy?"

Hilde laughed. "It has to do with your fadir."

"The troll?" Lately, they'd been having more and more trouble with trolls on the farm. They swaggered around, ruffled his hair, and told him he looked just like his fadir.

Hilde laughed again. "They are not really trolls. I just call them that. They are Sylvi's husband's relatives."

"I'm confused," Ivar said.

"The man, Sten, who killed your modir and was then killed by your brodir, Eiric, and systir, Liv, was not your fadir."

"That's a relief," Ivar said, "but–?"

"Your real fadir was an old friend of Sylvi's."

"Who was not her husband?" Ivar said.

"Who was not her husband," Hilde said, nodding. "She wanted another child, but by then she knew she did not want to have a child by Sten. She announced that she was divorcing him, but he would not leave.

"Then a friend came to visit when Sten was away, and one thing led to another. Sylvi was very happy when she realized that you were on the way, but she knew that Sten would be a threat to any child she had with another man. So she did what was necessary to convince him that he was the father.

"Any questions so far?" Hilde looked at Ivar.

Ivar shook his head, eager to hear the rest of the story.

"Sylvi was never sure that Sten really believed it–he was constantly making remarks that suggested he didn't. He wanted to believe it, though, and that goes a long way. Sylvi knew that elven children grow up quickly, so–"

"Wait–what about elven children?"

"Didn't I mention? Sylvi's old friend was a woodland elf," Hilde said. "She hoped that–"

"What was his name?" Ivar interrupted.

"Whose?"

"My real fadir."

"I don't know," Hilde said. "After you were born with the shake spells, all of Sten's doubts returned. He didn't want to claim parentage of a child he saw as damaged.

"It was then that Sylvi reached out to me."

"To you?"

Hilde nodded. "She feared for all three of you. She'd already spoken to my fadir about an apprenticeship in town for Eiric. She asked me to take you if anything happened to her. And she gave me this."

She handed Ivar a small silver amulet on a chain. He examined it, turning it over. On one side was inscribed a wide, spreading tree with an equally impressive web of roots below ground level.

"What's this?"

"It's a symbol for the elven."

"It looks like a tree," Ivar pointed out.

"It symbolizes the connection between root and branch–the light and the dark elves, both of which are necessary for survival."

On the other side were engraved *IVAR*, a series of runes, and another symbol.

"What's this?" Ivar held it up to show Hilde.

"My understanding is that it is a message of protection, of safe passage from your fadir."

"Is his name on here?" Ivar said.

Hilde shrugged. "I don't know. I don't read Elvish."

"So it could say, 'Put the bearer to death immediately.'"

Hilde rolled her eyes. "I suppose it could, but that seems unlikely."

"Why are you giving me this now–the pendant and the story?"

"Sten's family is here, more and more. I expect them to revive their claim on you as family, wait a while, and then lose you in a tragic accident. Or go straight to the accident."

"Why? I'm not bothering them."

"They want the farm."

"The farm doesn't belong to me. It belongs to the king."

"The king isn't here. And if you're gone, I don't really have any claim to be here."

"It's decided, then," Ivar said. "I'll leave tomorrow."

"What? And go where?"

"I will go on a quest to find my real fadir," Ivar said. "Isn't that what this is all about?"

"No!" Hilde was usually very patient with all his questions and comments, but she seemed to be reaching her limit. "You've been reading too many fantasy stories. I have come to an agreement with the king. I am putting you under his protection. The king is deeding the farm to me."

"You're trading me to Rikhard for the farm?" Ivar's voice rose until it nearly squeaked. He hated that.

"No, sweetheart," Hilde said, flustered. "I wouldn't trade you for a thousand farms. I am trying to keep the trolls away, and King Rikhard is powerful enough to do it. He doesn't really care about the farm."

"So I have to go and live with him?"

"Yes, for now," Hilde said, "until Sten's family gives up on their plan. But Kingshavn isn't far away from here, and I'm not going anywhere. So, in a way, you'll have two homes."

"Do I have any say in this?"

"Unfortunately, no, but what you do will determine whether this scheme is successful."

"What do you mean?"

"Rikhard is, I believe, a good man in most ways, but he is proud and stubborn and he can be vindictive. He's trying to find some kind of partnership with the Jotun–"

"The what?"

"The magically gifted," Hilde said. "Spinners and seers–and elves, of course. He was brought up to be suspicious of them, and whenever he has a bad experience with one of the gifted, he tends to blame all of them. Believe it or not, it would be better if Rikhard–and everyone else–believes that Sten was your fadir instead of a traveling elf. I know you can keep a secret, but the question is–will you?"

"What kind of magic can I do?" Ivar said.

"Magic?"

"You said the Jotun are magical, and elves are Jotun, so–"

"I don't know, Ivar. As I said, elvish children are very smart and grow up fast. They walk lightly on the earth. You have a grace and beauty that sets you apart. Maybe that's your gift."

Not impressive, Ivar wanted to say, but he was trying to practice being diplomatic.

"The king can offer many opportunities for schooling and to develop skills that I can't provide."

"Like fighting with swords and riding horses?"

"No doubt," Hilde said. "Elves are known to be excellent fighters." After a pause, she said, "Why are you so eager to learn to fight?"

"Someone has to fight the trolls," Ivar said.

Hilde embraced him. "I have no doubt that you will grow to become an excellent troll fighter," she said. "Now, this will be a big change for you. What are the truths I have taught you?"

"My modir, Sylvi, loved me very much. She gave her life to save mine."

"Correct. And?"

"My systir, Liv, and my brodir, Eiric, love me very much. They had to leave on a perilous journey, but they knew I would be safe and happy with you and Ulff."

"Good," Hilde said. "And finally?"

Ivar's lips moved against her overdress. "Hilde Stevenson loves me very much. Loving me has been the honor of her life."

72
BREAK-IN

EIRIC KNEW THE CHANNEL CROSSING to Klettrholm would be a challenge. The tides and currents that ran between the ocean and the sound were constantly changing, which meant that setting a predictable course was all but impossible.

Ordinarily, he might have sailed past the opening and landed from the sound side of the island, but the increasing traffic in the sound made that risky. He could approach from the west, but few braved the weather in the North Sea as the winter solstice approached if they had a choice.

So he put *Thistle* into the water at the western end of the passage, calculating that the inflowing tide, a bit of luck, and his sailing skills would land him on Klettrholm before he was spit out into the sound.

By now, the little boat was like an extension of his own body, if his body had a sail and a styrboard, and was half full of salt water at all times. *Thistle* was so wet, she seemed unlikely to burn, even if the dragons returned.

The crew of *Naglfar* had made a promise to Reginn to sail for her once their ship was repaired. The other crew was unrelenting in holding Eiric to his promise to free their families. The fiskers had given him two days to find out who held the fortress island before they took a run at it themselves.

Since when did a crew order their styrman around?

True, neither ship truly belonged to him, though he'd be willing to make a coaster's claim on the *Sylvi*. The king had offered it to him, after all, in exchange for a promise Eiric hadn't kept.

It didn't matter. He couldn't sail her without a crew. And he didn't want to see her burned to the waterline in a frontal assault on a fortress that had dragons on call.

He heard Liv's voice in his head. *So you're volunteering? Not a smart move, brodir.*

His gut twisted. What he wouldn't give to be scolded by that systir again.

The crossing was just as strenuous and miserable as he'd expected. One advantage of the foul weather was that nothing short of a low-flying eagle would have spotted him on the water.

It had been a long time since he'd sailed these waters (more than ten years, it turned out), but he'd once known this area well. The cities along the west coast were a good place to sell summer takings before sailing on to the mean and stingy markets in Selvagr.

Wave action along the cliffs of Sudreyjar had undercut them so that they resembled ladies lifting their skirts. Underneath were sea caves–some underwater at high tide, and others above the high tide line, or that at least led into dry chambers. His fadir had sometimes used them to store valuables if there was a risk of boarding by some other ship, or if he believed the markets would be more favorable the next year. He would not risk his farm and family by stowing valuables at Sundgard.

No doubt there were forgotten hoards of Halvorsen and Eiricsen silver and gold in the caves of Sudreyjar.

He was aiming, more or less, for a section of the coast that was unlikely to be closely watched, being rocky and dangerous and unforgiving of mistakes.

A lot can change in ten years.

His target was near the place where the channel met the sound. Winds and weather and tides ensured that conditions would never be the same twice. He'd timed it so that the stage of the tide and rush of waves would allow his little boat to clear the threshold of one of the largest caves on Klettrholm.

Once in the maelstrom boiling around the rocks, there was no good escape except into the cave. An error in timing would rip out the belly of a boat and throw its crew into the rocks.

He was six years old the first time he came here, aboard his fadir's ship. He was terrified, half-sick from the turbulence. The crew held the ship off the rocks with their oars, spray flying over them until Leif gave the signal. The force of the sea hurled the ship up and over the rocks into a pool inside the cliff.

Leif glanced at him before Eiric had time to scrape the alarm from his face. His fadir laughed and ruffled his hair. "Rest easy, Eiric, the Norns will decide whether we live or die."

That, in fact, did not help him rest easy.

"But what–what if a styrman makes a mistake, or an oar breaks, then–?"

"Then that was meant to be."

"But–couldn't you just store the takings someplace else?" Eiric said, trying to keep his voice from squeaking.

"It keeps away the amateur treasure hunters," Leif had said. "If a man steals from me, I want it to be a man with some skills."

He'd lost count of the number of times he'd been here since, eventually handling the styrboard himself, shouting out the orders. There was always that split second of doubt, the question of whether, this time, the Norns would deny him.

And so it was this time–the taste of metal on his tongue, the shock in his shoulders when the oars connected with rock, the hesitance on the stone threshold, and then relief as *Thistle* was hurled into the darkness of the cave.

He sat for a moment, his ship gently rocking, scanning his surroundings as his eyes adjusted to the light. It appeared to be unchanged from when he'd last been here, except that it was eerily quiet, broken only by the sound of water lapping on rock. In past times, the walls of the cave had echoed with voices, both family and crew.

The boat scraped bottom under his weight, so Eiric climbed out into the knee-deep water in the rocky pool, gathered up his weapons, and waded to the shore.

Though it had been years since he'd been here, it might have been yesterday, or a season ago. A small pile of kindling lay next to the wall, ready to feed new fires. A metal-strapped wooden box held a supply of torches–bundled sticks, the tips wrapped in hemp cloth stuffed with pitch and rendered fat. They were smoky and stank like an alehouse privy, but they gave good, consistent light.

Something in the dust at his feet caught his eye in the light from the cave entrance. It was his fadir's strike-steel, missing for years, now rusted over in the sea-damp air. He carefully tucked it into his carry bag, buckled on his mail shirt, followed with his coat, and finished by strapping on Gramr, his grandfadir's war axe, and as many torches as he could reasonably carry. He didn't look forward to navigating a cave with a sword on his back, but didn't want to risk leaving it behind.

He'd traveled light, since he'd most likely be dead or on his way back across the channel before he needed much in the way of supplies. Fortunately, the cave provided shelter from the cutting wind and sleet.

He closed his eyes, scraping at the hoarfrost of memory. This cave connected to a network of chambers and tunnels that honeycombed the island. There was an exit to the surface if he could find it. Hopefully it didn't lead straight into Grima's lockup.

Had there been a fortress or dwelling on this island fifteen years ago? Not that he remembered.

There was only one way out, aside from the sea gate, and Eiric lit the first of his torches and took it.

Several times, he came to places where tunnels branched off. Each time, he used his (admittedly flawed) internal compass to choose.

Reasoning that he had started at sea level, he walked an upslope whenever possible. Now and then, he felt reassuring drafts of cold air, suggesting the cave was well ventilated, by chance or design. Once he left the entry cave behind, he saw no further signs of human habitation. Also reassuring, to a point.

Abruptly, the tunnel opened into a good-sized chamber, its walls too far away for the torchlight to reach. Raising his torch, he circled the cave, close to the walls. The only opening he found was the one he'd entered through. Stumped, he made another circuit.

Sylvi always said that threes were lucky, but he wasn't sure that would help here. Air was moving–cold air pouring down from above, telling him there must be an opening up high. Riveted into the stone wall was a series of iron bars. Hand- and footholds for climbing.

Well then. He began to climb. By the time he reached the top, his fingers were numb and clumsy from contact with cold metal. He hauled himself up and onto the stone floor at the top. The floor was glazed with ice and slush, the ceiling too low for standing.

So he crawled forward on hands and knees until he finally reached the exit, in a jumble of rocks clotted with icy juniper.

He looked down on a courtyard surrounded by high rock walls, some natural and others intentionally built. It seemed that he had found the fortress. Some part of it, anyway.

Dawn was hours away. The sun had not yet risen, and the slaughter moon was shrouded in cloud, but in the light from torches burning in sconces on the walls, the courtyard appeared to be deserted. He waited. Still nothing. Yet he couldn't shake the notion that he was being watched.

Eiric couldn't stay here, clinging to the side of the cliff like a bat until the sun rose.

He jumped from the cave mouth, landing on his feet, knees bent, with his back to the cliff and within its shadow. From ground level, he could see archways spoking out from the central yard, what lay beyond shrouded in darkness.

He breathed in sharply, catching a musky, feral scent. Shadows shifted in the archways, shapes studded with yellow eyes.

Eiric lifted down a torch from a bracket on the wall and unhooked his axe, holding it close to his side.

There was more movement, some snapping and snarling, and finally a rush forward.

Issvargr. Ice wolves the size of horses, rimed with hoarfrost, silent as ghosts. And behind them, a rearguard of shape-shifting creatures trailing flame.

Fire and ice.

The wolf in the lead went straight for his throat, turning aside only when Eiric thrust the blazing torch in its face. He swung his axe in a wide arc, trying to create some space around himself, and wishing he'd inherited a long-handled axe. When the axe struck home, an explosion of ice splinters cut his skin and clattered on the stone.

Only a shred of flesh connected the vargr's head to its body, but it continued to try to drag itself toward him until overrun by the rest of the pack.

Two more wolves went down—decisively, Eiric thought, but soon they, too, were up and around again, though one was missing a foreleg.

He'd killed wolves before, on Muckleholm. It was never easy, but these seemed unkillable, and like they didn't even feel pain.

Eiric hadn't gone untouched. Now each axe stroke brought with it a spray of blood that steamed when it hit the cold stone. All the blood shed was his.

Maybe a sword forged by the gods might work. He considered drawing Gramr, but was afraid that he'd be dead by the time he freed it.

The courtyard was filled now with creatures of all kinds, fighting to get at him, howling for his blood. Some, frustrated, turned on each other.

Why did this keep happening? Constantly cornered, fighting for his life against impossible odds, whether it be on the cliff overlooking the Elivagar, in the Lundhof on Eimyrja, against bounty hunters in his hometown or trolls in caves. Would there ever come a time when he could stop fighting?

"That's enough!" someone shouted, by some miracle loud enough for all to hear. More miraculously, they listened.

"Don't let your bloodlust get ahead of you. Our lady said that all intruders should be taken alive."

Eiric couldn't tell who had spoken, since his view was blocked by a wall of wolves. Their snarling and snapping and growling said they were unhappy.

Eiric wasn't *exactly* happy. *All intruders should be taken alive* wasn't *exactly* reassuring. Maybe it would be better to go down fighting.

You're no good to anyone if you're dead, he thought. And if there was a chance Liv and Reginn were here, if he could see them again, save them somehow . . .

One of the wolves spoke, and, to Eiric's surprise, he understood it. "This is the first Asgardian we've seen who is big enough to share."

By now, the intercessor had elbowed his way forward. He was one of the flame creatures—a fire demon, like Asger Eldr. "If you disagree, I suggest that you take it up with her," he said. "But remember what happened to Finnulf."

Eiric did not know who Finnulf was but guessed he must have been the unlucky hero of a cautionary tale.

Grima. *Our lady* must be Grima, he thought.

Now an orc in the back spoke up. "He's trying to kill us," it said. "It's self-defense."

The demon rolled his eyes. "You're worried he might *kill* us," he said.

"You get stupider by the minute, Raghat. I get stupider just listening to you."

"He probably won't surrender," Raghat said with rekindled hope. "He'll probably fight to the death."

"I surrender," Eiric said. He returned the torch to its bracket, and set the axe down on the floor in front of him.

For a moment, the demon seemed stumped.

"The sword, too," he said finally.

Eiric laid Gramr next to Bjorn's axe, wondering how any hero ever held on to an heirloom sword for long.

Heroes don't lose, Leif would have said.

Admittedly, the weapons hadn't done him much good so far. He was the only one who looked like he'd been in a fight.

Where *was* that blood coming from?

He seemed to notice injuries more since he'd given his amulet to Ivar.

Ivar. He hoped the Asgardian amulet would protect him when he could not.

It would all be worth it if Ivar grew into the man he promised to be.

"Come with me," the demon said. And Eiric did.

73
THE INTRUDER

THE DAY AFTER THE SCENE at the strategy meeting, Reginn was mortified to find people tiptoeing around her, handling her like fragile Frankian glass, afraid of sparking another fit of pique. Her commanders hadn't asked for any of this, either, but she had called, and they had answered. They did their jobs, now with the added burden of tending a mercurial leader.

Hrym was right. The window was closing during which they could make a difference in the coming war. Doing nothing was a choice, too.

She met with the freed spinners, living and Risen, and found them eager to fight for whatever opposed Grima.

"She may be dead," Reginn said.

"She's alive," Keila said, "but not for long, if I have anything to do with it."

"Thank you. I'll let you know what the plan is."

When I've figured it out.

Finally, she called a meeting of her commanders and told them to present her with a proposal by the next morning outlining the best way to use their one ship and the fighters who elected to sail to Vandrgardr.

Reginn took her dinner alone by the hearth in the chamber in which she and Naima had been held captive. She saw no reason to move, and this room still had some reminders of her friend. The bit of cording Naima had used to practice knots still lay on a table, awaiting her return. The clothes she'd been captured in, washed and mended, waited on her bed.

The memory of Naima's words, when she persuaded Reginn not to take poison to escape another stint as a thrall.

Neither of us knows what's ahead. It's probably terrible, but maybe not. Maybe it's a fantastic surprise. Maybe Grima is going to crown us systir queens of the Archipelago.

Reginn raised her cup. "To the systir queens of the Archipelago," she said, a catch in her throat.

There came a knock at the door. "Your Grace?" It was Kåre.

Reginn sighed. She was well into her third cup of wine from Grima's stores, and her mood was just beginning to improve.

"Can it wait?" she said.

"No, ma'am."

"Come, then."

Kåre entered, flanked by a pair of demons.

"We've caught an intruder," he said.

Reginn's feeling of well-being dissipated as her suspicions went straight to Grima. "Who? Where?"

"He was on the rooftop of the barracks building," Kåre said. "The gods only know how he got there. It's a sheer face above, and a drop on both sides. We thought at first that he might be one of the upland giants that report to Hrym, but he is not Risen. We thought you could verify with that–that stone you have."

"He's dead?"

The two demons looked at each other. "Well, no," one said in his raspy-ash voice. "You said to take prisoners alive, if possible. He surrendered, so . . ."

"If you've changed your mind," the other one said, "we'll–"

"No," Reginn said hastily. "Of course not. Did you interrogate him? Did he say who he was or why he's here?"

"He said his name was Halvorsen. He asked for you, and someone named Liv," Kåre said. "He said he was told you were here."

Reginn's heart seemed to stop, quivering ineffectively. When it started up again, she still couldn't seem to get her breath. "Halvorsen? Are you sure?"

Kåre nodded. "He said that if you weren't here, then Grima would do. He said that he had a message for you from someone named Naima." He paused. "I suspect it's a trick."

"Where is he now?"

"We locked him in the Deeps for safekeeping."

"The Deeps!" That place still gave her the shudders. "There wasn't someplace else you could have–?"

"It's not like we've had the need for multiple dungeons," Kåre said, avoiding her eyes. "Most of our prisoners don't–well, anyway, we just have the one. Don't worry. It's been cleaned up since you saw it. Now it's more of a–more of a room for guests that we want to stay put. This way, you can have a look at him from the gallery and not get too close."

"Let's go, then," Reginn said. She scooped up her staff and was out of her room and halfway down the corridor before he followed.

Reginn had returned to the Deeps several times since the freeing of the prisoners, only because she had to cross the gallery to access the room housing Grima's stone. Every time, she kept her eyes fixed on the door ahead and held her breath as if she was trying to avoid breathing in some contagion.

The door to the gallery was locked, with a bar thrown across for good measure. By the time Kåre arrived, Reginn had removed the bar and fished out her key.

"Where are the others?" Reginn said, since Kåre had lost the demons somewhere.

"Given what's happened," Kåre said, "we're doubling our sentries. They had to go back to their posts."

Reginn unlocked the door, and stepped onto the gallery. When Kåre tried to follow her in, Reginn blocked his path. "You stay here."

"With all due respect, Your Grace, it's not safe," Kåre said. "You know that Grima's a shape-shifter. Her illusions are very, very convincing, and she knows this stronghold better than anyone. This Halvorsen could very well be Grima in disguise."

"If that's the case, I'll call you in," Reginn said. The dungeon-master was getting on her nerves. A spinner with a staff would not be looking to the likes of Kåre for protection.

"You keep agreeing with me," Kåre said, "but I'm not sure you're listening."

"You're the one that isn't listening," Reginn said, losing patience. "Stand down." With that, she shut the door in Kåre's face.

So much for slipping in unobserved.

She advanced to the railing and looked down into the room that had been used for bleeding spinners of their megin. The table, the collars, the cables, the jars of "mead" were gone. In their place was a small table with an oil lamp, a sleeping bench, a wash basin and chamber pot.

The commotion should have woken the dead, but apparently the prisoner was still sleeping. She could see the shape of him under a rough blanket, a shock of fair hair peeking out, his wrists manacled to the wall in what appeared to be an uncomfortable position. A blood-spattered rag lay next to the bed.

"Eiric," Reginn said. And then, louder, "Halvorsen!"

The figure stirred, rolled over, and fought with the blanket until his head poked out. He looked around, resembling an angry bird with his tousled hair. He reached for a weapon, but was caught up short by the chains. It was a move so typically Eiric that Reginn all but melted in place.

"Up here," she said.

He looked up. His face changed when he saw her, lit with joy, gratitude, and hope–as if he'd finally been ambushed by good news. No one had ever looked at her like that before.

"Reginn," he whispered. "Thank the gods." He struggled to sit up, tried the chains again. Looked around the room and back up at Reginn. She could tell he was trying to piece things together in a way that made sense.

His eyes narrowed. "Is it really you?" he said.

This Halvorsen could very well be Grima in disguise.

"Is it really *you*?" she said.

After an awkward pause, Eiric said, "Where did we meet?"

"In an alehouse in Langvik," Reginn said. "What did I give you to keep on the night we met?"

"A runestick," he said without hesitation. "What did you tell me about heroes that night?" When she didn't answer right away, he added, "It was when I asked you to come home with me."

Then she knew. Throat thick, she said, "I told you that there's no place for heroes in some stories. I was wrong. There are different heroes for different stories." She blotted away tears with the backs of her hands and fished in her neckline for the string of keys she kept there. "I don't know if I have the keys to unlock you, but I'll come down and–"

Reginn heard the door open and close behind her, rapid footsteps approaching. "Kåre," she said, turning, "good timing. Would you have the key for–?"

Kåre wrapped an arm around her, pinning her arms, twisted her staff out of her hand, and dropped it over the railing to the floor below. He gripped the chain of keys at her neck and broke it, palming the keys.

She could hear Eiric shouting from below.

Now Reginn was all knees and elbows and stomping feet. She'd been in her share of bar fights and knew that if she could inflict enough pain, he'd let go.

Either that or kill her.

Kåre swore, adjusting his grip, trying to find a safe hold. Then finally lifted her off her feet, avoiding her attempts to gouge his eyes out, and dropped her over the railing to the floor below.

That was the last she knew for a long time.

74
HARD LESSONS

EIRIC HAD NEVER FELT SO helpless. It was like one of those dreams where disaster is bearing down, and you can't move. He couldn't see exactly what was happening on the gallery above, but he knew Reginn was being attacked and fighting for her life. It seemed to be by someone she knew, since she'd called him by name.

He yanked at the chains tethering him to the wall, but they were good tempered steel and would not give way. All he got for his trouble was a pair of badly bruised wrists. Above, the assailant howled in rage, and he knew Reginn was giving some back, but without her staff, it seemed unlikely that she could fight him off.

He saw two figures struggling against the railing, and then the smaller one went over the railing and landed, hard, on the stone floor not far from Eiric's sleeping bench.

Reginn lay crumpled, half on her side, blood pooling around her head. She wasn't moving.

The attacker looked down at Reginn. "Like I said, you weren't listening, you stupid bitch. I've spent years building this place, and you've all but ruined it in the space of a few days."

Eiric blinked. The figure shifted, dwindled, changed, until someone else entirely was gloating down at him.

Grima.

"I'll be back in a few minutes, and then I'll see to both of you."

She disappeared, and Eiric could hear her footsteps continuing down the gallery, the sound of a key in a lock, and the door opening.

"Reginn!" he hissed. And then, louder, "Reginn. Can you hear me?

You have to get out of here."

There was no response.

He twisted around, braced his feet against the wall, and pushed backward, all but dislocating his shoulder. Rolling forward, he examined the place where the chain was attached to the wall. He wrapped one of the chains around his boot and slammed his foot into the connection, once, twice, three times, and then the chain fell free from the wall. He went to work on the other one, which went faster now that he knew what he was doing. It ended with him still wearing manacles, chains hanging free.

He crossed to where Reginn was lying. His hope rekindled when he found that she was breathing. He examined her skull with gentle fingers. The bone seemed intact, but the scalp was still bleeding heavily. One of her arms looked as if it might be broken.

I'll be back in a few minutes.

Eiric had to move Reginn out of danger, but the only way out he knew was via the gallery, and he didn't know how much time he had. He was also afraid to move quickly, for fear of making her injuries worse. He laid the blanket from his bed next to her and rolled her onto it, then dragged her under the gallery, out of sight, and set her staff beside her.

They were near water–he could hear it and smell it and taste it–there had to be a door out on this level. He soft-footed around the perimeter of the room until he found it–a metal-framed wooden door, hinges rusted from exposure to salt and moisture. His impatience lending him strength, he wrenched the door off its hinges. The metal shrieked, and he froze, but no one seemed to have heard.

The door let out into a sea cave, one he hadn't seen before. He assumed it must be the entrance off the sound they'd tried to approach before. He could hear water lapping, and voices on the other side of a rocky outcropping.

"I hope she doesn't take too much longer," somebody said. "It'll be light soon, and if we're spotted, we'll get cooked."

"I just hope she gets what she came for," another voice said. "I'd rather face a dragon than the Spider in a rage."

"Maybe it'll be both," the first sailor said with a braying laugh.

"Shut up! Sound carries over water, you know."

Eiric debated. It would be satisfying to dispose of Grima's crew and steal her ship, but he didn't know how many crew were on board. If it was one of her longships, it was too many, given that he had no weapons–yet.

There was a tunnel that branched off on this side of the outcropping that might provide some cover.

Meanwhile, Reginn lay in the dungeon, unprotected.

He hurried back into the building to find Reginn stirring, groaning. Her eyes fluttered open, still cloudy with confusion. When he leaned close, she reached up with her good hand and touched his face, tried to speak.

"Shhh," he said. "Grima's here, and we need to stay quiet. I'm going to try to move you to a safer place." He wrapped Reginn and her staff tightly in the blanket, slid his arms under, and lifted her, cradling her against him. Her breath hissed out, as if it hurt, but she seemed to understand that she needed to keep quiet.

Above their heads, a door banged open and he heard quick footsteps along the gallery. A purplish glow poured over the railing and into the cell below.

"What's this?" Grima said. "Have my birds flown? Even though I clipped their wings?"

Eiric put his lips to Reginn's ear and said again, "Shhh." Keeping under the shelter of the gallery, he carried her to the doorway to the cave, regretting the ruined door, which might as well have been a signpost pointing which way they had gone.

As he stepped across the threshold, he saw purple light spilling down the steps and heard Grima's tread on the stairs.

He carried Reginn into the branching tunnel just inside the door. As he suspected, it didn't go far, dead-ending into a rock face just out of sight of the main cave.

"Wait here," he said, kissing her on the forehead, knowing that it might be goodbye. He hurried back to the main cave, wondering if he could somehow lead Grima away from Reginn. There just wasn't much of anywhere to go.

He returned to the ruined doorway. Grima was stalking around the dungeon room, poking her staff into every hole to make sure nobody was hiding there. "Come out, come out, wherever you are," she crooned, as if they were playing hide-and-seek.

When she turned toward him, he could see where the purplish light was coming from. A large jewel swirling with color hung on a chain around her neck. Eiric didn't know what it was, but he assumed it was bad news.

All at once, she froze and looked up at the gallery. Eiric heard it, too—running feet, shouting, doors slamming, alarm bells ringing.

Grima swore and swung around, toward the cave entrance. Eiric leaped back, but not before she'd seen him.

Grima smiled. "Perhaps there's still time to take care of this bit of business, at least," she said, striding toward him. "You've been a thorn in my side for too long, and now I have the power I need to remove it."

Eiric flattened himself against the wall just inside the doorway. When the Spider stepped through, he swung his arm, wrapping the heavy chain around her neck and pulling it tight. He made a grab for the pendant, but she pivoted, smashing her staff against his shoulder. His entire arm went numb, and he lost hold of the chain, but whipped the other one across her face. She screamed as the blood poured down, blinding her as he scrambled away.

Grima mopped at her face with her sleeve, then took hold of her pendant and aimed the business end of the staff at him. Eiric waited until what he judged was the very last second, then lunged sideways and landed rolling. He narrowly evaded a blast of flame that reduced the rock outcropping to rubble, sending large chunks of limestone flying. Beyond the ruined wall, Eiric could see Grima's longship resting on the sand, and bewildered, bleeding crew members scrambling to their feet.

That was new. Now she had power beyond shape-shifting.

Grima's next blast all but brought the ceiling down on top of him.

If those sounding the alarm had any doubts as to where the trouble was, they knew now. Boots clattered down the stairs from the gallery, and he heard the yipping of wolves on the hunt.

"Better go," Eiric said. "Company's coming."

Swearing, Grima scrambled over the pile of rocks between her and her ship. "I've got what I came for," she said. "Let's go." She leaped aboard the longship, her momentum pushing it off the sand, her oarsmen already pulling for the open sea.

Eiric should have tried to stop her, but knew that without a sword or axe or even a knife, he was outmatched. Grima might get lucky on her third try. Eiric wasn't sure what it was she'd stolen, but he wasn't willing to trade his life for it.

At the moment, he was just glad to see Grima gone so that he could get back to Reginn.

He was intercepted before he reached the tunnel by a troop of guards, who slammed him up against the wall.

"I knew we should have killed you when we found you on the roof," one of them said, his breath burning his skin. "We could've said it was an accident." It was one of the demons that had apprehended him.

"This bastard murdered Kåre," one of the other soldiers said. "Now, what did you do with Her Grace?" he said to Eiric.

Before he could blurt out an answer, someone said, "Halvorsen! What are you doing here?"

It was Asger Eldr, flaming sword in hand.

What are you doing here?

"Grima was here, posing as a guard," Eiric said. "If you move quickly, you might be able to catch her in the sound. Reginn is hurt." He pointed up the side tunnel. "She's up there. Grima threw her off the gallery."

75
VANDRGARDR

The best way to honor someone you've lost is to remember and use the lessons that they taught you.

–Hilde Stevenson

HEIDIN'S SHIP LANDED AT VANDRGARDR the day after Ivar's shake spell. The New Jotunheim army seemed relieved to have their queen back. They were tired of camping along the coast in a place where the weather got colder and nastier by the day. They were ready to either fight or go home.

Ivar got the impression that "going home" was growing more popular by the day. But Tyra and Heidin seemed determined to wait and see how Rikhard responded to Heidin's terms.

The queen did not restrict Ivar's movements around camp, but she assigned four personal guards who went with him everywhere. They included two youngish spinners and two oldish and biggish, fully armed soldiers. He felt like a dragon with a long tail.

They even slept in his tent, which he didn't like at all, especially because the soldiers snored.

The spinners, called adepts, included a healer, Bryn, and one named Shelby. They treated him like a child, but Ivar didn't mind. They were friendly and informative. People let their guard down around children.

The guards had nothing to say to Ivar, so Ivar had trouble remembering which was which. He called them Grak and Grover, which might not have been their real names.

"Where are the rest of the Jotun?" Ivar asked one day as he was helping Bryn pound powders for medicines.

"What do you mean?" Bryn said, combing through his curly hair with his fingers to remove stray powder.

"I thought there would be dragons. And elves," Ivar said. "All I've seen are spinners and regular people. Soldiers."

"So many of the others were lost at Ragnarok," Bryn said. "Those that survived have scattered. We're hoping that as we take more and more territory, they'll come out of hiding and join us."

"We don't need the help of monsters to win this war," Grak said. "At the first sign of trouble, they'll turn tail and run. You saw what happened with the dead ones."

"The dead ones?" Ivar said.

Ivar could tell that Bryn was sorry Grak brought this up. "One of the queen's counselors was able to call up some of the Jotun who died at Ragnarok. She went missing recently, and her army went to search for her. That's all."

"Are you talking about Reginn?" Ivar said. Then instantly regretted it. The less his captors knew the better.

Bryn and Grak stared at him.

"What do you know about Reginn?" Bryn said.

"Nothing," Ivar said hastily. "Some strangers were looking for her is all."

"What strangers?" Bryn said.

The more you talk, the deeper the hole you're in. "Someone who came to Kingshavn," Ivar said. "I don't remember who. There's a lot of coming and going there. Speaking of, has anyone been into Vandrgardr?"

"There's nothing to see there," Grak said flatly.

"I always liked it," Ivar said. "We could go, wearing disguises, and I could show you around. There's a stall at their market that sells these delicious–"

"It's gone, Ivar," Bryn said. "Everything–and everyone–is gone."

"I don't understand," Ivar said, though he was beginning to. "Since when?"

"It happened not long after we arrived," Bryn said, "when we were trying to keep our presence here quiet. We wanted to access their storehouses for provisions."

Ivar refused to understand. "And so, all the people–?"

"Welcome to the war, princeling," Grak said, ruffling his hair.

If Ivar had been carrying his belt dagger, he would have gutted him.

Ivar never mentioned going to town again.

Ivar had been watching out for Tyra since they came ashore, remembering the overheard conversation aboard ship. But there is no avoiding a person on a mission. One evening after the nattmal, he was playing hnefatafl with Bryn when the tent flap was pulled aside, revealing a tall figure in the doorway, the glow at the tip of her staff uplighting her features.

It was not a good look. It was a monstrous look.

"Everyone out," Tyra said. "I need to speak to the little prince in private."

They left. Bryn took his time, obviously worried about leaving the two of them alone, but unable to find a hook to hang that on.

Ivar was sitting cross-legged on the floor of the tent, so Tyra sat down opposite him, her staff resting in the crook of her arm.

"Have you come to murder me?" Ivar said.

Tyra flinched back. "N-no, of course not! What gave you that idea?"

"I get the impression that you don't approve of me," Ivar said. "Is there something I'm doing that I shouldn't, or something that I should be doing that I'm not?"

"Not really, no," Tyra said, still a little flustered. "The queen has asked me to speak with you."

"You're worried about her," Ivar said.

"Every modir worries about her children."

"My modir doesn't worry about me," Ivar said. "She's dead."

"Enough!" Tyra all but shouted. "Shut up!"

Ivar did.

"King Rikhard's fleet has been spotted in the sound," Tyra said. "Queen Heidin asked me to speak with you because we want to make sure that everyone in her inner circle is loyal to her."

"Did she say that? That I'm in her inner circle?"

"You're here, aren't you?"

"I thought I was here as, you know, a prisoner."

"The quickest path to freedom is by proving that you are trustworthy," Tyra said.

Ivar still had other questions, such as whether everyone was being tested or just him, but he didn't ask. Instead, he said, "So, what do we do?"

Tyra let out a long sigh, as if relieved. "You don't need to do anything, really," she said. "Why don't you lie down on your sleeping bench and relax, and just be open to what I say."

Ivar lay down on his bed and pulled the woolen blanket up to his chin, as if that would protect him. Under the blanket, he took hold of the two pendants he wore–Eiric's pendant, with its Asgardian symbols, and the amulet of protection from his elvish fadir.

Tyra's staff began to spin, tendrils of magic reaching out for him, probing for a way in. Ivar fixed his inner eye on Hilde's face and hung on.

Your modir, Sylvi, loved you very much. . . .

76

ALL THINGS BROKEN

THE FORCES AT KLETTRHOLM DID not find Grima sailing the sound in a longship, or hidden in a back corridor, or clinging to a cliff on the far side of the island. They looked in all of those places. Nor was the longboat in the sea cave adjacent to the Deeps, though the damage there suggested that *something* had happened.

Others who might have verified his story were unavailable. The dungeon-master, Kåre, was dead. It had been a full day, and Reginn had not regained consciousness.

Even if Reginn came to, she hadn't actually *seen* Grima. As far as she knew, it was Kåre who threw her over the rail.

This left Eiric sailing a sea of suspicion. Her soldiers would not return his weapons, and they would not allow him to see Reginn. If not for the intervention of Asger Eldr, he might have been back in chains.

These are strange times, Eiric thought, when I look to a fire demon to speak up for me.

Lord Eldr had his reasons, as Eiric eventually found out.

Asger took him on a walking tour through the fortress and its surroundings. Apparently, he'd spent his time on Klettrholm exploring. He introduced him to the other commanders of the Risen army. They were polite, but distant. The line soldiers gazed at him with a virulent loathing that would have put a twist in his gut except that he was used to being viewed with visceral hatred, and this was only a small step up.

They ended on a viewpoint atop the fortress, the highest point on the island, where a person could survey the entire sweep of the sound, from Langvik to the most distant of the Sudreyjar Islands. In good weather, that is, and there wouldn't be much of that before the Disting.

"It seems likely that the most decisive fighting will happen at Vandrgardr," Asger said. "As far as we know, the queen is still there. You've said the king's departure was imminent some time ago, so he may be in the sound already. If we delay any further, it may limit our options.

"One of our issues is that we have relatively few ships. Some of the Risen can swim or fly across the sound, but the rest will need–"

"I may have access to two more ships," Eiric said, "but–"

"Two more ships!" Asger said with a rare flicker of enthusiasm. "That would be–"

"But it's up to the crews to decide whether to put themselves and their ships at risk."

"The *crews*?" Asger said, as if this notion was preposterous.

"One of the ships is *Naglfar*, which was damaged when it ran aground just to the west of these islands. If you'll recall, some of the crew stayed behind to make repairs. Reginn promised that if they would sail for her for a year, the ship was theirs."

Eiric knew that the fisker ships might already be on their way. His two days were up.

"If they come, they'll be flying the fisker banner." When Asger looked lost, Eiric inscribed the air with his forefinger. "Wavelets, like their skin art. I've asked the commanders to pass the word not to shoot at them. It would help if you said something as well."

Asger leaned his forearms on the railing and gazed out to sea. "You should know that the aldrnari is–troubled."

"What do you mean?"

Asger nodded. "She's full of doubt about a path forward."

"I don't blame her."

"She might be swayed by what you do."

"If you think I exert any influence over Reginn, you're mistaken.

Right now, I just want her to heal. After that she can make up her own mind."

"What will *you* do?"

"What do you mean?"

"Will you remain with the aldrnari and fight for the Jotun, or will you return to the king and fight for him?"

Maybe I'll go fishing, Eiric thought.

"I promised my brodir, Ivar, that I would fight by his side. Besides, the Jotun have done nothing to win me over. They've been trying to kill me since I set foot on Eimyrja."

"This is not about the Jotun," Asger said. "The aldrnari needs you. She needs someone who is focused on keeping her alive."

"I thought that was *you*," Eiric said. "That's been your claim all along."

"My skill is in breaking things, not in mending what is broken. My role here is–"

Asger stopped abruptly and gave a little shake of his head, as if to dislodge whatever mischief spirit had prompted this confession.

Who are you? Eiric thought. Where is the demon who tortured her in the alehouse in Langvik?

"Reginn is an attractive target for anyone who understands her role. If anything happens to her, the Risen go, too. All it would take is one traitor in our midst–one lucky shot from the enemy, and we'll have another Ragnarok."

"The Risen are still holding my weapons. They don't trust me in the same room with Reginn. I've not seen her since Grima–"

"I will see to it that your weapons are returned," Asger said, "and that the access issue is resolved. That done, I would expect that–"

Just then, one of the demons found them. "Lord Eldr," he said, "two ships are approaching from the south." He pointed.

It was *Naglfar* and *Sylvi*. The fiskers were coming.

* * *

Reginn opened her eyes, feeling a weight on her chest that had not been there before. She reached up and brushed her fingers over etched metal. It was the protective pendant she'd given Naima before Grima took her away. On the same chain was a runestick like the one she'd given Eiric Halvorsen at their first meeting.

In fact, it *was* the runestick she'd given Eiric.

How had they come back to her? Was this the afterworld where all lost things come back? Where all things broken are mended?

Her head still hurt–a dull ache–but the wound had an itchy quality that said it was finally healing. When she looked up at the ceiling, it rippled and swam, like she was underwater. Her left arm was stiff and useless, splinted to immobilize it.

Reginn propped on her right elbow, and her stomach lurched, threatening to empty all over her bedclothes. There were two other people in the room, both sleeping.

Eiric Halvorsen sprawled on his back against the wall, one leg bent, the other extended, weapons piled on the floor beside him. It appeared that he had been sitting up, leaning against the wall, but fell asleep and slid down to his present position.

The last she remembered, he was scruffy and bloody, bound in chains in the Deeps. Now he appeared freshly washed, in clean clothes, though he was still fighting in his dreams, his hands opening and closing on imaginary weapons.

On her other side was Naima, curled up in a chair, head pillowed on her arms, her face hidden by a fall of pale hair. She was thin and wan, as if it had been a long road that brought her here, but she was alive.

Reginn licked cracked lips. "Naima," she said, her voice hoarse from lack of use. When she didn't respond, she repeated, "NAIMA!"

Eiric scrambled to his feet. Naima all but rolled onto the floor before she was fully awake.

"Reginn!" Naima knelt beside her bed and gripped her hands. "Thank the gods," she said, tears sliding down her cheeks. "After all the trouble I took to stay alive, I would have been really put out if you'd died on me."

"I might die of thirst if I can't get some water," Reginn said.

Eiric grabbed a pitcher, poured a cup, and carried it to Reginn's bedside. "I dipped the water from the well myself, and drank some earlier. I'm still alive, so it's probably not poisoned," he said.

Reginn was so thirsty, she might have emptied the cup even if it *was* poisoned.

Together, Naima and Eiric helped her sit up, piling pillows behind her for support. She downed three cups of water before she was ready to talk. Even then, she held on to the cup just in case.

"How long has it been?" she said.

Naima and Eiric looked at each other. "Just a day," Eiric said, "but a lot has happened."

"I want to hear all of it, but, first–who attacked me and where are they now? Did Kåre go rogue, or was that Grima on the gallery?"

Eiric closed his hand over hers. "It was Grima, not Kåre. I don't know when the switch was made, but they found Kåre's body in the armory. Grima seemed to be after the keys you were carrying. She used them to get into a room at the end of the gallery."

"Skita," Reginn muttered, flooded with dread.

"What was she after?" Naima said.

"This is just a guess," Reginn said. "I believe she was making her own godstone. It was in that back room."

"Godstone?" Eiric said. "What do you mean?"

"Naima, remember the story I told on that last night in Vandrgardr? I think at least parts of it are true. Grima was making her own plans that were disrupted when Heidin showed up."

She turned to Eiric. "Grima was jealous of your systir's pendant and its legacy of power," Reginn said. "Grima's gift was that of shape-shifting–useful for a spy and assassin, but she's more ambitious than that. Apparently, she's not willing to bend the knee to either Rikhard or Heidin."

"That makes sense," Naima said. "At Vandrgardr, Grima was disrespectful, even insubordinate."

"Right," Reginn said. "She's been draining megin from the gifted and storing it in a jewel that was locked up in the back room."

"Was it purple? About this size?" Eiric formed a circle with his thumb and forefinger. "I didn't get a close look, but she had a stone hanging from a chain around her neck."

Reginn nodded. "It was a mixture of red and blue. She didn't discriminate. She harvested from both Asgardians and the Jotun."

"She was definitely more powerful than I remember," Eiric said. "Given a little more time, I think she would have brought the fortress down around our ears."

"I'm not surprised," Reginn said. "I suspect that if it comes to war, Grima will be there to break things and then pick up the pieces."

77

TOE TO TOE WITH THE FATES

AS WORD SPREAD THAT THE aldrnari was awake and talking, it seemed like everyone on Klettrholm found an excuse to stop by and see for themselves.

Eiric and Naima did their best to manage the stream of visitors who sought entry, but Reginn undermined their efforts.

"The Risen, especially, took a chance on me," Reginn said. "They need to know I'm not going anywhere."

The members of her Risen army were all but impossible to keep out anyway. If denied access through the door, they simply walked through the wall. They never stayed long, though, but simply paid their respects and moved on.

Svend Bondi came, and stayed, making himself useful in a hundred ways. He bent his knee to Reginn, but Eiric had the sense that he was really there to see Naima. They resembled two planets orbiting around each other.

Eiric was turning into the kind of person who noticed such things. Liv would be proud. No, amazed. No, amused.

Likewise, Asger came, but stayed only long enough to assure himself that Reginn was on the mend. On his way out, he leaned toward Eiric and said, "I'll set a guard outside and put a stop to this traveling circus so she can rest."

It was obvious that he thought Eiric and Naima could do better.

Asger was as good as his word. A phalanx of demons filled the corridor outside Reginn's chamber, challenging anyone who got too close. Eiric knew from experience how persuasive they could be.

With the constant traffic stopped, Reginn slept the rest of the afternoon, until long after the shy winter sun went down. Eiric lit the oil lamps and built up the fire on the hearth, while Naima and Svend brought food and drink up from the kitchen, enough for a small army. Or two people, depending.

"Will you be all right if I take the rest of the night off?" Naima said. "Svend and I would like to—you know—catch up."

"Some of the fiskers invited us for a drink," Svend said. "They really just want to meet Naima, but I'll be there for the introductions."

"We thought you and Reginn might want to catch up, too," Naima said, gazing up at the ceiling, a ghost of a smile tugging at her lips.

"We'll manage," Eiric said. "Now, go."

"Send word if you need us," Svend said, and they were out the door.

Reginn was still sleeping, so Eiric set the food on the hearth to try to keep it warm for her and poured himself a cup of cider. He returned to his seat by her bedside so that he could savor the miracle of her survival.

The purple bruises on her face were fading to shadows, perhaps due to the effect of the runestick. Naima had coaxed Reginn's unruly hair into a thick plait threaded with ivy and winterberry. The red berries stood out against her hair like drops of blood. He resisted the temptation to lean close or to touch her—to verify that she was real, and still breathing.

She was complex, intoxicating, powerful, principled—and yet vulnerable.

He'd fallen hard. He was not used to that.

Yule was coming on. He wondered if he'd ever see another. War seemed inevitable, but he could see no way to win it. By all rights, he should bend the knee to his king and fight alongside his brodir to assure his survival and the protection of Ivar's legacy.

But that would mean going to war against his systir and Reginn—

two people that he loved.

It would also mean losing, despite his best efforts. Even Rikhard's tested army would not prevail against the spinners and the Risen—an army with a grudge and no fear of dying.

Grima, now—it would be easy to go to war against Grima.

A pleasure, in fact.

If wishes were fishes . . .

The cider was warm and potent, its spicy scent reminding him of the night in Langvik when he'd stepped into a fight in an alehouse that had changed his life.

There's no place for heroes in some stories.

In the Deeps, she'd said she'd changed her mind.

Eiric wasn't sure that he could be the kind of hero she needed.

Restless, he rose, and made a circuit of the room. He could tell Reginn hadn't been here long; she'd only begun to make it her own. Here was her remedy bag, her flute—miraculously still with her. That ugly staff she carried. Promising that there were some things that a person could hold on to.

He sat down on the hearth and refilled his cup.

"Is that cider?"

Startled, he almost spilled it all over himself.

When he looked up, Reginn was sitting on the edge of the bed, bare legs poking out from under her linen shirt, her feet not reaching the floor.

"It is," he said. "Would you like some?"

"Yes, please." She slid off the bed, her shirt riding up until—

His face burning, Eiric busied himself with the cider, thinking, You are every bad thing Liv ever said about you. An untrustworthy scoundrel who thinks with his—

He heard a light step behind him. Reginn put her hand on his shoulder and kissed him on the back of the neck.

He all but spilled the cider again as gooseflesh pebbled his neck and shoulders.

"Should you be out of bed?" he said without turning around.

"I'm much better."

"Clearly," he said.

"I've missed you."

She sat down next to him, her hip touching his, and he handed her the cup of cider. She breathed in the scent, then drank deeply, half emptying the cup at a go.

"It's strong," he warned.

"Good," she said. Of course. "What's in the pot?"

"I haven't looked." He stood and lifted the lid. It was stew–chunks of pork, onion, turnips, golden beets, and lingonberry. There was also a plate of soft cheese, flatbread, honey, and hazelnuts.

Whoever was doing the cooking here was no slouch. Grima must have had plenty of food supplies stowed away.

It was cozy by the hearth, so Eiric dragged a small table over, and a bench. They sat, side by side, facing the fire, eating stew, drinking cider. Every now and then, Reginn rested her hand on his forearm, his thigh, as if to reassure herself that he was there, that he was real. It was distracting–in a good way.

Keep that up, he thought, and I won't make it through the meal.

The last thing Eiric wanted to do was to bring up the coming war. But, of course he eventually did.

"Asger's worried that if you don't sail soon, they'll have the war without you."

"That would be a shame," Reginn murmured.

"Rikhard blames Liv for Sundgard. Ivar's foster modir, Hilde, was killed in the attack. Hilde was carrying Rikhard's baby. Rikhard has vowed to hunt Liv to the ends of the earth if need be. He's out for blood."

Reginn frowned, thinking. "Talk to Naima. I haven't had much chance to sit with her, what with everything, but I believe she told Ivar that it was Grima, not Heidin, that attacked Sundgard. So hopefully Rikhard knows the truth by now."

"If true, that's good news," Eiric said, a faint hope kindling within him. Ivar would never have forgiven Liv for murdering the only modir he'd ever known. He remembered what his brodir had said when Eiric told him that their systir had taught him to sail in *Thistle*.

I don't have a systir.

The fact remained that if Rikhard's army faced off with Liv's forces, it would be a slaughter. Not to mention Grima, waiting in the wings.

Reginn must have read that in Eiric's expression, because she said, "Do you think you could convince Ivar to sit this war out? Surely there's a place the two of you can go until it's over, one way or another."

Eiric shook his head. "I suggested that, early on. Ivar said that he intended to stay and fight for his king. To be honest, Rikhard's done more for Ivar than I ever have. Now it's even more complicated. Since Hilde died, Rikhard has named Ivar as the heir to his throne."

Reginn stared at him. "What? Your little brodir is Rikhard's heir? Isn't he just ten years old?"

Eiric nodded. "Eleven, at the Solstice," he said. "Wise beyond his years. I hope you'll have the chance to meet him somewhere other than the battlefield."

"So you're determined to go and fight for Rikhard," Reginn said.

Eiric shook his head. "I'll go and fight for Ivar."

"You'll both die," Reginn said. "Rikhard, too."

Eiric shrugged. "If that's what the fates decree."

Reginn stood and started pacing back and forth. "No," she said. "That is not acceptable."

"You're going toe to toe with the fates?" Eiric rolled his eyes. "Good luck with that."

"What if we refuse to fight?"

"Who's 'we'? You and I?"

Reginn nodded.

"I've been accused of being arrogant, but I'm not so arrogant as to believe that my absence would stop this war. It would still be a bloodbath, and the people I care about would still die. The difference is that I would survive, and I'd have to live with that."

Reginn resumed pacing. "What if we refuse to let them fight?"

Eiric rested his hand on Reginn's cup. "That's enough cider."

"No, listen. It could work. The Risen are the key. They are the ones with nothing to lose."

Reginn was lit, burning brighter than midsummer, as if all her worries had fallen away. Where was the girl who had seemed near death just a short time ago?

If she was fire and ice, this was the fire part. He loved seeing her like this, even at the risk of catching fire himself.

She returned to the hearth and stood in front of him. With her standing and Eiric sitting, they were nearly eye to eye.

"We'll talk more about it tomorrow. In the meantime . . ." She stepped forward, between his knees, pressed against him, and kissed him as thoroughly as he'd ever been kissed. She pulled back, cradled his chin in her good hand, and studied his face. "In the meantime, I just want to be with you. Please."

Gently, he returned the kiss, walked his fingers down the bones of her spine until he found the hem of her linen shift. He slid his hands underneath, touching warm skin, wishing his hands weren't so rough. She wrapped her legs around him, and he lifted her and carried her back to her sleeping bench.

She sat on the edge of the bed and patted the ticking beside her.

Eiric hesitated. "Are you sure I won't hurt your arm?"

"I'm sure you'll be careful."

78

A NEW PLAN

WHEN REGINN WAS LITTLE, TOVE was never moved by complaints about having to learn this or that lesson. "Why do I need to know counting and numbers?" Reginn would say.

"Who will teach you when I am gone?" Tove said.

Fear washed over her. "Are you leaving?"

"Not for a long time," Tove said.

"So I have plenty of time to learn that later."

Herbs and plants were the same. "There are too many, and they all look alike," Reginn said. "You can tell me what's what."

"When you're on your own, you will need to know."

Again, that promise of leaving.

"I won't be a healer when I'm out on my own," Reginn said. "I'll be a musician and play in the great halls. I'll have servants."

"A person never knows what skills will be important in the future," Tove said. "You cannot learn everything, all at once."

Tove was right. Her skills as a healer and herbalist had served her well, and her experience as an entertainer, speaker, and performer also.

Never more so than when she enlisted the Risen and her commanders in her unlikely scheme.

She met with her commanders first. They were skeptical, but willing to put their trust in her, which seemed foolhardy. "I'll be asking for volunteers from among the Risen," she said.

"Why can't the living volunteer?" Katia said. She still seemed to feel the need to atone for her time in service to Modir Tyra.

"The Risen won't pay a blood price for this gambit. The living most certainly will. Those most likely to volunteer are the people I can least afford to lose." She smiled at Katia. "Remember, if you fight against the Jotun army, you may come up against your friends."

Stonebiter, commander of the dwarves, raised the next question. "How many sides can there be in a war?" She counted on her fingers. "There's Queen Heidin's side, King Rikhard's side, Grima's side–and now our side. Seems complicated."

"I suppose that's why we're having a war," Reginn said. "We don't get along." This was met with laughter and shouts of agreement. "Seriously, we'll be on everybody's side, and no one's. There is no one more despised than a peacemaker."

"What about him?" Hrym jerked a thumb at Eiric Halvorsen, who was lurking in the background, drawing speculative looks and whispers.

Reginn turned toward Eiric. "What about you?"

"I'm in, if the Risen agree," Eiric said.

Asger had his doubts about this "volunteer" business. Demons were authoritarian by nature.

"In effect, the Risen have already volunteered, when they answered your call to rise. They are obligated to do whatever you ask."

"The Risen have answered my call for a variety of reasons," Reginn said. "Most seem to believe that their deaths at Ragnarok accomplished nothing but turning the Nine Worlds to ash. They want to do something important, something that makes a difference. What I will ask of them is very different from what they might have envisioned. So I think they should have a choice."

"What will you do with those who say no?"

Admittedly, she hadn't thought much about that. "I suppose I'll thank them and send them back into the deadlands."

"What if they refuse?"

"Then I suppose I'll ask them to bring me the heads of opinionated and uncooperative fire demons," Reginn snapped.

Asger studied her for a long moment, then inclined his head. "So long as you have a plan," he said.

In many ways, the Risen were easier to convince. Reginn had earned considerable credit and goodwill simply by staying alive. Most mirrored Asger's view that they had risen to her call, and so they would follow her orders, whatever they were. That said, there was some grumbling among the wolves and demons. It seemed they had been looking forward to a fight after this long fallow time.

"We will not drink the blood of Asgard?" one said, eyeing Eiric with flattened ears and bared teeth.

Eiric straightened, broadening his stance, resting his hand on the haft of his axe in a "try me" sort of way.

The wolf took a step forward, hackles raised. "We will not rend the flesh from the bones of our enemies?"

"No," Reginn said. "Not if this goes according to plan. But you are welcome to leave my service and return to the deadlands. No one will hold it against you."

"This is not what was promised," the wolf snarled. It eased forward, and two orcs stepped between Reginn and the vargr.

"Remember what happened last time," one of them said in a voice that sounded rarely used. "Stand down."

"I don't want to hurt you," Reginn said. "Why would I? You answered when I called. But I cannot involve anyone who will not follow orders. The choice is yours–stay or go."

"I will stay," the wolf said grudgingly, and returned to his pack.

"Is there anyone else who would like to step away now?" Reginn scanned the gathering. No one responded. "If anyone wants to approach me privately, do so before day's end. We sail in the morning."

79

FAIR WINDS AND FOLLOWING SEAS

REGINN'S ARMY SET SAIL IN three ships on the nastiest of days, and Eiric sailed with them. The slate-gray waters of the sound thrashed under a biting northwest wind that drove rain and sleet and snow into their faces, and coated the decks and rigging and anyone aboard who stood still for too long.

Bjorn would have said that it was the kind of day that was good for sitting by the fire, drinking hot cider and telling summer tales. His grandfadir loved the sea, but respected its power. Hence Bjorn's best and most useful advice: *Don't set sail into a storm.*

Liv should know better, yet she'd chosen to launch an attack on the Archipelago in this vicious season.

Bjorn should have said, *Don't allow enemies to take the choice of timing out of your hands.*

Three ships seemed a paltry number compared to the many ships at Liv's disposal. Eiric had not seen Rikhard's entire fleet, but assumed it must be impressive, having been built over the years spent in the conquest of the Archipelago.

Eiric's fadir, Leif, claimed Tyr, god of war, as an ancestor. He would have shrugged off the mismatch. *Wars are not won at sea, Eiric. They are won on the land, by claiming territory and treasure and dominion over people. We are coasters, not pirates. Ships are a means of transporting us from one battle to another. Then the real work begins.*

Work that Reginn Eiklund aimed to take off the table.

All three ships had fisker styrmen, their crews a combination of fiskers and others with sailing skills.

Two groups of fiskers had a reunion of sorts—the ones Reginn had sailed with, on *Naglfar,* and Eiric's *Firebird* crew. Though none of them had much experience sailing in winter weather, they were more than happy to participate in a mission to defeat the spinners who had treated them so badly.

"Our ancestors sailed the blue ocean," Nils said, "before the spinners put up their walls. Our hearts remember."

Eiric sailed aboard *Naglfar,* with Rollo as styrman, along with Reginn and most of the Risen.

Reginn simply introduced Eiric to her Risen army as an ally. "He has a lot riding on the outcome of this plan."

The remaining Risen were divided among the other two ships, as were her living forces and recovering wraiths. Reginn had assigned Naima and Svend to *Sylvi,* with Reyna at the helm, knowing that they would look after each other.

Very few of the living had elected to stay behind, despite Reginn's best efforts to persuade them to stand down.

Eiric, Reginn, Reyna, and Rollo had studied a detailed map of Muckleholm and the surrounding waters before they set sail. Reyna, of course, had sailed both the east and west coasts of Muckleholm during her time crewing on *Firebird.* Neither she nor Rollo had sailed around the northern tip of the island.

"Would the king sail north or south, do you think?" the fiskers asked Eiric.

Eiric rocked his hand. "That's hard to say. The southern route is longer, but less risky in winter, since they can use the shelter of the sound. The northern route is shorter, leaving from Kingshavn, but you're out in the open sea the whole way. It's quicker, if they don't run into a storm."

"If they come from the north," Reginn said, "they may very well arrive and get into position ahead of us. I think we have to sail directly for Vandrgardr or risk arriving too late. Hopefully Katia's scouts can update us on the location of the king's fleet before too long."

They launched on the more sheltered sound side of the island, but immediately cut through to the seaward side. Katia sailed aboard *Naglfar* so that she could relay messages from her scouts, the dragon-like eldrvaettir. They swept back and forth across the sound, and then out to the open sea, watching for ships on the water.

It wasn't easy getting used to the comings and goings of the creatures that had burned Grima's ship to the waterline. They would materialize out of the freezing mist, heart-stoppingly close before they were visible. The first time that happened, Eiric threw himself facedown on the icy deck, much to the amusement of the Risen.

"You'll get used to it, Asgardian," one of the elves said. (Eiric might be a barbarian in New Jotunheim, but he was an Asgardian to the Risen.)

Eiric stuck close to Reginn, recalling Asger's warning. He gave the wolves special attention, after the meeting on Klettrholm. He had a natural wariness of the issvargr. They had been a constant threat in his childhood, the villain of every cautionary tale.

One of the vargr, noting his vigilance, said, "Don't be so jumpy, Asgardian. It makes us think of you as prey."

"It would help if you would smile more," Eiric said, "and wag your tail a little." When the wolf bared its teeth, he said, "There you go. That wasn't so hard, was it?"

Eiric half expected the wolf to charge, but, instead, the wolf looked him up and down, as if imprinting his appearance for later use.

Skita, Eiric thought, you're as bad as the rest. We'll be lucky if we're not fighting each other by the end of this.

He vowed to do better.

At least, these did not have the memory of the slaughter on Ithavoll, the murder of the council and the keeper. Their primary response was curiosity about why an Asgardian was aboard the aldrnari's flagship.

They discussed it as if he weren't there.

"What do you think he is, some kind of lookout?" Stonebiter said. "He *is* very tall."

"Maybe he's a bodyguard," Ursinus said. "Asgardians *are* fierce fighters, else we would have won at Ragnarok."

"Who says we didn't?" Stonebiter said. "Their skalds and storytellers are better, is all."

"Whoever won, the fact that we're headed for war again suggests that we accomplished nothing," Hrym said. "Our deaths made no difference."

"I've been told the Jotun welcome chaos," Eiric said. "By that measure, you're winning."

"That's a story told by Asgard," Dainn said. "Your chaos is our freedom, our magic, our grace–the light in the natural world that you've tried to extinguish. This world is livable because we exist."

Later that same day, the eldrvaettir returned with grim news–a fleet of ships carrying the fossegrim banner had been spotted sailing south along the west coast of Muckleholm, not far from Vandrgardr.

"The vaettir say they are sailing at top speed, under full sail in that northwest wind. It's as if they are running away from something, or running toward something."

If what they said was true, there was a chance Reginn's ships would be too late to intervene.

"Is there a way to slow them down?" one of the thursen said. "Could the dragons set fire to them like they did back at Klettrholm?"

Katia slid a look at Reginn. "That seems harsh," she said.

"Maybe just the sails?" the demon persisted.

"Those are wooden ships," Eiric said. "And my brodir is likely to be on one of them. So no."

"Ursinus," Reginn said. "Do you think the kraken could help?"

"Possibly," he said. "Though it would be a distance for them to travel."

"I can call on the Sjóvættir," Katia said. "The sea spirits. I don't have a relationship with the local guardians of these waters, but–"

"What would they do?" Eiric said.

"They can grab onto the ships, slow them down, yank the styrboard sideways. The larger ones can loom up in front of them, or kick water up so they can't see where they're going. Make mischief, in other words."

"That sounds perfect," Reginn said. "Can you see what you can do?"

Katia nodded, gripped her staff with both hands, and closed her eyes.

Eiric and the fiskers huddled to discuss their own strategy. They were sailing against the northwest wind, which meant that there was no straight line to where they needed to go. One more advantage of sailing south instead of north.

Again, Reginn turned to Ursinus. "Hafgufa helped us salvage this ship when it hit the reef west of these islands. Could the kraken push us along faster?"

"They are willing," Ursinus said grudgingly. "But three ships against the wind for that far? Even if they make it, they won't be fit for battle once they arrive."

"I understand," Reginn said. She looked around. "Does anyone know where Haki is? What ship she's on?"

Haki was one of Grima's freed spinners. She was aboard *Sylvi*, helmed by Reyna. They brought *Naglfar* up alongside, using their oars to hold a space between them.

"Haki!" Reginn shouted, trying to be heard above the wind. "We're going to have trouble reaching Vandrgardr in time, with this northwest wind working against us the whole time. Any way you could send us a good, fresh wind from the south?"

Haki took a deep breath. "I will try, Aldrnari," she said. "I just don't know what will happen when the two winds collide."

"We'll have to take that chance," Reginn said. "Do your best, and adjust as needed."

Eiric listened to this exchange with skepticism. A spinner who could control the winds? That, he'd like to see. Granted, the keeper had put up a weather wall to protect New Jotunheim, but–

"Reyna!" Eiric called. The fisker, who had been riveted by the conversation between the aldrnari and the spinner, turned toward him. "Send word down the line, so we don't take anyone by surprise."

Reyna nodded, and the two ships slipped apart.

The fiskers had a system of flagging that allowed crews to communicate with other ships within sight. This message, though, seemed to cause confusion, more than anything. If there was a signal for *Are you out of your mind?* he was sure it was deployed.

Rollo and his crew did his best to keep the two ships close enough so that they could see what was happening on *Sylvi.*

Naima handed Haki her staff. She rolled it between her hands, faster and faster, catching the wind, spinning it until the sleet and mist formed a funnel. Eiric could feel the movement of air against his cheek, marginally warmer.

Water witches erupted all around them, dancing on the surface of the thrashing ocean.

They'd been executing yet another tack against the unfavorable wind, when the ship lurched forward as the sails filled with the warm breath of the southlands. Those managing the sheets leaped to adjust to the change, while Rollo shifted course.

Their little fleet of three ships put on speed as the sleet turned to rain.

It was true. Haki was a spinner who could control the winds. What a difference it would make to the coasters and fishers of the Archipelago to have a weather witch as crew.

80

THE KING'S FLEET

THE FLEET THAT SET SAIL from Kingshavn was like none other ever seen in the Archipelago. The forces deployed to serve in the greatest battles of the past decade paled in comparison. King Rikhard had pulled resources from every part of his empire to meet the challenge of the Jotun army.

The weather was typical of that time of year–in other words, dreadful. Not as cold as it would be after Solstice, but fickle as a coaster's heart. It was *not* typical to launch a campaign in this season, but the spinners had struck at the king's heart and must be answered.

Drifa sailed aboard the king's flagship, the *Fossegrim*. Rikhard had sailed several ships over the years, of different sizes, but always called *Fossegrim*.

Many members of the king's army still expressed a cocky confidence about the outcome of the battle they faced. Eiric Halvorsen had tried to warn the commanders about the strength and weaponry the spinners wielded, but the line soldiers, especially, envisioned fighting hedge witches waving humble distaffs and muttering spells while veteran soldiers cut them down.

The fact that Halvorsen had deserted when faced with the prospect of war told them all they needed to know about the king's great champion.

They joked about completing this mission in a matter of days, rescuing the new prince, splitting the witch queen's treasure, and being home in time for Yule.

They have no idea what they're in for, Drifa thought with a shiver.

She and the king comprised a small pocket of gloom amid the cheer. The king had described this as a rescue mission, but it might be a mission of revenge.

Or a disaster.

When Drifa returned from Sundgard with the news about the Jotun attack and the abduction of Prince Ivar, she'd been worried the king might unleash his anger and grief on her—the sole survivor of the prince's personal guard. Instead, for some reason, Rikhard seemed to want to keep her close. She'd been assigned to his personal guard, alongside soldiers much more experienced than she. The only explanation she could think of was that she'd been close with Ivar, and because she was the last person to see him alive.

Rikhard had become a melancholy king. When he was deep in his cups, he would ricochet between pain and grief and rage. Drifa's role was to listen. And pour.

"Ivar was brave, wasn't he," Rikhard said, "when he met the witch queen."

"Of course he was," Drifa said. "Brave and well-spoken. You would have been proud of him."

"Still young, but with more courage than his traitorous brodir. A legendary sword is not enough."

"Yes, Lord," Drifa said.

"Ivar has always had a way about him," the king continued. "A way of winning people over. Even a witch would recognize that quality in him."

"Everyone loves Ivar," Drifa said, recalling the argument between the Jotun queen and her modir about whether to put Ivar to death on the spot. What if the modir had prevailed?

"The taking of hostages is a despicable act," Rikhard declared, although it was a tactic he'd used often enough himself. But it was not Drifa's job to argue with the king. She poured more of the wine he favored, knowing his mood was darkening.

"If they have harmed him, I will cleanse the world of witches," Rikhard declared, "from the herbalists in the markets to the ones that claim to see the future in the entrails of dead animals, from the ones that sell love charms and curses to the witch queen of the Jotun."

As the king tallied up his targets, Drifa thought of the midwife who'd saved her systir's life, and the healer at Sweinhavn who made the best ointment for the itches, and the volva her favorite aunt swore by when it came to making big decisions.

She'd never seen the king like this, and it frightened her.

"Perhaps if you ate something, Lord, you would feel better," Drifa said, since she was getting hungry herself. "There might be porridge on the firebox–"

The king waved a dismissive hand. "Later, perhaps."

A warning shout came from the midships lookout. "Dragons to port!"

Drifa turned to see the crew looking up, blinking against the freezing mist. She scanned the sky in time to see a serpentish creature pass low overhead, trailing smoke and flame. And then a second one, bright enough to light up the gloomy sky.

She turned to see the king still standing, hands on hips, following their progress across the sky.

"Dragons!" Drifa said. "Please, Lord, get down!"

"They aren't here to attack," Rikhard said, "or they'd have done that already."

"They're coming back!" the stern watch shouted.

Or maybe they were just scouting their targets on their first run, Drifa thought.

This time, some of the archers had their bows ready and launched a flurry of arrows at the beasts. The bolts seemed to pass right through them. Harmlessly.

After this second pass, they winged off south.

The appearance of the dragons dampened the soldiers' confidence somewhat.

"Your Majesty," the lookout said. "Do you think those dragons were flying witches?"

"They may have been conjured by the witches," Rikhard said, "but I believe that they are just shades or figments, meant to frighten us."

"Could they be spying on us?" Drifa said.

The king shrugged. "It's possible. The witch queen invited us to come, so no doubt they are expecting us."

Given the king's unruffled reaction, the off-duty soldiers settled in to sleep. The weather had cleared enough that they could see the setting sun bloodying the ocean to starboard.

"Will you need me, Lord?" Drifa asked the king.

Rikhard waved her off. "Go to sleep, if you can. Hopefully we'll reach Vandrgardr by sunrise."

Drifa curled up between the thwarts, hoping that her oilskins would keep her reasonably dry. When she looked aft, she saw the king, sitting alone.

Drifa awoke sometime in the middle of the night to a commotion all around her. The weather was clear–stars were pricking the night sky and the moon silvered the surface of the water. The sail strained under the force of a fair wind, and yet their ship seemed all but stalled on the water. Crew members scrambled fore and aft, as the water around them boiled and seethed.

The king stood midships, an oar in his hands, smacking it into the water.

"What's going on?" Drifa asked the nearest sailor.

The sailor turned, and Drifa saw that her face was pale with fright. "We don't know," she said. "Something is grabbing onto the boat."

When Drifa looked around, it seemed that the other ships in the fleet were grappling with the same problem. Their forward progress had all but stalled. And, yet, when she peered over the gunwales, she saw no tentacles, no many-eyed creatures, no web of sargassum—nothing that would explain it. It was as if the ocean itself was grabbing onto them and blocking their progress.

Drifa had heard stories about ships sailing to places so cold, the water froze around them and they couldn't move. That wasn't it. It was cold here, but not that cold.

Several of the crew had snatched up spears and war axes and leaned over the gunwales, stabbing into the dark waters.

But the king had stopped smacking the water. Instead, he surveyed his fleet, each ship centering a patch of turbulent water. Then looked up at the spangle of stars in the sky.

"Leave off!" he shouted to the frenzied crew. "Stop fighting it. You'll wear yourselves out, and you'll need your strength."

Leave off! The word was passed from ship to ship.

"The weather has cleared, and so we can verify that we are still on course. We're still moving, just more slowly than before. Whatever this demon magic is, the wind is stronger, and will prevail. If the spinners want to squander their magic this way, let them. We'll be fresh for battle, and they will not."

All around her, Drifa could see nodding heads and murmurs of agreement. Oars were returned to their racks, weapons sheathed, and the crew returned to their makeshift sleeping sections.

Whether the king was right or not, this was the king Drifa remembered.

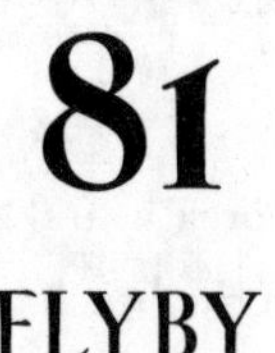

81

FLYBY

IN THE DAYS FOLLOWING TYRA'S "interview" with him, Ivar felt like a ship with a broken styrboard—never fully under control. He worried he might go sailing off in an unexpected direction, until he was lost at sea. Or run straight into a reef and be stuck there, thinking about things that he didn't want to think about.

You belong to the forest folk, the Alfar.

Long before Ragnarok, Asgard stole your forest home and set you wandering in the world.

You are the rightful king of the Midlands, named by Rikhard and raised by the thrice-risen goddess Heidin. You will be her hand in the world. All will kneel before you.

Only Asgard is in the way.

It didn't help that everyone was watching him like he was an egg about to hatch and they didn't know what species would emerge. Tyra and Heidin were a pair of hawks that might eat the hatchling if it didn't suit. Squalls blew up between them more and more often. When they shouted at each other, it seemed loud enough to be heard all over the Archipelago.

"Are you sure of him, Modir? Because if you are not, we stand to lose more than a valuable game piece."

And Tyra fired back. "This was your idea, remember? If I'd had my way, he'd be fish bait by now."

"If you have any doubts, give it another go and make sure."

After a brief pause, Tyra said, "I don't want to go there again."

Heidin scoffed. "*Now* you're losing your nerve? I've gone to the flame three times for you."

But Tyra held her ground. "What I can do, I have done. If you have doubts, then you handle it."

Bryn appeared, all out of breath, and tugged at Ivar's arm. "*There* you are, Ivar. Let's take a walk on the beach."

Ivar shook him off. "I need to hear this. Besides, I could probably still hear them on the beach."

Heidin was scary. It was as if Liv had totally disappeared. Ivar knew that if the goddess lost confidence in him, his days were numbered. She needed to believe that he'd been won over by Tyra's spellwork and would perform when the time came.

Maybe he had, and maybe he would. All his life, his mind was the one thing he had control of–the one place where he could safely be himself.

He could feel the spark of self still burning, but he wasn't sure who else was living there.

Meanwhile, Bryn brought him soothing teas, good things to eat, and no questions. He was a healer, tidying up around the margins of a gaping wound.

"The king should have arrived by now," Heidin grumbled. "Why isn't he here? He has to come–he will come." The delay was not improving Heidin's mood.

Why not just attack somebody or something? Ivar thought. Why do you have to wait for the king? It was as if this was a grudge match, and Heidin needed to see the king bend his knee.

The Jotun army sprawled around them like a beached whale, a massive beast with a ravenous appetite and nothing to do. The officers did their best to keep them busy. They built fortifications just inland from the beach from which to launch attacks on an enemy who might be landing from boats. They drilled them endlessly, organized archery tournaments, and sent them on miles-long patrols. Some never came back. Ivar suspected that, had the weather not been so cold, and they not conditioned to it, more would have deserted.

The officers met with Heidin, perhaps to urge some kind of action. After considerable shouting, they exited quickly, as if propelled by the force of her rage.

Heidin obsessed about Reginn Eiklund's absence and the disappearance of her Risen army. She seemed to view it as a personal betrayal.

"I thought she was my friend," Heidin said. "It was like we were systirs. And then, with everything on the line, she left."

But she was abducted, Ivar thought. Grima took Reginn and Naima back to her stronghold. It wasn't like she had a choice.

He wanted to say that, but knew that would open doors to places he didn't want to go and raise questions he didn't want to answer. Besides, what good would it do? He was beginning to realize that the thing about kings and queens and goddesses is that they are never wrong.

He didn't even know what to wish for.

The weather had improved, at least. The sleet and snow had stopped, and the wind slackened. Ivar put on his coat and walked down to the beach to watch the sunset, his guard trailing behind him.

He stood on a point of land overlooking the shallow bay. What if he just started walking, out into the ocean, and disappeared? He looked at his minders on either side, gauging his chances.

"Don't," Bryn said. "We'd have to go in after you, and it's too cold for swimming."

Who knew he was so readable? Or was Bryn just good at reading?

When he looked out at the harbor again, he saw two embers detach themselves from the bloody sun and fly straight toward them.

"What's that?" he said, pointing.

Bryn followed his gaze. "It's the eldrvaettir! Katia's eldrvaettir!"

Which was not all that helpful to Ivar. But Bryn seemed as happy as he'd ever seen him. Shelby, too.

"What are eldrvaettir?" Ivar looked from one to the other.

"They're like dragons," Shelby said. "Spirits that spew flame."

Ivar had read about landvaettir in one of the books from the Kingshavn library. But they were homebodies, protecting their particular mountain, or cave, or river.

"And . . . they're friendly?" Ivar said, shifting his feet. "We don't need to take cover?"

Grak and Grover leaned in to listen, apparently sharing Ivar's concern.

"They're on our side," Bryn said. "They went in search of Reginn Aldrnari. Perhaps they've found her."

"This might mean the Risen are returning," Shelby said.

As if in answer, a ship appeared on the horizon, a silhouette against the reddened sea. And then another. And another. Three in all.

"We don't need monsters to win this war," Grak (or was it Grover?) grumbled.

Bryn and Shelby ignored him. They stood fast, so Ivar did, too, as the winged vaettir grew closer and closer. They made a wide turn and flew, low to the ground, along the beachfront, spewing flame, incinerating everything in their path.

Shelby and Bryn slammed Ivar to the ground, covering him with their bodies as the dragons swept by. As soon as they were past, Shelby scooped him up and carried him inland, into the maze of tents that made up the army camp.

The camp was bedlam, with soldiers pouring out of their tents like ants in a flood, some running toward the waterfront, others fleeing landward.

Shelby refused to put Ivar down until they reached the command tent. Ivar guessed that he probably wanted to hand responsibility off before something happened to his charge.

Heidin, Tyra, and several army officers had emerged from the command tent, drawn by the commotion. Durinn, the army commander, charged toward the waterfront, leading a squad of heavily armed soldiers, with Heidin and her spinner court close behind.

When Ivar went to follow, Shelby grabbed his arm. "Stay back, where it's safe," he said.

"It's not safe here," Ivar said. "It's not safe anywhere. I would be with my queen."

Shelby had no answer for that, so he let go.

"We'll all go," Bryn said. So back they went, to the shingled beach, where the others stood, bristling with weapons, but the eldrvaettir had disappeared.

The three ships remained, neither coming nor going. A silent threat.

The only fight going on was among those onshore, arguing about who it was and what it meant.

"Who are they?" Tyra all but shouted at Durinn, though why Durinn would know, Ivar couldn't say.

Durinn looked to Caitilin Lund, skipari of the fleet, who had produced a sighting glass and was scanning the ships on the horizon. "Can you tell who it is?"

Caitilin lowered the glass. "I can't say for sure, but from the size, I would say one of the ships is *Naglfar.*"

"Maybe I can help," Stian said. Stian was an adept and council elder with an affinity for animals of all kinds. He never said much, but maybe he did all his talking to animals. He whistled, and a bird launched from a tall snag in the marsh behind them, winged over their heads, and flew toward the little offshore fleet.

A raven, Ivar thought. They are smart, and have good eyes.

While they were waiting, Ivar walked up and down the strip of beach that the dragons had scorched. The flames had been so hot that, in some places, grains of sand were fused together, and he could feel heat through the soles of his shoes. But there was no sign that any structures or people had been burned.

It seemed to take forever, but finally, Stian's emissary returned, landing on the head of his staff. For several minutes, they appeared to be communicating silently. Stian stood, head tilted, rubbing his chin with his free hand. Finally, he nodded, gave the bird its reward, and it flew back to the snag it had occupied earlier.

"Well?" Heidin said. "What did you find out?"

"Keep in mind, Rafi doesn't know who's who. He said the biggest ship was filled with many sorts of creatures he'd never seen before. They looked to be alive, but they didn't *smell* alive. They didn't smell dead, either."

Ivar didn't like the sound of that–was it a ship full of draugr–the walking dead? But nobody else seemed surprised or particularly frightened. Just puzzled.

Ivar leaned toward Bryn. "I don't understand. How can they be neither dead nor alive?"

"It sounds like one of the ships is carrying the Risen–the aldrnari's army," Bryn said. "If that's the case, their commander would be Reginn Eiklund, one of the elders, and counselor to the queen. I'm not sure who serves aboard the other ships."

This was interesting. Ivar kept hearing about the Risen, and Reginn Eiklund, who raised them, but this was the first time he might actually *see* one.

Bryn was still trying to solve the puzzle. "They should be our allies," he said. "Why would they attack? Why wouldn't they send a message?"

"They did send a message," Ivar said.

Bryn eyed him. "What do you mean?"

"They could have easily burned all our ships or set fire to our camp," Ivar said. "Instead, they scorched an empty beach. It wasn't an attack. It was a message. It was a warning to stay put."

82

HERO OF LOST CAUSES

THE WINDS REMAINED FAVORABLE, OUT of the northwest. All night long, the king's fleet continued its southward journey, though more slowly than expected. No doubt, more slowly than King Rikhard would have liked.

Even this experienced crew was understandably jumpy, reading sorcery into every unidentified sighting or unanticipated event. And there were plenty of those. The night watch reported firebirds flying high overhead, trailing embers. Sailors kept seeing (or imagining) creatures riding their wakes, tracking them through the trackless ocean.

Good, Drifa thought. A little fear was not misplaced.

Healthy respect was probably the wisest attitude.

Fortunately, this was a coast they knew well. As they passed by familiar landmarks, Drifa knew they must be getting close. The skipari set out his sun compass and confirmed it. But there was usually more ship's traffic between Grimsby and Vandrgardr.

Just after the midday, the bow lookout shouted, "Ships to port!"

Drifa had been bedded down in her section, but came to her feet, instantly wide awake. She could see the shoreline beyond, the river mouth that signified that they had reached Vandrgardr, but three ships lay between the king's fleet and the shoreline.

Three ships that flew no banners.

"What's this?" the king murmured. "Overconfident coasters or a witch welcoming committee?"

"Shall we approach, Lord?" the skipari said.

"Can you tell if they are fully crewed?"

The skipari pulled out his spotting glass and scanned the decks of the mystery ships for what seemed like a long time.

"Well?" the king said, impatient as always.

"Lord," the skipari said, his face pale as mare's milk. "They look to be fully crewed and fully armed–even crowded. The thing is . . ." The officer trailed off.

"What?" Rikhard snapped.

"They appear to be crewed by a mixture of men and monsters."

Monsters! That word was repeated the length of the ship, from bow to stern.

The king sighed. "What do you mean, monsters?"

"Well, issvargr and bjorn and demons and orcs and–the like," he finished lamely.

Visibly irritated, the king produced his own glass and scanned the line of ships. Scanned it again. He lowered the glass and slapped it against his opposite palm. Then swiveled to face his crew huddled aft.

"Some of you have been with me since the day I claimed the jarldom from my fadir. Consider everything we've accomplished since then. Not only have we cleared outlaws and predators from the forests of Muckleholm, we have done it for the rest of the Archipelago as well. We have built an empire to rival those of legend. Many of us have become rich in the process."

This was met with nods and murmurs of "Yes, Lord." The king was a fine speaker. Besides, it was always wise to agree with the king.

"This is the greatest fleet ever assembled in the Midlands, but we are not here to conquer, or to win riches, but to right a great wrong. The spinners from the Temple at the Grove across the sea launched an unprovoked attack on our manufactories at Sundgard, leaving not a soul alive. They have also kidnapped my adopted son and heir, using him as a bargaining chip to demand our surrender."

This was met with howls of outrage and shaking of fists.

"I will not surrender," Rikhard said, and a cheer went up.

"Though we have limited experience contending with the forces of magic, there are none that I would rather have at my back than all of you. I would also ask you to consider the fact that the volur are masters of subterfuge and illusion, having long ago mastered the tactics of fear and intimidation. The monsters you believe you see may be nothing more than sorcery and smoke."

That, too, was met with mingled enthusiasm and doubt.

"They've deployed three ships against us. Three ships! They must know that they are outmatched."

"May I look, Lord?" Drifa said. The king handed her the glass, and she took a good look at each of the ships. And then, looked beyond, to the shoreline. The enemy camp was huge, with a sea of tents extending all the way from the river to the fringes of the trees on either side. Ships were pulled up on the shore, along the river and the beach.

The land encampment was huge.

"Could it be a trap, Lord?" she said. "Or . . . do they mean to negotiate?"

As if prompted by her suggestion, the largest ship deployed a small oarboat flying a flag of truce.

"We will accept their surrender," the king said, his jaw set, "if they return what was taken from us–undamaged."

I think their plan is that *we* surrender to *them*, Drifa thought, recalling what the Jotun queen had said.

The oarboat crawled steadily toward them, tipping up and over the largest waves and plunging down into the troughs between. It roiled Drifa's stomach just to watch.

As they drew closer, Drifa could see that there were but four passengers and eight oarsmen. Or, rather, three passengers, a styrman, and eight oarsmen. Some of the oarsmen looked suspiciously like orcs. Others were lean and muscled, with sculpted features and markings like rivulets covering their exposed skin.

Three of the passengers were women. One Drifa recognized as Naima Bondi. She had last seen her at Sundgard, when she'd come with Ivar to warn Eiric Halvorsen that he was walking into a trap. She'd elected to stay and sail with Halvorsen's crew to try to intercept him.

Another was a tall, long-limbed woman with close-cropped hair and a spinner staff.

The third was small but striking, with lavish hair like spun gold and copper and copper skin. She drew the eye, like the glint of gold in a creek bed, or a bonefire atop a distant mountain. A bent and twisted staff rested in the crook of her arm, so Drifa guessed that she, too, was a spinner.

The male passenger was a lean and hungry wolf of a man who wore no coat or hat, despite the cold. Drifa had never seen him before.

"Asger Eldr," the king murmured.

The styrman stood out among them all, for his size and the force of his presence. His golden hair ignited in the timid winter sun as he called out the cadence for the oarsmen.

Eiric Halvorsen.

"So, it's true," the king said. "Halvorsen has joined his systir's army and betrayed his own brodir. He must have been behind the conspiracy to kidnap Ivar."

Drifa could sense the anger rising in the king, like boiling water and steam in a geysir before the blow. She knew she had to find a way to release or deflect it, or Rikhard would do something that couldn't be undone.

"Lord," she said. "I would do everything in my power to save the young prince, and I know you would, too. It seems obvious that they want to talk to us. Why don't we listen to what they have to say?"

"Why should we entertain the honeyed words of a traitor?" Rikhard said. "Why should we consider their demands?"

"It costs us nothing more than a little time," Drifa said, "against a lifetime of loss and regret. Isn't it worth it?"

After a moment that lived like days, Rikhard nodded. "All right," he said. He turned to his waiting crew. "Hold your fire," he said, "until we see what they have to say."

Which was good, because Drifa had seen what the king had not–the water all around them seethed with life–not the diaphanous water spirits from before–but tentacles, gray and studded with blue-black suckers like hungry mouths. Once, an eye broke the surface and regarded Drifa with calm intelligence. Shadows rippled over the water as immense winged creatures crossed the sun.

Had they wanted to launch an attack or refuse a conversation, it was probably already too late. This made the consequences of the wrong decision all too clear.

The rest of the crew, fixed on the king and the oncoming oarboat, had not seen the threat, either. Which was fortunate, because it would have caused widespread panic. So far, the panic was confined to Drifa's wildly beating heart.

The oarboat came alongside Rikhard's flagship, no more than a toy next to the longship. Up close, Drifa was struck once again by the resemblance between Halvorsen and his brodir. They shared the same straight noses and strong chins. Where Ivar's eyes were gray, Halvorsen's were a striking blue-green.

Halvorsen stood, balancing with the ease of long practice. "Your Majesty," he said, politely enough. "Requesting your oath of safe passage for my party to come aboard for a meeting and leave unharmed. In return, I offer my word that we will keep the peace."

"You have my word," the king said through gritted teeth. Drifa knew he wanted to say more, to qualify or undo the oath he had just given, but he did not.

Murmurs of disapproval rose all around them, and Rikhard said, "When I give my word, I expect all of you to honor it as well."

The complaints dwindled, and died away. As they closed the distance between the two vessels, Halvorsen hooked his battle axe over the gunwale of the king's flagship and pulled it closer still. He lashed the two ships together with cordage and vaulted into the *Fossegrim*.

He turned and extended his hand to Naima Bondi. Then the spinners, tall and small. The one called Asger Eldr declined assistance. He leaped lightly from the oarboat to the dragon ship.

The orc-ish crew remained at their stations aboard the oarboat. Drifa hoped they would stay there.

Both Halvorsen and Eldr carried sheathed swords on their backs. Drifa hoped they would stay sheathed.

Halvorsen inclined his head to Rikhard, who stood, flanked by his most trusted guards. "Your Majesty. I believe you've met Lord Eldr," he said with a hint of irony. "And Naima, the sole survivor of the attack at Sundgard."

Naima appeared much improved from the last time Drifa had seen her, when Ivar had brought her to Sundgard.

Halvorsen turned to the spinners. "Finally, this is Katia Elder, liaison to our vaettir allies, and Reginn Eiklund, counselor to Queen Heidin of New Jotunheim. You may remember her as Lord Eldr's thrall who set fire to your ship's boat in the harbor at Langvik."

Drifa did not know that story, but it sounded like one that would be well worth hearing. There was something almost deferential in the way the coaster put the spinner forward, taking a step back himself.

"Counselor," Rikhard said. "Do you speak for the witch queen?"

She studied him with ice-blue eyes framed by her fiery hair. "No, Your Majesty," she said. "I speak for myself, and those who fell at Ragnarok."

Drifa didn't know what to make of that. From his expression, neither did the king. "In the interest of time, I would prefer to speak with the queen's representative," the king said.

This little delegation didn't seem to know who that person would be. Finally, the spinner said, "We do not represent Queen Heidin."

Dangerous color came up in Rikhard's cheeks. "Then this would seem to be a waste of time." He made as if to turn away.

"Rikhard!" The spinner's voice was loud and sharp enough to carry the length of the ship. Those crew members who had been pretending not to watch turned and stared. "We need to speak, and it must be now. I promise that it will not be a waste of time."

She paused, the silence broken only by the wind, and the snap and clatter of sails and rigging. "Now. Is there someplace under shelter we could sit, and speak comfortably and privately? Some of us are not masters at balancing on a moving ship."

Grudgingly, Rikhard nodded to Drifa, who led them aft to the king's informal quarters midships. An oilcloth had been stretched across the ship and draped with the spare sail and the king's purple and gold. It was by no means plush, but it blocked the wind, and offered chests and casks to sit on.

The visitors did not ask permission to sit in the presence of the king, but sat wherever they could find room. Drifa wondered if she should offer refreshments, but the king seemed in no mood to entertain. He stood, arms crossed, waiting for the others to get settled.

Halvorsen remained standing, too. He seemed to be looking for someone–unsuccessfully. He scanned the faces around him, then looked forward and aft.

"Your Majesty," the spinner said. "Thank you for hearing us out. I told you that we are not here as representatives of Queen Heidin. We are here in hopes of preventing this catastrophic war."

With three ships? Drifa thought, just as a tentacle nosed its way over the gunwale. Then again, with an army of orcs, issvargr, and sea monsters, it might be that–

"If you were hoping for peace," Rikhard said, "then perhaps you should have taken that up with the witch queen before she brought an army to our shores and launched a cowardly, unprovoked attack on Sundgard, killing hundreds of people, including–"

"That was Grima," Naima said, speaking for the first time. "Grima is an assassin, executioner, and spy who–"

"–is in the employ of the queen of New Jotunheim, who is therefore responsible for what she's done," Rikhard cut in. "Just as I am responsible for what is done in my name."

"Does that include the hundreds of gifted Agata murdered at Langvik as your agent?" Halvorsen said.

Agata? Drifa had no idea what Halvorsen was talking about, but it was obvious that the king felt the hit.

The spinner seemed to feel the need to cool rising tempers. "This is not an opportunity to fling accusations at each other. Our purpose is to prevent a wholesale slaughter. And it will be a slaughter if this battle is joined. I've seen the forces the Jotun queen is fielding. Even without the Risen, it is–"

"With all due respect, *Counselor,*" the king broke in, "any talk of peace, truce, or negotiation is impossible so long as Prince Ivar remains the witch queen's hostage."

After a moment of shocked silence, Halvorsen said, "What do you mean?"

"Your systir, Queen Heidin, is holding Ivar prisoner at Vandrgardr. She has demanded that I surrender."

"Are you certain of this?" Halvorsen said. "Could it be another of Grima's tricks?"

"Unfortunately, you cannot blame this one on Grima," the king said. "We have a witness. Drifa–tell them what happened."

All at once, everyone was looking at her, something Drifa generally managed to avoid. She licked her lips. "It happened after we brought Naima to Sundgard to warn Halvorsen about Grima's trap, and to tell him that it was Grima, not–not the queen who had attacked Sundgard. Since Halvorsen was already gone, his crew–and Naima–went after him. When we were sailing back to Kingshavn, our ship was attacked at the seaward end of the sound. We made it to land before our ship broke up, but the prince and I were the only survivors. The queen recognized the prince, took him prisoner, and sent me back to Kingshavn with a demand that the king surrender."

"Are you certain that it was Queen Heidin?" Halvorsen said. There was no threat or anger about him, only the grim expectation of bad news.

"Yes, Lord, I would stake my life on it."

"Do you remember anything of what was said?" Halvorsen said.

Drifa nodded, keeping her eyes fixed on the ground. She was afraid that if she met the coaster's eyes, her courage would fail her. "Ivar–the prince–was soaked and shivering, and the queen wrapped him in her arms to warm him. After, she held him out at arm's length and said, 'This is not the first time that I have saved you from the cold. Has anyone ever told you that you have your modir's eyes?' The prince nodded, and she said, 'And, yet, in a way, you favor your brodir.'"

The coaster cleared his throat. "So she recognized him, even after all these years."

"Drifa," the king said, as if jealous. "This is much more detail than I've heard before."

"Aye, Your Majesty," Drifa said. "The coaster asks a great many questions."

"Was–was Ivar harmed?"

"No," Drifa said quickly, glad to deliver some good news. "Only the usual cuts and scrapes from climbing up the rocks. The queen seemed determined to keep him safe, even when her modir–" Drifa stopped.

"Go on," Halvorsen said.

"Another spinner—who seemed to be Heidin's modir—argued that the safest thing was to—to kill him now, since he was the heir to the throne."

The coaster swore softly.

"But the queen said no," Drifa said quickly. "She told her modir to stay out of her business. She said—she said that sometimes a live hostage is worth more than a dead rival."

To Drifa's astonishment, the coaster laughed. "That sounds about right."

When she looked up at him, he met her gaze and inclined his head a bit. "Thank you, Drifa, for your honesty and clear memory. In particular, thank you for your loyal service to my brodir." With that, he slid a gold arm ring off his left arm. Taking her hand, he slid it onto Drifa's.

"Lord," Drifa protested, feeling the weight of it. "That's too much. I serve the king, and so his adopted son and heir. I need no further reward than that."

"Take it, Drifa," King Rikhard said. "A soldier never knows when she may need a stake. That will buy you a fine farm if such a thing exists after the coming war."

He turned to Reginn Eiklund. To Drifa's surprise, the counselor's face was wet with tears.

"As you see, Counselor, there will be no peace. I will not surrender, and I cannot let this go unanswered. If what you say is true, I will fail. If that is what the fates decree, I will not be the first nor the last to die in a lost cause."

"Lord," Halvorsen said, going down on one knee. "Asking permission to speak."

"Halvorsen," the king said with a trace of a smile, "that would be a first. Speak, then."

"First, I offer my sword in your service," the coaster said. "I will do whatever I can to free my brodir and bring him back alive."

"A bit late, but I accept," Rikhard said dryly.

"Second, with due respect, dying in the name of a lost cause is all well and good, but I ask for your patience and partnership in figuring out a way to win."

83

STALEMATE

MAYBE THAT'S WHY THEY CALL it a stalemate, Ivar thought. It gets really stale after a while. To make matters worse, after the dragon incident, he was not allowed to wander about the camp as he had before–not even with his comet's tail guard. Every night, they moved him and his entourage to a different tent. Ivar had heard of nomads moving tents from place to place, but never people moving from tent to tent.

He was more used to cold weather than any of his Jotun companions/captors. Spending night and day in their overheated tents was like clinging to the inside wall of a fumarole. He spent much of his time half in and half out of a tent, like a fiddler crab in a borrowed shell, longing to taste fresh air.

Bryn and Shelby did their best to help him pass the time. They had a few books, but they seemed to think that Ivar wasn't old enough to read them. At first, they played endless games of hnefatafl until they got tired of losing and began making excuses.

Every night, they brought fresh fish and stale news for the nattmal. Night by night, the portions dwindled, until one night, he was offered only one small fish atop a bucket of barley.

Ivar broke the fish apart with his spoon to make it go further. "What's happened?" he said. "Is fishing season over already? Or have my rations been cut for bad behavior?"

"Be glad you're getting that much," Grover said. "All of us have had to tighten our belts."

If Grover had tightened his belt, it wasn't obvious.

"The grain stored at Vandrgardr doesn't go very far when it comes to feeding an army," Bryn said. "As for the fish, Stian thinks they are being netted by the ships offshore to feed their crews. Truth be told, we can't stay here too much longer without access to more provisions."

"It doesn't help that we're surrounded by a gods-forsaken swamp," Grak said. "We can't even raid a farm or pillage a village."

"There are many kinds of foods to be found in a swamp," Ivar said. "Well, maybe not so much this time of year, but my foster modir used to take me out and–"

"I'm not eating skita out of a swamp!" Grak said, and stalked out of the tent.

"Try not to make Grak angry, Ivar," Shelby said. "He's just stupid enough to hurt you."

"There's not much I can do," Ivar said. "My existence makes him angry. Besides, he's right–it makes no sense to stay here. It's not very defensible, and, as you've found, there's no way to replenish your supplies."

"The queen seems convinced that the king will bend his knee to her. She told him to come here, and she means to stay here until he does."

"We might be waiting a long time, then," Ivar said. "Why should the king give up anything for me? I'm not his blood. The heir he was waiting for died at Sundgard. I'm just filling the spot until he sires another son."

Bryn made shushing noises. "Even if that's what you believe, keep your mouth shut about it. You're still alive because the queen believes that you might be useful."

"I will be useful," Ivar said. "Just not in the way she thinks." With that, Ivar rolled up in his wool blankets and his wolf-pelt cover and fell asleep.

* * *

Shelby shook him awake as the sun was rising. "Get up," he said. "The king is here."

"The king?"

"Isn't that what I just said?" Tension edged Shelby's voice. "Hurry and get dressed."

The clothes they'd laid out for him were particularly fine–a green velvet tunic and narrow black trousers with a black woolen coat over top and soft leather boots. They must have been made to measure because they fit perfectly. The entire time he was dressing, though, he kept thinking, This doesn't make sense.

Maybe Rikhard had come with an army and an ultimatum. Maybe he'd come to say no in a threatening sort of way.

What he would not do is surrender to the witch queen–not after what happened to Hilde. He would not be outmaneuvered. His pride would not allow it.

As soon as Ivar was presentable, Bryn and Shelby hustled him down to the beach, where Queen Heidin, Tyra, and the rest of the spinner court stood waiting. The queen stood on one side of him, her hand on his shoulder as if to prevent him from bolting. Tyra stood on his other side.

The weather had cleared–a miracle this time of year–and Ivar could see that the Jotun ships were gone, replaced by the king's fleet, filling the mouth of the inlet and stretching as far as the eye could see. Just for a moment, pride elbowed aside Ivar's worry. This was the stuff of the sagas, even if his personal story came to a bad end.

A ship broke away from the rest and approached the landing just inside the mouth of the creek. Ivar recognized it as Rikhard's knifelike dragon ship, leading with its fossegrim figurehead.

The ship came to rest just offshore, and several crew members leaped over the sides and waded to shore, fastening the bowline to an iron ring set into the rock for that purpose. They all wore the king's purple and gold livery–some of it ill-fitting. Ivar did not recognize any of them.

One of them struck a pose just past the scrim line.

"Announcing–"

"Proclaiming–"

"Celebrating–the new king in the east!"

The king in the east?

A tall warrior vaulted over the gunwale and splashed toward shore, flanked by a handful of attendants. He was dressed finely, his gray wool coat embroidered at the hem and neckline, the custom fit displaying his broad shoulders and narrow waist. A black wolf fur mantle was fastened over his shoulders with a silver clasp, and the hilt of a great sword protruded above his back.

Sunlight glittered on his fair hair.

He was the very picture of a king, but he was not Rikhard Karlsen.

It was Eiric Halvorsen.

84

FINDING A WAY TO WIN

EIRIC STOOD AT THE SCRIM line on the beach, flanked by Reginn Eiklund and Asger Eldr. Behind them stood his crew, mostly fiskers, but including Drifa. All wore Rikhard's livery with the exception of Asger and Reginn.

Facing him were Heidin, Tyra, a handful of spinners he couldn't remember the names of, and some military officers.

Heidin was Liv as he'd never seen her–taller than most men, her gilded skin reflecting the rising sun, the staff Bjorn had given her resting in the crook of one arm. With every movement, she flung out showers of gold and flame. The goddess pendant shone brightest of all, just above her collarbone–the goddess that had stolen his systir from him.

Beside Heidin was Ivar, dressed in princely finery, his face pale under his shock of wayward hair. When he saw Eiric, his eyes widened a bit, but then he resumed his usual expression of watchful waiting.

Eiric looked him over carefully and could see no sign of abuse or injury. But he knew full well that the worst wounds are the ones that cannot be seen.

Behind them, the nearby tents had emptied, disgorging their occupants to gawk at the proceedings. Some appeared ready to fight, while others stood in their underclothes, yawning, but unwilling to miss history being made.

Tyra was *not* glad to see him–that came as no surprise. To Tyra, Eiric was the draugr Asgardian–the one that would not stay dead.

Heidin looked perplexed. And suspicious. "We had expected the king," she said. "Where's Rikhard?"

"King Rikhard has met with an unfortunate accident," Eiric said.

"What happened?"

"He ran into a sword," Eiric said.

"Whose sword?"

"My sword," Eiric said, watching Heidin closely, to see if she caught the reference. Her narrowed eyes said that she did.

Ivar's court face slipped a little. He looked as if he'd been clubbed over the head.

"And now *you* are king," Tyra said, her voice low and venomous. "How very convenient."

Eiric stared at Tyra—feigning surprise. "*Me* as king?" He turned to Heidin. "Systir, as you know well, I would be a miserable king."

"Yes," Heidin said carefully, as if playing a part that she'd never prepared for. "You would be a terrible king. So—why are you here?"

"I am here to crown the rightful king of the Archipelago—Ivar Karlsen." He extended his hand, displaying the gold circlet that Rikhard wore for court functions. Behind him, his crew beat their weapons against their shields, shouting, "Hail King Ivar!"

Eiric strode forward, followed closely by Reginn and Asger, the rest of his guard standing fast where they were.

Move quickly, and your enemy has less time to think.

Having crossed the distance between them, he stood before Heidin, the crown in his hands. "Systir, back on Eimyrja, you asked me to serve you. I would not commit, because I did not know how best to do that. Had I remained by your side, I would have been just another sword in your employ until someone knifed me in the back." He glanced at Tyra, then back at Heidin. "I knew that I could be most useful to you by returning home and preparing a place here."

Eiric paused, but then, hearing shouts and commotion coming from the rear of the camp, hurried on. "Heidin—you are a goddess, but the world is in need of kings and queens as well. Would you do us the honor of crowning our brodir king of the Archipelago?" He extended the crown toward his systir.

"Don't do it!" Tyra hissed. "It's a trick."

"This is what we planned, Modir–don't you remember?" Handing off her staff, she took the crown from Eiric and turned toward Ivar. "Kneel, Ivar Karlsen."

Ivar didn't move. "You killed him," Ivar said, fixed on Eiric. "You gave him your oath, and then you killed him."

"Ivar," Eiric said. "I am–"

"I told you once that I had no systir," Ivar said. "It seems that I've lost my brodir as well."

"Our brodir is only looking out for you," Heidin said.

"Is he?" Ivar said. "I'm not so sure that–"

"Traitor!" someone shouted. "Halvorsen! Stand down!"

Everyone turned to see King Rikhard approaching at a dead run from around the point, a blade in each hand, his hird following right behind.

Eiric had drawn his sword at the shouting. Now he stood, immobilized by confusion, the tip of his sword drooping while he waited for something to start making sense. The noise from the rear of the encampment was growing louder. Some of the spinners turned and looked, but the group surrounding the queen was focused on the drama unfolding in front of them.

"Well, well," Tyra said, "it seems it's trickery after all." She stood, smiling, as if looking forward to the show.

But Rikhard did not launch himself at Eiric, or try to maneuver around him to get to Ivar, or stop to make his case. Instead, he leaped toward Heidin, knocking her to the ground with his momentum, then slashed away at the base of her neck with his dagger.

He stood, then, holding something aloft in his bloody fist.

Something that glowed through his fingers.

Heidin's pendant. But why would Rikhard want to–?

"Heidin!" Tyra screamed, dropping to her knees next to the fallen queen.

But the king wasn't finished. Still clutching the pendant, he pivoted and wrapped an arm around Ivar, pinning his arms and pressing his dagger against the prince's throat.

"Now," Rikhard said, his cold blue eyes fixed on Eiric and his companions. "Drop your weapons or the boy dies."

For a long moment, nobody moved, frozen by surprise.

"Do not try my patience," Rikhard said. His knuckles whitened as he tightened his grip on the hilt of the blade.

Eiric allowed Gramr to slip from his hand and land in the dirt. Reginn and Asger followed suit with staff and sword.

The pieces of this puzzle were not fitting together. Why would Rikhard go after Heidin's pendant, with so many other targets? How much did he even know about it?

"My lord," Ivar whispered, swallowing hard. "I don't understand."

The pain and betrayal on Ivar's face ignited a geysir of rage in Eiric's heart.

"If it makes any difference, I don't understand, either," he said, his voice deceptively calm.

"You don't understand because you are stupid," Rikhard spat. "Did you really believe that I would name the half-breed son of a tar digger as my heir? It's simple–this gambit has allowed me to assemble all my enemies in one place so that they can be dispatched in an efficient manner.

"You first, Halvorsen," Rikhard said as his hird gathered around like carrion crows. "On your knees."

"Brodir," Ivar said. "You know how this ends." Their eyes met, held, a shared understanding.

Eiric dropped to his knees, spreading his arms like a courtier, a flamboyant move that distracted the king just as Ivar slammed his head back, smashing Rikhard's nose. He then gripped the king's shoulder, looped his foot around his ankle, and flung him to the ground, sending his blade flying one way and Heidin's bloody pendant the other.

Lausatok. Ivar was an apt student.

Rikhard lunged for the amulet, but Asger threw himself on top of it, curling around it, all flame and smoke and ember eyes. The king was trying to wrestle it away when Eiric ran him through with his reclaimed sword.

He freed his blade and turned, expecting to face the king's hird, but it had dissipated like a vapor in the freshening wind.

When Eiric went to give Asger a hand, the demon was gone, leaving behind a pile of gray ash. Eiric stirred it with his boot. There was no sign of the pendant.

Ivar had been standing as if frozen. Now he fell to his knees beside Rikhard's body. "It makes no sense," he whispered. "Hilde trusted you. I trusted Hilde."

Eiric squatted next to Ivar and rested his hand on his shoulder. "Ivar," he said. "What I can tell you is, we had a plan, and this was not the way it was supposed to go. If I'd thought that–" Eiric broke off as Ivar stiffened. "What is it?"

Ivar pointed down at the body with a shaking finger.

"Who is that?"

It was no longer Rikhard. It was a young woman, wiry and strong, with chin-length, honey-colored hair, and honed features. She wore a gold chain with a glowing purple stone hanging from it.

"It's Grima," Eiric said. "This is what she looks like when she is not glamoured."

"This is what she looks like when she is dead, as she deserves," Ivar said, his voice low and bitter.

Eiric wanted to offer some reassurance, but he knew that this probably meant that Grima had somehow killed the king and taken his place.

And Ivar was smart enough to know it, too.

He put his arm around his brodir and drew him close. This time, Ivar didn't flinch away. They looked to where Reginn was kneeling next to Heidin, trying to stanch the bleeding from her neck.

No, Liv. Her name was Liv.

"Is it bad?" Ivar said. "Do you think she'll survive?"

Eiric sighed. "I don't know. If anyone can save her, it's Reginn." He hesitated. "Would you like to go ask her what she thinks?"

Ivar stood, and Eiric did, too. But not before breaking the chain that held the purple godstone pendant and sliding it into his carry bag.

Eiric and Ivar knelt on one side of Liv, with Reginn on the other. Liv was semiconscious, mumbling, reacting to the painful bits. Eiric reached out and took Liv's hand carefully, as if he might break something.

Reginn was exploring the wound with her fingers. She looked up long enough to nod at them. "It's an ugly piece of work," she said, blotting away the blood that was welling up, "but at least he didn't cut the great vein."

"She," Ivar said.

"She?" Reginn looked up again.

"It was Grima," Eiric said. "Not Rikhard." Suddenly exhausted, he ground the heel of his free hand into his forehead. "How many times am I going to fall for that?"

"I think this is the last time," Reginn said, with a perfunctory glance at the assassin's body before returning to her work. Having assured herself that the wound was clean, she stitched it up, doing her best with the ragged edges. She covered the wound with a cream and inscribed healing runes all around it before wrapping it in linen.

Liv was already changing, her skin softening, darkening from gold to its usual copper, some of the scarring visible once again. Eiric leaned in and stroked her hair away from her forehead. All at once, her eyes flew open and she gripped his coat with both hands.

"I don't know," she whispered. "I don't know who I am. They keep asking, and I don't know what to tell them." She studied his face, her chestnut eyes clouded with confusion. "I don't know who you are, either."

"You are Liv Halvorsen, dottir of Leif Halvorsen, who was also my fadir. I am Eiric Halvorsen, and this is the healer, Reginn Eiklund."

"I am Ivar Karlsen," Ivar said. "I am your brodir."

"Ivar!" someone was shouting. "Where is Prince Ivar? Where is my son?"

Ivar brightened and looked up, recognizing the voice.

It was Rikhard, storming through the crowd, his bared sword by his side, his hird scarcely able to keep up. Behind him came the officers of Reginn's Risen army.

"Go," Eiric said, but Ivar was already gone. Eiric sighed, releasing one source of pain.

Reginn was still counting up casualties and survivors. "Where's Asger?" she said, looking around.

"He's gone," Eiric said.

"Gone?" Reginn stared at him with an expression of shocked disbelief. "Gone where?"

Eiric shook his head. "I don't know." He pointed at the demon's leavings. "Wherever he is, he took Heidin's pendant with him."

A shadow fell over them. Eiric looked up, and it was Tyra, looking as if she'd been clubbed. "How is she–how is Heidin doing?" she said diffidently.

Rage boiled up in Eiric, and he stood, fists clenched. "Get away from my systir, you selfish, manipulative witch," he growled.

Reginn stood also, and put a hand on Eiric's arm. "Heidin is gone," she said to Tyra. "I suggest that you find something else to do."

Rorik and Nils were standing nearby, awaiting orders. Recalling that they were resistant to Tyra's mind magic, and knowing that they would be motivated by this opportunity, Eiric said, "Take this prisoner to the far end of the beach and keep an eye on her."

THRUMS

Thrums: a fringe of warp threads left on the loom after the cloth has been removed. (2) one of these warp threads.

THE BATTLE OF VANDRGARDR HAD ended in an all but bloodless stalemate. Rikhard's forces had approached the Jotun camp from the swamps behind, to find that it was already surrounded by the Risen army, under Reginn's orders to keep the living armies apart.

Rikhard's soldiers were tested warriors, but they were not eager to confront orcs, demons, issvargr, elves, dwarves, bjorn, and the walking dead in such numbers. Especially since they were allies, of a sort.

The New Jotunheim soldiers had seen the Risen in action and knew there was no chance of winning against them. The goddess queen who had led them to war was gone. So they stood down as well.

Having saved thousands of lives and preserved the Midlands, the Risen retreated to lands north of Vandrgardr, where the bonefires blazed late into the night. On many nights, Reginn sat with them, playing the old songs on her flute. Often, Ivar slipped away from the king's camp to sit beside her, listening and watching and scribbling notes.

The young prince was like quicksilver–impossible to confine. The king had all but given up.

"I saw my systir," he said one night, poking a stick into the flames. "She is stronger every day."

Reginn nodded. "She is one of the strongest people I know. No one else could have held off the goddess for so long."

"I asked her to stay," he said, "but I don't think she will."

"Whether she stays, or goes, the ocean is not so wide, these days."

"Eiric is gone, as well," Ivar said. "He took *Sylvi*, and his fisker crew, and sailed for New Jotunheim. The king is not happy."

"Eiric left because he made a promise that he had to keep. Maybe one day the king will learn that your brodir is not biddable."

Ivar snorted. "Probably not."

They both laughed.

"One thing I know," Reginn said. "Eiric will come back, for you and for Liv."

"And for you," Ivar said.

When Rikhard asked Reginn what sort of reward might suit the Risen, she was momentarily stumped. They had no need of the usual spoils of war–treasure, hack silver, jewelry, or estates in the Midlands.

Then Reginn remembered what Hafgufa had said when she'd asked him that question.

Those who die in war live on as long as they are remembered, loved, mourned–as long as their true stories are told. To be honored and remembered is to be immortal.

"There is something we can do," she said. "Let me speak to Ivar."

So it was that a few days later, King Rikhard and Prince Ivar led a delegation to the Risen encampment, where Reginn and her commanders waited to welcome them on a small hill overlooking a sea of soldiers.

First, King Rikhard addressed the entire gathering. "I would like to offer you all–the Risen warriors of Jotunheim–a warm welcome to the Archipelago." He paused. "I must admit, I'm a little late."

This was met by a murmur of amusement.

Rikhard motioned Ivar forward and rested a hand on his shoulder. "This is my son and heir, Prince Ivar. While preparing for an invasion by Heidin, the queen of New Jotunheim, I received word that she had captured my son, and was holding him hostage, demanding my surrender. And, so, I sailed for Vandrgardr, intending to attack the queen's army, even though I knew this would likely result in the end of my line and the slaughter of my army."

Rikhard paused, sweeping his gaze across the assembled Risen soldiers. "That did not happen," he said, "and the credit belongs to you."

Rikhard's hird raised their spears and shouted their agreement.

"I am learning that there are many kinds of heroes, and many ways to win," Rikhard said. "Not all victories take place on the field. In fact, it can be argued that the bloodiest battles are not victories for anyone.

"They say that history is written by the victors, but in this case, mercy and justice and peace prevailed. I promise you this–you will be remembered, and honored in the Midlands from this day forward. I will raise a monument on this spot–not for the slain, but for you who triumphed here, and for all of those who survived because of what you did."

Now Ivar spoke up. "Your stories will be shared by the hearth for generations as long as stories are told. I have made a beginning, and I hope you will tell me how it can be improved."

He motioned to Reginn, and she stepped forward, raised her flute to her lips, and began to play as Ivar sang. As always, his voice was clear and high and almost otherworldly.

Once again, the storms of Fimbulwinter
Scour the land.
Crops fail, the fishing boats return empty.
Fruit shrivels on the branch
And babies die in the womb.
Wolves howl from the wilderness.
The Jotun are on the move again,
And the forges of the Aesir blaze once more.
Humans cast lots to choose which side to die on.

Now Reginn heard other voices—a wordless chorus that twined over and around the melody. She looked out over the Risen, and realized that it was the elves. Everyone else sat, transfixed.

When the aldrnari calls
the old heroes rise from their graves at Ithavoll.
Demons, elves, issvargr, dwarves, orcs, and trolls
The bjorn, the vargr, the human warriors who know too well the cost of war.
Forever marked by the calamity of Ragnarok
They stand astride the rifts that divide us.
The Risen deny us the sweat of battle and the eagles go hungry.

All wounds are healed.
All weapons are sheathed.
All gifts are honored—of Aesir, Vanir, and Jotun
Spinners, conjurers, and volva.
Of humans and beasts, birds and fishes
Connected by Yggdrasil, the tree of life
They bloom.

As the music died away, Ivar said, "It's a start, as I said."

Based on the response from the assembly, it was a good start.

Afterward, the king and prince met with each commander and representatives from among the soldiers themselves. The Risen seemed especially taken with Ivar, who had read all the available histories of the wars between Asgard and Jotunheim, and asked endless questions about the parts that had been left out. The prince also spent considerable time in quiet conversation with Dainn, the elven commander.

Growing weary, Reginn withdrew a short distance away and sat, her back against a tree, half dozing. She startled awake when a familiar voice intruded on her dreams. "Aldrnari," Asger Eldr said, "well done."

Reginn scrambled away on all fours, skinning both knees in the process, then spun to face him. "Get away from me," she said. "You're dead."

"Well, yes," Asger said, stretching out his long legs and leaning back himself. "Thank you for noticing. Finally." He paused. "I won't be staying long, but we need to talk, before I go. There are things you need to know."

"Fair enough," Reginn said, recovering. "Start with this–what did you do with Heidin's amulet?"

In stories, the amulet was the kind of dangerous magical object that always found its way back into the world.

"It is–*inaccessible*," Asger said.

"I want to hear that it's *destroyed*," Regir.n said.

The demon shrugged. "Gods are immortal. But they can be leashed."

He paused and, when Reginn didn't respond, continued. "It was no accident that you came into the world when you did. The fallen at Ragnarok could see that the seeds of the next apocalypse had been planted, and we were hurtling toward another world-ending war. This meant that everyone who died, all the blood that was shed, everything that was lost and destroyed–it was all for nothing. The cycle was beginning again."

"Isn't that the way it's always been?" Reginn said.

"Maybe," Asger said, "but the Jotun, in particular, were unhappy with it. We don't go to Valhalla after death and fight all day and feast all night. Instead, we brood, and plot, and plan. We thought, what if we could return to the Midlands, and use all the wisdom we'd gained in the run-up to Ragnarok? What if we could move forward, rather than circle endlessly through creation and destruction?

"We had heard of the aldrnari–this creature of fire and ice–an elemental who could cross the boundary between the dead and the living. Someone who could help us do the same.

"You were brought into this world as a baby. I was not involved in that decision, or I would have conjured someone older and more self-sufficient. Perhaps you needed time to connect with the people of the Midlands.

"You summoned a caregiver who could look after you and also teach you some skills so that you could make your way in the Midlands."

"Tove," Reginn whispered, entangled in spite of herself. "I . . . summoned?"

Asger nodded. "Tove was perfect, but the time came when you needed more protection than she could offer. That's where I came in."

"She didn't sell me to you?"

Asger shook his head. "That was a lie. She would never have done that. You summoned me, and she returned to the deadlands."

"You bastard," Reginn said, the heat rising in her. "You lied to me."

Asger shrugged. "I am not a bastard–I am a demon with an agenda. My instincts do not run to kindness, or mercy, or telling the truth. I lied to you because it was easier for me.

"What you need to know is that I am here because of you. You raised me when you needed me, just as you raised your army."

Reginn's racing thoughts froze. "Wait–you are blaming *me* for creating my own tormentor?"

"You did not *create* me, but you *raised* me, just as you raised Hrym, and Dainn, Ursinus and Stonebiter." He paused, frowning. "Perhaps a demon wasn't the best choice. But you survived, until this time came."

"You're saying that you are dead," Reginn said. "I mean, you've been dead all along."

"I am," Asger said, "and I never appreciated it. I was only able to remain here this long because of the life I stole from you. I am so very tired of dealing with the endlessly needy living."

"You're going back," Reginn said.

"I am, as are the rest of the Risen. Some of us have left already. We don't belong here, and it's time the living assume a little responsibility."

"What about me?" Reginn said, feeling like a selfish child.

"Stay or go–that's up to you," Asger said. "If it were me, I would leave before you become more hopelessly entangled with the Midlands."

"When do you go?"

"This is goodbye," Asger said.

Reginn was mortified to find her eyes filling with tears.

Asger rose to his feet and stood for a moment, looking down at her. "Don't worry," he said softly. "Nobody misses a demon once he's gone."

With Queen Heidin gone, Grima dead, and Tyra sent to a secure but pleasant lockup in the country, the lust for war dissipated quickly. King Rikhard proclaimed an armistice and reconciliation, along with new laws outlining the rights of the gifted, and penalties for mistreatment.

Any of the gifted in the Archipelago were free to take passage to New Jotunheim, but Rikhard made it clear that he hoped that some of them would stay, and partner with him to build the new realm. Many of Grima's wraiths, freed from their collars, chose to stay and develop the unique gifts that had been stifled under Grima's hard hand.

Some of Reginn's fellow elders decided to stay on in the Archipelago, despite the miserable weather. Bryn became a member of the king's council, in charge of the integration of magic and conventional healing. Shelby took on the challenge of turning Muckleholm green again. Katia chose to return to New Jotunheim, but promised to visit. "I'll come back in the summers," she said. "There's only so much snow, sleet, and ice I can take. I like to feel the warm sunshine on my shoulders now and then."

"Thank you, Katia," Reginn said, embracing her. "You and Bryn were my first real friends."

Eiric was wary of kings and their promises, but Ivar's influence was growing. The prince was nearly always at the king's side, asking questions, offering counsel, and moderating Rikhard's worst instincts.

The more the peoples of the Archipelago saw of their young prince, the more they loved him, and Eiric worried less and less that Rikhard might sire a rival.

Once Eiric was sure that Liv was on the mend, he kept his promise and sailed back to Fiskeholm with his crew to sort things out. The hostages were released, and reunited with their families. Eiric's presence helped, of course, but the fiskers themselves had acquired new skills with weaponry while in Barbaria. They would not be the soft targets they had been before.

Eiric was still there when Liv returned to Eimyrja with her own hird, a mixture of spinners and former bondi who comprised a new Council of Elders, temporarily, at least. Svend and Naima were among them, and their endorsement went a long way toward allaying the fears of those who worried that the old regime was returning.

Brodir and systir rode horseback from Wetherby in the south to the bondi villages in the north of Ithavoll—a redemption tour of sorts. They led a party of brave volunteers across the bridge into Vigrid, where they did *not* go up in flames, but discovered the hidden history of the Last Battle beneath the ground.

Plans were made to mine the riches there for the benefit of all who were harmed in the name of the temple.

Liv was much more like her old self, with an edged wit, impatience with fools, and a soft heart for those in need. She tried to persuade Eiric to stay and help with the rebuilding, but New Jotunheim still held dark memories for him. Many there still blamed him for the death of their beloved keeper.

"It seems that we are divided by the past, brodir," Liv said sadly. "I will never sleep easy in the Archipelago, and you can't abide New Jotunheim."

"I'm not sure I belong anywhere," Eiric said. "But as long as I have a ship, I won't be far away."

When Eiric returned to the Archipelago in spring, Muckleholm was greener than he'd seen it since before he sailed to find the Temple at the Grove. Rikhard and Ivar were everywhere, it seemed.

When he asked after Reginn, he was told that she'd gone to Sundgard. So he went there himself.

He found her puttering in Sylvi's old garden, clearing out weeds and replanting herbs and medicinals, along with the barley and cabbage that had kept Eiric's family alive in the winters. Now and then, she paused, leaned on her hoe, and looked out to sea.

"Reginn," he said.

She turned to face him and dropped her hoe.

"What are you doing here?" he said. "You're no farmer."

"Neither are you," she countered. "What are *you* doing here?"

"I came for you," Eiric said.

Truth be told, they accomplished very little farming over the next several days. One night, it was warm enough that they slept out on the headland, overlooking the sea. In the morning, they sat, snuggled together, wrapped in furs to watch the sun peek over the horizon, promising a fair day.

"So," Eiric said, his hand on her bare knee. That slight contact still ignited him like nothing else. "What do you plan to do?"

Reginn squirmed closer. "I don't know if I'm cut out for farming," she said. "Farming is more of a long-term effort, and I don't know how long I'll be here."

"None of us do," Eiric said.

"I'd like to see more of Rikhard's new kingdom. I've never traveled very far outside of Muckleholm. But for that, I would need a ship and a styrman."

"I happen to know a styrman who is looking for work," Eiric said. "I'll warn you–it's a small ship, and the food is bad, and the styrman is–"

"I accept," Reginn said.

ACKNOWLEDGMENTS

SO, HERE WE HAVE IT—my fifteenth novel. I've been publishing about a book a year since my first novel, *The Warrior Heir*, in 2006. All big fat fantasy books (*Warrior Heir* was the shortest at ~110,000 words). You'd think I'd have the hang of it by now.

But this one kicked my butt. This one took two years, even though it was the sequel in a duology—a two-book series. That should represent fewer literary messes to clean up.

When I missed my deadline, my editor, Donna Bray, was very kind. Much kinder than I was to myself. "But I don't miss deadlines," I said. "I'm a reliable person."

"Every book is different," she said. "Some books take more time."

So, many thanks to the editorial team at Balzer + Bray, Donna Bray and Paige Pagan, for their kindness and forbearance during this difficult birth. I wish them great success in their new endeavors at Harper and elsewhere and hope that, given the small world of publishing, our paths will cross again. Special blessings to Kristin Rens, who took the handoff from Donna and Paige with such grace that I knew immediately I was in good hands. Immense gratitude to Laura Mock and Joel Tipple for a spectacular package design, and to Kim Ekdahl for the jacket art. I always say that the best covers make a promise that the book keeps, and I believe this one succeeds on every level. Others on the Harper team included Vanessa Nuttry in production and Erika West and Gwen Morton in copyediting and managing editorial. Any errors that slipped through are my own deal.

I look forward to working with Audrey Diestelkamp and Lauren

Levite again in marketing and publicity, and Patty Rosati and her team in school and library promotion. Finally, thanks to Kerry Moynagh, Kathy Faber, Jen Wygand, and the rest of the sales team for their part in sending *Bane* out into the world.

To my literary agent, the imperturbable Christopher Schelling, who saw his low-maintenance client take a turn and joined the support group—thank you for the kind heart that beats under that cynical shell. Thanks also to my foreign rights agent, Chris Lotts.

Speaking of support groups, thanks to the writing communities I've been fortunate enough to be a part of. At this stage of the writing game, when classes and workshops are less helpful, their wisdom, experience, and commiseration is most useful. Thanks to the Stanford Fellows: Megan Whalen Turner, Tricia Springstubb, Michelle Houts, Shelley Pearsall, Rebecca Bohner, and Edie Pattou. Not a critique group—more of an eating and drinking group with a writing problem.

The same could be said about members of the Swashbooklers, a retreat in which I hang out with smart and savvy, mostly younger literati at the beach and share low-country boils, beach bonfires, dance parties, and tarot. Also Serious Literary Discussions, problem-solving, and industry gossip. Many thanks to friends I've made at Kindling Words East and West and the critique groups of the past. The groups may have succumbed to time and life changes, but the friendships live on.

Special thanks to my son Eric, the world's best beta reader and editor. Your notes go deep and your insights are always worthwhile. Also to my husband, Rod, technical advisor, webmaster, graphic designer, fixer, and finder of lost things.